I0642417

Hands
of the
Architects

Book Three

Broken Clocks and Amber Threads

A novel by

Brian Harmon

Hands of the Architects

Book Three

Broken Clocks and Amber Threads

Published by Brian Harmon

Cover Images and Design by Candorem

ISBN: 1-945559-13-6

ISBN-13: **978-1-945559-13-6**

Also by Brian Harmon

Rushed Series:

Rushed (Book 1)
Rushed: The Unseen (Book 2)
Rushed: Something Wicked (Book 3)
Rushed: Hedge Lake (Book 4)
Rushed: A Matter of Time (Book 5)
Rushed: All Fun and Games (Book 6)
Rushed: Something Wickeder (Book 7)
Rushed: Evancurt (Book 8)
Rushed: Relic (Book 9)

The Temple of the Blind series:

Book 1 – *The Box*
Book 2 – *Gilbert House*
Book 3 – *The Temple of the Blind*
Book 4 – *Road Beneath The Wood*
Book 5 – *Secret of the Labyrinth*
Book 6 – *The Judgment of the Sentinels*

Hands of the Architects trilogy:

Spirit Ears and Prophet Sight (Book 1)
Pretty Faces and Peculiar Places (Book 2)
Broken Clocks and Amber Threads (Book 3)

For Collin

Chapter 1

No, that wasn't right.

The shading was wrong. It was throwing off the whole scene. And there was still something bothering her about the anatomy, too. The whole thing just didn't look right.

Seph took off her glasses and rubbed her eyes. She was getting frustrated. She knew she was a much better artist than this. But she was having a hard time focusing. She didn't sleep very well last night. She had that nightmare again. The one about the giant worm.

She returned her glasses to her face and yawned. She reached for her coffee, but found it empty again. How many cups had she already drunk today? She'd lost count. And they were doing nothing to help her focus. Did she need something stronger?

This wasn't a good time for this sort of thing. There were deadlines coming up and she was behind schedule. They needed to be finished with the promotional material for Inky Net Games by the end of the week or they'd risk delaying the new *Fever Island* sequel. But she just couldn't seem to get it together today.

Her mind wouldn't stop wandering…

Mona Yenning gave her a polite smile as she walked by on her way back to her desk.

Seph watched her until she sat down in front of her computer, then she turned in her chair and looked around the office at her other coworkers, confused. What was she doing again? Wasn't she just somewhere else?

No… Of course she wasn't somewhere else. She'd been here all morning. What kind of odd thought was that?

Mr. Carrol, her boss, stepped into the doorway and looked out across the room. "Four o'clock tomorrow, Zeke."

Zeke Jenfir swiveled around in his chair and pointed back at him with one of his long, bony fingers. "Okay! Thank you!"

Mr. Carrol nodded and glanced once more over the room. When his eyes met hers, he gave her his usual, friendly nod and then turned and walked away.

Seph stared through the empty doorway after him for a moment, distracted. That was weird. For a moment there, she had the most intense feeling of déjà vu…

She turned and stared at her monitor. Seriously, what was she doing? Something wasn't right here. Where was Piper? She was just here.

Wasn't she?

No…that was…

That was *what*? She felt like she could almost remember something. It was right in the very back of her thoughts, lurking just out of reach, staring back at her from the shadows of her mind.

(…something cold and wet against her skin…)

Then, before she could quite grasp it, it was gone again.

No, Piper wasn't here. She'd *never* been here before. Not here in the studio. Seph was at work, and Piper never bothered her at work.

But she *would* be here soon. They were going to have lunch together. In fact, when she glanced at the clock on her computer screen, she found that it was *already* time for lunch. Piper was probably downstairs waiting for her right now.

That was what her weary mind was most likely trying to tell her, she decided.

Lunch sounded good. She was hungry. She needed a break. And maybe she could grab a coffee or two to perk herself up. She saved her work and cleaned up the reference materials scattered across her desk-top. Then she collected her purse, slipped it over her arm and made her way out into the hallway, her stubborn mind still wandering, dragging her back to Avelby for some reason, to those creepy tunnels that never seemed to go anywhere.

It wasn't that strange. She found herself thinking of Avelby a lot, actually. She supposed it'd be weird *not* to, after all that had happened there last summer.

She shook it off and checked her phone. Usually Piper texted her to tell her she was here, but all she had was a message from her mom.

Maybe she was running late.

The elevator doors slid open before she could push the button. Inside, staring back at her, stood Piper. "Oh!" she chirped, cheerful as ever. "Hi! That was easy."

Seph stared at her for a moment, surprised to see her there. Her long, blonde hair was shaped into a perfect bun. She was wearing her favorite skinny jeans, high-heel booties and a light, peach-colored, off-the-shoulder sweater. Her complexion and makeup were flawless. As usual, she was positively adorable.

Meanwhile, Seph's hair was falling out of her ponytail, her skirt was wrinkled, she never bothered putting on *any* makeup that morning and she was pretty sure her cardigan was adding about thirty pounds.

Life wasn't fair.

"What're you doing up here?" she asked as she stepped into the car beside her and pressed the button for the ground floor. Piper usually waited for her in the lobby.

"The lady downstairs said I should just come up and find you."

Seph frowned. "That's odd." They didn't usually want any unnecessary people in the studios. Distractions were kept to a minimum.

She slipped her phone back into her purse as the elevator doors slid shut and the car began to descend. She'd message her mom back later.

"She said your boss said I was okay," said Piper.

"Mr. Carrol?"

"Uh huh."

"I didn't know Mr. Carrol even knew who you were." A lot of the people in the office called him by his first name, but she'd always felt weird about that. He was, after all, the one who gave her the job, in spite of the fact that she totally botched her third job interview. (It really wasn't her fault, but no one would ever believe the real reason she was forced to cancel that day.) She felt like she owed him more respect than to call him "*Millard*."

Piper shrugged. "I didn't either."

She supposed it wasn't *that* odd. It wasn't unheard of for Mr. Carrol to do stuff like that. Mona's nine-year-old son sometimes came to work with her when she couldn't find a sitter. (He was a good kid. He pretty much just sat in the floor next to her desk with his nose in a handheld video game the whole time.) And Robert Lutzin's wife was always stopping by to check on him because he was severely diabetic. But Mona and Robert had been working here a long time. It was fairly well-understood that they had special privileges that didn't extend to everyone in the office.

She took off her glasses and rubbed her eyes again. It didn't matter. She didn't have the energy to think too much about it right now. He probably just saw her and Piper together a few times and recognized her. And it probably didn't hurt that Piper was a *very* attractive and *super* charming young woman. A lot of people took an instant liking to her. Even Mr. Carrol probably wasn't immune to her cuteness.

"Still not sleeping well?"

Seph glanced over at her without putting her glasses back on. "Woke up at about three o'clock and couldn't get back to sleep."

"Same dream?"

"Yeah." She was no stranger to nightmares, but this one was oddly unsettling, even by her standards. She woke up from it with such an overwhelming feeling of impending doom that her whole body had trembled.

"What do you think it means?" wondered Piper.

Seph returned her glasses to her face. "I'm not sure it has to *mean* anything. It's just a dream. And it's not like we don't have any good reasons to have nightmares."

It wasn't even as if she'd never encountered a giant worm before.

"True," Piper admitted. After all, she'd had her fair share of bad dreams, too. She wouldn't admit it to just anyone, but there were more than a few nights last summer, after that awful business with the incubus, that she had to crawl into bed with Seph in the middle of the night. She just couldn't seem to close her eyes without seeing those monstrous children closing in around her…or those hairy, alien zombie things…or the flickering men with their skeletal, screaming faces… Just thinking about it now gave her an icy shudder.

Seph did find it odd, however, that this particular dream had only been tormenting her for the past week or two. It'd been almost ten months since those horrific events in Avelby and in all that time she never saw so much as a glimpse of any of Gispuknya's shadow monsters. Things had been quiet. The horrors had subsided.

But maybe that was just it. Maybe it was *too* quiet. Maybe it was because she knew that this was merely the still before the storm. The monsters were still out there. *Janon Tane* was still out there. *Gispuknya* was still out there. It was only a matter of time until one of them came looking for them.

"Where do you want to eat?" asked Piper.

"I don't care. Where do you want to go?"

"You know what my answer to that always is."

"Right. Anywhere with the words 'meat-lovers' somewhere on the menu."

Piper flashed her that pretty smile. She was a cute little carnivore. That much was undeniable. Seph was annoyed by a lot of things about a lot of people, but strangely enough, her roommate's unusual obsession with *meat*, of all things, wasn't one of them. In fact, for some reason she found it sort of endearing.

For one thing, it wasn't really her fault. It wasn't as if she just decided one day that she really loved meat and couldn't live without it. Ever since she was a little girl, she'd had a strange condition that made her sick if she went too long without eating meat. Seph had never heard of anything like it before, but it was true. She'd seen it with her own eyes. It didn't seem to matter how much meat she ate, or what kind of meat, but it had to be real meat. A veggie burger just wouldn't do. It was the strangest thing. And also strangely adorable, given that she looked exactly like the sort of girl who lived off kale salad and vitamin water.

"So how's the project going?" asked Piper.

"Okay, I guess. When I can focus for more than five minutes.

How are things at Hot Topic?"

She shrugged. "Fine. My store manager seems like sort of a drama queen, but it's fun. I like it."

Seph kept asking her when she was going to quit bouncing around the mall like a teenager and actually find a job that utilized her hard-earned master's degree in journalism. But she *liked* working at the mall. She didn't want to be tied to one job for the rest of her life. She liked changing things up. It kept life interesting. And if she was going to be honest, the whole reason she stayed in school long enough to *earn* her masters was so that she had a good excuse to keep working at the mall.

She supposed she was just weird that way.

"Oh! Before I forget again, Kaitlyn texted me this morning. She wants to know if we want to get together with everyone in Madison this weekend."

Seph shrugged. "Sure. Why not?" She didn't have any plans. She hardly ever did. And she *did* enjoy getting together with Kaitlyn, Alton and Phoenix now and then. They'd been her friends since the beginning of her freshman year at college. They'd helped her through some difficult times.

"'Kay." Her purse hung at her hip. She plucked her phone out of it and lit up the screen. "I'll text her back and let her know."

Everyone took a liking to Piper as soon as Seph introduced them. She'd immediately fit right into the group. Now Kaitlyn texted Piper instead of Seph when she wanted to get everyone together for these coffee dates. Probably because Piper always texted her right back, whereas Seph had a bad habit of putting it off. It wasn't personal. She did that to everyone. She just wasn't always in the mood to talk to other people.

Piper frowned at her phone. "No service in here. I guess I'll wait until we get outside."

Seph looked up at the ceiling of the car. "I guess we *are* in a concrete shaft."

"Yeah…" She frowned at her phone. "You know, I haven't heard from Meg since, like, *Saturday*. You didn't reap her, did you?"

"No. You said I wasn't allowed."

Meg used to be Piper's roommate, before she moved in with her boyfriend and Seph took her place. Then, when she and her boyfriend inevitably broke up, she began a nasty crusade to try to get rid of Seph and move back into her old room. The girl was kind of unstable, in Seph's opinion. She was self-centered, hot-headed, impulsive and manipulative. Not to mention none too bright.

She never did succeed in getting rid of Seph, but she *did* manage to move back in. She just sort of kept moving her stuff in whenever they weren't looking until everything she owned was there. Then she just sort of took over their living room, transforming it into a makeshift third bedroom.

Seph hated it.

"It's odd, isn't it?" said Piper.

"It's *suspicious*. Her having the courtesy to not be home to annoy me for so long isn't like her. She's obviously up to something."

"She's not *that* bad," giggled Piper as she dropped her phone back into her purse. "But yeah… It's kind of weird her not blowing up my phone when I'm not home."

"I know. She's like a little kid. If she's too quiet for too long, it's definitely not going to end well."

Piper laughed. The girl *did* get into trouble a lot. She had that dangerous combination of idiotic fearlessness and unabashed shamelessness. She was like the villain in some lame cartoon. It boggled the mind.

Just this past December, Meg took a liking to some guy she met at a bar. When she discovered that he was already dating someone, she did what Meg always did when she encountered something that upset her selfish world and shifted all the way into crisis mode. She spent most of the following week stalking the poor girl on social media and spreading vicious rumors about her in hopes that he'd dump her.

It didn't go as she planned.

Her first mistake was assuming that this guy even had any interest in her. He didn't. And when he caught onto what she was up to, he immediately told his girlfriend who she was. *She* was Meg's second mistake. She was a lot smarter than Meg, a lot more popular, a lot more *liked* and a lot more plugged-in.

She never stood a chance. Within a few days, she was forced to deactivate most of her social media accounts to escape the backlash of cyber-hate. And as a bonus, she ended up banned from almost every bar in Cakwetak.

Meg still insisted that the whole thing was that other girl's fault. It was as if she truly couldn't comprehend the weight of her own actions.

There was something wrong with her. Seph was convinced of this.

"How about that Mexican place?" suggested Seph.

Piper's blue eyes lit up. "Ooh! The one with those *huge* steak burritos?" She made a sound that was no doubt supposed to sound like "yummy" but came out strangely erotic, instead.

"Oh my god! *Down*, girl. It's just a burrito."

Piper clapped her hands over her mouth, embarrassed. "Don't make fun of me!" she cried through her fingers.

Seph laughed.

"You're so mean!"

"I'm sorry."

"No, you're not."

"Fine, I'll buy you lunch."

Piper lowered her hands and pouted. "You already said you'd buy me lunch."

"Then stop acting like I'm the devil. You know I love you and your weird meat fetish."

"It's not a *fetish*!"

She laughed again.

"*So* rude."

Seph looked at her watch, distracted. "Is it just me, or is this elevator taking *forever*?"

Piper frowned up at the display. It was showing the number one, but for some reason they were still moving. They were only going down three floors. The entire building was only five. "It didn't take this long when I was going *up*."

Seph pressed the button for the ground floor again. They weren't stopped. She could feel the car moving. "Are we just, like, going *really* slow?" She pressed the button for the second floor. Then the stop button. Nothing was working.

"Is it broken?"

"I hope not. I *really* don't want to spend my lunch break trapped in a bad sitcom episode."

Now that she was thinking about it, she remembered hearing some of her coworkers complain about this elevator. She'd never noticed anything herself, but apparently it sometimes behaved erratically, taking forever to arrive and sometimes cruising right past the floor they were waiting on without even stopping.

Maybe the thing was just old and dying. It'd be just her luck to be inside it when it finally croaked.

But the elevator didn't die. The speaker dinged and the car finally rumbled to a stop.

"Here we are," said Piper, relieved. She didn't usually mind confined spaces, but she didn't care for the idea of being trapped.

The doors rumbled open. The hallway leading to the front entrance of the building lay before them, just like always.

"Huh," said Seph. "Weird." She made a mental note to use the stairs for a while, but otherwise dismissed the entire strange ordeal. "I'll buy you your meat-bomb burrito, but you're driving."

"Fair enough," agreed Piper.

But when they turned at the end of the hallway, Seph stopped, confused. "Wait…"

This wasn't the lobby. In fact, this wasn't any part of the building she'd ever seen before. Instead of the big, glass entrance and receptionist desk, they found an utterly empty space enclosed within large panes of frosted glass. The floor was naked concrete and there were no doors.

"This is the wrong floor," observed Piper.

Seph frowned. She wasn't wrong. This definitely wasn't where she wanted to be. But she'd been on every floor of this building and no part of any of them had ever looked like this.

Did the Vertical Design building have a secret sub-basement she'd never seen?

She couldn't even guess at the purpose of such a room.

"Come on. Let's go back and try again."

But when they turned the corner that should've taken them back to the elevator, they found themselves in another open space surrounded by more of those strange, frosted windows again.

"What the hell?" exclaimed Seph.

"Okay, I know we came this way," said Piper. "What's going on?"

Seph turned and went the other way, toward the back of the building. The logical part of her brain insisted that she was just confused. Clearly, she was doing something wrong. Maybe her sleep-deprived brain was short-circuiting on her.

Except that explanation never turned out to be the right one.

Again, they found themselves standing in another empty room, staring at those huge, frosted windows.

"Pea?" said Seph.

"Yes?" said Piper. (Nobody ever called her Piper. Not even her parents. She had no idea why.)

"Are you hearing anything right now?"

She wasn't talking about ordinary sounds. Her ears worked just fine. She could hear for herself that everything was quiet. *Eerily* quiet, in fact, now that she was listening. There were none of the muffled voices or hushed footsteps that she associated with business as usual. Not even the soft hum of office electronics. But Piper had *two* pairs of ears. One pair was just like everyone else's. They were on the sides of her head, just like they were supposed to be. They were pierced, with little, heart-shaped earrings in each lobe, and just as annoyingly perfect as the rest of the features on her pretty little head. They worked just like anyone else's. But she also had another pair of ears, a pair that only Seph could see. They were on the very top of her head, poking up through her hair, spectral and transparent, a ghostly, iridescent shade of gray. They looked a little like those cat ear headbands that some girls liked to wear. They were her spirit ears. And with *those*, she could hear things that other people couldn't.

Piper turned around. She cocked her head to one side and then the other. Her spirit ears twitched this way and that, searching for anything that her other ears couldn't detect. "I don't think so," she replied.

But it'd been a while since she'd last used them. She wasn't entirely sure she was doing it right. "What about you?"

"I don't see anything." Seph didn't have spectral ears on top of her head. Or if she did, she didn't know it. Piper's spirit ears didn't show up in mirrors or on film, they were intangible to the touch and Seph simply couldn't see the top of her own head to be sure there weren't any up there. But she probably didn't have any spirit ears because she couldn't hear any of the special things that Piper heard. Instead, she had an ability called "prophet sight" that allowed her to *see* things no one else could see.

Like Piper's spirit ears, for example.

She was already looking around, but like Piper, she couldn't be certain she was using them right. It was always a little tricky. Some things took a while to see. Other things, like Piper's ghostly ears, were always visible to her. Sometimes just walking into a place gave her a peculiar sensation that something was there and she only had to make herself see it. Other times, like now, for example, there was simply nothing.

She glanced over at Piper's spirit ears again. It was weird. When she first awoke to her prophet sight, the first unusual thing she saw was a pair of foxlike spirit ears sitting atop the head of a barista at a coffee shop in Madison. Soon after, she saw a man on the street in Cakwetak, and not long after that she found Piper. That was three in less than a month. And yet, in all the time between then and now, she'd only caught sight of one other person, a random glimpse of a woman on a crowded street with long, rabbit-like ears sticking straight up through her hat.

How many people in the world had spirit ears? Was it strange that she'd seen so many in those first few weeks? Or was it strange that she'd seen so few since then?

Piper took a step toward the glass, squinting at it. "What was that?"

"What was what?"

She took another step closer. Was it only her imagination?

Seph turned all the way around, searching the entire room. What was even the purpose of a place like this? Given the extra time it took to get here in the elevator, she'd guess that they were underground, in some sort of sub-basement. But why would there be windows in a place like that? Where was the light coming from that was illuminating all this frosted glass?

And why were there no doors?

This place smelled funny, she realized. Not like a basement, exactly. It reminded her of the hospital where her father died. Sterile. Chemical-like. With the faint stench of something sickly.

Piper doubted very much that it was only her imagination. When she was a little girl making her dad search her room top to bottom for lurking monsters, it was only her imagination. But she wasn't a little girl anymore. And real monsters didn't waste their time hiding in little girls' bedrooms. "We have to get out of here."

"You think?" grumbled Seph.

Something slammed against one of the windows. Both of them turned to see a blurry shape standing on the other side. The silhouettes of two hands were clearly visible against the frosted glass, behind which was a hazy, indistinct shadow.

Another appeared beside it. Then a third.

Within seconds, they were surrounded.

Chapter 2

"And now we're in a zombie movie..." croaked Seph as fresh, hot terror welled up within her, souring her stomach.

"I don't like zombies," whimpered Piper.

"I know you don't. I don't either."

They weren't talking about the *movies*. Zombies were a real thing. Or, at least, things that were supposed to be dead getting up and chasing you were a real thing. They'd encountered a lot of things like that. Whether they were actually zombies or mummies or some other variation of undead things wasn't really relevant. They were real. They were dangerous. And something very reminiscent of them was here right now, just on the other side of that glass...

A lot of very unpleasant memories were suddenly welling up inside both of them.

Seph forced herself to ignore the sick feeling in her gut and hurried back out the way they came. She must've missed something. If there was a way into this freaky place, then there had to be a way out.

Except there wasn't a way out. They seemed to be trapped here. There was no sign of the malfunctioning elevator that dropped them off, or even of the hallway that led back to it. There wasn't even a place where these things *used to be*.

It didn't make sense.

"What do we do?" squealed Piper.

Seph wasn't entirely sure. The silence of the mysterious floor was gone, replaced by the unnerving sounds of unearthly things pounding on glass. How long would it take something to break through it?

And *what* would come through it? The undead things they'd encountered in the past had never been human. They were monstrous, alien things, as if they'd not only been summoned from the dead, but from some distant planet.

"Keep it together!" snapped Seph, speaking as much to herself as to Piper. "We've been in worse situations than this before."

"Yeah, but those situations all started out just like this *right before they got worse*!"

She had a point there…

But they could handle this. It wasn't exactly a surprise, after all. They both knew that something like this was going to happen eventually. It was only a matter of time. That business with the Hands wasn't over yet. There was another one still out there somewhere, waiting to be claimed. And Janon Tane was almost certainly keeping a close watch on them.

The question was why *here*? This was her job. What would happen if Mr. Carrol found out the truth about her? That she was essentially a magnet for monsters, demons and all manner of otherworldly things? Could he fire her for that? She was, technically, something of a hazard to those around her…

And what *was* this place, anyway? Why was there an unmarked floor under the office building she'd been working at for the past year and a half with a vanishing elevator and a horde of ravenous zombie-things trapped behind panes of eerie, translucent glass like some kind of cheap Halloween spook house trick?

Had this always been here?

Was this some kind of weird, government research facility?

"Persephone..." squeaked Piper. (Everyone but Piper called her Seph. She was the only one who liked calling her by her full name. She insisted it was too pretty not to use.)

"I see it," said Seph.

The monsters were changing. They no longer looked like a horde of zombies. They were clustering together, those creepy hands clawing higher and higher up the glass, those eerie shadows merging into something bigger and even more frightening.

Seph looked back the way they came. When they were in that first room, they hadn't yet realized what was happening. She didn't look it over very well. She turned and ran back there, hoping to find something she missed. But it was the same as the other two.

The things behind the glass had now transformed into something horrible. She stood staring at them, her heart pounding in her chest. Long, shadowy shapes were slowly slithering across the surface on a multitude of human hands, like some hellish centipede.

Other, smaller shapes skittered up and out of sight among them, looking more like big, human-handed spiders.

The pounding on the glass had turned into a sort of rhythmic *scuttling* sound that made her skin crawl. If there were bugs in hell, she thought they'd probably have shadows that looked exactly like these things.

And Seph *detested* bugs.

"There has to be a way out of here," insisted Piper.

Seph wasn't so sure. The way *in* was the elevator. Without it, could they really be trapped in this place? "The universe always gives us a way," she said, recalling what the Ahns told them in that mysterious cabin back in July. But her voice lacked confidence. That was what they'd been told, but was it really true? Was there *always* a way out? Or was that just the stuff of suspense movies?

Above them, the ceiling tiles rattled as something scurried overhead.

"Persephone…?"

"I'm *trying*!"

It was hard to concentrate with her heart hammering and her inner voice screaming at her about the fact that the zombie shadows had turned into freakish *bug* shadows with human hands. She felt like every hair on her body was standing on end right now, as if a steady current of pure, electrified fear were coursing through her blood. She turned around and around, searching for something—*anything*—that might show them the way out of this nightmare.

From one of the other rooms came the sound of shattering glass.

Piper screamed.

Seph turned and looked back toward the useless little hallway, terrified. She tried to focus on the task of finding something unseen, but that screaming voice inside her head was now shrieking at her that maybe the way out was actually in whatever room was just breached by the nightmare-hand-bugs.

Somewhere, another pane of glass shattered.

A ceiling tile cracked, raining down a shower of white dust.

Then the eerie sound of bare hands slapping against concrete echoed from the far end of the hallway.

"*Persephone*!"

Seph turned around again, her dark eyes darting from one shadow to the next. She wanted to scream, but she was afraid of what might follow the sound of her voice.

Piper stared through the doorway leading back to the other rooms. Something was moving in there. She could see its shadow creeping across the floor.

One of the panes of glass in front of them cracked.

"There!" gasped Seph, pointing toward a place in the corner of the room.

It wasn't her prophet sight. It was her human eyes that saw it this time. The shadows were scurrying over every pane of glass except one. They kept turning away from it when they reached it, as if there were a wall separating the spaces behind them.

She didn't let herself hesitate. If she hesitated, she'd only convince herself that she was wrong, that she was only going to speed along her own demise. And then the rest of the glass would shatter and there would be no more time to save themselves. She hurried over to the suspicious pane, hiked up her skirt and kicked it with the sole of her ballet flat.

It gave easier than she expected. She nearly fell into the shattering glass, but managed somehow to keep her balance. And even better, she *didn't* find herself swarmed by monsters. Instead, a door stood before her.

She hoped desperately that it led out of this nightmare and not immediately into a new one.

There was no time to second guess it. As more panes of glass shattered and one of the ceiling tiles crashed to the floor behind them, the two of them fled through the newly revealed door and into the unknown beyond.

Chapter 3

The door didn't lead directly to freedom. But it also didn't lead to a horde of monstrous hell bugs with abundances of opposable thumbs, either, so Seph decided that it would do.

And even better, the door had a lock on it! Piper snapped the latch into place just as something heavy slammed against the other side, startling another scream from her.

"Come on!" said Seph. She took her by the hand and pulled her along, eager to get as far away from this place as possible.

Piper watched the door as she backed away, convinced that the things on the other side would burst through it before they had time to escape. Only after they'd retreated several yards did she dare turn her back on it and focus on where she was going.

"Faster!" urged Seph.

"I can't go any faster in these shoes!" she replied.

"Why are you wearing heels, anyway?"

"Because they're cute! We were just supposed to have lunch!"

"You're a seeker! Always assume something's going to end up chasing you!"

They were running through an extremely long, empty hallway that seemed to stretch on forever in front of them, with no other doors to be seen.

It was getting colder. (Seph was glad to be wearing her cardigan, even if it did make her look frumpy.) And that hospital-like stench was getting worse. Her creepy imagination was trying to convince her that it smelled less like a hospital than a morgue, but she refused to let it get the better of her. After all, she'd never been inside a morgue before. She didn't know what they smelled like. She was only guessing.

"What is this place?" gasped Piper.

"How should I know?"

"You *work here*, don't you?"

"I'm an artist! I don't work down here in the *hell department*!"

Seph, too, wasn't convinced that the locked door would actually stop the things in those creepy rooms from following them. Any second now, they'd break it down. Or else they'd burst through the walls. At the very least, the ones in the ceiling would continue chasing them, raining plaster down behind them as they scurried through the drop space. But none of that happened. Even the thing that slammed against the door when Piper first locked it gave up almost immediately.

The hallway remained as silent as it was endless.

And as she stared into the emptiness ahead of her, she realized that it was familiar to her. She'd been here once before. She was sure of it. But when? Surely, she would've remembered a place like this.

Was it something from a dream, maybe?

"How can it be this long?" asked Piper. "Where's it taking us?"

"You're doing that really annoying thing again where you keep asking me questions you can't possibly expect me to know the answer to."

"Sorry."

Seph glanced back over her shoulder. The door behind them had dwindled in the distance. It was strangely surreal to see that she'd gone so far from it that it could possibly look that small. It made her think of the tiny door in that Disney version of *Alice in Wonderland*. And something about that colorful, ridiculous image of Alice and the tiny door made her remember where she knew this place from.

It was ten months ago, in the cellar of the Old Avelby Inn. When she touched the slime on that concrete wall and was thrown into a vivid series of visions of her own past and future. At one point, she was running down an endless hallway exactly like this one.

It also explained that weird case of déjà vu when she was sitting at her desk, she realized. She saw that moment during that vision as well.

It seemed that today was always meant to be an important day.

She couldn't decide if that made her feel better or worse.

"I think I see something," said Piper.

Seph looked forward again. She was right. There was something ahead of them. The end of this maddening hallway? She picked up her pace, eager to find out.

Soon it became clear that it was, in fact, a doorway. Not a door with another lock they could put between them and those horrible things in those other rooms, but an opening. A way out of this ridiculous hallway, at least.

Or so she thought. But when they finally arrived there, they found that nothing awaited them on the other side. They found only a small room with no doors or windows.

A dead end.

"Oh come on!" groaned Piper. "This doesn't even make any sense!"

"I don't think it's supposed to," said Seph as she turned in a circle, searching every surface of every wall for anything that might be hidden here. But nothing jumped out at her. If there was something only her prophet sight could see, it was hidden well enough that she was completely blind to it.

Piper turned and looked back down the hallway again. She half-expected to see those weird hand-bugs crawling toward them, but the passage remained empty. "Why don't you use the scythe?"

Seph glanced back at her. "What?"

"The *scythe*," she said again.

The Grim Reaper's scythe. The first of the three Hands of the Architects. Seph had claimed it the first time their lives took a sudden detour through horror town. It was inside her somewhere right now. An object of unimaginable power, capable of striking anything from existence with a single slash of its incredible blade.

She looked down at her hand. It was suddenly wet, as if she'd just taken it from a tub of water. (That was the scythe's true form, after all: living water.) It was as if it'd heard Piper speak of it and was eager to be put to work again.

"Can't you just hack through one of these walls and let us out?"

"We have no idea if there's even anything on the other side of these walls," Seph replied. "We could be ten stories underground for all we know."

She spread her hands as if that were the stupidest argument she'd ever heard. "Then just carve us a tunnel out," she said, as if that solved it.

"I can't just whip it out and swing it around any time we get stuck somewhere. Wielding the scythe is a big responsibility!"

Piper wrinkled her nose at her. "I watched you open your *mail* with it the other day!"

Seph looked down at her wet hand again. The water clung to her, not dripping, not running down her arm. It defied gravity. Because it wasn't really water. It was a living thing. It was the physical manifestation of one of the three Architects.

For the first eight months she possessed it, she didn't realize it was still with her. She thought it left her. But it was slumbering inside her that whole time. Since then, she'd taught herself to use it. Now, it came to her like second nature. She could practically summon it in her sleep. But only in *little* ways. She hadn't been able to make the entire scythe appear again, as she did when she used it against the shepherd and the incubus. But then again, she hadn't tried all that hard. The truth was that it sort of terrified her. It wasn't just a blade, after all. If she were to accidently unleash it in a moment of confusion or surprise, the scythe wouldn't just cut someone. It would utterly destroy them. It would erase them from existence, soul and all.

But Piper was right. This was starting to look like one of those situations where she was running dangerously low on options.

She turned and looked at the blank walls of the tiny room at the end of the long corridor. Then she looked down at her hands again. "I guess I can try," she sighed, turning to face one of the walls. "But seriously, stand back. I have no idea what this is going to do."

She'd been using the power of the scythe for various little things since she discovered that she still possessed it. She considered it practice. Or maybe *research* was a better word for it. It was actually quite handy. Although it appeared to be nothing more than water, it seemed to have an intelligence about it. If she wanted to cut a wire tie or a loose string or the tape holding a box closed, all she had to do was drag her fingertip across it and the scythe formed a tiny blade exactly where she wanted it. If she wanted to cut something much stronger—like when she was snipping off pieces of steel pipe for a sculpture she was working on this past winter—she closed her whole hand around it and squeezed. The scythe created a blade in the palm of her hand that cut through the hard metal with the ease of a hydraulic bolt cuter. It was amazingly cool.

But those blades were tiny, nothing at all like the wicked business end of the reaper's legendary tool of choice as it had appeared when she wielded it against those two monsters. In both those instances, it left no trace of its victim.

She had no idea what was going to happen if she hacked at a wall with it. Would it make the entire surface disintegrate into nothing? Would it melt away the drywall and the studs? Would the entire room vanish? Would it erase the supports on which all of Vertical Design rested? Could the entire building come crashing down around them, burying them alive?

She wasn't at all sure that this was a good idea. But she couldn't deny that options were in short supply right now.

Piper stepped back and watched her from the doorway. She was nervously pinching her lower lip between her thumb and forefinger. If this didn't work, she had no idea what they were going to do. There was no way out of here.

Seph took a breath and then let it out in a long, uneasy sigh. Then she lifted her arms.

The water flowed. The scythe unfolded itself from her hands, forming a handle that shimmered like glass. Then a four-foot-long blade curved around her, gleaming in those harsh fluorescent lights. She'd never held it this long before. Those other two times, the entire ordeal was over in an instant. A flash of a crystal blade. A faint whoosh as it split the air. And then it was over. Standing there now, she realized that it had a strange sort of weight to it. Not heavy, exactly. It was amazingly easy for her to move it around. But it was also plenty heavy enough to feel formidable. No matter how she held it, it was perfectly balanced. And why shouldn't it be? It was hers, after all. It wasn't just that she found it. According to those who knew about these sorts of things, the scythe *chose her*. Whatever form it took, it would always be *just for her*.

She lifted it over her shoulder, like a baseball bat. She didn't have to worry about it hitting the ceiling. Or anything else she wasn't aiming at. The blade remained rigid, but also flowed like water. It bent itself as she moved it, automatically avoiding everything around her.

She took a breath, held it, steadied herself…then she swung it.

The water broke apart and splashed harmlessly against the wall.

For a moment, she stood there, motionless, trying to comprehend what just happened.

"Did you…mean to do that?" asked Piper.

"Uh…not…exactly. No."

"Oh."

She looked down at her hands. The water still covered them, still seemed to be waiting to serve her.

Was it supposed to do that? Had she triggered some sort of fail-safe?

"Is the safety on?" asked Piper.

Again, she held out her arms and focused on the shape of the scythe. The handle stretched into existence between her clenched fists.

This time, it came apart and splashed to the floor before it had time to even begin forming the blade.

"Are you unfocused?" asked Piper.

"I don't know." She frowned at her hands. They were still wet, they just weren't doing what she wanted them to do. She turned them around and looked at her palms.

Was it her imagination, or did the water look muddy for a second there?

"Do you need to change the batteries?"

"You're not helping."

"Like, use the force or whatever."

"I don't think it works that way."

"Well then I'm out of ideas."

Seph closed her eyes and took another deep breath. "I can do this," she muttered. "Just *focus.*"

Piper twisted her lower lip and remained silent.

Again, the scythe began to form. First the handle, then the blade, until she was again holding the entire weapon in her hands. Again, she willed herself to focus. She took another calming breath…then she swung it at the wall.

A long, silver streak of gleaming water flashed in the overhead lights as the blade arced before her eyes.

Then the scythe was gone again. Her hands were empty. And they were instantly dry, too, as if the water had never been there at all.

The wall didn't vanish. Instead, there was a long, narrow, diagonal slash in front of her, exactly as a real blade might've done.

And as she stood there, wondering why nothing more than that happened, the wall began to *bleed.*

It oozed from the crack and drizzled down the clean wall in gory streaks.

"Um…" said Seph. "That's not what I expected to happen."

"That's really unsettling," agreed Piper.

Then the room, itself, let out a long, agonized groan and the walls began to *writhe.*

Chapter 4

"*This place is alive?*" shrieked Piper.

They backed away, retreating into the hallway as the gash in the wall gaped open wider, pushed apart by the heavy mass of heaving tissue that was twisting and churning inside it. Blood gushed from the crack in thick, gory spurts, pooling on the floor below.

Something was inside the wound. A bloody, bulging thing was squirming around in there, pushing it apart, tearing its way free.

"I don't think you should've done that," decided Piper.

"It was *your* idea!"

"Why would you listen to me? You know I don't know anything about this stuff!"

It didn't smell like a hospital *or* a morgue now. All Seph could smell was *blood.* It filled the air, a thick and unnatural, overpowering stench that soured her stomach and made her cover her mouth and nose as she backed away.

As they watched, a gory hand wriggled its way out of the oozing, pulsating mass of meat revealed by the widening gash. It reached out and clawed at the wall, digging grooves into the drywall with its ragged nails.

Then another appeared, this one groping at the other side. Then another. Then more. Soon, there were a dozen of them in all, half of them on each side, pulling the wound open even wider and revealing the slimy, hemorrhaging flesh within.

Then something began to bulge outward from between the hands. The tissue stretched, then ripped. A gleaming mass of yellowish white pushed its way through, its glossy surface painted with fine, bloody veins. For a moment, Seph thought she was looking at a giant egg, but then it…*rolled…*

A second later, there was a huge, bulging eyeball staring back at her, its lens a ghastly, translucent white, its pupil a cloudy, cavernous hole.

"That is *so* wrong," groaned Piper.

"If it's alive," reasoned Seph, struggling to wrap her head around what was going on, "why didn't the scythe destroy it?" It destroyed the incubus. It destroyed the shepherd. It didn't leave a trace of either of them behind.

"Because it's *not* a living thing," came the reply from behind them.

They turned around, surprised, to find Millard Carrol standing there, his hands casually crossed behind his back, smiling at them with that friendly smile that Seph knew so well.

"It's a patchwork of *thousands* of living things."

"Mr. Carrol?" said Seph, confused. What was her boss doing here?

"At its current level, the Grim Reaper's scythe can only destroy what it physically touches," he explained. "Arranged as they are, you couldn't possibly take them all out with a single swing."

"How…?" She shook her head, flustered. This didn't make any sense. "You know about the scythe?"

"Of course," he replied, as if they were talking about almost anything else at all, as if she'd just said, "You know about beekeeping?" or,

"You know about motorcycle maintenance?" As if the Hands of the Architects were some ordinary hobby that anybody might have an interest in.

"I don't understand. Did…? Are you…? I mean, did the Keeper send you?"

Millard Carrol didn't reply. He merely smiled his usual, friendly smile at her and waited for it to properly sink in.

Piper tugged at her sleeve. "Um, Persephone?" she whispered. "I don't think he's one of the good guys."

Seph shook her head again. "No…"

"I'm afraid she's right," he said.

She shook her head again. More firmly this time. "No!" It was some kind of misunderstanding. It had to be.

Piper glanced behind them. That freaky eyeball was still staring at them, but it hadn't crawled out of the gaping wound in the wall. And neither had any of the other unspeakable things that were lurking behind that bloody gash.

Was Seph's boss holding them back? Was he controlling them?

"You can't…" breathed Seph. "You just…*can't* be."

"Look at what he's done," said Piper. "This whole floor… He's not your boss. He's one of Tane's monsters."

"Close," said Millard Carrol. That friendly smile spread into a smug grin. In an instant his familiar, kindly face became something sinister. He shifted his weight and brought his hands out from behind his back.

The right one was on fire.

Seph stared at the blood-red flames dancing upon his upturned palm. She knew that blaze. She saw it ten months ago, just before it rejected them and flew away to find its chosen master. "Noah's Hammer…" she sighed.

Piper felt her heart sink. "Not one of Tane's monsters…" she amended. "You *are* Janon Tane."

"In the flesh."

Seph clenched her fists at her side and set her jaw. "What did you do to the real Mr. Carrol?"

"Sorry, Seph. It's not going to be that easy. Millard Carrol never existed. *I* was the one who hired you a year and a half ago."

She stared at him, confused. That didn't add up at all. Mr. Carrol had been with the company for years, long before she ever even applied for the job.

"You didn't actually think that Shawbeck girl was the only one capable of seeing what you really were, did you?"

Lyla Shawbeck. Or as Seph thought she'd known her, Amethyst Wilhoit. The two of them literally bumped into each other by chance at a mall in Madison when Seph was still only a freshman in college. Amethyst—or Lyla or Eloise or whichever of her countless names she was using now—was able to see a glimpse of the future from that chance encounter. She knew that Seph would one day become a seeker and she dedicated the next few years of her life to watching over her and protecting her from things just like Tane.

For her part, Seph didn't even remember that fateful encounter at the mall. She didn't recognize Amethyst the following year when she thought they were randomly paired together in the dormitory. She had no idea she was anything more than another typical student like herself. Not until that business with the first Hand forced her to reveal the truth.

"She thought she was so clever," gloated Tane, "but I'd already found you. I've been watching you for a *very* long time. Since you were just a small girl. I inserted myself into your life long before the idea ever crossed her simple little mind."

Seph stared at him. It was so strange, having a conversation like this. That was the face of the man who gave her the job she worked so hard for. The man who gave her a second chance when the universe snatched her first one away from her. The man she looked up to and strove to impress. That face summarized all of her ambitions, all of her hopes and dreams as an artist. How could it be the same face as the monster that sought the power of the Hands of the Architects to re-make the next universe into another living hell?

She shook her head. "No…" It just didn't make sense. "How could…?"

Tane's face changed. He grew thinner. His hair receded. His nose grew more pronounced. Even his eyes changed color.

"No…" said Seph. She could feel the weight of her emotions draining the strength from her body.

"You have a very promising future ahead of you," he told her, re-peating the very words he told her years ago, just before she graduated high school. "It's yours as long as you're willing to work for it. Don't disappoint me."

She shook her head again. No… It couldn't be. It just couldn't be.

"Um…" said Piper, confused. "Who're you supposed to be now?"

He was Otis Pealmonger, Seph's high school art teacher. Like Mr. Carrol, he was an early source of inspiration for her. He was one of the first people to truly appreciate her talent as an artist. For four years, he offered her praise and encouragement. He was the one who convinced her that a future in art was not only possible, but unavoidable if she only wanted it. He was the one who told her about the art program in

Madison. And he was the one who first told her about Vertical Design and how it could open the door to any career she could ever want as an artist.

He was the reason she was here today…

Right where he wanted her…

"What do you want?" demanded Piper.

"You know what I want," replied Tane.

"The third Hand," she said. It wasn't a guess. They knew all along that he was going to come for it eventually.

Piper clung to Seph's arm. She wasn't entirely sure what was going on here, but she was smart enough to realize that he was dishing out some seriously emotional psychological warfare. Seph was usually the strong one, but right now she was struggling. She needed her. "Forget it," Piper told him. "We won't help you find it."

"Are you sure about that?" He cocked his head to one side and fixed his gaze on Seph. He was Millard Carrol again, though she couldn't recall exactly when he changed back. "I mean, Hands of the Architects aside, you still have your future to think about."

She stared back at him, confused. Wait… Was he threatening to fire her?

He shook his head. A deep frown pulled at his face, as if he were wracked with pity for her. "You didn't *really* think you were talented enough to get this job all on your own, did you? Just because of your 'stellar first impression'? Really?"

This hit her like a punch in the gut. Her face flushed red, her heart plunged into her belly.

"I mean, you're an *okay* artist. But *everyone* else who applied for your job was way more qualified than you."

"He's lying," said Piper. "You're a great artist. He's just messing with your head."

Tane shrugged. "Why not? Believe what you want. You should know, though, that you've been getting paid all this time through a dummy account. No one ever actually entered you into the system when you started. There's not going to be any record of you ever working for Vertical Design. You either work for me or you start over from scratch and find out how unemployable you really are."

Seph's head was spinning. If he was telling the truth, then everything she'd worked for since she graduated college was wasted.

"If you don't want to cooperate with me, that's fine. But know that I have your very *future* by the throat."

"Don't listen to him, Persephone!" said Piper. "Use the scythe!"

Tane chuckled. "The scythe is useless against me. Sorry. The wielders of the Hands of the Architects can't harm each other."

Piper stared at the red flames swirling around his hand. "If that's true, then the hammer is useless against us, too!"

He gave his head a little tilt and said, "No… It's useless against *her*." He nodded at Seph. "*You*, I can turn inside out and make you spend the rest of your life carrying your guts around in a bucket if I so choose."

Piper made a terrified squeaking noise in her throat and took a step backward.

A shaft of water swirled between Seph's outstretched fists, forming the shaft of the scythe, which she held in front of her like a fighting staff. At one end, the water bubbled impatiently, eager to unleash the blade as well. "*You stay away from her*," she growled.

Tane's grin widened again, this time into something both gleeful *and* sinister. The blood-red flames around his hand swirled into something resembling a handle. At one end, the tips of the blaze spread apart, forming the fleeting shape of the underside of a huge, invisible hammer. "There's that fighting spirit."

"Shut up!"

But Tane didn't flinch. All around them, the hallway began to groan. The drywall broke and buckled. Dark blood drizzled down from each crack. The floor trembled beneath their feet. Ceiling tiles rattled above them.

"How long do you think you can protect her?" he asked. "When the walls break open and all the little nightmares come pouring out, how long do you think she'll last?"

Piper stepped closer to Seph, trying to hide herself behind the safety of the scythe.

Another of those terrified squeaks escaped her.

Seph glared at Tane. Tane stared back at her, unfazed. Neither spoke.

Then Tane sighed. The hallway stopped trembling. The hammer withdrew back into his hand. The red flames winked out. For a fleeting moment there was a soft curl of black smoke rising from his palm. Then even that was gone. He looked like the same Mr. Carrol she'd always known. "Listen," he said, his voice softer. "This doesn't have to be like those last two times. I can help you. We can find it together. No more monsters. No more traps. No more of the Keeper's nasty surprises. I can protect you from all of that. We'll just go out there and get it. And then you can both just go on with your lives."

"And just let you walk away with *two* of the Hands?" challenged Seph.

"What does it matter to you if I do or not?" he countered. "It's not like it's going to change anything in *this* world."

This caught her off guard. She lowered the scythe a little. "What?"

"The outcome of this struggle doesn't have the slightest effect on this world. Whether you claim the third Hand or I do...it won't change a single thing here today."

"But it'll affect the next one," reasoned Piper.

"Sure. In a few million years, maybe. When the Architects finish their work and go back to sleep. When they start ushering the last of the people through the gateways. What does it matter to you what happens when you're nothing more than a forgotten speck in the endless cycle of human history?"

Seph stared at him. That...wasn't an entirely absurd point, actually. But still, she couldn't just let the fate of the next universe fall into the hands of Janon Tane. It didn't matter how small they were in the grand scheme of things. The last time Tane claimed two of the Hands, he created a world where humanity very nearly met its extinction. She wouldn't be the reason that happened again, no matter what.

"Besides," he added. "You can't win this time. Not on your own. You already know about the bug."

Gispuknya...the apocalyptic bug god determined to bring an end to the cycle of the universe and usher in an eternity of death and decay utterly devoid of life. And a direct result of the horrors wrought upon mankind the last time Tane acquired two of the three Hands.

He turned away from them and crossed his arms behind his back again. "For some reason, Gispuknya's grown extremely powerful in this universe. You got lucky last time. You managed to cripple it for a while. But that's only going to make it come back stronger. And it's already had plenty of time to recover. I should've done this months ago, while it was still weak, but I had to keep an eye on that business in Hedge Lake... That could've seriously crinkled things if it'd gone differently..." He looked back at them. "But that's nothing you should concern yourselves with. The important thing is that the bug's still out there. And it won't underestimate you a second time. You *need* me if you want to survive what's coming."

"We'll take our chances," said Seph. "Thanks."

He turned away again and sighed a heavy, dramatic sigh. "That's your final answer, then?"

"It is," said Seph. She tried to sound tough, but she couldn't hide the waver in her voice. She was terrified. He had them trapped, after all. There was nowhere for them to go.

He nodded. "Okay then."

There was a loud "ding" from right behind them. They turned to find a pair of elevator doors sliding open where there most certainly wasn't an elevator just a moment ago.

"You're free to go, then."

Seph and Piper exchanged an uncertain glance.

"That's it?" said Seph.

"That's it," said Tane. "If you're so determined that you'd rather take on Gispuknya without my help, then so be it." He turned and faced them again. "It's not like I'm going to kill you. I need you alive if you're going to find the Hand for me. So I guess we're at an impasse."

Neither of them dared to move.

It was a trap. It had to be. He wouldn't really let them go. He was trying to get them to lower their guard. Either that or the elevator was another trap. It was probably going to come to life the moment they stepped inside and devour them both.

Whatever it was, they had no intention of falling for it.

And yet… What *were* they supposed to do? Just keep standing here?

Tane lifted a finger. "There is *one* more little thing, actually."

They didn't have time to get their guard up. An ugly, shriveled thing burst from the concrete between them and began shrieking in an eerie, wailing voice. It had a big head that was almost entirely mouth and a body that looked like a worm covered in hundreds of tiny, undulating arms.

Both of them screamed and jumped away from the freaky thing, precisely as Tane intended. As soon as their backs hit the wall, a multitude of slimy, gray hands burst from it and seized them, holding them both in place.

All around them, the walls began to crack and crumble. Blood oozed and dripped down the paint. Above them, the ceiling tiles began to stain red and drip.

"I get the feeling you girls aren't taking me seriously," said Tane as the shrieking monster that had burst from the floor flopped onto its side and began to wriggle blindly away. Its gaping mouth was still open, but its shrieking had already died into a creepy sort of agonized howl.

"*Get off me*!" screamed Seph as she struggled to pull her arms free of the monstrous hands. The scythe was gone, dropped when that freaky thing scared her, and she couldn't seem to make it form again with these things holding her.

"Relax," said Tane. "I didn't lie. I have every intention of letting you go." He took a step toward Piper. "But first, I just want to give this one a little gift. Something to remember me by. A reminder of how I offered to play nice and you refused." Fire enveloped his hand again as he reached toward her face.

Her blue eyes grew wide with terror as she realized what he meant to do, and the reflection of those blood-red flames danced in them.

"Get away from her!" screamed Seph. She squirmed around and seized one of the arms that were holding her by the wrist. The scythe's mysterious blade closed with her hand and sliced through it. But as quickly as the hand fell away and thudded against the floor, another one reached out from the bleeding wall and took its place.

As she grabbed hold of another one, she saw movement from the corner of her eye. She turned her head in time to see something long and wriggly squirming out of an oozing crack only inches from her head.

The sight made her scream.

And it wasn't alone. Lots of squirming things were scuttling across the floor of the hallway, and more were crawling out of the cracked walls and dropping from the crumbling ceiling with each passing second.

They weren't precisely bugs. Not any kind of bugs she'd ever seen before. They looked soft and fleshy. But they were more than enough to trigger her phobia of all things creepy-crawly. She screamed again and struggled harder.

The hands that held her were strong, but they were only hands. They were no match for the scythe. One by one, the blade shredded them, snipping them away as easily as trimming a hedge. Foul, gray fingers rained down onto the floor around her feet and then dissolved into dust on the concrete.

But each time she cut one away another took its place.

They were endless.

"I'm thinking we'll just burn off a little piece," decided Tane. "That should get the message across."

Piper stared at those burning fingers as they drew closer and closer to her face, her heart racing. She could already feel the heat on her cheek. She had no hope. She had no scythe to cut these awful hands away and she wasn't strong enough to pull herself free. Whatever they were attached to had a monstrous grip.

"*Leave her alone*!" screamed Seph.

The faster she cut the hands away, the faster more reached out to grab her.

It was designed that way, she realized. The hammer and the scythe couldn't harm each other, but Tane could use the hammer to keep her busy so that she couldn't use it to protect Piper. This was his way of showing them that they were no match for him. This was his way of proving that the scythe might be able to protect her, but it couldn't always protect the people she cared about.

"Just a little bit of that nice, smooth cheek," he went on. "Mess up that charming smile of yours. Maybe an eye. We'll just experiment a little, I think. Get creative. That *is* what we do here, after all. We make *art*."

Piper stared at those red flames, horrified. A tear streaked down her face. The heat from those blistering flames was already burning her. "Please stop!" she whimpered.

"I'm not going to lie," said Tane. "This is going to hurt. A lot."

Piper screamed.

Chapter 5

"*Don't you dare touch her!*" screamed Seph.

Tane pulled his hand back a little and glanced over at her as she struggled to cut herself free from the endless monsters inside the wall. His eyebrows crept up a little, interested. "It doesn't have to be this way. We don't have to be on different sides on this."

Piper wanted to tell him she'd never work with him, but her voice had left her. She could do nothing but stare at that blazing hand, terrified of what this monster was going to do to her.

Another tear spilled down her cheek.

She couldn't lift her arm high enough to shield her exposed face. Absently, she reached up and clawed at her chest instead, pulling at the fabric of her sweater.

The locket was there, lying against her skin, the one Annalisa gave her in Avelby, the one she swore would protect her from evil.

And she was pretty certain this guy counted as evil.

She didn't know how it could possibly save her at this point, but it was the only thing she had, the only chance she could even grasp at.

…if only she could reach it…

More slimy, severed hands fell to the floor around Seph's feet.

Just as quickly, more reached out and took their place.

She cried out, frustrated.

Tane sighed. "Such pointlessness. You don't even really understand what you're fighting for. You can't possibly. You're both just children. If only you knew the truth about the cycle. Then you'd see who the monsters really were. But it doesn't really matter what I say, does it? You're not going to listen to me because I'm the bad guy." He shook his head. "I wish I had time to show you the truth, but I don't." He reached out again with his blazing hand. "Pity, really."

Piper felt the heat against her soft skin. She turned her head away and squeezed her eyes closed. More tears streaked down her face. She felt them hang for a moment on her chin, then fall away.

Seph was screaming at him to stop, but he had no intention of stopping again. He was going to make his point, one way or another.

Piper's hand closed around the small, golden circle under her sweater. She could feel the warmth of it through the fabric. "Please…" she whimpered as the heat began to burn the tender flesh of her cheek.

With her other hand, she groped blindly at the wall, desperately searching for a way out that she knew wasn't there.

…except there *was* something there. She opened her eyes and saw it. A small, red switch. IN CASE OF EMERGENCY: PULL. She didn't waste time thinking about it. This was certainly an emergency. She jabbed her fingers into the slot of the handle and yanked it down.

A shrill alarm began to sound around them.

Overhead, the sprinklers burst open, raining cold water down onto them.

Tane squinted up at them, confused. The hammer's flames winked out.

Around them, the hallway blurred. A strange mist began to roll off every surface. Inside the walls, things began to shriek, as if the water from the sprinklers were causing excruciating pain to all of the creepy creatures trapped in there. Even the hands that held them suddenly lost their strength.

Piper jerked herself free and rushed to Seph, who was finally managing to break away from Tane's wall monsters.

"What is this?" demanded Tane. He lowered his face and squinted at Piper, instead. "How did you do that?"

Seph stepped in front of her and unfurled the scythe. Its watery blade shimmered in the steam that was rapidly filling the hellish corridor.

Piper took hold of her arm with one hand and pulled her backward, through the open elevator door. Her other hand she kept at her heart, clutching the fabric of her sweater and the little, circular pendant that hung there, unseen.

When they were inside the car, she let go of Seph and mashed the button for the ground floor.

Not surprisingly, nothing happened.

This was Tane's elevator. He made it. He was in control of it. And he wasn't going to let them leave until he was done with them.

He took a step toward them, his head twisting to one side, a sinister sneer replacing his smug grin. "*What is that?*" he demanded in an evil snarl of a voice.

Seph glanced over her shoulder. Even she didn't understand what was happening right now.

Piper wasn't sure what else to do. She reached into her sweater and pulled out the pendant. She held it in front of her, desperately hoping it would shield her from this monster's wrath.

Tane's eyes grew wide the moment he saw it. "No…"

She glanced down at it. Tane recognized her good luck charm?

"How do you have that?" he growled. "*Where did you get it?*"

"None of your business!" she told him.

She closed her hand around it, squeezing it. Was it her imagination, or did it suddenly get a lot warmer? It was almost hot.

The elevator dinged. The light on the ground floor button lit up.

The doors began to slide closed.

Tane took another step toward them, a great, fiery hammer suddenly blazing in his fists. "You've cheated!" he snarled.

Seph held the scythe up in front of her. Its handle and blade stretched out to match the width of the elevator, blocking the doors and forcing him to stop.

The hammer and the scythe countered each other. He couldn't stop them now.

"I quit, by the way!" shouted Seph as the doors slid all the way closed.

Then they were alone in the elevator and it was moving upward again.

Seph let go of the scythe and it vanished back into her hands. She turned and grabbed Piper's face, turning her head back and forth, looking her over. "Are you okay? Did he hurt you?"

"I'm fine."

But there was a bright red mark on her left cheek where the flames had begun to burn her. Another few seconds and…

She took off her wet glasses and looked closer. "That bastard."

"I'll be okay," Piper promised, pushing her away. "Really."

Seph squinted down at the pendant. "What *is* that thing?"

She held it up and looked at it. It wasn't even all that pretty. It was just a ring of rough, shiny gold with stones of various colors and sizes molded into it. "It's my good luck charm," she replied.

Seph remembered Piper showing it to her after they returned

home from Avelby last July. It didn't look like much to her, but she had no intention of turning down any kind of lucky charm. They were going to need all the luck they could get. But what happened in that hellish corridor went far beyond mere luck. "Well, don't lose it," she said.

"Don't worry." She slipped it back into her sweater. It still felt warm against her skin. Unnaturally warm, it seemed, as if it were giving off a strange sort of power. "What did he mean when he said we cheated?"

"Just that he's a sore loser, I'm sure." She began cleaning her glasses with the tail of her shirt. "I can't believe that jerk!"

Piper felt horrible for her. Those were some really mean things he said about her. "Jerk" was too nice a word for a monster like him. But she knew Seph better than anyone, and she didn't like to talk about things that upset her, so she didn't push the subject. Instead, she said, "So Tane made his move. That's what we were waiting for, right?"

Seph nodded. "That's what we were waiting for."

"So now we follow the plan?"

"Now we follow the plan."

Somewhere below them, Tane stood staring at the closed elevator doors, his teeth clenched, his thoughts racing. The hallway was dissolving into steam all around him. The water from the sprinklers that were never a part of his design continued to rain down on him, drenching him. It ran down his face and dripped from his chin. It soaked his nice suit. It sizzled in the flames that engulfed his hand.

"That wasn't supposed to happen," he growled.

That little test was supposed to show him whether or not his clueless employee had any *real* control over the scythe. Instead, it showed him something infuriatingly unexpected about the *other* little bitch.

He turned his head and spoke to the shadowy figure lurking in the steam behind him. “Change of plans. Bring me that wheel.”

The figure began to turn away.

“And summon the sisters.”

The figure paused for a moment, then it nodded again and vanished into the mist.

Chapter 6

The elevator didn't take them to another of Tane's freaky monster floors, so Piper's good luck charm still seemed to be working. Instead, it dropped them off right where they wanted to be.

Of course, the elevator had seemed to drop them off in the right place the first time, too. The short hallway leading between the elevator and the lobby was identical to the one on that other floor. It wasn't until they turned the corner that things turned weird. But this time the hallway wasn't deserted. Gina Sarrelli was standing there as the doors slid open, waiting to go up, as if everything were perfectly normal.

"Hi Seph," she said in her timid, sleepy voice. "Um…why are you *wet?*"

Seph looked down at herself. In all the confusion, she'd forgotten about being wet, much less that she was dripping all over the elevator's floor. "Um… Kind of a long story?"

"Okay…" said Gina, her small face understandably scrunched into an expression of befuddlement. "If you say so…"

Gina had a slight build and an even slighter demeanor. She'd come to work here just a few weeks after Seph started. She was a sweet girl, just a little younger than her, and painfully shy. Pretty, in an unassuming sort of way. Her personality never really let her stand out in group projects, but her artistic talent was always impressive.

They didn't have time to stop and chat. Tane wasn't likely to just let them leave. He was probably already on his way up after them. But she also didn't want to just shove past Gina and leave her here now that she knew the truth about Millard Carrol.

What she wanted to do was take her by the hand and run out the door with her. And it was taking every ounce of willpower she had not to do just that. But she couldn't imagine it being any safer for her to be dragged into whatever mess they were running headlong into than it would be to leave her here. She was probably much safer not knowing anything about any of this.

Besides, there was no guarantee Gina would come quietly. This was her job, after all. And a very good job. She wasn't likely to just abandon it because some crazy coworker told her she needed to leave. They couldn't risk making a scene. They had to get out of here quickly.

She forced herself to walk past her. "Sorry, we have to go. There's…uh…been an emergency."

"Oh," said Gina. "Okay." She reached out and stopped the elevator doors from closing. "Bye, then."

"You should probably take the stairs!" blurted Piper.

Gina turned her inquisitive eyes on her. "Why?"

"It was making some really weird noises while we were coming down. It sounds like something's wrong with it."

"Oh." She turned and looked into the elevator car, uncertain.

"It kind of freaked us out a little bit," continued Piper. It never failed to amaze Seph how quickly and naturally Piper could spin a lie and make it believable. She even managed to say that they were coming *down*, rather than up. Seph never would've been able to do that. Her brain just didn't work that quickly. All she ever managed to do was blubber like an idiot. "It's probably nothing, but I wouldn't risk it if you don't have to."

"Okay," said Gina, withdrawing her hand and letting the doors slide shut. "I'll take the stairs then."

"I'll, uh…let someone know about it on my way out?" tried Seph, glancing up at Piper.

"Yeah," said Piper, every bit as confident and convincing as Seph was awkward. "Like I said, it's probably nothing. But it never hurts to be cautious."

"Okay," said Gina as she pushed open the door to the stairwell instead. "See you later, then."

Probably not, thought Seph as a sharp pang of sadness passed through her. It didn't look like she worked here anymore. There was a lot to regret about that alone, but Gina might've been her favorite of all the people she knew here. Aloud, however, she only said, "Yeah. See you."

For a moment, she stood there, watching after her, still fighting the urge to run after her. Then something inside the elevator slammed against the closed doors.

Piper pulled on her arm. "We have to go!"

Seph nodded. She knew Piper was right. The couldn't stay. But she found herself caught between two fears. The first, of course, was her fear of whatever monstrosity had just appeared inside the elevator without either the intelligence to open the doors or the need to call the car to whatever floor it originated from. The second was her fear for her friend, who hadn't yet had time to reach the second-floor landing.

Would the monsters that were pursuing them harm Gina if they stumbled across her? Would Tane take out his anger on her because she was her friend? It wouldn't be the first time someone she cared about was threatened.

As she turned away, she prayed that she was making the right decision leaving her behind.

The two of them fled from the hallway as the pounding inside the elevator grew more insistent.

They *did* seem to be where they wanted to be, at least. The front entrance of the building was right where it belonged, complete with receptionist's desk and matching receptionist.

Her name was Stacy Getledder. She was rather plain-looking, with a slightly too-big nose and eyes that seemed just a little too close together. She was the polar opposite of soft-spoken Gina: loud, boisterous and impossible to overlook. She was one of the gabbiest people Seph had ever known. She couldn't count the times she'd gotten caught in some ridiculously endless conversation on her way out the door.

She was a nice person, though, and she hated the thought of being rude to her, but she had no intention of stopping for a chat today. She'd already wasted too much time with Gina.

But Stacy didn't try to talk to Seph. Instead, she called out to Piper: "Are you Miss Holleworth?"

Piper stopped and looked back at her, surprised.

"You have a phone call."

"I do?" She stood there, confused. "Why would I have a phone call?"

Seph stared at her. That was strange. How would anyone have known to even look for her here?

"It sounds like an emergency," said Stacy, holding out the phone for her to take. "Something about your sister?"

Piper felt her heart flutter. "Penny?" She hurried over to the desk and reached for the phone.

"Pea! No!" shouted Seph.

Before Piper could take the phone, Stacy dropped it and launched herself over the desk. Her unremarkable face unfolded itself into something with far too many eyes and teeth and her hands became clusters of long, worm-like things ending in slimy, tooth-lined suckers.

Piper screamed and jumped back.

The Reaper's blade whistled through the air.

With a horrid screech, the monster that was once the receptionist melted into nothing and vanished.

Piper stood a few feet away, her heart still pounding, staring at the long, clean slash that ran down the middle of the wooden desk.

"Oh god…" gasped Seph. "I just reaped Stacy."

Piper stared at her, her heart still racing, unsure what to say. Personally, she wasn't that unhappy to see freaky Stacy go away.

Was it really Stacy? The same Stacy who told her in excruciating detail about the health problems of her dachshund, Chester, and her constant quarrels with her nosy next-door neighbor, Mr. Habershein, and her endless struggle to find a decent optometrist? Was every long-winded story a part of the lie, like Mr. Carrol? Or was there a real Stacy Getledder out there somewhere?

Was *anyone* in this building who they said they were?

She turned her wide eyes on Piper. "We've got to get out of here before I have to reap someone else I know!"

If this was the kind of people Seph knew, Piper didn't care for the idea of hanging around until more of them showed up, either.

But before either of them could move, a noise broke the silence.

It was the sound of the elevator dinging.

A moment later, they heard the patter of approaching footsteps.

"My Jeep's parked right out front!" squeaked Piper, already backing toward the door.

Seph nodded. "Uh huh."

"Come on!"

As Piper opened the door, a strange creature peered around the corner at them. It had a big, round, bald head and a face that was almost entirely comprised of a huge mouth with large, blocky teeth. The rest of its features, its eyes, nose and ears, were all tiny. Even its lips seemed too small for that enormous mouth. They were stretched tight around those teeth in a ghastly, exaggerated grin.

The two of them stood in the doorway, staring back at it, too surprised to even run away.

"What…am I looking at…?" asked Piper.

Seph, once again, had no answer for her.

The thing came around the corner and started loping toward them. It was only between three and four feet tall, with short little legs and arms and a stubby little torso, but its hands and feet, like its head and mouth, were grotesquely exaggerated, as was its belly. It drooped like a heavy, fleshy sack and swung back and forth as it moved toward them. Its flesh was pale pink with large splotches of bright red that looked like burns.

Seph held up her hands. The scythe's handle stretched between them. Its glistening blade curled into existence.

Then it fell apart and splashed onto the carpet at her feet.

"What the hell?" She looked down at her hands. Like in the basement, the water that enveloped them looked strangely muddy. But when she lifted them for a closer look, it was perfectly clear again.

It was probably just the lighting.

She looked up at the approaching monster again and found that three more had rounded the corner behind it.

"Yep!" yelped Piper. "Time to go!" She grabbed Seph by the arm and dragged her through the door and out into the bright sunlight.

Chapter 7

It was a lovely day out for early May. A little windy, but warm. Perfect weather, Piper supposed, for fleeing for their lives.

She unlocked the doors of her Jeep Grand Cherokee and quickly climbed behind the wheel. "What *are* those things?"

"Stop asking me what things are!"

"*Sorry*!"

She looked over her shoulder as she fastened her seatbelt, expecting those awful monsters to come running out of the building after them. Instead, they were all standing behind the doors, their huge hands, noses and bellies pressed against it. One of them was licking the glass with an obscenely wide tongue.

"That's not right…" groaned Seph.

Piper shifted the Jeep into gear and pulled away from the curb, her gaze repeatedly shifting to the rearview mirror.

The little monsters didn't chase after them. Were they not able to leave the building for some reason? Or did Tane stop them from running outside so they wouldn't cause a scene?

Did they really escape? Or did Tane let them get away? With the power of Noah's hammer at his fingertips, the entire building was literally his to command. It possessed the ability to change the form of anything in existence, all the way down to the atomic level. If he'd wanted, he could've turned all the exits into brick walls. Or all the carpets into boiling tar. Or the very air into poison. So why were they allowed to run through those doors?

She hated to think it, but that was entirely too easy.

Seph looked down at her hands, at the water that swirled around her fingers. Why did the scythe keep falling apart like that? Was she doing something wrong? She didn't understand.

There was *so much* she didn't understand.

"I don't like this."

"I don't think *anyone* would like this very much," replied Piper.

"About Stacy, I mean."

"That she was a *monster*?"

"That she knew to trick you by bringing up your sister," said Seph. "That seems a little strange, doesn't it?"

"Wouldn't anybody be concerned if they heard there was an emergency and their sister was involved?"

"Well yeah, but how'd she even know you had a sister?"

Piper reached up and pinched her lower lip as she considered this. Her eyes narrowed. Her eyebrows scrunched together. Seph called it her "thinking face."

"Why not your mom? Or your dad? I don't feel like she was guessing. It was like she knew the best way to make you drop your guard."

Piper glanced over at her. "You think they've been watching us?"

"It makes sense, I guess. I mean, obviously Tane's known who we are this whole time." She shook her head. She still couldn't believe that Tane was Mr. Carrol. *And* Mr. Pealmonger. It was mad. It was like a crappy plot twist in an even crappier movie. The whole thing was just stupid. If he was that close to her this whole time, why did he wait until now to reveal himself?

But she supposed it was pointless to try to understand the mind of a monster.

Piper turned down one of the side streets.

"Do you know where you're going?"

"I think so. I mean, I know where it is, but I always get a little confused on the streets in this part of town."

Seph knew exactly what she was talking about. The streets behind the Vertical Design building ran kind of wonky for some reason. She'd gotten confused on a number of occasions trying to avoid the Trawling Road traffic on her way home. But they needed to find Huntington Street. And this was the shortest route.

Piper wondered how long Seph thought it would take for Tane to regroup and come after them again, but she didn't get the chance to ask her. At that moment, one of those fat little monsters from the lobby came out of nowhere and threw itself onto the Jeep's hood. They both screamed as the little, naked beast rolled toward them and splattered itself against the windshield, its arms and legs splayed apart, its bloated, sagging belly shoved to one side and both its grinning, toothy face and hideous, exposed genitals squashed against the glass on full display before them.

"*Oh my god!*" screamed Seph, horrified.

Piper jerked the wheel left, then right, veering into the other lane, then back across and up onto the curb before straightening out again.

Seph grabbed her seatbelt and held on, still screaming.

The obscene little beast slid to one side, then the other, its fat, stubby hands groping for something to hold on to, its oversized teeth snapping pointlessly at the glass. Then, finally, it tumbled over the side and vanished.

"*That was highly inappropriate*!" shrieked Piper.

"*Look out*!"

Another of the foul little monsters appeared in front of them, seemingly from thin air. It stood in the middle of the street, those huge, square teeth looking like a big, stupid grin. If Seph had seen one of these things in the movies, she would've found it utterly absurd. Lazy and uncreative, she would've called it. But here in the real world, there was something astoundingly *creepy* about these awful things, as if they'd stepped right out of some forgotten nightmare.

This one was doing its best impression of a goalie. It was holding its freakish hands out at its sides and shuffling back and forth in the middle of the street as if it meant to *catch* the forty-five-hundred-pound vehicle that was speeding toward it. Its grotesque belly was swinging to and fro with the motion, like a pendulum on some hideous, flabby clock.

"Out of the way, you stupid, ugly troll!" shouted Piper, blaring her horn at it.

"Just run the stupid thing over!" yelled Seph.

She grimaced at the thought of one of these nasty things smeared all over her Jeep's undercarriage. "Ew!"

"It's either that or stop!"

Something heavy thudded against the roof. Piper screamed and looked back over her shoulder. "*Are they falling out of the sky*?"

A loud thump, followed by two hard bumps signaled the results of the goalie's absurd bluff.

"Oh my gosh!"

"Served it right!" snapped Seph. She leaned against the window to see if she could see what was on the roof in the side mirror, but as soon as her forehead touched the glass, a hideous, grinning face dropped from above and slammed against the other side, wrenching yet another scream from her.

Piper jerked the wheel again, veering back and forth. But this monster was more persistent than the first one. It clung to the mirror with one meaty hand and the luggage rack with the other as its over-sized head banged against the glass.

A fourth monster appeared on top of a parked minivan and tried to jump onto the Jeep as it sped by. Piper cried out, startled, and swerved away from it, so that the stupid creature missed the Jeep and instead belly-flopped onto the pavement. The same motion caused her to scrape the side of a parked box truck on the other side, taking out both the third monster and her passenger-side mirror. "*My car*!"

"Just keep driving!"

An intersection loomed ahead. "Which way?" asked Piper. In all the excitement, she couldn't seem to remember.

"Right!" said Seph. Then, "*No*! *I mean left*!"

Piper had already begun the turn, now she slammed on the brakes and jerked the wheel to the left, making the tires squeal.

Something struck the back of the Jeep and Piper looked up to see another hideous, grinning face staring back at her through the window. It was clinging to the rear windshield wiper and the spoiler and trying to figure out how to bite its way through the safety glass.

"*Where do they keep coming from*?"

She stomped on the gas pedal and sped onward, but the monster refused to let go.

"Turn right at the stop sign!" instructed Seph.

Piper didn't bother stopping for the sign.

"Left again!"

"Got it!" She swerved onto the next street, straightened the wheel and looked back to find that the monster was climbing up onto the roof. Its flabby belly was just disappearing from sight. "Hold onto something!"

"What?"

Piper stomped hard on the brake. The Jeep shuddered to a violent stop. Both of them were thrown against their seatbelts. And the foul little monster atop the vehicle flew forward, tumbled down the wind-shield, across the hood and onto the pavement. Then she stomped the gas pedal again. The Jeep lurched forward. The thuds of the tires were simultaneously sickening and satisfying.

"That's for messing up my car!"

"Jeez!" gasped Seph.

"What?"

"Nothing!" She sat up, adjusting her seatbelt. "Right at the next intersection."

"Got it." Piper glanced up at her rearview mirror. She could see a blotchy, pink and red lump lying in the street behind her and that was all. For the moment, they seemed to have lost the rest of the horrid pack, so she slowed down and ran the next stop sign at a much safer speed than she did the last few.

"Where do you think they went?" asked Seph, uncertain.

"Maybe we lost them?" hoped Piper. "I mean they seem pretty stupid."

But the words were barely out of her mouth when another one dropped out of the sky and buried the head of an axe in the Jeep's hood.

"*Not as stupid*!" screamed Piper.

"*Where did it get an axe*?" shrieked Seph.

The ugly little creature rose to its feet and began yanking at the axe's handle, trying to dislodge it from the hood.

"*Get rid of it!*" said Seph.

"*I'm trying!*" Piper swerved hard to one side, then the other, but the stuck axe was acting as a handle, allowing the beast to hold on. "Get *off*, you little freak!"

Another of the big-mouthed monsters landed on the roof with a heavy thump and then dropped down onto the windshield, where it immediately began attacking the glass with a stapler.

"*Where are they finding this stuff?*" squealed Piper.

Another monster dropped from the sky as she swerved into the other lane and back, this one absurdly armed with a large potted plant. Unfortunately for it, its aim was off. It missed the Jeep entirely and instead thudded onto the street directly in front of them, plant and all, and was promptly crushed under the tires like the two before it.

"Knock it off!" Piper screamed at the one banging on her windshield.

She turned on the windshield wipers and the little beast grabbed one and tried to bite it. As soon as both its hands were visible, she slammed on the brakes again and sent it sliding down the glass and across the hood, where it grabbed the axe-wielding monster's leg and bit it.

Up until now, the one with the axe had been completely unshakeable thanks to its grip on the handle and the fact that the axe was lodged in the Jeep's hood. But now it let go of the axe handle and attacked the other monster.

Piper stomped the accelerator again and both of the little creatures were thrown across the hood, against the windshield and then off the vehicle altogether.

"Huntington Street is right up there on the left!" said Seph.

"I see it!"

Seph turned and looked behind them. The two monsters were already back on their feet and loping after them, but they were too slow to catch them at this speed. She turned her attention up to the sky instead, to see if any more of the little freaks were raining down on them.

She didn't see any falling monsters, but for just an instant, she thought she saw something else. An enormous shadow loomed over them, something that wasn't there before…

And it wasn't there now, either. It was only for that one, fleeting instant. A fraction of a frantic heartbeat. A blink of an eye.

And now it was gone again.

Piper swerved hard onto Huntington Street and then pushed the pedal all the way down, letting the accelerator climb. "Did we lose them?"

Seph stared through the back window, her eyes peeled for any kind of movement, but Huntington Street was as deserted as it always was. "I think they're gone now." She kept watching for few more seconds, just to be sure, then she faced forward again and finally dared to relax a little.

She took off her cardigan and laid it in the seat beside her, then turned up the blower on the Jeep's air conditioner as she watched the road that stretched out in front of them.

Huntington Street had already transformed. The buildings had vanished. The sidewalks had ended. In spite of the fact that it was located deep within the city limits of Cakwetak, the city street had become a rural highway. The first of a great many trees had already begun to spring up here and there. In another few minutes, they'd be speeding through a pitch-black forest beneath an impenetrable canopy of deep branches.

"My car…" whined Piper.

Seph stared at the axe still lodged in the Jeep's hood. It looked like a fireman's axe, fairly small, with a bright, red blade. Where did the little monster get it? And why was this one so much better armed than its stapler- and plant-wielding comrades? "Sorry, Pea…"

"And my mirror…"

Seph grimaced. She'd already forgotten about the mirror. And she was quite sure the damage went considerably further than that. She could still hear the sound of that truck grinding down the length of the Grand Cherokee's side.

She knew how she felt. It wasn't that long ago that another monstrous creature banged up her pickup truck. And after she'd taken such good care of it, too. It still had those dents in the fender and tailgate.

Piper glanced over at her. "So…was that 'according to plan'?"

"The plan was to wait for Tane to make his move and then get to the nearest fringe road entrance." She turned and looked back once more to make sure those ugly little monsters still weren't chasing them. It shouldn't have been possible for anything to follow them here. The weird physics of the fringe roads prevented it. But she didn't dare make any assumptions. "We found the fringe road entrance and we didn't die. I'd say that's mission accomplished."

Piper nodded. "I guess so…"

Seph sighed and settled into her seat again. "Now we go see Amethyst."

Chapter 8

There was a trick to using the fringe roads. If you knew the trick, and were able to find a fringe road entrance—which was, itself, a lofty feat since most people couldn't see them—you could travel hundreds of miles in a fraction of the time it would ordinarily take. However, if you were to locate a fringe road entrance and then proceed *incorrectly*, you would only sink gradually into the strange depths of this dark forest, all the way down to where the monsters lurked.

The first time Seph and Piper ever used a fringe road, no one had bothered to tell them how it worked. They spent hours descending deeper and deeper into the forest. They were attacked by a tusker. They ran out of gas. And they were very nearly eaten by a fringe cat.

The trick was to clearly envision your destination and then find an emotional anchor to hold on to. Something precious to you. Something you desperately wouldn't want to lose. Something important enough to come back to. In Seph's case, the memory of her father was her emotional anchor. For Piper, it was her big sister, Penny, who now lived halfway around the world.

In less than an hour, the forest of the fringe road began to break apart and endless, rolling fields spread out before them. A few minutes more and they were driving through the back fields of Shawbeck Ranch in Northwest Nebraska, some eight or nine hundred miles from where they started in Cakwetak.

Jarrett Burchett, dressed in his cowboy attire, was standing in the driveway, securing the doors on a large livestock trailer when he caught sight of them. Immediately, he sprinted to the gate and opened it for them, letting them through.

Seph rolled down the window as Piper pulled up beside him.

"Hi, Jarrett," said Piper.

He tipped his cowboy hat at her and said, "Miss Holleworth," which for some reason made Piper giggle.

Seph rolled her eyes. "Is Amethyst here?"

"She's in the house. You girls okay?"

"We're fine. But we ran into a little trouble."

"I can see that," he replied, his eyes lingering on the axe handle sticking out of the hood. "Go on in. Make yourselves at home. Miss Lyla'll prob'ly be in the kitchen."

Piper pulled through and then parked in front of the porch while Jarrett closed the gate behind them.

On the other side of that gate, the road that brought them here had vanished. There was nothing over there but open fields as far as the eye could see. Many fringe roads exited there. Huntington Street in Cakwetak and Old Castle Road in Fathom Lake were only two of them. But the individual fringe roads were all one-way. To get back onto those strange paths, you had to go several miles down the highway to find Ugly Orchard Road.

The world, as it had turned out, was a very strange place, in lots of very strange ways.

Jarrett told her that she'd find Amethyst inside, but Seph didn't need to go looking for her. As soon as she stepped out of the vehicle, she found herself enveloped in her old roommate's arms (and practically smothered in her obnoxiously large breasts). Her smell was strangely nostalgic. Her perfume. Her conditioner. Her hand lotion. Her favorite brand of fabric softener. A second ago, she didn't even remember Amethyst *having* a smell, much less one so warm and familiar that it seemed to carry her back to a time before the world was weird and scary and enormous beyond scope.

"I'm so happy to see you again! You aren't hurt, are you?"

"I'm fine," mumbled Seph from the depths of her cleavage. "And you saw me, like, two weeks ago."

"It's been at least a month," insisted Amethyst.

Seph pushed her to arm's length and looked away. "Whatever."

Amethyst stood there for a moment, her hands resting on Seph's shoulders, looking her over as her long, brown hair fluttered about her lovely face in the breeze. She was dressed a lot like Jarrett. She wasn't wearing a hat, but she had the cowboy boots, blue jeans and a western shirt that she filled out *far* better than he did. "Look at you! You're not wearing all black!"

She glanced down at herself, embarrassed. Hidden under her cardigan had been a light, boat-neck shirt with three-quarter sleeves. It was *barely* not black. It was dark purple. "I *do* wear things other than black, you know? God, you sound just like Pea."

It wasn't like she was running around in a girly, yellow sundress or something…

Amethyst stared at her. "You're still mad at me, aren't you?"

Seph had to force herself to meet those pretty eyes. She couldn't help it. A hug from Amethyst was once one of the most natural things in the world. (She'd always been a hugger, after all.) But it didn't feel natural anymore.

Hugs were for people without open wounds, and hers hadn't finished healing yet.

"I'm working on it. Really."

She smiled. "That's all I can ask for."

Seph spent a lot of time being angry with Amethyst. She did, after all, lie to her for the first four years they knew each other. And not just about some little, pointless thing. Almost everything about her was a lie.

She thought she was just another college girl like herself, if an obnoxiously attractive one. She was a loveable goofball with strange, new-age ideas about karma and emotional energy and the power of clean auras. But her name wasn't really Amethyst Wilhoit. She wasn't from Green Bay. She didn't believe in any of that karmic nonsense. She wasn't even really vegan! All that stuff was just an elaborate lie to cover up how weird her *real* life was. In reality, she was the enigmatic head of a mysterious ranch hundreds of miles away where alien creatures roamed the otherworldly fields and the Grim Reaper's scythe slumbered beneath a transdimensional vault at the crossroads between multiple universes.

Oh, and she also had the power to glimpse the future and open portals to nearby, flying-worm-infested dimensions, just in case the whole otherworldly ranch thing wasn't odd enough.

Seph had every right to be angry. It wasn't as if she was merely an acquaintance. Amethyst passed herself off as her friend while lying about almost every detail about her life. She'd trusted her.

But in the end, that anger turned out to be a terrible mistake. If she'd only made an effort to forgive her and move on, the incubus that caused all that trouble back in July might not have been able to fool her so easily. A single phone call would've told her that Amethyst never sent someone named Ian Heffler to help her locate the second Hand of the Architects.

But she didn't want to talk to Amethyst.

After the ordeal in Avelby, however, when the strange, body-snatching creature that called itself Warner Harr was finally able to return to the ranch and let her know what had been going on, Amethyst immediately raced to Cakwetak and, with tears in those pretty eyes, literally *begged* her for a chance to talk.

Seph wanted to shrug it off as just another of her countless lies. She was obviously a gifted actress, after all. But she really didn't think it was an act. And she'd almost lost her mother that weekend. She found that she simply didn't have the heart to say no.

Amethyst swore that day that she wouldn't let something like this happen again. And she was determined to start by making up for all the lies she told. "I can't tell you everything," she'd said. "There're things I can't tell you for one reason or another. Things that I promised never to speak of. Things that would put you in danger. Things that're just too complicated to explain. And…while I'm being honest, things that I'm ashamed of. But I promise to be honest about everything I *can* tell you from now on."

And that didn't seem like a bad deal. She'd already discovered on her own that ignorance sometimes really was bliss. She could accept that there were things she was better off not knowing. As long as she was up-front about it.

She was still angry. But the fact was that the anger had gotten old. It'd gotten tiring. And she couldn't deny that she missed her friend.

And so she was working on it.

Maybe someday she'd find a way past the bitterness.

"Aw…" pouted Piper as she stood looking at the damage left by the box truck. The paint had been scraped away almost the entire length of the vehicle. Not a single piece of the passenger-side body had been spared. "My car…"

"Sorry, Pipe," said Seph. It was considerably worse than the dents the stupid tusker left in her truck way back on their first adventure together.

"What happened?" asked Amethyst, her eyes drawn to the axe still sticking out of the Jeep's hood.

"Monsters happened," pouted Piper. "Ugly little *troll* things with big heads and even bigger teeth."

Amethyst frowned. "This'll probably sound messed up, but that doesn't narrow it down much."

She glanced over at her, surprised. But on second thought, she realized she was right. Given that the primary business of Shawbeck Ranch revolved around exotic creatures from countless other worlds, she wasn't remotely surprised that "troll things" and "big heads and even bigger teeth" wasn't enough for her to identify the monsters that attacked them in Cakwetak.

"I might be able to patch some of that up for you," said Jarrett as he stepped up beside them and looked over the damage.

"You can do that?" asked Piper.

"There's not much Jarrett can't do," said Amethyst, proudly puffing her already impressive chest.

"I expect I won't have time for it today," he said, "but I bet I can patch it up pretty nice for you. Not perfect, prob'ly, but definitely not so noticeable. In the meantime, you can borrow the ranch truck."

"That won't be necessary," said Amethyst. "We'll be taking my car when we leave here."

"We?" said Seph.

"I'm not leaving your side today," she said. "I owe it to you after the way I botched everything last time."

Seph glanced at Piper, who just shrugged at her.

Last time wasn't really Amethyst's fault. If anything, it was Seph's fault for not getting over being mad and just calling her. She knew that.

Or maybe it was Warner's fault for not checking in regularly. It shouldn't have gone unnoticed that he'd been trapped inside that revenant for *three weeks*. That was more than a little careless of him.

A series of very strange cries erupted from the parked livestock trailer. It sounded a little like two children shrieking at each other, only louder and with a strange sort of almost-mechanical warble in their voices.

"That's one of our chackteets," said Jarrett.

"Just one?" Asked Seph. It sounded like there were at least two of whatever they were in there.

"Chackteets have two respiratory systems," he explained. "So they can carry on in *stereo*."

"That's…really *weird*…" said Piper.

The thing let out another pair of loud shrieks and the trailer rocked back and forth as it shifted around.

"She's not happy about her trip to Wisconsin," said Amethyst.

Seph glanced over at her, surprised. "You're sending that thing to Wisconsin?" She wasn't sure she liked the idea of *any* of Shawbeck Ranch's oddities being exported to her home state.

"To Weapony Island," said Amethyst. "We have a client there who runs a facility suitable for studying our…*uncommon* varieties of livestock."

"In exchange for getting to study our animals," explained Jarrett, "he provides veterinary services. And this one's been acting a bit hostile toward the rest of its herd lately."

Amethyst turned and looked at him. "We don't have much time.

Please find Reid and Vernon and start getting things ready, just like we planned."

"Yes ma'am." Jarrett gave her a nod and then set off toward the back of the property without hesitation.

Piper stared after him as he went. "I like it when he talks," she sighed.

"Ugh," groaned Seph.

Jarrett was in charge of the daily upkeep of the ranch. Besides Amethyst, herself, it was just Jarrett and his younger brother, Reid, Vernon Sealtor, the animal expert, and grouchy old Mr. Hallet. Seph had no idea how the five of them managed this entire ranch on their own. It seemed like the sort of job that would require at least a few dozen people, given the massive size of the place. But what did she know about it?

Amethyst smiled at Piper. "It's good to see you again, by the way."

Piper smiled back at her. Unlike Seph, she never knew her before she was Miss Lyla Shawbeck. She never had any reason to dislike her. "You too."

Amethyst crossed her arms in front of her. Her smile faded. "So Tane made his move…" she said, her gaze drifting toward the axe again. "Tell me exactly how it went."

The time they'd spent with Amethyst these past ten months weren't only about mending fences. It was also about preparing for the inevitable. During that time, Amethyst told them everything she knew about Tane, which wasn't a lot, unfortunately. And she taught them all she knew about the fringe roads, which was considerably more. She showed them all the places in Cakwetak where they could access Huntington Street as well as several other fringe road entrances in the surrounding areas. She even gave them practice using the fringe roads. The plan that brought them here, simple as it may have been, was hers. It was how they knew the shortest route here.

"Not as well as we'd hoped, honestly," replied Seph.

"He tried to burn my face off," pouted Piper, hugging herself against the frightful memory of those burning fingers hovering before her. She could still feel the heat from that hellish fire on her cheek.

"Oh no!" gasped Amethyst, she reached out and took hold of her face, much as Seph had done in the elevator, turning her head this way and that in her hands, taking a good look at her and that painful-looking red mark on her cheek.

"I'm fine," Piper assured her, her voice muffled a little because Amethyst was smushing her face. "He didn't hurt me."

"Not for a lack of trying, though," growled Seph.

"She was never in any real danger," came a new voice.

The three of them turned to find a smiling old woman in a long, blue skirt and a white sweater jacket walking toward them, her long, gray hair tied into a familiar braid and slung over her shoulder.

"Annalisa!" said Piper, delighted.

"She arrived just a few minutes ahead of you and told me you were coming," said Amethyst. "Her and another one showed up in the kitchen. Scared me half to death…"

Annalisa smiled. She never took her eyes off Piper. "You still have what I gave you, don't you?" she asked.

Piper reached into her sweater and pulled out the pendant. "I keep it on me all the time. Just like you told me."

"That thing really *is* a lucky charm," said Seph, remembering how Piper had escaped Tane by setting off a *fire alarm* of all things.

Amethyst squinted at it. "Wait… Let me see that." She took the pendant between her thumb and forefinger and leaned close to it, examining it. Then she looked up at Annalisa, her eyes wide. "Is that…?"

Annalisa smiled a wicked grin. "It is."

"But that's…"

"Cheating," she said, nodding. "Yes. It is." Then she giggled like a young girl. "And I'll bet old Tane is just mad as hell about that right about now."

Seph stared at the pendant. Tane said something about cheating, too. And he *was* mad as hell. "What is it?"

Annalisa was positively beaming when she replied, "It's the third Hand of the Architects."

Chapter 9

Although they'd now missed lunch, it wasn't so late that Piper had begun to get sick. If she let herself get that far along, then her table manners changed. Gone were those tiny, polite bites and the gratuitous dabbing with her napkin. Hell, she barely even bothered with her fork. Meat-deprived Piper was a vegan's nightmare. She was a savage. She could wolf down a cheeseburger or strip a steak to the bone in seconds.

It wasn't that she was utterly without manners at those times. Seph had known lots of *guys* who ate like that all the time. It was merely magnified by the juxtaposition of her usual, girlish personality and the experience of seeing her obliterate a plate of chicken wings like a school of starving piranhas.

It never failed to amuse Seph when it happened.

This wasn't one of those times, and yet there Piper sat, with barbeque sauce smeared almost from ear to ear, gnawing on a rib bone.

"Stop watching me eat!"

Seph chuckled. "Sorry."

"It's not my fault! They're just *so good*!"

"They're heavenly!" agreed Annalisa, who was almost as messy as Piper. Both of her wrinkled cheeks were smeared with sauce.

"Mr. Hallet's very proud of that recipe," said Amethyst. She was eating one, too, but she was managing it without making a mess.

It was still weird to see her enjoying meat. Apparently, she thought pretending to be vegan would make the made-up "Amethyst-from-Green-Bay" more believable. It went well with the whole new-age, emotional energy shtick she was going for.

She'd pretended to be a lot of things she wasn't. She wasn't really attending graduate school those last few months they lived together. She was either coming here to the ranch or else hanging out in her favorite coffee shops. In fact, she'd only actually attended any undergraduate classes during the two years they lived together in the dorms, and only then because it was the only practical way for her to live there.

"He certainly should be," said Annice as she dabbed at her mouth with a napkin. "We'll have to ask him if he'd be interested in providing some for our next charity dinner. These would fly off the buffet table."

"I'll have to mention it to him when he gets back," said Amethyst. "He's away on an errand right now."

"Please do."

They met Annalisa and Annice last summer while they were searching for Noah's hammer. They looked like sweet, ordinary old ladies. And for all practical purposes, they were just that. They were some of the nicest people Seph had ever met. They even ran a fairly large charity organization called The Anns Hearts Foundation that helped children in need all over the world. But the truth was that they weren't actually human. They were Ahns, also known as "little souls" or "whisper people" or "feints." They also sometimes called themselves "Anns," and all of them had chosen individual names containing "ann" somewhere in them, which Piper thought was positively adorable. Their appearance was nothing more than a clever disguise. Beneath those kindly old faces lurked unspeakable monsters capable of shredding and devouring *other* monsters (and probably humans, too, if they so took a notion).

There were dozens of Ahns throughout the world, all of them working tirelessly toward a greater good. And they didn't have to appear as old women. Another Ahn, a spunky and energetic old woman named Louann, once told her that they could be almost anything they wanted to be and had, at different points in history, spent time as little girls, beautiful women and even hideous hags. (She claimed that they were the original inspiration for the ugly old witches made famous in all sorts of literature, from the wicked witches of Oz to the weird sisters of *Macbeth*, and Seph found little reason to doubt her.)

After Seph and Piper helped them destroy the black council and take back their "playground," the Ahns returned the favor by traveling to Cakwetak and nursing Seph's mother back to health. It was then, as they were all gathered together in that cramped apartment, that they promised to watch over them while they waited for Tane to make his move.

It was also around that time that the Ahns began working with Amethyst and Shawbeck Ranch in preparation for this day.

"I can't believe Tane was *your boss*," said Amethyst. "Of all the people…"

"He said he's been watching me for years," said Seph. "Just like you did."

Amethyst managed to look ashamed, if only for a second.

"Except I guess he's been watching me since I was little. He was also my art teacher in high school! How messed up is *that*? I mean, he's been manipulating my life since before I can remember!"

"His cleverness can't be underestimated," said Annalisa. "He's one of the Great Enemy's Twelve Teeth. He's been around in some incarnation or another almost since the dawn of time. He's practically a god."

"But he's not infallible," said Annice. "He's only once managed to take control of two of the Hands. And we're pretty clever ourselves. We knew he was probably going to be *someone* in that building. And probably someone in a position of power directly over her."

Seph looked up at her, surprised. "You did?"

"Well Vertical Design *is* under the umbrella of Vertical Industries."

Seph stared at her, confused. Was that supposed to mean something to her?

"Vertical Industries is a massive, world-wide front for much darker business," explained Annalisa.

"*What?*"

She nodded. "Vertical Design, Vertical Foods, Vertical Publishing."

"Vertical Media," added Annice. "Vertical Logistics…"

"*Vertical Pharmaceuticals*," said Annalisa, grimacing at all the awful possibilities of that one alone.

(Seph, for one, had seen enough zombie movies to know that *that* sort of thing never turned out well.)

"They have facilities all over the world," Annalisa went on. "And all of them are airtight, legitimate businesses. But behind all the legal operations are some of the most sinister organizations in the world."

"Nameless, shadowy organizations," said Annice. "The kind you won't ever hear about on the news."

"They have their hands in every aspect of modern civilization. They control entire economies, governments, even religions. They control an entire army of monstrous agents, many of them possessing unspeakable powers."

"There was no chance you were there by coincidence," agreed Annice.

Seph looked back and forth between the two of them, shocked. Then she turned and looked at Amethyst. "Did *you* know about this?"

She stared back at her, her eyes wide. Then she shook her rib bone at the two Ahns on the other side of the table. "*They* told me I couldn't tell you about that."

"Sorry," said Annalisa. "We didn't want to risk tipping our hand to Tane or one of his monsters."

"But we were keeping a close eye on you," promised Annice. "Plus, we've had Warner watching over you the whole time, too. I expect he was the reason you got out of the building with as little trouble as you did."

Seph looked across the table at Piper, who sucked on the last of her rib bones and shrugged. *She* certainly didn't know anything about it.

She *did* wonder why they were allowed to leave the building. Was that Warner's doing, then? Or had Tane simply let them go?

"I'm sorry," said Amethyst. "I *want* to tell you everything. I really do. But I can only tell you so much. Too much information is dangerous. You know that."

She *did* know that. Two years ago she was living her life blissfully unaware that any of this craziness was real. She couldn't help but wonder where she'd be now if she'd never awakened to her prophet sight and never saw that first pair of ghostly ears in that coffee shop in Madison.

But her gaze drifted back to Piper. She was wiping herself clean with her napkin, but she'd missed a spot high up on her left cheekbone, just above where Tane burned her.

Not all the weird things she'd found were bad.

"What do we do next?" she asked. "I mean, I thought we were supposed to find the third Hand, but…"

Piper looked down at the golden wheel dangling from its chain around her neck. "Yeah. If I already have the third Hand…aren't we kind of *done*? I mean, isn't that what we were supposed to do?"

"You don't actually have it yet," explained Annalisa.

Piper stared back at her, confused. But…she *did* have it. It was right here…

"You have it in your possession, but you can't fully claim it yet."

"It hasn't *chosen you*, yet," said Annice. "It hasn't decided if you're worthy of it."

She looked down at it again. "It hasn't?"

Seph pointed at it. "But she's already used it. She made that fire alarm appear. And she made the elevator work."

"Sure," said Annice. "She can *use* it. It's not opposed to letting her have some of its power. But she can't fully claim it until she's proven herself to it."

"Ordinarily, you'd do that during the process of searching for it," explained Annalisa. She gestured at Seph with a bone. "Like *you* did on your quest for the scythe. But we cheated and skipped that part. So you'll have to prove yourself another way."

"Okay…" said Piper, not really understanding. "Then how do I do that?"

Annalisa smiled. "We can't really tell you that. That's something that's between you and the wheel."

"Wheel?"

Annice nodded. "Yes. Rumpelstiltskin's spinning wheel."

"Oh!" said Piper. "I know that story." She wrinkled her nose at it. "Doesn't *look* like a spinning wheel."

"Why would it be Rumpelstiltskin's spinning wheel?" asked Seph.

"The famous wheel that could spin straw into gold," said Annalisa.

Seph tilted her head to one side, confused. "Sure, I know the story. Just…isn't that what the hammer does? Take one thing and turn it into something else."

"Well, it's not literal," huffed Annice.

"Straw into gold is a metaphor for something from nothing," said Amethyst, nodding.

"Well it's a stupid metaphor," said Seph. "Straw isn't nothing. It's something."

Annalisa shrugged. "She's not wrong about that," she said to Annice.

"The original story, as I remember it," said Annice, sounding exasperated, "didn't have any straw in it. The wheel from *that* story spun riches out of thin air."

"Ah yes," said Annalisa. "I vaguely remember that, now that you mention it."

Annice nodded. "It *has* been a while. I'm fairly certain that first version's been lost to time, like so many other things."

Seph lifted her glasses and rubbed at her eye. This whole thing was crazy. How old *were* these women?

"So what do we do next?" asked Piper, finally putting her napkin down and pushing her plate aside. She still had that little smear of missed barbeque sauce on her cheek.

"The first thing to do," replied Annice, "is evaluate our situation. We've pissed off Tane, so we know he's going to throw everything he has at us."

"And since those creatures you described sound a lot like

teethers," reasoned Annalisa as she reached over with a clean napkin and dabbed away the missed spot on Piper's cheek, "I think it's safe to say that he's let the ringmaster off his leash."

"Ringmaster?" said Seph.

"Teethers?" said Piper.

"The ringmaster is a lot like the shepherd," explained Annice. "He's a twisted murderer who particularly enjoys terrorizing small towns."

"A conjurer," said Annalisa. "Like the shepherd, but whereas the shepherd was known for his vicious flock, the ringmaster has an entire menagerie of monsters at his disposal."

"Teethers have a tendency to spawn in large numbers and overwhelm their prey," said Annice. "They chase down their victims, corner them and then…well…that's where the teeth come in."

Piper shivered. It wasn't hard to picture those nasty little creatures sinking their teeth into their victims. Several of them had tried their best to bite her Jeep, after all.

"Usually there're a lot more of them than what you described," said Annalisa. "No doubt we have Warner to thank for that."

"He'll have his work cut out for him," sighed Annice. "Teethers are the least of our worries if the ringmaster has his sights set on you."

"He has an army at his disposal," agreed Annalisa. "It won't be easy."

"It's worse than that," said Amethyst.

Annalisa looked up at her and smiled. "Ah. Warner. You made it. Good to see you again. So to speak."

Seph and Piper turned and looked at Amethyst. Annalisa was right. Her pretty brown eyes had been replaced with an unsettling, but familiar darkness. This was no longer Amethyst. This was Warner Harr.

"He's sent for the white sisters," reported Warner.

"Oh dear," said Annalisa. "We really *did* piss him off, didn't we?"

"Um…who are the white sisters?" asked Piper.

"They're remnants," replied Annice. "Phantoms from one of the earliest universes."

"Very powerful," said Annalisa. "Very *evil*."

"Terrifying," agreed Annice. "Tane shouldn't be powerful enough to control those two, yet they seem to be loyal to him. It doesn't make sense."

"The fact remains that they *are* loyal to him," said Warner. He scrunched Amethyst's pretty face into a grim expression. "Loyal enough to fight his battles, anyway. But they don't play games like the shepherd and ringmaster. They'll destroy their opponents without mercy. If Tane's summoned them, he's not holding back. He means to take the wheel even if he has to kill the girl to get it."

Piper grasped the pendant and sank down in her chair, her eyes widening. "Can he do that?"

"Whether he can or he can't," said Warner, "he *has*. His objectives have changed. He means to have what he believes is his and deal with the consequences later."

"That moody old fart," grumbled Annalisa.

"But he can't just *take* the wheel," said Seph. She looked over at Piper, worried. "Can he? I thought the Hands were supposed to choose their owners."

"I believe he intends to claim it, even if it won't accept him, and hold it hostage until the Keeper and the Architects accept him as its rightful owner," replied Warner. "I think he's gambling that they'll choose him over letting the cycle end."

"*Will* they choose him over the end?" asked Piper.

"Hard to say," replied Annice. "But *I* wouldn't wager it."

"A dangerous gamble," agreed Annalisa. "*Very* dangerous."

"And we also have the bug to worry about," added Warner.

"Gispuknya?" Said Seph. "It's back, too?"

"Using the Hands attracts it," he explained.

"Seriously?" She glanced over at the Ahns, surprised. "I've been playing with mine since July!"

"You were only using a tiny fraction of the scythe's power," said Annice.

"The Hands are aware of the bug," said Warner. "They wouldn't risk luring it to you. That's why it was reluctant to manifest until today, when Tane forced your hand."

"Oh." She frowned. So that was why she'd never been able to shape the scythe into its full form? Granted, she'd never tried very hard because she was also a little afraid of it… "Wait…have you all been spying on us this whole time?"

"Not *spying*," said Annalisa. "That sounds so *sneaky*. We were just keeping watch for trouble, like we promised."

"*I* was spying a little," said Annice.

"Shush!" Laughed Annalisa.

"I *won't* shush. I'm nosy. Deal with it."

Seph glanced over at Piper, her eyebrows raised.

Piper merely shrugged and reached for another rib. She found that she didn't quite care if Warner and the Ahns spied on them. It wasn't like she did anything all that interesting or embarrassing. It was kind of nice knowing someone was keeping an eye out for monsters while they went about their lives.

"But today you used far more than a tiny fraction," continued Warner. He didn't seem remotely amused with the old women. "And so did Tane. I'm certain the bug noticed you. The shadows will already be searching for you."

"Tane *and* Gispuknya," sighed Seph. "Great."

"What do we do?" Asked Piper.

"Use it to your advantage," he replied.

"This is a three-way war," Annalisa reminded them. "Tane and Gispuknya don't like each other. *At all.*"

"They'll both be searching for you," said Annice. "If one's creeps show up, the other's won't be far behind. And if they get anywhere near each other, they'll be at each other's throats."

"And if they're fighting each other," continued Annalisa, "they won't be able to focus on the two of you."

"Gispuknya's shadows seem endless," said Annice, "but they're not. Only so many can manifest at a time. The same is true of the ring-master. There are limits to how many he can summon and control at once. They'll both defend against the greatest threat first, which will be each other."

"These are all weaknesses you can exploit," said Annalisa, nod-ding. "Remember, there's always a way. You just have to find it."

Seph wasn't sure if the whole "there's always a way" thing was some kind of higher power at work or just more of Amethyst's "power of positive thinking," but it was all they had sometimes. And so far they *had* always found a way. They wouldn't be here now if they hadn't.

In fact, sometimes it seemed like the way found *them.*

Piper's cell phone rang. She took it out of her purse and looked at the screen. "It's Kaitlyn. I never did get back to her about this week-end."

"I don't think we'll be making any plans for a while," sighed Seph.

She put the phone back into her purse without answering it. She'd have to remember to get back to her later, when she had more time.

"Speaking of the scythe…" said Seph, looking down at the water that swirled around her fingers. "I think something's wrong with it."

Annalisa frowned. "Something wrong with it?"

"Impossible," said Annice.

"Yeah," said Piper, pointing at Seph's hand. "It kept, like, coming apart when she was trying to use it."

"It's probably just that you're not used to using it yet," guessed Annalisa.

"The Hands are infallible," insisted Annice. "But their power is immeasurable. It's not unlikely that you just need more practice."

"I guess so…" said Seph, still staring at the water on her hand.

Annalisa leaned forward, squinting at it as she wiped her fingers with her napkin. "It wouldn't hurt to have a look at it, though."

Warner turned Amethyst's head and stared out the window. "The ringmaster's here."

"Already?" said Annice.

"The seekers need to leave immediately."

Annalisa dropped her napkin onto her plate and stood up. "Well then I guess we should stop dawdling."

Annice nodded. "Yes. Time to go."

Amethyst blinked at her. "Go where?" She glanced around the table. "What just…? Wait…was that Warner? That son of a bitch! I *hate* when he does that!" She crossed her arms over her huge bosom and clenched her teeth, furious. "What'd I miss this time?"

But before anyone could catch her up, a loud boom broke the silence of the ranch.

Chapter 10

"Flutters," said Annice as the five of them gathered on the front porch to find a smoking, basket-ball-sized hole in the roof of the stable.

Several red and black, moth-like creatures were flying around the yard. As they watched, one of them settled itself on top of a horse trailer, convulsed violently and then exploded, blowing a hole right through the metal and sending a ball of fire high into the air.

"What the hell?" said Seph. "Kamikaze butterflies?" She didn't even like *regular* butterflies. They were still bugs, after all. And bugs were gross. But *exploding* bugs?

Seriously, was the whole universe out to get her with the stupid bugs?

"Another of the ringmaster's pets," explained Annalisa.

"So he's here now?" asked Piper. She turned and looked around, those ghostly ears swiveling back and forth atop her head.

"The ringmaster never reveals himself," said Annice. "He's a coward. He'll let his monsters do all the work for him and then scurry off again."

Another explosion shredded one of the huge doors on the garage. A fourth explosion followed a second later, sending a ball of smoke up from behind the tool shed.

At least a dozen more of them were flying aimlessly about the yard, still looking for somewhere to detonate.

"We'll take out as many as we can," said Annalisa. She turned and looked at Amethyst, "*You* get them out of here. You know where to go."

She nodded.

The two old women stepped off the porch and transformed themselves. Seph and Piper had seen this twice before, but it was no less shocking the third time. Their mouths stretched open, splitting their faces in half and tipping back their heads like life-sized Pez dispensers to reveal impossibly cavernous, tooth-filled maws. Their bodies twisted and contorted with a series of sickening cracks and pops, as if all the bones in their bodies were breaking, their very skeletons disassembling and knitting themselves back together into a new and horrifying form. By the time they reached the bottom of the porch's three steps, they'd become monstrous, four-legged things somehow still dressed in Annalisa and Annice's disheveled clothing.

With blinding speed, their long, tentacle-like tongues lashed out and began snatching the explosive flutters out of the air. One after another, they slammed the little bugs onto the ground, where they exploded, leaving small, smoldering craters in the dirt.

"Follow me!" said Amethyst as she set off toward the garage. "Stay close!"

"Will they be all right?" asked Piper. "Those fluttery things aren't going to hurt them, are they?" She'd already seen that those nasty bugs could blow a hole through a steel horse trailer. She could only imagine what kind of damage they could do to the tentacles that were swatting them to the ground.

"Doubtful," replied Amethyst. "There aren't many things out there that can even scratch an Ahn. My car's parked next to the shed."

But the words were barely past her lips when a larger-than-average explosion blasted a hole in the corner of the shed's roof and sent debris raining down around them.

Amethyst turned away, shielding her face with one arm and Piper and Seph with the other.

"That looked like a *big* one!" exclaimed Seph.

"Probably two or three in a chain reaction," reasoned Amethyst, peering over at the smoldering hole in the shed. "Mr. Hallet's *not* gonna like this."

Another flutter landed in a nearby tree and exploded, blasting off a heavy branch and dropping it onto the little red Impala Amethyst had been leading them toward, caving in the windshield.

She cursed, then turned and nudged them toward the garage. "Ranch truck it is, then," she decided.

Around them, Shawbeck Ranch had become a war zone. Two more explosions blasted holes in the roof of the house. A third took out most of the bay window overlooking the yard. A fourth blew the gate leading back into the fields nearly in half, mangling the steel bars as if they were plastic.

An electric pole snapped and fell, dragging deadly power lines to the ground with it.

There were great billows of smoke pouring out of the stable.

And throughout it all there were two monsters dressed for an afternoon of bingo and senior-special brunch buffets swatting exploding butterflies out of the air and dashing them into cinders in the dirt.

"Keep up!" said Amethyst.

"I'm trying!" squealed Piper as she struggled to run across the thick lawn in her heels.

One of the little monsters fluttered across their path, forcing them to stop.

From this distance, Seph could see that they weren't simply butterflies. Their wings were similar in shape and function to a large butterfly or moth, but the body of the creature was significantly larger and stranger, more like a grotesquely fat slug with dozens of long, wavy legs dangling from its underside. It hung there, suspended by the flapping wings, weighing it down.

The sight made her skin crawl.

"Careful!" said Amethyst.

"No kidding," grumbled Seph, her eyes drifting to the holes the little monsters had blown all over the yard and in every building.

Were those fat, fleshy bodies filled with chemicals, she wondered. Or did these things defy any kind of scientific explanation and just…go boom?

Piper caught up to them and then turned around to find another flutter behind them, flapping its tiny wings and making its way slowly toward her. "Guys…"

"Keep moving!" ordered Amethyst. She made a wide path around the flutter, careful not to move too quickly and startle or agitate the little beast.

Seph glanced around at the damage they were causing. They didn't seem all that smart. They appeared to be attacking at random. If they had the capacity for a coordinated attack, they should've converged on the house from the start while they were all inside. Was this part of a greater plan? Was it just to flush them out? To separate and confuse them? Was the ringmaster up to something? Or had Warner simply thrown a wrench in the works by warning them of the impending attack before the ringmaster was ready? She supposed it didn't matter, as long as they got the hell out of here before something nastier than flutters showed up. But something about the whole situation was leaving a bad taste in her mouth. Being ushered from one place to the next without fully understanding what was happening? It was exactly the same thing the shepherd and the incubus did to them.

It felt like they were being herded.

Another flutter exploded on a bird feeder dangerously close to where they were running and Seph threw her arm up to shield her face from flying debris. Something cold landed on the back of her hand. It was a gross glob of grayish goo.

She cried out in disgust and wiped it on her skirt. It was bad enough the stupid things were *exploding*, but they were spraying their gross slug innards all over everything, too? She *hated* these things!

Piper's heel sank into a mole hill and she dropped into the grass with a startled cry.

Seph hurried back and heaved her back onto her feet. "No more heels!"

"But I *love* these shoes!" She got her feet under her, thankful not to have twisted her ankle, and looked back the way she came.

A flutter landed right on her forehead.

Chapter 11

For one terrible second, everything stopped. Time slowed to a crawl. The chaos around her became a deathly hush. Her whole body went numb. Her heart froze in her chest. The blood drained from her face. She stood there, her blue eyes wide open and crossed as she stared up at those softly twitching wings. She was only vaguely aware of the long, shrill noise she was making, like a balloon with a slow leak.

Seph, too, stood frozen for that second, her gaze fixed on that hideous bug, her heart filled with terror as the grotesque, slug-like body twitched and throbbed.

She'd watched the process before. First they convulsed a couple times. Then they detonated, destroying anything they were touching, whether it was wood, steel or flesh and bone.

The flutter's fat, slug body flexed.

Its wings jerked upright.

Then a tentacle lashed out, snatching the foul bug away, lightning fast, and dashing it against the trunk of a nearby tree, where it exploded.

The wind from the blast hit Piper's face hard enough to blow back her bangs.

She stared at the smoldering hole that was almost her skull, that terrified noise still escaping her.

Annalisa gave them an impatient roar and then whirled around and went back to exterminating flutters.

Piper's knees gave out. She slumped in Seph's arms.

"Move it!" grunted Seph.

Her feet started moving, but they didn't feel like they'd hold all of her weight. She clung to Seph, trembling. She turned and blinked up at her. "I think I peed myself a little," she squeaked.

Me too, thought Seph. But aloud, she just said, "*Run*!"

An explosion behind them snapped her out of it. She didn't quite dare to let go of Seph's arm, but she turned and hurried after Amethyst without having to be dragged there, which she thought was a solid win, considering how close she'd come to having the worst hair day imaginable.

The ranch truck was a badly rusted Dodge Ram with a cracked windshield and duct-taped upholstery. It was parked around the side of the garage, as if to keep the ugly thing out of sight. There was a twisted curl of smoldering tin from the garage's roof lying on the hood, but otherwise, it seemed to have remained untouched by the invading suicide bomber bugs.

Amethyst was already inside, starting the engine. Seph and Piper climbed into the cab with her and slammed the doors.

"Okay…" said Amethyst as she shifted the pickup into gear and started forward. "Now we just have to get out of here without hitting any bugs."

Seph thought that might be easier said than done. Looking around, she couldn't help but notice that there were more of them than there were when they first stepped out of the house. A *lot* more. There were more holes blown in the roof of the house. The stable was fully engulfed in flames now. And there was a smoldering hole in the lift gate of Piper's Jeep.

"Aw!" whined Piper.

"Jarrett can fix it!" promised Amethyst. "Just…one thing at a time!"

"They're everywhere!" exclaimed Seph as they drove around the garage to find the driveway swarming with exploding butterfly monsters.

There was no way to avoid all of them. Just looking around, it was clear that the ranch's aging pickup couldn't protect them from these things. They might as well be sitting in a cardboard box.

One was fluttering straight toward them, on a collision course with the old Ram's windshield.

Then something black streaked across their line of vision, impossibly fast, followed by a rapid-fire detonation of a dozen flutters.

"Was that Warner?" asked Seph.

Piper was looking around, confused. "What? Where?"

Another shadow streaked past them, zigzagging back and forth, followed by another delayed string of explosions.

"He's an asshole, but you can't deny he's impressive," said Amethyst.

When he wasn't taking control of someone's body, Warner Harr's true form was an impossibly black, featureless, nightmare-inducing shape. But he rarely moved slowly enough to actually be seen like that. Right now, he was little more than a darting shadow, an almost *imagined* thing passing before their eyes, much more shadow than flesh, a black blur streaking through the sunlight. Seph might've dismissed it as a trick of her mind if not for the explosions that followed in his wake, painting a blazing picture of his movements.

And as she watched, it occurred to her that she might only be able to see as much as she did because of her prophet sight, just as only she could see Piper's spirit ears and Amethyst's portals.

Then the Ahns were there, too. Those long, whipping tongues lashed out, snatching the exploding bugs out of the air and slamming them into the dirt, clearing a path for them.

Amethyst stomped the accelerator and sped through the opening.

Seph and Piper both turned and looked behind them.

"I really hope they're okay back there," said Piper.

"They're fine," insisted Amethyst. She glanced over at her. "And even if they weren't, we wouldn't exactly be any help to them."

Seph nodded. That was certainly true. They might look like two little old ladies and a pair of black eyes, but those were three of the most ferocious monsters she'd ever encountered.

Amethyst turned her attention to the driveway in front of them and suddenly sat up and stomped on the brake. "Oh shit."

Seph and Piper both turned, startled.

"What the hell is that?" blurted Seph.

Standing at the end of the driveway were two strange, white figures.

They appeared to be women, dressed in identical, brilliant-white clothes that were difficult to make out. Both of them had long, white hair and ghostly white faces.

"The white sisters…" breathed Amethyst.

"Seriously?" gasped Piper. "They're here, too?"

"What are they?" asked Seph. She put her hands on the dashboard and leaned forward, squinting at them, trying to make out the details of these strange, white specters blocking their path. It was strange. It was like the way some of Gispuknya's shadow things were hard to make out because they were black on black, except…*the opposite.* These two were so brilliantly *white* that it was difficult to differentiate between their shapes. They were like snow sculptures, except they even defied the blazing sunlight, casting no shadows at all.

What was it Annice called them? Remnants?

Phantoms from one of the earliest universes.

Very powerful. Very evil.

The memory gave her a shiver.

Piper sat up, her eyes flashing black. "Get out of here!" ordered Warner. "Don't stop for anything!"

Then she blinked and her eyes were blue again. "What was that?"

A black shadow streaked through the air and the white sisters vanished from the end of the driveway, becoming white streaks as they instantly met Warner's supernatural speed.

Amethyst stomped the accelerator again, kicking up gravel and dust as she shot out onto the pavement.

Seph and Piper turned to look behind them again.

White and black streaks darted in and out of view as Annalisa and Annice loped up the driveway to join the fray.

Then they were all vanishing into the distance as they sped down the highway, leaving Shawbeck Ranch to the monsters.

"You're going back to help them, right?" said Piper.

Amethyst glanced over at her. "What? No. I already told you, I'm staying with you guys."

Seph stared at her. "Are you sure?"

"First there was the shepherd and Pappy Stan's Diner. Then there was the incubus. Gispuknya broke one of the vault gates. The Ahns are violating the rules of the game." She bit her lip and brushed aside a strand of long, brown hair. "Ever since you came back from the scythe vault, everything's felt a little off. Nothing's happening quite like it should."

Seph remembered returning from the scythe vault after that awful final encounter with the shepherd. She recalled her saying something about things not feeling right, that she felt like she was missing something, but that she didn't yet know what it was.

"I'm not taking any chances this time," she insisted. "I'm staying with you guys to the end."

"But can you do that?" asked Piper. "I thought there were rules."

"Like the one the Ahns broke by just *giving you* the third Hand?"

"Right… I guess the rules sort of went right out the window, didn't they?"

"I promised myself when I found out about that incubus that I wouldn't let anything like that happen again. And it's a promise I intend to keep."

"Okay," said Seph. Although she had mixed feeling about the whole thing. "So where're we going first, then?"

"To see Sandy," replied Amethyst.

"Sandy?" Seph frowned. "Wait… You mean that hippy chick you used to go see all the time? The one that taught you how to cleanse your aura and channel positive energy? I thought you made all that up."

"I *did* make that stuff up," she replied. "But Sandy's real. She's actually my spirit guide. And it's time you finally met her."

Chapter 12

Ugly Orchard Road was just like Huntington Street and Old Castle Road. Besides not obeying the laws of nature or physics, it was invisible to most of the world. People drove right past it every day, without ever noticing its existence. Most people wouldn't be able to see it even if they knew to look for it. It was apparently a very rare ability, possessed by very few people in the world. And even fewer people had ever been shown how to identify and use them.

Amethyst had not only revealed the locations of all the nearest fringe road entrances to them, she'd spent several months training them to see through the illusions that kept everyone else out. Seph, with her prophet sight, had picked up the skill fairly fast, but Piper had taken considerably longer. She might have had those special ears, but the fringe roads, unlike some unseen places, didn't make any sounds. It'd seemed for a while that, in spite of her gifts, she might not be among the few who had the ability to see them without being physically taken onto one. But she was a smart girl and a good student. And she was a seeker. In time, she'd mastered it. Now she could theoretically see and use any fringe road in the world, assuming that she could tell them apart from the real roads.

After just a few minutes, the wide-open landscape of Northern Nebraska began to melt away. Trees sprang up across the empty plains.

Just one or two at first. Then small groves. As she'd done many times before, Seph tried to watch and see exactly where Nebraska turned into fringe, but like always, she couldn't quite comprehend the transition. It was both subtle and fast, like an extremely complicated optical illusion. Before she could wrap her head around it, they were already deep inside, speeding along an endless road with no curves or hills, bathed in eerie darkness beneath an impenetrable canopy of branches.

Seph once asked Amethyst why the fringe was a forest, of all things. Her response was as mysterious as the fringe road itself: "Because everything began with the forest. I can't really explain it any better than that because I don't really understand it all myself. It's just the way it is."

"I feel like I should be more prepared than this," said Piper, pulling Seph from her thoughts. "After all the work we did to be ready."

"We were never going to be prepared," replied Seph. "Not really."

"But we worked so hard."

They *had* worked hard. And not just with Amethyst.

Ten months ago, one of Piper's dearest friends, Wanda, was dragged into this weirdness with them. She was chased by monsters, captured, held captive by a demon and then bound, chained and locked in a wooden crate, where she came terrifyingly close to getting set on fire and burned alive. Seph had worried that such an ordeal would've been more than the poor woman could handle. She wasn't even sure if she, herself, would've been able to handle something like that without serious psychological damage. But far from being traumatized, Wanda had risen to the occasion. She made it her personal mission to whip the two of them into shape. "If you're going to go around pissing off *demons* and getting chased by *monsters*," she'd announced soon after they'd all returned from the weirdness of Avelby, "then you can't afford to not be in excellent physical shape." And from that day on, Wanda was their own personal fitness trainer. Whether they liked it or not. No amount of Seph's complaining or Piper's whining would dissuade her from working them ragged every chance she had.

Seph was positively *sick* of jogging.

But she had to admit…she *was* in the best shape of her life. And she would almost certainly be grateful for that before this new ordeal was over.

And Wanda wasn't the only one faring well after those horrific events of last July. Seph's own mother had been poisoned by an incubus. She never knew, of course. *She* thought she'd only had a passing flu. But for a while, Seph had really believed she was going to lose the last of her family.

But Buffy Kipp had no recollection of the man who called himself Travis and pretended to be her gentlemanly boyfriend. The Ahns had erased him from her memory somehow, sparing her the heartache and humiliation of losing someone she'd begun to truly care about.

Seph had worried that losing Travis would make her spiral back into one of her self-destructive depressions, whether she remembered him or not. But if anything, she was functioning better than ever. Many of the Ahns had befriended her that day. And they still visited her regularly. Now she was eating better. She was trying to quit smoking. She'd even taken up baking. She was pretty good at it, too.

"You're making me nervous," said Seph.

Amethyst glanced over at her. "What?"

"You keep checking your mirrors. I thought you said we were safe on the fringe roads."

"We should be. Even if something *did* manage to follow us, things have a way of getting displaced. If we were in separate cars, we would've lost sight of each other almost immediately. Things like distance and speed and time don't work the same in the fringe. And nothing's constant."

That much was true. She knew it from experience. It was at the same time a single road and many roads. It was no more than what you could see in either direction, and yet it was also infinite. Time became jumbled, moving inconsistently even between clocks in the same vehicle. Even now, the dashboard clock in the truck was malfunctioning. The ten-minute display was slowly running backward while the hours ticked forward every couple of seconds by threes and fours.

Just thinking too much about it was enough to make a person crazy.

"But when you're dealing with beings like Tane and the ringmaster," said Amethyst, looking up at the rearview mirror again, "you can never be too careful."

"Lovely," grumbled Seph.

"Just sit tight. We're almost there."

Around them, the trees began to thin, then to change. The shadowy, towering fringe trees gave way to smaller oaks and maples and pines. Underbrush sprang up around them, filling in the eerie, empty shadows of the forest floor. The darkness broke apart as the canopy began to open up. After a moment that might have been seconds or might have been minutes, they were again driving beneath a warm, blue sky. Except it wasn't the same sky. The last sky was wide open and clear. This sky was a deeper, prettier shade of blue and filled with soft, fluffy clouds.

Then, without any warning at all, the old truck was lumbering down a dusty gravel drive past rows and rows of crowded mobile homes.

Sandy the Spirit Guide lived in a trailer park?

"Where are we?" asked Seph.

"This is Nora's Lilac Grove," replied Amethyst. "Missouri."

"We're in Missouri?" She shook her head. They were just in Nebraska only a few minutes ago. Or was it closer to an hour ago? How much time had gone by? She looked at her watch, but she wasn't sure what time it was when they left the ranch. And thanks to the fringe road, her watch wasn't working right, anyway…

Piper stared out the window at the passing scenery. She didn't see any lilac groves. All she saw were trailer homes. And not the nicest collection of them she'd ever seen, either.

There was very little in the way of healthy lawns or even specific borders between yards. The vast majority of the ground here was bare earth, overgrown weeds and fingers of encroaching brush creeping out from the surrounding forest as it crowded in on everything. Whenever there was some attempt at landscaping, it was either done with garish lawn ornaments or with large rocks arranged in a way to add some semblance of intentional beautification. But most of these homes were either utterly devoid of any kind of decoration or littered with junk.

She saw paint cans stacked on porches, brooms and rakes lying abandoned in the dirt. Barbeque grills, propane tanks, broken lawn chairs and random car parts were as common as flower beds, satellite dishes and American flags.

Every third or fourth trailer came with an assortment of usually mismatched and badly sun-faded patio furniture, occasionally occupied by one or more overweight, middle-aged men with a beer in one hand and unfriendly sorts of looks on their faces as they watched them drive past.

Here and there, she saw clothes lines stretched across toy-littered patios. In other places, damp clothes were simply thrown over porch railings and chain-link fences to dry.

A sad-looking Cozy Coop was parked at the side of the road, its door open, seemingly abandoned by its tiny driver. Plastic dolls lay naked in the dirt. Half-hidden balls peeked out from tufts of weeds and overgrown grass along underpinnings and from under wooden porches. There were rickety swing sets, hazardous-looking trampolines and kiddie pools that had been sitting out since last summer.

There was something extra-creepy about all that stuff with no children anywhere to be seen.

Perhaps they were all in school.

In fact, the entire park was eerily quiet. No one was moving around. The few people she saw were just sitting in their yards, staring back at her from their sun-damaged yard furniture.

For some reason, she found herself reminded of those creepy, animatronic wax figures they used to decorate amusement rides or museum exhibits, and the thought was more than enough to elevate the already eerie atmosphere to something bordering on sheer horror.

Amethyst turned left and drove past an ugly old trailer that someone had converted into a church, identified by the large cross hung in the front window and the hand-scrawled sign mounted above the door. Someone had even gone to the trouble of adding a handicap ramp to the porch.

Seph didn't feel any urges to stop and pray.

The trailers went on and on. Each time they thought they'd gone as far as the park reached, Amethyst turned down another dusty drive and revealed even more.

It felt like it went on for miles.

And there was something dreadfully depressing about most of

these homes. Almost all of them were dirty white, dingy green, sickly yellow or muddy brown in color. Only occasionally did one stand out from the rest in bright, happy shades. She could almost imagine that there was some kind of force in this place that sucked the brightness out of everything, leaving the world, and the people, dingy and bland and joyless.

Adding to that illusion was the fact that some of these homes were clearly deserted. Doors hung open, revealing empty darkness within. Others had broken windows or leaned dramatically to one side. Many others were difficult to tell whether they were abandoned or simply neglected. They loomed behind the rest, half swallowed by the crowding trees and brush, but with tiny signs of life. A single chair. A welcome mat. A small patch of mown grass.

And just when it began to seem like more than she could stand, they passed an adorable little mobile home painted bright pink and adorned with paper lanterns, strings of lights and new wicker furniture complete with flowery cushions and colorful throws. A chubby, joyful-looking older woman sat amid it all, adorned in a flowing, yellow dress, sunglasses and big, straw hat, sipping on an iced tea as if she were on vacation, quite clearly living her very best life.

There was a strangely infectious sort of joyfulness about the woman and her happy little home. She seemed to brighten up all of Nora's Lilac Grove. Suddenly, the place didn't seem so dingy. It was just a little dusty, after all. It just needed a good Spring rain.

But only a few doors down from the happy woman, they passed the charred husk of a trailer surrounded by litter and piles of garbage and that strangely hopeless atmosphere came rolling back in again.

Tiny little outbuildings had been erected in places where there was room, some from aging wood and some from rusting tin. They were mostly garden sheds, but there were also carports, single-car garages and even a cramped chicken coop pushed back into the woods. Piper even spotted an outhouse.

"That's just for decoration, right?"

Amethyst shrugged. "Maybe. Hard to say."

Piper wrinkled her nose at the thought and went back to taking it all in.

There were signs everywhere in the winding tangle of drives. STOP. YIELD. NO EXIT. DEAD END. And on every few fences there could be found NO TRESPASSING and NO SOLICITING and BEWARE OF DOG.

Most of these homes were topped with useless old television antennas. Power lines crisscrossed from every direction so that every sizeable shade tree they passed had been hacked into ugly, stunted trunks to make room for them all.

Looming over all of this was a backdrop of high-tension power line towers that seemed strangely fitting to Seph. She found it easy to imagine a nuclear power plant chugging away in the distance. The perfect setting for whatever horror movie they were currently participating in.

Amethyst turned down another street. The trailers were getting older here. They were smaller. Rounder. More metal than plastic. Most of them were rusty as well as dusty.

And there were a lot of add-ons here. Closed-in porches were built on many of them. One had a wooden attic mounted onto its roof. And in one case there were five of them all strung together into a strange conglomeration that looked to Seph like some kind of redneck mobile *mansion*.

Around the next curve they found an old, converted school bus, of all things, complete with a built-on, covered porch.

"This place is enormous," said Seph.

"It's a lot like the ranch," explained Amethyst. "It only partially exists in our world. The rest stretches into the surrounding void. No one knows how big it really is. Some say it goes on forever."

"Why does it need to be so big?" asked Piper. "Is there really that big of a market for mobile homes in Missouri?"

Amethyst chuckled. "It's not like that, exactly. This place is special. People don't *choose* to settle down here. This is where people end up when they get lost. Like *really* lost. When everything you ever knew is utterly gone. When the world turns its back on you and you have nowhere left to go. When you're at the very end of your road… That's when *she* comes to find you."

"She?" asked Piper, intrigued.

"Sandy."

"Is that how you met her?"

"It is. I lived here for a while. Back before I found Shawbeck Ranch. That was a long time ago. A lot's changed since then."

Seph stared at her. It couldn't have been *that* long ago. She was only twenty-five.

…wasn't she?

"She comes to you in your dreams," Amethyst went on. "She gives you directions. Tells you where to go, what to look for. It's never not scary, but if you're brave and you follow her, you end up here." She pointed straight ahead. The jumbled drives were finally coming to an end. The trailers crowded closer and closer together, as if blocking the way forward. There appeared to be a clearing in the forest on the other side. "It doesn't look like much, but this is a sanctuary. The people here were all hurt by the world. Some emotionally. Some mentally. Some *physically.*"

Seph's gaze was drawn to the scar under her left eye. She'd told her that it was the result of a random fall when she was a little girl…but now she wondered if there was more to the story than that.

"But they're all safe here," she continued. "The world can't harm them here. Sandy makes sure of that. That's why it's so big. Almost no one ever leaves."

Piper looked out at the park again. Suddenly, all those muted colors and junky yards didn't seem quite so depressing. They were still homes, after all. If anything, they were a symbol of hope.

They passed one trailer that was sitting close to the road. The blinds were raised and an unremarkable young woman was sitting inside, staring out at them, as if bored. She watched them go by.

Seph stared back at her. Their eyes met. Something in this woman's expression spoke volumes.

"So why did *you* leave?" asked Piper.

Amethyst glanced over at her. "Sometimes we have to. Sometimes she tells us we have work to do and sends us back out."

"She sent you to the ranch?" guessed Seph.

"No, actually. She sent me…well…somewhere else," she finished, looking uncomfortable. "It's a long story. And a difficult one. I'll tell you someday, I promise. We just don't have time for it right now. But along the way I *did* find the ranch." She smiled. "But she knew I'd end up there. She knows lots of things. I could tell you all about it, but that'd be kind of redundant. You'll see for yourself in a few minutes."

Amethyst swerved around an ugly green trailer with a collapsing porch and parked in the middle of the largest patch of neatly mown lawn Seph had seen since they left the ranch. In front of them stood a twelve-foot-tall stone statue of an angel with spread wings guarding a set of stone steps leading down into the shadowy depths of the forest.

"Everyone lost that Sandy finds ends up here," said Amethyst. "At the feet of the angel."

Seph found herself in no hurry to jump out of the truck. She stared at the angel, its expressionless face, its empty eyes. And then there were the deep shadows that seemed to spiral down those steps and into the woods behind it. "Why do I feel like I'm about to be *judged*?"

"That's normal," Amethyst assured her. "Everyone gets that."

Somehow, that didn't comfort her.

Chapter 13

The steps beyond the angel descended the side of a very large, very steep hill, virtually *plunging* into the crowding forest so that it grew darker and darker the deeper it went, until they were bathed in eerie shadows.

Seph kept looking out into those shadowy woods as she made her way downward. She couldn't help but think about how many spiders and bugs were crawling around in all those trees and the thought made her skin crawl.

Inside Piper's purse, her phone buzzed at her, informing her of a new text message. She pulled it out and looked at the screen. "Oh good," she sighed. "It's Meg."

"She finally realize you're gone?"

"Wow… There's, like, *twenty* messages." And a dozen missed calls, too. "She must've started trying to get in touch with me about the time those flutters attacked." She wouldn't have heard the phone ring in all that noisy chaos. And there was no service on the fringe road.

"I can't believe she just moved herself into you guys' apartment," laughed Amethyst. Then she said, "No, forget that. I *do* believe she did that. I've met her. What I can't believe is that you didn't physically *throw* her out on her ass."

"Believe me," said Seph, her gaze still washing over those shadowy woods. "I *wanted* to." Actually, what she *really* wanted to do was put the dumb little bimbo on a bus with a one-way ticket to Alaska.

Piper scrolled through the messages, frowning. "Aw jeez…"

Seph glanced down at her. "What?"

In an almost comically bored tone, she replied, "Someone's trying to kill her."

"*What?*"

"She says someone tried to poison her with cranberries."

"Cranberries?" said Amethyst, confused.

Seph rolled her eyes. "Meg's allergic to cranberries."

"Oh."

"They make her break out in ugly rashes. But I'm pretty sure it's never been one of those *life-threatening* food allergies." It wasn't as if she carried around an EpiPen or anything.

"How does someone even go about trying to poison you with a cranberry?" wondered Amethyst.

Piper scrolled through the messages again. "Something about a box of candy someone sent to her. I guess it didn't have a name on it?"

"Why the hell would she eat something if she didn't know who…?" Seph put her hand up, cutting herself off. "You know what? Never mind. She's Meg. Why *wouldn't* she? She eats everything she sees."

Piper nodded. No leftovers were safe with Meg in the house. And she was especially bad around sweets. She had no self-control whatsoever. And then she'd usually bitch about how they were always ruining her diet. They'd both taken to hiding treats in their underwear drawers. "She says she thought they were from a 'mysterious admirer' or something."

"Well that was her first mistake," said Seph. "*Nobody* admires

Meg."

"Be nice."

Seph rolled her eyes again. She didn't have to be nice. Meg was *Piper's* friend. Not *hers.*

And for a second there, she thought Meg might *really* be in trouble. It wouldn't have been the first time that someone close to them had been put in danger, after all. Her mom and Wanda had both been targeted in July. Why *wouldn't* someone try going after their roommate?

But why would Tane and his army of evil henchmen use *cranberries* when they had ungodly supernatural powers? That was just stupid. No, this was just more of Meg's nonsense. She was sure of it.

Piper's cell phone rang in her hand. It was Meg, of course. Reluctantly, she accepted the call and lifted it to her ear. "Hello?"

"Finally!" blurted Meg. "Where *are* you?"

"I'm visiting some friends with Persephone. What's wrong?"

"What's wrong? I'll tell you what's wrong! While you two're out gallivanting around, someone's trying to *murder* me!"

Piper frowned. "*Gallivanting*? Who *gallivants*? Where do you get these words from? You don't read."

Amethyst had to cover her mouth to stifle a laugh.

"Oh my *god*, Pipes, will you *focus* already? My *life* is in danger, here."

Piper sighed. "Who would want to kill you?" she asked.

"Who *wouldn't*?" grumbled Seph.

Piper flapped her free hand at her. "Shut it!" the gesture said.

"Oh, I don't know. Maybe *Juliet Gilbenhousen*?"

Piper scrunched up her face, confused. "Who?" Then she shook her head. "No. Forget that." It wouldn't matter if she told her. She didn't know any of Meg's friends anymore. "*Why* would this Juliet girl want you dead?"

"*Duh.* Because I spent the weekend up north in my parents' cabin with *Rocky.*"

"Rocky?" Why would anyone want to spend a weekend with someone named "Rocky"?

"Her ex-boyfriend?" huffed Meg. "God, Pipes, try and keep up."

Piper rubbed her eyes. This conversation was even more exhausting than the usual conversations she had with the woman. But that at least explained where she'd been these past few days. "Okay… If he's her ex, then what does she care if you spent the weekend with him?"

Amethyst glanced over at Seph, one eyebrow raised.

Meg sighed. "*Obviously*, she's obsessed with him and doesn't want anyone else dating him."

"I see. So how long have they been broken up, then?"

"He just dumped her right before we hooked up. He told me so, himself."

"Oh." She looked back at Seph, an expression of "here she goes again" painted across her face. "I see."

Seph rolled her eyes.

"Can you *please* focus on the real issue here?" snapped Meg.

"Right," said Piper. "I'll *try* to keep up." She rubbed her eyes again. "But you're okay?"

"*No*, I'm not okay! I'm all splotchy and gross and itchy from those stupid cranberries! What kind of lunatic hides cranberries in cookies? This chick is seriously deranged."

Piper frowned. Cookies? She thought she said in her text message that it was a box of candy. Her first thought had been of a box of chocolates. Shouldn't she have been able to *see* if a cookie had cranberries in it? Not that it mattered. "Okay, well, until this blows over, maybe don't eat any more suspicious food, okay?"

"Don't be a smart ass, Pipes."

How was that being a smart ass? It was simple logic. You had to be a *dumbass* to eat a box of mystery sweets in the first place. Where did she even *get* mystery sweets. She was about to ask her when a better question popped into her head: "Wait a minute…I thought you were seeing that Greg guy. What happened to you and Greg?"

"Will you *please* stay on track. We are *obviously* dealing with a very disturbed woman here."

"*Obviously*," agreed Piper. The bottom of the steps was finally coming into view. There was a narrow, grassy path down there, leading deeper into the woods. It looked immensely creepy. And it was getting colder, too. The temperature had dropped at least ten degrees and they weren't even at the bottom yet. "You should probably stay home and keep your head down for a while."

"No way! This bitch is totally going down! She's going to wish she never messed with me."

"You just said you were all blotchy from the cranberries. Just stay on the couch tonight."

Meg groaned. "No offense, Pipes, but just stay out of this. You're way too naïve to understand how things like this work."

"*What*?" squeaked Piper, indignant. If she was supposed to "stay out of this" then why the heck did she call her in the first place?

"I'm just saying. It's not like you've ever had a serious relationship or anything."

Her mouth dropped open, insulted.

Seriously, why did Meg even call her? What was the purpose? Just so she'd have someone to flap her mouth at?

The three of them stepped onto the grassy path and Amethyst

walked on ahead. "Almost there," she said, gesturing down a long, narrow tunnel of dense foliage looming before them, long enough that they couldn't see what was at the far end.

Seph, for one, didn't think she liked it down here. Any other day, any other place, and she probably would've appreciated the beauty of such a place. But right now…in this place…under these circumstances…it was just *creepy.*

"When're you coming home?" blurted Meg.

"I don't know!"

"There's, like, no food in the apartment."

"There's lots of food. You just have to cook it."

"That's *obviously* what I meant."

Piper looked back at Seph again, her eyes wide in an expression that quite clearly read, "What is *wrong* with this woman?"

Seph replied with a shrug that said, "She's *your* friend."

"Whatever," groaned Meg. "Just keep your phone on. I hate it when you let me go to voice mail."

"I don't *let* you go to voice mail. There's no service out here." Then she frowned. "Hello?" She lowered the phone and looked at the screen. "I hate it when she just hangs up like that!" She dropped it back into her purse and growled, frustrated.

"I told you she was being too quiet," said Seph.

Piper sighed. "I know."

Chapter 14

Sandy's home wasn't even a mobile home. It was an old camper trailer. The kind that might've been found hooked up to the family station wagon in the nineteen fifties. The whole thing was only about twelve feet wide and half-swallowed by the dense foliage of the creepy, Missouri forest.

It didn't even have a color to it, except the reddish-brown hue of rust and a few lingering patches of dull metal. Its one visible window was covered in gray and rotting plywood. The only splash of color was the cracked and peeling paint on the trailer's mismatched door, and even that was only the ugly, orangish-brown of river mud.

There were no decorations, no flowers, no lights. There weren't even any power lines running down to it.

It looked like something long ago abandoned and forgotten.

Everything else was forest, and so thick and all-encompassing that it was impossible to see more than a few yards into it, so that even the sunlight didn't reach this place. Everything was bathed in shade so deep it was easy to forget that it was barely mid-afternoon on a bright and sunny day.

"Sandy's not much for gardening, is she?" observed Piper.

Seph glanced over at her and saw those ethereal ears atop her head laid all the way back. This place scared her. And it didn't take prophet sight to see why.

"Come on," said Amethyst, looking back over her shoulder. "I'm sure she's waiting for you."

Neither of them questioned the fact that someone they'd never met might already be waiting for them when even *they* didn't know they'd be leaving Cakwetak until a few short hours ago. That was the *least* of the weirdness these sorts of things faced them with. *Of course* a mysterious spirit guide who lived in a creepy forest trailer guarded by a stone angel at the far end of a vast, multidimensional trailer park would be expecting them. It'd be weird if she wasn't.

Amethyst opened the door and led them inside. Although it looked as if four people would barely be able to fit in the tiny trailer, they found themselves staring down a candlelit corridor that was at least twice as long as the largest trailers they passed on their way here.

It was a testament to the strange things she'd already seen that such a thing didn't even surprise Seph. Although she could logically argue that someone had simply attached more trailers to the back of this one and easily hid them in the dense foliage outside, she didn't think for a moment that that was the case here. Amethyst told them that Nora's Lilac Grove existed across more than one world and she had no reason to doubt her. After all, Shawbeck Ranch was the same way. She'd seen both sides of it for herself. And then there was the Keeper's vault, the Ahns' playground and even Tane's freaky basement. After seeing all those places, there was no reason to think for even a second that there should be some sort of logical explanation for the broken physics of the spirit guide's trailer.

This was the part where they just went with it.

Amethyst walked ahead of them, making her way fearlessly through the impossible hallway, no doubt just like she'd done countless times before.

There was something at the far end, Seph saw. Beyond the light of the last of the candles, bathed in darkness. A person. Or something resembling the shadowy *shape* of a person, anyway.

Sandy?

Seph had never spoken much to Amethyst about Sandy. She never asked questions. She'd merely pictured some wispy woman spouting nonsense about karmic energy flow and spiritual enlightenment. She never cared beyond that. She didn't believe in that sort of thing.

She didn't believe in a lot of things back then…

As they passed the last of the candles and walked into the deeper darkness beyond, it became apparent that there *was* a person waiting there. She appeared to be wrapped in an old blanket, her head covered in a hood, her face hidden behind a heavy veil. As they approached, Seph found that she could see a woman's eyes staring back. They were illuminated by a narrow strip of light that fell across her face so that they shined back at them from the darkness. They were the prettiest blue eyes she'd ever seen, almost turquoise.

And they were fixed on only *her*.

"Hi Sandy," said Amethyst.

"Bella," said the mystery woman, without looking away from Seph. "I've missed you."

"I've missed you, too."

"Bella?" whispered Seph.

"When I lived here, I was Bella Leval," said Amethyst, impatient.

Another fake name. Another lie. A fresh wave of bitterness swept through her.

"I know," she said. "I'll tell you all about it later. I promise." She turned her attention back to Sandy. "The Ahns asked me to bring the seekers to you. But I…probably don't need to explain it."

"No," said Sandy. Those piercing, blue eyes never moved from Seph's gaze. "I've been expecting you." Those dramatically illuminated eyes remained fixed on Seph. They were already making her uncomfortable.

She glanced over at Piper, but she was staring down at her feet, looking anxious. Those spectral ears were still laid back against her skull.

"Of course you were," said Amethyst. She didn't seem very intimidated by this woman. She glanced over at Seph. "Like I said, she knows *lots* of things. Which makes conversations kind of dull. She always knows what I'm going to say."

Seph couldn't see the woman's face, but those eyes seemed to smile at that.

"My apologies, Bella."

"No need," said Amethyst. (*Bella?*) "You know I love you."

"And I you. This is the one you told me about, correct?"

"Seph, yes. She's the one who awoke to the prophet sight."

Seph wasn't sure what to say. Was she supposed to bow or something? This whole thing was ridiculously surreal. Why was this woman hiding in the dark, with only her eyes visible?

"I'm the spirit guide of Nora's Lilac Grove. I'm a lot like you, in a way. I perceive things that are invisible to others. But what I possess is neither sight nor hearing. I perceive *threads*."

"Threads?" Asked Seph.

"Paths laid before you," explained Sandy. "Choices. Opportunities. Risks and rewards. Everything that *may be* looms in the mysterious darkness ahead of you, connected to the you who stands here now by fine threads of glistening amber."

"Fate," said Amethyst, impatient. "She sees your fate. Your future. Your fortune. Etcetera. I'm sorry, Sandy, but we're in kind of a hurry here."

Sandy sighed. "But I love telling people this part."

"I know," said Amethyst. "And I'm really sorry. But seriously…"

"Fine… Let's get to the point, then."

"They need to know where to go next. The markers are useless now."

"Yes," said Sandy. "The Ahns cheated. The wheel was given to its owner too soon."

"Now Tane's furious," continued Amethyst. "He's declaring war." She glanced over at Piper. "And the wheel hasn't bonded yet. Everything's a mess."

Seph glanced over at her again. Hearing her say it like that made her feel strangely small, as if she were just a speck floating about in a *much* larger picture.

"The wheel will bond with its owner in time," Sandy assured her. "All the threads lead to this."

Amethyst looked relieved. "Really?"

"The Ahns weren't wrong," explained Sandy. "The safety of the vaults were compromised. They foresaw the danger. One Hand was almost lost to the infestation, after all."

The infestation. She was talking about Gispuknya. The apocalyptic bug god that was born from the ashes of a dead and corrupted world and the sins of its people. At least, that was how the Ahns described it to them.

They'd seen the broken vault with their own eyes, cracked right down the middle by some unimaginable force.

"The preservation of the cycle comes first," Sandy went on.

"Even Tane knows this. The problem is that the wheel won't be enough to protect her as it is now. She was supposed to collect the wheel using the markers. It would've bonded naturally. And then it would've protected her on her way to Tartarus."

"Tartarus?" said Seph.

"Greek Mythology," recalled Piper, still looking at her feet. "Lowest level of the underworld, where the titans were imprisoned for all time. Basically hell."

"Oh," replied Seph, bewildered. "That sounds fun."

"It's also the name of the nexus," explained Sandy. "Where the Architects inserted the cornerstone on which they'll build the next world. It's a machine built into the very fabric of the universe. Think of it as a pottery wheel. It's the foundation on which the Hands of the Architects will begin shaping the future." Those eyes never looked away. They never even blinked. "The seekers will have to go there to activate the machine and open the nexus. Only then will they have completed their task. The rest will be as the Keeper wills it."

Seph nodded and looked away from those eyes. She couldn't help it. She couldn't take that intense stare any longer. But as soon as she shifted her gaze to the darkness looming behind the woman, she became aware of shapes moving back there. Something was behind her.

Were those…*wings*?

Her thoughts flashed back to the statue at the top of the steps outside. Was Sandy an *angel*?

Everyone lost that Sandy finds ends up here. At the feet of the angel.

She felt a fierce shudder rush through her body.

"To reach Tartarus, however," Sandy continued, "you'll need to open the three locks."

Seph stared into that darkness, distracted.

No. Not wings. Not the kind of wings that were on the angel statue, anyway. Whatever was behind this woman took up much more space than that. Something large and shadowy was piled up back there, slowly shifting, twisting, like the coils of some giant snake.

Her next thought was of the dreaded gorgon with the body of a great serpent and writhing snakes for hair whose magical gaze turned men to stone. The very thought seemed to drag her back to those beautiful eyes with the strength of a celestial force. There was no way to stop it…

No. Her stupid imagination was just getting the better of her. Sandy was no more a monster than the Ahns. She was on their side. If Amethyst trusted her, so did she. Regardless of how many lies she'd told and secrets she was keeping.

"The amber threads clearly point your path. The Keeper's gates are in Waybel Valley in Florida, Pobsick Spring in Texas and Fathom Lake in South Dakota."

Amethyst turned and looked at Seph and Piper. Both of them had just paled. And it wasn't at the idea of traveling all the way to Florida and Texas.

"Did you say Fathom Lake?" croaked Seph. She looked over at Piper, who looked back at her with the same, worried expression that she was sure was mirrored in her own face. Neither of them had ever wanted to have to go anywhere near the city of Fathom Lake ever again.

Those mysterious eyes never looked away from Seph, never dropped, never even blinked. "I understand your concern. You went through an ordeal in Fathom Lake."

"That's kind of a gross understatement," said Seph. The very memory still made her feel sick. She could still see the monstrous thing hiding behind Pappy Stan's fleshy mask. She could almost smell the acrid stench of the smoking sludge bubbling in those awful fryers. And she'd never forget the sounds of Piper's terrified pleading as the hideous thing forced her mouth open to stuff a fistful of foul, worm-ridden meat down her throat.

"Only the custodians can open the Keeper's gates and take you inside the compendium," she went on.

"Compendium?" asked Seph.

"Think of it as a sort of cosmic museum," explained Amethyst. "Or even a zoo. Fragments of the past salvaged and stored for all eternity."

Seph frowned. "You mean like Brainiac and the bottled city of Kandor?"

Amethyst scrunched her face up. "I…have no idea what that is."

"Really? The Superman villain. With the…" She shook her head. "Not important. Forget it."

"You'll need to seek out the custodians at all three locations in order to enter." She sighed. "Unfortunately…it seems that your guide in Fathom Lake is dead."

Amethyst gasped as if someone had slapped her. "What?"

"The threads have shown me. At the diner that harbors so many terrible memories for you, you'll find the custodian long dead."

Seph stared into those creepy, lovely eyes. Long dead…? Stan and Marsha… The *real* Stan and Marsha, the ones who were murdered and partially devoured by the monsters that later pretended to be them… Amethyst told them once that they were supposed to help them on their journey to find her and the scythe at Shawbeck Ranch, but those monsters messed everything up. But if they were the only ones who knew the exact location of the Keeper's gate…

"But how will they enter the Keeper's gate without a custodian?" asked Amethyst.

"There will be a way," Sandy assured her. "There *must* be. The Keeper may be bound by his rules, but it's his duty to preserve the cycle. He'll have a plan. I'm certain of that."

Seph couldn't help but notice that these people put an awful lot of trust in this Keeper guy for someone who liked dead things so much.

"Follow the threads," instructed Sandy. "Begin your search for the locks in Waybel Valley. The Keeper's custodian will find you there and show you the way. But be careful. Tane will already have something unpleasant waiting for you. He already knows the locations of the locks."

"He does?" said Seph, surprised.

"He knows much. His eyes are *everywhere*. He's always watching."

Seph glanced around, surprised. "He's not *here*, is he?"

"Not here," Sandy assured her. "He won't come to this place. I won't let him enter the grove. I *do* sense *something* approaching, however. Something *already* inside the grove."

"Impossible!" exclaimed Amethyst. "The grove is an absolute safe harbor! Nothing can get in without your permission!"

"Not nothing," she corrected. Those lovely, yet unsettling eyes narrowed a little. "Some things don't obey me."

Piper gasped.

Seph looked over to see those spectral ears standing straight up and twitching toward the door behind them. "What is it?"

Piper looked over at her, terrified. A familiar buzzing was rapidly growing inside her head, a sound she hadn't heard since the Ahns destroyed the black council.

"You can hear it, can't you?" said Sandy. "The *bug* draws near."

"Gispuknya!" breathed Seph.

"Your threads are woven through a tangle of pain and grief," sighed Sandy. "The devil and the wretch are only the first of many."

The devil and the wretch? What the hell was that? Pain and grief? Seph didn't like the sound of any of that. What did it mean?

"You'll want to give up before it's over," she warned. "There's no avoiding that. But no matter what happens, you must remember that not all your roads are short. If you keep pushing forward, you *will* find the light at the end of your amber threads."

Seph shook her head. "I don't understand any of that." She looked over at Piper. "Did you understand any of that?"

Piper didn't seem to have heard her. She was staring at the floor at her feet again. Those spectral ears had laid back against her skull, only occasionally twitching at some distant sound outside.

"You must go," said Sandy. "They're almost here."

"But we still don't—"

Amethyst took her by the arm and pulled her toward the front of the spirit guide's mysterious trailer. "Come on! If she says we have to go, *we have to go.*"

Chapter 15

Amethyst led the way back down the candlelit corridor to the door.

Seph looked back over her shoulder, but the creature that called itself Sandy didn't seem to be there anymore. It had withdrawn into the deeper darkness beyond where it'd been sitting. "My god, you guys, that woman's eyes were seriously unsettling. Why was she just staring at *me* the whole time?"

Amethyst and Piper both turned and stared at her.

"You could see her?" asked Piper.

Seph blinked, surprised. "Huh? Yeah. I mean, just her eyes, but… Wait…you couldn't see them?"

She shook her head. "It was too dark."

"Nobody's ever seen what Sandy looks like," said Amethyst. "Not even her eyes. It's always too dark."

Seph stared back at her, confused. But her eyes weren't in the darkness. They were illuminated by that warm beam of light…

Except…now that she was thinking about it…where did that beam even come from? She turned and looked back into that darkness again. The candles were the only source of light. Was it the eyes themselves that were illuminated? Or was it her prophet sight that showed her that turquoise stare?

Was that why she kept them on her? Because she knew she was the only one who could meet her gaze?

"So…" said Piper, her voice timid, "…does…that mean you didn't hear those awful noises she was making?"

Seph turned and stared at her. It suddenly occurred to her that those spirit ears were still laid back in fear. "What?"

"That scratching noise? And those weird *popping* sounds?"

Amethyst shook her head.

"And her *voice*… You guys seriously didn't hear that awful grinding in her voice?"

Seph and Amethyst exchanged a nervous glance.

Piper looked down at her feet again. She was ringing her hands. "And the…whispering…" she added, her voice getting smaller and smaller with each word she spoke.

"My god, Pea…"

She shook her head. "It's okay. I didn't feel like she was *trying* to scare me. If anything, that weird whispering seemed like it was trying to calm me. But…" She looked up, her eyes gleaming in the candlelight. "It was like listening to a voice from a nightmare. I felt so scared I thought I was going to throw up."

Seph reached out and squeezed her hand. She looked up at Amethyst, then back into that mysterious darkness again. "What *is* she?" she asked.

Amethyst shook her head. She didn't know. But it didn't matter. "Come on. We have to go."

The three of them stepped out of Sandy's mysterious trailer and made their way back through the eerie gloom of the grassy path.

Piper was concentrating on not falling down again in her cute-but-highly-inappropriate footwear when her phone rang again. She reached into her purse, swearing to herself that if it was Meg again, she was finally going to tell her off, but when she looked at the screen, she found that it was Kaitlyn again.

She bit her lip, uncertain. She liked Kaitlyn a lot. She was such a sweet girl, with a *huge* heart, but she had a bad habit of poking around in other people's business and an even worse habit of worrying herself over silly, unimportant things. Right now, she was undoubtedly concerned about the fact that she still hadn't gotten back to her about this weekend.

And in her defense, it *was* kind of unusual for Piper not to get back to people right away.

She first called last night, but Seph had gone to bed early because she hadn't been sleeping well. She promised to ask her in the morning and get right back to her, but she forgot. By the time she remembered to ask her, they were inside that elevator where she didn't have a signal and then…well then *everything else.*

That noise was telling her that Gispuknya's shadows were close, but it wasn't getting any louder. She might have a minute now, if she was quick, and who knew when she'd have time again?

She accepted the call. "Kaitlyn?"

"Hi Peeps!"

Piper turned and looked back the way they'd come. The forest down here was silent. Nothing was moving, not even the wind. "Sorry I didn't get back to you. It's been kind of a crazy day."

"It's okay. I was just a little worried. You know me."

She *did* know her.

"So did you talk to Seph about this weekend."

"Yeah. She totally wants to, but, uh…she thinks she'll have to get back to you about it later this week. She's got that huge project she's working on at work and might get stuck working."

"Bummer!"

"Yeah..." As bad as it sounded, lying was one of Piper's more impressive talents. She was surprisingly good at it, it seemed. And it'd come in handy quite a lot since she met Seph. Making up stories about doing research for a graduate thesis was much more productive than telling people you're looking for an ancient artifact capable of building a universe.

"Well let me know as soon as she knows, okay?"

"Sure."

"By the way, where *are* you?"

"Oh, I've been all over the place today," she lied. "Running errands. Nothing exciting. Getting my exercise for the day." That last part, at least, was definitely the truth. Her poor legs were already aching. She was *really* wishing now that she'd picked more practical shoes.

"So, you're in Cakwetak?"

"Yeah." She frowned. Something in Kaitlyn's tone seemed a little off. It felt strangely as if she were being interrogated. "Where else would I be?"

"Keep up!" called Seph. Unimpeded by their more sensible shoes, she and Amethyst were leaving her behind.

"Was that Seph?"

"Huh? Oh. Yeah. She's with me."

"She's not at work?"

She blinked, surprised. That's right, Seph was supposed to be at work right now. Thinking quickly, she replied, "No, she got the afternoon off."

"But she might have to work this weekend?"

Piper bit her lip. *Dammit.* What was the deal? Why was Kaitlyn acting so suspicious all of a sudden? "Well that's part of the problem," she explained. "There was some kind of crash in the computer system and everyone had to go home early."

"Huh."

Ahead of her, Amethyst and Seph abruptly stopped. She froze, startled, her spirit ears perked.

The buzzing had suddenly gotten louder while she was distracted with Kaitlyn.

Gispuknya's shadows were much closer now.

And they were still getting closer.

Something moved in the dense brush behind her and she twirled around, a startled cry escaping her.

"What's wrong?" asked Kaitlyn, worried. "Peeps? What's going on?"

"Nothing," she replied, staring into the woods where the noise had come from. Maybe it was just a squirrel. Or a bird. Or even just a falling branch. "I tripped was all. I'm fine."

But was she?

Something snapped in the woods to the left and Seph and Amethyst both twirled around, startled.

"See anything?" asked Amethyst.

Seph shook her head. "No, but I've got a bad feeling."

Amethyst nodded. "Me too." She looked back at Piper. "We have to hurry!" she called.

Piper didn't need to be told. She could feel it. A fresh panic was rapidly filling her, starting in her belly and worming its way outward.

"Who's that?" asked Kaitlyn.

She hurried forward, as fast as her heels would allow, struggling to catch up before Seph and Amethyst ran ahead again. "I'm sorry, I've got to go!"

"What?" gasped Kaitlyn. "Wait! What's going on? Why're you—?"

Piper disconnected the call and stuffed the phone back into her purse.

"Hurry!" snapped Seph.

"I'm sorry!"

The three of them pushed forward, their eyes peeled for danger.

The steps were just up ahead. At the top, the angel waited and watched over the truck.

But they stopped as soon as they reached the first of those concrete steps.

Halfway up, blocking their path, were three black creatures.

No. They were *more* than black. These things were unnaturally dark, like pools of living shadows stretched into monstrous shapes with jaws and teeth. They looked a little like greyhounds, with long legs and haunches, slender waists, and deep chests, but their heads were far too big, with teeth more resembling the tusks of a boar, except that they were the same impossible, deep black as the rest of the beasts' bodies. And they had long, bushy tails that dragged the ground behind them, stirring up dust as they swished back and forth.

"Gispuknya hounds," gasped Amethyst.

Seph's heart was pounding. This wasn't good. There was nowhere for them to go. They were trapped.

Somewhere off to their left, deep inside the dense woods, something rustled in the brush. A moment later, the same sound came from the other side.

"They're surrounding us." Amethyst turned and cocked her head, listening. "Now's probably a good time to show off that scythe."

The handle was already unfurling itself from her hands. She hoped it worked this time. Although, truth be told, even if it *did* work, she wasn't sure how confident she was about taking on a pack of shadow wolves with a giant, old-school *weed whacker.*

Why couldn't it have been the Grim Reaper's *assault rifle*?

Amethyst glanced back at Piper. "And you… The Ahns said you could use that wheel, even if it's not bonded yet."

Piper reached into her sweater and pulled out the pendant. "But I still don't know how to work it."

"Just do the same thing you did earlier," said Seph as the scythe's blade took form in front of her, glimmering like glass in the shade of the forest. "When you drenched Tane."

Piper stared back at her. "I don't *know* what I did!"

"You must've done *something*!"

"I started crying and I almost wet myself! Do you think it was one of those things?" She stared up at the snarling monsters making their way slowly down the steps toward them. "Because I think I might be moving in that direction again!"

"The spinning wheel is supposed to weave matter into existence," explained Amethyst. "It sounds like it produces things you need out of thin air. Especially when you need it the most."

Piper stared at the strange, little golden ring with its odd assortment of colorful crystals molded into it. Matter out of thin air… Weaving things into existence when she needed them most…. Like a fire alarm within arm's reach when a madman was trying to burn her face off? Or a clearly visible door to mark an unseen passage in a dead-end tunnel when something terrible was bearing down on her? Or an empty walkway in a zombie-infested marsh that just happened to lead straight toward the parking lot? Or even a conveniently timed portal to another world containing a crosser monstrous enough to scare away a murderous mob of terrifying, black-eyed children?

She stared at it as a chill crept up the nape of her neck.

Rumpelstiltskin's spinning wheel…

Now that she was really thinking about it, every single time she'd gotten herself into a pinch and reached for the pendant Annalisa told her would protect her, she always found some convenient thing to save herself. She'd thought those things were always there and that she just couldn't see them at first, like those things that only Seph could see. But the truth was that the wheel was *creating* those things for her.

It really was the third Hand of the Architects…

She was holding it in her hand right now…

But…it looked nothing like Seph's scythe or Tane's hammer. And all those things she did… She did them all subconsciously, in moments of sheer terror. She had no idea how to make it work on command. *Would* it even work if she wasn't in dire peril?

The three Gispuknya hounds on the steps drew closer.

Amethyst stepped in front of them and gestured toward the one in the lead.

Seph watched the stone beneath its paws bubble. A second later, the creature dropped through one of Amethyst's mysterious portals and vanished.

It was one of her more impressive abilities. Only Seph could actually see the portals. That weird, bubbling illusion was a product of her prophet sight. To everyone else, even Amethyst, they were invisible. To them, the beast had just vanished from sight like a stage magician through a trapdoor.

According to Amethyst, these portals led to whatever worlds happened to be nearby. Wherever the shadowy mutt had just gone, it wasn't likely to ever find its way back.

The other two creatures paused and sniffed at the concrete where their companion had just vanished. They seemed confused. But only for a moment. Then they dismissed the entire thing and turned their attention back to the prey at the bottom of the steps.

Another portal opened beneath the one on the left, but this time it leaped back and out of the way, avoiding the fate of the first one.

Amethyst cursed. "They're smarter than they look."

Another of the beasts burst through the brush and sprinted toward them.

Seph cried out, startled, and swung the scythe in a blind panic.

The monster was cut cleanly in two…but unfortunately, so were two tall pine trees, which crashed to the ground, one of them only narrowly missing Piper as she screamed and stumbled out of the way.

"Oops…" said Seph, cringing.

"What the heck, Persephone?"

"Sorry!"

Amethyst opened another portal at the second Gispuknya hound's feet. This time, when it jumped back, it only succeeded in falling through the second portal that she opened at the same time. "Not *that* smart, are you?" she chided.

A fifth monster appeared then, far more cautious than the one before it. It crawled out of the brush, its head low to the ground, its black eyes fixed on the crystal-like blade of the scythe.

Seph turned to face it and began slowly backing away. If she could just keep that blade between her and it, maybe it wouldn't risk pouncing. She wasn't at all confident that her aim would be lethal a second time. Or that the scythe wouldn't just burst like it did in Tane's basement and lobby. "We need to get out of here."

"Agreed," said Amethyst.

Another one leapt from the brush and bounded straight at Piper.

She clutched the pendant in her hands, but nothing was happening. She screamed.

Amethyst turned around and thrust her arm toward the monster, opening a portal directly in its path. In an instant, the beast vanished.

"Oh gosh…" gasped Piper, her heart thudding in her chest. She *really* didn't like this.

Amethyst turned back to find the last of the three on the stairs leaping at her. She jumped backward and opened another portal right where she was standing a second before.

The beast vanished with an almost comical yelp.

"Up the steps!" she shouted, sounding winded. "Now!"

"Little busy here!" grunted Seph, who was still locked in eye-contact with the monster crouched in front of her.

Amethyst opened another portal under it, but its reflexes were too fast. It leapt to the side, out of the way. She opened a second where it landed, with the same result. Then a third. The monster evaded it as well, but with its attention drawn to the portals, it never saw the scythe coming.

It cut through these creatures like smoke, leaving nothing behind.

And yet, for some reason those big pine trees were still lying where they fell. Weren't trees living things, too? Why didn't they disintegrate like the monsters? How did this thing work? She didn't understand it.

"Go!" shouted Amethyst.

Seph let go of the scythe, letting it splash back into her hands. Then she grabbed Piper's elbow and the two of them ran up the steps with Amethyst at their heels.

"I didn't get an owner's manual for this thing!" cried Piper, shaking the pendant at Seph.

"Just don't let go of it!" replied Seph. "And run faster!"

"This is as fast as I can go!"

"Ugh! You and those stupid heels!"

"They're fashionable!"

"Fantastic! You'll be an adorable *corpse*!" She glanced back down the steps to find that Amethyst had stopped. Two more hounds had crawled out of the woods behind her and bounded up the steps, forcing her to turn and face them. "Amethyst!"

"Keep going!" she shouted as she opened several bubbling portals in an attempt to box the monsters in. "I'll catch up in a minute!"

Seph didn't want to leave her. She'd seen more than enough horror movies to know that splitting up was never a good idea. But Amethyst knew how to take care of herself. Even as they stood there watching, one of the two hounds lost its footing and vanished into a portal, leaving only one stubborn monster.

Reluctantly, she turned and ran on.

A moment later, she and Piper reached the top of the steps, only to stumble to a stop beneath the outstretched wings of the angel statue.

Four more Gispuknya hounds were crouched between them and the truck, blocking their escape.

Seph cursed and unfurled the scythe again, letting the long, curved blade stretch between them and the monsters.

"What do we do?" squeaked Piper.

But Seph didn't know what to do. She might've been able to cut down one of them, especially out here in the open where she didn't have to worry about any more trees falling on them. Maybe. But she was sure she couldn't fend off four of them at once.

She dared a quick glance over her shoulder.

The other hound was giving Amethyst a hard time. It kept avoiding her portals.

"Now would be an excellent time to make that wheel work!" said Seph. Her voice was doing that squeaking thing that Piper's did when she was scared. She *really* hated that.

"I'm trying!" She was squeezing it as hard as she could. Her knuckles had turned white. She could feel her palm sweating. But it didn't seem to be working. It wasn't getting warm like it did in Tane's elevator.

She still didn't know how to turn it on!

The Gispuknya hounds crept toward them. They meant to go for it. They knew she couldn't take out all four of them. It was merely a game of numbers.

Seph and Piper took a step backward. They could run back the way they came, but the moment their back was turned, these monsters would pounce. And there was nowhere else to go anyway. They needed to get to the truck and get out of here. Otherwise, Gispuknya would only keep throwing things at them until they were finally overwhelmed.

But the monsters were moving faster now.

They meant to have their prey while the chance was theirs.

Seph didn't know what to do. Was this where it ended? Had they failed?

"Is that the only shape that thing can make?" asked Piper.

"What?"

"I mean, it's made of *water*, isn't it?"

Seph looked down at the weapon in her hands, surprised. She was right. It was in the shape of the Reaper's scythe, a long, crooked handle and an even longer, curved blade, but the whole thing was made out of water! There was absolutely no reason for it to remain in this cumbersome form.

She took a deep breath and thrust the handle forward.

The Gispuknya hounds spread out, intending to take her from separate directions. Working together and going on the offensive, they were more than capable of getting past a single blade. But when the scythe split into *four different blades*, all of them lashing outward like individual swords, they never saw it coming.

All four of them were hacked out of existence with a single slash.

"Wow…" said Seph as she watched the water vanish back into her hands. "I totally rock with this thing."

"Don't get cocky," grumbled Piper, looking down at the pendant in her hand. What was she doing wrong? Was it her state of mind?

"Get in the truck!" shouted Amethyst. She'd finally banished the stubborn hound and was running up the steps toward them.

But as soon as they turned around, they found one more Gispuknya hound racing toward them.

Seph shoved Piper out of the way and thrust her hand out at the thing, but the scythe came apart and splashed harmlessly around the beast.

It lunged at her, its huge jaws opening wide.

She had a split-second to register the bubbling ground around her, then she was falling. She felt her insides float up into her chest. She felt her heart stutter.

Then someone grabbed her hand and jolted her to a stop.

"*Seph*!"

Amethyst hovered above her, holding her, trying to pull her back up.

Below her, the Gispuknya hound was plunging into a queer darkness over an immense forest crowded with strange-looking, naked trees.

"I'm sorry!" gasped Amethyst. "I got tired! I couldn't control the size of the portal!"

Seph stared into the vast emptiness over which she was precariously dangling, a petrifying terror gripping her. It was at least a hundred feet down to the tops of those trees. If Amethyst were to lose her grip, there was no way she'd survive such a fall. But somehow that wasn't what terrified her about this situation.

This place felt *bad.* The air was stale and cold and thin. It had an unpleasant stench about it.

Wherever this was, it was nowhere she ever wanted to be stranded.

She reached up and grabbed Amethyst's wrist with her other hand. "What's down there?"

"That's the Wood! It's where all the worlds go when they die! *Help me! I don't know how long I can keep it open!*"

Piper was there, then. She reached into the portal and seized her wrist.

Seph looked down into that darkness again. Where worlds went when they died? Something about those words was incredibly creepy. It was as if she'd already known that, as if she'd seen this place before. Perhaps in a dream?

Slowly, Amethyst and Piper were pulling her back up.

This was so bizarre. She was dangling between two worlds. Empty darkness spread out beneath her. Open blue sky spread out above her. And in-between was *nothing.* The border revealed by Amethyst's bubbling portal was as thin as spider silk, virtually non-existent.

It was dizzying.

"*Hurry!*" cried Amethyst, a clear note of panic in her voice. "*Before*

I lose my grip on the portal!"

Seph couldn't help but wonder what that meant? Would she simply fall if the portal closed? Or would it tear her in half, leaving part of her to plummet into that black hell while the rest of her died an agonizing, bloody death under a sunny, Missouri sky?

Slowly, Seph felt herself lifted out of that cold, stale air. She kicked her leg out and hooked it over the paper-thin edge. There was literally nothing beneath the dirt she was digging her heel and elbows into. It shouldn't have been able to hold her weight, and yet it was perfectly solid.

Her mind was so strange. The only thing she should be focused on was climbing to safety, but half of her brain was obsessing over the mysterious properties of Amethyst's portal while the other half of her brain screamed at her that her skirt had ridden up and that she was now flashing her panties at everybody.

She thought her priorities were in better order than that.

Finally, Seph crawled out of the portal and Amethyst swallowed her in her arms. "Thank God!" she gasped. "Are you okay?"

"I'm fine."

"That was too close…"

"It's okay," said Seph. "I mean it *was* close. But I'm okay."

But Amethyst shook her head. "No. It's *not* okay. If you'd fallen…"

"I'm fine," she insisted, glancing over at Piper. It was a lie. She wasn't fine. Her heart was racing. She was trembling. Her legs were weak. But she felt weird being held by Amethyst like that. "Let's just get out of here."

Amethyst nodded. Together, they stood up.

Seph dusted herself off and looked up at her. She had a single second to register the towering shadow that was standing over her before a black, spade-shaped thing burst from the middle of Amethyst's chest.

Chapter 16

"Oh no..." gasped Piper.

Seph couldn't find any words.

Amethyst stared back at her, those big, brown eyes wide with shock.

Her lips moved, but no sound escaped her.

A blood-red stain blossomed on the front of her western shirt, around the thing sticking out of her chest.

No... This wasn't happening. It couldn't be. This wasn't how things were supposed to go.

The spade-shaped thing peeled apart into several long, pointed fingers. She watched the blood drip from them in silent horror. Then, with a sick, wet sound, it suddenly withdrew again.

Amethyst's body jerked backward. She took a single step, wavered there on her feet for a moment, then fell forward onto the ground.

Just like that, Amethyst was gone.

She was dead.

Her blood was soaking into the dirt beneath her.

Seph's whole body was numb. She stood frozen, staring at the shadowy figure that now loomed before her. It towered over her, with a great, barrel-like chest and long, strangely slender arms ending in those weird, spade-shaped hands. Like the hounds, it was entirely black, covered in a shaggy, oily-looking fur. And like those horrid teethers, it was freakishly proportioned. The upper half of its torso made up most of its mass. It stood on short, stubby legs that ended in wide, hairy, hoof-like feet. It had no neck; its unusually wide head sat directly on its shoulders. And great, branched horns, like the antlers of some massive, monstrous deer, towered over all of it.

A devil…

The devil and the wretch are only the first of many, Sandy had warned them. She said it right after she told them that their amber threads were woven through a tangle of pain and grief.

Was this what she meant? Was this the pain and the grief?

"Persephone…" breathed Piper.

The devil made a sound like gears clicking together on a bicycle, but long and slow. Eerie. For reasons she could never understand, it made Seph think of the threatening, guttural growl of an angry dog replayed in slow motion on a broken recorder. A hellish sort of sound, if ever she'd heard one.

It lifted its hands and spread those murderous, dagger-like fingers, half of them still dripping with Amethyst's blood.

Piper pulled at her jacket, tugging her backward. "Persephone!"

More Gispuknya hounds were approaching from the steps behind the devil monster. Two of them, their heads down, their black tusks glinting in the sun. And more were probably on their way.

They needed to leave.

And yet, Seph couldn't seem to make her feet move. She couldn't drag her eyes from Amethyst's motionless body.

How could this happen? She was supposed to stay with them this time. She was supposed to show them the way.

She promised…

They couldn't do this without her…

"*Persephone*!"

The devil lurched forward.

Piper screamed.

But Seph still couldn't move. She stared straight ahead and wide-eyed as the monster's deadly hands slammed against the glass.

She blinked, confused. "Wha…?"

"Come on!" Piper grabbed her hand and pulled at her.

The devil seemed equally confused. It stood on the other side of a large, free-standing window fitted with what could only be a thick pane of bulletproof glass.

It wasn't much of an obstacle. All the stupid thing had to do was walk around it. An entire cage to hold the beast might've been a better option, but it was all Piper had time to think of in that split second.

In fact, to say that she thought of it at all was something of a lie. It happened so fast that it was difficult to tell if it appeared because she thought of it or if she thought of it because it appeared.

And for the moment at least, it seemed as completely incapable of understanding what had happened as Seph was.

Even the hounds behind it seemed baffled.

"*Hurry up*!"

Seph took a couple steps backward, but that was all. Her brain didn't want to work. She was caught in a fog. She was numb.

It wasn't real.

That window was proof enough of that.

Windows didn't just appear from thin air.

And shadowy devils didn't stab people through the back in broad daylight.

That was…that was just how the world worked…it was crazy to

think otherwise…

The devil slammed its spade-shaped hand into the glass again. This time, it left a neat little hole, just like a bullet, but nothing more. The frame didn't even wobble. It was remarkably sturdy for a figment of her imagination…

Piper wasn't sure how long the glass would last any more than she was sure how she managed to conjure it. Did things the spinning wheel created last forever? Or did they fade away in time? Thinking back, she was pretty sure she'd conjured an entire walkway back in that marsh outside Avelby. Surely it wasn't still there. Wouldn't they have heard about a brand-new stretch of walking path appearing mysteriously overnight in a protected nature preserve?

That seemed like the sort of thing that would make the news.

But Avelby was pretty far from Cakwetak. Maybe she just didn't see it.

Or maybe, now that she was thinking about it, there was some sort of magic attached to the spinning wheel that made people ignore the new things it created. Maybe the wheel not only created new things, but also constructed a history to go with those things, adding them not only to the physical world, but into the very memories of the people who came across them. That would be the easiest scenario, though probably far too convenient.

It was funny how her brain worked. She shouldn't be thinking at all. She should just be running away. The whole of her attention should've been fixed only on getting Seph away from here and into the truck and driving away as fast as possible.

Not for the first time, she wondered if she might just be crazy.

Seph's gaze fell on the motionless form of the woman who was once her best friend. Countless memories raced through her mind. She never thought it would end like this. She never thought she'd run out of time to make things right between them. She had so many regrets.

A sudden and seething rage welled up within her. She looked up at the devil. It'd finally figured out that it could simply walk around the window. It was shuffling around it on those squatty devil legs, peering around the side of the frame with its empty, black eyes.

She barely even thought about it. She thrust her hand out at it. A long, watery blade shot from her palm and pierced the monster between those awful eyes.

It let out a strange, clockwork kind of cry, a weird, clicking, grinding sort of sound that seemed far more machine than creature, and with a great gushing of foul, black gore, it melted away and was gone.

But there was little to celebrate. Amethyst was still dead. And the Gispuknya hounds remained.

There were three of them now. They didn't seem fazed by the gruesome fate of their horned companion. They didn't even hesitate.

Piper was still clinging to her hand, still tugging at her. She pulled her backward, away from the approaching hounds, a series of terrified whimpers and squeaks bubbling up from somewhere near her pounding heart.

Even in her state of shock, Seph knew it was time to go. She didn't want to. She didn't want to leave Amethyst like that. But the monsters would only keep coming.

Annalisa told them that Gispuknya had limits to what it could summon, which was almost certainly why it didn't send everything it had at once to overwhelm them. But as long as they stayed here, it would only be a matter of time before they were exhausted and overwhelmed.

Piper opened the truck's passenger-side door and pushed Seph into it.

Still numb, Seph climbed up into the seat.

The hounds were moving more quickly now. Piper scrambled in after her, slamming and locking the door behind her as the monsters converged on the vehicle. Then she crawled over her and across the old Ram's bench seat and locked the driver-side door, too.

The hounds circled the truck like hungry sharks. They snarled. They growled. They jumped up on the doors, clawing and snapping at the glass, but that was all they were able to do.

They seemed to be safe…but only for the moment. It was only a matter of time before something else arrived. They needed to leave this place *now*.

But her eyes fell on Amethyst's body, lying on the ground in the shadow of the stone angel, and she couldn't help but pause. "Oh my gosh…" she whimpered. Why did *she* have to be the brave one? She couldn't handle this. She wasn't as strong as Seph.

The keys were still in the ignition, which was good. Perhaps the wheel might've made a key for her if the need had arisen, but she didn't like the thought of relying on it. So far, it'd only worked while she was in full-on panic mode. She started the engine and backed the truck up, pointing it back the way they came.

She hoped she could figure out how to get out of here. Nora's Lilac Grove was so big…

Seph turned and stared out the window at the motionless form of her ex-roommate.

That was her best friend, once upon a time. The person she felt closest to in the entire world.

Before all the lies unraveled…

Was she too hard on her? Was she being selfish that whole time?

Oh god…

The Gispuknya hounds followed them, still snarling and snapping at the tires, but only for about fifty yards or so. Then they simply gave up. The last Piper saw of them, they were standing in the middle of the drive in the rearview, watching them go.

Perhaps they weren't built for long-distance stalking, in spite of their greyhound-like bodies. Perhaps they were more suited to short bursts of speed. Or perhaps they simply understood that they had no hope of getting to them inside the safety of the truck cab.

Either way, Piper was glad to be rid of them. She glanced over at Seph, worried. "Are you okay?"

"Why didn't she tell us?"

"What?"

Seph turned and looked at her. Her eyes were oddly empty. "Sandy said she could see people's fates. Their possibilities. Their *future.* All that talk about amber threads… But if she could see what was going to happen…?" Tears streaked down her cheeks. "Why would she not say something? She told her she loved her…but she just let her…?" Her voice cracked. She couldn't say it aloud.

Piper didn't have an answer for her.

She turned and looked away. "None of this stuff ever makes any sense," she whispered.

No. It didn't. Piper turned her attention back to the road.

There was something there.

She stepped on the brake, bringing the old truck to a stop. "What the heck is *that* thing?"

Seph leaned forward and squinted at it.

It was just sitting there. A lump of darkness in the otherwise bright, sunlit day. At night, it might've been mistaken for a wadded-up tarp or an old, discarded blanket. But in this light, it didn't look like anything that should be lying there. It was *too* dark. *Too* shadowy. It was as if the sunlight falling all around it didn't even touch it.

It was…*wrong.*

Whatever it was, it didn't belong there. It didn't belong *anywhere.* Both of them felt it. A cold shiver crept through them at the very sight of it. Instinctively, they knew that it was bad.

And then it *moved.*

It lifted its head and turned a withered and hideous face toward them. It was human, she realized. Or…human-*shaped*, at least. It was lying in a sort of shadowy puddle, beneath greasy-looking, black rags, its limbs folded up beneath it, looking oddly *broken.* It was almost as if the unfortunate thing had fallen out of the sky and landed there, snapping every bone in its body when it struck the ground.

Unlike most of Gispuknya's shadows, it wasn't entirely black. Its flesh, where visible, was a dark and moldy shade of gray, giving it an eerie, corpse-like appearance. Its head was mostly bald, but what little hair it had was long, limp and silver when the sunlight hit it. Its face was sickly, with deep, dark, sunken eyes and whisper-thin lips. It was only the rags in which it was dressed that were black and shadowy.

And its eyes… It had the same black eyes as those creepy children Piper encountered in July. Except that the blackness extended *around* this thing's eyes, darkening most of its upper face, like a mask of dark bruises.

"Should I go around?" asked Piper.

"You should go around," affirmed Seph.

The thing unfolded its broken form, reached out with long, skeleton-thin hands and began dragging itself over the gravel toward them.

The tips of those bony hands were the same black as the top half of its face, withered and bony. They looked as if they'd been burned away in some awful accident.

"*Definitely go around*!" screamed Seph.

Piper didn't need any encouragement. She was already shifting the truck into reverse and backing away from the awful thing.

It was longer than it should've been. As it pulled itself along, its body seemed to stretch out, unfolding itself, revealing a shape far longer than it should've been. From its blackened fingertips to its dragging toes, it was at least fifteen feet long.

And the closer it came, the more corpse-like that awful face appeared.

The devil and the wretch are only the first of many, Seph thought, remembering Sandy's warning. This, she realized, was the thing she called the wretch. And it wasn't difficult to see why she chose such a name. The thing certainly *looked* wretched.

Piper shifted the truck back into drive and sped down another of the park's winding lanes, spinning gravel as she went. She hoped this didn't turn out to be a dead end. "Is it following us?"

Seph had already turned to look out the back window. "I don't know. I lost sight of it."

But as she watched, those long, black, skeletal fingertips reached up and curled around the rim of the tailgate.

Chapter 17

Seph stared at that hand, her eyes widening with horror. Her very mind felt numb. It didn't make sense. Piper couldn't drive very fast on these narrow, gravel drives, but she was certainly going faster than this thing was crawling. How did it catch up to them? And where was the rest of it? As long as it was, she should be able to see those black rags it was wrapped in dragging behind them.

But then again, she had a bad habit of trying to cling to logic in situations like this. And logic simply didn't apply to Gispuknya shadows in multi-dimensional trailer parks run by mysterious, darkness-dwelling, spirit guide monsters.

Piper turned at the end of the drive and made her way past several overgrown lawns and dilapidated trailers. "At least *that one* wasn't very fast."

Seph looked over at her. Her mouth was moving, but she couldn't seem to make the words. All that came out was one of those wimpy squeaks. She looked back and saw the other hand closing around the top of the tailgate.

"How do we get out of here?" asked Piper.

She tried again and this time managed a slightly louder squeak, enough to at least catch Piper's attention.

She glanced over at her, those blue eyes wide again. "*What's wrong?*" She leaned over and looked into the rearview in time to see those black eyes appear over the tailgate.

Her voice was working fine. Her scream was loud and piercing.

She stomped the accelerator. The truck lurched forward with a great revving of the engine and kicked up a spray of dust and gravel, but the wretch only continued to slowly pull itself up over the tailgate, those black-on-black eyes staring back at them.

"*It's not letting go!*" squeaked Seph.

"*I know!*" Piper squeaked back at her as she watched the creepy thing in the rearview mirror. "*What do I do?*"

"*I don't know!*"

Piper turned hard at the next drive, hoping to shake the foul thing. But although Seph was thrown hard against her, mashing her against the driver-side door, the wretch didn't even pause.

It just kept coming. Its shoulders were passing over the top of the tailgate now. In just a few more seconds, it was going to be inside the bed of the truck!

"*Get rid of it!*" screamed Piper.

Seph was still struggling to right herself after the sudden turn. "*What am* I *supposed to do?*"

"*Aren't you the grim reaper now? Use the scythe!*"

"*I'm not—*" She shook her head, flustered. She was no such thing. The grim reaper didn't even exist. It was nothing more than one of the many myths that evolved from the bizarre history of the Hands of the Architects. "Even if I could, I can't use the scythe from inside the truck!"

"So open the window!"

Seph stared at the latch that opened the old Ram's sliding rear window. "You're kidding, right?"

"*Do you have a better idea?*"

She didn't.

She stared out at the monster as it reached down and pressed those creepy, black fingers against the scarred metal of the truck bed.

"It's that or we ditch the truck," reasoned Piper. "And I really don't think we'll get very far on foot."

Seph cursed under her breath. That was a pretty solid argument. There were Gispuknya hounds out there. And any number of *other* horrors, too, she was sure.

She snapped the latch back and slid open the back window. She was immediately rewarded with a gust of air that reeked of death and decay. "*Oh my god*!" she gasped.

Piper choked and clasped her hand over her mouth. "What *is* that?"

The odorous creeper stared back with those black eyes, unashamed of its horrendous personal hygiene.

"Don't drive crazy!" snapped Seph.

"I don't drive crazy! I drive good! Those things *make* me drive crazy!"

"Whatever! Just don't let me die while I'm doing this!"

"What? *No*! No more dying! Be careful!"

"This was *your* idea!" Seph stood up on the seat and shimmied through the narrow window until the top half of her body was in the bed of the truck with the wretch and its awful stench and her back half was prominently aimed at the windshield.

"I thought you were just going to stick the *scythe* out the window!" shouted Piper.

"It's too big! I wouldn't be able to swing it like that!"

"Don't get stuck!"

"You're not helping!" Seph shouted back at her. Balancing there, with her hands clutching the rim of the truck bed, she suddenly realized that she had no idea how she was supposed to use the scythe without tumbling all the way out of the cab. She lifted her head and looked up at the monster.

It stared back at her, its chin nearly touching the floor of the bed, its blackened fingers clawing at the rusty metal, its strange torso stretched over the tailgate as if it were made of rubber.

It was only a few short feet from her face.

The closer she was to the awful thing, the more disturbing it was. From this distance, she could see that its gray flesh was covered in blisters and sores. There was a large knot protruding from one side of its skull. A greenish goo was oozing from its ears. And half of its nose had been eaten away.

The thing looked like the victim of some horrendous plague.

As she stared at it, the wretch opened its mouth in a wide, silent scream and a foul, black ichor spilled over its rotten teeth and down its chin, pooling on the floor of the truck bed.

Seph screamed.

"*What's going on?*" shouted Piper.

Seph wedged her knees against the back of the seat. With a loud and fairly unladylike grunt, she let go of the truck bed and thrust her fists out at the monster.

The scythe splashed harmlessly over the monster's head and onto the tailgate.

No! Not now!

Again, the wretch reached out with its skeletal fingers. Again it dragged itself a little closer to her.

She steadied herself with one hand and thrust the other one out at the monster again.

Again, it broke apart.

She cursed and grabbed the rim of the truck bed again. This time, she placed her hand in something slimy and slipped forward, scraping her belly on the window frame.

"*What's happening*?" cried Piper as Seph's feet flailed at the dashboard. She looked over and saw that her skirt was riding up. She grabbed the hem and yanked it back down for her. "Persephone?"

Seph grimaced and wiped the sludge off her hand. (It was probably engine grease or something; it *was* a work truck for the ranch, after all.) Then she pushed herself back up. "I'm okay!"

She looked up to see that the wretch had crawled closer now.

Did it even have a body? Or was it all arms and face and empty rags?

It raised a hand and reached out for her.

This was her last chance. If the scythe failed her again, things were going to go very badly. She was sure of it.

She clenched her teeth, tightened her muscles and thrust both her hands at the monster's hideous face.

The gleaming blade of the scythe shimmered in the sunlight as it lashed outward and buried itself in the tailgate.

She missed.

The wretch was much faster than the devil. As she hovered there, half-in and half-out of the pickup's cab, straining her muscles to remain upright, she saw it lying in the gravel drive behind them, its black eyes watching them as Piper drove away. Its long, freakish body lay stretched out behind it, looking eerily like the tail of a giant, black serpent.

Then Piper turned down another drive and the monster vanished from sight.

She began wriggling her way back into the cab, cursing under her breath as the frame pushed up her shirt and scraped against her bare belly.

"Is it dead?"

"No. But it's gone," she grunted. "Ouch! I think I'm stuck."

"Suck it in."

"It's not my gut! My bra's caught on something! Rude!"

"Take it off, then. I don't know. Jeez."

"I'm not taking my top off!" snapped Seph.

Piper glanced over at her. "You're mostly out of it anyway."

"Just get us out of here already!" She wedged her feet against the dashboard and pushed herself back through the window a couple of inches, allowing herself to untangle the cloth from the window latch. Once she was free, she wriggled back into the cab and slammed the window shut.

She was thankful no one but Piper was here to see her as she yanked down her shirt and started putting everything back where it belonged. Even her skirt was hiked all the way up to her waist. Plus, she'd scraped her belly and sides up on the stupid window frame during her struggle. That was probably going to sting for a while.

But at least the wretch seemed to be gone for now. She kept looking back at the tailgate, watching for those creepy black fingers to reach up and curl around it again, but it seemed to have given up for the moment.

"That was really freaky!" gasped Piper. "And *stinky*! My gosh that thing reeked!"

"At least you weren't out there *with* it," she retorted as she pushed her skirt back down where it belonged.

"What would *I* have done? *My* Hand only works when I'm about two seconds from peeing myself!" She lifted the pendant and looked at it. "I feel like I'm dangerously under-equipped for this job."

Seph finished tugging her shirt back into place and sat down, still keeping an eye on that tailgate. She felt exhausted. "Just get us out of here already."

Piper let go of the pendant and gripped the wheel with both hands. "I *hope* I can find my way out of here."

But strangely, the way back out of Nora's Lilac Grove seemed a lot shorter than the way in, once they finally got away from Gispuknya's shadow monsters. In just a short amount of time, she found the park's entrance and sped off down the highway.

Amethyst showed them all the useful fringe road entrances in Wisconsin, but they had no idea where to find one anywhere in Missouri. Since they looked just like any other road, they wouldn't know one even if they saw it.

Meaning they'd have to take the long way to Waybel Valley.

Piper checked her phone. They were in the middle of nowhere, heading toward a town called Dunnen. They were going to have to drive all night to get to Florida, and they didn't have so much as a change of clothes.

(So much for those survival kits Wanda stashed in their vehicles. Seph's Ford was still in the Vertical Design parking lot in Cakwetak and Piper's Jeep was in Nebraska with a bunch of holes in it.)

Meanwhile, Tane was sure to be preparing something nasty for them when they arrived.

This definitely wasn't going to be a Disney vacation.

Chapter 18

They stopped for dinner in Briar Hills, Missouri. Drive-through, naturally. Spending too long in one place wasn't a good idea. Just filling up the old Ram's gas tank took every ounce of patience Piper had. The pump seemed to take forever.

She probably looked like an escaped convict. She kept looking around, paranoid, jumping at every little noise. She eyed every single person who walked by as if they were a potential murderer. Her heart wouldn't stop pounding. It felt as if she were only one small "boo" from cardiac arrest.

And it wasn't just the thought of Gispuknya's shadows or Tane's monsters that made her nervous.

Something felt wrong about that city. She picked up on it several miles before they reached the first exit and it didn't subside until they were several miles down the road. It started as something like a ringing in her ears, then swelled into a low *throbbing*. Her head began to ache. She felt sick to her stomach. An almost overwhelming anxiousness swelled within her. But worst of all was the subtle, gnawing feeling that something deeply unpleasant was calling out to her.

Something *bad.*

By now, she knew how to recognize the "sounds" her spirit ears picked up. And something in that city was making a lot of that kind of noise. Although she couldn't explain exactly *how* she knew it, she was certain that, whatever it was, she should *never* follow it.

Seph didn't seem to notice anything. And Piper didn't mention it to her. She didn't want to add to her already-heavy emotional load. She was clearly upset. She hadn't said more than a few words since they left Nora's Lilac Grove. And she wasn't able to eat more than a few bites of her sandwich. The last thing she needed was something else to worry about.

The rest of the day was blissfully uneventful. Piper did all of the driving until well into the night. Seph continued to say very little and she didn't try to make her talk about it. It'd been an epically bad day for her. She lost her job. She found out her boss was an immortal lunatic. He even wrecked her *resume*! What kind of evil bastard would even think of that? And he almost certainly rattled her confidence all the way to the core with all that awful talk about how she wasn't really good enough to work there.

And now Amethyst was dead… She didn't have to be a therapist to know *that* was going to be a whole bunch of complicated feelings.

She felt guilty even thinking about what happened to her Jeep. Vehicles could be repaired or replaced. Amethyst was gone forever.

And so the evening passed into night in somber silence…until a little past ten o'clock in the evening, when Meg called again.

She glanced over at Seph, who'd fallen asleep. If she didn't answer it, Meg would just keep blowing up her phone and waking her up, so she accepted the call, hoping to get it over with.

"Where *are* you?"

"I'm in Madison with Persephone," she lied.

"You're coming home soon, right?"

"Not tonight."

"*Auuuuugh*!"

Piper winced. She hated when Meg made that noise on a *good* day. It was probably the most obnoxious sound she'd ever heard.

"What are you guys even *doing*?"

"Bachelorette party. One of Persephone's friends from college. We can't drive home tonight 'cause we've been drinking."

"That's just great. What am I supposed to do now?"

Piper sighed. "Cook your own dinner. You're a grown woman. You know where the kitchen is."

"Not *that*! God, Pipes, you're so hopeless sometimes."

She was starting to seriously regret telling Seph she couldn't reap Meg. "Okay, then *what*?"

"Only that there's still a *psychopath* stalking me."

"I don't think sneaking you cranberries actually constitutes attempted murder. You're not even *dangerously* allergic to them."

"Forget the *cranberries*! God! This is *way* past that!"

She sighed again. "Fine." She glance over at Seph. She hadn't moved. Hopefully this conversation didn't go on long enough to wake her. "What happened now?"

"Okay, so I went over to that Shiny's coffee place today to talk to Mandy, because I know Mandy's friends with Lori, who's *always* hanging around Juliet because she has, like, *no life*, I swear."

Kettle, meet Pot, thought Piper.

"And I was *way* uncomfortable, by the way, thanks to those stupid candies!"

Piper wrinkled her nose. Was it candies or cookies? She couldn't even keep her story straight. She still had no idea what it was she was stupid enough to eat!

"I had to dig out my big winter sweater. It was so stupid hot in there! And I couldn't stop itching!"

"*Or* you could've just *stayed home* like I told you to do."

"And I probably looked like I was high or something 'cause I couldn't take off my sunglasses," she went on, ignoring her. "It was *so* stupid!"

"Totally."

"But anyway," she continued, oblivious, "I told Mandy to tell Lori to tell Juliet that I knew what she was up to and to back off 'cause Rocky is totally over her and she just needs to get over it. But I guess it turns out that Lori is a total backstabbing bitch who was obviously trying to get her claws on Rocky this whole time because *she* turned around and told *Greg* a bunch of bull about me cheating on him."

"Wait…" said Piper, confused. "So you *are* still seeing Greg?" Then she scrunched her face up. "Are you dating Greg or are you dating Rocky?" And if she was dating Greg and she spent the weekend with Rocky, then didn't that mean she was *totally* cheating on him?

"Would you please *listen*?"

Piper rolled her eyes.

"So then later Sherry texted me and she says Greg's friend, Baker—or Bentley or Bart or… *Something*. I don't even know. It's not important. *Anyway*, she says he's on Facebook talking trash about me like he knows anything about anything, right? And then *Mandy* tells me—that's Mandy *P.*, not Mandy *S.*—*she* tells me that that bitch, Crystal, is talking shit about me again."

Piper was barely keeping up now. Who was Sherry? There were *two* Mandys? She didn't know *any* Mandys. "Which one was Crystal again?"

"Crystal Yawbeckner? The *cyberbully*?"

"Oh, right. Her." The girl from that idiotic business back in December. Technically, *Meg* was the cyberbully. Crystal never did anything to her except have the audacity to be dating a guy Meg decided to suddenly have a crush on. Everything that happened to Meg after that was only retaliation for the vicious and completely unwarranted attack *she* made against Crystal.

"So I called Hillary to see what Crystal's been saying and that's how I found out that her friend, Nina, overheard *River Lobnetter* talking to her friends about me."

Piper sat there a moment, waiting for her to go on. "*And?*"

"And *obviously* it was *River* who's trying to kill me. *Duh.*"

Piper frowned. Did she miss something? How did she jump from *talking about her* to *trying to murder her*? "Wait, so this River girl wants you dead, too?"

"Ugh. You can't *really* be this dense, can you?"

Piper puffed out her cheeks and glared at the phone. She didn't think she'd ever wanted so badly to call someone such a bad name before.

"*Obviously*, River's the one who tried to poison me. *Duh.*"

She forced herself to focus on the road. Why didn't she just say that to begin with? "I thought *Juliet* sent you the candy."

"Mandy told me—that's Mandy S.—that it sounds like Juliet didn't even know about the weekend up north until Lori opened her big mouth."

"But you're the one who told Lori to tell…" She trailed off. "Never mind." She rubbed at her temple, frustrated. So…Juliet didn't even know about Meg and Rocky until Meg basically *told her* about it?

"I guess she didn't even know that he'd dumped her. I mean, how dense can you be, right?"

"Right," replied Piper. She absolutely couldn't agree more.

"There's no way she could've come up with something like those cranberries. She's *way* too stupid."

This *conversation* was stupid. Why did she have to listen to the entire story about how Meg mouthed off to Juliet through some sort of gossip network with Lori and Sherry and the two Mandys and whoever else she mentioned? What did Crystal Yawbeckner even have to do with any of it. And for that matter, "So, why would *River* want to kill you?"

"Because her boyfriend, Shaun, got fired from Cak-Attack last month for getting caught having sex in the storeroom and she thinks *I* was the girl he got caught with."

Piper blinked, horrified. First of all, *ew*. She made a mental note to not order from Cakwetak Pizza Attack anytime soon. And secondly: "*Were* you the girl?"

"Of course not! Quit interrupting me!"

"*Sorry…*"

"But River's friend, Latasha, lied and told everyone it was me."

"Why would she lie on you?"

"Good question, right? If you ask me, it was *her* in that storeroom with Shaun."

"I see." Piper glanced up at the rearview mirror. They still had the road to themselves, which was good, but she'd almost rather be getting chased by wretches and teethers than have to sit through this idiotic conversation much longer.

"Obviously, it was River who sent me that candy."

Everything was always so *obvious* to Meg. Except for what a psychopath she was.

"Also, I talked to Vickie and she says she's seen River hanging out with Libby Voloner, too. You ask me, they were both in on it."

Libby Voloner, too? The one she accused of arranging a convoluted plot to steal Meg's laptop in order to destroy evidence that she'd been sleeping with Meg's boyfriend, Martin?

"Libby probably gave her the idea. She's such a shallow bitch. She totally refuses to get over that misunderstanding we had."

Misunderstanding? She ran out and had sex with Libby's boyfriend as revenge. And Libby was completely innocent. Meg's laptop was at Martin's apartment the whole time!

That went *way* beyond a "misunderstanding."

"River should've stayed out of my business. I mean, if she was any kind of girlfriend, Shaun wouldn't've *needed* to go in that closet with me in the first place, would he?"

"I thought you said it wasn't you."

"It *wasn't* me. I already told you, it was that Latasha bitch."

"But you just…" She shook her head. "Never mind," she sighed.

"I mean everyone knows what was going on there. She never cared anything about Shaun. The very next day I saw her at Killer Subs, getting all friendly with a *new* boyfriend. She's such a hypocrite. It's sickening."

"I *hate* people like that."

"I know, right! I guess we'll see how she likes having *two* boyfriends prefer me over her."

Piper groaned. "*No*. No more *revenge sex*. That *totally* didn't work out so well last time."

"I told you, that was a *misunderstanding*."

"It wasn't a—" She shook her head again. "Look, just don't go doing anything rash, okay. You don't even have any proof that…" She sighed. "You already did it, didn't you?"

"For someone who's *so* upset about someone screwing her boyfriends, she sure doesn't seem to take care of them. He was *so* eager. It was kind of pathetic, really."

"*Ugh*! *Stop*." What was *wrong* with this woman?

"I'm just *saying*. *God*. Don't be such a prude."

"So did you just call to brag about this, or…?"

"*No*. I called because River Lobnetter's a total *psycho*. Somehow she got ahold of my cell phone number and she won't stop calling me. I can't believe you two are at some stupid party, leaving me here all alone with this shit. I'm telling you, she's *dangerous*."

Piper groaned again. "Just turn off your phone and go to bed. Stay in for a while."

"That's so typical of you. You're such a princess."

"What?"

"I don't know why I bother. Of course *you* don't know what it's like to have your *life threatened*."

She took the phone away from her ear and gaped at it.

"Just come home first thing in the morning."

"We're not rushing home just for *you*," she snapped. "Hello? *Meg*?" But Meg was already gone. She growled and dropped her phone back into her purse.

"You okay?" asked Seph.

Piper glanced over at her, surprised. "Yeah… I'm sorry. I didn't mean to wake you."

"It's fine. Psycho Meg's back, I hear."

"Yeah." She shuddered. "Yuck. I think I need to disinfect my *ear* after that conversation."

Chapter 19

Around three o'clock in the morning, Seph insisted on taking over. She could tell that Piper was at her limit. Her eyes were drooping. She looked uncomfortable. She was struggling to stay awake.

Piper didn't want to burden her, but she also didn't refuse. She *was* pretty exhausted. And dying in a traffic accident *would* be downright undignified after all the crap they'd survived up to this point.

They pulled off the interstate at the next rest stop and swapped places. They didn't use the facilities, even though they both could've probably used a restroom break. Even as brightly lit as the place was, even with security cameras everywhere, it was far too terrifying at this time of night. It looked utterly deserted. And just beyond the reach of all those blinding halogen lamps, there was a looming wall of darkness from which any number of nightmare things could be watching them.

Piper pined for the days when thoughts like that were the immature and silly products of a little girl's overactive imagination, rather than legitimate and entirely rational fears based on the actual experiences of a grown woman.

They didn't even dare opening the doors for fear of what might be lurking out there. They just sort of crawled over each other.

Piper was asleep almost before the old truck had reached the end of the onramp.

Seph wasn't sure how she'd feel being left to herself. Even when Piper wasn't speaking to her, she was there, always glancing over at her, worrying about her. There was something comforting about that. She thought that her being asleep would leave her feeling completely and unbearably alone. But it was okay this way, too.

Just having Piper nearby always seemed to make everything a little easier.

Still…

She sighed and turned her attention to the road again.

Poor Amethyst… Sure, she was bitter about all those lies, but she never once wanted anything like this. The look on her face when it happened was going to haunt her forever. Her pretty, brown eyes so big…so full of pain and surprise… Her lips moving with silent, lost words…

…the blood dripping from that devil's freakish hand…

Oh god!

Why? Why did it have to be that way?

And why didn't Sandy say anything? Her mind kept returning to that. Was all that talk about amber threads and choices and opportunities nothing but a big crock of lies? Was she a fraud? No… That didn't feel right. She warned them about the devil and the wretch. She told them there would be pain. She told them it would be hard. Looking back, it seemed like she must've known what was going to happen.

Did she really just *choose* to let Amethyst die?

She felt so confused.

And guilty. She wished she'd found it in herself to just let go of those lies and forgive her when she had the chance. She wished she wasn't so damned stubborn.

And of course she felt *angry*.

All of those things together felt like a sickness deep in her gut. A low, queasy sort of aching, like she might have to pull over and throw up. But it wouldn't come to that, she knew. It wasn't that simple. This was the sort of sickness that was going to hurt for a long, long time.

But time was one thing she might have plenty of. Driving all the way to Florida seemed like trouble enough, but that they were then going to have to drive all the way to Texas and then all the way back to South Dakota? It was exhausting just to think about.

It'd almost be worth the price to stop and get them each an airline ticket. Except that would mean sitting around in some stuffy airport somewhere just waiting for Gispuknya or Tane to attack. And even if they *did* manage to get on a plane, what guarantee did they have that those monsters couldn't get to them there, too?

She kept looking over at Piper as she slept. It was a fitful sleep. Several times she heard her mumble something. And a few times she *whimpered.* But at least she was sleeping. It was better than nothing.

The night dragged on, lonely and uneventful, until eventually the sun came up. A new day began. And as Amethyst drifted away into yesterday, Seph wept a little in somber silence.

At about seven o'clock in the morning, Piper was startled awake by a nightmare about Gispuknya hounds and teethers and Tane's burning fingers snatching at her face. The first of many, she was certain.

They stopped at the next town for breakfast and a much-needed restroom break. Seph didn't feel remotely hungry, but she couldn't let Piper miss a meal. By now, it was safe to say that something unpleasant was waiting for them, so they couldn't count on having time to eat later. She ordered her a breakfast sandwich and both of them a large coffee. Then she sped on down the interstate, leaving no time for something awful to climb into the bed of the truck.

Not long after, they spotted the first sign for Waybel Valley. Only eleven miles away, it informed them. The dread she felt about the unknown horrors that must await them there was almost worse than the sick feeling about what she'd left behind.

Almost.

"What's that look for?"

Piper's eyebrows sprang up, those pretty, blue eyes widening. "Wha looh?" she asked around a mouthful of bagel and sausage.

"I wasn't hungry."

Piper swallowed and dabbed at her mouth with her napkin. "I didn't say anything."

"I know, but you keep looking over at me."

"I'm sorry."

Seph stared at the road in front of them.

Piper took another bite. Chewed. Swallowed. Dabbed at her mouth again. The whole time, she never took those pretty eyes off her.

Even those spectral ears seemed to be glued to her.

Seph sighed. "I'm confused, okay? I don't know what to feel. I'm exhausted. I'm messed up. I'm scared to death. I just want to go home and crawl under my covers, but I can't."

Piper gave her a sympathetic smile. "That's okay. I feel like that, too."

She shook her head. No one else ever did that to her. Amethyst used to pester her when she was in a bad mood until she finally told her what was wrong. Kaitlyn used to do the same, but she was a little sweeter and a lot more annoying about it. And way back in high school, her best friend, Valerie used to *sing* to her until she spilled it. Wherever they were, even if it was the middle of the cafeteria. God, but *that* was embarrassing.

Piper cared about her just as much as they did. But she didn't pester her about it. She didn't annoy it out of her. She didn't say a word. She just sat and stared at her with those big puppy eyes and those adorable, ghostly ears.

She just…*waited.*

Was it odd that she got through her defenses faster than anyone else ever did?

"But I know you'll protect me," said Piper. "So it's okay."

Seph glanced over at her. It was impossible to hide the worry in her eyes. "I wasn't able to protect Amethyst."

"But you *will* protect *me*," she insisted. "I know you will. So don't worry about it."

But she *did* worry about it. What if she lost Piper, too? What if she lost *everything*? What if she wasn't the person the Ahns believed she was?

What unspeakable horrors were waiting for them at the end of this highway?

Chapter 20

The sign at the exit pointed them left, down a three-mile stretch of rural, two-lane road past a boat dealership and a trailer park that looked nothing like Nora's Lilac Grove but still made Seph cringe when she saw it. Then, with very little warning, the two-lane road became Waybel Valley's Main Street. It stayed that way for about a third of a mile, and then they were at the end of it.

Seph turned around in a church parking lot and made her way back to the city's only intersection. She turned left, past a post office, a small gas station and about a dozen houses before the scenery gave way to a swampy-looking forest that she immediately assumed was haunted by the vengeful spirit of a vampire witch and her zombie boyfriend. She turned around in front of an old barn and tried the other way, where they found another dozen or so homes, a bank and a fire station.

That was it. There were only two streets.

The only thing that stood out in any way was a curiously familiar-looking bronze statue in front of the post office.

She made her way back into town and parked in front of a little bar with a number of other shoddy-looking vehicles in front of it. There, they stepped out of the truck and looked around.

Seph had never been to Florida before. It was a lot warmer here than it was in Missouri. A lot more humid. Which was pretty much what she'd always been told Florida was like. But she still found it difficult to wrap her head around the fact that she was even here. She always thought she'd be having a lot more fun if she ever found herself here.

"I don't think I dressed appropriately for this outing," lamented Piper, tugging at her sweater. It was ideal when she left the house yesterday morning in Wisconsin. Comfortable. Light. Cute. But instead of sitting in a cozy booth, sipping iced tea and enjoying an amazing steak burrito, she was kidnapped by a rogue elevator and assaulted by a monster basement. (Which, by the way, was *not* in her morning horoscope.) Her poor sweater had now been hosed down, dried and slept in. *And* it was dirty.

She wished she'd worn something under it so she could just take it off, but that wasn't an option. She couldn't go running around in her bra, no matter how much the fate of the next universe might depend on her.

She also wished she'd worn her cute *sneakers* instead of her cute booties. This was worse than last time, when she found herself fleeing from those black-eyed children while wearing flip-flops.

She peered into the truck's side mirror and made a face at herself. "Ugh! I do *not* look cute today." She had bags under her eyes, her hair was falling out of her bun and her makeup was a mess. She probably looked like a drug addict.

Seph rolled her eyes. "Can you hear anything?"

Piper stood up straight and cocked her head to one side. Her spirit ears perked up at once and began twitching back and forth.

Seph watched them, as she always did. On one hand, it was useful. If she *did* hear something with those ears, they'd point toward the source of the "sound." On the other hand…well…they were kind of adorable. They were so *expressive.*

"I don't think so…"

Seph turned and looked around. This shouldn't be that hard. From this one spot, she could practically see the whole town. It was nothing like trying to find the marker hidden in Avelby.

But then again, the markers weren't hard to find because of where they were. They were hard to find because they were designed to be invisible to everyone but the two of them.

Also, no one said they were looking for another marker. They were here to open the first lock of Tartarus. And she had no idea what a Tartarus lock looked like. Or even how big it was. It could be almost anything.

Her gaze drifted to the post office and that curious sculpture. She felt like she'd seen it somewhere before, but she couldn't quite place it. It was a spiraling arrangement of small, bronze shapes that gave an impression of golden, fall leaves caught in a whirlwind.

Did she see it in a dream once?

No… Not a dream. Not exactly…

It was like the endless hallway in Tane's freaky basement, she realized. And her weird episode of déjà vu in the office.

The slime lady showed it to her. The memory was a little hazy, but she was certain it was the same sculpture.

Hopefully that meant they were in the right place.

Piper reached up and took down her hair, then she quickly tied it back up into a much less sloppy ponytail. "Didn't Sandy say we were supposed to meet someone here? Some kind of guide?"

Seph glanced over at her. She'd nearly forgotten after all that had happened. "The Keeper's custodian," she recalled. That was what Sandy called him. Someone here was supposed to help them locate the lock. But…how were they supposed to find this custodian? Were they supposed to recognize him? Or was *he* supposed to recognize *them*?

(Or she, she supposed; Sandy never said if it was a man or a woman.)

Not that it mattered at the moment, she supposed. There was literally no one around. Waybel Valley looked utterly deserted.

No…not deserted. There was a young couple walking down the sidewalk on the other side of the street.

"You wanna just start here at this bar?" asked Piper as she rummaged through her purse for her makeup. "Come up with a story and start asking questions? Like in Avelby?"

But Seph barely heard her. She was staring at the couple across the street. Something seemed…*wrong*…about those two. It was like the project she was working on yesterday, just before everything went all Bizarro World. Something just wasn't right about them. Something about the way the sunlight played across their faces… Something about shading? The anatomy?

They just didn't *look* right…

They didn't seem to notice her. They walked on by, completely absorbed in their conversation. She was hanging on his arm, giggling. He was smiling. They had eyes only for each other. It should've been adorable, but…there was something distinctly *creepy* about those two.

As she watched them walk away, they suddenly and simultaneously turned and looked back at her.

She turned away, startled, and pretended not to have seen.

What was wrong with their faces?

"Persephone?"

Seph looked over at her, her eyes wide. "Did you see that?" she whispered.

Clearly, she didn't. She stared back at her, paused in the middle of removing the cap from her lipstick tube. "See what?"

Carefully, *causally*, she turned as if to look at the Ram's rear tire. As she did, she dared a quick glance at the strange couple. They were looking at each other again, still walking.

Did she only imagine that they'd turned and looked at her? She doubted it. It was never that simple.

"Those people over there," said Seph. "Did they look…*strange*…to you?"

Piper craned her neck and gawked at them.

"*Not so obvious*!"

"What is wrong with you?"

"You didn't see them?"

"They looked like a normal couple to me."

Seph turned and looked after them again. They turned at the lone intersection and disappeared from sight without another look back.

"Why? What did you see?"

She shook her head. "Nothing. I'm probably just tired."

Piper stared after the couple for a moment. She probably shouldn't leave it at that. It probably *wasn't* nothing. With Seph, seeing things was *literally* her thing. But she was so tired after that long drive… And they just got here. Surely it'd be okay to take just a few minutes to gather her thoughts.

She turned back to the truck's side mirror and went back to touching up her makeup.

Seph, meanwhile, looked out at the street. Something wasn't right about this town. Not just the people, but the town itself. It seemed…out of place somehow…but she couldn't quite put her finger on what it was.

Something about the cars parked on the street, maybe? Some subtle little *wrongness*?

Piper finished touching up her makeup and then admired her work. "Much better," she said.

Seph turned and stared at her. How did she even do that? It'd been, like, *thirty seconds* and she looked perfect again.

It wasn't fair!

"What?" said Piper. But before Seph had a chance to reply, her cell phone rang. She reached into her purse, hoping it wasn't Meg again. She was *definitely* not in the mood for any more of *that* slutty nonsense. "It's Violet."

Seph's expression lit up. "Oh, good!"

They met Violet Snubb and Corey Vano last summer in Avelby. They described themselves as "treasure hunters" who traveled all over the country in search of mysterious doorways they believed existed throughout this world. Gateways. Rifts between dimensions. Portals to other universes. It sounded kind of crazy, but who were they to judge? They were walking around with the Grim Reaper's scythe and Rumpelstiltskin's spinning wheel, after all. And it wasn't like they hadn't seen a few of these other universes with their own eyes.

After sharing a particularly terrifying experience in an Illinois marsh involving freaky alien zombies and a murderous Gispuknya shadow, it was pretty clear that Violet and Corey were the real deal. And lying about their own mission to locate and claim the Hands of the Architects seemed pretty pointless. A few weeks after Avelby, they came to visit them in Cakwetak and the four of them shared stories over dinner. They'd since become good friends. And they were invaluable sources of information regarding weird places in the world. Corey was even building a map of them. If anyone could tell them anything about Waybel Valley, it'd be them, so Piper texted Violet during night to ask what she knew.

She put the phone on speaker and stepped closer to Seph so they could both hear. "Hello?"

"Hey, Pippy."

Piper didn't understand everyone's obsession with calling her by all these silly nicknames, but it'd gotten so that she barely even noticed anymore. She answered to just about anything now. "Hi, Violet."

"Hey, Vi," said Seph. "What's up?"

"Hi, Seph. You guys getting into trouble again?"

"It's pretty messy, yeah," admitted Seph.

"You haven't run into any more freaky zombies, have you?"

"Not yet," said Piper.

"But there's still time," added Seph.

"Tell 'em I said hi, too," said a gruff voice in the background.

"Corey says hi, too," said Violet.

"Hi, Corey!" said Piper, raising her voice in case he could actually hear her.

"Seriously, though," said Violet, "you guys are okay, right?"

"We're fine," Piper assured her, though she couldn't help but think of poor Amethyst as she said it.

"That's good. You let us know if you need any help. We'll rush right down there if you need us."

"Thanks, Vi," said Seph. "We appreciate it. But I think we'll probably be gone again before you could get here."

"I guess so… We're in *Florida* this time, huh?"

"We're all over the place," sighed Seph.

"Where're *you guys*?" wondered Piper.

"Michigan," replied Violet. "We're investigating a ghost town called Cedric's Cove that apparently has a habit of moving around."

"Weird," said Seph.

"Towns usually don't do that," agreed Piper. "Ghost or not."

"I know, right? Every now and then I guess there's a report of someone stumbling across it, but when they try to show it to people, they can never find it again. We think it might be because it was built over a dimensional rift of some sort and so it might be shifting back and forth between worlds."

"Huh," said Seph. "Well…good luck with that."

"Thanks."

"So can you tell us anything about *this* place?" asked Piper.

"Okay, so we've never come across any Waybel Valley before," she began. "It hasn't shown up on our radar at all. That whole area seems to be pretty clean. But that might just be because we've never investigated around there before. A lot of times the *real* stuff is also the stuff the locals don't like to talk about."

Seph nodded. She could see that.

"There *is* a haunted alligator farm not too far from there," said Corey in the background.

Piper looked up at Seph. "Well *that* sounds awful."

"Yeah, let's not go there," agreed Seph. Bugs were her big phobia, but snakes and other scary reptiles were pretty high on the list, too.

"It's a little odd though," said Violet. "I can't find anything to suggest that there's any paranormal reports in the town, but I also can't find anything else, either."

Seph frowned. "What's that mean?"

"There's no city website. No news stories. No public records. No schedules of events. No police reports…"

"Well it's just a tiny little place," reasoned Piper.

"Yeah, but even so… There's no *census records*. It's weird. It's on maps…*some* maps, anyway…but there's almost no proof that Waybel Valley even exists."

"Well *that's* weird," said Seph.

Piper nodded and looked around. Clearly the city existed. She was standing in the middle of it, surrounded by it.

"Could be nothing," admitted Violet. "Just a small-town thing. Maybe they still keep paper records or something. Except of course that *you guys* are there, so obviously *something* must be going on."

"True," agreed Seph. And she hadn't expected much. Clearly, the locks to Tartarus weren't meant to be found by ordinary people. Chances were pretty good they'd be hidden in places that didn't draw much attention. That could explain the lack of information online.

The Keeper had that kind of power, after all.

She glanced up to see a tall man in his late thirties walking down the sidewalk toward them. He had his hands stuffed into his pants pockets and was staring at the ground in front of his feet as if contemplating all of life's troubles.

"I can keep digging, but I have a feeling we're not going to be much help with whatever you're doing there."

"That's okay," said Piper. "Thanks anyway. I'll probably text you again when we get to the next town."

"No problem. We're happy to help. You two be careful out there, okay?"

"We will. Bye."

Seph shaded her eyes and squinted at the stranger walking toward her. Once again, something seemed weirdly off.

Something about the man's face…

He lifted his head and looked at her.

She looked away. She would've liked to think that it was because of that weirdness, but the truth was that she would've looked away even if the guy hadn't looked weird. It was embarrassing to be caught staring at someone. *Anyone.* And she wasn't exactly the social queen that Piper was. Piper was the very model of poise and elegance at any get-together. Seph, meanwhile, was downright awkward around most people. She'd usually gravitate toward some empty corner somewhere and try her best to disappear. Eye contact didn't exactly come naturally to her.

But in that split second between him looking up and her looking away, she saw a little bit more of the man. There was something dreadfully wrong with his eyes and mouth.

She couldn't say exactly *what* was wrong. She couldn't quite comprehend it. It was like looking at a character in a poorly rendered video game, where all the three-dimensional components didn't fit together as smoothly as they should.

When she glanced back again, the man had turned and was disappearing into one of the buildings.

"So what do we do?" asked Piper.

Seph blinked, distracted, and looked over at her. "Huh? Oh. Um…" She looked down the sidewalk again, but the man was gone. Again, the town seemed to be deserted.

Was she just imagining it? She didn't get much sleep last night. And she hadn't been sleeping well before that. And it wasn't like she wasn't already paranoid.

Piper's cell phone alerted her to a new text message. She stuck out her tongue and made a face at it. "Meg's up." She was demanding to know when they'd be home. "I'm totally not dealing with her right now."

Another text message followed it. Then another. She switched her phone to Do Not Disturb mode and stuffed it back into her purse without reading them.

The bar's front door opened and an old man shuffled out into the sunshine.

Piper looked up at him, those iridescent ears twitching curiously. "Should we just ask someone if they know about this Tartarus thing?"

Seph grabbed her hand and pulled her in the opposite direction. "Nope!"

"Hey! What're you doing?"

"Just walk!" whispered Seph.

"What's going on?"

"You seriously don't see these people?"

Piper glanced back at the old man. He looked to her just like any other old man. "What's wrong with you?"

Seph didn't dare look back. She saw enough when he came out of the bar. He was dressed like a normal person. He *moved* like a normal person. But he was definitely *not* human. It was as if someone had taken an old man's *skin* and stretched it over a roughly human frame and brought the whole thing to life. His eyes and mouth were *empty*. There was nothing inside that man but shadowy darkness.

And yet Piper didn't seem to see anything unusual.

Whatever these things were, they were indistinguishable from normal people without her prophet sight.

Sandy warned them that Tane would be at least one step ahead of them. She warned them that he'd be watching their every move, that he'd be placing obstacles in their way. And without Amethyst to navigate the fringe roads for them, they'd given him plenty of time to set a trap for them.

Seph set off down the sidewalk, away from the creepy old man. But they didn't get far before two younger men stepped out of a building ahead of them and began walking toward them.

Like everyone else she'd seen, these men didn't seem to be looking at them. They were looking at each other, as if caught in an intense conversation. It looked strangely as if they were doing their best to not look directly at them. Were they just trying to look casual? If so, they were terrible at it.

Even from here, she could see that the two men weren't human. Their eyes and mouths had that same dark, hollow look.

Their lips didn't even move naturally. They just sort of flapped open and closed, as if whatever was lurking inside them had no idea how to act human.

She looked back over her shoulder, doing *her* best to look casual, and saw from the corner of her eye that the old man had stopped on the sidewalk behind them and was watching them.

And he wasn't alone. There was a stuffy-looking, middle-aged woman standing on the front porch of a house across from him, a teenage boy walking down the sidewalk and a woman on a bicycle slowly crossing the street. All of them seemed to be watching them. And all of them had that strange, shadowy darkness behind their faces.

"This way," she whispered, steering Piper into a narrow driveway and into a small parking lot behind one of the buildings.

There was a small auto shop back here, its two garage doors standing wide open, revealing a deep, shadowy gloom inside. There were several cars crowded into the small lot. Plus two inside the building, hoods raised.

Seph's father was a mechanic, back before the cancer took him. The sight and sound of men working in a garage was painfully nostalgic to her. Even the smell of an auto shop was enough to send a flood of bittersweet memories racing through her thoughts. But strangely, this one held no such charm.

There were no sounds of people working. No power tools. No clinking, clanging, ringing of metal. No slamming doors or turning engines.

Nothing but that deeply unsettling emptiness.

It was as if everyone had gone away.

Everyone but those hollow skins…

Someone was coming!

Again, she grabbed Piper's hand.

Piper wasn't entirely sure what was going on. She didn't see anything strange about these people. But if Seph said something was wrong with them, she believed her. She just wished she'd tell her *what* was wrong with them. She had no idea what they were running from.

They slipped between two parked cars, around the back of an old van, and then made their way around the side of the garage to the rear of the building, where a high, chain-link fence and a rough row of trees separated the property from a neatly mown lawn on the other side.

"This way!" hissed Seph, steering her along the back of the garage, through the trees on the other side and across the back lawn of a small church.

She had no idea where she was going. There was something off about this town. Something just didn't seem right. The more she saw of it, the more wrong it looked. Even the church didn't look quite right. It seemed…tilted somehow…*askew* in some slight way that she couldn't quite wrap her head around…

"Slow down!" whined Piper. "My heels!"

But she didn't dare slow down. She hurried around the back of the church and circled around the other side, heading back toward the street.

But here, she stopped.

There were dozens of people on the street now, of all ages and builds, as if the entire town had gathered there. Each one was standing motionless. Each one was staring directly at them. Each one had that eerie emptiness in their faces.

"Persephone!" squeaked Piper.

"Yeah…" Seph squeaked back at her. She took a step back, then turned and looked behind them.

More of the creepy townsfolk were crossing the back lawn of the church.

They were surrounded.

Chapter 21

"Hurry!" hissed Seph. She cut across the lawn and through the back yards of the neighboring houses, dodging swimming pools, lawn furniture and swing sets.

With each passing moment, more and more of her surroundings looked wrong. All the things in these back yards looked strangely like props, as if she were running across an absurdly large stage for some low-budget play. The same was true of the vehicles, she realized. Something about them, some small detail that she couldn't quite grasp, just didn't feel right. Even the houses were wrong. They didn't appear very well built. They didn't even look *realistic*! They were crooked. Twisted. From the corners of her eyes, some of them looked almost like *tents* that were merely *painted* to resemble houses, but when she looked directly at them, she couldn't quite understand why she would even think something as silly as that. Everything looked perfectly normal when viewed straight-on.

There's no city website, she remembered Violet telling them. *No public records. No schedules of events. No police reports…*

"I really don't understand what's going on here!" whimpered Piper.

"Just keep running!"

"I never said I was going to stop!"

It wasn't her imagination. It wasn't her fear at work. This was prophet sight. These were glimpses of the truth that was hidden from everyone else. If only her *real* eyes would stop getting in the way…

No census records, she thought.

There's almost no proof that Waybel Valley even exists.

She couldn't help but be reminded of that horrid diner in Fathom Lake. That place had looked much different to her prophet sight as well.

Was this the same sort of thing? Was this whole town a trap? Were these fake people the same kind of monster as the things that pretended to be Pappy Stan and his family?

The very thought made her sick.

A young boy strolled around the corner ahead of them, that eerie darkness pooled behind his eyes and lips.

They gave him plenty of room as they darted around him.

But the houses didn't go on forever. They were running out of back yards to flee through. And these "people" had completely stopped pretending to ignore them. They were actively following them now.

The last house was just ahead of them. Beyond it was a fence. From there, the only options were to flee into the trees or return to Main Street, where all the freaky people were gathering.

But before she could decide which option would be more foolish, the back door of the last house on the street opened and a stout man in jeans and a stiff western shirt squinted out at them from the gloom of the doorway.

This was the first person she'd seen who didn't have that strange darkness behind his face.

"This way!" he called out to them, just loud enough that they could hear him. "Hurry!"

Any other day and Seph would've had reservations about just blindly accepting a strange man's invitation into a dark house. That was just basic common sense. But given the circumstances, she decided to trust the fact that this man actually had *eyeballs*.

Maybe this was the custodian Sandy told them about.

The man stepped aside and let them in, then immediately slammed the door and engaged the deadbolt. "Quick!" he whispered. "Away from the window!" Then he turned and pressed his back to the wall next to the door.

They didn't hesitate. They backed into the corner of the room and huddled together against the counter, their hearts pounding.

Almost immediately, a shadowy face pressed against the glass, peering in.

The knob rattled as the thing pretending to be a person tried to open it.

The man held a finger to his lips.

Seph looked around, uneasy. They were standing in a small, darkened kitchen. It smelled strongly of coffee and more subtly of toast and bacon and more subtly still of lemon and bleach. Her eyes were drawn to the two doorways leading into even darker rooms of the house. Lots of gloomy spaces. Lots of places for something awful to hide.

Two more faces appeared at the window over the sink. Through the thin curtains, it was impossible to see if they had hollow skulls behind their faces, but Seph found that she knew they did without seeing.

Those things weren't human.

"Don't move," mouthed the stranger with his back to the wall.

Seph looked back at the open doorways with the darkness looming behind them. What if they were wrong? What if those *things* weren't the monsters? What if they were like the Ahns? What if they were the good guys and this man was the real monster?

She clenched her fist and felt the water envelop her hand. If all else failed, she had the scythe. She just had to keep her guard up.

Unless, of course, the scythe failed her again… But she didn't dare dwell on that grim possibility.

The thing at the door rattled the knob once more. Then, one by one, the shadows at the windows wandered away.

The stranger didn't move immediately. He stood there a long moment, his finger still pressed against his lips.

Neither of them dared to move before he did.

Then, finally, he relaxed. "We should be okay now," he said.

"How are we okay?" asked Seph. "I know they saw us come in here."

"Yeah, but they're stupid. They'll've already forgotten about you by now."

She looked him up and down, still uncertain. He appeared to be in his mid-sixties. He had the rather humorless look of a man who'd worked hard his whole life, with callused hands and sun-beaten skin. His expression was firm, confident, if a bit weary. "Who are you?" she asked.

He pulled back the curtain and peered out into the back yard. "Wilbur Rischt," he replied. "Custodian of Waybel Valley. I was starting to think you two were never showing up."

"Um…sorry?" said Piper.

Seph scowled. *She* wasn't sorry. "It's not like anybody bothered to send us an itinerary."

Wilbur only grunted. Satisfied that the monsters had forgotten about them, he turned from the window and walked past them, through the darkened doorway. "Come with me."

Seph and Piper hesitated only a second or two, time enough to exchange a quick, uncertain glance, then followed him out of the kitchen, through the dining room and into the living room of the little house.

The Reaper's scythe continued to swirl around Seph's clenched fist. "Where are we going?" she asked.

"Upstairs." But instead of walking to the stairs, he crossed the room and peered through the curtain at the front yard. "Who's out right now?"

Before either of them could ask him what he was talking about, a small voice startled them from the shadowy belly of an overstuffed armchair: "Just Wallace."

Piper pressed her hand against her chest and sighed. "You scared me…"

She scared Seph, too. The scythe's handle twitched and swirled, ready to lash out, but remained in check.

"Sorry about that," replied the old woman as she stood up. She looked to be about ten years older than Wilbur, small and frail, with a sweet smile and a long, flowery dress.

Piper stared at her. "Are you…?"

"I'm Hattie."

"Oh… For a second there… Um… Sorry."

The old woman gave her head an inquisitive tilt, but otherwise only continued smiling.

An old woman in a place like this, without a hint of fear in her beaming face in spite of the strange army of monsters lurking just beyond these walls… She'd thought for sure that she must be another Ahn. But her name was Hattie. And Louann had assured her once that while not every woman with "Ann" in her name was an Ahn, there were no Ahns without an "Ann" name.

Wilbur nodded and turned away from the window. "Call him back."

"Already have," replied Hattie.

"We'll start as soon as he gets here."

"Whatever you think is best." She just kept smiling. It was such a profoundly kind smile. Pure. Sweet. Calming. "I'll get Ross up, too."

"You two come with me," he said, already starting up the stairs.

"Hold on," said Seph. "You're the custodian Sandy sent us here to find?"

Wilbur didn't "hold on" at all. He continued on up the steps without pausing, forcing her to follow him if she wanted an answer to her question. "Don't know anyone named Sandy," he replied. "We were sent here by a goddess a long time ago."

"Goddess?" said Piper. Her spectral ears perked up. Didn't someone say something like that once before? A long time ago?

"Sandy might be a goddess…" considered Seph. She was mysterious, scary and weirdly all-knowing. She certainly wasn't *human.*

"Maybe," admitted Wilbur. "What do I know?"

Piper nodded. Now she remembered. It was the humming chicken. The one they found at Harvard Tottlestep's farm way back when this weirdness first started. Harv told them that night that a goddess gave him the strange bird to hold onto.

(That seemed like so long ago!)

Was this guy talking about the same goddess?

Seph pondered the matter. There was also that enigmatic slime lady she ran into last time… Could *she* have been a goddess? Or what about those strange sisters from that little gas station who rescued them from the depths of the fringe road? Nadia and Max. Were *they* goddesses?

What would a goddess actually look like? What was the difference between a goddess and all those other things they kept running into?

Wilbur opened the first door at the top of the stairs and gestured for them to enter first. They expected to find a bedroom. Instead, they found a cozy sitting area that should've been much more at home on the ground level. There were two coffee tables in the middle of the room, surrounded by an assortment of armchairs and loveseats that didn't quite go together, but also didn't clash. It wasn't a luxurious space, but it was homey. Comfortable. An extremely fat man of about seventy was taking up most of a plain red loveseat while a much older, much thinner man with a much more humorless sort of look on his face than even Wilber sat in a brown leather armchair, facing him. He appeared to be well past his mid-eighties, and not very happy about it.

"So these are the seekers, I take it?" said the fat one, eyeing them up. His voice was gentler than Wilbur's. Kinder.

"Took 'em long enough," grumbled the older one.

Seph shot him an irritated look. She was getting a little tired of everybody acting like they were supposed to know they were coming here. "Who are you people?"

"I'm Hugh," replied the fat one. "This is Lee."

Lee huffed and looked away, as if this whole situation were pissing him off for some reason.

"Lee's kind of an ass," apologized Hugh. "Don't pay any attention to him."

"Okay…" said Piper, distracted. She was still looking around, her thoughts still fumbling with the idea of real, live goddesses.

"Can we hurry up and get this over with?" growled Lee.

"We're waiting for Wallace," said Hattie as she shuffled into the room and carefully eased herself into an empty armchair. "Ross, too," she added.

Piper stared at her for a moment. She mentioned that she was going to "get Ross up" before they came upstairs, but as far as she could tell, the old woman had simply followed them into this room. Did she forget?

Maybe she texted him while she was walking up the steps or something…

Lee snorted as if she'd said something funny. "What the hell is *he* gonna do?"

"It's his job, too," she replied, as patient as she was sweet.

"Agreed," said Hugh.

Lee rolled his eyes.

Wilbur walked across the room and peered out through the curtains of one of the two windows. "How long?" he asked.

"He should be here in just a couple minutes."

"We should start without him," huffed Lee.

"We should wait," insisted Hugh. "We've waited all these years, you can wait two more minutes."

Lee looked like he was about to say something, but his gaze washed over Seph and Piper and he simply set his jaw and turned and looked off into the corner. Apparently, whatever was on his mind was too vulgar to say in front of a couple of young ladies.

"And Ross?" asked Wilbur.

"Maybe just a little more than a couple minutes," replied Hattie.

Again, he nodded. "We'll give them that long."

Lee muttered something that was probably offensive under his breath and shifted his weight, impatient.

"Wait…" said Piper, confused. "Just how long have you been expecting us?"

"Years," grunted Lee.

"We've been *waiting* years, sure," explained Hugh. "But we only learned that you were finally about to arrive *yesterday*."

"Yesterday?" said Seph.

"When *they* showed up," said Wilbur.

Seph and Piper walked across the room to the second window and pulled back the curtain. Those strange, not-quite-human things were still out there. They were disguised as people of all ages, but they weren't people. Seph could tell. Even from this distance, she could see the darkness behind their faces.

"There're more of them," said Lee. "They've nearly doubled just in the past hour. Probably because *they're* here."

"We knew that'd probably happen," said Hugh.

"What are they?" asked Seph.

"Empty people," growled Wilbur.

She glanced up at him, surprised. Empty people… What an eerily fitting name.

"They look just like ordinary people," explained Hugh. "But there's nothing inside them. They don't bleed. It's like they're just empty skins walking around."

Seph watched them as they wandered back and forth. They didn't shuffle or lurch or stagger. They walked just like ordinary people, if a bit aimless. Yet she couldn't help being reminded of every zombie movie she'd ever watched. Those things looked like people at first glance, but when you looked closer…

The thought made her shudder.

"So they just showed up yesterday?" asked Piper, confused. She still couldn't see any difference between them and real people. Except that they *really* didn't seem to like strangers.

"Sandy said Tane would probably set a trap for us," recalled Seph.

"So those things are his?" said Piper. She leaned closer to the window and squinted out at the so-called empty people. "I can't tell which monsters are on which side."

"Tell me about it," grumbled Seph. "This three-way war thing is confusing. They seriously need team uniforms."

Piper pinched her lower lip and considered the matter. Actually, she *did* know the difference, now that she was thinking about it. Every time those Gispuknya shadows appeared, they filled her head with that horrible buzzing noise, which she wasn't hearing at all right now.

Not that it really mattered, she supposed. Monsters were monsters.

Unless they were friendly monsters, like the Ahns…or Warner Harr…or Sandy…

Gosh this world was confusing!

"*There's* Wallace," grunted Wilbur.

They looked out to see an old man walking down the sidewalk. He looked to be in his early eighties, with a shiny, bald head and big, oversized sunglasses. He wasn't being sneaky at all. In fact, he appeared to be *whistling.*

He turned the corner at the sidewalk and made his way straight for the front door of the house.

None of the empty people seemed to be paying him any attention at all.

"Why aren't they attacking him?" asked Seph.

"They're not programed to attack locals," replied Wilbur.

"Programed? What, like robots?"

"Sort of."

"They're only here to stop the seekers from reaching the Keeper's gate," explained Hugh. "From what we can tell, they're not interested in anyone else."

"As long as we act like we don't know they're not human, they don't bother us," said Wilbur.

And Wallace was proving just that. He walked right up onto the porch and out of sight without any of the empty people so much as sparing him a glance. A moment later, they heard the front door open and close, then the overly cheerful sound of whistling marked the old man's progress through the house and up the stairs.

"That's what gives you away," explained Hugh. "If you see them for what they are, you might be a seeker."

"So everyone in this town is just *ignoring* these things?" said Seph.

"Pretty much," replied Wilbur. "Although almost no one but us lives in this town."

Seph turned to face him, confused.

"The Keeper put this town here specifically to hide the Tartarus lock," explained Hugh. "Pretty much the whole town is an illusion to keep anyone from building here and disturbing the gate."

She remembered catching strange glimpses of some of the buildings from the corners of her eyes when she was running from the empty people. They looked almost like poorly disguised tents, as if someone had simply *painted* the whole thing as a backdrop, like some lame cartoon gag.

The whistling drew closer. Now it was accompanied by the sharp footsteps of Wallace's loafers. Wilbur and Hugh both turned toward the doorway and watched as the cheerful, bald-headed man walked into the room. "Hello!" he said in a jolly sort of sing-song voice. He stopped next to Hattie and bent over her, giving the top of her head a quick kiss. "Hattie."

"Wallace," greeted the woman, still smiling that big, sweet smile.

"You're late," grumbled Lee.

"And you're as delightful as ever," returned Wallace as he straightened up again. Though he looked much older than the others—everyone except for grouchy old Lee—he had more energy than any of them. "So these're the seekers we've been waiting so long for." He looked them both over. "Huh. Didn't think you'd be so young. Or that you'd be girls. Not that there's anything wrong with being girls, of course. Just wasn't what I always pictured." He stroked the stubble on his old chin and furrowed his brow into a deeply thoughtful expression. "Not really sure why, now that I mention it…"

"Old men keep telling us that," grumbled Seph. Harv in Minnesota said the same thing. So did Mr. Hallet the first time they visited the ranch.

Wallace grinned. "We old men are just foolish like that, I suppose. I'm Wallace, by the way."

"They know already," grumbled Lee.

Like Hattie, Wallace's cheerful expression never faltered. "Of course they do."

"I'm Piper. This is Persephone."

"Seph," said Seph.

Piper wasn't sure why she always did that. Why would she rather be Seph than Persephone? Persephone was such a pretty name.

Wallace turned and looked around. "Are we still waiting on Ross?"

Before anyone could answer, the door behind Lee opened.

"Ah. Here he is now."

It opened very slowly. And very slowly, a very old, very frail-looking old man…

…stepped…

…into…

…the room…

He looked to be in his mid-nineties at least, bald except for a band of short-cropped, snow-white hair circling the lower half of the back of his head.

The old man took the tiniest, most careful steps Piper had ever seen, as if he might topple over and shatter a hip at any moment. And perhaps that was, indeed, a grim possibility. He was frightfully thin and he moved with a noticeable wobble in his joints.

"Take your time there, Ross," chuckled Wallace.

Ross' slow movements came to a complete halt at this, and he turned…ever so slowly…and looked at him.

"Aw Jesus!" groaned Lee. "Don't make him stop and *talk*!"

Ross stared at him for a moment. Then he licked his lips and said in the loud voice of a man whose hearing had been going for a long time, "What's that?"

"I said you dropped something," said Wallace.

"*Goddammit*!" snarled Lee.

Ross turned (…so…very…slowly…) and looked at the floor behind him.

"Nope," said Wallace. "I was wrong. My bad."

Ross stood there, looking back at the floor behind him, puzzled.

"He's just messing with you," said Hugh.

Wallace looked up at Wilbur. "Did you tell them about Horace yet?"

Wilbur sighed. "We don't need to talk about him. It'll just complicate everything. And it'll take too long to explain."

"I drop something?" said Ross.

Lee cursed. "You didn't drop anything! Sit down already!"

"Feels wrong to leave him out of this," said Hattie.

"This was his job," agreed Wallace. "The goddess gave it to *him*."

"It's what he's been waiting all these years for," said Hugh.

"I don't think I dropped anything," said Ross.

"Sit down!" shouted Lee.

"We don't have time for this!" growled Wilbur.

"It's nobody else's business," huffed Lee.

"There's enough time for *this*," insisted Hattie. "We owe that much to Horace."

"I'll just sit down over here," said Ross as he ever-so-slowly turned and continued his long trek across the floor to the chair.

"Good idea," said Wallace, grinning.

"Who's Horace?" asked Piper.

Wilbur turned away, frustrated.

"Horace is *us*," replied Hugh.

Seph turned and looked at him, baffled. "What?"

"We're *all* Horace," said Wallace, as if that did any better job of explaining what the hell these people were talking about.

"You're all…?" Piper scrunched up her face, confused. "*What*?"

Hugh looked up at Wilbur. "Take them to him. Let them see. It'll be easier."

He sighed another heavy sigh and nodded. "Follow me," he relented.

As Ross continued his slow pilgrimage across the room, Wilbur led them out of the sitting room and into a small bedroom across the hall.

There, they found a hospital bed, complete with monitors and IV racks and rubber tubes and machines they had no way of understanding. A withered old man lay beneath the sheets in the middle of it all, older than even poor, slow Ross. Seph thought he had to be at least a hundred years old.

Wilbur stepped up to the side of the bed and stared down at the ancient man. "This is Horace Rischt," he said. "He was the first of us."

Chapter 22

"I don't understand what you mean," said Seph. "He was the first of you? The first *what*?"

"The first," said Wilbur, as if that meant something. "The original." He turned to face them, frustrated. "You know how multiple personalities work, right?"

"Sure," replied Seph. "Or…as much as I've seen on television, I guess." She was no psychiatrist.

Piper nodded. She'd read about it in books. Dissociative Identity Disorder was a popular cliché in fiction. It seemed to be related to childhood abuse and trauma, like some kind of extreme self-defense mechanism. But she had no idea how realistic those fictional depictions of the disorder were. She'd never looked it up.

"Well, we're like that. Except we're not just personalities."

Seph frowned. "Huh?"

"Wait…" said Piper. "So…?"

"The six of us," he explained, "all split off from *him*."

Seph pushed up her glasses and rubbed her eye. "What, like when you get a gremlin wet?"

Wilbur's bushy eyebrows furrowed. "That's a weird way of putting it…but yeah, I guess so… Except it wasn't anything as simple as water. For Horace, it was *near-death experiences* that did it."

Piper stared at the old man. "So…?"

"Every time old Horace nearly croaked," said Wallace from the doorway behind them, "one of us sprang into existence."

"Don't be disrespectful," growled Wilbur.

"I have nothing but respect for that man," replied Wallace in a tone that was, for the first time, not at all cheerful. "You *know* that."

Wilbur *did* seem to know that, because he said nothing more about it. He turned his gaze back on the old man in the bed.

Seph struggled to understand it. "When you say, 'sprang into existence'…?"

"Just that," replied Wilbur. "None of us were ever born. We were just there one day, fully grown, fully functioning, fully aware adults."

"Horace Rischt wasn't so different from most people," explained Wallace. "He grew up thinking he was a perfectly normal human being. Then, one day, everything he thought he knew about the world just…*fell apart.* He suddenly had to accept the reality of things like monsters, alien worlds and even gods and devils."

Piper nodded. She could definitely relate to that.

"Things escalated," he went on. "He got in over his head. There was an *incident.* He ended up in a river and nearly drowned. Then Ross pulled him out of the water."

"Wow," sighed Piper. "And that's how all of you came into this world?"

Wallace grinned. "That's right."

"Hattie, too?"

He chuckled. "Now *that* really messed with old Horace's head. He was convinced that we were all some variation of his own mind. Just shadows of himself from different angles, even though none of us really looked anything like him. He was old-fashioned, even back then. The idea that any part of his brain identified as a woman…it *confused* him. And in his defense, he *was* desperately trying to rationalize the fact that he seemed to be spawning a new human being every time someone tried to kill him."

Seph nodded. She guessed she understood that.

"Also," he added, "there was the little matter of our peculiar abilities."

"Abilities?" asked Piper, her spirit ears perked again.

He nodded. "Little things, mostly. Like Hattie, for example. She can communicate with all of us telepathically."

"Seriously?" asked Seph.

"Seriously. It only works with us, though. It's weird that way."

Piper recalled Hattie saying she'd get Ross up, but not actually going anywhere. And she knew exactly how long it would take Wallace and Ross to arrive when Wilbur asked her, almost as if she could sense exactly where they were and what they were doing.

"Lee can sense danger," said Wallace. "He can see traps and other hidden danger. And he's always aware of the location of an enemy. That's why he's more hateful than usual today, by the way. Those empty people have him wound pretty tight. Although he's *always* something of an ass. Just in general."

Wilbur grunted, as if to say that he disapproved of Wallace badmouthing Lee, but again, he didn't say anything, suggesting that he didn't particularly disagree with the statement, either.

"Hugh sometimes gets flashes of the future," he went on. "They're brief and usually random, and most of them aren't very far out, so a lot of times it's not very helpful. But he does sometimes see things much farther out, especially in his dreams."

Seph couldn't help but think of Amethyst. Did her glimpses of the future work the same way? Then she realized that she'd probably never know and a deep pang of sadness hit her in the heart, forcing her to push the thought away.

"And Wilbur, here," Wallace went on, "can nudge things."

"What, like telekinesis?" asked Seph, curious.

"Sort of. Except it's not very strong. He can literally just *nudge* things."

Wilbur grunted again.

"It's extremely useful for distracting people," said Wallace. "He got us out of quite a few predicaments with that trick."

"That's really cool," said Piper.

Wilbur shifted his weight and cracked his neck, as if she'd embarrassed him.

"Ross was the most impressive, though," continued Wallace. "He used to be able to manipulate air pressure. He could make all sorts of things happen. I saw him crush an entire house once."

"Wow," said Seph.

"What about you?" asked Piper.

"Oh, I was *never* very impressive. All I could do was make people sort of confused for a couple seconds."

"That could be useful," argued Piper.

"It *could* be," he agreed. "And it *was* a few times. But timing is crucial. And it's hard to predict how people are going to act when they suddenly get confused. Sometimes they do the exact opposite of what you want them to do."

Piper pinched her lower lip and thought about that for a moment. "I can see how that would be tricky."

"So how'd you all end up in Waybel Valley?" asked Seph. She could almost feel Gispuknya's shadows creeping closer with each passing moment. She didn't want to be rude, but she also didn't think it was wise to linger too long in this house. And she wasn't sure why they needed to know all this. They were just here for the Tartarus lock.

"It was after we completed our mission," said Wilbur. "After we saved all those people. Almost fifty years ago now, it's been. No… *More* than fifty, I guess…" He shook his head as if he couldn't believe it'd been so long. "None of us had any idea what to do with our lives."

"Then a message came," recalled Wallace. "A new calling. Complete with room and board. Privacy. Peace."

"A good job," said Wilbur.

"Not even a job," said Wallace. "More of a reward, really. Where else would we have gone? I mean, legally none of us even exist. We have no birth records because we were never born."

Wilbur stared at Horace's still and frail form. "But we've been waiting a long time."

"These machines keep him alive," said Wallace. "Without them, he'd have died years ago. I know for a fact he wouldn't have wanted to linger like this…but we were afraid of what might happen to us if he passed away. Not so much for ourselves as for our mission. What if we all just disappear the moment his heart stops? Who would finish the job? What would happen?"

The four of them fell silent for a moment as that sank in.

"Lee and I…we didn't want to talk about all this," said Wilbur. "I don't think it's relevant. None of your business. Not to be rude, it's just…kind of *personal.* But the others all agreed that you should understand what this means to us."

"You have a right to know who we are," said Wallace. "Why we're here. We need you to trust us as completely as possible. Because those things outside aren't going to make it easy to get to the Keeper's gate."

Wilbur turned to face them. “And the gate’s the least of your problems. Once you’re inside the library, I have no doubt things are going to get very ugly.”

Chapter 23

"The majority of the enemy's numbers are stationed around the water tower," reported Lee once they were all gathered in the sitting room again.

Wilbur sat down on one side of an empty loveseat and scratched at the stubble on his chin. "So it's safe to say they already know where the gate's hidden," he reasoned.

"Water tower?" Seph tried to remember where the water tower was in this town, but she couldn't recall seeing it.

"It's backed into the woods a ways," explained Hugh. "Behind the post office, mostly out of sight."

"I thought you said the gate was in a library," said Piper, confused.

Wallace chuckled. He was standing in the doorway, leaning casually against the jamb, as if they weren't talking about a horde of monsters blocking the only way to the Keeper's gate. "No, the library's in the gate."

"Huh?"

"The gate is hidden in an underground chamber," said Hugh, "accessible by a stairwell behind a locked door inside the base of the town's water tower."

Ross had been dozing in his chair. Suddenly, he lifted his head and looked around. "We got company?"

"Those're the *seekers*, sweetie," explained Hattie.

"Sneakers?" said Ross.

"*Seekers*," she said, raising her voice a little. "They're here for the Tartarus lock."

The old man squinted at her, confused. "Tartar sauce?"

Hattie giggled. It was a delightfully *girlish* sound, almost childlike.

Wallace chuckled.

Lee closed his eyes and took a deep, calming breath. "The problem," he grumbled, "is going to be getting past those *things*." He jabbed an arthritic finger toward the window. "They—"

"I don't think we have any tartar sauce, do we?" asked Ross.

Lee gave a frustrated sigh.

"You want me to go check?" asked Wallace.

"Goddammit!" grumbled Lee.

Hattie giggled again. "I'll explain it to him," she promised. "You go on with what you were saying."

"I don't think we have any," decided Ross, fairly sure of himself.

"Ross, sweetie," said Hattie.

Seph watched as Ross turned to look at her. Immediately, his eyes grew distant and he nodded, as if listening to a voice inside his head.

This was Hattie's special ability that Wallace told them about. She was explaining the situation to him inside his head, where his bad hearing wouldn't distract him from the truth.

He nodded, his expression sharpening a little. "Seekers…" he said.

"Those things out there are what we need to focus on," continued Lee, frustrated.

Piper walked over and peered out through the curtains. There didn't appear to be more than there was last time, but then again, she could only see a little bit of the town. If he was right, then most of them were gathering around the water tower in anticipation of their next move.

They still looked like ordinary people to her, but if Seph said they were monsters, she believed her.

"I'm telling you, they're a *lot* more dangerous than they look. They intend to ambush anyone who gets near the gate. And every minute we waste," he shot a furious look at Wallace, "there're more and more of them we have to worry about."

"We're aware that we're pressed for time," growled Wilbur, "but we can't rush this."

"He's right," agreed Hattie. "We've waited all this time. We can't risk blowing it in the final hour. We owe that much to Horace."

"We risk blowing it if we sit around talking about it too long, too," argued Lee.

"Also true," admitted Hugh. "So let's stop arguing and come up with a of plan action."

"Oh…" said Hattie. "He's fallen asleep again."

Seph looked over at Ross. Sure enough, his head was down. He was softly snoring.

Lee rolled his eyes again. "Should've just left him in bed," he grumbled.

"Hey guys…" said Piper. She was still standing at the window, peering through the curtains. "One of those empty people things is acting really weird."

Seph crowded next to her and looked out. Sure enough, there was a man out there on the sidewalk. He appeared to be in his early forties, tall, lanky. He was wearing a blue baseball cap, cargo shorts, a baggy tee shirt and flip flops. He was pulling an old wagon and appeared to be *dancing* his way down the street.

Wallace walked over and peered out between them. "No, that's just Phil," he said. "He's always like that."

"Phil?" said Piper.

"He's this town's only real resident," explained Hugh. "He moved in about ten years ago. Lives in an old camper out past the edge of town."

"An artist," said Hugh. "He made that sculpture in front of the post office."

"Hm," said Seph. A fellow artist.

"He's kind of an odd duck," said Wallace as he watched him through the window. "No idea why he'd want to stick around here. It's not like anything happens here. The town was literally designed to *prevent* anything from happening here. But he's not dangerous. Lee would've known if he was."

"Spends most of his time wandering around the town, dancing like an idiot," grumbled Lee. "Or else sitting at the bar all day, pestering Wilbur and the handful of people who occasionally stop for a drink on their way to someplace out of the way."

"He's a sweet guy," said Hattie. "He stops by every Sunday afternoon. He brings me a flower and sits and talks with me for a while. I've grown kind of fond of him, to be honest."

"The guy's *nice* enough," admitted Lee. "But he's still a weirdo."

Hattie smiled and gave her head a little tilt as if to say, "So what if he is?"

"We're wasting time again," said Wilbur.

"Sorry, Chief," said Wallace, turning to face him.

Wilbur looked annoyed. "Getting *into* the gate is one thing. What you find on the other side of it is going to be something entirely different." He looked over at the girls, eyeing them up. "The goddess told us you'd come and that you'd be ready for what's waiting on the other side. I hope she was right."

"I hope so, too," said Seph. If it was like everything else they'd been through, she supposed they wouldn't know for certain until they'd done it. That seemed to be how the Keeper worked. "So tell us about this library."

"Lodblin's Library," said Hugh. "You'll find no records of it anywhere in this world. Any mention of it has been utterly lost to time. All we know for sure is that it existed once. A vast library, far larger than anything in *this* world, one of the largest collections of books ever assembled in the entire history of all the universes. The Keeper plucked it from its cycle in the last hours before the Wood consumed it and stored it in his compendium."

"That means you'll be stepping right into that world," explained Wallace. "The things you encounter on the other side of that gate are going to be ancient beyond imagining."

"How can anything last so long?" asked Piper.

"The Keeper's compendium exists outside the normal flow of time," replied Hugh. "So time doesn't work the same way in there. Once inside, we'll be completely isolated from everyone outside. We'll be on our own."

"We?" said Seph.

"I'll be coming with you. One of us has to. You'll need a guide to open the gate. Going in *and* going out. I won't be able to do it from this side."

"I still think *I* should go with them," said Wilbur. "I'm the youngest. The most capable."

"And I'm too fat, right?"

"I never said anything like that."

"You don't have to," countered Hugh. "I know what I look like. I know I can't get around as well as you. But I'm the only one who's actually *seen* the library." He reached up and tapped the side of his head. "In my mind. In my dreams. In the *future*." He leaned forward, his expression hardening. "It has to be me. You know it."

Wilbur stared back at him. He shook his head.

Ross snorted loudly and sat up in his chair. "Better tell 'em about the library," he said, scratching at his neck.

"We already *did* tell 'em that," snapped Lee. "Go back to sleep."

Ross nodded, satisfied. "Okay."

"It's not just that you're…*big*…" insisted Wilbur. "You know that. It's your overall health. You can barely get up a flight of steps without wheezing. And then there's the matter of your bad knee."

"I'm not going to *war*, Will," said Hugh. "I'm literally the doorman. I get them in. They do what they need to do. I get them out."

"I still don't like it," huffed Wilbur. "I feel like I should go, too."

"You know that's against the rules," grumbled Lee. "We've been over all this."

"Rules?" said Piper.

"The goddess was specific when she gave us the job," explained Wallace. "There're rules we have to follow. And one of those rules is that only one of us can go in with the seekers."

"Have to follow the rules," said Hattie, nodding. She still hadn't stopped smiling.

Hugh nodded. "I don't know for sure that the gate'll hold four people. We could all get trapped inside forever."

Wilbur grunted.

"Besides, I'll need you on the outside, in case there's trouble."

"Fine."

Hugh turned his attention to Seph and Piper. "As for you two…I honestly have no idea what you'll have to do once you're inside. But obviously you'll have to do *something*. There must be a switch or a lever or some sort of mechanism hidden in there. Something inside that library opens one of the locks of Tartarus."

"You're the seekers," growled Lee. "You'll figure it out."

"Sure," grumbled Seph, annoyed. "No problem. Send the two city girls blindly into the most terrifying place we can find without any instructions whatsoever and figure out how to do something completely random and stupid. Probably while being chased by monsters, demons and psychopaths. Sounds like business as usual for us."

For the first time, a shadow of a smile touched Lee's wrinkled face. "I think I like her," he decided.

Wallace turned and faced Lee. "So what's the plan for getting inside? I know you've been studying those things this whole time."

Lee sat up, eyebrows lifted. "They're concentrated around the front of the fence surrounding the water tower. A small distraction to draw them into the driveway should provide an opening large enough for you to get the girls inside the back. But getting through the wire will take time."

"Leave both of those things to me," said Wallace. "I've been studying those things. I can move around relatively unnoticed." He turned to Hugh. "You take the girls and get into position."

"I'll stay here and monitor the empty people," said Lee.

"I'll coordinate everyone," said Hattie, her smile brightening again. "Just like the old days."

Wilbur nodded. "Alright… I'll—"

"Don't forget!" huffed Ross. He lifted his old face and pointed a crooked finger at Wilbur. His eyes weren't droopy now. They were sharp and clear.

Wilbur stared back at him. *Everyone* stared back at him.

That finger trembled, but it remained there, fixed on Wilbur. Deliberate. Almost accusing.

They waited…

"Don't forget *what?*" growled Lee.

Ross turned his head and stared at him. "Forget wha?"

Lee cursed.

Hattie giggled.

Wallace chuckled.

Ross turned his face back to his still-outstretched hand and stared at it for a moment, confused as to why it was pointing at Wilbur like that.

Wilbur shook his head. "Let's get started before any more of those things show up." He pointed at the girls and then at Hugh. "You three come with me. There's a trail that leads back behind the tower. I'll take you around and drop you off."

Ross lowered his hand onto the arm of the chair and stared at it a moment longer, as if he expected it to rise up and start pointing at people on its own again. But after a few seconds, his head bobbed a couple times and he nodded off again.

Wallace was already crossing the room toward the door. "I'll take care of that fence. Give me about fifteen minutes."

"We'll be counting on you, Hattie," said Wilbur.

"You'd all be lost without me," she agreed, flashing Seph and Piper another cheerful smile.

"Let's get this over with," grumbled Lee. "Come on, Ross!"

Ross snapped his head up and opened his eyes. "Breakfast ready?"

Chapter 24

Wallace wasted no time getting out the door. Whistling, he set off through town as if he weren't surrounded by monstrous things pretending to be people.

Piper watched him from behind the curtains. Some of the empty people turned and eyed him as he walked by, but they didn't pursue him. Wilbur seemed to be right about their programming. They weren't interested in anyone that didn't obviously see them for what they really were. Perhaps they didn't want to blow their cover. Or perhaps they simply couldn't focus on more than one task at a time.

She had no idea how he was able to be so confident.

Wilbur walked into the room with a deer rifle in his hands and a holstered revolver on his hip. "My truck's parked right outside. We go out the door, casual-like. Walk to the truck. Get in. Drive off. Don't run. Don't make eye contact. Like they're not even there. If you show any sign that you know what they are, they'll attack. And we're probably not getting more than one shot at this."

"Sounds easy enough," said Piper, uncertain. "I guess."

"Yeah," said Seph. "What could go wrong?"

Wilbur turned and looked at Hattie. "Stay with Wallace."

"I know," she told him.

"These things don't seem like much right now, but I have a feeling as soon as they've verified their target, it'll be a different kind of ballgame."

"Tane's totally pissed off right now," said Seph. "In the past, he wouldn't risk killing us because he needs us to find the Hands. But it sounds like he might be past that now."

Piper pulled out the pendant Annalisa gave her and looked it over. Would Tane really kill her for it? What would happen if he did? Would the wheel just give up on her and accept Tane as its rightful owner? Or would it reject him and never awaken? Either way would be disastrous for this world, according to the Ahns.

"Let's get in position." Wilbur opened the door and walked out onto the porch.

Seph and Piper followed behind him, doing their best to appear oblivious to the fourteen strangers that were dawdling within sight along the quiet street.

All of them seemed to turn and look at them. Seph could feel those empty eyes on her as she concentrated hard on walking slowly and casually.

This was far too easy. Getting past all these monsters couldn't be anything so simple as acting nonchalant.

...could it?

It had to be a trap.

And yet, step by step, they drew closer to Wilbur's pickup truck. And while she saw several of them turn and look their way, not one of the empty people took a step toward them.

Why would Tane send these things here if they were no smarter than this? It took all night to drive here. He had plenty of time.

She didn't like it. It just didn't add up.

Piper glanced back at Hugh. He was lumbering along behind

them. Like the others, he didn't look even slightly afraid. But was he really okay to follow them into the library? He wasn't exactly in fighting shape…

The four of them climbed into Wilbur's truck. Seph and Piper crawled into the back seat and slammed the door behind them. Hugh struggled a little to pull his own bulk into the cab, but he eventually managed.

He was already out of breath. Everyone noticed it, but no one spoke of it.

More importantly, the empty people still weren't paying them any attention. They simply carried on with their strange patrol, seemingly unaware that the ones they were searching for were already here.

Seph didn't like it. More and more, the whole situation seemed wrong to her. She looked at the two men sitting in the front of the truck, wondering…

It wouldn't be the first time the enemy pretended to be their ally. Or even the second. As much as she didn't want to believe that these people could be just more of Tane's monsters, she didn't dare let her guard down.

The scythe bubbled in the palm of her hand, ready to be unleashed at any moment.

"What's *he* doing?" asked Piper.

Seph looked up to see Ross slowly making his way across the lawn. He was carrying a metal folding chair, using it sort of like a cane. He'd plant the chair's legs in the grass, then take three small, slow steps, then move the chair again.

"Who knows?" said Wilbur. He was already backing out of the driveway. "I never could make sense of what he was doing, even before he was senile."

"Is he going to be okay?" asked Piper.

"He'll be fine," said Wilbur.

"Hattie'll keep an eye on him," agreed Hugh.

Around them, dozens of empty people were wandering the sidewalks now. They weren't even being subtle about it, like they were when they first arrived. Each and every one of them turned and looked at them with their hollow eyes as they passed.

But the town was so tiny that Wilbur was past the city limit sign almost before Ross and his folding chair were out of sight. And less than a minute after that, he turned onto a rough trail and circled back through the dense, Florida brush.

The landscape here was so different from that of Wisconsin. The trees were different. The underbrush was different. It seemed sort of surreal. Seph couldn't help but wonder if this was really what Florida forests looked like or if they'd wandered onto another fringe road or some other alien world. Like that swamp they found behind a hidden gateway in the middle of an Illinois marsh last summer…

"Is that the water tower?" asked Piper.

"That's it," confirmed Hugh.

Seph leaned over and peered up through Piper's window. There was a large, white structure looming above the bushy canopy.

"There's a trail leading back to it up ahead," explained Wilbur. "We'll park there and make our way down to it when Hattie gives us the signal."

"And you really think it's going to be that simple?" asked Seph, meeting his gaze in the rearview.

"Of course it's not going to be that simple."

"Oh."

"It's never that simple. Something always goes sideways."

Hugh chuckled. "Ross used to say that if everything went according to plan, that's when you knew you were in real trouble."

"Ross knew about trouble," recalled Wilbur. "He got us out of more of it than anyone else."

"Usually by destroying things."

"He *was* good at that."

"Remember when he collapsed that bridge?"

Wilbur huffed. "How could I forget? I was still on the damn thing when he did it."

Hugh laughed. "Good times."

"You and I have very different criteria for what constitutes a good time."

"I suppose we do."

Wilbur brought the truck to a stop and killed the engine. "There's our path," he said, nodding toward the tower. A narrow trail had been worn through the trees. "I'll escort you down to the fence and stand guard while you three go inside."

"So we're just waiting on Hattie?" asked Seph.

Wilbur nodded.

"She says Wally's already finished securing our entrance," reported Hugh. "We're just waiting on the distraction."

Wilbur opened his door and stepped out of the truck. The rest of them followed his lead. A moment later the four of them had gathered at the top of the trail, ready to descend as soon as Hattie gave the signal.

Seph flexed her fingers, letting the water swirl between them. She hoped she wouldn't need it. She hoped even more that if she *did* need it that it would actually do what she wanted it to do.

Piper closed her hand around the pendant and hoped that it

would continue to protect her for as long as it took.

"Any second now…" said Hugh.

Seconds passed with nothing more than the sounds of the forest. Then a reverberating boom shattered the quiet and a fireball erupted on the far side of the tower. Birds broke into flight all around them and things in the forest that had been still darted away in fear.

"Gotta hand it to him," chuckled Hugh. "He knows how to make a distraction."

"Go!" hissed Wilbur. "Now!"

Together, they made their way down the path, toward the looming tower with its peeling, white paint.

But then both Wilbur and Hugh stopped.

Wilbur cursed.

"What is it?" asked Piper.

"Distraction didn't work," said Hugh.

"*What?*" said Seph.

"They're coming!" growled Wilbur.

"Why're they coming to *us*?" cried Piper.

"Did they know what we were planning the whole time?" asked Hugh. "A trap?"

Seph turned and looked around. Things were moving in the brush, human shapes with nothing inside pushing their way toward them. And not just in front of them, but on either side, too.

This was definitely *not* going according to plan.

Chapter 25

To Piper, the empty people still looked like ordinary people, except for the fact that they were tearing through the Florida underbrush with unsettling expressions on their faces. It wasn't rage, exactly. Instead, they looked like people *pretending* to be enraged, and doing a poor job of it, as if they didn't truly understand the emotion.

Seph was right. There was something truly *alien* about these people. She wondered how she didn't see it before.

"Back to the truck!" bellowed Wilbur. He lifted the rifle and fired at the nearest target. A thirty-something man in jeans and a tee shirt fell to the ground, motionless, with a hole in his forehead that didn't bleed.

None of the other monsters paused. It was impossible to tell if they even noticed that one of their numbers had fallen. Those creepy, unnatural expressions never changed, never faltered for even a second.

Luckily, they hadn't gone far. The empty people hadn't separated them from the pickup. They had time to get back to it, if only barely. Seph and Piper scurried into the back seat. Wilbur hurried around the front and climbed in behind the wheel, pausing only once to cut down a monster that looked like it might've been someone's grandmother, except that the bullet hole in her neck didn't bleed when she fell.

It was Hugh, with his extra bulk, that struggled to pull himself up into the cab. Wilbur grabbed one arm, Seph and Piper the other. He groaned and he cursed, but he managed to heave himself into the seat and slam the door closed a few seconds ahead of the empty people that crowded around the vehicle.

"What do we do now?" asked Piper as she struggled to repress the panic she felt welling up inside her.

"Plan B," replied Wilbur. He shifted the truck into gear and spun the wheel all the way to the right. Then he nosed the truck into the narrow trail, rolling over several empty people in the process. "This is going to be tight!" he groaned, steering the truck between the trees.

"Is this thing going to fit?" squealed Seph.

"I always hated it when you did stuff like this!" grunted Hugh, grabbing the handle over the door with one hand and the armrest with his other.

The path was wide enough, but not quite straight enough for the pickup. It rolled over several small trees, flattening them, their branches grinding against the undercarriage. The wheels bounced over an old stump. The driver-side mirror snapped off against the trunk of a large pine.

The empty people didn't seem to have any sense of self-preservation at all. Several of them wandered directly into to the truck's path, to be crushed beneath it, one by one.

Yet not one of them made a sound as they died.

Piper knew they were monsters, but she couldn't bear to watch. She buried her face in her hands and tried not to scream.

The water tower loomed overhead. The path widened. The truck picked up speed.

"Everyone needs to be ready to jump out when I say!"

"*What?*" gasped Piper.

"Aw, hell!" grunted Hugh.

Seph fumbled with the seatbelt as she watched the foliage part in front of them, revealing the eight-foot-tall, chain link fence that enclosed the water tower.

It was right in front of them. She could see the slit Wallace cut in it for them to sneak through, as part of their failed Plan A. It wasn't nearly big enough for the truck to fit through, but Wilbur clearly wasn't going to let that stop him.

She gave up on the seatbelt and grabbed the headrest on Hugh's seat, instead.

Piper screamed and threw her arms around Seph.

The truck ripped through the fence with relative ease. Then Wilbur spun the wheel and cut left, only narrowly avoiding the concrete wall of the tower's base and slamming Seph and Piper against the door.

"Sorry!" squeaked Piper.

"Get ready!" warned Wilbur. He spun the wheel back the other way, kicking up gravel as he swerved around the building. Then he stomped on the brake and skidded to a stop. "Go now!"

Hugh cursed and flung open the door.

Seph pushed Piper off of her and fumbled for the handle. She had to hand it to Wilbur. He thought the plan through, regardless of how crazy it may have seemed at the time. Not only did he circle around so that the passenger-side doors were next to the tower's door, he even managed to park the truck so that its bed was almost touching the building, creating a barrier between them and the empty people, knowing that the majority of those monsters were probably going to follow the truck, rather than try to head it off from the other direction.

But as she ran toward the door, she immediately saw that it was padlocked. "We need a key!" she shouted.

"I've got it!" grunted Hugh, but he was still fumbling to remove his formidable mass from the front seat of Wilbur's truck.

"Go, goddammit!" bellowed Wilbur.

"I'm trying!"

Piper ran back and took hold of his arm as he teetered perilously on the edge of the seat, searching with his foot for the running boards he couldn't see over his protruding belly.

"They're coming!" cried Seph as several empty people came running into view behind the truck.

Still cursing under his breath, Wilbur threw open his door and jumped out of the truck. He fired three shots at the approaching monsters, and three of them dropped. The man might have been a little past his prime, but he was still a damn good shot.

Finally finding his footing, Hugh lurched from the cab and stumbled forward, barely managing not to fall on his chubby face, even with Piper still clinging to his arm.

"Hugh!" shouted Wilbur as he cut down two more bloodless empty people.

"*I'm going*!" Hugh bellowed back, stuffing his chubby hand into his pocket and fumbling for the key. But he no sooner had them out than they slipped from his pudgy fingers and fell into the dirt. "*Dammit*!" He stooped down, groaning, but his plump fingertips stopped several inches short of the ground.

Seph knelt down and scooped them up.

"Persephone!"

She turned to find two empty people running toward her, having circled around from the other side of the water tower.

"Take these!" she said, tossing Piper the keys. Then she turned to face them. The scythe's handle sprang from her hands, the water gleaming in the sunlight like churning glass. She lifted it over her head and swung it at them. The long, gleaming blade slashed outward, a fluid, twisting shape, and snipped both of the monsters in two as easily as if she were pruning a rose bush.

But more empty people came around the tower to take their place. *Many* more.

She turned and looked behind her. There were dozens of them converging on the truck. Wilbur had already emptied the rifle and was now firing into the crowd with his revolver as he climbed back into the truck, overwhelmed.

"Pea!"

"I got it!" shouted Piper. She yanked the padlock off the door and pulled it open.

"Inside!" shouted Hugh.

Piper didn't hesitate. She ran inside and began searching the walls for a light switch.

Seph held out the scythe, using the long blade like a shield against the incoming horde of monsters as Hugh lumbered through the doorway behind her. Then she let go and darted inside, slamming the door behind her.

Almost immediately, something began yanking at the handle, trying to open it.

As Piper found the light and turned it on, Hugh grabbed a heavy wooden beam that was leaning against the wall and dropped it into a pair of steel brackets bolted to the door.

Seph stared at it, confused. It was like something out of a medieval castle! "Why does a water tower need something like that?"

Hugh was leaning against the wall, trying to catch his breath. "I asked…myself…the same thing…" he panted, "…the first time…I saw it in a vision…" He coughed and yanked at the collar of his shirt. It was stifling in here. They were *all* sweating now. There was a sheen of sweat on Piper's forehead. And Seph could already feel it stinging in those painful scratches left on her belly and beneath her breast from the ranch truck's rear window frame. But poor Hugh was practically *drenched.* "If there's one thing…I've learned…it's that there's…*always*…a reason for that sort of…thing."

"Makes sense," gasped Piper. She was lifting her sweater up, fanning her sweaty belly with it.

Seph supposed it did. As much as anything ever made sense anymore, anyway. She turned and looked at the door. She could hear Wilbur's truck out there. He was on the move, probably mowing down empty people *Grand Theft Auto* style. "Will he be okay out there?"

"Probably," panted Hugh. "He can…take care of himself." He swallowed and took a deep breath, trying to calm his great, pounding heart. "Besides…Wallace is out there with him somewhere."

As if on cue, there was a reverberating boom, as if someone had just detonated a bomb not too far away.

"See? There he is now."

Seph shook her head. This definitely wasn't your typical retirement community. She turned to look around and ran into a spiderweb. Her scream was piercing.

"Wow…" said Hugh.

Piper nodded. "I know, right?"

"Shut up," grumbled Seph. "I *hate* spiders."

"I know you do."

"Lee's afraid of spiders, too," said Hugh.

Piper looked up at him, surprised. "*Really*?"

"Oh yeah. *Deathly* afraid." Then his chubby features fell into a deeply concerned frown. "Don't tell him I told you so, though."

She made a locking gesture against her lips and giggled.

Seph shook her hair, making double-sure there was nothing crawling around in it. "So where do we go now?"

Hugh pointed at a door on the other side of the room. "Down there."

Piper stared at it. "Is it safe?"

"At the bottom of those steps is Keeper territory. Nothing goes there that he doesn't want there."

Seph wiped at the sweat on her forehead and then nodded. Keeper territory. Just like the markers in Messing Knob, Muntony, Sukmukwe and Avelby. Meaning there were probably monsters down there. Of the *undead* variety. The Keeper liked that sort of thing, it seemed. "Let's get it over with," she sighed.

Chapter 26

Beyond the door was a set of steep, narrow, concrete steps and a pervasive smell of dank, underground places. Seph couldn't help squealing in disgust at all the nasty little things that scurried about on the damp, concrete surfaces.

"Why are all the places associated with the Keeper like this?" she asked, shivering at the sight of a huge, hairy spider scurrying overhead. "The Ahns said he was the Keeper of all sorts of things, so why's he such a terrible *housekeeper*?"

Piper snorted, then quickly covered her mouth, embarrassed.

"I mean, it's just plain *lazy*, if you ask me." She let out another shrill scream and brushed something off her shoulder. "I'm *so* over this *Temple of Doom* crap. How much farther is it?"

"Not sure," replied Hugh. He was leading the way with a tiny, keychain flashlight that did little to push back the darkness. He moved slowly, and with a distinct limp. (Wilbur said something about a bad knee, Seph recalled.) He was leaning heavily on the wall as he descended. But he was also clearing out most of the cobwebs with his excessive bulk, for which she was very grateful. "I've never actually been down here before."

"You haven't?" said Piper. "I thought you knew the way."

"I know it's down here. But like I said, nobody comes down here unless the Keeper wants them down here. And we were explicitly told to only come down here to bring the seekers. I may've been curious, but I'm not stupid. Bad things happen to people who don't follow the Keeper's rules."

Seph shivered. It was true. The traps they encountered inside the marker chambers weren't just there to scare away intruders. Those things meant business.

"Besides," said Hugh. "There're rules you have to follow with all this ancient stuff. Only certain people are allowed to enter. Or only at certain times, or under certain conditions. There're places no one's allowed to enter unless they're naked."

"Ew!" gasped Seph. "No way!" She couldn't imagine trying to walk around these bug-infested chambers in her birthday suit. The very idea made her skin crawl.

"Yeah," agreed Piper. "I'm pretty sure I'd just die."

Seph squealed again and slapped at something that brushed against her cheek. Probably her own hair, but just as likely a black widow, she was sure. "I hate this place!"

"I see the bottom," reported Hugh.

"I don't hear anything outside anymore," observed Piper. "Is that just because we've gone down so far? I hope everyone's okay."

"Can you still talk to Hattie?" asked Seph.

Hugh glanced back over his shoulder. "I lost her shortly after we started down these steps."

"I don't like that," groaned Piper.

"I don't either," he said. "Hattie's not like a walkie talkie or a cell phone. If she can't reach me then I'm guessing we've essentially left our universe."

Seph and Piper exchanged an uncertain glance. This wasn't the first time they'd ventured into another world, but they hadn't yet done so without finding themselves in a frightening predicament.

He shined his light at the rough, stone walls on either side of them. "It feels weird, not being able to talk to her… Lonely… But we can't turn back. We have a job to do. It's the reason we're all here. They all knew that as well as I did."

At the bottom of the steps was a smooth, black archway framing a long, black tunnel.

It was the same material they'd encountered in the Keeper's marker chambers. Smooth and shiny, utterly flawless, sort of like onyx, but not quite.

Hugh nodded. "This is the place, all right. I've seen it before. In my dreams."

Piper supposed that was good news. It would probably be pretty bad if they'd found themselves in the *wrong* place. But she still wasn't very excited to be here. Every other time she'd seen this black stone, things had turned really scary, really fast.

He reached out and ran his chubby fingers over the smooth, black surface. "Tartarus stone."

Seph glanced up, surprised. "Tartarus stone?"

"I've never seen it outside of my dreams." He glanced back at her. "Very handy building material, if you happen to be an Architect. We humans would probably go insane just trying to comprehend how it works."

Seph turned her gaze back to the shiny surface. This was news to her. She'd just assumed that it was ordinary, black stone. She switched on her cell phone's flashlight and aimed it at the archway.

"Are there words?" asked Piper.

In all the other instances that they encountered this material, Piper was able to see only smooth, black stone, but Seph, with her prophet sight, was able to see ancient characters carved into the surface, spelling out mysterious messages or revealing the strange history of the cycle.

"Only one," said Seph, staring up at an ancient symbol that should've been utterly unreadable to her, but shined as clear as day.

"What's it say?"

"Uh…basically something along the lines of, 'by invitation only,' but with a really strong, 'by penalty of death' kind of tone."

Piper stared at her for a moment. "Oh." She looked up at the top of the archway where Seph was looking. "Well, good thing we're on the guest list."

Seph nodded. "Let's just hope this is the right party."

"Don't say that," she whined.

Hugh was already making his way to the far end of the tunnel.

Seph shined her light around, searching for creepy crawly things she wanted to avoid touching, but there didn't seem to be any here. For some reason, the cobwebs stopped at the archway behind them.

This should've delighted her, but instead, she found it very unnerving that she was now in a place where even the disgusting *bugs* refused to go.

She focused her attention on following Hugh and tried not to think too much about it.

The black stone seemed to devour the light, limiting visibility to only a few feet. If something nasty was blocking the way forward, they weren't going to have much warning before they saw it.

But nothing was blocking the way. After just a few minutes, a door emerged from the darkness in front of them. Big, heavy, wooden, like something that might've been found in a grand castle somewhere. A perfect match for Hugh's siege gate lock on the door upstairs, perhaps.

"This is *definitely* it," said Hugh. "I've been seeing this door for as far back as I can remember. It's haunted me for years."

"There's no handle," observed Piper.

"You don't open it with a handle." He reached out and touched the smooth surface. Immediately, he snatched his hand back, as if shocked.

"What's wrong?" gasped Piper.

"Nothing. I mean, nothing *serious*. Just… A strange sort of tingle. Like there's some kind of low-voltage energy flowing through it." He chuckled a little. "Makes sense, I guess. I mean…if this is what I've been led to believe it is, this isn't an ordinary door. On the other side…" he reached out again, carefully, and let his fingertips slide down the surface, "…everything is different. *Everything*."

"We shouldn't waste time," said Seph.

He glanced back at her. "Right. We don't know what's happening outside." He took a breath and placed his palm against it, but still he hesitated. Again, he glanced back at her. "I've stepped through this door more times than I can count in my dreams, and every time the dream ends right there. I have no idea what comes next. I only know that it scares me. Every time."

She nodded. "So…brace ourselves."

"Exactly."

"Got it."

"Take hold of my shirt and hold on. Don't get separated from me. I can only open it twice. Once on the way in and once on the way out."

They nodded and each took a fistful of sweaty fabric.

Hugh took a deep breath…held it… Then he stepped forward

and pushed.

The door didn't open. Instead, it rippled, like liquid, and he stepped *through* it, pulling them along with him.

Chapter 27

Hugh wasn't wrong. In an instant, everything was different. Gone was the dank, underground smell of the concrete stairs. In its place was the dry, musty scent of old books. Gone was the claustrophobic black tunnel. Now they were standing in a wide, open space, surrounded by large, white columns. The air was stuffy and humid before, but now it was lighter, thinner and much cooler. There was even a considerable change in the atmosphere, as if the space around them had suddenly depressurized. Their ears felt like they were going to pop. The only thing that remained the same was the darkness, and even that was different. While everything in that tunnel was perfect, light-devouring black, everything here was soft, subtle shades of white that *reflected* their lights and gave the whole scene an eerie, misty sort of glow.

Hugh grunted and dropped onto one knee.

"Are you okay?" asked Piper, startled.

"I think so. I guess that took a lot more out of me than I expected."

"Let me help you up."

But he shook his head. "Just…just give me a minute. I'm okay."

Seph turned around, taking in her strange, new surroundings. The floor appeared to be shiny, white marble under all the dust. The walls were mottled with grime and mold and riddled with cracks from which fine, black vines were growing, creeping and snaking their way across the surface so that they resembled delicate veins coursing just below the surface of pale, thin flesh.

However, just like in the black tunnel, there didn't appear to be any spiderwebs, which was fantastic news to her. Instead, there were tiny, black, seed-like things scattered all over the floor that crunched softly beneath their feet every time they took a step.

Seph sighed and brushed a loose strand of hair from her face. She, too, felt suddenly weary. Her body seemed heavy.

Piper felt it, too. A sudden, weighted sensation, as if something had sapped her strength as she passed through that peculiar door.

Did something in that black tunnel make her sick?

Was something *here* making her sick?

She looked around, concerned. Hugh warned them that this place was a remnant of another universe. Was it possible that the germs from that universe still remained here? Had they been exposed to something?

No… Surely the Keeper wouldn't be foolish enough to send them somewhere like that. He was the Keeper of the Cycle. Wasn't it his job to ensure the survival of the human race?

"This place *smells* like a library," said Seph, wrinkling her nose. "Sort of."

"A little bit," agreed Piper. "But also like…" She sniffed at the air. "Um… I don't really know…"

Seph knew what she meant. It was an odd sort of smell. Or maybe a few different smells. Fairly distinct, but utterly foreign. She didn't think she'd ever smelled anything like it before. She couldn't even decide if she liked it. One moment it was pleasant and the next it wasn't. Her mind couldn't seem to make itself up.

"This isn't the same universe we come from," Hugh reminded

them. "There's no reason it would smell the same. Different plants. Different building materials. Different kinds of dust particles. Even the fundamental laws of nature can change from universe to universe."

"Huh," said Piper, wrinkling her nose. "I never thought of that."

"The fact that books in this world smell anything like those in ours is probably a minor miracle." He looked up at the columns looming over them, at the unsettling darkness into which they reached. "But then again, I've heard that everything started with the trees…so maybe it's not so surprising…"

Seph turned and looked at him. Amethyst said something like that once, too. When she asked her why the fringe roads were a forest.

Because everything began with the forest.

The memory sent another painful pang through her heart.

That was probably going to happen a lot now, she realized…

Hugh grunted and rose to his feet. "Strange… Now that I'm here, I remember this place. I saw it in my dreams, like the door outside, but I'd forgotten." He turned and looked around. "I knew it had to be me who came here." He pointed into the darkness in front of them. "There's a door over this way."

They followed him through the wispy darkness, through the doorway he promised was there and into the largest library either of them had ever seen. The shelves towered over them, reaching as high as their lights would reach and beyond. Every wall was a skyscraper of dusty, old books rising up into eerie darkness, reachable only with the help of the dozens of ladders that were strategically bolted to the walls.

Here and there, throughout the room, individual shelves had sagged or snapped with age, spilling piles of books onto the filthy, marble floor, where hundreds more had been piled up in tall stacks, as if waiting for someone to come along and reshelve them.

Chunks of debris were littered around the floor with the books, apparently having rained down over the years from whatever ceiling loomed atop all that darkness that filled the cavernous space above them.

Directly in front of them stood a large, wooden desk, big enough to seat at least ten librarians if not for the fact that it was half-buried under a mountain of books, some of them neatly stacked and others seemingly tossed into haphazard piles that spilled off into the floor.

A strange, luminescent white globe hung from a thick, metal cable above the desk, casting an eerie glow over the entire mess.

"King Lodblin's Library," said Hugh, looking around. "Lodblin was a mad tyrant of a dictator who lived near the final days of a universe our ancestors had already long abandoned."

"You know that from your dreams?" asked Piper.

He nodded. "It would seem so. I feel almost like I've been here before. It's like every dream I never remembered when I woke up was about this place. Its history. Its legacy."

"Awesome," said Seph. "So where's the lock?"

Hugh frowned. "*That*, I don't seem to know."

"Typical."

Piper picked up one of the books on the desk and flipped through it. It was covered in dust and its spine was dry and cracked. Its pages were brittle and faded with time. She frowned at the text inside. "I can't read any of these." Then she looked up and said, "I have no idea why that surprised me."

Hugh chuckled. "You didn't think anything in here would be in English, did you?"

"I guess not…"

"English isn't even a very old language in *our* universe." He picked up one of the books and examined the writing on the cover. "Any languages found in this library are *beyond* dead. The last traces of their existence were forgotten by civilizations long forgotten by civilizations long forgotten again." He dropped the book back onto the desk, kicking up a cloud of dust around it. "The time that's passed since this place was alive is unfathomable. It's humbling."

She looked up at the towering shelves. There was something sad about seeing so many books and knowing she wouldn't be able to read a single one of them.

"You're really into this, aren't you," said Seph.

He looked over at her, surprised, then laughed. "Yes, I am. Aren't you? I mean, look around. Think about where we're standing. This is a place that existed so long ago that we don't even have any real concept of it. We're literally standing in a relic of a bygone *universe*."

"Yeah. I get it." She *did* look around. All these musty books, all written in languages no one alive could hope to ever understand... The last treasure trove of a dead world, containing all the accumulated knowledge and records of its people...saved...but still lost. What was the point? "Thing is, I'm not so sure how I feel about all this stuff. Dead universes? Forgotten worlds?"

"It doesn't make you feel exhilarated?"

"It makes me feel *small*. Like..." her gaze swept over the books strewn across the floor, left to rot forever, "...like I can barely hope to be somebody in *my* little world... Are all of us...and everything we ever do...just going to end up like this place someday? Forgotten by everyone? As if it never existed?"

Hugh stared at her for a moment, taken aback. "I see. That's...certainly a legitimate way of looking at it." He turned around and looked at the books on the desk, taking it all in again. "I see your point. We *are* all but specks in the greater scheme of things, I suppose. And looked at that way, it *is* quite overwhelming. I apologize."

Seph shrugged. "It's fine. I guess I've just spent a lot of time thinking about it. I mean, if I accept all this stuff about the cycle, then how do I hope to understand the rest of the universe? I mean, there are countless other planets floating around out there. Are *they* all a part of the cycle, too?"

"It's confusing, I admit. And I don't have all the answers."

"How do you know so much about stuff?" asked Piper. "Is it because you can see the future?"

"Partly. But I've also met a lot of…*interesting* people since I was ejected from Hector's subconscious. Maybe someday I'll get the chance to tell you some of the stories I've…" He blinked, confused and then swayed on his feet.

"Are you okay?"

He leaned on the desk and shook his head. "I think so. I just…feel kind of lightheaded."

"We should probably get moving," said Seph. "Get this over with and then leave."

Hugh nodded. "Yeah. I think you might be right."

"So where do we go from here?" asked Piper.

He stood up straight again and cleared his throat. "Lodblin's Library was built onto again and again over the course of many centuries. We're standing in the newest part of it. The farther back you go, the older things get. Not just the building, but the books, too. Deep inside its guts is a convoluted labyrinth of book-filled chambers. Above all else, this place was designed by a madman, not only as a repository for the accumulated knowledge of the world, but as a place of *secrets*. Legend has it that *anything* could be hidden here."

"So we've got our work cut out for us," grumbled Seph.

"Also, we'll do well to remember that the Keeper snatched this place away in the final hours before the universe sank into the Wood. That means the world that existed outside these walls was a terribly dark place. I'm not sure how far out the Keeper's strange magic extends, but I'd warn strongly against leaving the building or approaching anything that might have come from outside."

"Good safety tip," said Seph. "Got it."

Hugh turned and walked around the desk, moving deeper into the open chamber. Near the back of the room was a large archway. He led them through it and onto an elegant walkway overlooking a much larger room filled with more towering shelves and illuminated by several more of those strange, glowing orbs. Then he sighed heavily and leaned on the wooden railing.

Seph and Piper each took one of his arms.

"You don't look so good," said Piper.

"I wouldn't put too much faith in that railing," said Seph.

Hugh chuckled. "I suppose not…" He rubbed at his eyes. "Strange. I don't know what's wrong with me." He looked around. "Maybe the air? Are you two feeling all right?"

"I'm okay," replied Piper. "I think…"

"I'm fine," said Seph. "I mean, I feel a little heavy, but otherwise…"

"That's the atmosphere. Also the planet might be bigger in this universe."

Piper looked down at her feet, as if she could somehow see the difference in the size of the planet she was standing on.

He shook his head. "I don't get it."

"Maybe you should just wait here," said Seph. "This is supposed to be our thing. Maybe you're just not supposed to help us. You know…rules and stuff."

He swayed on his feet, making them grab tighter to his chubby arms. "Maybe you're right. I just don't get it. I never saw anything like this in any of my visions."

"Rules," said Piper, as if that explained everything.

"Over there," said Seph, pointing at a door to the right of where they came in. It looked like an office of some sort. "I see a chair."

The two of them led him in that direction.

"Just for a minute," he conceded. "Then I'm sure I'll feel better."

"Right," said Seph. "And we'll take a look around this area, see if we can find any clues. Maybe a visitor's map or something."

He sighed. "Yeah. Okay."

Seph didn't like this one bit. She'd already lost Amethyst. She didn't know Hugh all that well, but she didn't care for the thought of losing him, too. They needed to find the lock and get out of this place before something happened.

Besides…who knew what was going on back in Waybel Valley right now. She desperately hoped that Wilbur and the others were safe.

"Listen," said Hugh. "I don't know what the lock is, what it looks like, but I'm sure it's hidden deep inside this library. I think we need to follow the decay. Look for the oldest books."

Seph nodded. "Sure. That sounds right. No pro—"

From somewhere in the endless darkness came a loud, rumbling groan.

Hugh froze in his tracks. His eyes grew wide. "Oh my god…"

"What is it?" asked Piper.

"I just remembered it…"

"Another dream?" asked Seph, looking around, nervous.

He shook his head. "Nightmare." He turned and stared out into the darkness of the library. "Something lives here. Something big. Something terrible." He backed away from the railing, rubbing at his mouth.

"What is it?" she pressed.

"Teeth..." he whispered as he gazed out over the library's endless books with an unsettling fear in his eyes. "Claws... A crawling shape in the darkness..." He shook his head as if to clear it. "It's not a creature of our world. It doesn't have a name. Call it anything you want. Call it..." He flapped a chubby hand at the open expanse of the library as he fumbled with the thought. "I don't know...the...*jabberwock*." He dropped his hand and nodded. "Why not?"

Seph stared at him. "What's a jabberwock?"

He turned those terrified eyes on her and blurted, "'Beware the Jabberwock, my son! The jaws that bite, the claws that catch!'"

She stared back at him, afraid *and* confused. "*What*?"

"Isn't that from *Alice in Wonderland*?" asked Piper.

"It's *Through the Looking Glass*, actually," Hugh replied absently as he stared across the emptiness of the library again.

Seph frowned. "Isn't that the same thing?"

"*Through the Looking Glass* was the sequel," said Piper, also absently. "It's a fairy tale."

"Not real..." agreed Hugh.

Another of those loud, rumbling groans rolled through the library. There was something indescribably eerie about the sound. It made the hair on the back of her neck stand up.

Hugh turned and met her gaze again. "*Lots* of things aren't supposed to be real."

She stared back at him. She was too terrified to think of a reply, but she understood perfectly what he was telling her. It didn't matter that there was never a real jabberwock. There also weren't any black-eyed children or undead revenants or relentless mall wraiths. Not until they discovered otherwise…

"Come on," said Seph, urging him forward again. "Sit down. Rest."

He let them lead him to a dusty, wooden chair. Piper brushed away the dust and more of those strange, little seeds and then he eased himself into it. "I'm sorry. I forgot until just now."

Piper pinched her lower lip nervously and looked out through the doorway.

"It's okay," said Seph. "We can handle big and terrible. We've done it before." But when she looked down at her hands, the water wasn't there. "Uh…where's my scythe?"

Piper looked up, surprised. "What?"

"It's not coming out." She gave her hands a hard shake, but there wasn't so much as a drop. "Where is it?"

Piper reached into her sweater and pulled out the wheel. It was just as it usually was, meaning it was just sort of hanging there, not doing anything. If it had stopped working, she probably wouldn't know it.

Seph shook her hands again. She didn't know what else to do. This wasn't supposed to happen. Her heart was pounding. "Where is it? What's happening?"

Hugh lifted his head. "I see…"

"What?" said Seph. "What do you see? Why my scythe won't work?"

"Not the air. The *time*."

She squinted at him, confused. "What?"

"This place exists outside the normal flow of time. It's what allows it to still exist after all these ages. But people *need* time. It's like air and water." He looked at Seph. "You're not going to be able to use the Hands in here because they're busy protecting you, making sure the Keeper's time magic doesn't kill you."

"It can kill us?" said Piper, staring at the wheel again.

"Eventually," said Hugh.

"Wait a minute…" Seph turned and looked at him.

He chuckled. "That's right. I'm the only one without protection. That's why I'm feeling so weak right now."

"We have to get you out of here!" exclaimed Piper.

"No. You have to find the lock. It's our only chance."

"But—"

"I told you, I can only open the door twice. Once on the way in and once on the way out. If we leave without finding the lock, it'll all be over. You're just going to have to find it before my…uh…time runs out." He chuckled at himself. Then he frowned at the horrified looks on their faces. "Sorry."

Seph and Piper looked at each other, uncertain.

"Rules," said Hugh, nodding.

"Rules…" sighed Piper.

Chapter 28

They left Hugh in the office and set off, as he'd instructed, to find the deepest bowels of the mad king's ancient superlibrary.

Seph was pretty sure they'd now surpassed the realm of "crappy B movie" and were now deep in "cheesy comic book" territory. The whole concept was utterly insane. And yet…there were things about this place… Like those strange smells she couldn't identify. And the weird, heavy atmosphere. And the deep, deep silence of this place, as if there were absolutely nothing beyond the walls, not even wind…as if the whole, unearthly thing were deep underground…or adrift in the endless expanse of space.

And then there was the absence of any cobwebs. How could something be this old and not be overrun with spiders? Wasn't that what happened to places that sat for any length of time?

Did this universe not have spiders?

There was a lovely concept.

They crossed the floor to the top of the staircase, where Seph paused to examine the tiny, black seeds that were scattered on the railing. She could hear them crunching beneath her feet with each step, but what were they? They looked like small peppercorns. Or maybe big poppy seeds? Where did they come from? The only plants she saw were those fine, black vines creeping up through the cracks in the floor and walls, and she didn't see any seeds on them. Were they falling from the ceiling? She picked one up and brought it close to her face, examining it.

Then she saw the tiny legs sticking out of it. She screamed, revolted, and threw the little beast away.

Piper giggled.

Seph glared at her as she wiped her hand on her skirt. "What?"

"You have such a girlish scream. You know that, right?"

"I do not! Shut up."

But she wasn't wrong. It wasn't a dignified scream at all. It was more of an, "Eek!" than anything. It was embarrassing.

Stupid bugs.

Piper picked one of them up and examined it. "Some kind of tiny beetle. A type of pill bug, maybe?" She looked down at the floor. "They're all dead." They were only empty exoskeletons.

"Good," grumbled Seph. Her skin was crawling. There were literally millions of these things in here. They were littered across every horizontal surface.

Was this what replaced spiders in this universe?

Why were there so many? And why were they all dead?

Piper tossed the tiny carcass aside and looked back the way they came. "Do you think he'll be all right in there?"

Seph was *still* wiping her hand on her skirt. "He should be safe in that office until we get back."

Another of those loud, rumbling groans rolled through the library like distant thunder. Seph could even feel it reverberating through the marble beneath her feet.

"And then there's that thing..." said Piper, her voice wavering. She was clutching the pendant through her sweater, her eyes wide.

The jabberwock…

"Doesn't sound very close, at least," observed Seph.

She nodded. "That's good."

"But knowing our luck, the stupid thing's probably exactly where the lock is."

Piper replied with one of those terrified squeaking noises in her throat.

"We should probably just save ourselves the time and trouble and just follow the sound of it."

Piper shook her head. "I don't like that plan."

Seph sighed and started down the steps. "Neither do I, but we can't just stand here all day."

Reluctantly, Piper followed her.

The floor of the lower level was far more littered with books than the last room. Whole sections of shelves had collapsed in here, spilling books onto the floor in huge piles.

In the middle of the room were dozens of wooden desks, most of which were covered in piles of books and papers and dust.

Piper tried to imagine this grand library in its prime, the people who were here. Was it once a bustling place, filled with people diligently studying? Did scholars walk these towering aisles in search of resources? Did great discoveries take place here? She could almost imagine a small army of librarians wandering about, returning books to the shelves as quickly as they were taken away. The sounds of squeaking cart wheels, hushed murmurings, the subtle shuffling of pages…

She'd always liked libraries. And this was the sort of library that book lovers like her always dreamed of.

But there clearly hadn't been any librarians working these shelves in a very, very long time. Maybe there never were. Hugh told her that

King Lodblin was a tyrant. A dictator. That probably meant he wasn't interested in the greater enlightenment of his people. This was probably his private collection, off limits to the general public, shared only with the people he trusted most.

Or maybe not even them.

Looking at it from this perspective, she found it all too easy to imagine the old king wandering these empty corridors, collecting piles of books and sitting alone for endless hours under those eerie, hanging lights, perhaps searching for answers that eluded him his whole, long life.

She couldn't help but appreciate that, for all the countless books on all these shelves, the most fascinating story of them all might be the library itself.

There were lots of books left sitting in small stacks on the floor in front of the shelves, as if someone had intended to come back and put them away later, but never did. Most of these stacks were fairly small, but a few of them were quite tall, reaching eight or nine feet in height. Seph stopped next to one of these tall stacks and looked at it for a moment. Then she turned and stared at Piper, her expression serious. "Symmetrical book stacking,"

Piper stared at her, confused.

"Just like the Philadelphia mass turbulence of 1947."

Still, she only stared at her. "Um…?"

Seph raised her eyebrows. "No *human being* would stack books like this?"

"*What?*"

"*Seriously*? Not even *Ghostbusters*?" She turned away, disgusted. "I have *seriously* failed you as your roommate. If we get out of this alive, I am *making* you get some real culture."

Piper watched her go, bemused, and then looked at the stack of books again. "*Huh?*"

"Ugh! Forget it!"

Somewhere in the depths of the library, something fell to the floor.

Both of them froze and listened, expecting to hear something terrible moving toward them in the eerie silence…something with jaws that bit and claws that caught…but nothing else moved.

Piper picked up a book, flipped through its alien pages, then put it back down again.

Seph turned her attention to those glowing, white orbs hanging overhead. "How do you think they work?" she wondered. "They can't be electric…"

"Hugh said things were different in this universe," recalled Piper. "Even the laws of nature. Maybe they had glowing rocks?"

Seph shrugged. That was as good an explanation as any, she supposed.

There were probably books about it here somewhere, if she only knew where to look for them.

And if she only knew how to read them, of course.

She plucked a book off one of the desks at random and opened it up. She'd thought for a fleeting moment that maybe she'd actually be able to read it. After all, her prophet sight allowed her to read the mysterious writing on the ancient, black Tartarus stone of the Keeper's various, underground vaults. But the writing was like nothing she'd ever seen before. A strange mix of dots, squiggles and circles of various sizes and arrangements. She flipped through the pages, but found no pictures or illustrations to help make sense of what the book might've been about. Was it a history book? A novel? A self-help manual? Senseless smut?

She'd never know.

"I wonder what the people who used these desks were studying," said Piper as she walked over to a desk directly under one of those big, glowing orbs and picked through the dusty books.

"Maybe they were trying to find a way to save their dying universe."

Piper picked up a book and opened it to a random page. "Oh my!" she gasped, and dropped it back onto the table.

"What is it?"

"Um..." She rubbed at the back of her neck, embarrassed. "Not...universe-saving stuff."

Seph walked over and picked up one of the books. As soon as she opened it, she started laughing. She flipped through it, then put it down and picked up another one. Every book was filled with pornographic photographs. "*Or* they were just ogling dirty pictures. Nice."

"That's just *wrong*."

Seph found it profoundly amusing that some ancient perv once sat at this desk, eons and eons ago, surrounding himself with stacks and stacks of porn. "I guess that's one way to whittle away the time while waiting for the world to end."

Piper wrinkled her nose at her. "Why are you still looking at that?"

Seph was still flipping through the pages. "These are actual pictures of people."

"Uh, *yeah*. *Dirty* pictures of people."

Seph rolled her eyes. "Yes, but *aside* from that...these are *people*. As in, the people of *this universe*."

Piper's eyes widened. "Wait...you mean...?"

She stopped at a page with a relatively tasteful picture of a woman stretched out on some sort of bed. At first glance, she looked like any other naked woman. She had dark skin and a muscular build, an attractive body. But a closer look revealed a number of subtle things about her. Her eyes seemed just a tad small, her nose just a tad big, her forehead just a tad high.

Whoever this person was, they'd been dead far longer than the oldest fossils on their world. She'd lived her life in another universe in a time so long ago it defied the imagination, utterly forgotten by time, exactly as Hugh had described.

The more she realized what she was looking at, the more she felt the hairs on the back of her neck tingle.

How long had it been since anyone even saw this woman's face?

Piper leaned over and peered at the picture. "So…women in this universe didn't shave?"

Seph shrugged, distracted. "Maybe." The woman in the picture had very hairy legs and arms. She also had very thick, very bushy black hair on her head and between her closed thighs. "Or maybe the pervo who used this desk was just into hairy chicks. Who knows?"

Seph flipped through the pages again. Most of the pictures were extreme closeups, and not very useful, but whenever there was a clear view of someone's face or hands, they all looked the same. Bushy hair. Dark skin. Small eyes.

Was this a specific race of people? Or was this what everyone looked like when they lived in this world?

She closed the dirty book and dropped it back onto the desk. She could nose through more of these books and see if there were more informative photographs, but she didn't care to. There'd probably be plenty of opportunities to look at pictures in less offensive media.

That eerie groan rolled through the library again, like a grim reminder of the task they still had to finish.

"Come on," said Seph. "Let's find that stupid lock and get out of here."

"Are we going to be able to?" Piper looked back up toward the office where they left Hugh. "What if we can't find it before this place poisons him? What if we get trapped here?"

"We won't. Remember what the Ahns are always telling us. There's always a way. Besides, how big can this place possibly be?"

Chapter 29

As it turned out, the place was *astonishingly* big.

Each chamber led into another, which led into another, which led into *another*, on and on and on, it seemed, until Seph feared that getting lost was inevitable. And the farther in they went, the more *rotten* the library was. More and more books were strewn across the floor until they covered the dusty marble tiles like a moldering carpet. Gone now was the elegant, smooth walls, replaced with something more resembling crumbling stucco, which littered the floors along with the countless tattered books and those disgusting little bug carcasses. Soon they discovered walls that had been reduced to their skeletal frames and ceilings that sagged almost all the way to the floor, until it seemed that the books might be the only thing holding the place up.

And the books, themselves, were faring no better. By the time they finally found a dead end and had to double back, those both on the shelves and on the floor had all begun to turn the same rotten shades of mottled gray, some of them so completely molded over that they were *mossy* with it. Other books appeared to have been partially *eaten.* Still others had simply fallen apart with time, seemingly under their own weight, their pages strewn throughout the room, forever detached from their bindings.

Piper found it dismaying to see so many books left to rot this way.

She couldn't help but wonder what treasures might be entombed in this place, irretrievable, forever lost.

Seph, however, was far more horrified by the massive, greenish structure in the far corner that appeared to be some kind of enormous insect nest covered in shimmering, green-shelled, crawling things that didn't look like bees, but almost certainly wanted to sting her.

It was almost as dismaying as the small, unseen thing that knocked over a stack of books as it darted from the room when they first entered. A rat, she told herself. Or at the very least this universe's equivalent. Nothing dangerous, or it would've run *at* them rather than *away* from them.

Hugh suggested they seek out the oldest books, and they were doing fine at that. At least a few hundred years seemed to have passed since they left him behind. But there were a lot more doors in this part of the library, too, a lot more places to explore. And just as he warned, the rooms were getting more labyrinth-like.

Seph stopped and looked back the way they came. How far had they walked now? How long had it been since they left him in that musty office? Her watch wouldn't tell her anything. It'd stopped. And her cell phone was telling her it was the middle of the night, two days ago.

It was like the fringe roads. Time was broken here. Worse than broken. Without the power of the Hands to protect them, they'd both be just like Hugh. They never would've had a chance of completing this task.

She wasn't sure what kind of chances they had anyway. This place was enormous beyond anything she ever could've imagined. And these dark, inner chambers were strange in other ways, too. In the next room they explored, the books were stacked like bricks into eight-foot-high walls, making it nearly impossible to remove most of them. A lot of them couldn't even be *seen* without removing the ones in front of them.

It was as if someone had grown bored and decided to build the world's biggest book fort.

In the next room, and in stark contrast, the books had simply been thrown into a single, towering pile in one corner. Most of these were falling apart. Loose pages littered the room, half-burying a small desk.

Was this where damaged books were brought to be discarded, perhaps? Or was this just senseless book violence? It was difficult to tell what kind of logic reigned in this place.

On and on they went, up a tight, winding staircase with books stacked on every step so that they had to turn sideways several times just to squeeze between them, over piles of overturned bookshelves and through a maze of cramped desks covered in books and scroll-like rolls of brittle paper.

And to make things even more difficult, most of these smaller rooms didn't even have those glowing orb lights in them, leaving them with only their cell phones to light the way.

And those batteries weren't going to last forever.

"What are we even looking for?" asked Piper as she thumbed through a large stack of yellowed paper bound in ancient, rotten twine.

It was a good question. What did a Tartarus lock look like? Hugh had described it as a button or a switch, but there was nothing like that in any of the rooms they'd seen so far. This place didn't even appear to have light switches. The library was pretty old-school, for having existed at the very end of its universe. Shouldn't this place be more futuristic? If this world was old enough to be near its end, they'd had more than enough time to back all this crap up onto computers.

But for all she knew, computers didn't work in the alien physics of this universe.

This whole thing was so surreal.

"Maybe we're looking for some kind of control room?" suggested Seph.

"Why would a library have a control room?"

"Why would a library have a Tartarus lock?"

Piper opened her mouth to reply, but closed it again when she realized she didn't have an answer. She scrunched up her face and pinched her lower lip between her thumb and forefinger.

"Maybe it's in some kind of *utility room*, then?"

Piper's face scrunched up a little more. "Would that be in, like, the basement, then?" She looked back the way they came and tried to remember. "I didn't see any stairs going down."

"I don't even know how a Tartarus lock works," said Seph. "If it's sealed up in this weird, bottled library, how can it unlock *anything*? Wouldn't it have to be *connected* to Tartarus somehow?"

"Maybe it's more like a key?" suggested Piper.

"Then why call it a lock?"

"Now you're doing it to *me*."

Seph glanced over at her, confused. "What?"

"You're asking me things you know I don't know the answer to."

She took off her glasses and rubbed her eyes. "This is stupid. We need more information."

Before Piper could reply, another of those thunderous groans shattered the eerie silence.

Both of them cringed. It was much closer this time. The reverberations of it were strong enough to shake dust from the cracked ceiling above them.

The jabberwock. But not the *real* jabberwock, because that was just a monster from an old children's book. It was only the thing that Hugh decided to *call* a jabberwock.

Seph wished she knew what it was. Or even *where* it was. But she couldn't even tell which direction the noise was coming from. "Come on," she said. "There's light in the next room."

Piper didn't quite dare speak aloud for fear that the monster might hear her, so she bit her lip and nodded. She followed Seph through the next door, down a short hallway with books strewn the entire length of it, and into a huge, four-story room illuminated by dozens of those dangling, white balls. "Whoa…" she sighed as she walked up to the railing and looked down at the vast space beneath them.

"Unbelievable," agreed Seph.

Below them was spread a vast network of walls comprised almost entirely of stacked books, most of them more than thirty feet high, with more of those towering shelves reaching up from the midst of it all like enormous, ancient trees. From this angle, the narrow walkways between those stacks looked like cramped streets in a tiny city.

"That's a *lot* of books," said Piper.

Seph stared at it. There was something strangely familiar about it. It reminded her of something… Something from a dream she had once… A fleeting image passed through her mind. A dark labyrinth of tight, narrow, crumbling walls…viewed from just such an angle…somewhere dark and scary… Looking at it made her feel…strangely afraid. *Vulnerable.* And *cold.*

But the memory was gone as quickly as it'd come.

Maybe it was nothing. Her imagination was running a little wild down here. How could it not? They were in an ancient, sprawling library in some long-forgotten time capsule of a universe.

And yet, for some reason she found herself thinking about what

Warner Harr told them the first time they met him. Something about a doorway having been opened and a struggle for balance…

"So do we have to go down there?" asked Piper.

"I don't think I want to," replied Seph. It looked like a very unpleasant place to get lost. And there didn't seem to be a way down there from here anyway. The walkway they were standing on circled the entire room, but there weren't any stairs or ladders that she could see, except for the ones mounted to those towering shelves, allowing access to all the books that would otherwise be impossible to reach.

"It's like a maze down there," observed Piper. "A labyrinth." She looked up at Seph, her blue eyes shining. "A library labyrinth. It's a *libyrinth*."

Seph rolled her eyes. There was another doorway around the nearest corner, to the right. She could see more light beyond it. "Let's see what's over there."

"Oh come on, that's good." She looked down over the rail as she followed her. "Libyrinth," she said again, proud of herself.

They walked through a darkened hallway and emerged near the top of a set of steps in a very familiar room.

"Wait…" Piper looked back the way they came. "We're back here again?"

Seph didn't understand it either. She thought they'd been moving *away* from here this whole time. How did they circle all the way back again? She tried to remember the path they took, but the layout of the library was so confusing and twisted…

On the far side of the room was the other stairwell they descended when they began their journey deeper into the library after leaving Hugh behind. He should still be behind that door over there, right where they left him. "I guess we should check in on him as long as we're back here."

Piper agreed that that was a good idea. She was worried about him. He'd looked so drained the last time she saw him. Plus, he was their only way back out of this freaky library. She shivered to think what would become of them if something happened to him.

Hugh was slumped in the chair when they opened the door, but he was still alive. It was easy to tell because he was snoring quite loudly.

Seph walked over and gave his shoulder a gentle shake. "Hey. Wake up."

His eyes fluttered open and he looked up at her. "You're back…" He sat up. "Did you find it?"

"Not yet…" She frowned and stepped back, looking at him. Were her eyes playing tricks on her? It *was* pretty dark in here. The only light was what came through the window in the door overlooking the orb-lit room outside.

"Not yet?" His old face scrunched in on itself, his furry eyebrows seeming to bristle. The lines in his face were deeper than they were before. "But you were gone so long…"

"We were?" Seph pulled out her flashlight and shined it on him. "Um…?"

"Uh…? Is it just me…" said Piper, "…or is he *shrinking*?"

Seph nodded. "I think he is."

Hugh stared at them, confused. "Huh?"

It definitely wasn't her imagination. He looked at least fifty pounds lighter than he did when they left him here, as if they'd abandoned him without food for a whole week instead of just the hour or two they were gone.

"What's happening?" asked Piper.

Hugh tugged at his shirt, seemingly noticing for the first time how loose his clothes had become. "Broken time…" he breathed.

Seph leaned closer. "What?"

"I'm not a part of this world." He looked up, his eyes distant and distracted. "That's why I'm so weak. This place is standing still, outside the normal flow of time. But I'm still inside the stream…" He frowned. "Time is passing all around me, accelerated by this stalled place…aging me…" He turned his eyes back to Seph. "My metabolism must be speeding out of control. It's like I haven't eaten in weeks. I'm literally wasting away…*starving…*"

Seph shook her head. "That doesn't make any sense. How can you starve in just a few hours? I mean, wouldn't you dehydrate first?"

"Different universe, different rules…" he muttered.

"What?"

He shook his head. "It doesn't matter. It doesn't change anything in the least. We already established that I only have a limited amount of time in this place. *How* it's going to kill me is irrelevant."

"I guess so… But—"

"You need to *hurry*."

"This place is enormous! We don't even know what we're looking for!"

Hugh looked down and frowned again as he considered it. "Well…it's a library, isn't it?" He looked up and met her gaze again. "Maybe you're looking for a *book*."

She stared at him, shocked.

"Okay, *that's* not helpful *at all*!" exclaimed Piper.

He chuckled. "I suppose not. But I'm sure you'll know it when you see it. You're the seekers, right? Your job is to seek these things. And their only job is to be sought. You'll find it. Or it'll find you." He closed his eyes and lowered his head. "Damn I'm tired."

Seph turned and looked at Piper. The Tartarus lock was a book? How could a book be a lock? That didn't make any sense.

Hugh leaned back in his chair, his eyes still closed. "I had a dream while you were out," he said, his voice weary. "Heavy stories… Obsession… Skeleton… Tree…" His voice trailed off. He fell silent for a moment. Then: "Reading…hole…"

Piper leaned closer, trying to hear. "What?"

"You'll find it," he mumbled. "I know you will. Just…hurry…"

Seph nodded. "We'd better go."

"What do you think that stuff he said meant?"

"I don't know. Maybe he's just delirious. Or maybe we'll find out for ourselves. But we should let him sleep for now."

Piper nodded. "So where do we go from here?"

She wasn't sure, but she knew they couldn't just stand here. Hugh was counting on them.

They left the room, leaving poor Hugh to sleep, and then made their way back down the steps to the main floor below.

"He's right," Seph decided as she looked out at the immense task before her. "It's like the markers. We'll know it when we see it. Or hear it… Or whatever. We've just got to keep covering ground. That's all." She turned and looked at Piper. Immediately, her expression darkened. "What's wrong?"

Piper looked back at her, her eyes filled with worry. She was grimacing. "I feel…"

Seph looked down at her hands. She was rubbing her belly, as if soothing a dull ache. "You haven't eaten…" If she went too long without eating meat… "You need to eat *now*. You didn't forget to bring some jerky, did you?"

Jerky was a perfect emergency snack for Piper. It kept a long time and it did the trick in a pinch, but sometimes she forgot. Especially when things were weird.

"I only brought one," she said, pouting. "But I already ate it."

"When?"

"A while ago… I don't know. I started to feel sick, so I ate it. But now I feel sick again."

"Why would you feel sick earlier?" She looked at her watch, but of course it told her nothing. It'd stopped a long time ago.

Piper was conditioned to eat three times a day. As long as she had meat with her meals those three times, even if a little bit of meat was all she ate, she never got sick. If she *were* to feel sick, it could only be because it was past time for her to eat. Since she had breakfast before they came here…and if she felt sick and had to eat her jerky…and now she was feeling sick *again*…that could only mean that it was already past *dinner time.*

But there was no way they'd been in here that long!

Or had they…?

But you were gone so long, Hugh told them when she reported that they hadn't found the lock yet.

Her heart sank. Time was messed up here. There was no telling how long they'd been wandering around this place, and if Hugh was able to drop fifty pounds in that time, Piper's body could easily have cycled through two mealtimes.

"I'm sorry," groaned Piper. "It never occurred to me that I'd need to bring more than one."

"No. It's okay." She turned and looked around. She'd never wished so badly for a vending machine in all her life.

"What're we going to do?"

Another of the jabberwock's eerie groans rolled through the library.

Seph set her jaw and nodded. "The only thing we *can* do," she replied. "We go in there, get that stupid lock and get you and Hugh out of this place."

Piper groaned. "Right. I'm sure it'll be just that easy."

"Optimism, Pi."

"Right. Because *you're* the optimist."

Seph set off toward the back of the library again. "Someone's going to have to be."

Chapter 30

"I really don't feel good…" groaned Piper.

"You have to hang in there," said Seph. "It can't be too much longer."

But that was a lie. It could very well be much, *much* longer. This place went on forever, room after room after room of nothing but damned *books. Unreadable* books, even. Could there be anything more pointless?

She'd never had the patience for reading. She liked *visual* stimulation. She liked colors. She liked *art.* Comic books. Movies. Games. She wasn't interested in black and white words. She wanted to *see* the story. That was how she felt it. That was how it reached her soul.

Had it been an hour since they left Hugh in that office and set out again? Or two hours? Or six? She couldn't tell. Lodblin's library was as mad as the king, himself. And the Keeper's time magic, as Hugh called it, was equally nuts.

This was bad. Piper was clearly in distress. She looked pale. She kept clutching at her cramping belly. She wasn't crying yet, but there were tears shimmering in her eyes. She was in pain. And there was nothing she could do about it.

She'd never seen what happened if Piper waited too long to eat. She was good about taking care of herself. But she'd heard both from

Piper *and* from Piper's parents about how deathly ill she used to get when she was a young girl and they still didn't understand what was happening to her. She used to curl up in the floor and sob, the pain was so bad.

How bad would it get if they couldn't get her out of here in time? Could she really die from it? It seemed ridiculous that anyone could die from *meat withdrawal*, of all things…but it would be far from the strangest thing she'd ever seen.

And this damned library refused to end so that she could get her out of here! It was so frustrating!

But the books were getting older again. The ones in this room were so badly molded that entire shelves had practically fused into single, fuzzy blocks.

Was it even safe for them to be here? Even in *their* world, moldy places like this were hazardous to walk around in without masks. And *these* molds were literally *alien*. Again, she wondered if their bodies had any immunity to the things in this world.

But the Keeper would know about that, wouldn't he? He seemed to know everything else. He apparently had the ability to construct an entire *city* to hide the gateway to this library, lasting hundreds of years. He wouldn't overlook something as basic as *germs*.

Would he?

She shined Piper's cell phone light into the next doorway, illuminating more moldy books and strewn pages. Her own cell phone had gone dead a while ago, but only after lasting much longer than it honestly should have. Time wasn't just slowed or stalled in this place. It behaved erratically, affecting different things in different ways.

The first time they used the fringe road, their bodies felt the passage of time, but not their minds. They grew hungry and thirsty, their bladders continued to fill, they became tired, but they weren't *aware* of the passing hours. Meanwhile, in stark contrast, there was the gas gauge that miraculously quit moving, allowing them to drive on and on through that endless forest, far longer than should've been possible. The same thing was happening here, she realized. Piper had grown hungry, as if far more time had passed than they realized, and yet the drain on their cell phone batteries had slowed, suggesting that time was, instead, compressed. It made no sense, no matter how she tried to rationalize it.

Piper stumbled over a book and dropped to her knees.

"Are you okay?" asked Seph.

"Yeah… Just my shoes…"

She kept thinking that she should just take the silly booties off, but that would just be asking to step on something sharp in all this mess. A single nail or screw from one of those broken bookshelves would be the perfect end to this terrible adventure.

Seph helped her to her feet again.

"Thanks…" She looked down at the floor, distracted. There was something there, under the book she'd tripped over. She bent down and plucked it from the mess.

It was a little doll with curly hair, wearing a pretty, yellow dress. It wasn't new, but it didn't look nearly as old as the other things in this place. "What's this doing here?"

Seph wrinkled her nose at the thing. Maybe it was all the horror movies she'd watched, but she wasn't a huge fan of dolls in general. Dolls cradled by little girls was one thing. Left on their own, unsupervised, they quickly became sort of terrifying.

And aside from that, she didn't really want to think about all the ways a doll might end up stranded in a place like *this*. The first question that came to mind, after all, was what happened to this doll's little girl?

Piper found herself stuck on the fact that the doll didn't look nearly old enough to be a part of the library. What did that mean? Had other people been here before them? And if so, what became of those people?

Her gaze drifted to the gloomy room around her, to the open doorways, to the deep shadows between the closely packed bookshelves, half-expecting to see a small, terrified face looking back at her.

For some reason, she found that she didn't want to put the doll back down on the floor. She didn't even want to leave it in this room. It'd already been lost once. Abandoned. She didn't have the heart to do it again. Instead, she hugged it against her chest.

Seph watched her. "You…plan on keeping it?"

"Just for now," she replied, her voice weary. It was strange, but it made her feel a little better. It made her stomach hurt a little less.

Seph stared at it for a moment, uncertain. "Okay… But if that thing possesses you or something, I'll leave your butt here."

"Fair enough," sighed Piper. She didn't feel well enough to argue right now. And she certainly couldn't explain why she felt the need to hold onto the stupid doll. Maybe she just wanted a distraction from the pain.

Or maybe the meat deprivation was starting to affect her brain.

Seph continued into the next room. She kept glancing back at Piper, uncertain about the doll, but she didn't say anything more. If it made her feel better, then so be it. But she'd grown wary of unfamiliar things these past couple years, and couldn't help imagining something horrible lurking inside it, just waiting for her to drop her guard.

For all they knew, it could be Hugh's jabberwock in disguise.

But when she entered the next room, she forgot about the doll.

A portion of the wall in here had collapsed. She found herself staring out into an empty, black abyss.

"Is that…?"

"I think so," whispered Seph. She wasn't entirely sure why she felt the need to whisper, but she did.

They hadn't seen any windows since they arrived here. This was the first either of them had seen of what existed outside these moldy walls.

Out there was another universe. A fragment of a world that died long, long ago. She shined her light out into that darkness. She even took a step toward it, but only that one step. Hugh warned them not to leave the building. He said that in these final hours the world outside this library had become a very dark place.

It was literally Armageddon out there.

She didn't dare tempt fate by disobeying Hugh on this subject. But she was also *very* curious.

What *did* the end of the world look like? Was this it? Was it just darkness? Emptiness? An encroaching void? Silent and creeping and gradual? Or was that just because everything here was stopped?

She leaned forward, squinting into that darkness. Were those *trees* looming in the gloom? Strange, coiled branches? Alien plants?

What was it Hugh said about this world's final hours? Something about…just before it sank into the woods?

She didn't understand exactly what he was talking about, but for some reason it gave her a terrible chill.

Did something just move out there?

"We shouldn't be here," groaned Piper. She clutched the doll a little tighter to her chest.

"Yeah…" But still she found herself watching that darkness, curious. "We should check the next room."

Piper grunted, finally tearing Seph's attention away from the haunting breach.

"How're you feeling?"

"My belly hurts…"

"Come on. Bear with it a little longer, okay?"

"I don't think I have any choice."

Seph took her hand and led her back into the previous room and to the next door.

She hadn't heard the monster in a while. Maybe it'd crawled off somewhere to sleep for a few days.

(Sure. And maybe they'd find the Tartarus lock waiting for them in a box full of hundred-dollar bills, too.)

A short corridor led to a narrow stairwell, which in turn led them down to *another* corridor and then into an even older chamber, where they stopped and stared.

"Big books," grunted Piper.

Seph nodded. Both sides of this room were lined with the biggest books she'd ever seen. There were dozens of them, shelved on a raised platform so that they were off the ground, their spines facing out. They ranged from three feet to six feet in height and up to three feet thick.

"Wow…" sighed Seph. This was insane. What kind of book needed to be that big? What could possibly be written in them? She doubted she could even lug the smallest of these monstrous tomes off the shelf to open it. And she almost certainly wouldn't be able to put it back when she was done *not* being able to read it.

Once again, she found herself reminded that this was the way of things. It wasn't just *this* universe that ended. *All* universes would eventually come to an end. Including theirs.

Someone went to a lot of trouble to make these books. And even though they were still here, it was doubtful that anyone would ever even see them again, much less read the words that were written inside.

When the world she knew finally died, how much of it would be forgotten? Would *anything* survive? Would all the knowledge and art and literature and accomplishments of the world just fade away with everything else? The Ahns told them that people would continue on. They'd survive, probably taking things with them. But how much could humanity carry? And how long could it survive in the next world?

She thought of her own art and suddenly felt so small, so *pointless.*

"Heavy…" grunted Piper.

"I'm sure they are," said Seph, distracted.

"No… Heavy stories."

"Huh?"

"What Hugh said. Heavy stories. In his dream."

Seph gasped. "That's right!" She thought the old man was just delirious, but he must've saw them come here in his dreams. It wasn't just nonsense. It was a *map.*

Did that mean, then, that they were going in the right direction?

Piper groaned and leaned against the doorjamb, still clinging to her lost doll.

"Just hang in there a little longer, okay?"

"You keep saying that…"

"Sorry."

"S'okay… I'm not trying to be—*ungh*!"

Seph twirled around, her heart leaping. "Pea!"

"I'm…m'okay…" she groaned, clutching at her belly. "Just…*ow*…just hurts… Can't…remember the last time…*uh*…the last time I went this long…"

"We're gonna get you out of here. *Soon.* I promise."

"Okay…"

Seph took her arm and led her forward, between the gargantuan tomes that would probably never be read again, and through the next doorway.

The next room looked a lot like those first rooms of the library, with their towering bookshelves reaching up into darkness, except much more cramped and without any of those big, glowing orbs to light the way. It was also much older. More of the shelves had collapsed, so that there were thousands of books strewn across the floor, along with large chunks of debris from the crumbling ceiling, making it difficult to walk, especially for Piper.

Maybe you're looking for a book, Seph thought, recalling Hugh's words. It almost made her angry to think about. If someone really wanted to hide a book…*really* hide it, so that no one…*no one*…would ever, *ever* find it…then this place was utterly perfect. But to suggest, for even a moment, that they were actually supposed to *find* such a book in here… It was *preposterous.*

Utterly impossible.

Still clinging to Piper's arm, holding her so she didn't fall down in those silly heels, she made her way deeper into the room, shining her light on every surface, trying to decide where to go next.

There were more of those huge insect nests in here. At least three of them. They were built right onto the shelves, themselves, like great mounds of hardened plaster smeared across the books, the biggest one nearly fifteen feet in height. The very sight made her skin crawl.

There was a passageway between two of the nests, leading into a dark corridor. She quickly decided that she didn't want to go that way.

But when she turned to look for another way out of this room, she was frozen by another of those unearthly groans.

And this one was *close.*

"*Persephone*!" squeaked Piper.

Something was moving at the far end of the room. Something *large.* There was a loud crash, followed by the thunderous sound of a great many books falling to the floor.

It was coming this way.

She didn't *know* the bugs in those nests were the stinging sort. For all she knew, they were as harmless as houseflies. It was, after all, the nearest exit, the quickest possible way *away* from whatever was approaching. The logical decision should've been to go that way. At this point, it was a more than acceptable risk. And yet, when she looked back at those enormous, papery constructions crawling with greenish bugs, she knew she couldn't do it. She wasn't strong enough to make her feet move in that direction.

Her heart pounding, she pulled Piper *away* from the infested doorway.

If there was a corridor on this side of the room, she reasoned, maybe there was one on the other side of the room, too. One that wasn't guarded by a swarm of killer alien hornets.

It was ironic, she knew. She kept choosing to take risks with truly dangerous things to avoid things that were probably harmless. She was so desperately afraid of bugs, but it was the *fear* that was far more likely to end up getting her killed.

Why was she like this?

The jabberwock groaned again, even louder than before, shaking the entire building around them. Books crashed to the floor. Dust rained down from the ceiling.

Piper barely managed to stifle a scream behind the palm of her hand.

Ahead of them, another passageway appeared in her flashlight beam, just as she'd hoped. And it wasn't flanked by two enormous alien beehives.

As another crash of falling books rang out from behind them, she led Piper into the corridor and out of the room.

But she didn't make it very far before she stopped, her eyes widening with mounting terror as her gaze slowly crept toward the ceiling.

She didn't avoid the bugs at all.

The biggest nest she'd yet seen was right there, covering the entire ceiling of the corridor.

Oh god…

"Persephone?" whispered Piper. "We have to keep moving. Perseph—*ungh*!" She crouched down, clutching at her stomach.

But Seph couldn't move. Behind her, the monster of the library let out another unearthly groan. Above her, those strange, greenish bugs were becoming agitated. They were buzzing all around her head. And beneath her, her feet were frozen to the floor. She couldn't move. She could barely even think. Her heart was pounding. She was starting to sweat.

She was going to die in this awful place.

Chapter 31

"Snap out of it…" groaned Piper. She grabbed a handful of Seph's shirt and pulled as hard as she could.

Seph stumbled, surprised, and they both fell onto their hands and knees. Little dead things crunched beneath her bare palms and knees. She screamed and sat up, revolted.

"*Oh my gosh*! *Shhh*!"

Her skin crawling, Seph shook her hands and wiped them on her skirt. Then she frantically brushed off her knees and then wiped her hands again.

Then something buzzed past her ear and she *screamed* again.

"*Stop screaming*! *It's going to hear you*!" Piper rose to her feet, swaying a little, still clutching the lost doll beneath her arm. She felt nauseous. Her vision blurred. Why did her stomach hurt so much? What was wrong with her? Why was she like this? Again, she grabbed Seph's shirt and pulled. "Please come on!"

It was so hard to think. There were disgusting bugs flying around her head. There were equally disgusting *dead* bugs all over the floor. She was surrounded by things that she hated and her stupid brain refused to work.

There was an *actual freaking monster* behind her! A thing that probably would *actually kill her*, and yet she was frozen in place by a bunch of buzzing insects that hadn't even stung her yet! And still her brain wouldn't work!

Deep down, she *knew* she was being stupid, but she just couldn't get control of herself.

And the worst part was that it wasn't just *herself* she was letting down. Piper needed her. She was in pain.

She realized that she was starting to cry. She *hated* that. It made her feel so weak. So *useless.*

Just move your feet, said her father somewhere in the back of her mind. *Don't worry about what your head's doing. Let it cry. Just concentrate on moving your feet.*

She took a shaky step forward. Then another. Piper pulled her along, tugging her toward the end of the corridor, moaning at the pain in her stomach.

Please don't sting me! Seph thought, gritting her teeth against the terror that just kept welling up inside her until she felt she would burst.

And somehow those hideous little green bugs didn't sting her. They buzzed around her head, they landed on her face, they crawled in her hair, making it so hard not to scream again, but they didn't sting her. They didn't bite. They just…*buzzed.*

Behind her, however, she could hear more books crashing to the floor.

The jabberwock was at the doorway.

She blinked away the tears and forced herself to focus on just the path in front of her feet.

They were almost out of the corridor. The doorway was just ahead.

She could do this!

But then Piper groaned and dropped to her knees.

Seph knelt over her, fresh panic filling her. "Pea!"

"Hurts…" she whimpered.

Seph shined her light into the next room. The walls and ceiling in there weren't covered in insect hives. She could actually *think* in there. She only had to go a few more steps. She slipped under Piper's arm, forcing herself to ignore the stupid, buzzing bugs, and heaved her to her feet.

She was heavier than she looked. But that was because of this universe's strange gravity. It made *everything* heavier. It didn't matter one bit. Piper wasn't going to leave her side when she was acting like an idiot, so she wasn't going to leave Piper's side now. She dragged her through the doorway and looked around.

Almost immediately, that crippling, irrational panic began to melt away and reveal the two much more *rational* terrors that she was facing.

There was another, much smaller doorway in the corner just to their left. An office of some kind. Or maybe a study room? Not that it mattered. Grunting, she tightened her grip on Piper and half-carried her to it, stumbling over a pile of spilled books in the process.

Behind them, the library's monster let out another fearsome groan.

What was that noise, anyway? It wasn't exactly a roar. It wasn't a growl, either. Or a snarl. In fact, she couldn't say for sure that she'd ever heard a sound quite like that before.

She'd never been much of a reader. What *was* a jabberwock, anyway? What did it look like? What did it do? Did they kill it? And if so, *how*?

Why didn't she just read the damn book?

Except even if she *had* read it, it wouldn't do her any good. She'd forgotten in her blind panic that "jabberwock" was only a silly name

Hugh had given the beast. No children's book was going to tell her how to defeat this monster.

She took Piper into the far corner of the little room and eased her onto the paper-littered floor. Then she turned around to see if she could make the door close.

That was when she saw it.

A great, monstrous shape emerged from the corridor. It was little more than an enormous, writhing shape in the darkness, a slick, shadowy thing dragging itself across the floor on deadly claws, its body rippling with terrible muscles, dragging a long, serpent-like tail behind it.

She backed away from the door until her back struck the desk, her wide eyes fixed on the behemoth as it crawled past them and out of sight, a cloud of buzzing, greenish bugs trailing after it.

It let out another of those awful, earth-trembling groans.

And then it was gone.

Seph didn't dare move for a moment. She stood there, her back pressed against the desk, her dark eyes wide behind the lenses of her glasses, her entire body trembling with terror.

Finally, she turned her head and looked at Piper. She didn't have to ask if she'd seen it, too. Her blue eyes were open wide, staring through the doorway. She looked like a terrified little girl, especially with the doll clutched against her breast like that.

"What…was…?" she squeaked.

Seph sank down to the floor and took a deep, ragged breath. When she went to let it out, it burst from her lips in a terrified sob.

What were they thinking? Why would they come to a place like this? They didn't belong here. They couldn't do these things.

Piper crawled over to her and wrapped her arms around her.

Neither of them said a word.

Several minutes passed like that. They might've both remained that way for hours, even, if Piper's stomach didn't cramp again, making her groan.

"I'm sorry," whispered Piper.

"Don't," said Seph, wiping at her eyes. "I'm the one who acts like an idiot when I see a bug."

"At least there're lots of people like you out there." She took a deep breath and rubbed at her stomach. "I'm just a *freak*."

"Don't say that."

"It's true."

"Don't."

Piper said nothing more. She closed her eyes and concentrated on letting a fresh wave of nausea pass.

Seph stared through the open office door.

Now that the monster was gone, she couldn't help but wonder why it didn't try to get in here. Could it not see her light? Could it not smell where they'd gone? It'd followed them this far. Why would it just walk right past them like that?

"I *really* don't feel good," groaned Piper.

"Hang in there," said Seph. "There's got to be a way. The Ahns said there'd be a way..." She rubbed at her temples, trying to make herself think. What was it Hugh said? Heavy stories, then...what? What came next? Obsession, was it?

What did that even mean?

She closed her eyes and leaned back, resting her head against the desk.

Obsession...

Obsession wasn't even a thing. It wasn't tangible. How did you find something that was basically a state of mind?

She opened her eyes and stared up at the ceiling.

A moment passed before she finally began to notice the room around her.

This place wasn't like the other parts of the library.

There were books everywhere, of course. *That* was the same. They were stacked on the floor next to the walls. They clung to deteriorating shelves, biding their time before the wood finally rotted and snapped from under them. But for some inexplicable reason, they were also nailed to the walls like some kind of bizarre artwork, tacked up like sticky notes, along with hundreds of loose pages.

"What is this place?" she asked as she rose to her feet.

It looked like someone had been working here. And not just a little light studying.

Obsession.

Her eyes widened. Was this it? Had she been here this whole time without realizing it?

She turned and sifted through the papers left littered all over the top of the desk. There were handwritten notes scribbled everywhere. She looked up at the walls. Strange diagrams and alien symbols stared back at her.

One particular arrangement of symbols was repeated over and over again. And in spite of the fact that it'd been written in an age she had no way of even imagining, she found that she could read it.

"Tartarus…" she sighed.

Piper looked up at her.

"Someone was looking for Tartarus." But who? Was it the seekers of the last universe? Had the Keeper been sending people here every cycle? Or was it someone from this library's original universe? Perhaps King Lodblin, himself? Was he trying to find the Tartarus of *his* world?

Maybe he built this library so he could escape the looming demise.

She supposed she'd never know. She could only read that one word. The rest of it was as alien as everything else in this library. But she couldn't help wondering if this person, whoever he might've been, managed to find any clues about the whereabouts of the lock.

Piper groaned again, pulling her back from her thoughts. She knelt down beside her and brushed back her hair. She didn't seem to have a fever. She wasn't sweating. But she looked pale. She was breathing hard. And she was clearly in pain.

What was going on inside her body?

She looked around once more at all the books that had been mounted to the walls. If she poured through every page in this room, would she find more characters that she could read? Or would it only be a colossal waste of time? Even if she did manage to find something else she could actually read, it wouldn't necessarily tell her what to do next. Meanwhile, Piper was getting worse by the minute. And how long did they have before that *thing* came back?

She hated this! She didn't know what to do. Why couldn't the Keeper just tell them what they were supposed to do?

She closed her eyes and tried to think.

After "obsession," Hugh said something about a skeleton… And after that, a tree. A "reading hole" was the last thing he mentioned.

Again, she looked down at Piper. If they were really supposed to find all those things and still get out of here in time to save both Piper *and* Hugh, then there was no way she could sift through all this mess.

She made up her mind.

They had to keep moving.

Chapter 32

The monster was nowhere to be seen when they crept out of the office. It couldn't have gone back the way it came, or Seph was certain she would've seen it. It wasn't exactly light on its feet. But she had no intention of going back into that bug-infested hallway for *any* reason. That left only two other ways out of this room. One was another corridor the same size as the last. The other was a much narrower hallway leading off to the left. She didn't get a good look at the beast, but she was pretty sure it was too big to fit through that one. And since it didn't seem to contain any massive insect hives, that was their way out of here.

"Hang in there," she whispered.

Piper nodded. She didn't dare open her mouth to reply. It felt like she might throw up if she did. Her whole body felt heavy. And that deep aching in her gut was almost more than she could bear. It felt like something was tearing her open from the inside.

Seph paused at the end of the narrow corridor and peered into the next room. There was another broken wall in here, revealing more of the unsettling, end-of-the-world void that loomed outside.

She'd grown accustomed to the strange, subtle smells of this new world already, but this room had a new smell to it, much stronger, and much, *much* more unpleasant. Was this new smell coming from outside, she wondered, or was it something in this room?

It was different than the other rooms. The books in here were all locked up in cabinets, behind filthy glass. Only a few of the cabinet doors stood open. Only one was broken, and even it had only one crack in a single pane.

Seph couldn't help wondering what these books were. Were these more valuable than the books in the rest of the library? Were they special in some way? Were they crazy King Lodblin's personal collection? The oldest and rarest? Or maybe the glass cabinets meant nothing at all. Maybe it was just the way this particular room was designed.

She wiped the dust away from one of the panes and peered in at the spines of the old books inside, but she still couldn't read anything that was written on them.

Maybe you're looking for a book.

Impossible. The old man had to have been joking. Or delirious. There was no way she had time to search for just one book in all of this. She refused. The Keeper wouldn't be so stupid as to actually expect them to search through every volume in this building.

They continued on.

The new smell wasn't unique to that one room. The next one smelled of it even more. It was pungent, but also weirdly sweet…something between cigar smoke and rotting compost, perhaps. It was too weird to accurately describe. She didn't think there was a word in her world to describe it.

This part of the building looked less like a vast library than a sprawling house that had simply been stuffed with as many books as it could fit. The rooms were smaller, but more elaborate, with orange-colored wood finish and strange, ornate patterns carved into the trim. There were fewer and fewer actual bookshelves and more and more stacks of books sitting on the bare floor.

At some point, the marble floors had given way to scarred hardwood, but she couldn't remember exactly when.

The rooms grew smaller. The hallways grew narrower. There were more stairs in this part of the building, leading both up and down, further complicating what was already a near-impossible labyrinth.

Seph decided to try one of the staircases and found a strangely out-of-place doorway halfway down.

It didn't even have a landing. It simply opened right onto the stairs without any warning, a safety hazard if she'd ever seen one.

She shined her light inside and discovered a small room that didn't seem to belong with the rest of building. There were no bookshelves, for one thing. Or stacks of books. Or book-littered desks or tables. The walls inside were completely bare, made entirely of red brick, which she hadn't seen anywhere else. And in spite of the fact that the layout of the floor above them made it extremely unlikely that there were any external walls anywhere near this part of the building, there were two windows on two different walls overlooking an empty darkness that she was quite sure wasn't a part of the library.

But what captured her attention wasn't the windows. It was the one piece of furniture occupying this room.

It was a strange, wooden cabinet with twelve mismatched glass doors containing what looked like a bunch of junk. There was a well-worn baseball in one and an old revolver that looked like something from a Hollywood western in another. Another contained what appeared to be a modern housekey. There was a weird, glowing lantern of some sort and a rusty pair of wire cutters. There was a mirror and a single piece of folded paper, a chunk of black rock, a golden bracelet, a little cloth sack and a small, wooden chest. And, of course, there was a book.

She stopped for a moment to stare at these things. A lot of it was stuff from *her* world. Did this world even have such a thing as baseball? Would this world's guns look just like her world's revolvers? And that housekey was about as modern as it got. Even the book was an old copy of *The Hobbit.* What was *that* doing here?

She was especially drawn to the book. *Maybe you're looking for a* book, she thought again. Could this be the book? Why would it be a copy of *The Hobbit*, of all things? She tried to open the door with the book in it, but it wouldn't budge.

There were strange symbols carved into the wood of the cabinet. She couldn't read them any more than she could read any of the writing on all these countless books, but somehow she was certain that this writing was different.

Piper stared at it. "What is that?"

Seph didn't know what it was. But the longer she stared at it, the more certain she was that it didn't belong here. This cabinet wasn't from the same world that built this library. And she didn't think it was from their world, either.

There was something very *otherworldly* about it.

"Can you…hear it?"

She looked over at her, surprised. "What?"

Piper reached out and touched the scarred wood. "It's talking…"

"It is?" She cocked her head and tried to listen, but she couldn't hear anything.

Piper's ears, however, were perked straight up, fixated on the cabinet.

"What's it saying?"

She dragged her fingertips along the surface, feeling the symbols that were carved there. "We have to give it something…"

"What kind of something?"

"Something…important."

"We don't have anything important." Nothing they were willing to give up, anyway. The only truly important thing they had was Piper's locket, and they couldn't give that up.

"Anything can be important…" whispered Piper. She looked down at the doll she was still clutching. "Maybe this?"

Seph stared at the doll. That thing? What would a magic cabinet want with a lost doll?

Piper held it up. "Try it."

She sighed. "If you say so." She reached out and tried to open the door with the book in it again, but still it wouldn't open. "Nope."

"Not that one," said Piper. She looked it over, then pointed to another door, the one with the rusty tool in it. "That one."

Seph raised an eyebrow at her. "Um…am I talking to you right now…or the cabinet? Or the doll?"

Piper blinked and squinted at her. "Huh?"

"Just checking." Seph reached out and tried the other door. Just as Piper said, it opened right up. She reached in and took the wire cutters. "What're we supposed to do with these?"

Piper shrugged. "Dunno. The cabinet just told me to take them."

"You talk to furniture now?"

She pointed to the ears on top of her head. "I hear what I hear. I dunno." She held the doll out for her to take. "Here."

Seph eyed the doll. She still thought it was more creepy than cute. Not because it wasn't a cute doll, but because they found it in a place like this. But she took it from her and placed it inside the mysterious cabinet. Then she closed the door. Almost immediately, she attempted to open the door again, but it wouldn't budge.

Apparently, the exchange was acceptable.

"That was weird," said Seph, looking at the rusty pair of cutters again.

Piper swayed on her feet.

Seph grabbed her arm. "Pea!"

"M'okay…"

She didn't *sound* okay. She sounded like she might pass out. Seph stuffed the wire cutters into her purse and steered her out of the strange, little room. "Come on. We have to be getting close now."

Piper nodded.

At the bottom of the steps was a narrow corridor made even narrower by the books stacked up against each wall. And beyond that was a room where the books appeared to have been dumped onto the floor, where they lay torn and tattered, forcing them to climb over them just to reach the next doorway. Piper, between her heels and the meat sickness, found this to be a particularly difficult task. She slipped four times before giving it up entirely and crawling to the doorway on her hands and knees.

"Don' make fun," she groaned.

"I'm not making fun," promised Seph. And she wasn't. At this point, she was far too worried to crack jokes.

The next room wasn't as bad. The books in here weren't piled so deep that she couldn't step between them.

In the next room, they found more books. In the room after that, they found even more books. And after that, not surprisingly, more books.

Books.

Books.

More books.

Oh, and *more damned books*!

Seph was sick of books. It was obvious that the guy who built this place was mad. You had to be crazy to want *this many freaking books*!

The only book she'd been able to find in this whole *universe* that she could actually read was locked inside some kind of *magic cabinet*, and the stupid thing decided that what they needed was a cruddy old pair of pliers!

She kept expecting to see something with her prophet sight. Some small detail that jumped out at her. Some tiny clue. Wasn't that how this stuff was supposed to work? Just when she became too frustrated to go on, she'd glimpse something out of place and it would turn out to be just what she needed.

But that wasn't happening here. She hadn't even once felt that odd sensation that something was here that she could almost, but not quite see.

There was nothing here at all but these god-forsaken *books*.

Piper stepped on one of them and slipped as the cover tore away from the spine. She dropped to her knees and yelped.

"You okay?"

She shook her head. "I'm so tired…"

"Come on. Just a little farther."

"No it's not…"

Seph stared at her. She wasn't sure what to say. It was true. She kept saying, "Just a little farther," and, "Hang in there just a little longer," but she had no idea how much farther it was or how much longer it was going to be.

"Hurts…" she whimpered. "So much…"

"You can do this."

But she shook her head. "I can't…"

"Just lean on me." Seph took her arm and hooked it over her shoulder, then hoisted her to her feet. "We'll do this together. It'll be okay."

But again, she had no way of knowing it'd be okay. And as if to prove it, the cell phone battery finally went dead, plunging them into darkness.

Chapter 33

"No, no, no, no, *no*!" squealed Seph. "Not now!" The battery indicator had been stuck on eighteen percent for what felt like hours and now it was suddenly *dead*?

"Persephone…" squeaked Piper.

"It's okay. I've got you. We just…we need to find the light." She turned around, searching for the familiar glow of one of those big orbs. They'd been scattered all over the place earlier, but suddenly she couldn't find one. Had they really ventured so far? "There has to be light somewhere!" she exclaimed, her voice cracking with panic.

"Persephone…"

"I'm here."

"I can't do it anymore…"

"Yes, you can. Don't say stuff like that."

"I can't…"

Seph could feel herself starting to cry again. She hated that so much. "Please, Pea…"

"M'sorry…"

She wiped at her tears. She hated feeling weak. But she didn't know what to do. She could hear Piper's breathing. It was heavy and ragged. She was struggling against the pain.

It didn't even make sense! That was the worst part of it all. Whoever heard of someone getting this sick because they didn't eat meat? She'd heard that people could be the opposite. Sometimes people who were vegetarians for a long time became *intolerant* of meat. But *this*? It just didn't make sense!

She stuffed the cell phone into her purse with her own—they were both useless now—and tightened her grip on Piper. She held her free hand out in front of herself to shield against any unexpected obstacles and began walking, dragging Piper along with her.

She didn't know what else to do.

The Keeper was a fool to think they were his seekers. They were just two dumb, useless girls. One of them couldn't miss a meal and the other was deathly afraid of bugs.

Would he be mad, she wondered? Or just disappointed? Surely he wouldn't be surprised. Even he must realize by now that he'd made a mistake trusting such an important task to the two of them.

Her hand brushed against something. More books. She could feel the dusty spines. The shelves. She kept her hand on it and followed it to the left until it ended. Here, she found a doorway. Another room?

Piper was slipping. Seph hoisted her up again and carried on. She couldn't stop. Stopping meant dying. It meant lying down with all those little black bug carcasses and never getting back up.

What happened to someone who died in a place like this? Would your soul move on? Or would you be trapped here forever, endlessly wandering this awful darkness, constantly lost and afraid?

Her hand brushed against more books. This time, it was one of those free-standing stacks. It tumbled over and crashed to the floor, making at least enough noise to let every monster in what was left of this universe know exactly where they were. *And* one of them struck the back of her wrist on its way down, hard enough to leave a bruise.

She cursed, frustrated.

"Persephone…"

"It's okay. I'm not leaving you."

"I always wondered…"

Seph reached out, more gingerly this time, and felt another stack of books a little to the right of the one she knocked over.

"…your prophet sight…all those things you can see…"

"Uh huh." A lot of good it'd done her in this place.

"…if you can see all those…all those things…do you really *need* a light?"

Seph stopped. Did she really need light? She turned and looked at Piper. Even in the dark, she could see those gray, iridescent ears. They were droopy, but they were clearly there. It was the only thing she *could* see.

"…it just…just seems like you should…be able to see…see *something.*"

Seph wiped at her eye again. That was stupid. She couldn't see *anything.* She couldn't even see *Piper.* Only her spirit ears. Everything else was utter blackness.

…wasn't it?

She turned her head and looked around. The room was pitch black. She was standing in perfect darkness with nothing but a pair of droopy cat ears hovering at her side.

"Sometimes," whispered Piper, "it's hard for me to…to hear things…with *those* ears…over all the noise I hear…with my other ears."

She considered this. It *had* occurred to her before that her prophet sight might be hindered by her *real* sight. After all, she was accustomed to using her human eyes. Her brain might only be able to process her prophet sight by treating what she saw like visible light.

But if that were true, she'd be able to see something now. Wouldn't she?

And there was nothing here.

Except… She squinted. *Was* there something there? A subtle shape in the darkness? A fleeting movement?

Piper groaned. "Why does it have to hurt so much?" she whimpered.

"Keep it together. We're going to get out of this."

Now that she was thinking about it, there seemed to be lots of things moving about in the darkness. *Was* it just her imagination?

She reached out and immediately knocked over another stack of books, startling herself again. She tried to take a step, but her foot fell on more books. It was so hard to move around in this place. It was frustrating. She didn't have time for this nonsense.

She closed her eyes and took a calming breath. She could do this. She just had to relax a little.

Something fluttered past her face in the darkness.

She opened her eyes and looked around, but all she could see was Piper's glowing ears.

No…that wasn't quite right. She could see something else, too. It was incredibly faint, but it was there. A shape flittering in the darkness. A shadow within a shadow. Darkness on top of darkness.

She reached out her hand, but it was too far away to touch. She took a step toward it, then another, using her hand to feel for obstacles at eye-level and her toes to watch for litter in her path.

One moment she was sure there was something there. The next moment she was convinced it was only her imagination. Back and forth again.

Her hand touched something. Wood. A door frame.

She felt her way into the next room.

Was she able to find her way here because she followed the fluttering, half-imagined thing? Or was it only a happy coincidence?

Piper groaned again.

"Hang on," pleaded Seph. She stuck her arm out again, but stopped herself halfway and pulled her hand back. She paused, confused, then reached out more carefully. Her fingers brushed against paper.

Books.

Another stack of them.

She frowned. Did she just sense that it was there? Was it possible that she saw it?

She glanced around the room again. There seemed to be two of the faint, fluttering things now. She could see them best from the corners of her eyes. What were they? What did they mean?

Curious, she turned and reached to the left. She imagined another stack of books over here…but no. There wasn't anything.

No, wait… She moved her hand a little farther to the left, then reached out again.

Books.

How did she do that?

Piper suddenly stiffened in her arm. "*Hunnnnnngh*!"

"*Pea*!"

"Oh gosh…!" she gasped. "Oh guh—*unnngh*!"

"*What is it*?"

"It *huuuurts*!"

Seph's heart was racing again. She didn't know what to do. How did this even work? She knew a little bit about first aid, but this wasn't something anyone had ever taught her about.

Piper threw her head back and groaned again. "*Ouchieeeeee*!"

"Just breathe! Breathe! It'll be okay!"

She grunted and relaxed again, sobbing. "*Make it stop*!" she whimpered.

Seph wished desperately that she could. She lifted her head and looked around again. The door was right over there. They just had to squeeze through these stupid stacks of books…

Wait… She reached up under her glasses and rubbed her eye. Had it gotten lighter in here? Had her eyes adjusted to the deeper darkness? How was she able to suddenly see the way out?

Does it matter? she thought in the voice of her father.

No, it didn't.

She tightened her grip on Piper and made her way across the room and through the doorway. This next room was much larger, with a great many more stupid, unreadable books stacked on either side of her so that she was making her way through a narrow valley between them.

There was another door on the far side of the room, and somewhere beyond that she could finally see the faint glow from one of those dangling orbs.

Please be the room where we left Hugh, she thought.

She was almost halfway across the room when she saw it. An unmoving shape in the darkness, black on top of black, a shadow within a shadow. It was stretched across the room, blocking her path, long and motionless.

Her wide eyes followed the length of it. To the left. On top of the pile of books. Half buried in the mountain of pages. Somehow, her mind unraveled the shapes, revealing a massive *claw* resting on the books.

She could feel the blood draining from her face as the weight of the realization sank in.

The jabberwock was here.

It was waiting in the darkness, motionless, invisible, ready to ambush them as they stumbled blindly toward the light.

Her legs trembled beneath her, threatening to spill them both onto the floor.

Piper groaned again. Somewhere behind her and to the left, Seph heard something shift in the darkness.

She pressed her lips against Piper's ear and whispered, "Don't…make…a sound…"

Piper stiffened in her grip. Her heart began to pound.

"Slowly…" She took a step backward, careful not to trip over any books. She turned her wide eyes toward the sound she heard a moment ago and found that she could make out another claw pressed against the wall.

It wasn't her imagination. Several small, moth-like things were fluttering around the room. And as she turned, she caught sight of something small and sleek scurrying across the floor.

But she didn't have time to think about these things. She was still fixated on the *big* shape, still following the long line of its neck all the way around the room and up to the ceiling, where the monster's enormous head hovered.

They'd walked directly beneath it when they entered the room.

She couldn't have screamed if she'd wanted to. Her throat was instantly dry. Her whole body trembled.

She took a step back, still clinging to Piper, and bumped into another stack of books.

The next few seconds were a blur. The books knocked into another stack, creating a domino effect that knocked down two more stacks.

The monster moved in the darkness, its head lashing out at them.

Seph thought they were dead where they stood, but instead of sinking its teeth into them, it struck where the books landed instead. An avalanche of books followed as the monster launched itself from its perch, claws flailing, jaws snapping and tail whipping, shredding pages and flinging books across the room.

Seph heaved Piper backward as a heavy claw came crashing down in front of them, only narrowly missing them.

Then, at this most inopportune time, Piper suddenly went limp and slumped to the floor, unconscious.

No!

Seph stooped down and hooked her arms around her.

Not now! This was the worst possible time for this!

Then something strange happened. Something about the horror of the moment seemed to flip a switch inside her. It was like the mysterious eye that allowed her to use her prophet sight suddenly opened wide, revealing *everything.*

The monster was right in front of her, slick and black, with blood-red horns and claws. It had no visible eyes or nose, only an enormous mouth lined with razor-sharp teeth. It was half-crawling, half-slithering across the floor, snapping at the falling books, instantly shredding any that it managed to scoop into its deadly maw.

And it wasn't alone.

Those other things she'd been seeing *did* look like large moths, but with extra-frilly wings and long, trailing tails. There were several fluttering about the room, some of them tossed around by the wind stirred up by the jabberwock's furious movements, but far more were clinging to the ceiling and walls. Dozens of them.

She didn't have time to look very closely at them, or even to decide whether these things counted as bugs or not. That monster was sure to turn its deadly teeth in her direction at any moment. She looked behind her and found a gap between the bookstacks, just wide enough to squeeze through.

She dragged Piper into it, backing all the way to the back, and curled up with her there on the floor.

The strangely illuminated world began to fade to black again, leaving them once more shrouded in darkness. And as books began to rain down on top of them, battering her, she shielded Piper as best she could and tried not to scream.

Chapter 34

Seph wasn't sure how much time passed before the monster gave up and wandered off, its terrible, earth-trembling groans following it into the black depths of the library. She also didn't know how long she spent sitting there in the dark, half buried in useless, dusty tomes and struggling to silence her sobbing. She didn't know if Piper was going to be okay. She didn't know if Hugh was still alive. She didn't know *anything* anymore.

How many hours had they been trapped down here? Was it still Wednesday? What happened to Wilbur and the others outside the water tower?

She'd never felt so afraid and helpless in her entire life.

She brushed Piper's hair from her face. She still didn't feel feverish. In fact, she was cool to the touch, almost clammy. Her breathing was shallow and ragged. Every now and then she'd make a pitiful whimpering sound in her sleep.

Seph clenched her teeth. Another tear streaked down her face. This whole thing was stupid and pointless. She didn't care about the Tartarus lock anymore. To hell with the Keeper and his stupid schemes. For all she knew, her best friend could be dying!

She'd already lost Amethyst. She couldn't bear to lose Piper, too.

They needed to get back to Hugh before it was too late—if it wasn't *already* too late—and get out of this nightmare library.

She lifted her face and looked up into the darkness. That strange vision that came to her before had completely faded. She couldn't seem to make it work again. Maybe it was a one-time kind of thing. Or maybe it only happened because that monster was nearby for some reason. If she ventured out of this hiding spot now, she had no guarantee that she wouldn't be left completely blind again.

But she didn't have a choice.

She was getting Piper out of here.

It was a struggle just to stand up. At least a few dozen books had fallen onto them during the monster's rampage—several of them, she was sure, leaving bruises on her shoulders and arms. There was nothing to use for leverage except more books, and those kept falling over. It was as if the library were determined to swallow them whole.

Piper groaned.

"Come on," whispered Seph, lifting her to her feet. "We're getting out of here."

"Can't see…"

"I know. We're going to go find some light. Just hang in there a little longer."

"Don't feel good…"

"I know."

"Like I'm gonna throw up…"

"That's okay. We're almost done."

They stumbled forward, knocking down more books in the darkness.

Piper looked up. Slowly, the encounter with the jabberwock came back to her. Although, there wasn't much to remember. It was extremely dark. She never saw anything. But she heard the books falling all around them. She thought a few of them hit her. The back of her hand still hurt. Her thigh, too. But that was all. "Did we win?"

"Yeah. Something like that." Seph squinted into the darkness as she made her way back out into the main room. When she first entered this area, she saw a faint light through one of the doorways. But she couldn't remember which way she was facing. "Just try to relax. We're going to go see Hugh."

"Is he all right?"

"I don't know. We're going to check on him now, okay?"

"Okay…"

No matter how hard she tried, she couldn't seem to make that weird night vision thing work again. She couldn't even see those moth-shaped things anymore. For all she knew, the monster could've circled back while they were cowering in the books. It could be right back where it was before, looming over them, watching them.

Although, it didn't seem to be able to see them. Or smell them. It only reacted to the falling books. Did it hunt solely by sound? Or maybe by vibrations?

She didn't care to think about the ordeal, but when she did, she couldn't help but think that they shouldn't have escaped so easily. A creature like that should've had far better hunting instincts.

How were they still alive?

She took another step into the open room and finally saw it. The faint glow of one of those curious, hanging orbs somewhere well beyond the next doorway. "This way!" she whispered. "Hurry!"

Beyond the doorway was a hallway, and beyond that another room, this one slightly more illuminated by that distant glow. It wasn't *much* more light, but it was enough to see that the leftmost wall had collapsed. The eerie, doomsday void of the dying universe loomed just on the other side. A faint, ominous mist was drifting in over the crumbled bricks.

That unpleasant smell was much stronger here, she realized.

There was something here, a dark shape filling the breach. A mere tree, she quickly realized…but like no tree she'd ever seen before. It had strange, slick bark and twisted, coiled branches. And for some reason it wasn't content with standing out in the apocalyptic weather. It was bent ninety degrees, reaching through the hole, filling the far half of the room with those strange, alien branches.

And were some of those branches…*moving*?

She took a step toward it, squinting to see it better, and something crunched under her feet. Looking down, she discovered a scattering of small bones.

The hair on the back of her neck stood up. With the exception of those little black bugs, she hadn't seen any dead animals in this place. She'd glimpsed something very much alive darting out of the room once—hours and hours ago, it seemed—proving that there were things living here, but there weren't any dead rats or other vermin carcasses lying around.

So why *here*?

Her gaze drifted back up to the tree. Now that she was looking…were those *more* bones tangled in those eerie, alien branches?

"Hold on…" she breathed. Hugh's mysterious dream words came back to her. Heavy stories…obsession…then skeleton…and tree… "Not skeleton and tree," she whispered. "*Skeleton tree.*"

She took a step backward, her every instinct screaming at her that she shouldn't be here, and felt something tug at her shirt.

She looked down to find a long, black tendril coiled around her shirttail. She yanked herself free and tried to back away, but Piper cried out.

Something had her hair!

Seph grabbed a handful of it and ripped it from the tree's grasp, only to find that several more had seized Piper's sweater.

"What's happening?" groaned Piper, her voice rising with panic.

"We have to get out of here!"

"I'm stuck!"

Seph wrapped her arms around her and pulled, but the tree was tangled in the knitted fabric. And when she looked up, she saw more of them slinking toward them from the darkness. *Bigger ones.* The tree was waking up. Its limbs were twisting and coiling like some deep-sea, Lovecraftian monstrosity come to life. Bones that had been clutched in those unmoving coils began to drop to the floor in a morbid, skeletal rain.

If that thing got ahold of them, they'd never escape.

Panic welling up inside her, she grabbed Piper's sweater and yanked it up over her head.

Piper cried out, surprised. "What're you doing!"

"No choice! Trust me!" She grabbed her around her waist and pulled her backward, out of her tangled sweater. Already, another tendril had seized Piper's hair. Another groped at her ankle. Another was snatching at Seph's shirttail again.

Piper cried out in pain as the coiling branch tore out a lock of her hair, but the two of them managed to break free and flee the room.

"My sweater!" pouted Piper, crossing her arms over her exposed bra, as if there were anyone around to see her.

"I'll buy you a new one! Just come on!" She looked back over her shoulder as they ran, making sure those snaking tendrils weren't still following them all the way down the hall.

What the hell was that thing? Was it really a tree? It moved more like some kind of animal.

But it didn't seem to be able to reach much farther than where they were standing when it attacked them, which was fortunate because Piper wasn't able to run. She stumbled along, barely keeping up with Seph as she dragged her toward the light, until she finally lost her footing altogether and fell.

"Get up!" gasped Seph.

"I'm trying…"

Seph knelt down and pulled at her arm, but Piper cried out as another wave of pain tore through her body. Then she collapsed back onto the floor, exhausted and sobbing.

"Pips…" She turned and looked behind her, then ahead, toward the light. They seemed to be alone in this corridor. There weren't even any of those awful insect nests in here. Maybe they'd be able to spare a moment.

Maybe…

She sat down on the floor, panting, and wiped at another tear under her glasses. Had she been crying this whole time? She didn't think so, but she couldn't quite remember.

What an epic failure.

Although…she *did* manage to find Hugh's third dream clue… Did that mean they were getting closer? She wasn't sure how that could be. All she'd done so far was wander blindly through the dark, repeatedly almost getting them both killed. She was literally trying to find her way back to the exit so she could give up when she found that damned tree thing.

What more could they possibly do?

She pushed all that aside and took hold of Piper again. "There's light up ahead," she said. "Let's just focus on getting that far, okay? Then we'll find somewhere for you to rest. I promise I'll get you out of here."

Piper nodded.

Together, they stood up and made their way toward the light again.

Chapter 35

The light that Seph was following turned out to be the same room they came across earlier, the one with the labyrinth of books. (The *libyrinth*, Piper had called it.) Except last time they were looking down at it from the highest level. Now they were on the floor, looking up.

She stared at the railings of that uppermost level. If they could go straight up to that fourth floor, they'd only be one room over from where they left Hugh. It would only be a matter of figuring out which corner of the room they were looking down from before. But there were no visible stairs and it had to be almost fifty feet to that railing.

All of the doorways at this end of the room led to either small reading rooms with no way out or to long corridors that stretched back into the unknown darkness where the jabberwock was lurking. With no light and no idea how to use that weird night-vision trick with her prophet sight, that just seemed like a bad idea. But the rest of the doors, including any that might lead to a convenient stairwell, were somewhere inside that libyrinth. And from what she'd seen of it when she was looking down from above, that was not going to be easy to navigate. If the stairs were at the very farthest end of the room from here, they might not be able to find it by simply wandering the narrow aisles between those towering stacks. For all she knew, there *wasn't* a way through the maze. She might have to climb over the books, and that could be dangerous. Most of them were stacked thirty feet high. And they were old and brittle. If just one of them shifted or tore beneath their weight, one or both of them could be seriously injured. Or worse.

And besides that, Piper was in pain. She wasn't in any condition to *climb* anything. And she also couldn't just keep blindly wandering these dangerous halls. She was already exhausted. She was at her limit. The next time something attacked them, she wouldn't be able to flee, much less defend herself.

She'd already fainted once when the jabberwock attacked.

She needed somewhere safe to go while Seph searched for the fastest way back to Hugh.

"Persephone…" groaned Piper.

"Just hold on. You're going to be okay." To their left, in the nearest corner of the room, a number of shorter bookshelves jutted out from the wall, half-buried in a landslide of books. Clinging tightly to Piper, she stumbled her way over the pile and into a dirty little space deep in the shadows against the wall. Here, she eased her down onto the floor. "You should be safe here while I find a way upstairs. Just stay as still as you can. Don't make any noise."

But as she stood up, Piper looked up at her. Her eyes were bloodshot and bulging. She was gasping for breath, her lips quivering. She was clutching at her stomach. A steady stream of drool was pouring from her lips. "*What's wrong with me?*" she gasped.

Seph didn't have the answer for her. She didn't know what was happening to her. She didn't know how to make it better. She didn't even know if it was really going to be all right. She wished desperately that she did, because she was far more terrified, she found, of losing Piper than she was of any monster in this library.

"Just try to relax. I'm going to get you out of here. I promise."

Piper slumped forward, groaning, as another wave of pain crawled through her guts, twisting and grinding inside her.

Seph didn't want to leave her side. She was deathly afraid that she wouldn't be here when she got back. And then what would she do? How would she go on?

But she definitely had no chance of surviving this if she couldn't get her out of this awful library.

She couldn't believe she was like this just because she hadn't eaten any *meat.*

Then something occurred to her. *Bugs* were meat, weren't they?

She looked out across the room, remembering those nasty insect hives. If she broke one of those open, would it spill out a bunch of bug larva? If she forced Piper to swallow a squirming handful of those, would it make her better?

But the idea was far too gruesome to even consider. No way she had that kind of courage. Maybe if her father was here. He was the kind of man who would probably do just that.

But she wasn't her father. She couldn't even stand the thought of it. Even if she could somehow force herself to handle bugs, there was no way she could make someone *eat* the hideous things.

There had to be another way.

"I'll be right back. I promise."

It was hard to tell if Piper even heard her. She was stooped forward, cringing against the pain, drooling onto the filthy floor in only her powder blue bra. There were light bruises on her exposed arms from those falling books and her hair was unraveling from her ponytail. Her usually flawless makeup was smeared and smudged. She looked so…*victimized.* Turning away and leaving her there was one of the hardest things Seph had ever done. But she couldn't just keep dragging the poor girl around without knowing where they were going.

She'd only be gone a few minutes.

She left Piper there and walked back out into the libyrinth.

It was all so overwhelming. If she managed to get out of this, she was never setting foot in another library ever again. Between this place and the one in Muntony with that giant zombie worm, she didn't care if she never saw another book. She looked around at the countless, unreadable volumes that filled this room alone and she decided she could happily throw a match on the whole stupid thing on her way out the door and never look back.

She hated this place so much.

Forget Tartarus. Forget the Keeper. Forget Tane. What was important right now was taking care of Piper. She didn't care what happened after that.

And the fastest way out of here, without risk of getting lost again, was straight up.

She turned her gaze to those towering bookshelves in the middle of the room, and the equally enormous, wooden ladders that were leaning against them.

One of those would be tall enough to reach straight to the highest floor.

But first, she needed to get to one.

The nearest wasn't too far inside. The walls of books standing between it and her were shorter than those deeper in, only between six and ten feet tall. And some of these shorter stacks had fallen over in places, providing gaps for her to climb through.

She made her way into the libyrinth, squeezing between closely stacked books, slipping over broken pages, climbing over shifting slopes of musty, disintegrating tomes, always keeping one eye on that nearest ladder, until finally she was standing at the bottom of it.

It was tall enough to allow them to climb to safety without venturing back into the dark parts of the library, but of course it wouldn't budge. It was mounted to the bookshelf way up at the top. She was going to have to climb up and disconnect it somehow. And if she was going to do that, she was going to need a tool…

Then she remembered the mysterious cabinet, where Piper exchanged that curious doll for the rusty pair of wire cutters.

This must've been what those were for!

She opened her purse and reached in for them, excited for *something* to finally go right in this God-forsaken place…only to find them gone.

She rummaged through her purse. She checked the other pocket. She turned the whole thing over and dumped it on the floor, her heart racing.

Nothing.

She turned and searched the area around her feet, as if, perchance, she weren't so utterly unlucky that she'd only dropped them in the past few seconds.

But they were gone.

They could've fallen out of her purse when that monster attacked them, when she was dragging Piper into their hiding place among the books. Or maybe she left them behind along with Piper's sweater when they fled the skeleton tree. Or she could've dropped them literally anywhere else between here and that cabinet.

She fell to her knees and took a ragged breath.

It was like this library was fighting them, resisting them every step they took, like it *wanted* them to fail.

Fresh tears welled up in her eyes and spilled down her cheeks.

How many times had she done this now? How many times had this place reduced her to tears?

She clenched her teeth and balled up her fists. *No.* She wasn't giving up. She gathered up her belongings, stuffed them back into her purse and then stood up and began to climb the ladder. She wasn't going to let a stupid *library* beat her.

The rungs were sturdy enough. They held her weight without sagging. That was a stroke of luck, at least. But the higher she climbed, the more of the libyrinth she saw, the bigger and more intimidating the library became, and the more she realized just how tall this ladder was.

And then there was that curious *heaviness* of this ancient universe. For the most part, she'd gotten used to it. It wasn't very noticeable after a while, except when she was carrying most of Piper's weight. Now, however, she was becoming keenly aware of it. The higher she climbed, the more the ground seemed to try to pull her back down.

At least she wasn't afraid of heights. That was one thing not stacked against her. But the thought had barely crossed her mind when she looked up and caught sight of another of those huge insect nests built right between the books and the ladder she was climbing.

She stopped and said a very bad word.

There were more ladders. She could just try a different one. But she'd have to wander father out into the *liberynth* to reach one. She was high enough now to see the layout of the maze. There wasn't a path that would take her straight to any of them. She was likely to get lost if she ventured any deeper.

Her eyes drifted to the corner of the room where she left Piper…

Every second she spent retracing her steps because of her idiotic fears was another second her best friend was suffering while she whimpered about a bunch of stupid *bugs.*

She looked up again. The nest was built on the bookshelves, not the ladder. She wouldn't even have to touch it. She just had to climb past it.

She could do this.

She set her jaw, made one of Piper's signature squeaking noises deep in her throat, and kept climbing.

"Oh god…" she groaned. "Oh god, oh god, oh god…"

Her knuckles were only inches away from the surface of the nest. Nasty little green things were crawling all over it. They were crawling on the ladder, too, most of them taking flight as she approached and buzzing around her head.

One landed on her arm and she let out a stifled cry and gave it a violent shake.

She looked down. It was much higher than she anticipated. If she did something like that and lost her grip, she could break her neck. Or worse, break everything else and have to lie there in this bug-infested nightmare until she died of dehydration or some horrendous, agonizing infection.

The thought was enough to make her woozy. The world swayed a little and she clung to the ladder until it passed.

For Pi, she thought. *Do it to save Pi.*

She took a deep breath and willed herself to calm down. And she almost did it, too. Then a bug landed on her face and she cried out in horror.

Her father would be so ashamed of her right now. Screaming and crying about some stupid bugs when people's *lives* were on the line.

She forced herself to open her eyes and look up.

There was the bracket, just a few feet above her head. She was almost there.

She could hear herself whimpering and hated it with every fiber of her being, but she climbed those last few feet and examined the bracket. She was hoping the ladder was sitting on a simple hook, or affixed by an easy-to-remove pin, or some other simple mechanism, but King Lodblin, while obviously crazy as a convention of cat ladies, apparently didn't screw around when it came to ladder safety. A heavy, rusted bolt with a strange, triangular head held it in place.

With no tools whatsoever, much less one that might actually fit this strange hardware, her only choice was going to be to break it. And the only way to do that that she could think of was to use *herself* as leverage. And that…really didn't seem like a good plan.

Clinging to the ladder, her heart pounding, she turned and looked out across the room.

The higher she climbed, the more she could see of the libyrinth, and the more complicated it became. If she went in there, it could take hours to find her way out.

Maybe she should give up and take one of those dark hallways after all. It'd be better than throwing herself to her death off a seventy-foot ladder.

She'd almost convinced herself to climb back down when another of those awful groans shattered the eerie silence of the library.

The jabberwock. Or…whatever the stupid thing really was…

She couldn't tell where it was coming from, but it wasn't far.

Was it coming this way?

Was it in here with them?

She waved away the bugs flying around her head and looked at the bracket again.

She had no choice. Squealing, she reached out and pressed the toe of her shoe through the hive and against the shelf beneath it. Predictably, the bugs began pouring out.

She was going to have to be quick. She knew for a fact that she didn't have the strength to keep this up long.

She wrapped her arms around the ladder and kicked out, yanking on it.

It came easier than she expected. The rotten wood snapped. The latch came off. The ladder lurched. And her heart leapt into her throat.

But somehow, she didn't fall.

The bugs were swarming now. There were so many of them. They still didn't sting her, which was a blessing, but they beat themselves against her skin, making it harder and harder for her to stay calm.

One more.

Just one more bracket.

She focused her thoughts on Piper and forced herself to keep moving. She shifted her weight to the other side, held on tight, set her foot against the shelf, and pulled.

This time, it was the shelf beneath her foot that snapped. A downpour of books rained to the floor far beneath her, tearing an enormous hole in the nest from which an endless cloud of bugs began to spew, rapidly filling the air.

She cried out, terrified.

Just a little longer. That was all.

But every second was pure torture. They were *touching* her. They were crawling all over her. They were buzzing in her ears. They were on her face. They were under her skirt.

It took everything she had just to cling to the ladder.

Don't you let those things beat you, said her father through the chaos and terror in her head. *You're stronger than this.*

She squinted through the cloud of bugs and looked out over the libyrinth. It was strange, the way her mind brought him back at times like this. Sometimes she couldn't quite be sure it was really all in her mind.

Was it possible that he…?

She clenched her teeth and reset her foot, this time against the back of the shelf, forcing herself to ignore those foul insects, and pulled at the ladder again.

Nothing moved.

She tried again.

It was taking everything she had not to scream as the bugs battered her. Was it her imagination, or were they getting bigger and more aggressive?

Something big and icky was crawling up her inner thigh.

This was supposed to be the easy way out of this mess. Why was everything so stupidly difficult?

She set her foot once more, a little higher this time, then she gripped as the ladder as tightly as she could and pulled. This time, the bracket snapped free. Immediately, the ladder jerked to the side and Seph lost her footing.

Her scream was deafening in the silence.

Chapter 36

Seph hung by her arms, her feet dangling over a deadly drop, this universe's strange gravity pulling at her and a swarm of green insects buzzing around her. They crawled on her exposed skin. They landed on her mouth. They tickled her nose. They threatened to crawl into her ears.

And she couldn't even swat at them.

The bottom of the ladder was hooked onto the base of the towering bookshelf to steady it, and that and the protruding brackets wedging themselves against the next row of shelves was the only reason she hadn't tipped all the way over.

She reached out with her foot, searching for the rungs. For a dreadful few seconds, she couldn't find it. Panic overwhelmed her. She cried out, terrified, her heart thundering as she stared down at the book-strewn floor far below.

This was really how it was all going to end? This was the moment her whole life had led up to?

It wasn't fair.

Not to her. Not to Piper. Not to Hugh.

Her fingers were slipping.

She couldn't hold on much longer…

Then, finally, she found the rung. She hooked her toe over it as a great, wet sob escaped her.

She thought she was going to die for sure there…

Her relief, however, was dampened by the fact that the ladder was now leaning precariously to the right and was no longer securely bolted to the shelf. It was wedged against the wooden shelf on top and the bracket far below. If it broke free from either of those things before she reached the ground, she was certain she wouldn't be so lucky a second time.

Best case scenario, she'd land on one of those huge stacks of books, and she doubted very much that the landing would be any softer at this height than hitting the marble floor.

In hindsight, she might've been better off chancing another encounter with the jabberwock than with these kinds of bright ideas.

Slowly, carefully, she made her way down, her heart racing, her body trembling.

Too fast and she'd surely shake the ladder loose and fall. But the longer she was up here, the more bugs assaulted her.

After what felt like an hour, but was probably only a minute or two—or maybe not, given the Keeper's weird time magic—her feet finally touched the floor again and she dropped to her hands and knees, shaking.

God, what an ordeal.

But she was safe, at least.

When the shaking in her knees had eased enough for them to hold her weight, she rose to her feet and took hold of the ladder. Now it was time to make it fall. She pulled it away from the shelf and tried to lower it gently, but it was so enormous that its weight was more than she could handle. It fell like lead, pushing her back as the top of it sailed across the room and crashed down against the fourth-floor railing and the bottom half kicked back, wedging itself against the base of the towering bookshelf hard enough to send a hailstorm of books crashing down around her.

She stumbled backward, covering her head, half expecting one of those falling tomes to finally do what the jabberwock and that freaky tree and the stupid ladder hadn't accomplished. But somehow she survived again.

When everything had gone still again, she coughed on the stirred dust and frowned up at the ladder. It wasn't exactly the perfect fit she imagined. It didn't look all that safe. It sagged a little. And there was an unsettling "crack" when it struck the railing, suggesting that some of its structural integrity might have been lost in the fall… But it seemed sturdy enough.

All she had to do now was go back and get Piper.

She felt it first, a prickling up her spine, a hot fear welling up deep in her belly. Her mouth went dry. She felt the blood slowly draining from her face. Then she heard it. Books shifting. Sliding. Old pages tearing beneath the weight of monstrous claws.

It was right behind her.

Slowly, her knees trembling beneath her, she turned to face the monster that was crawling over the freshly spilled pile of books, like a great dragon perched atop its hoard of precious gold. Except this was nothing as pleasant as a dragon.

At first, she thought it must be different from the one that attacked them in the dark. It looked nothing like that black and crimson thing. Then she remembered the way her prophet sight shifted into overdrive just before it struck, allowing her to see even in that utter darkness.

That was what the thing looked like to her prophet sight. And this was what it looked like with her real eyes.

It wasn't black and red, but rather *every* color. Its scales shifted and turned and twisted, changing colors like pixels on a computer screen. It was hardly invisible, but it would be hard to notice sitting motionless in a gloomy corner, surveying the room.

And while the prophet sight version had no eyes or nose, only an enormous maw with razor-sharp teeth, this thing had a strangely horse-like face attached to its enormous maw with razor-sharp teeth.

It had the same long neck and tail, the same powerful claws, but was as if it were naked the first time she saw it and now it was fully dressed.

And in this light, with her human eyes, she could see why the thing seemed to be blind. It was because it *was* blind. Where its eyes should've been, there were two festering wounds.

Perhaps it had a run-in with that nasty tree down the hall.

Slowly, carefully, she took a step backward.

No sudden movements. Last time, this monster reacted to the falling books. It might be blind, but it was clearly able to *hear* her. And it wasn't any wonder, really, considering how much of a racket she'd been making. Between the screaming and the crashing ladder, she must've been impossible to miss.

It wouldn't let her get away again.

The thing half-crawled, half-slithered over the piles of books, spilling them onto the floor.

She was terrified. Not just for herself, but for Piper. If this thing killed her…what would become of Piper? Would it eventually hunt her down as well? Or would the meat sickness kill her before it could get the chance?

There was nowhere to run. She couldn't outpace this thing. She saw how fast it was the first time. She took another step back and the toe of her shoe touched a book. She paused, never taking her eyes off the approaching beast, and stepped over the book.

The monster was moving toward her faster than she was backing away. If she tried to move any faster, it was going to charge her. She was sure of it.

Her mind was racing, but there was no way out of this one. She was going to die in this room. And it was going to hurt. A lot.

She should've just let go of the ladder. It probably would've been a less horrible way to die.

The beast reared back, let out another of those fearsome groans, and then, with a hard shake of its horse-like head, it launched itself at her.

She couldn't stop the scream that erupted from her any more than she could stop her heart from racing, even though she knew the monster would only find it that much easier to sink its teeth into her.

And as those terrible jaws opened wide to take her, one of those huge, glowing orbs fell from above and crushed the foul beast.

She stood there, her scream caught in her throat, her eyes wide, her knees wobbling, staring at the pitiful shape of the broken monster lying beneath the shattered remains of the orb as the light slowly faded from it and the last of the cable from which it had been hanging rained down.

What kind of freakish luck was this?

Even for her, that was unnatural. If this were a movie, she'd scoff at such lazy writing.

And yet, she didn't dare complain. She was alive, after all. She felt like she was going to pass out. Her heart was still hammering against her ribcage. And she might've wet herself a little, she wasn't entirely sure yet…

But she was alive!

Somehow.

Then a voice called out to her: "You okay?"

She turned and looked around, a drunken sort of confusion bogging her down. Just trying to think was like trying to run underwater. Then, slowly, she lifted her face and looked up.

A man was waving at her from the railing up there.

"Hugh?"

"I was asleep in the office, when I had the clearest vision I'd had in ages!" He turned and pointed to something behind him. "I opened a door right over there, and I cut the third cable from the left. Then I woke up and found *these* in my hand." He held up a very familiar pair of rusty wire cutters. "God works in mysterious ways, doesn't He?"

Seph stared up at him, unsure what to even say. *Was* it God who kept saving her? Or was it the Keeper? She stared at the rusty tool Hugh was still holding up. Was it possible that the Keeper *was* God? Or at the very least a messenger of God?

In fact, now that she was thinking about it, there was no way those cutters would've done her any good at the top of that ladder. Those were made for cutting wires and cables, not for loosening bolts. The only purpose that rusty old tool had was to free that orb and kill the jabberwock.

Did the Keeper plan every detail of this trip?

If so, why hadn't she found the lock?

What was that strange, old cabinet, anyway?

She shook it off. There'd be time to think about all of that later. Right now, she needed to focus. "Are you all right?" she shouted up at him.

"I'm *exhausted*!" he shouted back. Then he held his arms out and gestured at his own body, which she could tell even from here was considerably smaller than it was the last time she saw him. "And I'm wasting away up here! Did you find it yet?"

"No! I still can't find it! And my friend is really sick! She needs help!"

He seemed distressed. He rubbed his stubbly beard and paced back and forth, but he didn't argue with her. "Let's get her up here into the office."

Seph nodded and hurried over to the bookshelves where she left Piper. "Please be okay," she muttered. "Please, *please* be okay…"

She clambered over the pile of books to find Piper right where she left her, curled up on the floor, her hair covering her face, in her powder blue bra and dirty skinny jeans. She was definitely alive, because she was breathing in heavy, rasping breaths. "Oh, thank God…" she sighed. "Come on, we're getting you out of here."

Piper's heavy breathing suddenly stopped. Slowly, she lifted her head and looked at her. Her eyes were wide and bloodshot and…*yellow*. Drool oozed from her chin. There was *foam* on her lips.

Seph stared at her, her heart sinking. "Pea?" she whispered.

With a wild yell, Piper barred her teeth and launched herself at Seph.

Chapter 37

She was fast. *Amazingly* fast, given that she was on death's doorstep when Seph left her there. Now she was all hands and spit and gnashing teeth and seething hatred.

Seph screamed and fell backward, sliding down the huge pile of books with Piper on top of her, her hands, once gentle and delicately manicured, now hooked into lethal talons that slashed at her face.

And she was *strong.* Seph grabbed her dainty wrists and tried to pry those dangerous claws away from her, but it was like fighting with someone twice her size.

And then there was her *teeth*! She *snapped* at her. And it wasn't an idle threat. She seemed to be trying to bite her face! She *growled.* She *snarled* like a wild animal.

"*What the hell is wrong with you*?" she shrieked.

But if Piper still had the ability to speak, she gave no indication of it.

What was happening? It was like she'd been thrown into the opening scene of an episode of *Supernatural.*

Seph forced her knee up and between them, pushing her back, then managed to roll her over, pinning her down. "Snap out of it!" she screamed. "I'm trying to help you!"

Piper's eyes bulged. She opened her mouth wide. *Too* wide. The corners of her mouth stretched.

She *hissed.*

Were her teeth always that sharp?

Seph stared down at her with wide, horrified eyes. Was this *thing* really Piper?

She twisted her head to one side, making a series of loud, sickening popping sounds, and then lunged forward, snapping her teeth at her again.

Seph screamed and jumped back, letting go of her wrists. She rolled away and scrambled to her feet, intending to run away, but Piper was on her in an instant, her nails digging into her forearm hard enough to draw blood, those awful teeth snapping at her.

In a panic, she picked up a heavy book and swung it, striking her in the side of the head with it. Then she fled into the libyrinth.

This couldn't be real. It couldn't. Piper wasn't a monster. Piper wouldn't even hurt a spider. Literally. Every time she asked her to kill one, she did that annoying thing where she trapped it in a cup and took it outside, where Seph, for one, was convinced it just walked back inside the same way it got in the first time. She'd begun to joke that it was the same spider every time. She'd started calling them all Jerry.

Was this some kind of mimic? A shapeshifter of some sort? Was it just a monster *pretending* to be Piper?

Maybe the real Piper wandered off somewhere while she was fooling with that ladder and she didn't notice.

She turned right and rounded a corner, only to find a wall of books blocking her path. A dead end.

She turned to retrace her steps and froze as Piper darted past her, the sound of her heels clopping against the marble trailing after her.

She was only there for a second, perhaps less, but it was long enough to see how little of her best friend was left there. She looked more animal than woman, as if she were possessed.

Seph crept forward and peered around the corner, but she was already out of sight.

The sound of those hard heels was all that remained.

She turned and ran back the other way. She'd climb up the ladder and leave Piper down here. If she was quick, maybe she wouldn't realize where she'd gone. Maybe the libyrinth would keep her busy for a little bit while she and Hugh figured out what to do.

But what if there wasn't anything they could do? What if Piper was gone, replaced forever by that yellow-eyed monster? What then?

The thought of leaving her down here to prowl this awful library for the rest of her life was unbearable. How could she go on knowing that something so terrible had happened to her best friend? What would she tell her parents? Her beloved sister, Penny?

She turned a corner and stopped. Wasn't this the way she came? She should've been back to the ladder by now.

She turned around to retrace her steps again, but froze as she heard Piper's heels approaching.

She turned and ran on, choosing directions at random until she stepped out into a wide aisle flanked by thirty-foot high walls of stacked books.

Which way?

There were several narrow passages framed by Lodblin's books. Any one of them could take her back out to the ladder and to freedom. And any one of them could take her right into Piper's murderous path.

She ran left, then chose a passage at random.

On and on the libyrinth went. She lost track of which direction she was going. After a while, she wasn't even sure how long she'd been running, but her legs had begun to hurt and she had a stitch in her side.

She'd been able to hear the ghostly clopping of Piper's heels in the silence around her the entire time, occasionally distant, occasionally just on the other side of a wall of books, but now even that had fallen silent.

Had she wandered off somewhere? Did she wear herself out and go to sleep?

If she could just find her way back to the ladder, she could get a bird's-eye view of the librynth. Hopefully from there she'd be able to keep track of where Piper was.

If she could find her way back.

This place was stupid. She was glad King Lodblin was long dead and forgotten. Insane bastard. She hoped his death was as unpleasant as possible, preferably by being slowly crushed to death under a landslide of his own, stupid books.

Why would the Keeper want to save a place like this? He should've just let it go when the universe died. Surely there was something nicer he could've kept. This universe's version of Disneyworld, maybe?

She had some choice words for *that* lunatic, too, when she saw him again.

Stupid Keeper and his stupid traps.

She realized she was crying again. Had she been doing that this whole time? She couldn't remember.

Ahead of her, the libyrinth finally opened up. The stacks here had fallen over and she could see the ladder leaning against the fourth-floor railing. Desperate, she scrambled to the top of the overturned pile and peered over it.

There was her way out. It was just on the other side of the next pile.

But she heard a book tumble to the floor behind her and turned.

Piper was there, crouched at the top of the wall of books, glaring down at her with those creepy, yellow eyes.

She was even filthier now. Her face was covered in dirt. Dust and grime covered her chest and belly. There was a bruise blossoming under her right eye where she hit her with the book.

Seph stood up and took a step back. "Pea?" she squeaked.

Piper barred her teeth again. Those were definitely *not* Piper's teeth. Piper's teeth were perfect. She'd worn braces all through middle school. They were straight and white and as annoyingly pretty and perfect as every other part of her face. *These* teeth were yellow and crooked and sharp. And they were too big for her mouth. Her jaws opened too wide, her lips stretched way too far, the corners of her mouth practically tearing open.

Even her body seemed wrong. Her muscles were bigger. Her thighs bulged beneath the denim of her skinny jeans. Her arms and shoulders had swelled.

It wasn't Piper. It *couldn't* be Piper.

Piper threw herself at her.

Seph jumped back. She slipped and fell backward, tumbling and sliding down the pile of books as Piper scurried after her.

Books crashed to the floor all around them in a landslide of paper and dust and torn bindings.

Seph came to a stop on her back, looking up at the thing that used to be her best friend as it bounded after her, already almost on top of her.

She couldn't defend herself. And even if she could, would she really be able to hurt Piper? Even to save herself?

She groped at the books around her, looking for something to use as a shield.

Then something heavy landed hard on the floor between them with a great, wet slap. A large, ragged hunk of raw meat lay there, dark blood splattered around it, soaking into the torn pages beneath it.

Piper leapt onto it, tearing chunks out of it with those inhuman teeth and gulping it down like a feral beast in the wild.

"Don't just lie there!" shouted Hugh.

Seph looked up to see him crouched atop the next pile of books. He was covered in blood. His shirt was stained with it.

"Come on!"

She didn't waste another moment. She turned and scurried up the pile of books, her feet slipping the whole way.

She looked over her shoulder as she reached the top. "Where did that come from?"

"Your friend over there," replied Hugh.

She looked over at the monster that lay under the shattered orb. A large, bloody hole had been carved into its flank. "How did you know how to stop her?"

"Another vision." He took hold of the ladder and began to climb.

She paused and looked back one last time. She couldn't see Piper from here, but she knew she was still there.

She wished she knew what to do.

It was as she was turning to start up the ladder that her prophet sight shifted into overdrive again. The room flashed brighter. Those strange, black moths fluttered into existence all around her. Small shapes scurried among the fallen books.

And on one side of the room, something was glowing.

She stepped off the ladder and walked toward it.

"What're you doing?" called Hugh.

"Go on," she told him. "I'll be there in a minute."

The glow was coming from behind the books stacked against the far wall. There was something there. A hole, barely visible in the gloom.

A reading hole, she thought, her eyes widening.

She walked up to the books blocking the hole and began pulling them down, spilling them onto the floor.

The hole was a door. Only the top left corner was visible, and only that because some of the books had fallen over at some point.

On the other side of the door was a small room with only a table and two chairs in it. And on the table was an open book.

The book was what was glowing.

Maybe you're looking for a book.

Seph stepped over the last of the stack and walked into the room. She pulled out the chair and sat down. Then she bent forward and began to read what was written there.

Chapter 38

Seph blinked and rubbed at her eyes.

What just happened?

The book she was just looking at was lying in front of her, closed.

It wasn't glowing anymore.

In fact, her super prophet sight had faded. Everything looked normal again.

How long had she been sitting here?

And why hadn't she looked at the glowing book yet? She reached out to open it again, but froze when someone said, "Don't bother."

She looked up. There was a man sitting across from her. Or…he *looked* like a man… A very…*small*…man.

He had the face, stubble and hairy arms of a man in his late thirties or early forties, but was only the size of a boy, a small ten-year-old, at most.

"It would only be a waste of time," he explained. "You've already read what's written in it."

She looked down at the book again. "I have?"

He nodded. "There's power in knowledge. And there's more power in some knowledge than in others." He reached out and placed a small hand on the book. "The knowledge in this book is a special kind of knowledge. Not many people can handle the truths that are written in here. Most would be struck dead the moment they read it."

She stared at the book. His words were making the hairs on the back of her neck stand up. "I could've died…?"

"No. Not you. You're a seeker. You're the heir of the eyes of the goddess."

She blinked, confused. "I'm the what now?"

"Your prophet sight. No *ordinary* human being could handle that sort of power. That makes you more than qualified to survive what you read in this ancient tome. In fact, you can *thrive* on it."

She looked up at him, her head spinning. "Okay… So then…why don't I remember reading it?"

The little man kept smiling at her. There was something strangely calming about that smile. And his eyes held a strange sort of wisdom. "Because even people like you can't handle this knowledge *consciously*," he replied. "It would drive you mad, like the man who built this library."

She frowned. "Mad King Lodblin… You mean…he was mad because…"

He nodded. "Because he found what he so desperately searched for." He looked down at the book between them. "But there are things you simply can't take by force. And this knowledge was never *his*."

"But it's mine?"

"It is. And that's why I took the knowledge and buried it for you. It now lies deep in your subconscious, where no one can be hurt by it."

"So…you *memory wiped* me? *Men in Black* style?"

He looked amused. "That's one way of putting it. It's not gone. It'll always be in there. I've pushed it deep into your subconscious. You may glimpse it occasionally in your dreams from now on. But it won't be able to hurt you."

"Okay." Again, she looked down at the book. "Thanks, I guess."

What was written in that book could kill a normal person, and drive even a seeker insane… Was it crazy that her curiosity was almost more than she could stand? What kind of *knowledge* could *kill* a person?

"If you *really* want, I can let you read it again," he offered. "But you'd only beg me to make you forget it again. And then we'd be right back here, having this same conversation again, wasting time."

He had a point. She guessed.

She looked up at him. "Who *are* you?"

That smile never faltered. "I'm merely the attendant," he replied. "I attend to people when they are in need. And you were most certainly in need."

Again, she lowered her eyes to the book. What happened to her when she read it? Did she really beg him to take it away? Did what was written in there frighten her? Did it *hurt*? She could barely comprehend such a thing.

"I apologize for the impersonal nature of this meeting. Ordinarily, I'd offer you a Coke…"

"It's fine…" She rubbed at her eyes, weary. A Coke? Why did that give her a twinge of déjà vu? A memory flashed through her mind. A cluttered office. A smell that reminded her of her father. But she was so tired that she couldn't seem to hold onto it for more than that fleeting second. "I don't understand any of this…"

"That's okay. Some things simply can't be understood. And some things that *can* be understood *shouldn't*. Sometimes understanding gets in the way of doing."

She opened her eyes again and stared at him. "Was I supposed to understand *that*?"

The attendant shrugged.

She gave up. She turned her gaze back down to the book. "So…is that the lock to Tartarus or not?"

"The book itself? No. The information inside? Yes. In a manner of speaking."

"Huh?"

The little man chuckled. "The first lock is undone," he assured her. "You're free to leave the library now. The trial is finished."

"Trial? Is that what all this was?"

"Everything is a trial. Every day of one's life is a trial. You either succeed and you go on or you don't…and you don't."

She leaned forward. "I just don't understand why it has to be so *hard.* Why couldn't someone just tell us that this book was here, in this room? Why did we have to wander all over this disgusting library?" She turned in her seat and pointed out into the room. "My friends are *dying* out there!"

"They'll be fine. You have my word on that."

She stared at him, her thoughts racing. On one hand, she was relieved to hear that Piper and Hugh were going to be okay…but why did they have to suffer through all this at all? What was the point?

"There are reasons why things have to be like they are. And there are reasons I can't explain all those reasons to you. You just have to trust me on that. But I promise you, no matter how grim things look, you will always have everything you need to succeed."

"It's getting hard to trust *anyone*," said Seph.

"And that is just another trial for you to overcome."

"Of course it is."

"Your friend should be coming around about now."

"Huh?" She turned and looked through the door. "Pea? Is she really going to be okay?"

But when she turned back, the attendant was gone. Only the book remained.

She stared at it for a moment, curious. What was the profound secret that was written there? How could something written in a book drive a person crazy? It was almost more than she could stand.

She stood up and walked out of the room, leaving the book behind, and made her way to the top of the pile of books behind which she left Piper.

She was lying on the floor next to the ragged chunk of raw meat, her face buried in her arms.

Was she sleeping?

"Pea?" whispered Seph, bracing herself for another attack.

But Piper lifted her head and looked up at her. Her eyes were blue again, but filled with tears. Her face and chest and arms were covered in jabberwock blood. She looked ill. "Persephone…?" she squeaked. "What's wrong with me?"

Chapter 39

"I think I'm gonna throw up…" groaned Piper.

"Please don't do that," begged Seph. "You *seriously* need that protein."

"Don't say things like that! I *will* hurl!"

"Fine, just *be careful*."

"Are you sure this thing's safe?"

"It's fine." But of course that was a lie. She knew no such thing. She stared down at the floor as she made her way up the ladder behind Piper, praying it wouldn't break or slip and spill them both back into that bibliophobic nightmare. Hugh had managed to make his way down it and back up again, but Hugh was suddenly a lot smaller than he used to be, and the two of them together might have outweighed him now.

After what felt like an agonizing hour of slow climbing—and might've been even longer for all she knew, Piper finally reached the top and managed to climb over the railing. With her scuffed heels finally under her, she walked a few steps, then plopped down on the floor and just sat there, hugging herself against the weight of everything that had happened.

Seph stepped down onto the floor and knelt beside her. She gave Piper her shirt before they started the climb. She seemed to need it more. She looked so distressed sitting there, half-naked and covered in blood and grime. She looked so *vulnerable.*

If Hugh turned out to be the kind of perv who liked to ogle half-naked girls, then he could ogle Seph. She didn't care at this point. She just wanted Piper to be okay. That was all that mattered.

Where *was* Hugh, anyway?

Before she could look for him, he draped his own shirt over her bare shoulders, surprising her. It was blood-stained, damp with sweat and *enormous* on her, but it covered her, and she appreciated the gesture.

Clearly, Hugh was *not* a perv. In fact, he was a gentleman.

"You get what you came for?" he asked.

She turned and looked at him. He'd shrunk inside his own skin so that his flesh drooped from his body like a baggy suit. Given just how big he was when he started, it probably wasn't the worst thing that could've happened to him, but such a rapid loss of body weight couldn't possibly have been good for him, either. And it showed. He had dark circles under his eyes. He was wheezing. Even his hair had thinned. He was two hundred pounds lighter, *at least*, but he also looked at least ten years older. "Yeah," she said. "I got it."

"Good." He tugged at his belt and then sat down on the floor beside them with a weary groan.

"Are you okay?" She slipped her arms into the bloody sleeves of his shirt and started to button it, but it was so enormous on her that there was no way she could keep it on. She pulled it tight and knotted it instead.

"Don't worry about me," he assured her. "How's *she*?"

"Probably traumatized. You *did* feed her a giant, raw monster steak."

"*Oh gosh…*" groaned Piper. She buried her face in her hands again. "Please don't…"

Hugh turned his bloodshot eyes on her, looking her over. "You didn't tell me she was one of them."

Both of them turned and looked at him.

"Huh?" said Seph. "Them who?"

"Ah. I see. You didn't know. That explains some things."

"What didn't I know?" asked Piper.

He gave her a sympathetic smile. "That you're an Ahn."

She stared back at him, confused. "What…?"

"Wait…" said Seph. "An Ahn? Those old women who've been helping us? *Those* Ahns?"

Piper looked down at her hands, horrified. "Wait…how long have we been down here?"

Hugh chuckled. "Not nearly as long as you think. Don't worry. You're not a full Ahn. I'd say you're a descendant. Maybe third or fourth generation. Any farther up than that and your genes would be too diluted to affect you."

She scrunched up her face, confused. "So…one of my grandma's…or great grandmas was…?"

"Afraid so." He coughed and rubbed at the stubble on his chin. He was clean-shaven when they came in here, but he had at least a couple day's beard growth now. "You should probably ask them about it next time you see them. Ahns aren't exactly a one-night-stand kind of monster. I highly doubt they didn't know."

"You mean they've been lying to us this whole time?" said Seph, infuriated.

"More likely just…withholding information."

"What's the difference? She could've killed me down there! I think that's information I should've been given ahead of time, don't you?"

"I'm sorry…" whimpered Piper.

"No, it's…" She sighed. "It's not *your* fault. You didn't know."

"I didn't."

"Well this isn't the place to discuss it," said Hugh. "I'm literally wasting away in here. Can you girls go on?"

"I'm fine," said Seph, standing up.

"I'm okay," replied Piper.

It was Hugh who couldn't get his feet under him. Each of them had to take an arm and help him stand. And just as he was finally getting upright, his pants slipped over his shrinking hips and dropped to the floor around his feet.

"*Oh my gosh*!" cried Piper.

"Oh no!" moaned Hugh.

"This is *not* improving our situation!" exclaimed Seph.

He stooped over and grabbed at his belt, but almost lost his balance in the process, forcing the girls to grab his arms again. "*That's* embarrassing…" And he certainly *did* look embarrassed. Seph didn't think she'd ever seen a grown man's face flush like that before. "Dang belt won't go any tighter… Not enough holes." He grimaced and looked over at Seph. "Please don't tell Wallace that happened."

"We won't," promised Piper as he yanked up his pants. This time, he didn't let go of the belt, but kept it firmly clutched in one hand.

"Why would we ever speak of this again?" grumbled Seph.

Still clinging to Hugh's arms like a couple of dirty, disheveled escorts, they made their way back to the room through which they first entered this nightmare and Hugh opened the door back to Waybel Valley. By the time they reached the end of the black tunnel leading back to the concrete steps of the water tower, they were thankful for his rapid weight loss, because they were practically carrying him. And by the time they were at the top of those steps, he was finished. He was gasping for breath and struggling just to remain conscious.

They eased him onto the floor, with his back propped against the wall.

Somewhere outside, an engine revved. A loud explosion echoed somewhere in the distance. Seph looked around. "Are they still fighting out there?"

"Of course," gasped Hugh. He lifted his arm, his flesh dangling from his bones, and pointed at a dusty clock on the wall. "We've only been gone…about fifteen…minutes."

"No way!" exclaimed Seph. "It's been…I mean…" How long *had* it been? Hugh looked like he'd been wasting away for weeks, and yet he had only about two days' worth of beard growth and he didn't die of dehydration during all that time. In fact, she hadn't felt hungry or thirsty, herself, even once. Nor did she ever feel the need to find a restroom—which was good because now that she was thinking about it, she never saw one the whole time she was in that building. And yet Piper went into a catastrophic meat-deprivation *meltdown*.

All of that in only fifteen minutes… And that included the walk to the door at the bottom of the steps and back.

Time was complicated. She couldn't think too hard about it right now. It was too exhausting.

(And now that it'd occurred to her, she couldn't help feeling bothered by the library's lack of bathroom facilities… Where did people in that universe do their business?)

"My part's done," said Hugh. "Now get out of here."

"But the empty people…" said Piper, looking warily at the bolted door.

"You should have your tools back," he reminded them.

Seph looked down at her hands. At merely the thought of it, the scythe's water enveloped them both, ready for action.

"Wilbur should've cut a path for you by now, too," he added, listening to that roaring engine outside.

"What about you?" asked Seph.

"I'll be fine. They're not interested in me, remember. I'll just rest here for a while. Besides…" He tapped the side of his head. "Hattie knows where I am."

Seph looked up at Piper, uncertain.

Piper returned the look.

"Keep the shirt," he added. "Just throw it out when you find a proper change." He chuckled again. "Pretty sure it's not going to fit me anymore."

Seph looked down at it. It was probably ruined anyway. It was stained with the jabberwock's blood.

"Go!" huffed Hugh. "Get out of here. Hurry!"

They hesitated a moment longer, then stood up and walked to the door.

"It was a pleasure to meet you," he called after them. "By the way."

"You, too," said Piper.

Seph listened to the noises beyond the door. The action seemed to have moved away from the water tower. She lifted the wooden beam out of the brackets and leaned it against the wall. "You take care of yourself, okay?" she called back to Hugh.

"Don't you worry," he assured her. "Hattie says if you girls are ever in Waybel Valley again, be sure to stop by and see us."

"We will," promised Piper.

Seph took a deep breath and opened the door. She squinted out into the bright sunlight to find that chaos had erupted in Waybel Valley while they were gone.

Chapter 40

The Ahns warned them that they were in the middle of a three-way war.

As they looked out into the tower yard, they found that Tane's empty people were locked in an epic battle with Gispuknya's flickering men!

They were everywhere. Black, featureless shadows twitched in and out of existence, hundreds of them, swarming the hollow skins of the empty people.

"Oh gosh," whispered Piper. Now that she was looking at the flickering men, she was suddenly aware of that strange buzzing sensation in her head. How had she not noticed it before? Was the water tower shielded from it somehow? Or was she merely too distracted by her ordeal in the library to notice its gradual onset as she helped Hugh out of that black tunnel and up all those steps?

Not that it mattered one bit. Her gaze drifted out past the monsters to the surrounding forest. Almost all of the chain link fence had been knocked down. There was a fire burning in the nearby woods. Bloodless corpses and smoldering pools of black gore littered the ground. Somewhere behind the tower, Wilbur's truck roared and gunshots rang out. And somewhere in town, there was a series of explosions, one after another.

Had it really only been fifteen minutes?

Two empty people slaughtered a flickering man and then turned those hollow gazes on them.

"Oh no," gasped Piper.

Another flickering man glitched into existence and dragged one of the two empty people to the ground, but the other ran straight toward them, a strange sort of emotionless expression on its hollow face, like something out of an old zombie movie.

Seph was about to slam the door closed again when someone darted in front of them and cut down the monster with a kitchen knife.

It was that odd man who Wallace said lived in this town. Phil, his name was. The man they saw dancing down the sidewalk like an idiot from the window of the sitting room. Except it *wasn't* Phil. He turned and faced them, his eyes empty and black. "Gispuknya is here," he said. "*And* the ringmaster."

"Warner!" gasped Piper.

The ringmaster was here? Seph looked up at the smoke still rising into the sky. That meant those explosions probably weren't Wallace's distractions, but more of those destructive flutters. "How're we supposed to get through all that?"

"This is a war," he reminded them. "It's like we told you at the ranch. You're the targets, but you're also the lesser of the two threats for *both of them*." He turned around and buried his knife in the throat of a flickering man who'd just twitched into existence behind him. "Hurry!"

Seph said nothing more. She grabbed Piper's hand and ran.

But they didn't make it very far before they both stumbled to a stop.

A strange creature was moving toward them through the weedy

grass. It looked like an enormous centipede, except…well…*dead.* Like the *skeleton* of an enormous centipede. *If* centipedes had skeletons rather than *exoskeletons*, Piper supposed. Its three-foot-long body appeared to be comprised of dingy, bone-colored plates that were about a foot wide near its head and narrowed into a long, snake-like tail. At either end of each plate were short, skeletal legs. Hundreds of them in all. The thing's head was a round, disk-like protrusion with small, but quite painful-looking mandibles jutting out from the front beneath two black, sunken eyes.

"Skitters!" shouted Phil/Warner as he plunged his knife into the bloodless heart of an empty person in the shape of an overweight woman who was for some reason dressed in a bathrobe. "One of the ringmaster's scouts! Don't let them bite you!"

Piper gasped and took a step backward.

Seph squeezed her hand and led her around the base of the water tower, away from the skeletal skitter.

Wilbur's truck plowed into view, mowing down a trio of empty teenagers, then skidded to a stop. It was covered in scratches and dust. The windshield was broken. And it was dragging around a sizable tree limb that had become lodged in the undercarriage.

A flickering man appeared at the open window and Wilbur promptly fired a bullet into the monster's face.

Seph glanced back and saw *more* flickering men moving toward them, multiplying as they twitched nearer and nearer. "Go!"

Wilbur saw them coming and fired several shots at the chasing monsters. "What're you doing back out here?" he bellowed as they climbed into the back of the cab and slammed the door behind them.

"We found the lock!" said Seph as she climbed over the console and into the passenger's seat.

"Already?" He fired several more shots at the approaching flickering men and then shifted the truck into reverse. "Yeah, yeah! I'm going! Jesus, woman, I was just asking!"

Seph stared at him, confused. "What?"

"Sorry. Not you." He tapped his temple. "Hattie."

"Oh…"

He shifted the truck back into drive and took off again, kicking up gravel and dust as he circled back around the water tower.

One of the empty people ran out of the woods and rushed them. It was in the shape of a young boy, perhaps ten years old. Wilbur gestured at it and it stumbled and fell.

Seph watched it roll across the grass. That was Wilbur's special power, she recalled. Wallace said he could *nudge* things. Not much, he'd said. Just a little. Enough to make for a good distraction. Or to trip up an approaching enemy.

"Can you get us to our truck?"

"I can try, but Hattie says the whole town's under attack. Monsters everywhere. Never seen anything like it before, and I've seen some shit!" He looked up at Piper in the rearview mirror. "My god, what happened to *you*?"

"I don't want to talk about it!" she snapped.

"Alright then…"

"Is everyone okay?" she asked, worried.

"We're holding our own. These things aren't that interested in us. They're only attacking when we provoke 'em, so they aren't overwhelming us."

He veered hard to the right, plowing through a group of flickering men and empty people that were locked in combat, then he cut hard to the left and sped over the broken gate and down the hill.

"If we leave town, maybe they'll leave everybody here alone," hoped Piper.

"Probably," reasoned Wilbur. "*Whoa*!" He slammed on the brakes and skidded to a halt, carving up a cloud of dust beneath them.

A group of strange-looking children stood in the middle of the road, staring back at them and blocking the path. They were quite young, between four and six, dressed in strange, heavy clothing that was far too warm for May in Florida, and with thick, bushy hair covering most of their heads.

"Black-eyed children!" gasped Piper.

"*Those* are the black-eyed children?" said Seph. This was the first time she'd actually seen them. Piper had described them to her on several occasions. Aside from their strange clothes and long, bushy hair, their only distinguishing feature was those creepy black eyes. But as she looked at them, she knew that she could see more with her prophet sight than Piper did with her normal vision.

It wasn't just their eyes that were black. That empty void covered their entire faces. They were nothing but soulless darkness under that hair and inside those clothes.

"You're saying those things ain't human," said Wilbur.

"Definitely not human," replied Piper.

"Not even remotely," confirmed Seph.

"Do you *promise* me those ain't real kids?"

"Those're definitely *not* children," said Seph. Then she glanced over at him. "Wait…*why*?"

"Because if I have any doubt in my mind about that, I'm never going to sleep again after what I'm about to do."

"*What're you about to do*?" squealed Piper.

He didn't answer. He took his foot off the brake and stomped the accelerator. The pickup lurched forward and plowed through the small crowd of black-eyed children, rolling right over most of them and scattering the few that remained back into the woods from which they came.

Seph and Piper both screamed. Real kids or not, *that* was a terrifying thing to witness.

Seph started to turn around, but Wilber grabbed her shoulder. "Don't look back!" he said, his own eyes glued to the road in front of them. "Just don't do it. They weren't real kids. They never were."

"They weren't," promised Piper. Then, as if to convince herself: "They *weren't*."

Wilbur sped down the road, never looking back, just as he'd promised. "Where're you parked?" he asked as they approached Main Street.

"The bar," said Seph. But as he turned onto the pavement, a jarring blast blew the right, front tire out from under them and the truck ground to a halt.

"What happened?" squealed Piper.

"Flutters!" said Seph, pointing at the street. There were dozens of them flittering about, turning Waybel Valley's Main Street into a moving minefield. There were several smoking craters in the asphalt and two of the houses were on fire. As they watched, an explosion cut a streetlamp in two. It crashed to the ground, where the battle between Tane and Gispuknya raged on. Everywhere they looked, flickering men were dragging empty people to the ground and empty people were bludgeoning flickering men into shadowy goop.

Several of those skeleton-like skitters were slithering across the ground, too, snapping at the flickering men as they searched for the seekers.

"This isn't good," groaned Seph.

Another blast rocked the truck from behind. The three of them turned to find that the tailgate had been torn almost in half by a flutter blast.

If that thing had landed on the roof instead of the tailgate… Or the windshield…

Seph didn't want to think too much about it.

"They're concentrated on the streets," said Wilbur. "They have the roads leading out of town clogged."

"How do you know?" asked Seph.

He tapped his temple again. Hattie. She was transmitting everything Lee sensed about the monsters that were springing up all over town. It was the perfect information network.

"So what do we do?" asked Piper.

Wilbur pointed at the empty yard next to them. "You two go around behind those houses, like you were doing when I first spotted you. I'll make some noise, keep them distracted."

"No!" said Piper.

"I'll be okay," he assured them. "I know what I'm doing. Now go!"

Seph hated this. They kept having to rely on people to protect them. Wilbur. Hugh. *Amethyst*… It wasn't fair. She didn't want people to have to put themselves in harm's way for her. It was too much to bear. How was she ever supposed to sleep again if someone got hurt trying to protect her?

"Go! Before they swarm the whole damn town!"

Frustrated, she opened the door and jumped out of the truck.

"I'm seriously over this crap," grumbled Piper as she slammed the door behind her.

The two of them darted into the yard as the truck's engine revved and the wheels began to spin and screech, kicking up smoke and dust and sparks as the broken tire ground forward, plowing into empty people and flickering men and exploding flutters alike.

"I hope he'll be okay!" squealed Piper.

Seph did, too. She didn't want to see anyone else get hurt. But the quickest way to make sure of it was to leave as quickly as possible and never look back.

But as they ran around the corner of the house, they found the lawn crawling with skitters.

Piper screamed at the sight, and the skitters heard her. Each one of them turned and began slithering toward them, those deadly mandibles snapping.

Don't let them bite you!

Seph grabbed her hand and turned to go back the way they came, only to find the wretch that attacked them in Nora's Lilac Grove slithering toward them in the grass.

Chapter 41

Seph and Piper froze.

The wretched thing dragged itself across the ground, clawing at the grass with the black tips of its finger bones, pulling its impossibly long and strangely broken body behind it.

"I forgot about that thing!" whispered Piper as it stared back at her from the unnatural blackness that enveloped those creepy eyes.

So did Seph. She looked back the other way. The skeletal skitters were slithering around the corner of the building, blocking their path. There was nowhere to go. They were trapped between the two.

She reached out toward the wretch with one hand and closed her fingers around the handle of the scythe. But as the glass-like blade materialized between her and it, the monster reared up and twisted itself around. An instant later, it was thirty feet away, staring back at them from a pile of shadows coiled at the base of an old maple tree.

Seph blinked. Right. This thing was fast. Or it was able to…teleport…or something. That creepy, dragging thing it did was apparently only a ruse to catch them off guard.

"Persephone!" hissed Piper.

Seph turned to see the skitters closing in on them.

When she turned back again, the wretch's hideous, diseased face was right in front of her, its black, withered fingertips almost touching her throat.

She screamed and thrust her hands forward, lashing out with the blade of the scythe. But like when she struck at it in the back of the truck in Nora's Lilac Grove, the awful thing was too fast. It snapped away like a stretched rubber band, retreating back into its shadow puddle in the shade of the old maple.

That foul, rotten stench, however, lingered around her like a putrid cloud, strong enough to bring tears to her eyes.

"*What do we do?*" cried Piper.

Seph wasn't sure. She turned sideways, keeping her right hand stretched out toward the wretch, and reached out behind her with the other hand. Suddenly, she was wielding *two* scythes, each of the blades shielding them from one of the two dangers.

"I didn't know you could do that," whispered Piper.

"Neither did I," she replied.

It wasn't much of a defense. Seph couldn't help but feel a little bit like she was trying to fend off a firing squad with a knife.

The skitters clearly weren't concerned about the weapon. They kept coming, scuttling closer on those bony little legs. She lowered the scythe in an attempt to stop them from simply slithering under it and Piper watched as the grass burned away at the blade's watery touch, painting an arc of bare, dead earth between them and the approaching swarm.

The wretch, too, wasn't particularly deterred. Again, it began crawling toward them on those blackened fingertips, that awful, disfigured visage dragging in the grass, those empty black eyes fixed on her.

She lowered the blade on that side, threatening it, but the tip of the blade began to melt. Water dripped into the grass.

Seph's heart leaped. No! Not now! She furrowed her brow and

thrust it toward the wretch. The blade obeyed. It lengthened. Sunlight flashed off its watery surface. But it lasted only a second before it began to melt again, more rapidly this time.

The wretch seized its chance and launched itself at her with lightning speed. But instead of reappearing right in front of her face again, it turned ninety degrees and slammed itself into the wall of the house.

Seph and Piper watched, confused, as it backed away and shook its head.

"Get out of there!" shouted Wallace.

He was on the roof of one of the buildings, overlooking the lawn where they stood staring back at him.

Piper recalled him mentioning that he had the ability to make people briefly confused. He also said that it often led to unexpected results. He'd just done that to the wretch, buying them a little more time.

The wretch turned its black eyes on Wallace and then vanished. In almost the same instant, Seph saw it slithering up the side of the house.

It was going for him.

"Look out!" she shouted.

But it turned out she didn't need to worry about Wallace. He wasn't alone up there.

A monster leapt over the peak of the roof and descended on the wretch. It had four legs, two tentacle-like tongues, enormous, gaping, tooth-lined jaws and a semi-casual, beige pantsuit.

The Ahns were here, too?

The wretch and the Ahn rolled off the roof and crashed into the grass, both of them thrashing around, making awful, snarling noises. It was like watching some epic nature battle, the fearsome crocodile versus the giant anaconda, perhaps.

Seph couldn't pull her eyes away.

Piper watched the Ahn, too, her thoughts whirling through her head. Hugh had told her that one of her grandmothers was an Ahn, explaining her monstrous transformation in the library. But which one was it? It couldn't be one of her parents' mothers. She knew them. They were both still alive. And neither of them had an "ann" in her name. So it had to be one of her *great* grandmothers…

"Go!" shouted Wallace from his rooftop.

Seph snapped out of it and looked down at her hands. Both scythes had vanished. She was just standing there with her arms outstretched, looking like an idiot.

"This way!" shouted Lee from behind them. He was standing in the doorway of the next house, gesturing impatiently for them to follow him.

Seph stared at him, confused. Was that door even there a second ago?

"Hurry up!" he snapped at her.

She didn't dare waste any more time. She took Piper by the arm and hurried into the house with her, slamming and locking the door behind them.

"Follow me," whispered Lee, a bony finger pressed to his lips. "But stay quiet."

Seph glanced back at the door they just entered through, wondering if Wallace and the Ahn would be okay, but she paused and frowned at the it. Something seemed off.

The door didn't look right.

In fact, *nothing* looked right. She turned and looked around her. She was standing in a small laundry room. There was a washroom next to her and a hallway behind her. And yet, it didn't *feel* like a small laundry room. It felt much bigger than that. She turned around again, half-convinced that she'd find a wide-open space behind her, but she was only staring out into that narrow hallway. There was a pantry door on the right and the kitchen at the other end.

Lee and Piper were already making their way through the kitchen.

She shook it off and hurried after them.

They followed Lee into the dining room, to a set of sliding doors overlooking the back yard where the skitters had been gathered. Slowly, he slid the door open. He looked back at them, pressed his finger to his lips again and gestured for them to follow him. Then, without waiting for them to respond, he stepped out of the building and back into the sunlight.

Seph peered out the door to find that the skitters were all slithering around the side of the house, leaving this part of the yard open.

Lee didn't seem concerned by them at all. He stood by the corner of the house, his back pressed against the wall. He had one crooked hand out, warning them to stop, while he stood motionless, as if waiting for something.

He remained like that for a moment, listening, and Seph turned and looked nervously back at where those skeletal creeps had gone.

Again, that odd feeling of something wrong crept over her. From the corner of her eye, she saw a great, empty space inside the house she'd just walked through. But when she turned to look, it was only an ordinary dining room again. She stared at it for a moment, thinking about what Wilbur said about the town being fake….

When she looked back again, Lee was gesturing for them to follow him, his finger again pressed to his lips.

Yeah, she thought. *We get it. Loose lips sink ships.*

She followed him past the corner of the building and barely managed to hold back a scream when she saw the two empty people standing with their backs to them in the side yard only a few paces away.

Seph recalled as she followed him that Lee's power was being able to sense danger, including the exact location and movement of the enemy. This was why he didn't seem to need to look where he was going.

There was a loud shriek from the direction of the street. When they turned to look, they caught a brief glimpse of another four-legged, two-tentacled monstrosity loping past them, this one wearing a loud, knitted sweater, khaki pants and bright orange sneakers.

Piper wondered how many Ahns were here.

And was it possible that she was related to one of them?

Lee crossed behind the next house, cut through the next yard and slipped into the side door of the house beyond it.

As soon as she closed the door behind her, Seph again felt that strong sense of wrongness.

Not wrong as in dangerous. If anything, the houses in this town felt distinctly safer in comparison to the monster-infested outdoors. But she was instantly convinced that what she was seeing was something drastically different from what her eyes were showing her.

As she passed through a cozy living room, she closed her eyes for a moment and tried to make herself relax. When she opened them again, she found herself walking through what appeared to be an enormous, empty *crate* with a few doors and windows cut into it.

The ceiling was low and covered in cobwebs. The ground was bare, dry earth.

This was what she'd glimpsed from the corners of her eyes the first time she ran behind these buildings. These were the true forms of the fake houses of Waybel Valley, what the Keeper's strange illusion hid from the world to convince it that this was a real city.

Lee made his way across the shadowy emptiness of the false house and opened the door on the other side. He paused for a moment, seemed to consider whatever he felt out there, then nodded and made his way across the next lawn and into the next building in line, which was revealed by Seph's prophet sight to be little more than a boarded-up frame with no interior walls. It was entirely hollow inside, and covered in cloth.

She remembered how some of the buildings had looked almost like poorly painted tents as she hurried past them. This was one of *those* buildings, she realized.

Lee opened the next door and gestured for them to stop. Then he looked down at the ground, where Seph followed his gaze and caught sight of a long, skeletal tail slowly slithering through the grass.

When it was gone, he led them out the door, along a tall, concrete wall, and then into a weedy lot behind an old, brick building. Here, he peered around the corner and then turned and gestured for them to look.

Seph and Piper stepped forward. There, only about a hundred feet away, was Amethyst's ranch truck.

They were almost there!

"You go on," whispered Lee. "There're more heading this way. I'll distract them."

"Thank you," whispered Seph.

"Be careful!" fretted Piper.

"I'll be fine," he insisted. "Just get your butts out of Waybel Valley and find those other two Tartarus locks." And with that, he turned and hurried off.

"You really think they'll be okay?" worried Piper.

"They'll be even more okay once we're gone," whispered Seph.

"Right."

"Let's get out of here."

Together, they crept along the side of the building and peered around the next corner. There was an empty person in front of the bar, an overweight, middle-aged woman with short hair, but she was locked in combat with two flickering men, and not faring well. They hurried past them, ducked behind an old Toyota and then darted behind a white van with a flat tire.

In fact, as Seph glanced around, she realized that *all* the vehicles parked around Waybel Valley had flat tires. They were nothing more than derelicts staged to look like there were people living and working here. Most of them were faded and dusty, outdated and broken down. They clearly hadn't been moved in years.

Just beyond the ranch truck was Waybel Valley's Main Street. There, the war between the bug god and Tane's monster breeder was raging. And as she looked out over this chaos, Seph finally saw the town for what it was. All but a very few of the buildings were real. The Rischt's house was real, as were the businesses. The bar and the post office and the gas station. The rest looked like lazily painted, cardboard cutouts, little more than placeholders for the Keeper's illusion. Some were great, wooden boxes. Some were framed tents. One was nothing more than a twelve-foot-high, wooden fence with a door and some windows half-heartedly painted on the front. It looked like the sort of thing a cartoon character might draw to fool a particularly stupid villain.

"What do we do?" whispered Piper, who didn't seem to notice that the city was little more than rough cutouts from a giant toddler's coloring book.

"Just go for it!" Seph whispered back.

They ran the last several yards and jumped into the truck, slamming and locking the door behind them.

They made it. They were inside the truck. But now what? There were monsters everywhere, including those stupid suicide bomber butterflies. There was no way they were getting out of here on these roads.

And the slamming door had drawn the attention of quite a few of the surrounding monsters. Black and empty eyes had turned their way.

But before they could even ponder any other options, something very bizarre happened.

The truck shuddered, as if something had just shoved it from behind.

Every monster on Main Street suddenly staggered and came to a stop.

Then, in an instant, their ears popped and the street and everything on it was instantly crushed flat, as if a giant, invisible foot had just stomped down on top of it all.

"What just happened?" asked Seph.

Piper stared for a moment at the carnage before them, horrified. Even the pavement had been crushed into gravel. The remains of flickering men and empty people alike had been pounded into it in the most gruesome manner. Then she shook it off. "Who cares?" she blurted. "Just get us out of here!"

She was right. Seph shifted the truck into gear and then sped onto the street before those things began flooding the roads again, especially those flutters. She aimed the truck away from town and took off.

"What's that?" asked Piper.

Seph slowed down as they approached it. "Is that…?"

Sitting in the middle of the street in the folding chair he was carrying the last time they saw him, with his back to the city limits, was *Ross*.

Ross was the most impressive, though, she remembered Wallace telling them. *He used to be able to manipulate air pressure. He could make all sorts of things happen. I saw him crush an entire house once.*

It appeared that "was" was the wrong word. Ross was still very much the most impressive of the group.

He smiled and gave them a friendly wave as they passed, not bothering to get up.

He looked so pleased with himself.

And…was that a *wink*?

"You know," said Seph as she left Ross and all of Waybel Valley in her rearview and accelerated down the road, "I'm starting to think Ross wasn't as senile as he was pretending to be."

Piper nodded. She was starting to think the same thing. "Those people were nice and all, but I don't think I ever want to go back there again."

Seph wasn't going to argue with that. "So, where do we go now?"

"Texas, isn't it?"

She sighed. "Right. Pobsick Spring." She hoped all the locks weren't like this first one. She was *not* in the mood to deal with another library. But she also wasn't in the mood to keep being chased by empty people, black-eyed children and skitters. "So how do we get there?"

Piper reached for her phone, but it wasn't there. "Oh yeah. You have it."

"Right. Sorry." She reached into her purse and pulled both of them out. "And they're dead," she remembered.

Piper took her phone and frowned at it. Not much use like this. And they didn't even have a charger in this truck. "Now what?" she asked.

Seph sat up in her seat. "Who's *this*, now?"

A man was standing by the side of the road, shielding his eyes from the sun as they approached.

For a moment, Seph thought it was Wallace. She wondered how he managed to get all the way here. But then she realized that it wasn't him. The build was wrong. This guy was a bit more heavyset than Wallace, but not as much so as Wilbur. And he had a beard.

As they drew closer, the man reached out and pointed into the woods.

Then Seph saw it. There was a little road, hidden away behind the high grass. "Fringe road," she realized. She turned on her blinker and slowed down. As the old truck lumbered over the ditch, she glanced over at the man and realized that she'd seen him before. "Is that…?"

She lost sight of him for a split-second as she pulled up next to him, and just like that, he was gone.

"What…?"

Piper leaned over her and looked out the window. "Where'd he go?"

Seph shook her head. She didn't have an answer for her.

"Who was that guy?"

"You didn't recognize him?"

Piper stared at her. "Who?"

"*Horace.*"

Her blue eyes widened. "Wait…you mean the guy in the hospital bed?"

Seph turned and looked out the window again. He didn't look much like the frail old man who was lying in that room. The man who showed them this road was considerably younger and more vibrant looking. "I guess he finally completed his work."

Piper's eyes widened. "You mean he's…?"

Seph nodded. It was the only explanation she could find.

"What about the others?" asked Piper. "Are they…?"

"No. They're fine. I mean, we literally just saw Ross." But she turned and looked back toward the smoke rising from Waybel Valley. "…right?"

Piper stared off in that direction, too. "Yeah. You're right."

"Yeah…"

"We should get out of here before any of those things figure out which way we went."

Seph nodded. She didn't like not knowing for sure, but going back was downright stupid. She leaned back in her seat and set off down the nameless road, mentally preparing herself for a journey through the fringe.

Pobsick Spring, Texas…

She just knew this was going to suck.

Chapter 42

Seph switched on the truck's headlights as they entered the dark expanse of the fringe road, then glanced over at Piper. "How're you feeling?"

She was slumped down in the seat, pinching her lower lip and staring off into space. She dropped her hand into her lap and glanced over at her. "I think I'm okay. I mean, you know… *Physically*."

"Well you did get a nap and a snack."

Piper shuddered and made a gagging face. "Please don't ever bring that up again. I've never wanted to brush my teeth so badly in my life…"

Seph still couldn't help but wonder if that whole situation could've been avoided if only she'd been brave enough to gather up a bunch of those bugs and make her eat them. They *were* technically meat, right? Sure, it was hideously disgusting, but it wasn't entirely *unnatural.* Lots of cultures around the world ate bugs. It was probably a staple in the diets of their distant ancestors. And it wasn't like the situation wasn't *dire.* She'd really believed for a while there that her best friend might actually *die.* And then the truth of the situation turned out to be even stranger and more terrifying by far.

If all it would've taken to avoid *Feral Piper* was a single handful of stupid, squirming bugs…

And yet, even knowing what happened, the idea horrified her. She couldn't stand the thought of it. She couldn't have done it. And not just the part about *touching* the bugs. The idea of forcing someone to *eat bugs* was *beyond* disgusting.

Her heart sank as she found herself wondering if she could've let her best friend die because of her stupid phobias.

No. She couldn't think about that right now. For all she knew, bugs didn't count. It could've made no difference whatsoever.

She shoved the awful thought out of her mind and hoped it never came back.

"Do you think Hugh was right?" asked Piper. "About me being an Ahn?"

Seph glanced over at her. "Well, you have to be *something.* You tried to eat my face back there, remember?"

She turned away, embarrassed. "Not very much of it, no. It was all kind of a blur."

"Well, *I* sure won't forget."

"I'm sorry."

"Not your fault. You're apparently one-quarter monster or something." She considered it for a moment. "It does *kind of* make sense. I mean…we've seen those women eat. They're definitely not vegetarians."

Piper nodded. She'd noticed before that the Ahns didn't have little grandma appetites like most of the old ladies she'd known. Every time she saw them eat, they all had big portions, with extra meat. She never thought much about it because she knew what they were. It probably required a lot of protein to maintain those freakishly powerful monster forms they took. But it never occurred to her that it might have any kind of connection to her strange meat condition. "I didn't turn into a monster like they did, though," she pondered. She was twisting her lower lip again, thinking. "I mean I didn't, did I?"

Seph cringed a little. "Not…not exactly…"

Piper turned and looked at her, concerned.

"Your eyes turned really yellow."

She lowered the sun visor and looked at herself in the vanity mirror. But her eyes were their normal bright and pretty shade of blue. Her sclera were a little bloodshot, still, but perfectly white. There was no sign of the monster that emerged in the library. The rest of her, however… "Ugh! I look disgusting!"

Seph's usual response to things like that was to roll her eyes and tell her she was fine. She'd literally seen Piper roll out of bed in the morning with a hangover and look prettier than she could ever manage. (She was kind of a lightweight; two or three glasses of wine and she was an annoyingly cute mess the next morning.) But in this case, she wasn't exactly wrong.

It was mostly the dried blood caked on her face. They hadn't had a chance yet to clean up, so she still looked sort of monstrous, in a freshly risen zombie sort of way.

Piper began rummaging through the glove box and console, looking for napkins or tissue to clean herself off with.

Seph focused on the dark road before them. She decided not to mention the other things she saw when Piper was hulked out back there, how her mouth and jaw stretched open wider than it should've been able to without tearing her face in half. How her teeth changed. How her muscles swelled. Mostly because she wasn't entirely sure she didn't imagine that part. She *was* terrified out of her mind at the moment. But now she couldn't stop thinking about the way the Ahns transformed. It began at their mouths, which split open from ear to ear and then flipped back like a giant Pez dispenser before those two tentacle-like tongues came slithering out.

Piper turned around, still looking for something to clean herself up with, and peered behind the truck's seat. "Hey, what's this?" There was a zippered bag stuffed back there. She pulled it out and laid it on the seat between them. Inside, she found two complete changes of clothes, including undergarments and two pairs of comfortable running shoes, some bottles of water, a first aid kit, disinfecting wipes, flashlights with extra batteries, a phone charger, sunscreen, bug spray and some granola bars and beef jerky. "Isn't this one of Wanda's survival kits?"

Seph looked over at it, confused. "Why would she put one in here?" Wanda knew about Amethyst. The two of them had even met once or twice after her ordeal in Avelby. But she'd never been to the ranch.

And yet, this looked exactly like the bags Wanda stashed in Seph's Ford and Piper's Jeep.

"Whatever," said Piper, pulling out the clothes and laying them beside her in the seat. "*I'm* not complaining."

"No. Me neither."

Maybe Amethyst was inspired by Wanda's mission to prepare them for any contingency. Maybe she stashed one of these in every vehicle at the ranch, just in case. It didn't really matter. She was just happy to have it.

Piper plugged her phone into the charger and laid it on the seat. Then she took off the shirt Seph loaned her and began cleaning the blood and dirt off her skin with the disinfecting wipes.

It was an ideal time for it, Seph supposed. No one was going to see them here on the fringe road. She, too, shrugged out of Hugh's enormous shirt and stuffed it behind the truck seat.

There were clean socks and panties for both of them, two sports bras, two light tee shirts, two pairs of athletic capris leggings and two running jackets. Whoever it was that packed these things obviously knew how much *running* they did on these trips. Even more impressive, they knew their sizes and even their color preferences: all black for Seph, pink and light gray for Piper.

"I'm still a little bummed about my sweater," grumbled Piper as she stuffed her soiled bra and Seph's purple shirt into the bag.

"*I'm* not," grumbled Seph. "Better than being eaten by that freaky *tree*."

"I didn't say it *wasn't*," huffed Piper. "I just liked that sweater. That's all." She looked herself over, wiping at several dark spots on her arms and chest, trying to distinguish the smudges from the bruises. "It just wouldn't've been my first pick if I had to choose something out of my closet to throw at a monster."

Seph pulled the black tee shirt over her head and then stuffed her arms through the sleeves, careful not to lose her glasses in the process. (She didn't dare take her eyes off the fringe road for more than a second.) She didn't bother changing bras like Piper. It was too much trouble while she was driving and she certainly had no intention of stopping the truck in this monster-infested wilderness. The same was true of her panties. But she *did* wriggle out of her shoes and skirt and into the new leggings. She'd put on the new socks and shoes after they arrived in Pobsick Spring.

Piper, on the other hand, wasn't hindered in any way in the passenger's seat and was thrilled to have a complete change of clean clothes. It'd been bothering her that she'd been wearing the same underwear since she got dressed to go out to lunch yesterday.

(Was that really only yesterday?)

By the time the fringe road's endless forest began to thin, they both looked pretty much normal again.

Well, *Seph* looked normal. She thought Piper looked ready for a date with a hot fitness coach. She had absolutely no idea how she managed to get her hair so cute without so much as a brush. Was that an Ahn thing, too? Or was she also part *witch*?

Either way, Seph found it kind of annoying.

The fringe road came to an end on a two-lane, country road. There were buildings visible off to the right, so Seph turned and drove there first. The sooner they figured out where they were, the sooner they could figure out where they were going.

"Hugh said the Ahns must've known the whole time," recalled Piper, returning to the subject of her strange, monster heritage. "Do you think he's right?"

Seph glanced over at her. "He might be. It's not like they've never strung us along before."

"Yeah…" The Ahns didn't get in any hurry about introducing themselves. How long did they spend watching them from the shadows, content to let them fumble along, ignorant of all the dangers out there?

What would they say if she asked them about it, she wondered. Would they come clean? Or would they lie to her? What reason did they even have to hide it from her? It seemed like good information to have. Seeing as how it made her turn into a monster and all…

The buildings Seph saw from the fringe road turned out to be a sprawling farm.

Maybe she should've gone the other way. But she decided to keep going until she at least found a useful road sign.

Piper's cell phone had booted back up. There were *dozens* of missed messages and phone calls waiting for her. All of them from Meg. "Ugh," she groaned. "Take a freaking *hint*, woman!"

It rang in her hands, startling a surprised, "Whaa!" from her that made Seph chuckle.

"Might as well answer it. She's only going to keep calling."

Piper sighed. She *really* wasn't in the mood for Meg right now, but Seph was right. She accepted the call and held the phone to her ear, careful not to pull the cord out of the charger. "Hello?"

"Where *are* you guys?" blurted Meg. "I've been trying to call you all morning!"

"We had a breakfast date," she lied. "What do you want?"

"Don't be so bitchy! This is an emergency!"

Piper made a face at her, offended. *She* wasn't the one being bitchy! "What's wrong *now*?" she groaned.

"River Lobnetter's gone off the deep end this time! I think she's having me followed!"

She rolled her eyes. "Why would she have you *followed*?"

"She's obviously out of her mind! She wouldn't stop calling me last night."

"What did she say to you?"

"I didn't *answer* it! What do you think I am? Stupid?"

Piper had to bite her tongue. This was definitely one of those "if you can't say anything nice" moments her mom used to warn her about.

"She kept texting me, too, saying she needed to talk to me. Asking me where I was. She wanted to meet me somewhere, as if *that* would ever happen. Then she got *weird*. Started getting super threatening, telling me she couldn't stop thinking about what I did to her and shit. I mean, what the freaking *hell*? I turned my phone off after that. I think she's actually psychotic!"

Piper frowned. That *did* seem like a weird thing to say… But then again, Meg *did* have sex with *two* of her boyfriends… She'd read more than a few murder mysteries that had half that much motive…

"And then this morning I woke up to someone banging on the door at eight o'clock!"

"Who was it?"

"I don't know! I didn't open it!"

"You didn't even look through the peephole?"

"Why? So someone could *stab me in the eye*? No thank you!"

Piper rubbed her eyes, tired. Where did she come up with this stuff? "I don't…think…that would happen."

"That was when I started trying to call you, but you wouldn't pick up!"

"What would *I* have done? I'm all the way in *Madison*."

Seph shook her head. How did she do that? That right there was where *she* would've messed up and said she was in Texas. Was making up lies and keeping track of your fake alibis an inheritable Ahn trait, too?

Meg probably wouldn't have noticed anyway. She was too busy starring in her own little horror story. "Anyway," she went on, "since it was obviously not safe at home anymore, I waited until they were gone and then I snuck out. I went to Starbucks, 'cause I *seriously* needed a frappe after all that, right? And get this! There was this *guy* there. He kept staring at me and talking on his phone. And when I left, he *followed* me out of the building! I'm telling you, that girl's having me followed. I wouldn't be surprised if she put a hit on me!"

Piper groaned. "I *really* don't think somebody put a *hit* on you."

Seph snorted. "Seriously?"

"The Lobnetters have a ton of money!" snapped Meg. "I've heard they're in bed with the mob. It wouldn't even be that hard for her. She probably has her own hitman."

"*Or* maybe you're jumping to conclusions again? Like you *always* are?"

"God, Pipes, how dense can you possibly be? Did you hear *any* of what I've been saying? Are you listening to me at all?"

"I heard you just fine," Piper growled. She was starting to hope someone really *was* trying to kill her.

(Okay, not really *kill* her…but she wouldn't necessarily be opposed to someone tying her up and gagging her for a few hours or a day or two.)

"I'm telling you this woman is deranged! And she's out to get me. Auuuuugh! I don't know why I bother talking to you. You can't possibly understand any of this. You've never had to deal with any *real* problems."

"*Excuse me?*"

"Oh come on. You wouldn't last two days in the real world. You have no idea what it's like to have your life threatened."

Piper took the phone from her ear and glared at it.

"I'm just saying."

She put the phone back to her ear and said, "Well have fun with that. I have to go. I'm about to lose service for a while."

"How long a while?"

"Don't know. A while."

"That's just stupid. Where *are* you?"

"I think I'm already losing you. What did you say?"

"*Where are you?*"

"We're in—" She stopped mid-sentence and ended the call. She dropped the phone back onto the seat and glanced over at Seph. "*So* not dealing with any more of *that*."

"Next time you turn into an Ahn, maybe you should eat *her*."

Piper looked horrified at the thought. "Are you kidding? Heaven knows where *she's* been."

Seph snorted and turned her attention back to the road. She could see more buildings looming ahead of them. It was bigger than any farm. An actual town. Was it their destination? Pobsick Spring?

She wasn't sure she was ready for this so soon. They'd only just left Waybel Valley.

Would it be another library, she wondered. Would it be more dangerous than the last one? She wasn't looking forward to it, whatever it was. Whatever awaited them, she was sure it was going to really, *really* suck.

"Why does this place look so familiar?" asked Piper, looking around for the first time. "I've never been to Texas before."

Neither had Seph, but she was right. Something about this landscape and the buildings up ahead were very familiar. She felt like she'd been here before.

Then she caught sight of the city limit sign. "Pea…"

Piper saw it too. She stared at the green sign as they drove past it, then turned and looked at Seph. "We're not in Texas." A special kind of dread was rising inside her, souring her stomach, making her feel sick.

They were in Fathom Lake, South Dakota.

"I thought we were going to Texas first!" said Piper.

"I thought so too. But this is where the fringe road spit us out."

"I thought the fringe road took us to the place we were thinking about. Isn't that how they work?"

Seph considered it. "Well, the first time we used them, we didn't *know* where we were going. No one told us."

"Oh yeah."

"We just…sort of assumed it would take us where we needed to go. And it took us to Shawbeck Ranch. Maybe that's what happened this time, too?" She was pretty distracted after their ordeal in the library. They were supposed to focus on their destination, but was she really focused on Pobsick Spring? Or was she just focusing on getting wherever they were supposed to go next? She'd never been to Pobsick Spring before, after all.

Or maybe it had something to do with the ghostly old man who showed them the entrance to the fringe road. Did *he* make them come here instead?

Piper looked up at her, worried. "Remember what Sandy told us? She said we were supposed to find the custodians of the Keeper's gates. Like Hugh and the others in Waybel Valley. But the custodians of Fathom Lake…"

"Stan and Marsha," recalled Seph. The owners of Pappy Stan's Diner. Long dead now, murdered by the very monsters who tried to eat them the last time they were in Fathom Lake, a year and a half ago.

"What do we do?"

Seph sighed. "As much as I hate it…the only place I can think to even start is…"

"The diner," finished Piper.

Chapter 43

"Fathom Lake we've actually heard of before," said Violet. "We haven't been out there to investigate, but Corey's collected *lots* of reports from that area. Their big claim to fame is supposed to be a lake monster named Old Fred. I guess there's this really goofy-looking statue of it in the middle of the town somewhere."

Piper nodded and looked out across the street. "Yeah. I'm literally looking at that right now."

"Oh! That's cool."

She chewed her lip and stared at the twelve-foot-tall, lime-green monstrosity. She guessed it was cool. In a "hey, I've been there before" kind of way. The first time she ever saw the thing, she couldn't decide if the concrete creature was supposed to be cute or scary, and after all this time, she found that she was no closer to telling. Those bright, cartoonish colors were impossible to take too seriously, and yet there was something eerily creepy about its yellow, blank-eyed stare and blood-red, gaping mouth.

Just looking at it sort of made her feel uneasy. It was an unnecessarily eerie reminder of the awful ordeal she suffered the last time she came to this awful little town.

She wished Seph would hurry back.

They'd stopped at the gas station right across the street from the city hall and its hideous mascot for a restroom break and to top off the tank. Seph took the opportunity to stock up on some supplies at the convenience store while Piper called Violet to see if she knew anything about the town that might be of use to them.

What was taking her so long?

"Fathom Lake is a seriously weird place," reported Violet. "Both the town *and* the actual lake. We first heard about it years ago, actually. It was one of the first places that turned up in our research. The area's a hot spot for all sorts of weird stories, ranging from ghosts to vampires to cryptids, but nothing anyone's ever been able to substantiate. Tons of eye-witness accounts. A handful of blurry photos and shaky, poorly lit cell phone videos. But we've never actually investigated there. Everything about it stinks of a hoax, to be honest. The leading theory is that the whole thing's a scheme to turn the town into a tourist trap."

Piper frowned. That wasn't helpful at all. "There *has* to be *something* here," she insisted.

"Right," agreed Violet. "If you guys are there, then there *has* to be *something*. That's why I was so surprised when you asked about it. Now we're digging up all our old information and looking at it again. But there's just so much of it. I mean, they're claiming bigfoot sightings all over the place. There's supposed to be a wendigo living somewhere in the area… I could keep going, but I think it's a waste of time. It just never stops."

"Tell 'em 'bout the aliens," said Corey from somewhere in the background.

"I'm getting to it!" insisted Violet.

"Aliens?" asked Piper.

"This one *is* kind of interesting," admitted Violet. "There're *two* locations within ten miles of Fathom Lake that are famous for their frequent UFO sightings. Like, *major* UFO enthusiast playgrounds."

"Strange lights in the sky," said Corey. "Weird electric storms. Abduction claims. All sorts of cool stuff."

"I'm telling her!" insisted Violet.

"Do you think that has anything to do with what *we're* looking for?" asked Piper.

"I'm not sure," replied Violet. "I mean one of the sites, Hodge Field, is only active around the winter solstice. There's no record of any activity the rest of the year. And the other, Canchester Road, is only known for a rash of strange sightings, unexplained radio interference and cattle mutilations every three years or so."

"Ew…" said Piper, wrinkling her nose at the idea of *cattle mutilations.*

"And this isn't a peak year," added Violet.

Piper pinched her lip and stared out at Old Fred. It was still possible that those places were related somehow. Perhaps the so-called UFO activity was caused by the Keeper's gate. Like, maybe the time magic was leaking out or something? But what did she know? "Did you find anything about that couple who ran the diner outside of town?"

"*No*, actually. I haven't been able to find any reports of any deaths or disappearances in the past two years of anyone named Stan or Marsha. Or any other suspicious or unusual deaths. There were no homicide reports of any kind, in fact. And I also can't find any record of a 'Pappy Stan's Diner,' either. It's like they never existed."

Piper pushed her mouth to one side and considered this. Amethyst *did* say something about taking care of that mess. Had they covered the whole ordeal up? Did they somehow erase Stan and Marsha's very *lives*? The idea was almost as frightening as the monsters that killed them.

"We may not be of much help here, unfortunately," lamented Violet. "Corey has this theory that maybe the hoaxes and other activity might be there to help hide what you're actually looking for."

Piper nodded. "I think he's probably right about that." After all, that was precisely what Ian told them last summer about Avelby, that the whole city, including its people and all their crazy stories, was one big "machine" designed specifically to hide the Keeper's marker that was hidden in Fibbel Marsh. And it wouldn't be all that different from Waybel Valley, which was an entire fake town designed to hide the entrance to Lodblin's Library.

"We'll keep digging, though," promised Violet. "If we spot anything we think might be helpful we'll let you know."

"Thanks. I'm sure it's another one of those things we're just going to have to figure out for ourselves."

"It kind of sounds that way. Sorry."

"It's okay. Thanks for helping."

"No problem. We're happy to do it. Stay safe out there, okay. No getting yourselves killed before you can tell us about all the cool stuff you found."

"We'll do our best. Promise. Bye."

She disconnected the call and stared at the hideous statue of Old Fred. It would've been nice if Violet had been able to give them something solid to go on, but she'd be lying if she said she expected anything more. If the Keeper's gates were easy enough for a couple of Missouri treasure hunters to find, then they would've been found ages ago.

The driver-side door opened, startling a scream from her.

"Calm down," said Seph as she slid behind the wheel. "It's just me."

Piper pressed her hands over her pounding heart. "Sorry…"

Seph took a bottle of Coke and a granola bar out of a plastic bag and dropped the rest into Piper's lap. "For you," she said.

Piper opened the bag and looked inside. It was stuffed full of jerky and smoked meat sticks. "Oh my gosh! How much did you *spend* in there? And how much of this stuff do you think I can *eat*?"

Seph fastened her seatbelt and then twisted the cap off her Coke. "I'm not taking any chances, *Cujo*."

Piper glared at her. "You be nice to me. We both know now that I *can* bite your face off."

Seph choked on her cola laughing.

Piper laughed too. She looked down at her giant bag of meat. It *was* ridiculous...but maybe not *that* ridiculous. Time was broken in that library. It moved strangely. Although they were only gone for fifteen minutes, her body seemed to think they were in there for *hours*, maybe even *days*.

"I got you an iced tea, too," said Seph, gesturing at the bag.

"Thanks."

"Did you talk to Violet?"

"Uh huh."

"Any help?"

Piper shook her head. "Not really."

"Didn't figure so."

"Me neither."

They sat there for a moment, silent. They needed to get moving again, but it was hard to get in any kind of hurry. With no other leads to follow, there was only one place they *could* go.

Pappy Stan's Diner...

It was the only place in town they visited last time they were here. And Sandy told them that the real Stan and Marsha were supposed to be the ones to guide them to the Keeper's gate. If anyone else in this town knew the location of the second gate, they had no idea where to look for them.

This town was nothing like Waybel Valley. It wasn't a fake town. It was small, but it was fully populated. None of the buildings here looked fake, not even from the corners of Seph's eyes. This was a real community, filled with thousands of real people with real jobs and real lives.

The only sensible place to start, as much as they both hated the idea, was where the custodians were last seen. Maybe they left something at the diner that would point them in the direction of the lock.

"That thing is hideous," said Seph between sips of Coke.

Piper looked up at the statue on the other side of the street. "I know. It looks like a cheap water park decoration or something."

Seph nodded. It did, didn't it?

Piper's cell phone buzzed in her hand. A new text message. She glanced down at the screen, expecting it to be Meg again. Instead, it was Kaitlyn. She was asking where she was.

She barely thought about it. She quickly texted back that she was at the mall.

Seph sighed. "I guess we should go before something awful shows up."

Piper turned and looked around at the quiet street, expecting to see black-eyed children or teethers or a creeping wretch watching them from every corner. "Yeah."

Seph took a bite from her granola bar and then shifted the old truck into gear. She really hated the thought of it, but she didn't appear to have any choice.

It was time to go back.

Chapter 44

In just a few, far-too-short minutes, they were pulling into the dusty, deserted parking lot of Pappy Stan's Diner.

"God, I hate this place."

"Me too," said Piper. She was pinching her lower lip again, nervous.

The windows and doors had been boarded up since they were last here. Amethyst once told them that the bodies had been removed and respectfully interred, without letting any of the locals know that anything had happened there. She didn't explain how it was done or who took care of everything, or how they kept it out of the media given that there were quite a few corpses lying around the last time she was in there. And Seph hadn't asked. She didn't care to think too much about this place. She never dreamed she'd ever come back here.

She drove around to the back of the building and parked the truck next to the rear door, out of sight from the road. They might have to break in, and it'd be better if no one saw the vehicle and decided to be nosy. A run-in with the local police would be very bad. If they were stuck in some local jail cell when Tane or Gispuknya inevitably showed up, they'd be utterly helpless.

"I can't believe we're actually doing this," sighed Piper. And so soon after escaping that library, too… "We must be insane."

"We must be," agreed Seph. She stepped out of the truck and looked around. There was no one in sight from back here, which wasn't surprising because there was nothing in sight but the empty road even from the front.

Piper put on her running jacket and started to get out of the truck, too, but her phone, still connected to the charger, began ringing. She paused and looked at the screen. It was Alton. What could *he* be wanting in the middle of the day? She accepted the call, grateful for any reason to procrastinate a little longer. "Hello?"

"Hey, it's me."

"Hi. What's up?"

"Nothing. Just wondering what you were doing."

"Nothing interesting," she lied. "Hanging out at the mall."

"In Cakwetak?"

"Yeah." Piper pushed her mouth to one side and furrowed her brow. What was with the third-degree? Last time she talked to Kaitlyn she did the same thing.

"Is Seph with you?"

She glanced over at Seph. She was standing by the door, looking impatient. She considered lying. Seph should've been at work, after all. But it seemed like a bad idea. "Yeah. She's here."

"Kaitlyn said they were having computer problems at the studio."

So Kaitlyn put him up to this? "Yeah. It's not looking like she's going to have off this weekend."

"Bummer."

"I know, right?"

"Well, if she's off we could all get together this evening instead," suggested Alton.

Piper blinked. "Oh. Uh… No, I don't think we can make it tonight…" She glanced over at Seph. "We promised Seph's mom we'd have dinner with her."

"Oh. Too bad."

"Yeah. Sorry."

"It's really quiet there."

"Huh?"

"You said you were at the mall. It must not be very busy."

Piper chewed her lip. This conversation was weird. It felt like Alton was fishing. Did she say something to make him suspicious? She didn't *like* lying to them, but she couldn't very well tell them the truth. It was dangerous. "Yeah. It's not very busy today. And we're way back by the Dick's." She leaned back in the seat, forgetting about the charger, and pulled the cord out of the phone. "Hey…is everything okay? You seem a little…I don't know. You just don't sound like yourself."

"Really? I don't know what you mean. I'm fine."

Piper frowned. Why did that sound so insincere?

Seph turned and looked at her, her eyebrows raised in a "wrap it up, already" sort of look.

Piper replied with an "I'm trying!" look.

"Anyway, Kaitlyn's totally sad that Seph has to work this weekend."

"Well, it's not decided yet, but it kinda looks that way. We'll have to see."

"Fingers crossed," said Alton.

"Yeah. Totally. Hey, sorry, but I've got to go."

"Yeah. No problem. But before you go, can I ask you something? Real quick?"

"Sure."

"Have you ever been to South Dakota?"

Piper froze, startled. "Um…" What the heck? "Uh, yeah. Couple times. Uh…" She scratched absently at an itch on her nose. "Why?"

"My mom said my cousin's thinking about moving out there. I was wondering what it was like. I've been asking everyone."

"Oh. Well, I haven't seen much of it." She looked up at the old diner looming before her. "Can't say I love it there."

"Yeah. Doesn't sound like my first choice, either. But whatever, I guess."

"Yeah." Piper's thoughts were racing now. Was that really just a coincidence?

"Anyway, I'll let you go."

"Okay. Bye."

"Bye."

Piper ended the call and then sat there and stared at the phone for a moment. That was weird…

"Are you coming?" asked Seph.

"Yeah." She plugged her phone back into the charger, then hopped out of the truck and closed the door behind her.

"You okay?"

She walked around the front of the truck and stopped in front of the diner's back door. She was pinching her lip, distracted, and staring at the ground. "How long have you known Kaitlyn and Alton?"

Seph stared at her, surprised. "I met them my first semester of college. Along with Phoenix. They were all friends already. They went to high school together. Why?"

Piper shook her head. "Nothing. Just…" It was unsettling. Why would Alton know anything about them being in South Dakota? And why would he have any reason to even think that she'd be lying to them?

Well…she *was* lying…but why would he *think* it?

She recalled how Amethyst Wilhoit turned out to be Lyla Shawbeck and how both Mr. Carrol and Seph's old high school art teacher turned out to be Janon Tane. Was it possible there were more? Could Kaitlyn Jernam and Alton Ripna also have been someone else in disguise this whole time?

The idea was unsettling.

"Come on. I want to get this over with so we can hurry up and get the hell out of here."

"Yeah. Okay." She couldn't argue with that. She pushed Alton and his weird behavior out of her mind and focused on the locked door in front of her. "So how do we get in?"

"I have a key."

"You do?"

Seph reached out her hand and shoved the scythe's watery blade through the lock, breaking it.

"Oh. I see." She looked down at her pendant. "You know, if I knew how to use this thing, I could probably make *actual* keys."

"What's the fun in that?" Seph pushed the door open and peered inside with one of the flashlights Piper found in the survival kit. (Her cell phone was still dead and waiting for its turn on the charger.)

This was the kitchen. Over there, near the door leading into the dining room, was the exact spot they almost died, caught in the monstrous grip of the things pretending to be Stan and his family.

She stood there a moment, frozen in place, unable to believe that she'd actually come back here. What was she thinking?

Piper peered in over her shoulder. The place was filthy. There were cobwebs and dust everywhere. But there was no evidence of any dead bodies. No dried blood. No sign of any struggles. Even the soiled appliances where they prepared their foul food had been removed. The only proof that they didn't imagine that entire, horrible encounter was the scorch marks on the walls and ceiling from the fires set by the exploding fryer. "What're we looking for again?"

Seph wasn't even sure. Logically, she couldn't imagine finding *anything* in this place. But she didn't know where else to go. If the original Stan and Marsha who owned this place were the custodians of the gate to the second Tartarus lock, then this diner was as close as they could hope to get to it. If they didn't leave any clues about it here, then she had no idea where else to look.

A roach skittered across the floor in front of her and she jumped back with a girlish yelp.

Piper sighed. "Let me go first."

"Thank you," whimpered Seph.

She stepped into the kitchen and took a few steps, but then she paused. "Oh my gosh…" she breathed. "I seriously can't believe I'm in this room again."

"I know."

"I must be *so* out of my mind right now."

Seph nodded. She felt the same way. She took another step and then let out a short scream as her foot slid forward, nearly sending her to the floor.

Piper twirled around. "You okay?"

"I'm fine." She looked down at the floor, at the smear of gray, congealed goop that she'd stepped in. "Just some old grease." She dragged her foot across the dirty tiles a few times.

"This place is so gross."

"Nasty," agreed Seph.

Piper pushed the door open and stepped out into the dining room. All those awful memories came rushing back to her. It all looked the same as it did that day, after the illusion was broken. The only thing missing was the body in the corner of the room and the various blood stains. Even their plates and cups from that awful breakfast were still sitting on the table, covered in eighteen months of creeping, black mold.

So gross!

"It just doesn't feel like they would've left us a message or something," reasoned Piper. "I mean, Hugh and the others in Waybel Valley were pretty serious about their duty as custodians. They were literally keeping Horace alive in that room just so they could be sure to complete their mission."

"True," agreed Seph. And there was something just a little bit terrifying about that fact, even if they *had* proven to be good people. "But Sandy said there must be a way, remember? Besides, I find it really hard to believe that the Keeper didn't have some kind of backup plan. He knew we were going to need to find the lock hidden here and he knew a year and a half ago that Stan and Marsha were dead. Even if he wasn't able to predict their deaths—which I kind of doubt at this point—he's had plenty of time to find new custodians. And he *knew* we'd have to come back to this diner. He *had* to have."

"So…what? The answer's just supposed to present itself to us if we wander around long enough?"

"Isn't that how things usually work?"

Piper shrugged. "Point taken, I guess."

Seph shivered. It was cold in here, in spite of the jacket, and she hugged herself against a chill.

She'd had a lot of horrifying experiences since she awakened to her prophet sight, but this place was, by far, one of the worst.

Was it because those monsters nearly tricked them? Because they came so close to falling into their deadly trap? Or was it merely the gruesomeness of the whole ordeal? Everything about their first visit here was horrific. The illusion of a warm and pleasant diner concealing the filthy, blood-soaked truth. The foul, rotten food that they very nearly put into their own mouths. The cold, vicious nature of the monsters with their ill-fitting skins. The half-eaten bodies…

She almost would've preferred to venture back down into Lodblin's mad library rather than come here. But if there was one thing she'd learned it was that she couldn't avoid what had to be done. And if they ever wanted these horrors to end, their only choice was to keep pushing forward.

Piper turned and looked at her, eyebrows raised. "Huh?"

Seph stared back at her. "What?"

"I thought you said something."

"No."

She stood there a moment, those iridescent ears perked and twitching. "You weren't muttering to yourself just now?"

"No. I didn't make a sound."

"Hm." She turned her head to one side, then the other. Her spirit ears turned this way and that, as if trying to home in on something.

"What do you hear?" whispered Seph.

"Nothing now." She turned and looked the other way. "Might've been my imagination. I'm pretty nervous right now."

"But it might not have been," said Seph.

"What about you? See anything?"

"Nothing out of place."

Piper thought for a moment. "How many doors can you see?"

Seph glanced around. She pointed at the boarded-up entrance. "Front door." Then she pointed to the doorway they entered through and the one behind the counter. "Kitchen doors. Restrooms and office," she finished, pointing to the little hallway opposite the main entrance.

Piper nodded. "Me too."

In the past, sometimes Seph hadn't been able to differentiate the things that only she could see from the rest of the world. If she'd pointed out a fifth doorway that Piper couldn't see, she'd have known right away that it was a place they should investigate.

But it wouldn't be that simple this time.

A loud creak from somewhere in the kitchen broke the eerie silence. Piper grabbed at her pendant. Seph held up her hands, the scythe's handle churning between them, ready to defend herself.

But several seconds passed and nothing moved.

"Probably the wind at the back door," reasoned Seph.

Piper nodded. "Yeah. Probably that."

Yet neither of them dared move for another moment, convinced that something was back there, just waiting for them to drop their guard.

Piper's ears twitched. She turned her head and looked at Seph.

"What?"

"You didn't just whisper something, did you?"

"No, I didn't."

Piper frowned and tilted her head to one side, struggling to hear.

"Is something there?"

"I don't know," she replied, frustrated.

Seph turned all the way around, trying see if there was something she was missing, but nothing stood out to her. Again, there was no sense that she was missing something. Everything seemed to be just what she could see with her human eyes and nothing more.

She wished she knew how to activate that super prophet sight like she did in the library. She had a feeling that would reveal even the most stubborn of hidden things.

Piper took a couple steps toward the little hallway, her ears perked straight up. "It's dark back there," she noted. "Scary."

Seph nodded.

"Probably means we're supposed to check it out."

"Probably." And yet, she found that she wasn't moving yet. She had to force herself to follow Piper toward that dark corner of the diner.

Nothing ever happened back here last time. They didn't use the restrooms. Everything happened in the kitchen and the corner of the dining room between the kitchen and the front entrance.

Piper shined her flashlight into the hallway. It was extra dirty back here. There were cobwebs everywhere. Unfazed, she reached out with her hand and swept them clean for Seph, then wiped them absently on the thigh of her leggings as she peered into both restrooms.

They were empty.

Seph turned and looked back the way they came, half-convinced something must be sneaking up behind her. It'd been too quiet for too long. Something terrifying was bound to happen soon. That was just the way things worked.

"What about it?" asked Piper.

Seph turned around, confused. "What about what?"

Piper looked back at her. "The bulletin board." It was mounted on the wall next to the office door. She shined her light onto it, revealing a number of old, dusty pages tacked up with pushpins.

"I didn't say anything about the bulletin board…"

Piper turned and looked around. "Somebody just whispered something about the bulletin board."

Before they could discuss the mysterious, whispering voice any further, a loud bang startled them.

Again, it seemed to come from the kitchen.

They both stood frozen, listening.

"Is something in here with us?" whispered Piper.

Seph desperately hoped it was the wind pushing the broken back door open and closed, but she couldn't quite make herself believe it.

Piper turned her attention back to the bulletin board. "Old Fred," she said, pointing to a big, blurry picture in a newspaper clipping from a decade before.

Seph glanced out into the dining room once more, just to be sure, and then aimed her flashlight at the board, too. "This town is fond of its lake monster." She remembered Marsha speaking so passionately about it when they were here last time, before they found out she was only a monster *pretending* to be Marsha.

Piper shined her light over the other articles. There were some old fliers for local businesses tacked up here, along with some notices for employees. But most of the board was covered with newspaper articles about various oddities related to the nearby lake.

"Fathom Lake…" she whispered. She turned and looked at Seph. "Remember in Muntiny? Archie called it a *sanctuary*. He said it was a remnant from a lost age or something?"

Seph nodded.

"That sounds a lot like Lodblin's library, doesn't it?"

It did. She shined her light over the other articles. *Is This Fathom Lake's Hairy Man? Mysterious Lights Spotted Over Fathom Lake. Who Was*

Fathom Lake's White Ghost? Psychic Claims Lake is Transmitting Messages from the Dead. "Wow…"

"Marsha said something about a hairy man and a white ghost, too, right?" recalled Piper.

The white lady's ghost… She also said they had a werewolf, as if the rest of it wasn't absurd enough. "Don't forget, that *wasn't* Marsha. *Or* Archie."

"That doesn't mean they were lying," Piper countered. "I mean, maybe they knew better than anyone."

That was a good point, actually.

Piper gasped and spun around.

"What's wrong?"

"Someone just whispered in my ear."

Seph stared at her, the hairs on the back of her neck prickling. "What did they say?"

"They said, 'They're coming.'"

"Who's coming?"

On the other side of the dining room, something rattled the front door. Shadows moved behind the boarded windows. From the kitchen came the loud creak of old hinges, followed by the bang of a door slamming against the wall. Then footsteps on tile.

Piper backed away from the dining area and opened the office door. "In here!" she whispered.

Seph didn't hesitate. She stepped inside and backed away from the door as Piper eased it shut behind them.

Something crinkled under her heel. She looked down to find a strange, black paper carpeting half of the floor. She turned, her eyes following it. It'd swallowed the back wall and most of the old desk and computer. A big, gaping hole, like a great, black eye, stared down at her from the old light fixture. The blood drained from her face as her brain finally pieced together what she was looking at.

It was like the sprawling, papery masses that covered the book-shelves in the library.

It was a *nest.*

Huge, black wasps were crawling on it, each one at least six inches long.

She tried to say something, but all that would come out was a long, quiet, pitiful sort of soft screech.

Piper turned around, expecting to find a hairy spider or some other harmless thing, and froze.

One by one, the enormous, black wasps took to the air.

Chapter 45

Most of the time, Seph's fear of bugs was utterly irrational. This wasn't one of those times.

Piper grabbed her hand and yanked her out of the office, slamming the door behind them.

That wouldn't stop them, of course. All they had to do was crawl under the door. There was plenty of room down there. But it might buy them enough time to get back to the truck.

When they ran back out into the dining room, however, they found five fat, naked teethers waiting for them, blocking the exit through the kitchen.

"*Pea*!" squealed Seph.

"I know!" squeaked Piper.

The nasty little monsters were already moving toward them. Each one was armed, though none of them very well. One had a dirty, wooden spoon. Another had a rusty spatula. The third was wielding a dusty coffee pot. The fourth had a fork in one hand and a napkin dispenser in the other. And the fifth was dragging a large sheet pan behind it.

Piper couldn't decide which of the little monsters she'd rather have to take on.

Seph heard the loud buzzing of an approaching wasp behind her. She screamed and darted to the empty corner across the room, forcing

Piper to chase after her.

One after another, the insects flew into the room, fanning out, threatening everything that moved.

"Those aren't normal wasps!" breathed Piper.

"You think?" snapped Seph. Those things were *huge*! They were like *death incarnate*!

The wasps and the teethers were both moving toward them, cornering them.

Then the teether with the spatula swung it at one of the wasps, trying to knock it out of the air. It wasn't a particularly *smart* move. The wasps responded with textbook hive mentality, changing direction and converging on the offending teether instead. The little beast swatted at them again, but quickly flew into a panic as they began to sting it.

The spatula clattered to the floor and the monster fled, screaming its strange, high-pitched screams.

Seph watched in horror as more and more wasps swarmed the little beast. Its screams became more frantic, its arms flailing.

It didn't make it halfway across the room before it collapsed onto the floor, still shrieking.

"Gispuknya wasps," breathed Piper. She could hear them. That familiar buzzing sensation that all of Gispuknya's shadowy things made, distinctly *different* from the *actual* buzzing of these monster wasps' wings. And it was fainter than it was with all the other shadows. She didn't hear it at all before they found the nest. Was that because they were so much smaller than the other things?

Now probably wasn't the time to ponder it.

The rest of the teethers lost interest in them as more and more of Gispuknya's terrible bugs filled the room. They were crawling out of the heating vents now, too. Hundreds of them.

"Your scythe!" squealed Piper.

Seph was trying, but it kept splashing apart before the handle was fully formed. "Come on!" she cried. She glanced around the room, desperate.

That's when she saw her. She was standing in the doorway to the kitchen, the same one they entered through a moment ago, and the same one those monsters dragged them through last time they were here.

A teenage girl with long, black hair and a sad sort of expression on her face.

Seph grabbed Piper's hand and pulled her toward the doorway. "Come on!"

Piper ducked as one of the Gispuknya wasps swooped at her. "I could really use a flyswatter right about now!" she whined. "A really *big* flyswatter!"

The girl smiled a familiar, sad smile and turned and disappeared into the kitchen.

It was the same girl she saw last time she was here, the one who saved them from ending up as two more naked, half-devoured corpses rotting in this bug-infested hellhole.

No one but Seph saw her last time, because she wasn't really here. Not physically.

The girl was a ghost.

She must've been the one who was whispering to Piper, communicating with her through her spirit ears.

Another of the wasps swooped down at her, scattering her thoughts. She screamed and ducked down, shielding her face.

Again, the scythe's handle sprang from her hand and immediately fell apart, splashing onto the filthy tiles at her feet.

What was she doing wrong?

Piper jumped forward and smacked the little beast with a tennis racket, knocking it to the floor where it writhed in the dust, broken.

Seph looked over at her, confused. "Where'd you get that?"

"*I have no idea*!" shrieked Piper. She turned and swatted another one out of the air. "*Just keep going*!"

For the moment, the majority of Gispuknya's swarm was occupied with the teethers, who were too stupid to run away until after the wasps began stinging them. But if the first one to fall was any indication, it wouldn't be long before the entire hive could turn its deadly attention on the two of them.

Piper knocked two more out of the air with her mystery tennis racket.

Another swooped in from the other direction. Seph panicked and lashed out with her hands. This time, the scythe slashed through the air, twisting as it went, as fluid as the water that comprised it, and easily chopped the little monster in two.

Why wouldn't it just do that *all the time*?

They had to get out of here. They couldn't fend these things off for long. Sheer numbers would overpower them in seconds.

They darted through the kitchen door and stumbled to a stop.

"What the hell?" stammered Seph.

The kitchen had suddenly become a freezer. The walls and countertops were frosting over. An icy mist was rising from the floor.

The girl with the long, black hair was standing in the doorway, the brilliant daylight shining behind her.

She cast no shadow on the floor.

"What's going on?" asked Piper. "Why is it suddenly winter?"

She made no indication whatsoever that she even saw the black-haired girl.

As Seph watched, the girl slowly disappeared and another teether ran through the doorway where she was just standing, its mouth wide open, ready to bite her.

Seph screamed and thrust her fists forward. The watery blade shot straight out like a spear, impaling the monster.

Piper yelped and stumbled forward. “Something just pushed me!” she cried, looking behind her.

Seph grabbed her hand. “She’s telling you to move your ass!”

“What? *Who*?”

The wasps were swarming into the kitchen around them, but they drooped as soon as they hit the cold.

Piper stared at them as Seph dragged her toward the door. Did these things act like real bugs? Did the cold make them lethargic? She wouldn’t have thought that Gispuknya’s strange creations worked that way.

Seph ran out the door, gasping at the sudden change of temperature again. “Get in the truck! Hurry!”

But the words were barely out of her mouth when a teether jumped out of the bed of the truck, of all places, and crouched by the driver-side door, blocking her path.

She groaned, frustrated. “I *hate* these little freaks!” she shouted.

She thrust her hands out, hoping to impale the little monster like she did the last one, but only succeeded in hitting it in the face with a great splash of water.

It stood there, blinking back at her, confused.

Seph cursed.

Piper was running around the front of the truck when another teether jumped up onto the vehicle’s roof and threw a rock at her, striking her in the head.

"*Ow*!" She stumbled backward, her hand pressed to the stinging spot on her forehead. Then she spat a very unladylike curse at the little monster and flung the racket at it. She couldn't have said whether it was sheer luck or if it was because the racket was created by the spinning wheel specifically to protect her, but it struck the teether right in its oversized forehead, knocking it back into the bed of the truck with a resounding bang. "That's what you get!" she screamed at it.

She turned around to see three more of the little monsters running toward her from the side of the building. With a startled yelp, she ran to the passenger-side door and jumped into the truck, slamming and locking it behind her.

Seph tried to form the scythe again. Again, it came apart in her hands.

The teether didn't rush her. Instead, it seemed to take a perverse pleasure in realizing that she was having trouble. It made a weird, high-pitched cackling noise at her, then grabbed its swollen belly and lifted it, waggling its filthy genitals at her.

"Oh, *very mature*!" she shouted at it.

Again, it laughed its high-pitched cackle at her.

Frustrated, she thrust her hands out once more, praying it would work. This time, the blade unfolded and cut through the air, the crystal-like blade flashing in the sunlight.

The little beast cackled one more time, but this time it was a half-hearted, confused sort of noise. Then its body broke apart and it fell into the dirt in two different directions.

"*Persephone*!"

She felt something on her arm and turned, the scythe raised and ready to reap another disgusting teether before it, too, decided to flash its junk at her.

But it wasn't a teether.

A sharp, searing pain shot through her arm where the Gispuknya wasp landed. She screamed and slapped at it, mangling it and knocking it to the ground. Almost immediately, she felt another bolt of pain on the back of her shoulder and she screamed again.

"*Get in the truck*!" shrieked Piper, opening the door.

Seph slapped at the buzzing monsters, but they kept coming. One stung her on the back of her wrist. Another stung her left arm, just beneath her elbow. Then again on the back of her shoulder.

"*Hurry*!"

Terror gripped her. She stumbled toward the truck, still screaming. That searing pain tore through her back again and again. Then the back of her thigh. Then the back of her *head*.

Something pierced her right through the seat of her leggings.

Were these things going to kill her? Was this how she was going to die? Needles of white-hot agony stabbed the back of her neck. Her thigh again. The top of her head. Her left ear. Her back felt like it was on fire! It hurt so much! She couldn't stand it!

Piper grabbed her arm and pulled her into the cab. Three of the giant wasps were clinging to her back. She thrust her arm out and hosed them off with a can of hornet spray that had suddenly appeared in her hand.

She didn't question it. It didn't matter. All that mattered was saving Seph.

The giant insects curled up and tumbled to the ground, where they lay twitching in agony. Several more dropped right out of the air. Still others changed course and veered away, flying rather drunkenly.

But she didn't have time to admire the effectiveness of Rumpelstiltskin's personal recipe for insect repellant. She tossed the mysterious can into the floorboard, then yanked the door shut and locked it. "*Persephone*!"

"*It hurts*!" she sobbed.

The teether in the back of the truck began banging on the back window. Another was trying to open the passenger-side door. Three more were already writhing on the ground, under attack by the growing swarm of angry Gispuknya wasps.

"We've got to get out of here!" gasped Piper. She climbed over Seph, squeezed in behind the wheel and quickly started the engine.

The teether in the bed began to shriek as the swarm enveloped it. It thrashed around for a few seconds, then threw itself over the side and onto the ground, where it writhed in agony beneath a crawling, black blanket of stinging death.

Piper slammed the truck into gear and sped away. "How bad is it?" she asked as they bounced over the ditch and onto the dusty road.

But Seph couldn't answer her. She didn't even hear the question. It felt like she was dying. Her body was on *fire*. She was *burning*. She'd never felt so much pain before. She cried out, her voice shrill, desperate. Tears streamed down her face.

Piper's heart was racing. Icy panic was welling up inside her, threatening to overflow. "Oh gosh…" she gasped. She, too, was beginning to cry. She didn't know what to do. "Oh my gosh… Oh no… Please be okay… *Please*…"

The danger was behind them again, but Seph's screams on that quiet stretch of South Dakota highway were terrible.

Chapter 46

Piper had no idea what to do. She drove until well after the last of the horrors of Pappy Stan's Diner were gone from her rearview, not daring to give anything a chance to catch up. But that was only half the trouble at the moment.

Seph was in terrible pain.

She probably needed a hospital, but that wasn't an option. Tane's and Gispuknya's monsters would eventually find them again. She had no doubt about that. And when it happened, they couldn't be caught in an emergency room. They needed to be able to run. Better yet, they needed to find the lock and be long gone from this whole, awful town before then.

But they weren't getting *anywhere* if Seph couldn't even *walk*.

She found a stretch of road where the terrain was flat and open for a good ways in every direction and pulled off onto the shoulder. From here, she should be able to see if something unpleasant was approaching while she checked on Seph's injuries.

The first aid kit was well stocked. It had bandages and antiseptic wipes and, best of all, insect sting ointment. "Let me see," she said, taking Seph's left arm and turning it so she could examine it. She gasped. On the back of her wrist was a bright red, swollen knot with an oozing puncture wound at the center. "Oh gosh…" She sat up and glanced around, making sure they were still alone, and then went to work treating the injury, unsure if she could even make a difference.

Seph moaned. The pain numbed her mind. She couldn't think clearly. She was vaguely aware that Piper was trying to help her, but everything was so foggy. The only thing that was clear to her was the searing, all-encompassing pain.

Piper removed Seph's jacket and then her shirt. There was another swollen puncture wound just below her elbow. One on her upper right arm and two on her chest, one just above her left breast and one a few inches below it that had gone right through the cup of her bra.

The top half of her left ear was badly swollen. The two earrings she was wearing there looked painful, but she couldn't get them off without Seph crying out in pain, so she left them.

Then she turned her around and looked at her back.

Again, she gasped. She counted *fourteen* stings. Plus another one right on the back of her neck. She remembered the three wasps that had landed on her back, stinging her right through her shirt and jacket. "Oh gosh… Okay… Just… Just relax. I've got you."

She wiped away another tear and opened another package of insect sting ointment. She hoped there was enough.

Please be okay… Please…

She looked out every window. They were still alone.

Please…

Was the ointment even doing anything? Was it easing the pain even a little? It was impossible to tell. Seph was still sobbing too hard to tell her.

She finished treating the multitude of stings on her back and then tugged down her leggings. "Sorry, Persephone. I just need to be sure." She found two more painful stings on her butt and three more on the back and side of her left thigh.

Did she miss any? The seat of an old pickup truck wasn't exactly the best place for a thorough examination. She counted nearly *thirty* stings, and she was sure she could've easily missed a few.

She pulled Seph's leggings back up and helped her back into her shirt, then ran her hands over her head, where she found two more swollen knots hidden under her hair.

She managed to give her some acetaminophen and an antihistamine, which she downed with her Coke, but would it be enough? Her ear was still swelling. It looked positively *frightful.* Should she have tried harder to get those earrings out? She wasn't sure what was the right thing to do!

How powerful was the venom? What if she had an allergic reaction? What if she went into anaphylactic shock? There was nothing in the first aid kit for that!

She was growing more terrified by the second. She felt like she was about to hyperventilate. She needed to calm down.

"They're coming," whispered a voice in her ear.

She cried out, startled, and looked around. "Who's there?"

"Hurry."

She clapped her hands over her ears. "*Who are you*?"

"To the lake."

What was going on? Who was speaking to her? Was this another of Tane's wicked tricks? Was he inside her head now?

"They're coming," the voice said again.

She looked out the window and saw small shapes moving toward her from the hill in the distance. They were little more than shadows, but she found that she knew them as soon as she saw them. She could hear them, that eerie, familiar buzzing sensation in her spirit ears.

Black-eyed children.

She turned and looked in the other direction. They were there, too, closing in from both sides.

Dozens of them.

Maybe *hundreds.*

Quickly, she shifted the truck into gear and sped on down the road, kicking up gravel from the shoulder.

Beside her, Seph groaned and struggled to sit up.

"How're you doing?" asked Piper.

"Hurts like hell…" It took everything she had just to think through the pain. "Ow…" Her ear was throbbing. Her back still felt like it was on fire. And her butt and thigh hurt when she tried to sit up. But something was wrong. She could sense it. Were they running from the bugs again? Please don't let there be more bugs…

She looked up and saw the girl from the diner standing beside the road ahead of them. She was pointing at a wooden sign. "Fathom Lake…" she read.

"I see it," said Piper. The voice a moment ago said something about the lake. Was that where she was supposed to go? She slowed down and turned off onto the next road.

"It was her," Seph grunted.

She glanced over at her. "Her who?"

"The girl from the diner. The one who helped us last time."

She frowned. "You mean the ghost girl?"

Seph nodded. "Saw her back there." Three times now, actually. Twice in the diner and once just now beside that sign. But she didn't feel well enough to explain it. "Helped us." She clenched her teeth and lowered her head. "Ow, ow, ow, *ow*!" Why did it have to hurt so much? It was so hard to focus. Her thoughts were scattered. She couldn't concentrate on anything.

Stupid bugs!

Piper considered this. She never saw the girl at the diner. From her perspective, there was no one there that day except the two of them and the three monsters. (Except for all those dead bodies, of course.) Only Seph had ever been able to see her, which wasn't that strange when you remembered that seeing things no one else could see was what Seph did.

But Seph told her that the girl was silent. She never spoke a word, even when Seph realized what she was and begged her for help.

Hearing things that others couldn't hear was *Piper's* thing. Was it possible that only Seph could see the girl in the diner and only Piper could *hear* her? Was that what was going on? Was the girl from the diner the voice that kept whispering to her?

"Left," whispered the mystery voice.

Piper jumped and let out a startled, "Eep!" She was too on edge for this sort of thing. But she obeyed the mysterious voice and turned left onto a narrow stretch of patchy blacktop.

She couldn't see those black-eyed children anymore, but they were still there. Or, at least, *something* was still there. She could still hear that faint buzzing noise Gispuknya's shadows made.

About a mile and a half past that, the disembodied voice of her ghostly navigator told her to go right and she turned onto a gravel road. Three quarters of a mile after that, the voice informed her to turn left again when the road forked.

She glanced over at Seph, who was bent forward, her head hanging between her knees, silent. "Still with me?"

"Uh huh."

"How're you feeling?"

"Delightful. I just love being *stabbed* multiple times by giant, disgusting *bugs* with *butt swords*."

Piper returned her attention to the road. "Yeah, you'll be fine."

Seph groaned. "Why does it hurt so much?"

Having seen the size of the puncture wounds those nasty Gispuknya wasps left, she could only imagine that those stings must be *agonizing*. Personally, she thought Seph's pain tolerance must be considerably higher than her own. The bellyache she experienced inside the library seemed like such a small thing compared to all those stings.

"I feel really queasy…"

"We'll be there soon," Piper assured her.

Seph groaned.

Another mile passed. Piper was just beginning to wonder if the ghostly voice had led her astray when she crested a hill and was finally awarded her first look at Fathom Lake.

It wasn't very impressive. It lay in a small depression, surrounded by a ring of trees and brush, maybe half a mile across at its widest.

The gravel road ended at an old, wooden boat dock that reached out into the water. An old, green jon boat was tied to it.

Piper killed the engine and stared out across the lake.

This was Fathom Lake? It looked more like a pond to her.

This body of water was supposed to be an ancient place, far older than all the other lakes, and hiding a vast ocean somewhere beneath its still surface, perhaps even an entire universe. None of this made any sense, of course. How could this lake be older than all the others? It was a natural lake, certainly older than anything man-made, but weren't most lakes just…there? A part of the earth, itself?

Thinking about it now, though, she supposed the landscape was always changing. Floods, earthquakes, volcanic eruptions, even meteor impacts could all reshape the land, giving birth to new lakes, not to mention natural erosion of the earth. But did that mean that *this* one little lake had been here since the beginning, exactly like this, unchanged for hundreds of millions of years?

Or was that all just local superstition?

Then again…if the Keeper really did hide another gateway here, it probably *did* mean that it hadn't changed since the beginning of the universe. And if there was another library hidden down there, it definitely explained the legends about a secret ocean.

Seph sat up and blinked out at the lake. "We here?"

"I think so."

She nodded. Was the pain medicine finally starting to work? Or was she just getting used to the pain? It was difficult to tell for sure. It was difficult to be sure of *anything*. Everything felt so fuzzy….

Piper jumped at the ghostly voice in her ear again. "Okay!" she snapped.

Seph turned and stared at her. "What?"

She rubbed at her ear, wincing at the weird feel of that disembodied voice. Was she only imagining that she could feel a cold breath on her skin? "The creepy ghost voice says to get in the boat."

She squinted at her as if she'd just…well…told her she was hearing voices. Then she bent forward and groaned again. "Whatever. Let's just get it over with."

Chapter 47

Piper filled her jacket pockets with all the jerky and beef sticks she could carry. After what happened inside the library, she wasn't taking any chances in *that* department. Then she added two flashlights and an entire package of spare batteries to her already bulging pockets, because getting caught blind and defenseless in the dark was *also* something she'd rather not risk happening again. Then she removed anything she thought they could do without from the zippered bag and left it in the truck seat. She stashed their purses under the seat, out of sight, and then stuffed the rest of the snacks Seph bought her into the bag. She zipped it, slung the strap over her shoulder and jumped out of the truck.

She regretted leaving their phones, but hers had only barely begun to charge and Seph's was still stone dead. They'd be useless to them.

And they didn't have time to wait around. That buzzing noise was already growing louder.

The old boat didn't look in great shape, but it floated. She dropped the bag into it, and then helped Seph out of the truck and on-to one of the seats. Immediately, she slumped forward and clutched at the side of the boat, dizzy, and her glasses slipped off her face.

Piper grabbed them before they could fall and started to put them back on, but decided to zip them safely in her jacket pocket instead.

"I'll take care of these for now, okay?" The last thing they needed was for Seph to lose her glasses at the bottom of this stupid lake and end up blind for the rest of the trip.

Finally, she stepped into the boat, untied it and began fumbling with the old trolling motor.

"Do you even know how to work that thing?" grumbled Seph as she struggled to find a way to sit in the stupid little boat that didn't hurt. The stings on her butt were making it difficult.

"How hard can it be? I just tug on the rope thingy, right?" She looked at one side and then the other. "Where's the little rope thingy? I've seen them do it on TV."

Seph groaned. "We're gonna die out here. I know it."

Piper slapped at her ear and yelped. "Stop doing that!"

She looked up, confused. "What?"

"Not you…" She bent over the motor. "What wire? Where?"

Seph squinted at her. "What's wrong with you?"

"You can't just say, 'Right there,' if I can't see where you're pointing!"

She rubbed her eyes. She couldn't seem to clear her vision. Everything was doubled. When she looked up again, the girl from the diner was standing in the boat in front of her, smiling her sad smile.

The rest of the world was blurry without her glasses, but the girl was perfectly clear, even to her nearsighted eyes. She blinked hard, confused, and when she looked up again, the girl was gone.

That was weird…

"You mean this?" asked Piper. "What? Like this?"

Seph squeezed her eyes closed. Something wasn't right. She was sure of it.

The motor started and Piper sat down, pleased with herself.

"There we go."

"The girl from the diner…" said Seph, pointing at the empty space between them where the girl stood just a moment ago.

"She says her name's Maria."

She stared at her. The diner ghost's name was Maria? She turned and looked around at the silent lake. "She can take us to the gate?"

Piper shrugged. "I guess so. I mean, she's taking us *somewhere*."

Seph couldn't handle this. Those stings hurt so bad she couldn't focus on such complicated revelations. "Fine," she said, closing her eyes. She felt dizzy again. The motion of the boat on the water was nauseating.

"She just said to take the boat out to the middle of the lake."

She turned and squinted across the surface of the water. "So…to some kind of hidden island or something?"

Piper shrugged again. "She didn't say."

"Let's just get out there and get it over with." She shifted her weight and winced. "Ouch…"

"Any better?" worried Piper.

Seph glanced up at her. "A little…I think…" It was only partially a lie. She *did* think the pain had eased a little. (Although it still hurt like hell.) But she didn't feel very good at all. Her heart was pounding. Her vision was doubled. Her body felt heavy. And she felt like she might throw up soon.

She was beginning to fear that those Gispuknya wasps were more venomous than she first anticipated. But she couldn't let Piper worry about such things when there was nothing she could do about it.

It didn't take long to reach the middle of the lake, but having reached it, they found that nothing was here. It wasn't even very deep. Piper thought she could almost touch the bottom, even way out here.

She turned and looked around. "Now what?" she asked.

But the voice didn't come to her this time.

She pushed her mouth to one side and puckered her lips. "Maria?"

Seph lifted her head and looked out across the lake again. But her eyes wouldn't focus. The world was spinning. She had to grip the side of the boat to steady herself.

Piper turned and looked the other way. "Maria?"

Where'd she go?

Seph tugged at the collar of her jacket. It was so hot. And why was it so hard to breathe?

"I don't get it…" said Piper. "I came to the middle of the lake, like she said. Where's the gate?" She turned and looked the other way. "Oh! Is that her?" She shielded her eyes and squinted. There was a woman over there, near the shore, looking back at them. But she couldn't tell what she looked like. She was just a shadow from this distance.

"Pea…" whispered Seph. "I don't…"

Piper barely heard her. She leaned forward. There was something off about that woman. Why did she look so shadowy? She was standing in the sunshine. Was she dressed all in black?

Then the woman sank straight down in the water and Piper felt her heart stutter in her chest.

"Oh no…" she squeaked. "Not *her*…"

It was the marsh woman. The Gispuknya ghoul who attacked them in that marsh last July. The one who hijacked the Keeper's undead guardians and unleashed a mini zombie apocalypse on them. The one who would've succeeded in dragging them into the stinking, muddy water to rot if not for Corey and Violet.

Something in the water was moving toward them, creating a wake on the calm surface. It was just a little disturbance at first, but it was rapidly growing larger.

Serpent-like tendrils of water rose up on either side of the wake, glistening in the sunshine.

She was back to finish what she started last July.

And Piper had no idea how they were going to escape her this time.

"…don't…feel so…" Seph felt the world spin out of control. Her hand slipped. She tipped over.

Piper looked back in time to see her tumble out of the boat and into the water. "*Persephone!*"

She didn't hesitate. She dived into the water after her.

It was cold. *Much* colder than she expected it to be, but she barely noticed. She focused on the blurry shape sinking before her. She had to get her back into the boat and off this lake before the marsh woman caught up to them.

Never in her life had she ever been so thankful for her good swimming skills.

Down and down she went, reaching…reaching…

She could feel the pressure of the water on her ears.

How far down could she go? It was only six or seven feet deep here at most. Wasn't it…?

Somewhere in the eerie, underwater silence, she heard the buzzing of Gispuknya's shadows. Time was running out. The marsh woman was closing in.

Then the weeds parted around them, revealing a deep, dark hole lined with smooth, black stone. It was as if they were slowly descending into a bottomless, black well, like Alice tumbling down the rabbit hole on her way to Wonderland.

Finally, she closed her hand around Seph's and tried to swim back up. But instead of pulling her up, she found herself being pulled down.

What was going on?

Why was it getting so dark?

She was running out of breath!

And something was coming. She could feel it bearing down on her. A large, *dark* presence loomed in the murky depths above them.

The buzzing in her spirit ears was almost deafening.

She looked up and saw her there, an ominous, black shadow silhouetted against the circle of sunlight at the top of the well, with long, flowing hair floating in the gloom.

She opened her mouth to scream…and then everything went dark.

Chapter 48

The next thing she knew, she was lying on a rough floor, dripping wet, coughing up lake water and enveloped in a cold, eerie darkness.

She could hear Seph next to her, gagging and choking and gasping for breath.

"Persephone?" she coughed. "Are you okay?"

"What happened?"

Piper had no idea. She sat up and brushed her dripping hair out of her face. She couldn't see anything—it was utterly dark—but it had an unusual smell to it, a subtle, rotting stench mixed with a strange bouquet of odors she couldn't identify. Earthy, yet sweet, but at the same time bitter and acrid. And the air felt thinner in this place. It was harder to catch her breath. And it was so cold. She was shivering. "Where are we?"

The marsh woman had vanished, along with the entire lake, it seemed. One second they were rapidly sinking into the impossible depths and the next second they were here.

She took the flashlight from her pocket and stood up, shining it into the darkness as her jaw trembled in the cold. They were in a spacious room that might've been a luxurious space once upon a long-forgotten time. But now the walls were crumbling with age. The ceiling was sagging in some places and completely collapsed onto the floor in others. Strange, low-to-the-ground furniture was arranged around the room, all of it ancient and moldy and collapsing in on itself. There were also large, rotten, long-deflated pillows. Or maybe they were cushions…or some sort of old beanbag chairs? Several portraits hung in heavy frames on the walls and several more lay broken on the floor below where they once hung, all of them so old and faded that the people in them were little more than featureless silhouettes, as if even the memory of these people had turned to ghosts.

Every surface of the room was mottled with strange patterns of a thick, gray mold.

Was this a house? Someone's home?

"They called it Covengale."

She turned, startled, to find a teenage girl with long, black hair standing behind her, staring at the decay that surrounded them.

"It was a beautiful, sprawling estate once. But terrible things happened here…and those things are still echoing through these walls today…"

"You…" sniffed Seph as she sat hugging herself against the cold. "You're her…"

"Maria?" asked Piper. She'd never seen this girl before, but she recognized her voice. She'd been talking to her since she entered the diner. "How…?"

The girl smiled that sad smile and looked down at her hands. "This universe was overflowing with spiritual energy. It fills me. Makes me stronger. I can…almost be real here…"

"So you *are* a ghost…" whispered Piper.

Maria met her gaze. "I am."

She might've felt a chill, but it was difficult to tell through the physical shivering.

Why did it have to be so cold here?

"How? What happened to you?"

"It's a very long story. The short version is that I...messed things up. In a really bad way." She stared off into the darkness, distracted. "I did something really bad. And I died. I should've gone to hell..." She blinked and turned her gaze back to Piper. "But then *he* found me. The Keeper of the Dead. He made me an offer. A chance to make up for what I'd done and avoid going to hell."

Keeper of the Dead... thought Piper. The Keeper of *lots of things...* She felt a shiver race through her as she wondered again just what the Keeper really was. Was he an angel? A *god?* "So he asked you to replace Stan and Marsha as our guide when they were killed by those monsters?"

Maria tilted her head to one side, as if that were the silliest thing she'd ever heard. "No. They were never your guides. They were just messengers. Their job was only to show you the fringe road and send you to the first vault."

"Oh..." said Piper, confused. "But Sandy said..." She frowned. What *did* Sandy say? Now that she was thinking about it...did she ever actually *say* that Stan and Marsha were the custodians? It was hard to remember clearly while her teeth were chattering so hard, but thinking about it, she was pretty sure that what Sandy actually said was that at the diner they'd "find the custodian long dead."

And...she supposed they did.

They'd just *assumed* she was talking about Stan and Marsha.

"*I'm* the custodian of Fathom Lake," said Maria. "I always have been. I only haunted that diner because I knew you'd pass through there on your way to the first Hand. And that you'd eventually go there to look for me."

Piper stared at her, surprised. "Huh," was all she could think to say. It was too cold to think very hard, after all. She rubbed her hands together. She hoped she didn't catch cold down here in this frigid place.

Seph rubbed at her eyes. Between the cold and the pain, she couldn't think clearly enough to even follow what was being said. But the pain *did* seem to be easing a little. She'd stopped sobbing uncontrollably, at least. Maybe the medicine Piper gave her was finally kicking in. But her thoughts were still so cloudy. She felt so sleepy…

She looked up and blinked. "Where're my glasses…?"

"I have them," Piper assured her. She took them from her pocket and handed them to her.

Seph squinted up at her as she took them back. She was little more than a blurry, blonde shape in the gloom. In contrast, the girl she called Maria was perfectly clear. She could make out every detail of her young face. "Okay…" was all she could manage to say. She slipped them back onto her face and looked down at the throbbing sting on the back of her wrist.

Why did they have to hurt so much?

"So the Keeper's gate was at the bottom of the lake," realized Piper. She remembered that deep, black well she swam into trying to save Seph. Not unlike the black tunnel leading to the gate under the Waybel Valley water tower. Only…*vertical.*

Maria gave her that same, sad smile. "That's right."

"So this is where the lock is."

She nodded. "Somewhere inside the rotting walls of Covengale, along with all its other terrible secrets."

"So is there another monster in this place?" She shined her light around the room again, nervous. "Like there was in the library?"

"No monsters, I don't think," replied Maria. "Although we *are* standing at the final moments of this world. Outside these walls is eminent doom. It's the ultimate finality out there, and all the horrors that come with it."

Piper recalled Ian telling them something about the end of the universe last July, something about how evil grew stronger as the worlds died. "Horrors like that tree that stole my sweater?"

Another sad smile touched her pale lips. "The night trees of the Wood… Deadly when not hibernating. You don't want to expose one to light for too long. Even a little flashlight like that one."

Piper shivered again. "There's a whole forest of those things?"

"Not just a forest. The Wood is practically a universe unto itself. It goes on almost forever. It's swallowed countless worlds. The ruins of entire cities can be found in that forest, some of them older than you can ever imagine. And there're few fates more unpleasant than death in the Wood, because those who die out there never leave it. *Not ever.* It's eternity. Endless, hopeless suffering."

"Don't leave the house," said Piper. "Got it." She pinched her lip and stared down at the floor for a moment as what she said sank in. She recalled Seph dangling from that open portal in Nora's Lilac Grove…the one Amethyst told them opened over the Wood. Suddenly, she remembered the panic in her voice when she pulled Seph to safety.

"That was too close…" she'd gasped. And it *was.* It was terrifying. But Seph had assured her it was okay. "No," Amethyst had said. "It's *not* okay. If you'd fallen…"

She never finished that sentence and Piper had never thought more about it. She'd assumed that it was something like, "If you'd fallen, I never would've forgiven myself," but if this ghost girl was telling the truth, then if she'd fallen…

Those who die out there never leave it. Not ever. *It's eternity. Endless, hope-*

less suffering.

She looked over at Seph, horrified.

"But it's not safe inside, either," warned Maria. "We're not alone. This place is one of the most haunted places that ever existed, in *any* universe. I can feel it. The energy isn't just strong, it's *alive.* And it's *aware.* You're going to have to be *very* careful here."

"Any idea what we're looking for, at least?" pressed Piper. "Is it another book?"

"I don't know that, either. I'm sorry. I only know that you'll know it when you find it." She turned and looked at the doorway leading deeper into Covengale's mysterious depths. "Unfortunately, I can't help you explore. If I leave this room, I'll run the risk of being absorbed into these walls with the other spirits in this house. I'll have to wait for you here or none of us may ever leave."

Piper made another of her high-pitched whining noises in her throat.

Like in the boat, Seph slumped over and passed out.

"Persephone!" Piper knelt over her, worried. "Will she be okay? She was stung a *lot*…" She brushed her hair out of her face and frowned. "She has a fever."

Maria bent over them, her dark eyes washing over Seph. "She's ill. Gispuknya wasp venom is very toxic. Given how many times she was stung, I'm surprised her heart hasn't stopped."

Piper looked up, terrified.

"I'm guessing her Hand is protecting her."

Her eyes lit up. "It can do that?"

"The Hands are very protective of their chosen owners. They can protect against many dangers."

"Oh, thank goodness…" she sighed.

"But that'll come with a trade-off. If the Hand is using a portion of its power to help her fight off the venom, then it can't fully protect her from the effects of the time shift inside these walls. She'll probably suffer some effects from it." She stood up straight again and turned her gaze back to Piper. "I doubt if she'll be a lot of help to you in here, but if it's allowed to run its course, I'm sure she'll be fine."

Piper took her hand and squeezed it. She wanted so badly to help, but she didn't know what to do. She packed the first aid kit, but she left it in the boat when she dived in after Seph. She never expected to get sucked through the Keeper's gate without a chance to grab it.

It was a good thing she thought to stuff the flashlights and batteries into her pockets with those snacks.

She took a deep breath and closed her eyes. There was no other choice. Seph was in no condition to face whatever lurked in this new nightmare. She was on her own. And she had no idea how she was going to do it.

"Any suggestion where I should start, at least?"

But when she looked up again, Maria was gone.

The two of them were alone.

"Of course not…" she sighed.

Chapter 49

Some time passed before Piper was able to gather the nerve to get up off the floor and even explore the room they were in. She wasn't entirely sure *how much* time passed. Her watch wasn't working. Here, inside one of the Keeper's ridiculous science projects, it could've been just a minute or two or it could've been hours.

Was she feeling the first twinges of a missed meal, or was it only her nerves? It was hard to tell, especially since she had no idea how far her internal schedule might've been thrown off by the twisted flow of time in the library.

She decided to give it a little longer, just to be safe. Surely she wouldn't be here long enough to run out of rations, but she wasn't going to take any chances.

Slowly, she circled the room, shining her light at every surface, taking it all in. There were windows all along one wall. The world outside was just as black and empty as the one beyond the walls of Lodblin's library. They appeared to be on the second floor, overlooking a dead lawn. More of those strange, twisted trees loomed in the darkness, just at the limit of her flashlight's reach. A pair of grimy glass doors led out onto a sagging death-trap of a balcony.

The only other way out of the room was on the opposite side, where a second pair of doors—wooden instead of glass, splintered and cracked and covered in that foul, gray mold—stood open and sagging, one of them barely clinging to its hinges, with an unsettling darkness waiting beyond them.

Her heart thumping, her teeth still chattering from the cold, she walked across the room toward this doorway. Along the way, she shined her light on the wall, where a strange, shiny disk was mounted. Some sort of art? Some style of sculpture that was popular at the end of this particular universe? It was silver—or some material resembling silver, anyway—with five small, black balls mounted to its front on short, metal rods.

If Seph were feeling better, maybe she could make something of it. Probably not, seeing as how it was a product of a civilization neither of them had any way of even beginning to understand, but one never knew. Seph had a great eye for art in her own world. Maybe that was something that never changed.

She continued on to the open doors and shined her light out into a long, debris-strewn hallway. The floor was warped. The ceiling had fallen onto it in places. The walls were cracked and peeling. More of that oppressive darkness waited at the far end of the corridor and behind every door, concealing any number of unimaginable horrors for her to walk into.

"Sure," she muttered. "It's only one of the most haunted places in the history of *forever.* Just send the girl who can't even get through a *commercial* for a horror movie without hiding her eyes. What could possibly go wrong?"

It was only fair, she supposed. Poor Seph had to face that library monster all by herself because of her stupid condition. And then there was that minor little matter of her turning into a yellow-eyed monster and *trying to eat her*!

Hugh said she was part Ahn. Could that really be true? And if it was, what manner of creature *were* the Ahns, anyway?

She wished Annalisa were here. She had some questions she was dying to ask her.

She turned and looked back at Seph. She was sleeping for the moment. It was a fitful sleep, but it was probably good for her.

Was it really okay to leave her there? Maria was here. She talked like this was a safe place, at least for her. And she'd only be gone a minute or two. She was just going to take a little look around. Not too far. Just enough to get a feel for the layout. Enough to formulate a plan, to see if her spirit ears could tell her anything, maybe give her a place to start. (As if it would ever be that easy.) Then she'd come right back to check on Seph. She could do this.

She stepped through the doorway and winced as the floorboards creaked beneath her toe. To her own ears in this silence, it sounded at least as loud as an air horn, as if she might as well start jumping up and down and shouting to every horrible thing that might be lurking out there to come and get her.

She took a deep breath, trying to steady her frantic nerves and ease her pounding heart.

She could do this. She'd faced much worse things than a bunch of *ghosts.* Could this really be any worse than the Avelby Marsh? How many times did she think she was going to die that night?

She took another step into the hallway, forcing herself to ignore those screaming floorboards, and shined her light around.

Yes. She had this. It was just a little survey mission.

She wasn't afraid.

She was strong.

Something somewhere crashed to the floor. It wasn't even a loud crash. It was almost certainly the sound of another piece of the crumbling ceiling dropping to the floor. But it was enough to wrench a terrified scream from her and send her darting back to Seph's side.

Okay…so maybe she wasn't that strong. She was absolutely *terrified.* She needed Seph for this! She couldn't do it on her own! She choked back a sob and forced herself to breathe.

"Wow," said Maria. "*You're* the seekers I've been waiting for all this time?"

"Oh, shut up!" snapped Piper, sniffling. "If you're not going to help, just…just stay quiet!"

Maria said no more. The room was silent except for the soft sounds of her weeping.

She had to pull herself together. This was no time to be Crybaby Piper. She wiped at her eyes and fought back the tears.

She could do this. She just…needed a minute… That was all.

Maybe a *few* minutes…

She shivered and rubbed her arms. At least she could be thankful that the clothes she found in the truck were quick-drying. She'd have been twice as miserable in her skinny jeans and sweater. If she survived this, she'd have to find out who packed that bag so she could thank them properly.

More time passed. She had no idea if it was minutes or hours or even days. It was hard to be sure. At times, she felt strangely as if she'd been sitting there a long, long time, staring off into the darkness, trying to gather her strength.

After a while, she realized that the thing on the wall was a clock. Those little black balls had changed position. They were moving left and right, like hands. But she couldn't make any sense of it. If it was anything like her watch, it wouldn't work correctly in the twisted time-flow of the Keeper's compendium. And even if it *did*, she had no way of knowing how it was *supposed* to work.

What would a clock in a different universe look like? Would the days still have been divided into hours? Would the days have been the same length? Thinking about it now, there was no reason to think that any measurement of time in any two universes would be the same.

Additionally, the mechanics of any timepiece might have to be drastically different. Hugh told them that even the fundamental laws of nature could change from universe to universe. The basic properties on which the clocks of her universe functioned might not even work here.

It was all so confusing!

She closed her eyes and took another deep breath. The air was so thin. The smell of this place was so strange. She didn't like any of it. It all felt so *wrong*.

And why shouldn't it feel wrong? She might as well be on an alien planet. This wasn't her world.

She took a bite of a meat stick. She couldn't remember opening it. She remembered feeling as if she needed one, as if she were dangerously close to getting sick again, and then she was chewing it. She looked down at it. "Ugh… I'm *pathetic*."

"Kind of, yeah," said Maria.

Piper rolled her eyes. "Thanks."

"You know you're going to have to go out there eventually."

"I know." She looked down at Seph. She wished she'd wake up. She needed her. She wasn't brave like she was. She couldn't do this on her own.

"I may be dead," said Maria, "but even I know you're braver than this. I mean, come on. How can you be scared of a few ghosts after everything you've seen? The monsters that pretended to be Stan and his family? Those ugly things with the huge teeth? Gispuknya wasps and that creepy woman in the lake? There's no way a bunch of dead people are worse than those swamp zombies."

"I know..." Piper took another bite of her meat stick, then scrunched her face up, confused. "Wait...how did you know about the swamp zombies?" She turned to look at her, but there was no one there.

She went back to chewing. Had Maria been following them around since the day she saved them from the fake Pappy Stan family?

Who *was* she, anyway?

She finished her meat stick and dropped the wrapper on the floor. She didn't like to litter, but what did it really matter in this place? It was already a dump.

She stood up, feeling a little better.

She sighed and looked down at Seph. "You'll stay with her, right?"

"I don't really have a choice," replied Maria. "I'm kind of stuck in this room. But with or without me, she should be safe as long as she stays here. The gate keeps the spirits in check."

Piper nodded. Okay then. She stared at Seph for a moment longer, then turned and looked at the doorway. "I'll be back in a minute," she said. She walked out into the hallway and shined her light around again.

She could do this.

It was only ghosts. Ghosts were only dead people. How scary could they possibly be?

Then a blood-curdling scream echoed through Covengale's silent halls and Piper had to lean against the wall to keep her trembling legs from giving out from under her.

Chapter 50

This was *not* Piper's idea of a good time.

She couldn't even stand the idea of those stupid haunted house attractions they had around Halloween. Dark passageways. People in silly, rubber masks jumping out and screaming at her. She'd certainly never had any desire whatsoever to enter a *real* haunted house. She didn't care if she never had the chance to hear real disembodied voices or footsteps. She'd had friends who were into that sort of stuff. They sought out haunted tours of abandoned hospitals and prisons. They went on those silly ghost hunts every fall. But she would've been perfectly happy to never experience a real, paranormal phenomenon in her lifetime.

And *this* place was inventing whole new levels of freaky!

She peered into each room with her flashlight as she made her way down the hallway, looking for anything that might be a Tartarus lock. (As if she had any idea what one might look like.) She was especially on the lookout for bookshelves, since Seph told her the last one turned out to be a book. (Though she still didn't understand any of what she told her about that little man pushing whatever she read in the book into the dream part of her brain...) Unfortunately, she didn't see any books of any kind in this place. She saw a number of strange, blocky devices mounted to pipes protruding from the walls, and a number of odd, metal bars that looked a little like ladders, except that they were mounted sideways on the walls. She found strange, ceramic basins set directly into the floor. She found large, black slabs of various sizes of something that looked like a strange merging of marble and iron protruding from the walls. She saw curious glass balls, vertical, multi-colored glass tubes and empty, rusted boxes with no apparent purpose. She saw *lots* more of that low furniture, chairs, tables, beds, all of them without legs, sitting directly on the floor, most of them collapsing under their own weight.

Was this universe even older than the library? Everything here was much less familiar and far more deteriorated. Of course, the building's horrid condition could just have been that it was already old and rotting when the Keeper snatched it away in its universe's final hours.

Either way, the place was a hole.

With each step she took, the air seemed to grow thinner and colder. The strange, alien smells that accosted her nose when she first arrived in this house were joined by other, equally alien smells. Something flowery and sweet. Something strong and metallic. Something sour and at the same time earthy. One was *almost* familiar, but not, like something half-remembered from a dream. Another reminded her a little bit of someone's perfume, but she couldn't quite recall whose. Each of these things took turns wafting through the chilly, suffocating air, then vanishing again.

And then there were the sounds… They came only occasionally, and then only faintly, so that she had trouble distinguishing them from the sounds of her own footfalls in the scattered debris. But they were there. Sighs. Sobs. Gasps. Faint whispers in a forgotten language that made her stop and listen, only for them to suddenly fall silent again.

Try as she might, she couldn't quite determine whether she heard these sounds with her human ears or with her spirit ears, but she was quite sure she wasn't imagining them.

She wanted so desperately to tell herself that none of it was real, that it was all in her head, that she didn't believe in ghosts…but it was a ghost who brought her here!

Her hand was shaking so badly she could barely aim the flashlight straight. This place was terrifying. It wasn't even a house. It was more like a hotel. There were hallways branching off in every direction, each one more dangerously deteriorated than the last. Some were so littered with debris from the collapsing ceiling that they were nearly impossible to walk through. Others were so completely overgrown with that gross, gray mold that she didn't dare go any farther for fear of poisoning herself.

She peered down one and found that the entire floor had fallen in, leaving nothing but a gaping hole overlooking the corridor beneath her.

Forget the ghosts. She made a mental note to be careful where she stepped!

She looked back the way she came. It was important that she kept track of where she'd been or she might never find her way back to Seph and Maria. This place was enormous. So far, she hadn't strayed far from the first hallway, but eventually she was probably going to have to explore farther.

She glanced back once more at the gaping hole in the floor as she turned to continue on and jumped at the sight of a dark figure standing on the lower level, staring up at her.

But when she shined her light down onto it, there was nothing there.

Her imagination?

Somehow, she doubted it.

The hairs on the back of her neck were standing straight up as she backed away from the hole and retreated to the previous corridor.

She really, *really* hated it here.

She closed her free hand around her pendant. It couldn't create things for her in this place. It was too busy protecting her from the Keeper's time magic. But it gave her comfort, nonetheless. When Annalisa first gave it to her, she'd called it a good luck charm and claimed it would ward off evil. She liked to think that it had those properties in addition to being a Hand of the Architects. She needed to believe that she wasn't utterly vulnerable in a place like this.

As she peered into the all-encompassing darkness in front of her, something ran at her from behind. She could clearly hear it, heavy footfalls on the hardwood floor, racing straight toward her, already almost upon her. She turned, a startled scream escaping her lips…but there was nothing there. The footsteps seemed to pass right beneath her—attached to nothing she could see or feel—and then rapidly faded back into the silence.

She stood where she was, her eyes wide with fright, her heart racing, a series of short, terrified squeaks rising from her throat like hiccups as she gasped for breath in the thin atmosphere of this strange, alien universe.

It wasn't too bad before, but now she *really* felt like she needed to pee.

Trembling with fear, she turned and searched the area directly around her with her flashlight again, half-convinced that something was standing in the darkness somewhere, just waiting to make eye contact before it pounced. But for the moment, at least, she seemed to still be alone.

Her gaze lingered on the soft glow of the flashlight she left with

Seph. It framed the doorway at the end of the hall, a comforting beacon to lead her back.

She wanted to go back *now*. She wanted to go and sit by Seph and not be terrified of what might be lurking within arm's reach of her at any given second, if only for just a little while. But she couldn't keep running away from this. The only way either of them were ever getting out of here was by finding the Tartarus lock. And she wasn't going to find it if she didn't look for it.

She made herself turn and walk away from the light.

Just a few paces ahead, she froze as the sound of a whimpering child drifted to her from behind a closed door just ahead of her.

She stood there, not moving, her big eyes fixed on that door.

She'd been through *this* crap before. Last July, when she first encountered the black-eyed children. A creepy little girl lured her out to the dumpsters behind her apartment with just such a trick.

There weren't supposed to be any black-eyed children here. She didn't think Gispuknya was able to enter the Keeper's gates. But neither should there be any children in this awful place.

She stared at the door, unable to move. In spite of all that logic, she couldn't help wondering… What if there really was a child locked in there? What if someone really did need help? Even if that *was* a ghost in there, it didn't mean it was something monstrous. Maria was a ghost and she wasn't evil.

Shouldn't she make sure?

Besides…what if the lock was inside that room?

Quietly, she stepped toward the door, her hand reaching out for the old knob.

The weeping faded.

Everything fell silent.

She hesitated.

Maria did warn her that it was dangerous in here. She made it clear that there were things inside these walls that could harm her. She didn't say anything about any innocent souls trapped here. Even if there *was* the lost spirit of a child weeping behind this door, was there anything she could realistically do for it?

She wasn't sure about this.

She withdrew her hand and clutched it against her chest, where she could feel her heart racing.

Bad idea. She was sure of it.

She took a step back.

Inside the room, the whimpering thing let out a deafening shriek, infuriated, and began violently shaking the door.

She screamed and fled down the hallway.

Definitely a bad idea!

The screaming and banging carried on until she'd passed several more doors, then, as suddenly as it began, it stopped. She didn't even consider opening any others. She reminded herself of the collapsed floor in that one hallway and forced herself to slow to a walk. Then she focused her attention on the hallway in front of her. "Just keep going…" she whispered to herself. She didn't even turn to look at the comforting glow of Seph's flashlight behind her. If she did, she might not be able to stop herself from fleeing back to it. She kept her eyes forward and made herself walk. "Just keep going… Just keep going…"

When something whispered alien words to her in the dark, she kept walking.

When she heard footsteps cross in front of her, she kept walking.

Even when one of the doors creaked open as she passed, she kept walking.

She was shaking. Her heart was pounding. She was whimpering under her breath. But she *kept walking.*

Then, *finally*, she reached the end of the hallway. A large, elaborate stairway stood before her, leading down to the lower level.

Now she allowed herself to look back. The light looked so far away now, the doorway so small… And if she descended these stairs, she wouldn't be able to see the light anymore. There'd be nothing to look to when she became scared. And she was quite sure that, in spite of the fact that she was trembling with fear, she hadn't *begun* to experience the true terror of Covengale.

She closed her eyes and tried to swallow, but her mouth was dry. The air was thinner than ever here. She felt like she was struggling for every breath.

Slowly, she made her way down the steps, careful not to slip on any of the debris that had rained down from the ceiling over the many twisted years.

There was water on the floor below her. And that thick, gray mold was everywhere. It hung from the railings like furry stalactites and covered the last few steps in a fuzzy, squishy carpet.

There was another stairwell leading back up across from her. A wide, open space was on her left. And another wide hallway led into the darkness to her right. One of those odd timepieces was mounted above the doorway leading into that hallway, its five orbs revealing a time that no one could read and probably wasn't right anyway.

Just another broken clock.

She stepped off the last step and into the still water. It soaked through her shoes and into her still-damp socks, cold and dirty and *icky*. It was only half an inch deep, but still she couldn't help thinking that something in it would reach out at any second and snatch her ankle.

Then she'd probably drop dead of fright right then and there.

And why wouldn't something like that be possible? It'd be no different than the gate that brought her here, really. A deep, black well hidden in the middle of a shallow lake.

Somewhere in the hallway to her right, a door slammed shut. She cried out, startled, and thrust her light in that direction, revealing nothing.

From somewhere in the darkness behind her came the sound of a woman crying. She twirled around, splashing water up onto her leggings, and pointed her light in *that* direction, revealing *more* nothing.

Calm down, she thought to herself. *Don't panic. You're fine.*

She turned around again, letting her flashlight peel back the darkness all around her, proving to herself that she was still alone. But as she came back around to where she started, she caught a glimpse of a dark, human-like shape scurrying up the wall and out of sight.

She screamed again and stumbled backward, away from the mysterious wall-climber.

She closed her eyes and shook her free hand as if shaking something gross off her fingers, as if she could simply shake away the crippling fear. She forced herself to breathe. She needed to get ahold of herself. If Seph were here, she'd tell her to stop being such a girl.

She took a deep, slow breath…then she opened her eyes again, a fresh wave of fear washing over her. Why did it suddenly smell so much like *blood*?

The hairs on the back of her neck were prickling again. Slowly, she turned and looked behind her.

A woman was standing there, staring back at her with pale, green eyes. She was dressed in a thin, white gown and drenched in blood.

It dripped from her fingertips, but never reached the water at her feet.

Piper made another of those terrified squeaking noises in her throat.

Then the woman lunged forward and wrapped her bloody fingers around her neck.

Chapter 51

Piper gasped and opened her eyes. She was lying on the floor, clutching at her neck. Gone was the bloody woman. Gone was the stagnant water and mold. Even the eerie darkness was gone. A soft, orange light filled the room and she was suddenly much warmer.

She placed her hands on the floor and pushed herself up. The wood was smooth and shiny. And it was beautiful. Dark and reddish, with wispy streaks of shining green and orange and yellow woven through the grain.

She looked up to see that the staircases were right where she left them, but they were shining and new. The steps were a different kind of wood, stark crimson with bold streaks of black, utterly contrasted against the railings, which were almost translucent and the color of the moon.

The walls were white and gray, adorned with subtle but beautiful patterns of sparkling silver.

There didn't appear to be any light fixtures. The orange light seemed to be radiating from the entire ceiling high above her, which was ablaze with all the colors of a brilliant sunset.

Was this the beauty of Covengale in its prime?

Slowly, she rose to her feet. To one side was a long, white hallway, a startling contrast to the dank, black corridor that was there when she first came down the stairs. On the other side was a spacious, open room with two long, low tables.

She walked that way, drawn to the flowers that someone had placed on the tables as centerpieces. They looked a little like lilies, except they were enormous. Each flower was big enough to fit her head inside, if she'd so chosen. Three of them filled each globe-like vase, and each one was a different color of the rainbow.

Also decorating the table were several glowing balls, each of them, like the flowers, a different color. She bent over one and looked more closely at it. It was a deep, calming shade of blue with little, almost imperceptible streaks of brightest green.

She straightened up again and looked around at the rest of the room. Large, bushy ferns occupied the corners of the room. Between them, along the walls, there were more of those legless pieces of furniture and large, luxurious-looking pillows.

She didn't think she'd ever seen such an alien-looking place. And yet it was absolutely beautiful. Like something from a fantasy novel.

But as beautiful as it all was, she couldn't help but wonder *why* she was in this place. How did she get here? Why was it all new again?

Was she dead? Did the bloody woman kill her? Was this the ghost version of Covengale?

The far side of the room was lined with windows, like those overlooking the death-trap balcony in that first room. These windows, however, were covered in soft, pinkish curtains. The sunlight filtering through them made them glow like the ceiling above her.

She looked up again. Was that artificial light, she wondered, or was the roof made of some kind of translucent material that let the sunlight filter through it like it did with the curtains?

Was the sunlight in this world naturally that color?

Slowly, she became aware of a soft ticking noise. She turned and looked back at the hallway. Above the door, that mysterious clock was brand new again, too. Its silver surface was shined to a mirror finish. She walked toward it, her head tilted to one side as she watched it. The bottommost ball was slowly moving from right to left each time she heard it tick, like a second hand, except it only ticked every three or four seconds. As she watched it, it reached its leftmost limit and, with another tick, swung all the way back to the right as the one above it ticked one more space to the left.

Simple, enough, she realized. To one familiar with the device, the time would be evident at a glance. There wasn't even any need for numbers.

But even if she *could* read the time on that thing, it wouldn't help her. It made no difference. It had no relevance to the moldy, rotten place she'd come from. There, time remained broken.

Why was she here? Did this have something to do with the Tartarus lock?

She heard voices approaching from above her and quickly backed away from the stairs.

A group of people were coming down the steps, seemingly in the middle of a serious discussion. They talked back and forth, but Piper could understand none of it. It didn't sound like any language she'd ever heard before.

Her instincts told her to hide, but there wasn't anywhere to go. She was standing in plain sight, too far away to duck behind any of those big ferns or flee down the white hallway. She backed away until she bumped into the table.

There were five of them in all, four of them men, one of them a woman, all of them with very dark complexions and curiously distinct features. They were dressed very strangely. Two of the men were wearing what appeared to be long skirts and heavy boots with what looked sort of like fancy, mini ponchos draped over their shoulders. The third man wore a vest and something that resembled a furry pair of bicycle shorts with flashy sandals. The fourth was naked except for a shorter variation of the first two men's skirts. The woman trailed behind the men, not speaking. Unlike the men, she wore long pants, but she was topless, with only a glittering, beaded sash that only covered one breast, and that only partially. Her hands, dripping with jewelry, were clasped in front of her, her head lowered, looking rather meek in comparison to the men.

Was this what people looked like in this universe? Was that what they wore?

Then she recalled that people dressed drastically different throughout her own universe, depending on the time period and where they were in the world.

She apparently didn't need to worry about hiding. The five of them reached the bottom of the stairs and then turned and walked right past her, without sparing her even a passing glance.

She watched them as they crossed the room and seated themselves on the furniture and pillows, curling their legs under them like children on a kindergarten classroom rug.

Wait… Was *she* the ghost now?

Cautiously, she crept toward them, examining them more closely. Their eyes looked a little big. The men had curiously trimmed beards. Their noses were a little flat.

She realized that two of them, the larger-built men with the little ponchos, had pointed ears. Not like a Vulcan or an elf. Nothing that pronounced. They were narrower than the ears she was used to seeing on people, and a little longer, with a soft, rounded sort of point at the top. And their lobes dangled a little lower, too.

She wondered if she could take a picture of them, but then she remembered that her phone was still charging in the truck, back at the dock.

Then she realized that her pockets were empty. Even her flash-light was gone, now that she was thinking about it. She looked down at herself. Her clothes were dry and clean, as if she'd never gone into that lake to save Seph.

She looked around again. "This isn't real…" she whispered.

She turned away from the people and came face to face with the bloody woman again.

She screamed and jumped back. But she quickly realized that the bloody woman didn't look like a nightmarish monster. Instead, she looked *desperate*. She was crying. Tears streaked down her face, carving lines through the blood smeared on her cheeks. She was fidgeting, wringing her bloody hands. She pointed to the girl.

Piper turned and looked again. Now that she was looking more closely, she realized that they were one and the same. The girl curled up on the pillow was a few years younger, her hair was beautifully done and she wasn't covered in blood and looking half mad, of course, but she was clearly the same person.

The bloody version of the woman on the pillow spoke. Her voice was strange. Less spoken than carried on the wind. But although she spoke words she'd never heard before, Piper found that she could understand two of them.

"Nonya shoy," was the phrase that stood out from the rest.

"Help her."

Piper stared at her, confused. How could she help her? If this was a real scene, then it all happened in a very distant past. What power did she have over something that already happened?

The bloody woman spoke again, growing more agitated.

"I'm sorry!" said Piper. She looked back at the girl on the pillow. Nothing was even happening. These four men were just sitting around talking and she was just…sitting there with them. Looking pretty. Help her what? Help her get out of listening to this boring conversation? "I don't know what to do? What do you want me to do?"

"Nonya shoy," said the woman in her ghostly, alien tongue.

"How? How do I help her?"

The girl on the pillow kept looking over at the nearly naked man. Was he someone special to her? Was he her lover? All she knew about these people was that they looked strange and they all came down the stairs together. How was she supposed to change anything?

"*Nonya shoy*!"

Piper was beginning to have a bad feeling about this conversation. "I don't understand. Please explain it to me. Help me understand."

"Nonya shoy!" shouted the woman, her pale, green eyes blazing. "*Nonya shoy*!"

"I can't!" She took a step back, afraid, and the bloody woman lunged forward and grabbed her by the throat again.

Everything went black.

When she opened her eyes next, it was dark again, but not the same kind of dark it was before the bloody woman first appeared. This darkness flickered and surged. This darkness was filled with smoke.

She sat up and looked around. The room was trashed. There appeared to have been a struggle. A fire was burning outside the window, casting that eerie light into the room.

Someone was sobbing behind her. She turned, startled, to find the woman who was sitting on the pillow in that last flashback kneeling over the body of the nearly naked man. Except he was no longer nearly naked. He was wearing a long, gray coat of some sort. He'd also grown one of those peculiarly trimmed beards, like those other men were wearing, meaning more than a little time had passed.

The woman was wearing an eerily familiar, thin, white gown. She was covered in blood.

There was a knife in her hand.

And even as she sobbed for him, she was still cutting him open.

Terrified, Piper rose to her feet and began to back away from the crazy woman carving up her boyfriend.

At least the people here weren't able to see her. She did *not* want to deal with what was going on over there.

But as she turned away, she came face to face with the bloody woman's ghost again.

"*Nonya shoy*!" she screamed in that strange, alien language that she had no business understanding. "*Nonya shoy*!" (*Help her*! *Help her*!) She threw herself at Piper, her bloody hands reaching for her neck again. "*Nonya shoy*! *Nonya shoy*! *Nonya shoy*!"

Piper screamed and backed away, shielding herself. "*Leave me alone*!"

The bloody woman suddenly froze. Her eyes grew even wider. Her lips quivered for a moment. Then she vanished.

In an instant, Piper was standing in the original darkness again, blinking at the sudden change. Her clothes were freshly soaked. Her hair clung to her face. She was shivering harder than ever, her breath billowing before her eyes.

Her flashlight was lying on the floor between the two staircases, where she was first attacked. Unnerved, she splashed through the dirty water and snatched it up.

What just happened? Why did the bloody woman suddenly flee? It almost looked as if something had frightened her.

The thought had barely crossed her mind when she felt the hairs on the back of her neck stand up again. Slowly, she turned. It was behind her. It'd been behind her the whole time. Not just something scary. Something scary enough to frighten away the crazy ghost of that woman with serious regrets about hacking up her boyfriend.

She lifted her light and shined it into the darkness of that dining room. She could still see those long, low tables in the gloom. She could still make out some of those pretty, glass balls.

And she could see something else, too: the shadow of a tall man staring back at her from the depths of that gloom.

She didn't want to see any more. She left the mysterious figure where it stood and bolted back up the stairs.

She'd check on Seph. That's what she'd do.

She could see the glow of her flashlight as soon as she neared the top of the steps. The sight was comforting.

She shined hers back the way she came, confirming that the hallway behind her was still deserted, then she turned her attention forward again. She wouldn't run. Running was dangerous. There was a lot of debris on the floor to slip on. The last thing she needed was a sprained ankle.

But almost immediately, she heard an unsettling noise behind her. A heavy thumping sound. She turned and shined her light back at the stairs again.

The tall man was there, slowly walking toward her. He was holding something, carrying it like a walking stick.

Thump… Thump… Thump…

The reflection of her light glinted off something metal.

A blade. A really *big* blade.

Sometimes you had no choice but to risk a sprained ankle.

She sprinted the rest of the way down that long hallway, not daring to look back until she reached that far room. As soon as she stepped through the doorway, however, she twirled around and shined her light back into that terrible darkness, panting and shivering and fighting back an urge to vomit from the fear.

But the tall man was gone.

The hallway was silent.

She was safe again.

"Oh gosh…" she gasped, finally relaxing. "I really don't like this place."

But when she turned around, Seph was gone.

Chapter 52

"Persephone?" Piper's heart was racing again. Where'd she go? She circled the room, shining her light into the dark corners, hoping to find her curled up just out of sight, but she was nowhere to be found. "*Persephone*?" She checked the balcony doors, but they were locked. There was no sign of her having gone out there.

Why would she leave? Did she wake up and go searching for her? If so, why would she leave her light behind? It didn't make sense.

"Maria?"

"Did you find what you were looking for?" asked Maria.

Piper jumped and twirled around to find her standing behind her as if nothing were wrong. "No! I didn't! Where's Persephone?"

"She left," she replied.

Piper stared at her. "What? *Why*? I thought you were watching her!"

"I *was* watching her." She pointed at the doors through which she'd just come. "She left through there."

"Why didn't you stop her?"

"I can't do much," said Maria. "I'm not that sort of spirit. She didn't seem to be able to hear me. And I couldn't follow."

Piper snatched Seph's flashlight off the floor and ran to the doorway. She had to find her.

"I'm sorry," said Maria. "I didn't expect you to be gone for such a long time."

She looked back at her, confused. "I was gone, like, *ten minutes*!" Or maybe it was twenty, or even closer to an hour. Time was broken, here, she reminded herself again.

Maria looked confused. "No, it was *much* longer than that."

As if to confirm, Piper's stomach gurgled loudly, indicating that it was past time for her next meal.

She frowned. What time was it? How long was she caught in that insane woman's memories?

No. She couldn't think about that right now. There was no time for that. She needed to find Seph. She was out there somewhere, roaming around these nightmarish halls. She tucked the extra flashlight into her pocket and then pulled out a beef jerky stick and stuffed it into her cheeks.

She didn't want to eat. Her stomach was still in knots from her repeated scares. But she couldn't risk getting sick. If she really had been gone a lot longer than she realized, then Seph could be anywhere in the building by now.

Why leave the flashlight? Her thoughts kept circling back to that question. It didn't make sense. And she didn't like it.

She stepped out into the hallway, shining her light back and forth, her heart pounding.

Could something in this place have possessed her? Was she *forced* to leave? Abducted by a vengeful spirit?

These terrible thoughts just kept pouring into her head. She couldn't make it stop.

Maria told her that room was safe. The ghosts of Covengale weren't supposed to have any power in there. Was it possible she was mistaken? Were the spirits of this universe more powerful than she anticipated?

Something glinted in the reflection of her light and she froze.

Seph's glasses were lying on the floor next to the wall, seemingly abandoned.

A terrified whine escaped her. An awful, gut-wrenching fear filled her chest, squeezing her heart. "Persephone?" she squeaked, shining her light around.

She snatched up the glasses and zippered them safely into her jacket pocket again.

She had to find her. Wherever she was, she was in terrible danger. And there were so many places for her to have gone. There were at least six different hallways branching off this main one. Without a light, Piper wouldn't have seen her fumbling around in the dark. She could've run right past her and never known she was there.

She could already be dead, for all she knew, brutally slaughtered by some insane specter and left to die an agonizing death all alone in the darkness.

Piper stopped and shook her head. Why would she think such things? *What was wrong with her?*

Already dead… Too late…

She stopped and closed her eyes. She could almost feel her spirit ears twitching as they zeroed in on something. This time, she could hear the words that were whispered to her, faint but clear: "Already dead…"

She opened her eyes and turned around, quickly shining her light behind her.

She caught only a glimpse of the shadowy thing as it darted away, its ghostly voice trailing behind it: "Too late…"

"What a nasty little ghost," she murmured, irritated. "Stupid dead people…"

She turned around again, her eyes peeled for bloody women or tall men with huge, heavy blades, and paused as a different sort of sound drifted to her.

She tipped her head to one side, then the other. Was that…someone *humming*? She turned around, straining to hear.

That way.

She tiptoed through a heavy scattering of fallen ceiling and peered into one of the adjacent hallways. She couldn't see anything, but the humming was louder here. Was it another ghost?

She'd didn't explore these corridors very far the first time she walked through here. She didn't want to stray too far and get lost. She had no idea what might be waiting for her down there. Something could be trying to lead her into a trap.

Slowly, she stepped through the debris, wincing at every creak of the floorboards, her muscles tense.

She hated this. She wasn't cut out for things like this. She had no stomach at all for scary things. Even as a child, she was a scaredy-cat. She used to run her poor father ragged every night making him turn her room upside down to prove there were no monsters waiting to eat her up.

That was why she needed Seph. Seph was so much stronger than she was.

She had to find her.

Footsteps behind her. Approaching quickly. She turned, barely stifling a loud squeal of terror, but once again, there was nothing there. The owner of the unseen feet seemed to pass right by her without so much as stirring the stagnant air.

She clasped her hand over her heart and took a deep, ragged breath. She held it a few seconds, willing herself to calm down, then turned and continued on.

The humming was louder now. She was getting closer to the source. But the deterioration of the building was growing worse, as well. Larger chunks of the ceiling had fallen in here. The walls were crumbling. The floor felt all wrong in places, springy, soft. If she wasn't careful, she was going to find herself crashing through it, probably breaking her legs in the process. Or her neck.

She stopped and shined her light into the darkness behind her. Someone, somewhere, was weeping again.

Seph?

No… That didn't sound like Seph.

She peered into each of the doorways as she passed, shining her light into each corner to make sure no one was there. As she swept her light across the floor of one of them, she was startled by a glimpse of a small, dirty child curled up there, weeping. But it was only a glimpse, there for only a fraction of a second as her light swept over the small form. Then it was just gone, as if nothing had ever been there.

Piper lingered here for a moment, uncertain, then continued on in search of the source of the mysterious humming.

A little farther along, and the entire ceiling had fallen in, leaving a large, gaping hole overhead, revealing a third-floor hallway above them. A pair of doors hung on the wall there, disembodied from the floor. It was a strangely surreal sight.

The humming stopped.

Piper swept her flashlight around. What happened? What did it mean? She swallowed and tightened the grip on her flashlight. Then she continued onward, stepping cautiously over the fallen debris.

The floor was sagging dangerously on the left side. She bit her lip and pressed herself to the wall on her right, carefully testing the warped floorboards with her toes before each step.

"Oh my gosh…" she whispered. "Oh…my gosh…"

Please, God, don't let this place come crashing down on top of her. *Please.*

She should turn back now. That humming was probably another stupid ghost trying to lure her to her doom. But she needed to be sure that she wasn't here. Just a little farther…

She was almost convinced that Seph couldn't have come this way when she heard the humming again. Much closer this time. Just ahead of her, it seemed.

The floor grew worse. The left side had finally given out. The boards had pulled away from the wall and sagged into the darkness beneath it.

Still prodding the boards with her toes, she crept forward. One step. Two. Three. Then something materialized from the darkness. A shape moved in the gloom.

One more step and she saw her.

Seph was walking toward her, head down, one hand on the wall, the other held out for balance. One foot in front of the other, she was balancing on the narrow strip of floor that was all that remained there. The rest had been swallowed by the gaping hole.

"Persephone!"

Seph stopped and looked up at her. She looked so strange, standing there without her glasses. "Hi, Pi!" she sighed. "Where've you been?"

Piper squinted at her, confused. "Are you okay?"

"M'hm," she said. Her voice sounded strange. Sort of sleepy, slurred, as if she were drunk.

Piper's eyes dropped to the floor again. She could hear those old boards creaking and groaning with each step Seph took. "Whatcha doing?" she asked.

Seph shrugged. "Dunno." She looked down at her feet again and continued her drunken tightrope walk along the failing hallway floor. One step. Two. Then she tilted dangerously to the left, her arm pinwheeling for a heart-stopping second.

"*Persephone*!"

Her voice echoed back to her from the far ends of the hallway.

Seph righted herself again, her hand pressed against the cracked wall for balance. Then she giggled.

"Oh my gosh…" Piper clutched at her chest, her heart pounding again. She felt dizzy, as if she might pass out. That was utterly *terrifying*!

Then, unbelievably, Seph continued walking toward her!

"*Please stop*!"

Seph looked up at her, her mouth drooping open. "Huh?"

She wasn't okay. The Gispuknya wasp toxins must have left her delirious. It was as if she'd been drugged. She had no idea what was going on.

"It's dangerous. You were supposed to stay in that room where it's safe. You were supposed to be sleeping."

"I *was* sleeping," she said, her voice disturbingly girlish, as if her mind had reverted to a small child in her feverish delirium. "But then I woke up 'cause I heard a voice calling me."

"A voice?" Piper didn't like the sound of that. What *good* reason could anything in this place have for luring her out of the only safe room?

"It told me to come here…so I come here…" She giggled and

took another step. "Look," she said. "The floor's *bouncy* here!"

To Piper's horror, she began bouncing up and down, the crumbling floor springing up and down with her weight, the rotting wood creaking loudly.

"*Oh my gosh please stop*!"

Seph stopped bouncing and looked up at her as if *she* were the one behaving like a clueless drunk.

Piper clutched at her chest again. She seriously didn't know how much more of this she could stand. Her heart was racing. She couldn't stop shaking. And she was seriously going to need to find a bathroom in this place before very much longer!

She thought of Seph's flashlight in her pocket. Had she wandered all this way blind? "How did you even find your way here in the dark?"

Seph tilted her head to the side. The motion made her whole body lean that way, closer and closer to that gaping hole in the floor.

"Don't do that!"

Seph didn't seem to hear her. "It's not dark in here," she said. Then her gaze shifted to Piper's hand. She wrinkled her nose and furrowed her brow in an exaggerated expression of bewilderment. "Why do you have a flashlight?"

She stared back at her, confused. It wasn't dark? She could see?

Was she doing that thing again that let her see in the library?

Seph straightened up again, wobbling a little as she did.

"Come on over here, okay?" urged Piper, holding out her hand. "It's dangerous over there. You could fall. *Please*."

Seph leaned forward, squinting at her. "Who's that?"

Piper froze. An icy shiver crept all the way up her back. Very slowly, she turned and shined her light behind her.

The tall man stood there, dressed in filthy, torn clothes. The blade at his side looked like an enormous saw, with sharp teeth jutting off it at odd angles. She couldn't tell if it was supposed to be a tool or a weapon, but she knew immediately that it wouldn't just carve her up. It would hack her into chunky, flying pieces.

She couldn't see the man's face. Her light didn't seem to pierce the darkness that concealed his head.

She screamed and backed away from the tall man, forgetting about the rotten floor until she heard the old boards crack and groan.

She tipped backward.

Seph laughed and threw herself at Piper, wrapping her arms around her, knocking her off balance as the floor broke away, spilling them both into the darkness below.

Chapter 53

The lower hallway was flooded. And not like the floor at the bottom of the staircases was flooded. The water here was chest deep.

Piper, Seph and a few hundred pounds of rotten wood came crashing down into this frigid, stagnant water.

It wasn't a graceful descent by any definition. It wasn't like in the movies where the heroes splashed down and then swam to safety without a scratch. There were streaks of stinging pain painted across Piper's back and butt and elbow and both her legs that burned hot against the cold of the water.

Icy panic filled her as she struggled to stand. How badly was she hurt? Had she broken anything? Did she catch a rusty nail? Did she need stitches? Had she been *impaled* by the jagged end of a broken board?

She couldn't move. Her foot was caught in the waterlogged rubble. She couldn't seem to stand up. She couldn't come up for air!

For a few frantic seconds she reached for something to pull herself up with, but nothing her hands closed around was attached to anything. Nothing offered any leverage at all.

Then she changed her strategy and grabbed for something beneath her instead, pushing against it, prying at the ensnaring lumber. This time, her foot slid out of her shoe and she finally managed to stand.

Coughing and gasping, she turned around, her hands out and grasping, trying to see in the dismal gloom of this soggy corridor. "*Persephone*?"

"Ouchy…" whimpered Seph.

Piper turned toward her voice, her arms outstretched. "Where are you? Are you okay?"

"I hurt my ankle…"

"Are you okay?" she asked again. "Can you walk on it?"

"I think so…"

She moved toward her, but tripped over the debris at her feet and tumbled forward, crashing into her.

"*Ouch*!" cried Seph.

"Sorry!"

"Inappropriate touching!"

"I'm sorry! Just hold on a second! I'm stuck again!" She couldn't seem to find a place to put her foot where she could put her weight on it.

Finally, she found her balance. She stood up, her teeth chattering with the cold, and looked around. Her eyes were adjusting to the dull glow of her flashlight, which she'd dropped on her way down. It was lying on the submerged floor a few feet away, casting a faint and eerie glow up through the filthy, churning water and floating debris, painting creepy shadows on the walls around them. She had to close her eyes and go back down into the water to retrieve it, but even blind, she managed it on her first try.

She came back up with it and shined it back and forth, making sure they were alone in this flooded nightmare. Then she aimed it up through the hole overhead.

The cloud of dust stirred up by the collapse made it difficult to see very far. It caught the light as it passed through, turning it into a narrow, laser-like beam. But the tall, blade-wielding man wasn't staring back at her from up there, so she decided she should merely be thankful for the moment that neither of them had been killed in that collapse.

She turned her attention to the floor beneath her and used the light to locate her lost shoe. She found it wedged in a tangle of boards. Another quick dive and she had it.

"Hey, Pea…?"

"Yeah?"

"I don't think that place we were in just now was very safe."

"You *think*?"

"M'hm. 'S'dangerous… You gotta be more careful."

"Just go!" snapped Piper.

They needed to get out of this frigid water as quickly as possible. She had no idea how cold it needed to be before hypothermia became a real concern, but this was definitely well below her comfort level. She was shivering.

It wasn't easy making their way through this mess, though. More of the upper floor had collapsed ahead of them. They kept tripping over jumbled knots of twisted wood. And that pain in her back and legs lingered, worrying her. She couldn't tell if she was bleeding or not. She hoped not. She had no idea what sort of ancient bacteria or parasites might thrive in a place like this. The last thing she needed was a nasty, alien infection.

And she kept expecting one of them to step on a nail or a screw, adding tetanus to her already-long list of things to worry about.

"This is *so* not my idea of a good time," she grumbled through chattering teeth.

"S'like a sunken city in a video game," observed Seph. Then she giggled and shouted, "Imma *ninja turtle*!" her voice echoing through the building.

"*Oh my gosh*!" hissed Piper. "*Be quiet*!" She turned and shined her light behind them. Every specter in this *universe* probably heard that. They'd be lucky if they weren't *swarmed* by the dead in the next few seconds.

"Don't yell at me," pouted Seph. "I don't like it when people yell at me."

"Since when do you care what people say?"

"I *always* care…"

Piper glanced over at her, surprised. Was this just more of drunk Seph being weird? Or was this the *real* Seph that she kept hidden under her tough exterior the rest of the time? Was this how she *really* felt? It was hard to imagine Seph being so sensitive. But she couldn't think about it now. As she watched, something moved in the gloom behind Seph. The water back there was churning.

"Come on…" she whispered, her voice wavering with the motion of her chattering teeth. "Keep moving."

Were those *eyes* staring back at her from the darkness? Or was that only her imagination?

She looked forward again and gasped as her light passed over the pale form of a bloated body floating in front of her. But even as she jumped back, she found that it was gone again.

Her imagination? She very much doubted it.

She really didn't know how much more of this her poor heart could take.

Ahead of them, the hallway ended. The room beyond was open and spacious. It was also set a lot higher than the hallway. Several steps transitioned between the two, so that the water here was only a few inches deep instead of a few feet.

Piper did a quick check to make sure they were alone, then sat down with Seph in the middle of the room and looked her over. She didn't seem to be bleeding anywhere that she could see. And she didn't appear to be in any real pain. She just looked cold. She was shivering. "How's your ankle?"

She looked down at her foot. "Still hurts."

Piper looked it over. "How bad?"

"Not very." She flexed it back and forth, wincing a little.

Just twisted, probably. Not sprained or broken. That was a relief. "Anywhere else hurt?"

She thought about it for a few seconds, then looked down at her hand. "Here." There was a painful-looking scrape on her palm. It was bleeding, but only a little.

"Anything else?"

She shook her head. Then she turned her hand over, showing her the back of her wrist. "Just these," she replied, pointing to one of the wasp stings.

The swelling had gone down considerably, but there was still a painful-looking welt surrounding it, as well as a fairly large bruise.

She brushed back Seph's hair and looked at her ear. It was still red and swollen, but even it looked better than it did when she examined it in the truck.

She wondered how long they'd been here now.

She let her hair fall back into place and looked into her eyes. "Can you still see?"

"Uh huh. S'bright in here."

"Huh..." Her eyes didn't agree with her. Her pupils were fully dilated. And when she shined her light at them, they reacted properly. Whatever her prophet sight was, it seemed to be completely separate from her human eyes.

She put her hand over her pocket, where Seph's glasses were resting. If she could see just fine without them, maybe she'd keep them where they were for now. They might not be lucky enough to find them again.

She turned her attention to her own body, instead. Her legs still hurt, mostly in the back, but her leggings weren't torn anywhere. She wasn't bleeding through the fabric. She probably just scraped against the splintered wood on her way down. She pulled them up and winced at the raw scrapes running down her right shin and on both her calves.

She lifted her shirt and reached behind her, prodding at her stinging back. It was tender to the touch, but only a light smear of blood came back on her fingertips. She decided that if there were a piece of rotten lumber or a large, rusty nail jutting out of her back that there'd probably be more blood than that, so she tugged her shirt back down and ignored it.

Her thighs and the left side of her butt were also burning.

She was going to be *so* sore in the morning…

She sat there a moment, cross-legged in the water, exhausted and sore and shivering, and stared at Seph, who was sitting with her legs spread out in front of her like a child, lightly slapping at the water between her legs.

She didn't like this. Why was she acting so weird? Was it really just a reaction to the Gispuknya wasp venom?

She sighed. "I really wish you'd come back to me. I'm not sure I can do this by myself."

Seph stared down at the water, as if she hadn't heard a word she'd just said. "I got water all over the floor again…" she whispered.

Piper stared at her. "What?"

"Daddy's gonna be mad." She looked up and met Piper's gaze. Her eyes shined with tears. Her lower lip was quivering. "I didn't mean to." She shook her head. A tear slipped down her wet cheek. "I didn't."

Piper nodded. Her heart was breaking. She'd never seen Seph look so upset before. "I know you didn't."

Seph leaned forward, her glistening eyes opening wide, and whispered, "He's coming!"

Piper felt that icy chill wash over her again.

Then something unseen grabbed her foot and dragged her across the floor, back into the flooded hallway.

Chapter 54

For a few frantic seconds, everything was chaos. Piper had no idea how many people were holding her. There were cold, clammy hands everywhere. They closed around her ankles, her wrists, her legs, her throat, all of them as unyielding as steel traps. They dragged her down beneath the surface of the filthy water and refused to let go.

She tried to scream, but she couldn't breathe. She was going to drown!

Then, all at once, the hands simply vanished. She scrambled to her feet, coughing and gasping, her hands flailing at her unseen assailants, determined to defend herself.

Except no one was here. She was alone in that empty corridor.

And everything had changed again.

Covengale wasn't brand new, as it'd been in the time of the blood-soaked ghost's happier years. But not nearly as far gone as it was in the present. (Or whatever you might call that broken, moldy age that separated these bouts of insanity she was suffering.) The hallway was still flooded, but the water was only up to her ankles. The ceiling wasn't falling down yet.

It was even colder now. The temperature had dropped considerably. And she was still drenched from being dragged into that filthy water. In that other Covengale, she'd been getting enough exercise to just barely keep up with the cold, but she was shivering uncontrollably now. Her teeth were chattering loudly. She could see her breath clearly in the orange-tinted light that was glowing at either end of the shadowy hallway.

Her flashlight was gone again, along with the contents of her pockets.

Those painful scrapes from falling through that rotten floor were stinging worse than ever.

But the worst part was the embarrassing realization that she no longer had to pee…

Her full bladder, the cold water, the terror of being dragged to a watery death by all those deathly hands… Well, no one ever had to know, she supposed. But still… It was kind of mortifying, even in spite of the danger she was in.

She didn't have time to dwell on it, though. Someone was coming.

She turned to see a man in tattered clothes splashing through the water, rushing straight toward her.

She cried out and shrank away from him, but like the last time, she didn't seem to be a tangible part of this flashback. The man stalked right past her without any indication that he noticed her. Even the water kicked up by his boots ignored her. Not a drop touched her, in spite of the fact that it splashed the wall behind her.

She turned and watched him go. Like the other people she'd seen in these queer glimpses of the past, he was dressed strangely. Many layers of dirty fabric were draped over his broad shoulders, giving him a shape sort of like a football player in shoulder pads. He wore what looked like a short skirt with a long, loincloth-like flap in the front and old, leather boots that covered his entire legs.

He had a dirty, bushy beard, wild, unkempt hair and a very unfriendly expression.

Whatever business he had here, he clearly wasn't happy about it. He stormed down the hallway and up the steps into the next room, where heated voices immediately began drifting back to her.

Hugging herself against the gnawing cold, she followed him, hoping he'd lead her somewhere warmer.

The room at the end of the hallway was the same room she and Seph were sitting in when those hands grabbed her and dragged her into this flashback. It wasn't any warmer, unfortunately, but it was *dryer*. She walked up the steps, her feet numb, her teeth hammering together, and looked around.

The man from the hallway was arguing with a second man in front of what looked like a large whiteboard, except it was purple and the writing glowed bright, fluorescent yellow. She couldn't read what was written on it any more than she could understand the words they were shouting at each other, but it was clear by the steadily increasing volume of their voices that they weren't merely here to discuss lunch.

The second man was dressed slightly nicer than the first. He was wearing a long, red coat that was open on top, revealing much of his hairy chest in spite of the cold. He was pudgy and short and neatly trimmed, and he looked as if he didn't have time for whatever the angry man was angry about.

She turned and surveyed the rest of the room. Was someone trying to show her something? If so, she wasn't sure she'd be able to get much out of an argument between two long-dead men in an equally long-dead language. Especially when she could barely think for being so cold!

She couldn't even distinguish the purpose of this room. It was pretty much empty except for the purple whiteboard, a few more of those big, fluffy pillows and another of those strange clocks on the wall. There was another wall of windows at the far back, but again they were covered by those wispy, glowing curtains.

The walls were cracked. The floor had long ago lost its lustrous shine. This argument obviously took place sometime long after the bloody woman murdered her boyfriend…or whatever that nightmare was that she saw before.

She turned her attention back to the two men. Their argument was getting more heated. The unfriendly-looking man was getting agitated. His voice was rising.

Maybe it was because of her spirit ears, but she realized that not every word they said was entirely alien. Right now, the raggedy man was saying something about a bridge, she thought. And a…last chance?

She rubbed her hands together and thought hard. They were told that the Keeper snatched these places from the very ends of their respective universes, in the eleventh hour of their imminent doom. Was it possible he was referring to the last gate leading out of this world and into the next?

Were these people on the verge of missing the exodus?

The angry man turned and stormed off, shouting something about…the last…*mailbox*? She shook her head. That wasn't right. That last part didn't translate properly. It was too hard to think clearly in this cold.

How was she even able to understand *that* much? She could get that her spirit ears could pick up things that her human ears couldn't. But just being able to *hear* something didn't make you able to understand it. And yet…when she thought about it, was it any different than Seph being able to read the writing on those Architects' disks?

This conversation was obviously significant to whoever was

showing this to her, but she couldn't understand most of what was being said. The vast majority of it, she was sure, had been utterly lost on her.

She watched the pudgy man return to his purple whiteboard, then turned to watch the angry man as he splashed off back down the flooded hallway. Was she supposed to follow him? Or stay here? Whose story was she supposed to witness?

Then everything changed again. It was darker now. The angry man was nowhere to be seen. She turned to find the pudgy man sitting on the floor behind her. The purple whiteboard was completely filled with that strange writing and now he was scribbling directly onto the scuffed tiles.

That was one question answered, she supposed.

She walked toward the scribbling man, curious.

Time had passed. A *lot* of time. A moment ago, he had short hair and a clean-shaven face. Now his hair was long and tangled and greasy. His beard was shaggy and graying. His long, red coat was gone and the clothes he now wore were filthy and tattered. And he wasn't nearly as pudgy as he was a moment ago.

What was he working so hard on?

These symbols still made no sense to her. She wondered if Seph would've been able to read any of them with her prophet sight. But of course Seph wasn't here. And even if she *was* here, she wasn't exactly…*herself.*

There was no one else here, nothing else to see.

Piper walked around the room, looking over the alien symbols scribbled on the floor.

Now that she was looking, she could see that he'd scribbled these markings on most of the walls as well, as high as he could reach on almost every surface before moving on to the floor. How long had he been at this? And what was it he was writing?

Unable to comprehend any of it, she walked over to the curtains. One was ripped, revealing a sliver of the dirty glass behind it. She leaned out, curious about the world outside this place, but there was nothing to see in that darkness but a gentle, rocky slope leading down to the rippling surface of a large pond or lake. Everything else was shadows.

Behind her, the scribbling man grunted and then muttered something incomprehensible.

She turned to look at him again and froze as she found him staring right back at her, his bloodshot eyes startlingly wide.

He spoke a single word in his alien language and her spirit ears translated it for her: "*Oblivion.*"

From somewhere outside the windows came a long and terrible series of screams, as if someone somewhere nearby were being brutally murdered.

The scribbling man's wild eyes twitched about the room, nervous. Then, as the awful screams died away, he lowered his head and went back to his scribbling.

Piper stared at him for a moment, wondering if he'd actually seen her or if she just happened to be in the way of his crazy, distant gazing. Then she turned toward the window again, concerned about all the terrible things that might be prowling out there.

But as she turned, she blinked, and the world turned darker still.

Suddenly, the curtains were gone.

An unsettling mist had risen, turning everything on the other side of the filthy glass into a horror movie scene. Strange shapes were moving around out there, slithering through the fog.

She looked down at her feet and found that the entire floor had been covered in those strange markings.

How long had it been now?

Days? Months? Years?

She turned around, looking at it all, and found herself staring at a dirty young woman. She was sitting on the floor, her hands and feet bound with chains that had been bolted to the floor next to her.

She was battered and bruised, her face swollen. Her clothes were stained with blood.

She knelt over her, horrified, and tried to touch her, but there was nothing there. The moment her fingers met the woman's skin, everything seemed to turn inside out. Her stomach gave a sickening lurch and the world swam out of focus.

She stood up, startled, and almost fell down again. She was dizzy.

What was that about?

What was going on?

She backed away from the woman, shaking her head. This was the past? This happened? How? Where did this woman even come from? What was she doing here? Where was the scribbling man?

The woman whimpered and shook her head. She said something that sounded to her human ears like, "Womva…"

There was a light approaching. Piper turned to see a lantern floating toward her in the gloom. A hand held the lantern. A few seconds more and she could see that the hand was attached to the scribbling man.

He was stark naked now. At some point he'd chopped off all of his hair and his beard. He was extremely thin, barely even a shadow of the pudgy man in the red coat she first witnessed in this room. He was filthy. And he looked utterly *insane.*

"Womva…" groaned the woman, struggling with her chains as he approached her. "Womva…womva…"

The scribbling lunatic placed the old lantern down on the floor and turned up the light, better illuminating the abused woman. Then he stood up and walked toward her.

Piper was filled with fresh horror as she realized what was about to happen. She cried out for the man to stop, but of course he couldn't hear her. She reached out to grab him, to hold him back, but her hands found nothing. All she caught was another jarring wave of vertigo.

Because there was nothing there. *He* wasn't there. None of what she was seeing existed in the same time and place she did.

And yet here she was, cursed to witness the atrocities that occurred in this place countless ages ago.

"*Womva*! *Womva*! *Womvaaaa!*"

Piper didn't need her spirit ears to tell her that "womva" translated to "no" in this language.

She was begging him.

Unable to do anything, she turned away and tried to cover her ears against the screams of the chained woman.

But the screams came anyway.

And worse…now that she'd turned away, she could see all the *other* women that the scribbling man's lantern illuminated when he turned up the flame.

Dead, bulging eyes stared back at her from bloated, purple faces.

She fell to her knees and squeezed her eyes shut.

Why? Why were these awful things happening? What was *wrong* with this world?

Do you see it yet? asked a voice inside her head.

Before she could question where this voice came from, the woman in the chains screamed again.

And Piper joined her.

Chapter 55

When she opened her eyes again, she was kneeling in ankle-deep water. Everything was dark except for the muted glow of her submerged flashlight.

She looked around, confused. The scribbling man and the chained women were gone. She was back in the present again. (Or whatever this was.)

But…was it real?

She snatched the flashlight out of the water and aimed it at the submerged floor. Then she reached down and wiped away the gathered silt.

The bright yellow scribblings had faded, but they were still there, and as soon as she saw them, she had to stifle another scream.

It *was* real… That man… Those women… Those horrors…

She stood up and looked around at the empty room. The purple whiteboard was there, unnoticed until now. It'd collapsed ages ago and was little more than a ruined lump of moldy garbage sticking up out of the water near the wall.

And where she last saw the woman—*womva!*—she found the long-rusted links of an old chain.

She shivered at the horror of it all.

What was wrong with this house? Was it cursed? Was there something evil lurking here that drove people mad?

She turned and looked around again.

It suddenly occurred to her that she was alone.

"Persephone?" Her heart leaped in her chest. An icy spring of fresh fear opened up inside her. Where did she go this time? How far could she have gone?

She remembered Maria telling her last time that she'd been gone for a long time. How long had it been this time?

"*Persephone?*"

What if one of those psycho ghosts found her while she was alone and delirious, unable to protect herself?

She looked back down the flooded tunnel from which she and Seph had entered this nightmare-filled chamber and couldn't help but imagine finding her in there, face-down in the water, her body beaten and battered like the scribbling man's victims.

But then she heard a noise that didn't belong. Somewhere in the darkness, someone was sobbing.

Seph?

She cocked her head to one side, then the other, and determined that it was coming from a doorway to the left. Following it, she found a wide, spiraling stairwell leading up two levels.

The steps were rotten. They sagged beneath her weight, threatening to collapse. She clung to the railing and kept her feet close to the wall, the better to distribute her weight.

It seemed unlikely that Seph, drunken and oblivious as she was when she last saw her, could've made it up these steps without them swallowing her up, and yet as she drew closer, she became more and more confident that it was her voice she was hearing.

A *new* terrible thought occurred to her then. Not Seph at all, but

Seph's sobbing spirit, trapped forever in this hideous nightmare dimension.

But when she reached the top of the steps, Seph was there. Not a ghostly Seph. Not a beaten and bloody Seph. Not even a possessed, vomit-spewing, head-spinning Seph.

Just Seph.

She was sitting on the top step, still wet and shivering, sobbing.

"Persephone?"

"He's gone…" she wept.

Piper glanced around, confused. "What?"

"Forever… He's never coming back…"

She sat down next to her and put her arm around her. "Who's gone?"

Seph lifted her face and looked at her. Her eyes were puffy with tears. Her nose was running. Her lip quivered. "My daddy… He's gone…"

Piper frowned. "I know," she said. "I'm sorry."

Seph's father had been gone almost six years now. Piper knew she took it hard, but was now really the time? They were kind of in the middle of something here.

Still, she didn't dare treat the situation carelessly. Seph was in pain.

"Gone…"

"*I'm* here," said Piper. "I'm not going anywhere."

Seph sniffled and wiped at her nose. "Okay…"

A couple minutes passed as they sat there like that, waiting for the grief to pass. Then Piper's stomach gave a loud gurgle. Was it already time for another meal?

She fished another piece of jerky from her pocket and peeled the wrapper open. She shared it with Seph, uncertain anymore whether this was breakfast, lunch or dinner. How many minutes had passed in the outside world? How many days had passed in *this one*?

She didn't care for these worlds of broken clocks. It made it hard to understand her own body. And if she didn't understand her own body, how was she supposed to understand *anything*?

Seph laid her head against Piper's shoulder and muttered something unintelligible.

Piper looked down at her, surprised. "Don't fall asleep. We have to get out of here."

"Gimme a minute…" she mumbled.

"We don't *have* a minute. Come on." She grabbed Seph's arm and stood up, pulling her to her feet.

"But I'm sleepy…"

"Just move!"

"Don't yell at me!"

Wow. Gispuknya wasp venom and time magic were a potent combination. Seph was cycling through moods even faster than Meg.

This was no good. She was still acting crazy. And Piper couldn't trust that she wouldn't get separated from her again.

Seph might be able to see in this darkness, but *she* couldn't. And next time she had one of those freaky episodes she might not be able to find her, especially if she curled up in some dark place and went to sleep again. She needed to be able to *see* her. If she was carrying a light, she could just look for that, but if she gave her the flashlight now, in the state she was in, she'd probably just drop it somewhere and lose it.

Then an idea popped into her head. "Turn around!"

She took Seph's hair out of her loose ponytail and pulled it tight. Then she took the flashlight out of her pocket and used the elastic tie to pin it directly into a new ponytail, with the light pointing up. She even took down her own hair and used the extra elastic to make double-sure it didn't go anywhere.

Now she turned her around and looked at her.

She was cute *and* functional. With the flashlight on, she now shined a light straight up at the ceiling, directly above where she was standing. It would go with her wherever she went, creating a sort of beacon for her to look for the next time one of these freaky ghosts separated them.

As long as the batteries held out, that was… Back in the library, their cell phone batteries held out for a really long time. But what happened there with their phones wasn't necessarily what would happen here with their flashlights.

Still, it was the best plan she could come up with, given the situation.

She shined her own light down the third-floor hallway, wondering where they were and how far it was back to the safe room. Would she even be able to find her way back there with so much of Covengale in ruins? It wasn't safe to take Seph with her, but would she even stay in the safe room if she took her there?

In the end, it didn't matter. When she shined her light back down those decrepit stairs, she saw a ghastly figure crawling up the steps toward them and immediately decided it was time to go.

Chapter 56

The third-floor hallway leading away from the stairs off the scribbling man's psycho study was in much better shape than the second-floor hallway that spilled them into that nightmare, perhaps because it was well above the waterline.

She passed door after door, looking back over her shoulder every few seconds to see if the crawling thing she saw on the stairs was catching up to them.

Did she really see something on those stairs, she wondered now, thinking back, or had she only imagined it? It was only there for a second before she grabbed Seph's hand and bolted down the hallway. A part of her insisted that there wasn't anything there. It was the same part of her, she was certain, that kept telling her that those sinister, murmured voices were nothing but wind whispering through Covengale's drafty corridors, that those shadows flittering about in the corners of her eyes were only her imagination and that it couldn't possibly get any worse.

She'd stopped listening to that part of her. That part of her was stupid and going to get her killed. Clearly, the part of her that was screaming, "Run away! You're going to die!" was the only one with sense enough to keep her alive.

If anything, the activity inside these walls had just spiked. A horrid, blood-covered face peered back at her through a cracked door. Glowing, white eyes stared down from the darkness above a gaping hole in the ceiling. Something black and strangely slimy-looking darted across her bouncing flashlight beam, out of one room and into another. And as she passed an adjacent hallway, she caught just a glimpse of a man engulfed in flames staggering through the darkness.

She thought she heard a child weeping again at one point. (She ignored it, of course.) Then she was sure she heard someone screaming somewhere in the darkness. (She ignored that, too.). And once she even heard the chilling sound of crazed laughter. (She *definitely* ignored that.)

A heavy door materialized out of the gloom in front of them. It stood partially open, as if waiting for them.

She turned and swept her flashlight across the hallway behind them. Was someone back there? She couldn't hear anything, but it *felt* like they were being followed.

She pulled Seph into the room and shoved the door closed, then turned and looked around. It appeared to be some sort of tower room. It was fairly small, round, with two sets of steps built against the wall to the left of the door as they entered, one leading down and the other up. There were windows in here overlooking the black void that loomed outside, and several small, legless tables covered in an assortment of strange, rusty objects that looked like parts to a machine of some sort. More parts were strewn about the floor and stacked in piles against the wall.

Her heart still pounding, she walked over and shined her light down into the darkness at the bottom of the staircase, half-expecting to see the ghostly crawler making its way up toward them again.

Seph, meanwhile, didn't seem the least bit fazed by any of this. It was difficult to tell if she even noticed it. "You're so *pretty*!" she cooed.

"Why do you have to be so much prettier than me?"

Piper glanced back at her, confused. She was standing behind her, the flashlight tied into her ponytail cast a halo onto the ceiling above her. "I'm *so* not prettier than you. Stop it. You're being weird."

"I wish I was as pretty as you."

She turned and shined her light toward the nearest window. Was someone there? She thought she saw a face peering back at them. She didn't think they were on the ground floor, but why would something like that matter in a world like this? "I think you're *very* pretty."

"Really?"

She turned and looked at her, annoyed. "*Yes.*"

Seph leaned toward her, a strange little smile on her lips. "You wanna make out with me?"

Piper stared at her. "Oh my gosh, you're just like Phoenix when you're drunk!"

She blinked, surprised. "Did you make out with *her*, too?"

"*No*! Wait, what do mean, '*too*'? I never made out with *anybody*!" She shook her head, flustered.

"Not even with a boy?"

"That's not…I don't…*Stop it*!"

From somewhere in the endless darkness came another of those blood-curdling screams.

Seph tilted her head to one side and frowned. "D'you hear somethin'?"

"Yeah," said Piper. "I did." She took Seph by the hand and led her down the steps.

"M'startin' to think this place might be haunted."

"No! Really? You think so?"

"I dunno… Maybe."

Piper almost didn't see what was in front of her. "Careful!" she shouted, throwing her hand out to stop Seph.

The floor here had collapsed, taking a portion of the wall and the last few steps with it. In front of her was a sheer drop into black, shadowy water. There were splintered boards jutting up toward her, threatening to impale anyone careless enough to come running down those steps without looking.

Even more unsettling was the tangle of black, coiled branches that reached in through the broken wall.

Another of the Wood's night trees.

In spite of being able to see in the dark, Seph didn't seem to notice any of this. "My boobs're a lot bigger'n yours," she said, looking down at them. "That's the only thing I got going for me."

"Quit it."

"S'true though… Wanna feel 'em?"

"*Oh my gosh*! *Shut up*!" She grabbed Seph's hand and ran back up the steps to the previous room.

Never mind getting Seph back to the safe room. She had no idea how she was going to get *herself* back to it. Even if she found the stupid lock, she had no idea how to find her way home from here.

Dragging Seph and her flashlight halo behind her, she tried the steps going up.

She reminded herself to try to remember to thank Wanda for the workouts. She was pretty sure the steps alone in this place would've killed her a year ago.

The top floor of the tower was completely different from the one below it. Almost every inch of the floor was covered in the long-deflated remains of those large pillows. A handful of small, legless tables held displays of strangely shaped jars and bowls. Another of those odd-looking boxes was mounted to the wall between two windows on the far side of the room.

Was this a bedroom?

Everything was so *strange* in this world.

There was another door in here. She hurried toward it and tried the handle. At first she thought it was locked, but when she pulled harder, it began to move. The old hinges ground together, the rusty metal screaming in the silence.

Then she felt a shiver creep up her back again.

She really hated that feeling…

She turned and looked behind her.

The room was new again. The pillows were clean and fluffy and brightly colored. Moonlight glowed softly behind fluttering curtains. A soft glow emanated from a series of concentric glass rings in the ceiling.

Lounging on the pillows were five women, each of them pale and thin and naked. They were also quite small. But they weren't little girls. They were mature, but petite, almost elf-like, with fine, white hair and eyes that were strikingly *black*.

They were like the men with the pointed ears, she realized. A lost race, perhaps?

Like the two times before this, no one seemed to be able to see her.

Unlike the times before, however, none of them were speaking. They just sat there, silent, with strange, haunted looks on their slight faces.

Piper had a really bad feeling about this. She shook her head and took a step backward. If this was anything like those last two flash-backs, something terrible must've happened in this place. Something *gruesome*. And she didn't want to see it.

From behind her came the sound of approaching footsteps. Heavy and echoing in the stillness. At the same moment, all five of the women sat up, their frightened eyes all turned toward the door behind her in anxious anticipation.

One of them began to cry.

She turned to face the door, already backing away from it, her heart pounding.

But the room had already changed. It was gloomier than it was before. The glowing rings overhead were dark. The curtains fluttered in the wind, illuminated by an eerie, twilight sky.

She stood there in an eerie silence for a moment, afraid to turn around, afraid to look.

But she had to look. Somehow she knew that she wasn't going to be allowed to leave until she saw what she was brought here to see.

She braced herself for whatever horror awaited her…but it wasn't enough. When she turned around, she found the five women not just dead, but *strewn* about the room in bloody *pieces*! She clasped her hands over her mouth, horrified.

You must see it by now, whispered a voice in the silence.

She turned around, her hands still pressed to her mouth, afraid that if she let go she might vomit.

The truth is here. It's written in all the blood spilled inside these walls.

"Who's there?" she asked through her fingers.

But when she turned around again, she was back where she started.

The room had aged countless lifetimes since those atrocities were committed, yet if she looked closely, she could still see disturbing shapes tattooed onto the rotting fabric of those pillows.

The truth is here, she thought, recalling the words of that mysterious voice. Who said that? And what did it mean?

But before she could ponder the matter, she realized that Seph was gone again.

The door was open. Somewhere on the other side of it, she could see the faint glow of a flashlight. She stepped toward it, then froze. That awful, creeping chill was slithering up her back again. She turned and looked behind her.

The five small women stood staring back at her, pale and thin, their eyes black as coal, their fine, white hair blowing about their faces in a breeze that Piper couldn't feel.

They didn't attack her. They didn't attempt to speak to her.

They just stood there, surrounded by the haunting shadows of their own, gruesome murders, staring at her.

She backed away from them, expecting them to give chase, but they only stood there and watched, an eerie sort of sadness on their ghostly faces. She wished she could help them, but she was certain she couldn't. They were already gone, after all. Already lost. Seph, on the other hand, still wasn't among them.

At least, she desperately hoped she wasn't.

She ran from the room, praying she wouldn't find the flashlight abandoned on the floor with Seph nowhere to be seen. Instead, she found Seph lying on the dirty floor, the flashlight still bound in her ponytail, casting a grayish, yellow circle on the moldy wall. She stopped, her heart skipping a beat in her chest. "Persephone?"

Seph turned her head and looked at her as she approached. "Pips…?" she sighed.

Piper felt a wave of relief flow through her. "Oh my gosh…" She rubbed her eyes and tried to calm herself. That was quite a scare. For a second there, she thought…

"Where'd you go? I was all alone."

"I'm sorry. There was something I had to do."

"I don't…feel so good…"

"It's okay," Piper assured her. But when she opened her eyes again, the tall man was standing over Seph's body.

Chapter 57

"*No!*" screamed Piper.

The tall man lifted the blade. The metal glinted in the flashlight's beam as it rose.

"*Persephone! Move!*"

But Seph didn't seem able to move. She looked exhausted.

Piper ran toward her, but it was pointless. She couldn't get to her in time. Even if she could, what could she possibly do? She had no way of defending against that weapon.

It slashed through the air, the metal flashing in the reflected flashlight beam as it fell.

Piper screamed.

The tip of the blade buried itself in the splintered wood floor and a terrifying shriek cut through the air.

Piper stood there, horrified.

But Seph was fine. The blade didn't even graze her.

The tall man missed?

No…

As she watched, ghostly hands crept up the long blade, grasping at it. A twisted, corpse-like thing emerged, as if it had been trapped under Seph when she fell over. It tilted its head back and let out a chilling wail, then rolled its face toward Piper. Dead, cataract eyes stared at her, a strange, frozen fury on the thing's rotten face.

It was a woman. Long, white, corpselike hair hung from her head.

Piper watched, horrified as the ghastly corpse climbed up the shaft of the tall man's wicked weapon, dragging herself up it.

Was this…*thing*…inside Seph? Maria told her that the scythe wouldn't be able to fully protect her from the Keeper's time magic while it was working to save her from the Gispuknya wasp venom. But did that mean it also wasn't able to fully protect her from the spirits of Covengale, either?

Was this why Seph had been acting so strange? Was she dealing with not two, but *three* invading forces on her body?

Before she could even begin to understand what she was supposed to do next, the old woman reached out with a long, shriveled arm and closed her skeletal hands around Piper's ankle.

Everything changed again.

But this time, she didn't find herself in a younger version of the same place she'd just been standing. Instead, she was sitting on one of those overstuffed pillows, staring out an open window at a night sky.

A mostly full moon hung there, but not the moon she knew. This moon was much bigger and much brighter. It shined like a gold coin, filling the sprawling lake beneath it with shimmering light.

It was beautiful.

Was this what this universe looked like before it died and was swallowed by the encroaching Wood?

And yet, strangely, she felt no peace as she sat there.

In fact, as the seconds passed…or perhaps they were minutes, or even hours…she found herself feeling uneasy…then agitated…then *angry*…

And why shouldn't she be angry? After what they'd done to her…

Then she frowned. Wait… What? Who?

She turned and looked around. The room was similar to the tower room where she saw the five terrified women, but bigger, with a single, enormous pillow in the middle of the floor like some kind of giant, beanbag bed, and with much more stuff lying around. There were tables against every wall, covered in little, variously shaped pots and bowls, strange-looking little dolls and decorative boxes in different sizes.

Again, her eyes were drawn to the window.

There was an ominous sort of energy in the air. She'd been feeling it for weeks now.

She shook her head. That wasn't true. She hadn't been here weeks.

Had she?

No… She would've run out of snacks by then and turned into a feral Ahn hybrid.

No. It was the woman, she realized. The owner of this bedroom. And the one whose corpse crawled out from under Seph's body a moment ago. *She'd* been feeling it for weeks now. Or…she'd been feeling it for weeks whenever *this* day was…

Gosh this stuff was confusing…

Why was this happening? This wasn't how it happened before. Why was she *inside* this woman? She'd only had to observe the other horrors. What manner of atrocity was going to happen this time? And what role would she be forced to play?

She stared up at that golden moon, mesmerized by its alien beauty.

This world was dying, she realized. It'd been dying for a long, long time. Almost since it began, really. That was the fate of all worlds. But through this woman's eyes, she saw that it was recently becoming much worse. The cancer that was eating this world was becoming *visible*, even to those who insisted on ignoring it. There were cracks now. Sores. The world was beginning to *bleed.*

Except what bled out of the universe when it died was not blood, but malice and madness. It oozed the foul, black ichor of the Oblivion that waited at the end of all things and brought with it unthinkable horrors that even now were clawing their way through the rotting skin that separated them from us.

Dark things were coming. Dark and terrible things. Unstoppable things.

Piper covered her face, horrified.

Was *this* what the end of the world was really like? Reality was simply going to crack open and spill out hordes of horrible monsters? No bloody wars? No fiery meteorites? No festering plagues? Just…a literal *hell* unleashed upon the world?

It was like the plot of some really lame book.

What the hell kind of design was that? The Architects were smart enough to craft an entire universe from nothing but they couldn't stop it from eventually falling apart and *devouring* the last of its remaining inhabitants?

When she lowered her hands again, she was no longer sitting in front of the window. Instead, she was standing in front of a shiny, green-tinted mirror mounted on the wall.

She had no memory of standing up or of crossing the room, but she didn't waste time dwelling on that minor detail. Much more concerning at the moment was that the reflection staring back at her wasn't her own.

The woman there was old and withered, battered by time, hardened by a life in a world on the brink of destruction. Staring at her, Piper could almost see the thing she would become someday, the thing that was impaled by the tall man's scary blade…the thing that crawled out from under her best friend.

She turned away from the mirror and looked around.

Time had passed again. Days, maybe. Or years. It was impossible to be certain. But the calm, peaceful night had been replaced by a dark, stormy day. Rain was falling in a heavy downpour outside. A cold wind whipped at the curtains. And beneath that, a soft, almost constant rumbling of thunder.

She stared out into the storm. Something else was out there, too. A strange, greenish luminescence that seemed to fall with the rain, beautiful but also somehow unsettling.

Was that a normal occurrence in this universe? Or was it something related to the approaching doom?

Even the fundamental laws of nature can change from universe to universe.

What wonders existed in these worlds before they died?

She turned away from the window, daydreaming a bit, and walked over to one of the tables. A silver box was sitting there. She opened it and took out a long, narrow-bladed knife. Then she opened the door and stepped out into the dark hallway.

He'd be sleeping by now. The rain wouldn't disturb him. On the contrary, he liked the sound of the rain. It soothed him. It drowned out all the other noises. He never slept more deeply than when the long rains came.

He'd never hear her until it was too late.

She reached for his doorknob, then paused.

What was she doing?

Was she about to…murder someone?

She looked down at the strange little blade, horrified. What was going on? Was she trapped inside the old woman's head?

She stared at the blade, more confused than ever. There was blood dripping from it. Did she cut herself with it?

But when she looked up, she was no longer standing outside the door. She was standing over one of those huge pillows. A man lay before her, twitching and gurgling as blood bubbled out of several puncture wounds in his throat.

What did…? How? *When*?

But as she stared down at the man's bulging eyes, she found that her horror was quickly melting away.

He deserved it.

He wasn't a man at all. He was a *monster*. He'd *always* been a monster. He'd done terrible, terrible things. Not just to her, either. To so many people.

He was especially fond of young girls.

She clenched her teeth, a great, seething fury rising in her, and plunged the blade deep into one of those hideous, bulging eyes.

Then the anger was gone, replaced by mounting horror. She clamped her hand over her mouth and staggered backward. What did she do? What was happening to her?

She was going to be sick!

She turned to run…but she was no longer in that room. She was sitting on one of those pillows in a much smaller room, a bowl of bright green little things that looked like nuts or seeds resting in her lap.

More time had passed. She didn't know how much time, but the rain had stopped. The sky outside the window was the blazing orange of a fiery sunset.

She didn't feel disturbed anymore. In fact, she felt at peace for the first time in many years.

He was gone now. He could never hurt her again. He could never hurt *anyone* ever again.

And neither could his evil brothers.

One by one, she'd slaughtered each of them. Eight in all. Before the rain stopped falling, each one of them died strangling on his own blood, gurgling and twitching like helpless babies. And each time the life left one of their remaining eyes, she was filled with such an electric sensation of thrilling satisfaction that it was almost *sexual.* She'd never felt so intoxicatingly *alive.*

Piper smiled at the memory.

The last one was the best. With the others done, she didn't have to be so quick. She was able to take her time. Just thinking about it now made her feel…

She shuddered at the memory of that dark, encompassing bliss.

The ones that came after that were good, too.

All of them.

Dozens of them.

And every one of them pure *ecstasy*!

She turned and looked at herself in the mirror. She was much older than she used to be. Her hair was so thin now she could see through it. Her face had sagged. Her body had withered. Her gnarled hands trembled.

For a moment, something about that reflection seemed wrong. Like it didn't belong to her…

But that was just the years. They piled up after a while, clogging things, cluttering the thoughts. It was to be expected.

Her time here was short.

There was just one last job that needed done.

She looked down at the bowl in front of her. With a smile on her crooked lips, she took a handful of the green seeds and stuffed them into her mouth.

The poison burned. Her tongue swelled. Her lips blistered. Almost immediately, her face began to swell.

She made up her mind a long time ago. She was never leaving this place.

She'd stay here forever, blessing her beloved Covengale to know the joy she'd discovered again and again.

Let the world end. Let the monsters come.

She was going to be the queen of them all!

And this would *always* be her castle!

The bowl clattered to the floor, spilling the deadly seeds. Her face went numb. Her throat swelled closed. She couldn't breathe.

But as she fell back onto the pillow, she smiled.

It was just as exquisite as she expected it to be…

Then Piper gasped for breath and opened her eyes.

She was sitting on the floor in that dark, moldy hallway, next to Seph. That scary blade was still wedged in the rotten floorboards, but the old hag had vanished.

Was she…*dead*? Did the tall man kill her? Or…*re*-kill her, she guessed…?

"That woman was a curse on Covengale," said the tall man. He was sitting on the floor on the other side of Seph, his knees bent, his arms resting casually on top of them, his long fingers dangling over the floor. His face remained stubbornly concealed in the darkness, in defiance of the two flashlights that illuminated the space around him. "A curse that refused to die with her. Every terrible thing that happened here began with her."

Piper felt at her lips, distracted. That flashback was so realistic that they still felt swollen.

"Do you see it yet?" he asked her.

She'd heard that voice before, asking that same question. In previous flashbacks.

"See what?" she asked.

"The truth."

She stared at him. What truth? What was he talking about? And who was he?

The tall man stood up. He grasped the handle of his weapon—such a strange and violent-looking blade—and yanked it from the floor. "You will," he promised her. "For now, go back to where you started. The lock waits for you there."

The lock was waiting for them back at the beginning? Did he mean the safe room?

That didn't make any sense.

But the tall man said no more. He turned and walked away, vanishing back into the darkness from which he'd come.

She watched after him for a moment, still confused by the whole ordeal, and then knelt over Seph.

Her eyes fluttered open. "Pea…?"

"Yeah. I'm here."

"I've been having the craziest dreams…"

Piper recalled the horrid form of the old woman's corpse crawling out from under her and shuddered a little at the thought. "I believe it," she replied.

Chapter 58

It took a while to navigate their way back to the safe room. Covengale's hallways were a confusing labyrinth to begin with, and a large portion of them were submerged or had collapsed. Piper lost count of how many times she had to backtrack and circle around. And the entire time the walls kept whispering and groaning and murmuring at her. Shadows kept moving. Ghostly faces kept watching them. And of course there were those occasional, blood-curdling screams.

She had to eat another piece of beef jerky. How many times was that now? Four? Five? Half a dozen? She wasn't sure. She'd lost count. And strangely, she didn't even actually feel hungry. She was only a little bit thirsty, and probably only that because of the saltiness of the jerky.

She tried not to think about why she didn't need to use the bathroom…

It was all so confusing. Her body didn't seem to think she'd been here but a few hours at most. Maria acted as if she'd been gone all day when she first returned to the safe room. And the ravenous Ahn in her seemed to think she'd been trapped here for a considerable portion of the week.

She didn't understand *anything* in this place.

Seph seemed to be doing better, at least. She was worn-out, but she'd stopped talking crazy, which was a huge improvement. She walked in silence beside her, their arms linked, determined not to get separated again.

The flashlight was still in her ponytail, still casting a halo of light onto the ceiling above her head wherever she went.

And so far nothing too concerning had happened. There was a moment there when the floor began to creak dangerously beneath them and they had to quickly turn back. And then there were a few frantic minutes where something child-sized with glowing, white eyes wouldn't stop following them, but it had finally lost interest and disappeared. And that damned *scream* kept making her jump.

Who the hell was doing that, anyway? Shut up already. You're dead. Probably murdered. She got it. Quit being such a drama queen.

Finally, she found the room with the two staircases, where she experienced her first flashback. From here, the safe room was just up those steps and at the far end of the hallway.

It seemed too easy. This was the part in the story where something terrifying jumped out to impede their progress. But step after step, nothing happened.

Maybe it was the tall man. He told them to go back to the beginning. Maybe he was ahead of them, clearing a path for them. He was clearly more than a match for these spirits.

She wondered who he was. He didn't seem like the other ghosts in this place.

Seph told her that a tiny little man who called himself "the attendant" was waiting for her in the room with the lock back in the library. Maybe the tall man was like him?

It didn't matter. They reached the safe room without any more *real* scares and looked around.

"Maria?" called Piper.

Seph looked up at her. "Who?"

"The custodian? The ghost girl from the diner?"

She furrowed her eyebrows and thought hard about it for a second. It took a little more effort than it usually did. Her head was still cloudy. "Oh yeah… I think I remember that."

"Maria!"

"Welcome back."

She turned around to find the black-haired girl standing right behind her.

"Did you find what you were looking for?"

"No."

"What's she saying?" whispered Seph.

Piper glanced over at her. "What?"

"You can understand her?"

This was confusing. "Of course I can understand her. Can't you?"

Seph stared at her. "No. I don't even know what language that is."

"Huh?"

"She's right," said Maria.

Or…*did* she say that? Now that she was paying attention…

"I'm guessing your spirit ears are translating it for you. I've been speaking like this the whole time."

It was true. She understood the words, so she'd never paid much attention, but that was definitely not English. Or any other language she'd ever heard before.

"So what's she saying?" Seph asked again.

"She was asking if we'd found the lock," replied Piper. "And I said no." She stared at Maria. "But you already knew that, didn't you?"

Maria smiled that sad smile of hers and said nothing.

"You've had it all along."

Seph looked back and forth between them, confused. "What?"

"You had to play by the rules," explained Maria. "You can't just *have* the lock. That's not how these things work."

"What'd she say that time?" whispered Seph.

"Shh!"

Seph shrugged and turned away.

Piper gnawed at her lip, annoyed. The rules… She was *sick* of the stupid rules. Who the heck even *made* all these rules? They were idiotic. "Do you have any idea what I've been through?"

"I know exactly what you've been through."

She stared at the girl for a moment. All the pieces were finally starting to fall into place. "You're one of them…aren't you?"

She gave her another of those sad smiles. For a moment, she changed. Her features shifted a little, making her more resemble some of the people in those flashbacks. Her eyes grew larger. Her nose flattened a little. Her skin darkened. Then, so abruptly it was difficult to tell for sure that it wasn't just a figment of her imagination, she looked like she did before again. "I told you I did something really bad."

"Really bad" was a phrase that probably had a whole different meaning out in the living world than it did here in this awful place. So many things had happened here that went well beyond "really bad" and even well past "really *depraved*."

"It happened in this very room. Would you like to see it?" All around them, the room began to turn back. The dust and grime and mold seemed to roll away. A dismal, red glow swelled in the windows.

"What's happening?" asked Seph.

"I can show it to you," said Maria, "just like the others did. You can see it with your own eyes."

Everything was splashed with blood. It was splattered on the floor. It dripped down the walls. It was soaked into the cushions.

As shadows began to materialize before her, ready to show her every gruesome detail of the horrific thing that Maria once did, Piper covered her eyes. "No!" She didn't want to see any more. She'd already seen enough to fuel her nightmares for years to come. The last thing she wanted was to see more of the same committed by someone with a familiar face. "No more! Please!"

When she peeked through her fingers, everything was back to the way it was before.

Maria stood there, smiling her sad smile at her.

"What just happened?" asked Seph.

"This place was cursed," said Piper. "That old woman… What she did. What she *became*. It wasn't your fault."

But Maria shook her head. "No. That's not how the curse worked. Covengale didn't turn people evil. It didn't *breed* darkness. It *attracted* it. The people who did those awful things…they already had that capacity for evil inside them when they first came here. The curse only helped us realize our true nature."

Piper stared at her, horrified.

"I'm not sorry for what I did. I *enjoyed* it. And not because of some old, dead witch's curse." She smiled that sad smile again. "I told you I should've gone to hell."

She shook her head. "But…you *helped* us. You saved us from those monsters in the diner. *Twice*."

"I couldn't fulfill my end of the deal if you'd died, could I?"

"No…" She didn't believe her. It was the guilt talking. That was all. She'd resigned herself to thinking she was one of Covengale's evils instead of one of its victims.

"What's happening?" asked Seph.

But Piper only shook her head again. It was absurd. Of course Maria was one of the good guys. The Keeper chose her for this job. He made her the custodian of the gate to Covengale.

"I'm on your side in this," explained Maria, "because I made a deal with the Keeper of the Dead. Not because I'm a good person. If I hadn't helped you, he would've sent me to hell, where I belong. You should be careful who you trust. Things are rarely black and white."

"Pea…?" prodded Seph.

Piper's head was spinning. None of this made any sense. Why would she say these things?

"You've completed your trial," said Maria. "I have only one last job to do and then I'll be free."

"The lock," breathed Piper.

She nodded. "Are you ready for it?"

Was she? She glanced over at Seph, who was merely standing there, watching them, able to understand only half the conversation. She looked understandably lost.

Back in the library, Seph told her that the first lock of Tartarus was in a book. It wasn't a switch or a button or a latch. It wasn't a physical thing at all. It was *information.* And it was apparently such overwhelmingly important information that she couldn't even handle remembering it. The attendant had to stuff the information deep into her subconscious mind and erase the memory of it just to keep her from going mad like King Lodblin.

Was she ready for something like that?

"What do I have to do?"

Why did she have such a sad smile? If she wasn't sorry for the things she did…if she really was the terrible person she claimed to be…then why did she smile like that?

"You just have to see one more thing. The most important thing of all. The secret that's been kept hidden here in Covengale, waiting for the day you'd come for it."

"Will it…drive me mad?"

"Almost certainly."

"Oh…"

"But don't worry. The Keeper showed me how to fix you. Just like the attendant fixed *her*."

She looked over at Seph again. "Okay. Let's get it over with then. I guess…"

"I'm going to say goodbye now, if that's okay."

"What?"

"The Keeper said I'd be free to go after I finished my job. I've waited a *really* long time for this day." This time, when she smiled, it was far less sad than it was *hungry*. "There're *so* many things I want to do."

Piper stared at her. She felt an unsettling chill that had nothing to do with the cold. "Where will you go?" she asked, not sure if she really wanted to know. "I mean, you're still *dead*, right?" Even if she *was* evil, what harm could she do now?

"I can go anywhere I want once this is over. I can *do* anything I want." Now her smile was positively *sinister*. "*Anything*. Death is only the beginning. There's a whole other world out there, lying just beneath the surface. You'll see it someday. Everyone does, eventually."

She rubbed her eyes. *Another* world? Weren't there enough of those out there already?

Maria held out her hand. "I'm ready to go whenever you are. I don't know about you, but I'd like to never see *this* universe again."

Piper stared at her for a moment longer, uncertain. They'd already established that the custodian possessed the only way in and out of the Keeper's gates. If she didn't do this, they'd be trapped here forever. And yet, if Maria really was what she claimed to be… Should she really set her free into the world?

Why would the Keeper make a deal like this? Why *her*? Why not one of the *victims* of Covengale? Why not one of those five poor women she left standing in that blood-soaked bedroom?

She glanced over at Seph, who merely shrugged at her. (She still didn't know what was going on.)

What choice did she really have? They had a job to do. And they certainly couldn't stay *here* forever.

She took a deep breath. She sighed. And then she reached out for Maria's hand.

Chapter 59

The next thing Piper was aware of was drowning.

The water was cold and black, all-enveloping. Startled and confused, she cried out and lost half her breath in a great belch of bubbles. She clasped her hand over her mouth and nose, trying to stifle herself. That was bad. She couldn't waste breath like that. She didn't know where she was or how she got here, but the water was deep. She could feel the pressure on her ears and chest.

She swam upward, chasing the bubbles.

The last thing she remembered was reaching for Maria's hand. Then everything became a white, blinding blur.

It was so dark. How deep was she? Her chest began to ache. She was going to run out of air! Fresh panic welled up inside her.

But then she broke the surface and gasped for air.

Seph was here. She was calling out to her. The flashlight in her hair was a bobbing beacon in the darkness.

"What happened?" panted Piper. "Where are we?"

"We're back," said Seph. "We're on the other side of the Keeper's gate."

They'd escaped Covengale? She looked around, confused. She was treading water in an open lake beneath an ocean of shining stars.

This was Fathom Lake… But it was nighttime? Why was it dark

out? How long were they in there? And…

"Wait…" She turned and looked around. Where was Maria? Was she already gone?

"My glasses!" gasped Seph. "I think I dropped them!"

"I have them," Piper assured her. She turned around again and then pointed. "Over there! The boat!" It was drifting about thirty feet away, barely visible in the darkness.

They swam over to it and climbed in, careful not to capsize it in the process. The bag Piper packed was still inside, untouched.

"What happened down there?" gasped Piper as she seated herself in the boat and began looking for her flashlight. She wasn't holding it anymore. Did she put it in one of her pockets? She didn't leave it back in Covengale, did she? Or drop it when she thought she was drowning?

She peered over the side of the boat, but saw no sign of it glowing at the bottom of the lake.

But then again, it'd probably be at the bottom of that black well…if it had a bottom at all…

"No idea," replied Seph. She was sitting across from her, rubbing her ankle. "That ghost girl took your hand and then…I don't even know. You kind of went away for a while. You just stood there for a long time with this kind of…*stoned* expression on your face."

Piper shot her a dirty look as she handed her glasses back to her. "I'm sure I didn't look *stoned*!"

"No, you definitely did." She returned them to her face and blinked out at the dark lake around her. "You were totally wasted." It would've been funny if it hadn't been so scary. For a moment there, she thought something had happened to her.

"Whatever." She unzipped the bag and began digging around in it. It didn't matter if she lost the flashlight. There were more in here.

"Don't make fun of me. Especially after the way *you* behaved down there."

"What're you talking about?"

"You really don't remember? Miss 'feel my boobs'?"

Seph gasped. "*I said no such thing*!"

"Whatever you say." She found another flashlight and switched it on. Now she could see to start the motor. "But you better not pick on me for turning into a were-Ahn in that library anymore."

"I never picked on you." She was looking around, confused. Was she glowing or something? Where was that light coming from?

Piper leaned over the motor, looking for the plug. "I'm glad you're feeling better, at least."

"Those stings still hurt, but yeah. I don't feel nearly so yucky anymore." She fumbled with her hair, confused. "Why is there a flashlight stuck to my head?"

"You kept wandering off. And I didn't have a leash."

Seph scowled at her as she untangled the elastic and pried the light free.

Piper started the trolling motor. So far, so good. She turned it all the way to the left and throttled it up, spinning the boat back toward the truck. She made it only a few yards, however, before the bottom of the boat thudded against the lakebed.

"What just happened?"

She leaned over the side of the boat and looked down. The water here was only a couple inches deep. Had they run aground on a submerged hill?

"Say, Pea?" said Seph. "Are you seeing this, too? Or is my brain still out to lunch?"

Piper looked up to see that the water all around them had inexplicably pulled away from them, creating an impossible depression, like a sinkhole, except…on *water*?

It made no sense. It was like something out of a bizarre dream.

Then she remembered what they were running from when she first dived into the water after Seph.

"Oh crap," she gasped.

In all the excitement, she hadn't even noticed the buzzing in her spirit ears.

The marsh woman was still here. She must've been waiting for them all this time, knowing they'd have to leave the same way they entered.

As she watched, the shadowy woman walked out of the water, emerging from it head-first, slowly, her empty, shadowy face invisible in the darkness, even when they aimed their flashlights at her head.

This was no good. There was nowhere to run. The boat wouldn't go. They were stranded.

The marsh woman raised her dripping hands, reaching out for them. Around her, shadowy water began to rise like the tentacles of some great sea monster.

Seph stood up in the boat and unfurled the scythe. Its handle sprang out in front of her, its long, flowing blade cutting through the air.

The marsh woman paused, but not because of Seph.

A strange, white glow had appeared behind her. She turned her shadowy head, distracted.

Something was coming.

Something as bright as she was dark.

Two somethings. They moved independently of each other, criss-crossing through the murky depths of the silent lake. The glow became a brilliant shine. An icy wind suddenly blew across the lake.

Even in the darkness, Piper saw the marsh woman panic. She turned away from the light and began to sink back into the water. But two shining figures rose up on either side of her, seizing her by her arms and lifting her into the air and out of the water.

The white sisters had found them!

They shined so brightly in this darkness that it hurt to look at them.

The marsh woman had always been silent before, but now she let out an unearthly scream. Her naked, shadowy form kicked and thrashed above the waves. Those black, watery tendrils snatched at the feet of the white figures.

The water came rushing back to them, tossing the boat, nearly knocking Seph overboard. She dropped to the deck and grabbed onto the seat.

Piper took advantage and seized the motor's handle, steering them away from the struggling figures as they rose up out of the lake.

"*What's going on*?" screamed Seph.

Piper focused on aiming the boat toward the parked truck as it rocked back and forth in the waves.

The marsh woman's horrible screaming grew only louder. She was shrieking now.

She looked back. She wished she didn't, but she did. She was watching as the marsh woman let out her most terrible shriek yet and was ripped in two like an old ragdoll.

"That...probably doesn't bode well for us, does it?" groaned Seph. She was still kneeling in the boat, clinging to the sides and staring back at the sisters.

"I really wish this thing would go faster!" cried Piper.

"They're coming this way!"

She looked back over her shoulder. Those white figures were gliding toward them, their feet dragging along the surface of the water, moving considerably faster than the stupid trolling motor.

One of them came up alongside them, but hovered a few yards away, seemingly looking them over, as if evaluating them.

Seph rose into a crouch and drew the scythe. It stretched out between them and it, shielding them.

Piper took the opportunity to look behind them again. "Where'd the other one go?" It'd vanished. She turned to look the other way, only to find the second one leaning over the side of the boat, staring directly into her face.

Beneath the radiant, white shine, the thing was, indeed, a woman. She was tall, and old, but strangely elegant. She had long, white hair, extremely pale skin and pure, white eyes.

It was as if she were created to be the exact opposite of Gispuknya's monsters.

Except there was something dreadfully *evil* about the woman's face.

She reached out with a ghostly sort of hand, long and pale, slender, with extremely long, glass-like nails, and snatched at the pendant that hung around her neck.

Piper screamed and leaned away, clutching at the wheel.

Seph turned, startled, and lashed out at the white woman, but she vanished into the lake. Her sister took advantage of the distraction and charged her.

She turned again and slashed at her, forcing her back.

This was only going to get her so far. She wasn't exactly trained to wield this thing. Or any weapon for that matter. It might be a supernatural tool, perfectly designed for her hands, able to evolve in any way she needed…but she was still pretty much just hacking at whatever it was she wanted to make go away. Plus, she was still feeling woozy from her ordeal in Covengale.

She wasn't going to be able to keep these things off them for long.

One of the white sisters was hovering over them, out of range of the scythe. The other was circling beneath the water, little more than an eerie glow in the murk of the lake.

And the whole while the little jon boat was putting along, taking its sweet time, still thirty yards from the relative safety of the shore.

"Pea?" said Seph.

"Yeah?" said Piper.

"This is bad."

"I know."

The white sisters came at them. One from above and one from below.

Seph couldn't defend against both of them. She held up the scythe and braced herself.

Piper squeezed the wheel in one fist and held onto the side of the boat with the other.

Both of them screamed.

Chapter 60

The white sisters converged on the boat. One swooped down from the air, gliding like a terrible angel on the wind. She dodged the scythe's deadly blade with ease and reached toward Seph's face with those long, glass nails. The second exploded from the water and thrust her hands toward Piper's heart.

At the same time, the lake, itself, awoke.

Something huge rose up, pushing the water with it, a great mountain of a thing forcing its way up out of the earth.

The waves thrust the little boat forward, away from the ghostly sisters.

And then a great, scaly shape was rising into the air.

"You've got to be kidding me…" breathed Seph. She stared at it as it rose higher and higher into the air, its enormous, toothy maw dripping mud and water, its long, serpent-like tongue slithering through the sky, great, yellow eyes burning in the gloom. A horned tail whipped overhead.

Old Fred… His statue in front of the courthouse absolutely did *not* do him justice.

She gaped at the monstrous form. "That thing's *real*?"

Piper could think of no words at all. She'd seen a lot of things since the day she met Seph, but this was definitely one of the most terrifying.

"How does something like that even fit in a lake this size?" stammered Seph.

She didn't have an answer for that, but as she watched it, she realized that the white sisters seemed to have forgotten about them for the moment. They'd turned their full attention to the lake monster. Also, the waves that thing kicked up when it emerged were pushing the boat much faster toward the shore.

In fact… She turned and looked ahead of them. "Look out!"

The boat slammed against the shore and Seph, her gaze still fixed on Old Fred, was thrown backward. She cried out, startled, and landed on her back on the ground.

Piper crawled forward and peered over the bow. "*Are you okay*?"

Seph stared back at her, dazed, her glasses askew. "I think so…" she groaned.

"Hurry up!" She grabbed the bag from the bottom of the boat and looked back out at the lake. She couldn't believe what she was seeing out there. It was a scene right out of a giant monster movie.

Seph straightened her glasses and then rolled over and pushed herself up onto her hands and knees. Then she screamed again.

Piper turned and jumped out of the boat. "*What's wrong*?" But she saw it for herself a moment later.

A small form was lying there on the ground, dressed in strange clothing, with a thick, brown mop of curly hair. It was twisted and mangled and motionless.

Seph looked up at her. "Black-eyed children…"

There were two more of them lying a little farther along the waterline.

Piper shined her light over them. "Did the white sisters do this?"

She couldn't hear that creepy buzzing noise, but it was also difficult to hear anything with a giant lake monster thrashing around right next to them.

"Who cares?" grumbled Seph. It wasn't as if these things were actual children. And the last thing she wanted was to think of them as such. "Let's just get out of here already!" She stood up, limping a little.

What did she do to her ankle?

"You okay?" asked Piper.

"I'm fine." And she *was* fine. It felt a little stiff was all. "Just keep moving."

Old Fred let out a terrible roar, seemingly urging her along as well.

They were parked about twenty yards farther up the shoreline. They ran for it, keeping one eye on the insane battle raging in the lake. It was difficult to see what was happening in the darkness. The white sisters glowed like torches, but Old Fred was little more than a giant, raging shadow kicking water high into the air and sending giant waves crashing around them as they ran.

Seph felt numb. This couldn't really be happening. It was ridiculous! It made no sense! Maybe she was still sick from the wasp stings. Maybe she was hallucinating all this. Maybe she'd hallucinated *everything* and was actually lying in a hospital bed somewhere. Maybe none of this had ever happened and she'd really just had an accident and was in a coma.

Yeah. That'd be great.

She nearly tripped over another dead child.

No! Not a child. A black-eyed, child-shaped monstrosity sent by Gispuknya to slaughter them. She only had to look at them to see it. Even their blood was black.

They ran around them, careful not to get too close, just in case any of them weren't quite dead.

Piper could see the truck now.

She could also see something else. A slick, oozing form perched on the roof of the truck, a writhing mass of oily blackness.

The two of them stopped, their flashlights shining up at it.

It turned its head toward them, a faint, skull-like pattern of lighter gray shapes peering back at them from the blackness of its face.

Piper felt a fresh chill wash over her. It couldn't be…

Seph shook her head. Amethyst said they'd never come back. But there it was, staring back at them.

Just like the first time, way back in the Cakwetak mall.

And yet, before she could even form the scythe's handle, the wraith twisted its gooey form around and darted off into the night, dropping something onto the truck's hood as it fled.

"Oh god…" sighed Seph.

Piper covered her mouth.

The thing it dropped was another of the black-eyed children.

The *wraiths* did that? But…*why*? What reason could the mall wraiths have for helping them?

Old Fred let out another mighty roar.

Lake water fell like rain around them.

Piper tossed her bag into the truck seat and then used a tree branch to push the small, broken corpse off the hood.

That felt *icky*.

(They're not really children! They're not!)

Both of them climbed into the truck and locked the doors behind them. Piper started the engine. She turned on the headlights. Then the two of them sat there, gawking through the gore-smeared windshield at the monstrous form writhing in the lake.

"How is that even possible?" sighed Seph.

Piper reached up and touched the pendant. "Maybe it wasn't…" She lifted it and looked down at it. She remembered grabbing it when the white sisters attacked and praying for a miracle…

Seph stared at it. "Wait…*you* made that thing?"

"I don't know! Maybe? How am I supposed to know?" Neither possibility seemed any less plausible to her, really.

Old Fred roared. That horned tail whipped through the air overhead. A deluge of lake water splashed onto the truck, washing away most of the black gore the mall wraith dripped down the windshield.

Piper turned on the windshield wipers. They swept across the glass, revealing a small figure standing in front of the truck that wasn't there a few seconds before.

One of the black-eyed children stared back at them.

Both of them screamed.

Piper slammed the truck into reverse and turned the truck around.

More black-eyed children were blocking the road back out.

"They're not real…" she whimpered as she shifted the truck into drive. "They're not real…"

They were walking toward them. More of them appeared each second, stepping out of the gloom.

"They're not real!"

She stomped the accelerator and plowed through the little monsters.

She and Seph both screamed.

They weren't real. They were just shadows of Gispuknya. But it didn't make the sounds of their small bodies slamming against the grill of the Ram any less sickening.

"They didn't have faces," said Seph. She looked over at Piper as she clutched the wheel, her eyes wide with horror. "They couldn't be real if they didn't have faces."

Piper nodded. She wished she saw them like Seph did, without faces. That might've made it easier.

Behind them, Old Fred let out another terrifying roar. It rolled over the truck like thunder.

"I'm so over this…" sighed Seph.

Chapter 61

It was well past eleven o'clock at night when they were far enough from Fathom Lake and all its nightmares to finally relax a little.

Piper took her phone off the charger and Seph plugged hers in.

Neither of them could even guess at how they only spent fifteen minutes in Lodblin's library, but half a day inside Covengale.

But then again, only one of them had been fully aware of what took place inside either of the Keeper's gates. Maybe they simply spent that much more time inside the rotting walls of Covengale. More likely, however, was that the Keeper's time magic simply made no damn sense. They could just as easily have been gone a week, for all they knew.

And it almost seemed like they had, given how many messages there were from Meg. And they were still coming. A new message arrived while she was looking at the screen.

"Oh my gosh, does she not sleep anymore?"

"Her crazy is evolving," said Seph. "Maybe I *should* reap her."

"If it'll get me some gosh darn peace and quiet…" grumbled Piper.

Seph's phone finished booting up and immediately informed her of dozens of missed calls and texts from Meg, too. "Why's she blowing up *my* phone? She doesn't even like me." Plus there were several messages and missed calls from both Kaitlyn and Alton. What did those two want?

Piper sighed. She really didn't want to deal with Meg's special brand of crazy right now. She was way too tired. Besides, she was driving. She dropped the phone onto the seat beside her without reading any of the messages.

Seph was exhausted, too. She felt like she could sleep for days, even though she'd pretty much already slept through the entire haunted house ride portion of the trip. She had almost no recollection of Covengale whatsoever, up until they were making their way back to the safe room where Maria was waiting for them. And even that was kind of a blur. All she remembered with any kind of clarity was Piper talking to the ghost girl from Pappy Stan's Diner and somehow understanding that strange language she was speaking. All that remained of the rest of the ordeal were snippets of strange, muddled dreams.

And now that she had time to really think about it, they might not have all been dreams. The ones about her dad were obviously dreams. And that part about Alton and Kaitlyn playing Pokémon in a bathtub probably wasn't real. Some of it, she was sure, was just delirious nonsense. But she also dreamed that she fell into a river and twisted her ankle, and that felt strangely real. She could still occasionally feel a twinge of pain from it.

She had another dream, too, though. One that stood out from all the others. It was extremely vivid, more realistic in her addled memory than Covengale, itself.

She remembered standing in a dark room, surrounded by crawling shadows and unable to find a door or a window. She had no idea where she was, how to get out or even how she got in. It was stiflingly hot, which was weird because everything else in that mental haze had been so cold… And there was an almost overpowering stench of something dead.

Those crawling shadows were creeping closer and closer, circling around her on scuttling little bug legs.

But the biggest shadow was on the ceiling. She looked up at it as it twisted and churned, oozing downward, staring at her with oily, dripping eyes.

"Hello?" said a voice.

She turned, startled, to find a strange, glowing door that wasn't there before. Someone was standing in front of it, a stark silhouette against the blinding light shining through the opening.

A little girl?

"Who are you?" she asked. Then, "You're not supposed to be here."

When she turned around again, the shadows had all gone. Even the big one.

There was something awful about it. That wasn't Gispuknya, or one of its many creatures. That was something else. Something older. Something far *greater.*

She didn't know how she got out of that room any more than she knew how she got in. It was probably the same way all dreams came and went. Except there was something about it…something about that little girl…and something about that big shadow. Even now, looking back on it, she found it unsettling.

And that name that kept swimming around in her thoughts…the one she heard deep inside her head when she was staring into that thing's oozing eyes…the one that chilled her even more than Gispuknya's name the first time she heard it…

Who…or *what*…was *Altrusk*?

"You okay?" asked Piper.

Seph glanced over at her, distracted. "Huh? *Yeah.* I'm fine. Just…you know…"

"Yeah. Those Gispuknya wasps did a real number on you. And the Keeper's time magic, too. And that old hag that possessed you, I guess…"

"Got it, thanks." She shivered and turned the Ram's heater vents so that they blew directly onto her gooseflesh-covered arms.

She wished they each had another change of clothes, but they were lucky they had this one. What were the odds that Amethyst would think to stash a bag behind the seat of this truck to begin with?

And with that one thought, she felt an agonizing pang of regret pierce her like a blade.

She'd forgotten about poor Amethyst. Remembering it hit her so hard it nearly took her breath away. She turned and stared out the window at the passing darkness.

A few minutes passed as emotions raged through her head.

Then Piper's cell phone rang.

"Meg," she groaned as she looked down at the screen beside her.

"Might as well answer it," said Seph without looking over. "She'll just keep calling until you do." And just maybe it would take her mind off things.

Piper sighed a defeated sort of sigh and accepted the call.

"You said you'd be back this morning!" shouted Meg.

"I said no such thing," snapped Piper. "I said I didn't know when we'd be back. You just don't listen."

"Where are you now?" she demanded, not listening.

"Still in Madison."

"*Auuuuugh*! What are you even *doing*? I need you back here *now*!"

"Are you still freaking out about River Lobnetter?"

"Did *neither* of you read *any* of my messages?"

"We didn't have service most of the day. I *told* you we weren't going to have service."

"How do you not have service in *Madison*? What part of Madison doesn't have cell service?"

Piper opened her mouth, but found that she didn't have an answer for that one. "Uh…"

"*Auuuuugh*! Forget it! Just come home right now! Someone broke into our apartment!"

She sat bolt-upright in her seat at that, startled. "*What*?"

Seph looked over, surprised by Piper's sudden change of tone.

"Yeah! *Now* do I have your fucking attention?"

"What do you mean someone broke in?"

"What?" said Seph, sitting up. "Broke in where? What's she saying?" She grabbed her phone and took another look at her messages.

"I was out all day trying not to *die*," huffed Meg, "and when I went home this afternoon to see if you two ever came back, the door was open!"

"Someone broke into the apartment?" exclaimed Seph, staring at Meg's frantic message.

"Was someone there?" asked Piper.

"I don't know. I peeked in the door and there was another box of candy sitting on the table! And there was a big *knife* lying next to it!"

Piper looked over at Seph, worried. That *did* sound more than a little threatening…

"I got the hell out of there when I saw that. I *told* you that bitch was trying to kill me!"

"Another box of candy and a knife?" said Seph, reading the same story on her phone.

Piper stared straight ahead. She didn't dare take her eyes off the road for fear that a black-eyed child or a glowing white hag might run out in front of them. But most of her attention was focused on Meg's voice. She was being as bitchy as ever, but there was a strange shrillness to her voice that she didn't think she'd ever heard before. Meg was actually *scared.* "Did you call the police?"

"Of course not! They're not going to believe me!"

"Why wouldn't they believe you?"

"Because Crystal Yawbeckner's *dad* is a police officer!"

Piper sighed. The so-called cyberbully.

"She'll have made sure they won't listen to anything I say."

"She can't do that. They still have to listen to you. It's their *job.*"

"No way!"

She groaned. "Fine. Where are you now?"

"I've just been sitting in my car outside the Verti-Go on Lodwyn Road for the past hour and a half waiting for you two to get home! At least there's surveillance cameras on me here."

Piper gnawed at her lower lip. It wasn't bad thinking, she supposed. It was a very public location. Even the most inexperienced murderer should be wary of making a move with security cameras watching. And if her assailant was too crazy to care about any of that, she could always just speed away in her car. But she highly doubted that Meg was dealing with a mob hitman or a jealous, jilted girlfriend with a bag of loose screws. Before now, she would've bet money that the whole ordeal was inside her head. But if someone really did break into their apartment and leave a threatening package for her… That was a pretty scary thing. And she couldn't help but think about how that incubus last summer attacked both Wanda and Seph's mom in an effort to steal the second Hand.

"So did they break the door?" wondered Seph. Meg never said how the intruder managed to get into the apartment. "And did she just leave it open?" The idea of their apartment door standing open for anyone to walk in was more than a little unsettling.

Piper shook her head. One thing at a time. "Listen, head over to Banned Dave's Bar. Wanda should be working tonight. I'll give her a call and she'll look after you, okay?"

"Banned Dave's…" Meg repeated. "I *think* I'm allowed in that one."

"Probably." She'd nearly forgotten about Meg getting banned from all those bars after pissing off Crystal Yawbeckner, but, "Nobody ever gets banned from Banned Dave's." After Dave Leeverd was, himself, banned from his favorite bar, he sank his life savings into opening his *own* bar right across the street, eventually putting it out of business. Dave *never* banned anyone from his bar on principle. He was known to have thrown more than a few people out on their butts for the night, but everyone was welcome to come back again the next night, once they'd sobered up.

Dave was crude, rowdy and loud, but Wanda said he was a fantastic boss. He was surprisingly kind, generous and always concerned for the well-being of his employees and customers. He'd been known to beat the snot out of more than a few drunks for being disrespectful to women.

And since Wanda knew all about the Hands of the Architects and just how dangerous it could be for people close to them, Piper couldn't think of a safer place for Meg to go.

"You know Wanda doesn't like me," she huffed.

"*Nobody* likes you," Piper snapped.

"*Rude*!"

"But at least *she's* not trying to kill you."

Meg was uncharacteristically silent after that.

"Drive over there and get inside. I'll let her know you're coming. And once you're there, just do what she tells you to do and don't piss off any more deranged lunatics for a while, okay? Can you do that for just one night?"

There was such a long silence on the phone then that she thought Meg hung up on her again. Then, strangely, she just said, "Okay."

Piper frowned. No bitchy retorts? No bossy, obnoxious remarks?

In a very small and un-Meg-like voice, she said, "Tell her to be nice to me, okay?"

She glanced over at Seph. "Yeah. Sure."

Meg disconnected the call without another word.

"Wow… I think this might *really* have freaked her out."

"It *is* kind of unsettling," admitted Seph. The idea of someone breaking into their apartment and leaving a second box of candy and a knife was just the sort of nasty, threatening thing Tane might do. But why? Did he want to use her as a hostage, like the incubus did last summer? And if so, then why bother with candy and knives at all? Why not just grab her, the way Ian grabbed Wanda?

Piper brought up Wanda's cell phone number. She always had it on, even at work. As long as she didn't stand around chatting all night, Dave never cared.

She answered on the third ring and Piper quickly told her the abridged version of what had been going on the past two days and that Meg was on her way there and if she could watch over her. Oh, and if she could possibly be nice to her, too.

Wanda, for her part, didn't question a word of it. She knew this was coming, after all. She'd literally *trained* them for this. She only seemed surprised that it had already started without her realizing it. She didn't even sound remotely surprised that the bad guys might be going after Meg. "I'll watch after her," she promised. "And I'll see if I can find someone to go check on your apartment for you, too."

"That'd be great," said Piper. "Thanks."

"Keep me informed, if you can, okay Babs?"

"I'll try." *No one* ever called her Piper, but only *Wanda* called her *Babs*. And no one knew why. She refused to tell anyone why. "Thanks a lot."

"Take care out there."

"I will. Bye."

She ended the call and laid the phone in the seat next to her again. Then she sat and stared at the road in front of them, pinching her lip, thinking about Meg and threatening knives and Wanda chained up in a box and so nearly set on fire…

Seph watched her for a moment. "Are you okay?"

"Yeah. Just… Meg."

"Yeah."

"And…*everything*."

"Yeah. I'm sorry I left you to deal with all that scary stuff on your own."

Piper shrugged. "It's only fair, I guess. I kind of did the same thing to you in that library. Plus, you know, I tried to *eat* you."

"You *did* do that."

"I'm okay. Just a little tired. Remind me to thank Wanda when we get home. For *everything*. I think her training is really paying off. If we survive this, I might owe her a steak dinner or something."

"I'll buy her dessert," decided Seph.

Piper smiled. "Looks like it'll be tomorrow by the time we get to Pobsick Spring. Try to get some sleep. Then we can switch."

Seph nodded. "Okay." She nuzzled into the pickup's musty seat and stared out the window. "Hey, Pepper?"

"Hm?"

"I didn't *really* ask you to feel my boobs, did I?"

"*Oh* yeah," laughed Piper. "You're kinda freaky when you're all drugged up."

Seph groaned and laid her head against the window. How embarrassing...

Piper smirked at her. "So I'm taking it you don't want to make out with me anymore?"

"Oh god... Please stop."

Piper giggled. "Okay. I promise." She turned her attention back to the empty road stretching out before them. Slowly, her smile faded. She could laugh *now* about Seph's state of mind, now that she knew she was okay. But it was kind of scary at the time. She had no idea what was going on. She was deathly afraid that the Gispuknya wasp venom might really kill her.

She glanced over at Seph. She was *still* worried. She seemed like she was back to normal, if exhausted, but how could she be certain?

No. The scythe protected her. That was its job. Just like the wheel had protected Piper.

She glanced down at it. Did she *really* summon Old Fred? Was the wheel really capable of creating something like that? It *was* supposed to be one of the three most powerful tools in existence. It was supposed to be able to spin *anything* into existence from nothing. Why not an eighty-foot-tall lake monster?

Or maybe Old Fred had been real the whole time and all she did was awaken him.

She might never know for sure. And it didn't really matter. She needed to focus on what awaited them at the end of this road.

The location of the third lock was definitely going to be someplace utterly terrifying. There was absolutely no reason to think otherwise. They'd already dealt with a library monster and an army of psychotic ghosts. What could possibly be waiting for them in Texas?

She already knew that Pobsick Spring wasn't going to be nearly as nice as it sounded.

Chapter 62

Pobsick Spring was a dump.

Literally.

It wasn't even a city. It was a ten-foot-tall, barbwire-topped fence surrounding the largest scrapyard either of them had ever seen. There was nothing else here. There was only an endless expanse of mostly flat desert scrub stretching all the way to the horizon in every direction.

Piper brought up the map on her phone and frowned at the screen. "This place is *literally* in the middle of nowhere."

"And that surprises you?"

She shrugged and lowered the phone. "I guess not..." She pinched her lip and stared out at the mountains of junk as they passed, her ghostly ears twitching nervously. She couldn't help noticing a suspicious lack of springs. Unless they meant the metal kind that were rusting away in those scrap piles...

They each took a turn trying to get some sleep, but neither of them had managed to get very much. They were both too worried about what was waiting for them in Pobsick Spring.

And now they were worried about Meg, too. An hour after Piper first called her, Wanda called back with the disturbing news that Meg never made it to the bar.

She never answered her phone the rest of the night.

Wanda sent a friend of hers from the bar to their apartment with her spare key. He reported no signs of a break-in. The door was closed and locked, without any damage. None of the windows were broken. And nothing seemed to be missing or noticeably out-of-place. There *was*, apparently, a box of cookies on the table, just as Meg described, but there weren't any knives lying around.

Everything seemed perfectly normal.

Except that Meg had apparently vanished off the face of the earth.

They stopped again for breakfast at a little past nine in the morning. Or maybe it was lunch. Or dinner… It was hard to tell for sure. But Piper's stomach had let them know that it was time for them to eat *something* and Seph had no intention of *ever* not feeding Piper when her stomach said it was time to eat again.

While they ate, Piper called everyone she could think of who still talked to Meg, which wasn't very many. And the vast majority of them not only didn't know where she was, they made it quite clear that they didn't *care*.

It was now approaching noon, and there was still no word from her.

Even Seph had become concerned about the situation, but she was doing her best to focus on the task in front of them.

She followed the endless scrapyard fence all the way to its end. Then, having confirmed that there was absolutely *nothing* else here, she made a U-turn and headed back again.

The gate stood open. Seph pulled into the drive, but stopped short of entering the scrapyard. She sat behind the wheel, surveying the scene before her. There was a squatty little tin shack of an office to the left. There was an old, blue and white, dust-covered tow truck parked next to it, the words "Pobsick Spring Towing" printed on its door. She stared at the mountains of scrap metal looming in the background, the walls of old cars towering like canyon walls carved through the endless junk. Was this where they were supposed to be? Was this where the custodian was supposed to meet them? It *did* make sense. What better place to hide the gate to the final Tartarus lock? The cliché, "needle in a haystack," immediately came to mind.

But then again, since when did any of this stuff ever have to make sense? Maybe this was just where they'd find the custodian. Or just some stupid clue telling them to go to some other stupid place. She glanced out at the endlessly sprawling scrub. For all she knew, the Keeper's gate could be out there somewhere, probably guarded by a pack of rabid Gispuknya coyotes and Tane's favorite homicidal pet clown.

It didn't really matter. They couldn't open the gate by themselves. Only the custodian could do that. Before they did anything else, they had to find *him.*

Or her. Or *it.* So far, she reminded herself, it'd been a group of elderly clones and a ghost from a dead and distant universe. It could be a talking goat this time and she honestly didn't think she'd be surprised.

"It's quiet," observed Piper. Her ears were still twitching back and forth, searching. She couldn't hear any buzzing noises, but that didn't always mean there weren't shadows nearby. Sometimes it was difficult to detect. And sometimes, like in the diner, they simply didn't seem to make any noise until they began to attack.

Seph nodded. There wasn't a soul to be seen. The office was dark and silent. The scrapyard looked deserted. There were no sounds of trucks or machinery. Even the road was devoid of traffic. She hadn't seen a single vehicle since she turned onto it more than twenty miles north of here.

The only sound was the rumble of the pickup's engine and the slight howl of the wind.

"Spooky…" sighed Piper.

It was. The silence was eerie. The place had a zombie apocalypse kind of feel about it. And there were dark clouds to the north. It looked like a storm might be brewing, just to add to the already creepy atmosphere.

Seph turned and looked out over the desert. Was it her imagination, or did she just see a dark shape dart by from the corner of her eye?

She was pretty tired. And she was totally on edge. It easily could've been her imagination.

But it could just as easily *not* be her imagination.

Piper's phone rang. She snatched it up, hoping for once that it was Meg. But it was Violet.

She'd texted Violet just a little while ago, asking for any information they might have on Pobsick Spring. She'd texted back right away that they'd look into it, and here they were, just in time. She put the phone on speaker and held it between them.

"Hello?"

"Hey Pippy. You guys still safe?"

"We're still *alive*," replied Seph, glancing down at her scratched palm and stung wrist.

"Well that's better than the alternative," reasoned Violet.

"True…"

"I'm dying to know what you found at Fathom Lake, by the way."

"We found the gate at the bottom of the lake," said Piper. "Big, scary mansion thingy. Lots of ghosts with *serious* psychological issues."

"*Very* cool," said Violet.

"Not so much, actually," said Seph.

"Well, we can't wait to hear all about it."

"Ever heard of Pobsick Spring before?" asked Piper.

"Never. There doesn't seem to be a city named Pobsick Spring. All searches point to a salvage yard by that name instead."

"That's the one," said Seph. "We're looking at it now."

"As far as we can tell, it's a normal business. Nothing suspicious about it at all."

"What about the surrounding area?" asked Seph.

"Nothing within a hundred-mile radius that we could find. Of course, it doesn't look like there's any *people* within a hundred-mile radius to *report* anything, so it's not that surprising."

"They *are* in chupacabra territory, though," said Corey from somewhere in the background.

"Hey, I know what those are," said Piper, proud of herself. Then she quickly frowned. "Oh…wait… I don't think I like those."

"I don't think you have to worry," grumbled Seph. "Chupacabras are probably smart enough to stay well away from whatever *we're* probably going to find here."

"That doesn't make me not worry," she whined.

"Sorry guys," said Violet. "Most of our field experience has been limited to the Midwest. Beyond that, it's mostly just second-hand reports."

"Could be they're near Regaza's Doorway," suggested Corey.

"No," said Violet. "That's *way* farther south, isn't it?"

"Not necessarily. One report claimed it to be as far north as Amarillo."

"Hmm… Still seems like a longshot to me."

"Regaza's Doorway?" asked Piper.

"A gateway to hell," explained Violet. "Named after George Regaza, who claimed to have stumbled across it way back in the nineteen twenties. He said it was an enormous stone door, set into a hillside, with a long, sloping tunnel behind it. The far end of the tunnel was supposed to be loaded with a vast fortune in gold and jewels, but emanated a terrible heat, the stench of brimstone and awful sounds that he insisted were the tortured wailings of the souls of the damned."

"Creepy," said Piper.

Seph nodded. She hoped that wasn't what they were here to find. The first two gates were bad enough, but literally walking into hell?

"But Regaza was never able to find the door again to prove his story. Since then, there've been other reports of people finding it. They describe it the same way. Huge door in the side of a hill. Long tunnel. Treasure. Heat and sulfur. Terrible screaming and moaning noises. Everyone who's ever claimed to see it has always turned back, too afraid to venture all the way to the end of the tunnel."

"And just like Regaza," said Corey in the background, "no one can ever find it again after they leave. So no one knows exactly where it is."

Seph and Piper exchanged an uneasy look. A mysterious doorway that seemed to disappear? A tunnel leading into a hellish nightmare world? It *did* sort of sound like the kind of thing they might be looking for.

"That's all we've got on Pobsick Spring, unfortunately," said Violet. "Sorry."

"It's fine," Piper assured her. "Thanks for looking into it for us."

"No problem. Let us know if you need anything else."

"We will," replied Seph. "Thanks."

"Bye!" said Piper.

Seph stared out at the mountains of scrap metal. Now she couldn't stop imagining some great, stone door buried under all that junk, and a long tunnel filled with the blistering winds and wailing sorrows of hell.

And why *not* hell? They'd been everywhere *else.*

Piper checked her messages again, but there was nothing new. "I really hope Meg's okay."

Seph could hardly believe it, but she hoped so, too. She couldn't stand the woman, but she didn't really want any harm to come to her. If Tane had hurt her in any way… She still couldn't get over the guilt of the incubus nearly murdering her mom and Wanda.

She pushed the thought away. It wouldn't do any good to linger on it. Besides, it was *Meg.* She'd turn up. This would turn out to be something *stupid*, like every other mess she'd gotten herself into. "Right now we need to figure out where to go next," she decided.

"That way," said Piper, pointing through the open gate to a litter-strewn aisle between two walls of stacked cars.

Seph shaded her eyes from the bright sunlight and squinted in that direction. It didn't look any different to her than the other two aisles leading deeper into the scrapyard. "You think so?"

"Hurry up. They're already here."

"*Who's* here?"

Piper looked over at her. "Who's where?"

"What?"

"What?"

Seph shook her head, baffled. "You said—"

"Stop wasting time and drive," growled Piper, her eyes flashing black.

"Warner!" gasped Seph.

"Warner?" Piper, her eyes already blue again, turned and looked out the window. "Where?"

"He was just—*ugh*! Never mind!" She shifted the old truck back into gear and steered the old pickup toward the indicated path.

"Wait… Was Warner *inside me* again?"

Seph wrinkled her nose. "Please don't say it like that. It's…*weird*."

"He was, wasn't he? He was inside me!"

"Stop it."

"I *hate* that! Why does he always pick *me*? He's never been inside *you*."

"Oh my god! Shut up!"

"Well he hasn't!"

"Probably because he knows what's good for him." She looked out at the towering piles of wrecked cars. She felt uneasy here. This place had the same kind of labyrinth-like feel to it that the library had, only brighter and dirtier.

A giant shadow passed overhead and was gone before Seph could turn to see it. "What was that?"

"Sugnog," said Piper. No… Said *Warner*. Piper wasn't at the wheel right now.

Seph looked over at him. Or her. Or…*it*? (Everyone called Warner "him," but did he actually have a gender of his own? Or did he just borrow that along with the bodies?)

"If you're going to think of Gispuknya as a bug, then the Sugnog would be its stinger. It's the most dangerous of all its shadows, the one you hope to avoid at any cost."

Seph shivered. She couldn't help it. Why did it always have to be bugs? She hated bugs! "So what is it, exactly?"

"A terror of the skies. A darkness that blots out the sun. The ultimate predator."

"Dramatic much?" she scoffed, but she leaned forward and looked up through the windshield, nervous.

That must've been the dark shape she saw from the corner of her eye right before Violet called. It was the monster's shadow sliding across the ground as it circled high overhead.

He reached out with Piper's arm and pointed her dainty finger at a narrow path she was about to drive past. "Turn left here."

Seph had to hit the brakes hard to make the turn. "Little more warning, please?"

"What?"

"Pea?"

Piper looked down at her outstretched hand, confused. Then she snatched it back and crossed her arms over her chest as if she'd just discovered that she were naked. "Ew! Get him off me! I hate being his puppet! It's creepy!"

"You'll be fine."

"And it's a blatant violation of my personal privacy!" she added.

"He has to tell me where we're going."

"Right," said Warner, pointing again.

Again, she had to stomp the brakes to make the turn.

Piper squealed as she was thrown against the seatbelt. "Stop it!"

"It's not me!" snapped Seph.

Another shadow flashed over them. A second later, a stiff, ominous wind washed across the scrapyard, sending dust and litter billowing across the windshield.

Again, she looked up to see what was there, but again, it was already gone.

"It'll try to stop you," warned Warner. "Whatever happens, you have to reach the warehouse at the center. He's waiting for you there."

"Who's waiting?"

"Turn right."

Seph stomped the brake and turned hard again.

Piper squealed and grabbed at her seatbelt. "Here's an idea!" she cried. "Maybe you should possess *her* and drive us there *yourself*!"

"Quiet!" snapped Seph. "We have a system."

"You just don't want him inside you!"

"*I said stop saying it like that*!"

Piper crossed her arms over her chest again and glared at her, those spectral ears laid flat against her head.

Her cell phone buzzed. She snatched it out of her purse, but again it wasn't Meg. It was Alton, asking what she was doing today.

She put it back in her purse without responding. She still wasn't sure what that last conversation was about and she didn't have time to deal with more of the same right now. She'd have to get back to him later.

Suddenly, she looked up. Those spectral ears were standing straight up again. "Gispuknya!" she gasped.

Seph glanced over at her. "What?"

"The buzzing!" she exclaimed, pointing at the top of her head, where her ears were twitching back and forth. "Gispuknya's here!"

"*Duh*!"

Piper stared at her, confused.

"Warner already told me!" She looked up through the windshield again. The Sugnog must've been flying high up in the sky, out of Piper's range. The fact that she'd just now heard that ominous buzzing was probably a really bad sign.

"Ugh!" Piper crossed her arms over her chest and turned away, pouting. "Why don't *you and Warner* just go get the stupid Tartarus lock then? Since you *obviously* don't need *me* anymore?"

Seph looked over at her, baffled. "What're you talking about?"

Then that dark shadow flashed overhead again, followed by a thunderous crash.

A landslide of wrecked vehicles and loose parts spilled down the side of one of the scrapyard's massive piles and slammed into the side of the truck.

Chapter 63

The impact knocked the truck sideways, pushing it into the scrap pile on the other side of the aisle and pinning it there.

"Are you okay?" asked Seph.

"It'll be coming back around!" said Warner. He didn't bother with the door. There was a crushed sedan pressed against it. Instead, he broke the window out with his elbow.

More accurately, he broke the window with *Piper's* elbow, since he was using *her* body. "Careful with her!" shouted Seph. That was the kind of thing you saw in movies all the time, but shouldn't work in real life without serious risk of hurting yourself.

But she found that she already knew he hadn't harmed her. First of all, Warner wasn't stupid enough to forget how fragile a human body was. Plus, she was pretty sure she saw Piper's arm turn black for a split-second as her elbow struck the glass, suggesting that Warner shielded her body with his own black form. Still, it'd startled her to see him handling her so rough.

He turned in the seat and grabbed Seph by her shoulders. "Gispuknya's shadows are everywhere," he warned as he leaned close to her, nearly touching Piper's nose to hers. "As are the ringmaster's scouts. We're outnumbered and our backs are to the wall."

Seph stared back at those empty, black eyes, unnerved by the gravity of his words.

"Get to the warehouse," he said. "Take the first left, then right, then left again."

She nodded.

"I'll hold them off as long as I can."

Then Piper blinked. Suddenly, she was staring back at her with her own eyes. They were blue and they were wide and they were utterly confused. "You didn't kiss me, did you?"

Seph pushed her away. "Just go! Before it gets back!"

"Before *what* gets back?" She grabbed the survival bag, stuffed their jackets and purses into it and then tossed it through the window. Then she crawled out after it, careful not to cut herself on any of the broken chunks of safety glass.

"The Sugnog."

"What the heck's a Sugnog?"

"Just *go*!"

"*I'm going*!"

Seph stuffed her phone into her pocket and crawled out the window after her. She felt bad leaving the truck behind. It wasn't hers, after all. It belonged to Shawbeck Ranch. To Amethyst… But there was nothing she could do about it.

As she clambered over the spilled junk behind Piper, she planted her hand in something goopy and cried out in disgust.

Piper turned and looked at her, worried. "You okay?"

"I'm fine," she grunted. "Keep going!"

She turned and continued on.

Seph wiped her hand on the sedan's fender. Just some grease, she was sure. It was a junk yard, after all. It was hardly clean. She stepped over the last of the spilled scrap and fled after Piper, wiping the rest of the gunk on the tail of her tee shirt.

They were barely out of the way when that huge, black shadow passed over them again and a fresh pile of heavy junk came crashing down from the other side of the aisle, burying the old Ram.

Seph looked over her shoulder in time to see an enormous, black shape vanishing over the top of the scrap pile.

"*What was that?*" cried Piper. She was backing away, clutching at the bag slung over her shoulder.

"Sugnog!"

Warner had called it the bug god's stinger. Gispuknya's ultimate weapon. She wasn't able to get more than a fleeting glimpse of the thing, but it was definitely *big.* To something that size, they were little more than bugs, themselves.

"I don't like Sugnogs!"

"Just run!"

"I don't even know where we're going!"

"This way!" said Seph, following Warner's directions and veering left into a narrow canyon of old tires.

The Sugnog made another pass overhead. It was lower this time, close enough to pull a wind behind it that stirred up the dust under their feet and threatened to bring the towering walls of tires on either side crashing down on top of them.

"What *is* that thing?" coughed Piper as she shielded her face against the gust. "Some kind of bird?"

Seph thought it more likely to be some kind of giant bug. Maybe a gargantuan dragonfly. Or a mammoth bumblebee. Wasn't that its thing? Bugs?

That, and shadow people, she guessed.

Piper screamed and jumped back, slapping at the air in front of her face. "Did you just see that?"

"See what?" asked Seph. But the words weren't fully out of her mouth yet when something small and white twitched into existence between the two of them.

She stumbled to a stop, surprised.

It was there for only an instant, gone before she could get a good look at it. Before she could even try dismissing it as a figment of her imagination, another one appeared, this one in front of her, closer to the ground. It, too, vanished almost as soon as it appeared. Then she saw two more. One higher in the air, the other to one side, barely glimpsed in her peripheral vision.

Or were they all the same one? It was difficult to be entirely sure. They moved sort of like the flickering men, twitching in and out of view like one of those ghosts in creepy horror movies. Except she was pretty sure that the flickering men actually flickered in and out of existence, passing through iron gates in the process, and even multiplying themselves. These things, however, were simply moving too fast to see. She could tell because she could hear them. They whistled past her head, making an eerie sort of buzzing noise that kept shifting from one direction to another. They darted through the air, pausing just barely long enough to be seen, reminding her of hummingbirds, but faster...and almost certainly far more dangerous.

She was definitely hearing more than one.

"Flits," said Piper.

Seph glanced over at her, confused. "What?"

But Piper wasn't Piper again. She reached out, lightning fast, and snagged one of the little creatures from the air, crushing it in her bare hand. Then she turned and looked at Seph with Warner's black eyes. He held the unfortunate little creature out for her to see.

Seph stared at it. It was broken, its tiny body mangled and mashed by Piper's grip and covered in muddy, orange-tinted gore, but it was whole enough that she could still make out its shape. As strange as it seemed, it almost looked like a *fairy*. As in, right out of a children's picture book. Miniature, somewhat human-shaped things, only about two inches long from head to toe, with delicate, nearly invisible wings. But as she leaned closer, she saw that it looked nothing like Tinkerbell. It was neither cute nor beautiful in any sense of the word. These were nightmarish things. They looked like tiny skeletons, white and bony, with several pairs of tiny arms. Their heads, at first glance, looked like little doll heads, complete with little ponytails, but those faces were rigid, with big, soulless eyes and even bigger mouths. Those ponytails appeared to be some kind of backward-curling antenna.

"The ringmaster," growled Warner. "Keep moving. Guard your faces." Then he was gone again.

Piper blinked and looked down at her open hand. Then she screamed and flung the tiny corpse away. "*What was that thing?*"

"Flit," said Seph. "Hurry!" She turned and ran onward.

Piper followed after her. "What's a flit?" But the question had barely escaped her lips when another one appeared in front of her face. She cried out and slapped at it, but it was gone before she could reach it.

"Warner says they go for the face!"

"*What?*"

"I'm just telling you what he told me!"

One darted past Piper's head, leaving a sharp pain on her right cheek and wrenching a startled scream from her.

An instant later, Seph felt a stinging pain over her left temple. She slapped at it, but the tiny monster had already done its damage and was gone. Her hand came away with a small smear of blood on it. "Ouch!"

"*So not cool!*" cried Piper.

They ran faster, both of them shielding their faces behind their arms, wary of the invisible little monsters.

Another one appeared in front of Seph, snapping at her nose as she peered between her upraised arms. She turned away, shielding herself just enough to exchange a painful bite on her face for an equally painful bite on her forearm.

Then it was gone, leaving only that one, bleeding bite mark behind.

How did something so small have such big bites? Their mouths were several times smaller than the wounds they left!

Piper cried out as one yanked at her hair.

Seph clenched her fists in front of her face. She could feel the water enveloping them, ready to unleash the reaper's scythe. But...how was she supposed to fight something like this? There was no room to wield it in its familiar scythe form in this canyon of old tires. She'd need it to become something more compact. But even if she came up with the perfect weapon, these things were so small and fast... She might be the wielder of the Grim Reaper's scythe, but she wasn't a *ninja.* She didn't have any kind of training. She certainly didn't possess the skills to knock something that small moving that fast out of the air.

And that was all assuming the silly thing actually *worked* when she needed it to...

The Sugnog swooped by overhead again. This time, it was moving *with* them, passing directly over the canyon of tires. Seph looked up to see a massive, manta-ray shape gliding through the air. Except instead of a long, manta-ray tail, it had a short, stubby one. And it had a long, thick neck attached to a small, horned head. And there were grotesque, wriggling things dangling from its belly like greasy, black tentacles.

She didn't have much time to process the strange sight, however, as another flit bit her upraised elbow.

Then Piper cried out as something bit her left cheek, then her thumb.

Seph peered between her arms again. The aisle they were in intersected another path ahead of them. Warner told her to go left, then right, then left again. They'd already gone left, so now they had to go right.

Another flit appeared and tried to bite Seph's hand. This time, when she flinched, the scythe reacted. Several short, gleaming blades shot out from around her hands, creating a sort of spiked shield in front of her face. She stared at it, surprised. "Okay, *that's* pretty cool!"

"What?" said Piper, her voice suddenly muffled.

Seph glanced over at her, surprised. "Where'd you get that?"

"I don't know!" she cried from inside the pink motorcycle helmet she was inexplicably wearing. One second, she was just running, trying her best to protect her face from these eyeball-eating little monsters, and the next she was wearing *this*! There wasn't even any transition that she'd been aware of between not wearing it and wearing it. It was just *there*! As if she'd been wearing it the whole time!

Did she wish it into existence with the spinning wheel?

Seph didn't have time to contemplate the bizarre abilities of Piper's necklace. While she was looking away, a flit appeared in front of her face and chomped down on the bridge of her nose. She let out an unladylike curse and slapped at it, forgetting about the scythe. If those had been real blades, they probably would've cut her up far worse than the stupid flit. But the scythe was alive, and apparently far more skilled at cutting down enemies than she was, because instead of breaking her glasses or chopping off her nose or putting out one or both of her eyes, they simply snipped the little skeletal beast in two. Both halves of it fluttered to the ground and landed in the dust behind her.

"*I can't see out of this thing*!" yelled Piper.

They were approaching the end of the aisle when a Gispuknya hound appeared in front of them, blocking their path.

Seph and Piper both stumbled to a halt.

"Oh no…" gasped Piper.

Then a black shape streaked through the air in front of them and the hound was knocked into the air with a painful yelp.

It was back up in an instant, but not nearly quick enough. A strange, black shape blossomed into view. Thin and oily, black as obsidian, its features lost in its own darkness, like something that crawled out of the darkest pits of hell.

Except this monster was on *their* side.

Several long, black spines shot out of the monster-shaped void, piercing the beast. It let out another startled yelp and then went limp.

Seph stared at the queer shape before them. She'd seen it only one other time, deep inside the first of the Architects' vaults, back when she first acquired the scythe.

"*Ow, bitch*!" shouted Piper, rubbing at a fresh flit bite on her arm.

Seph turned around, suddenly remembering the nasty little skeleton fairies. Almost immediately, one of the bloodthirsty freaks bit her ear. The same ear, unfortunately, where the stupid Gispuknya wasp stung her the day before, making it *far* more painful than the other bites. She cried out in pain.

"Persephone!"

Warner's monstrous form vanished from sight. In the same instant, Piper turned and shouted, "What're you waiting for? *Get out of here*!"

"*We're going*!" Seph bellowed back at him, still rubbing her stinging ear.

"What?" yelled Piper.

Three more Gispuknya hounds appeared from the labyrinth of junk, all of them running straight at them, teeth bared. One by one, the black streak that was Warner struck at them, knocking them back, clearing the way for them.

Seph grabbed Piper's hand and ran, leaving him to take care of Gispuknya's mutts. Almost immediately, however, she spotted several skitters crawling out of the scrap piles and slithering toward them.

At the same time, the Sugnog circled back around and sent two cars from the top of the stack crashing to the ground dangerously close to Warner and the hounds.

And while Piper was fumbling with the visor of the stupid motorcycle helmet, trying to see what was going on, one of the flits bit her right on her butt, making her say a *very* bad word.

"Just keep running!" shouted Seph.

"I hate this place!" Piper shouted back.

The skitters kept coming. Hundreds of them. They wriggled out from the gaps in the garbage and slithered through the dirt, their heads raised, their bony mandibles opening, ready to strike.

Warner told them to take the next left and it was coming up. They were almost there. But the skitters were getting closer and closer. The space in front of them was rapidly shrinking. *Too* rapidly. They weren't going to make it!

"Persephone!"

"I see them!"

"Do something!"

Seph wasn't sure what to do. There were hundreds of them. They were extremely low to the ground. And they were quick. What manner of weapon could take out enough of them to let them safely through?

"*Hurry*!" cried Piper.

Sometimes it seemed like the scythe made decisions on its own. With no other ideas, she thrust her arm out and left it to the Hand.

What emerged was not a mere scythe. Faced with a battlefield of enemies, the Architect's tool upgraded accordingly. A spinning whirlwind of blades stretched out in front of her, reaching the entire width of the aisle, far less a scythe than an enormous, twirling *lawnmower*!

The skitters were no match. They were chopped into bony pieces before their eyes, clearing a twenty-five-foot-wide path splattered with bits and pieces of skitter carcasses.

"*Holy crap*!" stammered Seph.

"*What the heck was that*?" shrieked Piper.

Seph squeezed her hand and hurried around the corner. But she stopped again when she found a dozen black-eyed children blocking their path.

Chapter 64

The skitters were already crowding in behind them again. They were surrounded.

"Well…" said Seph, stretching out her arm again. "No reason it won't work on these little freaks, too."

"Oh my gosh!" cried Piper, covering her visor with her free hand. "This is going to be *so gross*!"

The scythe unraveled itself into another whirling set of mower blades and stretched the entire width of the aisle. The idea of what was about to happen made Seph feel sick. But after all she'd been through, she was pretty confident that she'd get over it. The black-eyed children weren't *really* black-eyed children. That was just what they looked like to everyone else, everyone without prophet sight. To her, they'd always been featureless monsters dressed in creepy doll clothes and bushy brown wigs. They didn't even *have* eyes. It made this sort of thing a little easier, to be honest.

Except it wasn't going to be easy at all.

As she started toward them, the reaper's scythe set to Super Mass-Murder Mode, the little freaks suddenly changed. Great, shadowy, bat-like wings sprouted from their backs and they took to the air, hovering well above the deadly, churning blades of the scythe.

"*Oh, come on*!"

"They can *fly* now?" sputtered Piper.

The first of the flying children swooped toward them.

Seph reeled in the mower and reverted it back into the familiar shape of the scythe, its long blade held out in front of them, shielding them, forcing the monster back again.

She looked back over her shoulder. Those skitters were getting closer. She didn't think she could plow through them again and still defend against the flying freak-children.

What did she do?

But before anything could come to her, an old refrigerator dropped out of the sky and flattened one of the winged, black-eyed children.

Seph and Piper—as well as the other eleven monster children—stood there a few seconds, staring at the limp, twitching wings sticking out from under the fridge, unable to completely process the absurd randomness that kept happening around them. Then they all lifted their heads and looked up above them, at the top of the scrap pile, where several squatty, naked little figures were rummaging through the junk.

Teethers.

"Those things're *strong*..." observed Piper.

One of them chucked a metal bar at the hovering children. Then a tire axel flew from the top of the stack on the other side. A second later it was raining scrap metal and the children flapped their freakish wings and flew up to confront the teethers.

"Not good!" shouted Seph. She glanced back, startled to see that the skitters were a lot closer now than she'd expected. She squeezed Piper's hand again and ran, pulling her along. "Watch for falling appliances!"

A bent bicycle frame landed in front of them and to the left, followed by part of an old folding chair, then a muffler. A little farther ahead, a huge tire rim buried itself in the packed earth. To their right, a water heater crashed to the ground, close enough to make them both scream.

"Seriously, why can they *fly* now?" shrieked Piper. "That's just *stupid*! I *hate* this stuff!"

A car door slammed into the dirt in front of them. A second later, one of the monster children thudded to the ground next to it, its small form broken.

"I'm more concerned about the falling car parts at the moment!" shouted Seph.

An old Radio Flyer wagon fell from the sky, followed by a rusty, twin-sized headboard and a pair of motorcycle handlebars.

Something *very* heavy hit the ground behind them hard enough to shake the earth beneath their feet.

A fan blade sailed through the air overhead and buried itself in the dirt.

An empty propane canister bounced over their heads.

Then a mighty wind gusted through the aisle, kicking up dust and litter. The Sugnog. Seph had almost forgotten about *that* freaky thing. She looked up in time to see it drag its hideous underside along the top of the scrap pile, sending both teethers and junk careening down the slope.

Piper yanked on her hand, pulling her back just in time to avoid being crushed by an old vending machine.

Her heart stuttered in her chest. That was *way* too close.

"Come on!" shouted Piper, dragging her around the machine on their way. "We have to get out of here!"

A rusty sheet of tin fluttered through the air and slammed into the ground with enough force to have easily decapitated a person. It was a grisly reminder that the longer it took them to get out of here, the more likely it was that one or both of them were going to die a gory, horror-movie-worthy death.

Something crashed into the ground behind them again and Piper felt something smack the back of her helmet. (Apparently, it was a good thing she didn't take it off so she could see better…) She tugged at the strap of the bag and willed herself to run even faster.

Seph caught sight of more skitters crawling out of the scrap on either side of them and cursed. She didn't think they could handle any more of this nonsense.

But she was going to have to, because several fiery explosions announced the arrival of the ringmaster's flutters.

Now much smaller pieces of scrap were raining down around them, some of them still trailing smoke as they fell.

Seph felt a hard gust of wind at her back and looked over her shoulder in time to see the Sugnog sweeping low through the aisle, already almost on top of them. She grabbed Piper and shoved her to the ground as it swept over them, leaving a series of explosions in its wake as its powerful wind tossed and detonated the flutters.

"Ow!" yelled Piper.

"*Shut* up and *get* up!" shouted Seph.

"*Bossy*!"

"Just go!" She jumped up and looked behind her. There was a teether running at them, its ugly little gut sloshing back and forth. It was swinging a length of thick, rusty cable over its head. She thrust her hand out, unimpressed, and plunged the scythe's blade into its flabby chest. Immediately, the thing fell face-first into the dirt, dead.

She stood there a moment, her gaze washing over the war zone from which the little monster had come. There were only a few black-eyed children remaining by now and a number of teethers were bounding down the sides of the scrap piles, each of them armed with something heavy and probably quite deadly.

She didn't think she could take them all on.

She turned and ran after Piper.

Meanwhile, the skitters were still closing in on them.

Seph thrust her hands out in front of her. The scythe unraveled itself into another whirling lawnmower blade and began hacking away at the creepy little monsters. But when it hit a rusty truck bumper the Sugnog had knocked into the aisle, the blades shattered against it and splashed harmlessly into the dirt. "*Seriously*?" she shouted at it. "You're supposed to be able to cut through the freaking *universe*!"

Piper turned and looked back. The teethers and skitters were getting closer.

Seph thrust her arm out again. The scythe sprang into existence again, only to immediately come apart again.

Meanwhile, the ringmaster's monsters drew closer.

Why was it doing this? What was wrong with it? She *did* recall being told that the full power of the Hands wouldn't be restored until they reached Tartarus and awakened the Architects. Was this what they were talking about? It was so unreliable! What if it'd done this the first time she used it, when the shepherd lashed out at her? Or when she cut down the incubus? Or even a moment ago when she speared the teether that was charging her with that rusty cable?

Was it only by sheer luck that she'd survived this long?

She stared down at her hands, confused. This was wrong. Even if it wasn't at full power, the scythe shouldn't be like this. It was as if something were interfering with it.

"Persephone!"

She looked up to see the Sugnog circling back for another run, this time from the front. It was already swooping in low. From this angle, she could see that its face was a great, black, bird-like skull, filled with empty, cavernous eyes and massive, monstrous teeth, like a shadowy, prehistoric nightmare.

There was nowhere to go. The skitters and teethers blocked the way back.

They were trapped.

Chapter 65

The Sugnog swept through the sky, a cloud of dust and litter billowing in its wake. Seph stared as it barreled toward them on those impossible, oily wings, terrified. What should she do? How did she defend against something like that? It was at least as big as a full-sized passenger jet. The tips of its wings dug into the scrap piles on either side of it, slinging rusted metal and shrieking teethers into the air.

The last of those demonic children were flapping off into the sky, retreating from the monstrous creature's path, but the ringmaster's menagerie of horrors remained. The skitters were closing in, lifting their skeletal heads like vipers, their bony, venomous mandibles clicking together, threatening them. Flutters continued to explode all around them, raining a shower of smoking shrapnel down from above. And any second now those nasty little teethers would catch up to them, too. Seph could hear their approaching footsteps behind them.

What did she do?

She couldn't think of anything!

Then the air around them crackled. She felt a static charge pass over her. Her hair stood up. The burning stench of ozone filled her nostrils. And before she had time to fully understand what was happening, there was a tremendous crash of thunder and a violent storm of black lightning rained down around them.

Piper turned and grabbed her, hugging her as the strange, black storm raged.

Then it simply stopped. The air stilled as quickly as it had ignited. Cautiously, they both opened their eyes and looked around to find the skitters blown to bits, the flutters incinerated, the teethers smoldering in the dirt and the Sugnog swooping back up into the sky, shaking its great, bird-like head.

"I told you to keep moving!" shouted Piper, who was, of course, not Piper again. "Don't just stand there like idiots!"

Seph didn't bother telling him where he could stuff it. He was already gone again, first of all. Also, they didn't have a second to spare. Warner had slaughtered *these* monsters, but more would come. *Many* more. They were endless. And the Sugnog wasn't even gone. It was already circling around for another run.

Still clinging to Piper's hand, she turned and ran.

Ahead of them, the scrap piles were getting smaller. There was a large clearing in the junk where several aisles intersected. A crossroads in the endless, sunbaked garbage. And at the center of it, visible now over the rolling hills of the dwindling garbage heaps, was a large, square building.

The warehouse.

They were almost there.

Seph stared at it as she ran. It appeared to be a simple wood and tin structure. How was *that* supposed to be safe? It looked like the Sugnog could just tear through it like it was nothing.

And as she rounded the last corner and stepped into the clearing, she saw that a small army of fat teethers had gathered around it.

"Ugh!" groaned Piper. "I *hate* those guys!"

The gross little beasts were already running toward them. Like the others they'd encountered, they'd armed themselves with whatever they'd found lying around, anything from metal rods and lead pipes to broken lamps, hubcaps and glass bottles. Some of these weapons were more concerning than others, like the length of chain one of the little beasts was swinging around as it waddled toward them. Others, not as much. One was trying its best to drag a broken car axel along behind it, with the wheel still attached, and having a terrible time with it. Another was running with a torn sheet of rusty tin raised up over its head. Another of the stupid little creatures was waving an old toilet seat around.

Seph thrust her arm out, praying that the stupid thing would actually work this time, and watched as the scythe's watery blade cut through the air, hacking apart the three nearest teethers.

Inside her helmet, Piper's spirit ears stood up in alarm. She turned and threw herself at Seph, knocking her to the ground.

The Sugnog swooped low behind them, the tips of its oily wings tearing into the scrap piles, raining heavy junk down around them and sending the teethers fleeing in terror.

Piper sat up and looked around, her heart racing. The Sugnog was soaring away again, probably with the intention of circling back around for another dive. And those teethers would be back again, too. They had to move.

"Ow!" shouted Seph, rubbing at the spot on her forehead where Piper's helmet knocked against her when she was tackled.

Piper stood up and grabbed her hands, helping her to her feet. "I'm sorry!"

"Will you take that stupid thing off?"

She reached up and yanked at it, but it didn't budge. "I don't know how!"

"You have to undo the chin strap."

"No time!" Piper heaved the survival bag back up over her shoulder and then yanked on her hand, dragging her toward the warehouse door. "Hurry!"

"I'm hurrying!" She still didn't like the idea of going in there, but they didn't seem to have any other options at the moment. Some of the teethers had *already* regained their courage and were running back again, their makeshift weapons raised over their ugly heads.

By some miracle, the door was unlocked. Piper flung it open and ran inside. "*Oh my gosh that was terrifying*!"

Seph slammed the door behind her and snapped the deadbolt shut.

Almost immediately, something began banging on it.

She backed away, her hands instinctively raised, ready to reap anything that might burst through.

But the teether on the other side apparently had a very short attention span, because after just a few seconds, it stopped.

Both of them stood there, holding their breath, listening…

Finally, Seph sighed. Then she turned to Piper and rubbed at her forehead again. "That really hurt."

Piper found the latch on the chin strap and lifted the helmet off her head. "I said I was sorry!" She held it out and looked at it. "Aw, it's *pink*! Cute!"

Seph wasn't sure how she managed to conjure the stupid thing without knowing how the chin strap worked or even what color it was, but she was too tired to think too much about it right now. She walked over to the window and peered out through a set of dust-coated blinds.

The teethers were still out there. She could see several of them wandering aimlessly around, dragging their makeshift clubs along behind them, looking confused. They were like stupid video game enemies. Did the ringmaster *intend* for them to be that stupid? Did it make them easier to control or something?

The nearest one stopped and scratched its saggy butt.

"Ugh… Disgusting things."

"I know, right?" Piper placed the helmet on one of the desks and began fussing with her hair.

Seph pulled the slat down a little lower and peered up into the sky. "Do you think we're safe from that Sugnog thing in here?" She didn't want to come out and say it, but it seemed like that monster would be able to simply flatten this building with them inside it. Job done. Time to go home.

Piper opened the selfie camera on her cell phone and checked her hair in it. (*After* quickly checking to make sure Meg hadn't tried to contact her while she was running for her life.) "This is where Warner told us to go, right? Ugh…I look *awful*."

It *was* where Warner told them to go. But she still didn't like it. She leaned closer to the window. She didn't see the monster, but she caught a glimpse of its shadow as it passed overhead.

She turned and looked around. They were standing in a cluttered office. There were three desks, a bunch of filing cabinets, a printer on a shaky-looking old table and dozens of grimy binders on a bookshelf in one corner. There was even an old refrigerator, remarkably like the one that fell on that freaky, flying monster child. There were two other doors in this room. The first opened onto a small bathroom. The second, she assumed, led deeper into the warehouse.

The lights were on. A ceiling fan was turning lazily overhead. But no one was here. "Okay…" she said. "So where's the custodian?"

Piper pocketed her phone again. "Maybe it's his lunch time?"

Seph turned and peered through the blinds again. One of the

teethers was there, its hideous face pressed against the glass, its slimy, gray tongue oozing through the caked dust like a fat slug.

Barely managing to stifle a scream, she backed away, her hand clasped over her mouth.

For a moment, both of them stood silently, staring at the shadow behind the blinds.

"What's it doing?" whispered Piper.

"Who cares? Let's just get out of here."

Chapter 66

Piper hurried to the warehouse door and opened it. The space there was much larger than the one they'd just left. Aisles upon aisles of shelves containing all manner of scavenged parts stretched out before them.

Like in the office, everything was silent. The lights were on. Huge, metal fans slowly churned beneath the exposed rafters, circulating the stale air. But there didn't appear to be anyone working back here. It was eerily silent.

Seph closed the door firmly behind them and looked around. "Warner told us to come here. So where's the custodian?"

Before Piper could even make a guess, her cell phone announced a new text message. She withdrew it from her pocket and frowned at the screen. "Kaitlyn again." She was asking if Seph was with her. She hesitated to reply. What was the correct answer?

"Just tell her we can't see them this weekend," said Seph. "Maybe she'll quit pestering you. If I ever make it home, I'm not going to want to leave the apartment for a *month*."

"Yeah… You're right." But as soon as she began typing a response, her phone began ringing. "That's Phoenix… Why's *she* calling me?"

"Kaitlyn probably put her up to it," reasoned Seph. "Just answer it and tell her you're busy."

Piper accepted the call. "Hi, Phoenix."

"Hi Peppy. What're you doing?"

"Getting ready for work," Piper lied. Surely they wouldn't keep bothering her if she was working today. And it wasn't all that big of a lie. She *would* have been working had it not been for Tane and all this Hands of the Architects business. She had to call in this morning and tell her boss she was sick.

Seph walked out into the warehouse, looking it over. She supposed they should have a look around. She wasn't sure what else they *could* do. They couldn't just stand around and wait for those monsters to find their way inside.

She didn't care for it here. It was dark and it was kind of spooky. And worst of all, there were spider webs. She could see them in the rafters and on the shelves.

There were probably all sorts of other nasty things crawling around in here, too.

A gust of wind passed over the building and she froze, her gaze rising up to the ceiling high above.

"So you're at home?" asked Phoenix.

"Yep." Again with the questions? What was up with these guys?

"Is Seph there, too?"

"Uh…" She looked up at Seph, unsure what the correct answer was.

Before she could decide on an answer, Phoenix said, "I really need to talk to her. It's important."

She frowned. If it was so important, why didn't she call Seph's phone?

"Please?"

"Um… Sure. Yeah. Here." She held the phone out for Seph, who just sort of stared at it for a second. "Phoenix wants to talk to you."

"Why?" Seph mouthed.

Piper shrugged. How the heck should *she* know?

Frustrated, Seph took the phone and said, "Little busy today, Pho."

"Don't be huffy. I just wanted to see what you were doing."

She glanced over at Piper, confused. "Uh…nothing…really. Hanging out with Pea. What…uh…are *you* doing?"

"I've just been hanging out with Kaitlyn. Playing with our phones. Wondering if you were going to keep blowing us off for this weekend. Where're you guys at?"

"Where're we at?" She looked over at Piper. She hated lying. She was awful at it.

Piper mouthed the word "home" at her.

"We're at home."

"Why'd you repeat my question?"

Seph blinked. "What?"

"I asked you where you were and you said it back to me. It was kinda weird."

"No it wasn't. I just…wasn't…sure I heard you…?"

"Whatever. Bummer about the computers at work, huh?"

"Yeah. Total bummer." She turned and raised her eyebrows at Piper. Piper shrugged.

"Kaitlyn said it was, like, a fire in the server room or something?"

"Yeah. I guess so."

"Huh…"

Seph bit her lip. Wait… *Did* Piper ever say anything about a fire? She should've paid more attention to her side of the conversation when she was talking to Kaitlyn and Alton. She was starting to get a seriously bad vibe from this conversation. "Hey, we're kind of busy right now, so…"

"Which is it?"

Seph scratched at the wasp sting on the back of her neck, confused. "Huh?"

"Are you busy? Or are you just hanging out with Peppy?"

"Uh…" She winced. What was happening? She stared at Piper, pleading, but Piper didn't know what to do. "Both, I guess…"

"Are you really at home?"

Seph shook her head. "Yeah. I just said we were, didn't I?"

"In Cakwetak."

"That…*is* where we live."

"Huh. So then…you're definitely not in Texas right now?"

Seph's eyes grew very wide then. "*What*?"

Piper spread her hands open. "What'd she say?" she mouthed.

"Which is it? Cakwetak or Texas?"

"Why would we be in Texas?"

Piper gawked at her.

"I don't know. That's what I was wondering. Kaitlyn and Alton said that Peppy kept insisting you guys were in Cakwetak, but first you were in Nebraska. Then you were in *Missouri* for some reason…"

Seph felt her stomach sour as she listened. A deep, awful dread was spreading in her belly.

"Then you drove all the way to *Florida*," Phoenix went on. "Then all the way back to South Dakota… And now Texas."

Seph stared at Piper. She was so confused right now. "How do you know all this?" she asked. Her mind was racing. How was it possible for Phoenix of all people to know all the places they'd been?

"Huh. You know, it's tricky with Peppy, because I can never really tell if she's lying or not, but you've always been a *terrible* liar."

Which was obviously why she wanted to talk to her instead of Piper. Seph felt like an idiot. She never should've taken the phone. "Sorry, I have to go!" she blurted, panicking. Then she ended the call and stood staring at Piper.

"How does she know where we are?"

Seph shook her head. "She shouldn't know *anything*! She's *Phoenix*!"

"*Is* she?" asked Piper.

Seph stared at her. Something hot was churning inside her gut. *Was* she Phoenix? Was Kaitlyn Kaitlyn? Was Alton Alton? Her boss, Millard Carrol, wasn't Millard Carrol. The receptionist, Stacy Getledder wasn't Stacy Getledder. Her high school art teacher, Otis Pealmonger, wasn't Otis Pealmonger. Even *Amethyst* wasn't really Amethyst!

Her thoughts drifted back to that first week of college when she first laid eyes on Kaitlyn, Alton and Phoenix. They were already friends. They'd gone to the same high school. They were so free-spirited with their colorful hair and tattoos and piercings. So *relaxed*. She remembered thinking that there was no way she'd ever have friends like *those* three. She'd never fit in with people like them. She wouldn't even try. All she'd do was embarrass herself if she did.

It was Kaitlyn that popped up at her desk a few minutes later, attracted by the open sketchbook in front of her, telling her how amazing her art was.

Was it all another lie? Like Mr. Pealmonger telling her that art was her calling and she should seize it.

Now that she was thinking about it, why *wouldn't* Tane have surrounded her with people who would pretend to be her friends while steering her toward a career that would place her directly under his evil gaze on a daily basis?

Was *everything* a lie?

Piper took back her phone and returned it to her pocket. She didn't like this. If Kaitlyn and the others were working for Tane…could *they* have done something to Meg? "Come on," she said. "We should keep moving."

Seph nodded. She was right. There'd be time for processing this later. For now, they needed to find the custodian. She turned and looked around at the silent warehouse. She wanted to call out and ask if anyone was here, but she was too afraid of what might answer.

Another hard gust of wind washed over the building.

Was the Sugnog getting impatient? She kept expecting the monstrous thing to come crashing through the roof at any second, burying them under a pile of rubble.

"Where's Warner?" asked Piper.

Seph turned and looked at her. It was a good question. If *anyone* knew what they were supposed to do next, it'd be him. "Warner?" she called.

Piper scrunched her face up at her. "Don't look at *me* while you're talking to him!"

"Where else am I supposed to look? I can't talk to *myself*."

"Why do *you* always get to be the one who talks to him? *I* can talk to him, too."

Seph opened her mouth to tell her that she wasn't going to argue about this, but she froze as a loud scraping noise cut through the silence.

"What's that?" whispered Piper.

"How should I know?" Seph whispered back at her.

It was coming from the far corner of the room.

They turned and watched, their hearts racing, as the noise drew closer and closer.

Maybe it was the custodian.

But the thing that came lumbering around the corner didn't look like a custodian. It was a six-foot-tall, hunched, emaciated-looking thing with long, bony arms and three-foot-long, hooked claws that it dragged along behind it, making the scraping noise that announced its approach. It stepped into view and then stood there, staring back at them. Like the teethers outside, it was completely naked, with the same sort of blotchy, diseased-looking skin, except that this thing was a deathly shade of pale gray. It had an unnaturally long neck and a weird, droopy face that should've looked more *goofy* than scary…but *didn't*.

A moment passed between them in silence.

Then it darted at them with impossible speed.

Chapter 67

In an instant, the monster was standing over them, those wicked claws slashing through the air.

Seph barely managed to lift the scythe in time to block them.

The thing's droopy mouth sagged open and a terrible, ear-splitting wail washed over them, sending needles of piercing pain deep into their skulls.

Piper covered her ears and screamed.

Seph couldn't even do that. Her hands were busy holding back those murderous claws. She cried out in pain and tried to push the monster back, but it was strong. It wasn't budging.

It stared down at her with the glazed, cataract eyes of a festering corpse.

She needed to use the scythe. She needed to form the blade. She tried to imagine it snapping out of the handle like a switchblade knife, slicing the hideous beast in two as it unfolded itself. But it was so hard to concentrate through that awful wailing. It felt as if it were reverberating through her very skull, shaking her brain to pieces.

Then a thunderous boom shook the building and the side of the monster's head blew apart before her eyes.

In the silence that followed, the monster fell into a crumpled heap on the floor, those wicked claws clattering uselessly against the concrete.

A stout, muscular man whose bushy, reddish beard didn't quite match the curly, blond hair on the top of his head was standing at the end of one of the aisles, a large-caliber rifle aimed at the monster's motionless corpse.

"I totally had that under control," gasped Seph as she eyed the weapon.

"Maybe you did," admitted the stranger in a soft, Texas drawl. He was wearing dirty jeans, work boots and a blue, button-down shirt that was soaked with blood on one side. His left hand and forearm were covered in blood. "You want me to let you handle the rest of 'em by yourself?"

Seph glanced down at the monster again. She could still see those awful claws bearing down on her face. "No. I'm good."

"Come on," said the stranger. He turned and started back the way he came. "There won't be just one of them things."

She hesitated. She had no idea who this guy was. She let the scythe withdraw from her hands and then grimaced at a smear of monster gore splattered on the back of her hand. She wiped it on her dirty leggings and called after him, "Who *are* you?"

He looked back at her. He seemed confused for a moment. "Huh? Oh. Right… Uh…I'm Connor. Connor Stenzar." He stared at her for a moment, a strange look on his face. Then he turned and walked away. "I own Pobsick Spring Salvage. People call me the Trash Man."

"That's not a very flattering handle," remarked Seph.

"It may not be flatterin'," he admitted, "but it's *accurate*."

Piper nodded. She couldn't argue with that.

"I'm also the custodian of Zarechuff."

"Wait…" Seph hurried after him. "*You're* the custodian?"

"Zarechuff?" said Piper.

"The third trial of the Keeper of Tartarus. The reason you're here, ain't it? Keep movin' please."

From the next aisle over came the sound of heavy claws dragging across the concrete.

Connor, the Trash Man, Custodian of Zarechuff, turned and squinted through the stacks of junk on the shelves for a few seconds, then he lifted the rifle, aimed through a gap between two piles of old fan blades, and fired.

Piper covered her ears again and cringed at the thunderous sound of the report.

There was a heavy thump on the other side of the shelves, followed by silence.

Connor nodded, satisfied, and lowered the weapon again. "Let's keep it movin'."

"What *are* those things?" asked Piper.

Again, he looked back at her, that strange expression on his face. "Scrapers," he replied.

"Scrapers?"

Connor shrugged. "On account of 'em…scrapin' their claws on things, I reckon."

"Teethers and scrapers," said Seph, recalling the fat little freaks that were surrounding the building. "Is he a ringmaster or a dentist?"

Piper shivered. "I don't like dentists," she said in a small voice.

"I know you don't," said Seph. She tried to peer through the junk as she walked, searching for more lurking monsters.

"*I* didn't name 'em," said Connor, shaking his head.

Seph followed along behind him. Really, though? Scrapers? Flutters and skitters? Teethers and flits? The ringmaster wasn't much for naming his horrors, was he? It was downright lazy, if you asked her.

"What happened to your arm?" asked Piper.

"Teether," replied Connor. "Little bastards're everywhere out there. 'Course, you already know that…"

Piper glanced over at Seph. A teether did that? Did that mean he got hurt because of *them*? That *was* why the teethers were here, right? They came to this place hoping to stop them and steal the spinning wheel.

A third scraper began making that horrid noise somewhere to their right. Connor paused, considering it, but he must've decided it wasn't close enough to bother shooting because he continued on, ignoring it.

Somewhere far to the left, something crashed to the ground, announcing the presence of a fourth lurking scraper. Or perhaps it was one of the ringmaster's *other* monsters.

Connor reached the back of the warehouse and peered around the end of the aisle.

Nothing was here.

He walked up to a door and peered through the small window. "Jesus Christ," he muttered. "You weren't kiddin', were ya?"

Seph glanced up at him. "What?"

"Nothin'," he replied, his voice hushed. "Just takin' it in. The Keeper's gate is right out there."

"Okay," whispered Seph. "So let's go already." She turned and looked around. That scraping noise was getting closer. The monster was coming this way.

"Not yet," said Connor. "We need to wait for the storm. It's almost here."

"The storm?" said Piper. She recalled the dark clouds on the northern horizon. Again, a hard gust of wind rushed over the building and she looked up at the dark rafters overhead. She'd assumed that was the Sugnog circling low overhead, but perhaps it was instead the wind from the coming storm.

He stepped back away from the window and looked around. "Take a look."

Seph and Piper crowded together and peered out.

The door opened onto the mountain of garbage behind the warehouse. But for a moment, all either of them saw was the giant, black form of the Sugnog. It was perched on top of the garbage, its strange wings stretched out on either side of it, undulating in that weird, sea-creature sort of way. Those freaky, wriggling things that she'd seen dangling from its belly had oozed outward and snaked through the garbage like giant, slimy eels, almost as if its legs had melted and oozed down into the scrap pile.

That hideous, skeletal face stared blankly back at them, almost as if it knew exactly where they were.

"Do you see the doors?" asked Connor.

Seph had forgotten about the Gate. All she saw was Gispuknya's titanic monster. Now she lowered her gaze to the base of the junk pile. The rear end of an old, Dodge van was sticking out of it. Both doors stood open, a gaping, black hole loomed behind them. "In there?" she asked.

Piper stared at those rusty, metal doors. A gateway to an ancient world was waiting just beyond them, like some junkyard version of the wardrobe to Narnia.

"The only way in or out of the Keeper's gate," affirmed Warner. He lifted the gun and fired as a scraper shuffled into view several aisles down.

Piper covered her ears and bit back an urge to scream.

"So how do we get past that thing?" asked Seph.

"I told you, we wait for the storm."

"What's the storm going to do?" She turned and peered out the window again. It was much darker than it was before. The wind had picked up considerably.

A soft rumble of thunder crept across the desert.

The Sugnog stretched its queer wings and lifted its head. It looked agitated.

There was another crash as something was knocked to the floor again, followed by another of those terrible shrieks.

Suddenly, there were scraping noises coming from everywhere. Dark shadows were moving around behind the shelves.

"We need to get out of here," groaned Seph.

Piper was clutching the pendant, her blue eyes wide with terror.

"Just a little longer," breathed Connor. "Almost time."

A thin, freaky shape shuffled into view in the corner of the warehouse and then stopped and turned its droopy face toward them.

Seph held the scythe out in front of her, its long, glistening blade curving around her. "Any time now."

A flash of lightning illuminated the window, followed by an earth-shaking crash of thunder that made all of them jump.

"That's one…" said Connor. He lifted his rifle and shot the scraper. Almost immediately, another one shuffled into view.

Piper made a noise in her throat, a long, terrified sort of squeal.

Seph turned and looked the other way. Another one was over there. "Connor…?"

"Almost…" He had the gun trained on the next scraper, ready to fire again. He took his time. He pulled the trigger.

Piper was clutching the pendant at her chest. "I *really* don't like this…"

There were four scrapers now, all of them shuffling toward them. Seph recalled the way the first one closed the distance between it and her in the blink of an eye. "Connor!"

There was another flash of lightning, followed immediately by a deafening crack of thunder.

"Two!" shouted Connor. He lowered the rifle and threw open the door. "Go! Now!"

The warehouse was filled with those horrid, wailing screams as the three of them darted through the door, slammed it shut and pressed their backs to it.

The monsters banged and clawed and wailed and the three of them stood there, staring out at the scene before them.

The Sugnog was flapping those great, fishy wings and snapping its toothy, skeletal jaws. The wind howled. It stirred the dust and tore at their hair. The temperature had plummeted. And the sky had turned into a dangerous, churning sea of dark gray clouds.

"Now what?" screamed Piper.

Seph stared up into that sky. She'd seen a sky like that once before. And as she stood here, looking up into those writhing, flickering clouds, she finally understood what was happening. "The storm!" she shouted over the howling of the wind. She lifted her hand and pointed up at the sky. "It's here!"

Piper looked up. A fantastic, shape was soaring overhead, invisible except for the way the lightning traced its incredible form. Great, churning wings stretched across the sky, its long, elegant tail tracing a trail of lightning in its wake.

The thunderbird.

Shawbeck Ranch's most prized resident, a sentient stormfront of such unimaginable power that it defied imagination.

But what was it doing in Texas?

"Go!" shouted Connor.

Seph looked down to see the Sugnog rising into the air and finally realized what was about to happen. The titans were going to fight. An epic showdown was about to take place in the skies over Pobsick Spring.

...and they had no time whatsoever to enjoy the show.

"Move it!" shouted Connor.

She unfurled the scythe again and held it in front of them as they hurried across the empty space separating them from the Keeper's gate.

They were almost there when the wretch appeared out of nowhere and sprang at them, its withered, black fingers reaching for Piper's heart.

Chapter 68

The scythe sliced through the air just as another blinding bolt of lightning lit up the sky above them, close enough that the thunderclap was virtually instantaneous. And in that briefest of moments, the wretch moved, withdrawing with its uncanny speed into an unnatural puddle of shadows thirty feet away, leaving only that awful stench behind.

Piper stood there, clutching the pendant against her pounding heart.

Seph glared at the monster as it stared back at her from the empty darkness where its eyes should've been. The thing didn't even obey the laws of nature. Though the wind was whipping past it, those straggly clumps of hair didn't blow with it. They just hung there, defiant and *wrong*.

The first raindrops finally began to fall around them, but Seph didn't dare take her eyes off the thing. If her last two encounters with this thing had taught her anything it was that that was when it attacked. Instead, she began to back away, her eyes locked on the monster.

Connor aimed the rifle and fired…but nothing happened. The wretch never moved.

He squinted at it. "Did I miss it?"

"I don't think bullets can hurt shadows," said Seph.

"Guys…" said Piper, "…I think we have worse problems."

Seph glanced up to see teethers running toward them. When she looked back a second later, the wretch was closer than it was before.

She clenched her teeth. What should she do?

The rain fell harder. It was cold on her bare arms. Her vision began to blur as it dripped down the lenses of her glasses, threatening to blind her at this most inopportune of moments.

Connor turned and ran the last few yards to the base of the scrap pile. "Inside," he shouted.

But she couldn't just turn and run. She'd never make it. This monster was too fast.

It reached out with those awful, black fingers and began crawling toward her, slowly, purposefully, the lower half of its body uncoiling itself from its puddle of shadows.

Seph continued backing away from it, her eyes still locked on the monster. She shook her head, trying to clear the raindrops without losing sight of the awful thing, but it was a struggle to keep her eyes on it. The rain was dripping down her forehead. Sooner or later she was going to have to blink. And then it would attack.

Except…she *didn't* take her eyes off the wretch. It took its eyes off *her*. It turned, still crouched in that predatory crawling position, and stared off in the other direction. A few seconds later, she saw what had drawn its attention.

A stampede of familiar creatures thundered into view, large and woolly, each with four great tusks protruding from their snouts. They were followed by two massive semi-trailer trucks bearing the Shawbeck Ranch logo.

Seph and Piper stared in amazement as the half-dozen tuskers plowed through the teethers, whipping their shaggy heads back and forth.

One of those things banged up Seph's truck on her first journey through the fringe roads. Now, as she watched them stomp the life out of those little naked freaks, she found herself taking back some of the things she'd said about those cranky, overgrown hairballs.

So this was how the thunderbird got to Texas. In the back of one of Amethyst's trucks, just like these tuskers.

And they weren't alone.

Three more four-legged creatures galloped into view behind the truck. They were a little smaller than the tuskers, but hairless, with slimy-looking, red and black flesh and dragging long, lizard-like tails behind them. They had enormous claws and two large, horn-like things protruding from the backs of their skulls and curving over their shoulders. They had huge, yellow eyes and long, gray tongues hanging from flat, dripping snouts that looked sort of bat-like.

One of them shook its strange head and let out a loud, reverberating cry…but not from its snout. Instead, the sound came from those two horns. It was a strange sound, an almost mechanical warbling noise that sort of resembled two children shrieking at each other.

They'd heard that cry before. When they first showed up at Shawbeck Ranch, Jarrett had one of them loaded into a truck. They didn't see what it looked like, but they heard it calling out. He called it a chackteet and explained that they had two respiratory systems.

Apparently, they were a formidable beast, because one of them was dragging a scraper's corpse in its drooling jaws.

This was why Connor was waiting for the storm to arrive. It was *reinforcements.*

The trucks skidded to a halt and their doors flew open. Vernon and Jarrett, armed with two of the biggest rifles she'd ever seen, jumped out and began firing into the panicked pack of teethers.

The wretch, however, seemed utterly unimpressed by the strange army that had just arrived. It turned its shadowy face back to Seph again and, undeterred, continued crawling toward her.

Seph lifted the scythe, only to discover that it had melted while she was looking at the stampeding tuskers. She thrust her hands out again, reforming the handle, but again it broke apart. "Come on!" she grunted.

The wretch lunged at her.

She screamed.

The Ahns came out of nowhere, bounding down the side of the scrap pile in their monster forms. There were three of them. And unlike the single Ahn in Waybel Valley, from which this monster had clearly escaped, these terrifying ladies were more than a match for it.

They knocked it back before it could sink its withered fingers into Seph's startled face and were on it before it had time to flee.

Piper watched them, three monsters, two crammed into brightly colored, flower-print dresses and one in a familiar, beige pantsuit, as the wretch tried and failed to slither away, its fingers clawing at the dirt as the monstrous trio pinned down its broken, deformed legs and began tearing the ghoulish thing to pieces as easily as they'd dismembered the black council back in July.

For a moment, she couldn't turn away. The savagery of the scene… Was that what she was? Was that what she could've done to Seph if Hugh hadn't thrown that hunk of meat at her?

She was horrified by the thought! And yet…she still couldn't look away…

Seph glanced around. The grounds around the warehouse were in utter chaos. Most of the tuskers had vanished, having pursued the fleeing teethers into the depths of the scrapyard. The few that remained were being picked off one-by-one by the sharpshooting skills of Vernon and Jarrett.

The creature in the beige pantsuit turned its monstrous maw toward them and let out a series of short shrieks.

Piper stared at the Ahn. Was it only her imagination…or did she sort of understand that? Something very much like, "We've got this! Get moving!"

No… That was silly. It was just…body language.

Right?

But she didn't have time to ponder the thought. As she stood staring at the Ahn, a brilliant-white figure seemed to blossom like a flower from the very dirt beside the creature. In an instant, the pantsuit-wearing monster was knocked across the clearing and into a pile of car parts with a tremendous crash.

Piper clasped her hands over her mouth and backed away.

The white figure was standing right in front of her, its ghastly face only a few short feet away. It was like staring into a washed-out photograph.

Those snowy white eyes were utterly creepy.

The other two Ahns turned to face this new threat, but the second of the white sisters appeared and sent another one crashing into one of the ranch trailers.

Seph grabbed Piper by her arm and pulled her back toward the van doors. "We have to go!"

"But the Ahns!"

"They're way more capable of handling those things than we are!"

And indeed, the pantsuit Ahn had already shaken off the phantom witch's sucker punch and was charging back into the fray.

"Hurry!" shouted Connor.

"Come on!" urged Seph.

Piper nodded. She was right. There was nothing they could do here. They'd only put themselves in danger. Besides, the Ahns were fighting this fight for them, specifically so they could enter the Keeper's gate and finish the job they came here to do.

As the skies opened up entirely and the rain came pouring down, Connor ushered them into the back of the van. Then he climbed in after them and yanked the doors shut behind him.

Chapter 69

Instantly, the chaos outside was reduced to a hush.

Connor fumbled in the dark for a moment, then switched on a flashlight that had apparently been stashed in here for this exact purpose. Then he gestured for them to follow and set off into the darkness that loomed before them.

"They'll be okay out there, right?" said Piper.

Seph took off her glasses and wiped them clean. "They know what they're doing," she assured her. And they did. She was sure of it. She'd never seen monsters as ferocious as the Ahns. And Jarrett and the others regularly wrangled some of the universe's most deadly creatures. These were the men who kept a freaking *thunderbird* for a ranch mascot. They were more than a match for a bunch of stupid teethers and some shadow monsters.

Piper looked over her shoulder at the inside of the van doors as they faded into darkness behind them.

She hoped so.

The tunnel was dark and creepy. It looked as if someone had constructed it piece-by-piece by welding together various hunks of scrap metal, then buried it under years of accumulated garbage.

Seph eyed the welded joints as she walked. Was this all that was holding up the millions of tons of metal resting on top of them? What happened if one of those should fail?

"I'm seriously over tunnels," grumbled Piper. "Why is it always tunnels? I'm starting to question the creativity of whoever designed all these stupid places."

And it was starting to leak, too. The pouring rain outside was filtering through the rusty garbage above them and dripping down around them in a muddy, blood-tinted rain.

"The original entrance is just ahead," said Connor.

The welded metal walls gave way to the same Tartarus stone they found under Waybel Valley's water tower and in the well under Fathom Lake. This one was slanted downward, leading into the earth at a shallow slope.

"I've never been beyond this point," he said, pausing at the rim of the black opening. "I've only heard stories 'bout what's past here. And not the 'happily ever after' kind of stories, neither. They say the old folks who used to guard it, way back before the white settlers arrived, used to claim it was a gate to the underworld. One of the doorways to hell."

"That's not too far off, I don't think," reasoned Piper.

Seph shivered at the memory of Violet and Corey's story about Regaza's Doorway. (And also at the chill that was creeping through her drenched clothing.)

"I can't believe I'm actually here," sighed Connor.

She recalled Hugh having a similar reaction to finding the door of King Lodblin's library. It was understandable. She probably would've felt the same way. "I wish I could say you didn't have to come, but we kind of need you on the other side."

"Yeah," said Piper. "Time's all wonky in these places. You won't know when to open it for us if you wait out here."

He looked back at them, surprised. "I'm not *afraid.* I'm going in. I *have* to go in. I made a promise a long time ago that I won't break. I just..." He reached up with his good arm and ran his fingertips down the smooth stone. "I just needed a minute to let it soak in, I guess."

"Who did you make a promise to?" asked Piper, intrigued.

He stared off into space for a moment, distracted. "It's...a long story," he seemed to decide. "We don't really have time for it now. Maybe on the way out."

She stared at him a moment longer. She remembered Hugh and the other clones telling her about Horace's crazy adventures, how he almost died *six times*, but instead called into existence a brand-new version of himself. She also remembered Harv Tottlestep at his Minnesota farm with his humming chicken and his tales of a goddess and a troll and a young girl destined to be a hero. So many wonderous things had already happened long before they began this weird journey.

It was humbling. They were by no means the beginning of this wild story they were trapped inside. They were merely a single chapter. So much had happened before they were even born...

Were things like this *always* going on? Was there always some sort of struggle taking place?

Was this what the universe truly was? Just one long struggle for balance?

It wouldn't end with them, either, she realized. Things like this would be happening long after they were dead and gone...

Connor turned his attention to the black tunnel and began walking. It was dry beyond this point. That rusty rain stopped where the Tartarus stone began. "What'd'ya say we go see what hell looks like?" he said. "I *have* always wondered."

Seph supposed she would've wondered, too. The man would've

been mad to not be at least a *little* curious. It was only human nature.

Piper clutched the bag closer to her. This time she wasn't going through the gate unprepared.

A couple minutes passed in silence. The outside world grew more and more distant until nothing could be heard of whatever struggles were going on aboveground. Had they gone too deep? Or just too far? Or had they already left the world they knew and ventured into one of those in-between places? It was difficult to be sure.

Anything was possible, after all.

Anything at all.

Finally, a door emerged from the darkness. It was big and heavy, made of rusted steel, with a wheel lock, resembling something out of a submarine, except much bigger.

Piper recalled what Violet and Corey told them, about Regaza's Doorway.

Was it really possible that this was the place those old stories described? The scrapyard couldn't have always been here. Before Pobsick Spring, was this tunnel just sitting out here in the desert for anyone to stumble across?

She wasn't sure that made sense. There was no stone door set into a hillside. And there were no treasures. It wasn't sweltering down here, either.

None of the details matched the story.

Maybe there was another mysterious doorway out there in the desert somewhere.

Or maybe Regaza's Doorway was nothing more than a hoax all along and any resemblance to this place was utter coincidence.

"Zarechuff," sighed Connor as he stood staring at the door before them. "A place of unthinkable suffering and torment. *Hell.*"

"Been there," said Seph. "Twice in the past few days, actually. Let's just open it and get this over with."

He stared at her for a moment, surprised. "Whatever you say." He reached out and grasped the wheel. For a moment, it didn't want to turn. He grunted and strained, his muscles tightening under his drenched tee shirt. (Not that Piper noticed such things…) Then it broke free with a great, grinding of metal and the three of them were instantly swept into a new darkness.

Chapter 70

Seph switched on the flashlight she took out of her hair on Fathom Lake and swept it across the room. For a moment, she wasn't entirely sure if they'd arrived in Zarechuff or not. She was still surrounded by steel and rust. But as she took more of it in, it became clear that this was no scrap pile. There was much more order to *this* chaos. She was sitting on a corroded, metal floor inside some kind of sprawling industrial facility. Metal pipes of all sizes ran in every direction, snaking up the walls and along the ceiling. There were huge bundles of cables stretched overhead. Hoses and wires ran between steel boxes and rusty valves. Huge, silver tanks protruded from the steel walls. Mysterious panels, boxes and canisters were mounted to almost every surface, many of them connected by tangles of fine, colorful wires.

Again, everything was different. This place was hot and humid, the air so thick she could feel it pressing against her skin. And it *reeked.* Almost immediately, her mouth and nose were filled with a sour, chemical stench that irritated her throat and made her cough.

It took a surprising amount of effort just to stand up. Her body felt heavy, as if she'd suddenly gained fifty pounds. Her clothes were still wet from being caught in the downpour, but they weighed on her as if she'd just dragged herself out of that lake again.

"Ow..." groaned Piper. "I should've brought my helmet."

Seph shined her light onto her. She was sprawled on the floor, her feet stuck out in front of her, rubbing her head. "You okay?"

She covered her eyes. "I will be if you stop blinding me."

"Sorry." She stood up and shined the light behind her. Connor was there, pushing himself up on his one good arm. Behind him was a short corridor lined on either side by dozens of rotting hoses and corroded valves. The floor there was steel mesh with nothing but darkness beneath it. And at the far end was a dark, empty shaft.

She walked past him and shined her light down into it. There were no stairs, no ladders and no *floor*, just a sheer drop into a mysterious and probably very deadly darkness.

They wouldn't be going that way. She turned and shined her light onto the grimy metal stairs leading up to the next floor in the opposite direction.

Piper coughed. "What's that awful smell? Is there a gas leak in here or something?"

"It's Zarechuff…" sighed Connor. "The gateway to hell. The festerin' monument of mankind's capacity for unbridled *evil*."

"Charming," grumbled Seph. "They should definitely put that on the brochures."

"It's definitely *hot* as hell in here," huffed Piper, fanning herself as she shined her flashlight around, taking in her surroundings. A sheen of sweat had already appeared on her forehead. "My gosh!"

Seph sniffed at the air and grimaced. Those fumes weren't precisely sulfuric, but she could definitely sense a brimstone-like quality to the air here. It wasn't hard to imagine that a place just like this really could've spawned generations of stories about a great, fiery damnation just waiting to consume the souls of the wicked. Especially combined with this awful heat.

This wasn't going to be pleasant any way you looked at it.

"So, basically…" said Piper as she tugged at her damp tee shirt, "…this is the *industrial* version of Covengale."

"Sounds like it," said Seph. Although what little she remembered of that place was much colder than this. And not nearly so *heavy*. "Is it even safe to be here? You don't think the air is toxic, do you?" It was far too easy to imagine, given what they'd already experienced.

"You'll be fine," insisted Connor. He unshouldered the rifle and laid it on the floor beside him. "The Hands should protect you."

Piper looked over at her. "Like with the wasp venom."

Seph nodded and rubbed at one of the knots on her arm. Those *still* hurt. "Right. I guess the Keeper wouldn't have sent us here if it wasn't safe for us."

She just kept telling herself that like she knew it for a fact…

She looked down at her hands. They were a little sweaty now, but otherwise perfectly dry. The scythe was already busy protecting her. The spinning wheel was no doubt doing the same thing for Piper. But…

Connor groaned and rubbed his eyes. He had no such protection.

Piper bent over him, concerned. "Even if the air isn't poisonous, he'll be exposed to the Keeper's time magic." She looked up at Seph. "Just like Hugh."

Seph knew what she was thinking. As ironic as it seemed, Hugh's obesity had probably saved his life, buying him a lot of extra time. It was almost as if some greater, cosmic force had intended it that way. But Connor wasn't overweight. He was a fairly big guy, but muscular, not fat. Would he be able to last as long as Hugh did? And then there was the matter of his injured arm… How would the screwed-up time of this place affect the wound?

And if the air in Zarechuff really *was* poisonous…

"We'll have to hurry," said Seph.

"Will he be okay here alone?" worried Piper.

"I'll be fine," said Connor. "This's the job I was given. I wouldn't be here if I wasn't able to finish what I started. Besides…" He put his hand on the rifle next to him. "I came prepared."

Seph nodded. He had a point. "We should go then. The longer we wait the longer it'll take us to get back."

He rubbed at his irritated throat. "Yeah… I'd appreciate a little hustle, to be honest."

"We'll hurry back," promised Piper. "Just hang in there, okay?"

He nodded. "I'll just be here, then…wishin' I'd brought a cooler…"

"Amen," grumbled Seph as she shined her light back toward those mysterious steps and the no-doubt monstrous, mechanical labyrinth that loomed beyond it. The idea of saying, "Screw it," and just sitting down and drinking herself numb for a couple days sounded pretty nice at this point.

"Take care of yourself," said Piper. "We'll get you out of here before you know it."

"Pretty sure I already know it," he grumbled. He tried to clear his throat, but didn't seem to have much luck. He grimaced and rubbed at his neck again. "Be careful out there. I don't know what kinds of things went on in this place, but I know they were terrible beyond imaginin'."

"Believe me, I know," sighed Piper as she slung her survival kit back over her shoulder. "Ugh… When did this thing get so heavy?"

"I think the gravity's different in this world." Things were heavier in the library, too, she recalled, but not nearly like this.

Piper handed Connor a flashlight. "Just stay alive, okay?"

"Yes, ma'am. I'll be doin' my best."

She hesitated for a moment, looking him over, worrying that this would be the last time she ever saw the Trash Man alive…and of course wondering what would happen to her and Seph if it was.

"Let's go," said Seph. "So we can get back."

They left Connor there and set off up the steps, feeling as if they were each wearing lead weights.

"I really hope he'll be okay," worried Piper.

"All we can do is find the lock and get out of here as quick as we can," said Seph. She coughed and rubbed at her throat. "Before we suffocate in this nasty place."

Piper looked down at her arms, at the sweat that was clinging to her skin. "Why is it so hot here?"

"Maybe it was a hot universe. Or just a hot *region* of that universe. Or even just a really hot *day*. I don't know."

"Is this awful smell a part of the universe, too? Or just this place?"

Seph wasn't sure. It was always possible that this universe simply had an abrasive atmosphere that mankind adapted to live in. Humans were nothing if not resilient. But it seemed far more likely that it was just this place.

Or maybe places like this had polluted the air of this world.

Piper looked over at her. "By the way, why do *you* need a flash-light?"

She looked back at her, confused. "Uh…because it's *dark*. Duh."

"But you wandered all over Covengale without one. You said you could see just fine."

Seph squinted at her, confused. "It wasn't dark in Covengale."

"Uh…yeah it was. Like, pitch black. The whole time." Then she frowned. "Well, except when I was in those flashback thingies…but that was just me. You weren't there."

She stared at her, confused. She didn't remember much about that place. Hardly anything, really. But what little snippets she could remember were all well-lit. She didn't remember it ever being dark at all.

"You were using your prophet sight. Like you said you used in the library when I was sick."

"Really?"

"Yeah."

Seph looked down at her flashlight. She *did* make it work that way in the library. It was what allowed her to see the monster before it could ambush her. But it stopped working shortly after that and she couldn't figure out how to turn it back on. "Must've had something to do with me being poisoned or whatever."

"Well, if you could figure it out really quick, it might be a big help."

They reached the top of the steps and crossed a disturbingly shaky walkway through a tunnel of crisscrossing hoses affixed to rusty wheels and broken pressure gauges. Beyond that was a narrow corridor made even narrower by a massive, segmented pipe and several large machines with excessive amounts of switches, knobs and levers, all entangled in a nest of countless black wires. They squeezed past the ancient contraptions, ducked under heavy bundles of cable and stepped over a dangerously placed drainage pipe on the floor before Piper caught the strap of her bag on a protruding valve and had to stop to untangle herself.

"So the third lock of Tartarus is hidden inside the Temple of Tetanus," grumbled Seph as she wiped the fog from her glasses and eyed several jagged corners and protruding bolts. "Nice."

A tall doorway loomed ahead of them. On the other side was a narrow chasm of a room, only about twelve feet wide. A labyrinth of ladders and walkways stretched up, down and straight ahead as far as their lights would reach between the towering walls of steel plates and iron beams. Hundreds of fat, rusty pipes rose up from the bottomless darkness beneath them, curving around the walkways and snaking up into the equally endless darkness above.

"Well *this* seems unnecessarily complicated," grumbled Seph.

"Which way do we go? Can you see anything?"

She was already trying, but nothing stood out. "I don't think so. You?"

Piper shook her head. She couldn't hear anything with either pair of ears. The place was deathly quiet. All she could hear was the sound of her own beating heart and the unsettling creaks and groans of the deathtrap walkways beneath their feet.

Seph stared up into the darkness above her. She didn't like this. They didn't have time to wander blindly around like they did in the library. They had no guarantee that Connor could last that long. And if anything happened to him, they'd be stuck here forever.

Or at least until Piper ran out of snacks and ate her…

Piper took hold of the old handrail and started up the first ladder. Maybe if she climbed higher she'd be able to hear something. But she became immediately aware of her extra weight. It felt as if she were taxing the corroded metal to its limits. She could almost feel the rungs bending beneath her feet.

So not cool!

Seph stood at the bottom of the ladder and shined her light down into the darkness below her. If she could only make her prophet sight shift into overdrive like she did in the library—and apparently in Covengale—then she'd probably be able to see how far up and down this place went. But how did she make it work?

She tried to remember how it happened in the library. The battery finally died on Piper's cell phone, stranding them in that chilling darkness. Then she just sort of...pushed onward. She didn't even really see anything at first. She merely sensed those stacks of books she was about to bump into.

After that, it slowly became clearer. She found that she could picture the things she sensed. That was how she found the doorway out of that room. It wasn't until the jabberwock attacked that it turned all the way on.

But in Covengale, her advanced prophet sight just sort of happened on its own. Was it a natural reaction to danger? Or was it more of a state of mind sort of thing?

She looked up to see where Piper was, but she'd stopped on the topmost rung and was standing there, her head tilted to one side, listening. "You okay up there?"

She looked down at her. She opened her mouth to say something, but paused and listened some more. *Was* that her heartbeat she was hearing? The more she listened, the more there seemed to be *two* of those sounds.

She climbed back down, careful not to slip and fall—with all this awful, added weight, she might bring this whole, rusty place down around them—and then walked farther ahead, her spirit ears twitching in the darkness.

Seph stood back and watched her, curious.

Piper stopped at one of those big, winding steel pipes and placed her hand on it. For a moment she stood that way, silent, her head tilted, her spectral ears fixed on it. "Here..." she said after a moment. "There's something in here."

Seph shined her light up the pipe as far as it would reach. "What kind of something?" she asked, uncertain.

Piper peered down into the darkness below them. "I don't know… But I feel like we should follow it."

"Okay." It was fine by her. It was better than just wandering aimlessly. "Follow it *up*? Or *down*?"

"Uh… Down?"

Chapter 71

Seph wiped at the sweat on her face and looked up into the darkness above. This place was endless! It felt as if they'd been descending for hours already, and still there was no bottom.

She hoped they'd be able to find their way back to Connor when this was over. And that he could hold on for that long. This already wasn't going exactly as she'd hoped.

And her glasses kept fogging up in this awful humidity.

She paused for the third or fourth time now and leaned against the railing. She was out of breath, gasping for air only to choke on that foul chemical taste. She couldn't remember the last time she'd sweat this much. She felt positively *slimy* with it. Her shirt was clinging to her. If it wasn't so *icky* in here, she might've considered stripping all the way down to her bra and panties. It wasn't like there was anyone here to see her. But she wasn't *quite* that desperate yet.

She glanced over at Piper. She was standing there fanning herself, her shirt pulled up and knotted, exposing her lean, wet belly. Her hair was plastered to her face. Her cheeks were flushed. There were drops of sweat dangling from her chin.

How was she still so pretty? Seph was convinced she looked like something that crawled out of a sewer and her roommate looked ready for a Sports Illustrated photo shoot. It wasn't fair!

She squinted at her, suspicious. It was her monster DNA. It had to be.

Piper didn't notice her. She coughed at the sour air and stared up into the darkness above them. Were they ever going to reach the bottom? Three times now they'd had to backtrack and find a safer way down, once because of a ladder that had broken loose from its rusted frame, once because of a broken walkway and once because their path was blocked by some sort of monstrous conglomeration of steel bars, wheels, gears and hydraulic clamps that looked to her like an excellent tool for obtaining disability pay but otherwise was completely beyond her understanding.

It was taking far too long.

She kept telling herself that the Keeper had a plan. He *must* have had a plan, one for every possible contingency. It was what he did. He was the Keeper. The Keeper of the Vaults. The Keeper of the Tartarus Locks. He was literally the *Keeper of the Plan.*

Right?

But they *were* getting closer to something. The deeper they went, the more distinct the noise in the pipe grew. Not louder—Piper's spirit ears didn't work that way—but certainly more *intense.* By now, she was convinced that it wasn't something in the pipe itself, but rather some sort of vibration caused by something at the bottom of the pipe.

"We should keep going," coughed Seph. Again, she wiped the fog from her glasses and returned them to her face.

Piper tugged at the heavy bag and continued down the steps.

As it was in both the library and Covengale, there were no cobwebs here in Zarechuff. The only thing Seph had seen were a number of lazily floating things that sort of resembled very large mosquitoes, but showed no interest in trying to bite them. With a simple wave of the hand, they merely floated off in some other direction and left her be, which she very much appreciated.

A few times they heard noises from somewhere in the expansive darkness above them that Seph swore sounded like flapping bats, though she was hardly an expert on the little beasts. (Bats were yet another thing on her "nope" list, just beneath snakes and worms.) But like the lazy mosquito things, they didn't seem to be very interested in drinking their blood.

Still, she couldn't seem to relax. It was just a matter of time before they found something horrible. She was sure of it. Especially since the air in this place continued to irritate their throats and make them cough. If there *was* something dangerous in this endless darkness, they weren't likely to sneak by it unnoticed. They might as well be wearing bells.

But time slipped by in its weird way and nothing jumped out at them. Nothing tried to eat them.

Piper, however, had to reach for another piece of jerky. That was two now. Had she really been here that long? Or was the weird time messing up her internal clock? It was impossible to know for sure.

After a while, they both became aware of a familiar smell wafting through the harsh, chemical taste of the sour air. It was the unmistakable scent of water. Did that mean they were finally approaching the bottom of this iron chasm? Seph shined her light down into the darkness, searching for a reflection to tell her how far it was and hoping the lower levels weren't flooded like Covengale's ground floor.

Instead, she caught sight of something completely unexpected. She stopped and stared, her flashlight fixed on the thing as it floated in the air in front of her.

"What is it?" asked Piper.

"Do you see this?" she asked.

"See what?"

"Right in front of me." She pointed with her free hand. "Right in front of my finger. It's *tiny*."

Piper crowded next to her and peered down at it. "What is it?"

She had no idea. It *looked* a lot like a tiny little jellyfish, no bigger than a pea, with faint little tendrils, like fine hairs, dangling from it. It was transparent, like glass, and floating almost motionless in the air, barely moving at all.

She turned and shined the flashlight around. Now that she was looking for them, she saw several more hovering in the air all around her. They could've walked past hundreds of them without noticing them in this darkness. "Do you think they're dangerous?"

Piper shined her light onto the back of her wrist, where one of them had landed. It lay crumpled there, no more solid than a faint tuft of fine hair. She gently blew on it and it floated away into the darkness. "I don't think so."

Seph watched it vanish. "I don't like it," she decided. "Nothing's tried to kill us yet."

"Neither did any of the bugs in the library," Piper reminded her. "It only had the one monster." Then she puckered her lips and added, "Oh, and that tree that stole my sweater." She tilted her head to one side and wiped at her sweaty forehead. "And the only dangerous thing I encountered in Covengale was the ghosts." There were some night trees, she recalled, but they'd steered clear of those.

"I still don't trust it," said Seph, giving the little jellyfish thing a wide berth.

Piper shook her head and followed after her.

The smell of water grew stronger. Seph thought it would make the air of this world a little less foul, but if anything, it only made them cough worse. Like the air, there was something wrong with it. She couldn't even begin to describe *how* it was wrong, but she was quite certain she never wanted to drink it.

And the added humidity only made her glasses fog up more quickly.

After a few more minutes, the steel chasm opened up and they found themselves descending into a wide tunnel with a reservoir running through it. Two walkways ran the length of either side, connected by small bridges that crossed the water at regular intervals.

The water, itself, though bad, was deep and clear and still as glass, its surface as perfect as a mirror.

The little jellyfish creatures seemed to like the water. They were everywhere down here.

Piper found it hauntingly beautiful.

Seph couldn't decide what to think about it. On one hand, she'd never found jellyfish to be all that frightening. Probably because she'd spent almost her entire life in Wisconsin and had never been anywhere near a beach where she could possibly be stung by one. But these things weren't swimming in the water. They were flying in the air. And that was something *bugs* did.

She couldn't help but think that enough of them in one place would probably turn into a deadly, stinging swarm and try to kill them, just like those horrid Gispuknya wasps.

But as they descended onto the walkway, the tiny creatures still paid them no mind.

The pipe Piper was following stretched out over the water and through a hole in the wall on the other side. They crossed the first bridge and walked through the door nearest to it. Along the way, no shark-crocodile hybrid leapt out of the water to snap either of them in half. No man-eating snake plants swooped down from the darkness above. No hockey-mask-wearing ghosts or maintenance-worker zombies attacked them. And most surprising of all, no cloud of tiny jellyfish monsters swarmed over them and devoured their flesh.

Zarechuff remained suspiciously unthreatening. And Seph didn't care much for it at all. There *had* to be *something* terrifying down here. She just couldn't make herself believe there wasn't.

Beyond the doorway was a vast room filled with enormous machinery and several deep pools of that clear, but foul-smelling water.

Seph wandered through the room, doing her best to avoid the tiny jellyfish bugs while shining her light up at the towering machines. She couldn't even imagine what such monstrous things could be used for. There were pipes coming off some of them that were big enough to drive her truck through.

A massive tank, almost as big as Waybel Valley's entire water tower, stood on one side of the room with hundreds of fat, black hoses leading off the top of it and stretching up into the darkness, making it resemble some giant, mechanical Medusa. Across from it, a huge, silver shaft descended from the unseen ceiling with a great, metal ring, like a giant innertube raft, hanging horizontally beneath it. A bundle of cables twelve feet in diameter led down from the underside of the ring and disappeared into a hole in the floor. Looming behind both of those machines was a gigantic contraption, most of it little more than shadows among shadows high above them, that looked like a great, four-legged beast, with enormous, concrete tubes rising out of the water for legs and a gigantic, steel body dripping with cables. There was even a smaller tube running down the end of the contraption that sort of resembled a tail…or maybe an elephant-like trunk. And just beyond that monstrosity was a contraption that resembled a massive stack of steel waffles welded together and laid on its side.

Most of the floor and lower surfaces of the machinery were covered in some kind of hard, rocky substance, like a limestone crust.

"Over here," said Piper, pointing up at the rusty pipe she was following. It passed over the Medusa's snakes, curved around the giant, silver shaft, twisted to avoid the four-legged colossus and then passed through another wall directly over another doorway. She made her way around the pools of water, across a small, metal footbridge and past the waffle machine, then ducked under what looked suspiciously like a parked flying saucer. Then she made her way through the open doorway into the next room, where they finally stopped.

"That's it," said Piper. The pipe she'd been following ran across the ceiling and then curved downward, where it connected to a huge, rusting machine that looked to her like something that belonged on a space station. It consisted mainly of a large, cylindrical tank protruding from the wall, with a funnel-shaped cap on the end, leading to another large pipe that curved down and disappeared into a hole in the floor. A second, smaller tank was suspended above the first, one end curving down to merge with the lower one at the point where it met the wall and the other end attached to a large, hornet's nest-shaped device hanging from the ceiling. There were dozens of sturdy steel pipes and thick rubber hoses protruding from both tanks, most of them leading to large, metal boxes mounted on the walls. Huge bundles of heavy, white cables extended from the machine, connecting it to several locked panels, dozens of gages and meters and a few small display screens. Centered in the side of the larger tank facing them was a heavy, insulated door that stood wide open, as if inviting them to step inside.

"What do you hear?" asked Seph. She hesitated to step any closer. There was something strangely unsettling about this machine. It had a sort of aura about it that she couldn't quite describe, except that it was deeply, *deeply* unpleasant.

Plus, it kind of looked like the sort of thing that might be leaking radiation.

"It's just sort of…" She shook her head, uncertain how to explain it. "Kind of like when you forget to turn the oven off and I hear it making that ticking sound…" She frowned and pinched her lower lip as she stared at it. "But different," she added. "I'm not sure how to explain it."

"Gotcha," said Seph, although she didn't. Not really. She turned and looked at a large, locked panel next to the door. There was some sort of warning sign on it, written in a language she'd never seen before. There was a zigzaggy sort of symbol that seemed to indicate an electrical danger, but otherwise, there wasn't anything on it that she could read, even with her prophet sight.

Piper walked over and leaned through the doorway, shining her light inside the machine. There were large, mesh screens on both ends and the walls of the tank, though dusty, were oddly shiny and smooth for how old they were. Some sort of glass or ceramic, perhaps?

"Be careful," said Seph.

She stepped back and shined her light over the front of the machine. There was a box mounted a few feet from the door, connected to the rest of the machine by several dozen of those heavy, white cables. On the front of the box was a small video screen.

She walked over and placed her hand on the top of the box. The noise she'd been following was coming from here. She could feel it. A faint, almost thrumming sensation.

She placed the heavy bag on the floor beside her, relieved for an excuse to take a break from hauling it around in this weird gravity, and looked the contraption over. There was a confounding array of dials and switches and knobs under the screen, but one switch had a piece of wire twisted around it. She reached out and flipped it.

Immediately, the screen crackled to life.

Seph stepped closer, curious.

There was no sound and the picture wasn't very good, but they could distinctly see that the interior of that lower tank was displayed there.

Piper shined her light over to the open door. It wasn't a live feed. A recording?

After a few seconds, the light on the screen changed. The tank interior brightened. Then shadows appeared. Then a deathly skinny, naked man stumbled into view and fell onto the floor.

They both watched in horror as the sickly-looking man scrambled to his feet and began banging on the door, screaming.

"Oh my gosh…" sighed Piper.

Lights flickered on inside the machine. The man turned and looked around, clearly terrified. He banged on the locked door again, then turned away and covered his ears. His hair began to blow about his face.

The scene went on for almost a minute as the man grew increasingly desperate. He pounded on the door. He screamed. He sobbed. Then the screen began to flicker in and out.

He clawed at his ears and fell to his knees.

He convulsed.

He vomited onto the floor.

He crawled a few feet, then collapsed and began twitching.

Seph wanted to reach out and turn the thing back off, but she was frozen in horror.

The man on the screen rolled onto his back and wailed. There was blood on his face. It dripped from his nose and ears. Even his eyes were bleeding.

The screen flickered faster.

They watched in horror as the man on the screen writhed in pain.

Then Seph and Piper both realized that the screen wasn't flickering at all. The interior of the chamber never changed. It was only the *man.*

With a final, agonizing shriek, the unfortunate man vanished completely.

The screen stayed on. The video went on without him.

Did they disintegrate the poor man? Did they teleport him somewhere?

Piper reached out to turn off the screen, but before her finger touched it, the man flickered back into existence, his withered, corpse-like face pressed right against the camera, screaming out at them.

Even without sound, it scared the hell out of both of them.

Piper screamed and jumped back.

Seph let out an embarrassingly girlish shriek and backed away so quickly that she banged the back of her head against the wall.

The screen turned itself off then.

"*What the heck was that?*" squealed Piper, her heart pounding.

Seph didn't even know where to begin guessing.

"Was that *real?*"

Seph shook her head. Her gaze washed over the machine in front of them. She remembered watching Piper lean through that door to look into it. Did it still work? If one of them had stepped inside, could it still do what it did that poor man?

"I mean, what the actual *hell?*" croaked Piper.

Seph looked out at the rest of the building. In her mind, she remembered Connor's warning that Zarechuff was the gateway to hell. "The festering monument of mankind's capacity for unbridled *evil*," he'd called it.

What was this place?

Chapter 72

There was a door to the right of the monstrous death machine. Seph and Piper wasted no time leaving through it. It didn't matter that they still didn't know where they were going or what they were looking for. They just wanted to put as much space between them and Dr. Frankenstein's lab as they possibly could.

The next room contained a towering structure of steel beams, stairways, mesh walkways and countless pipes of every size, twisting and winding their way up into the darkness.

Piper tugged at the bag and looked around. She didn't feel anything from any of these pipes like she did the one that led them to the horror show, but that was fine by her. Clearly, that wasn't where they really wanted to be. There was no lock in that room. There was nothing there but lingering memories of the horrors of Zarechuff.

They started up the steps, slowly climbing the tower, making their way back up through the towering structure. Maybe they went the wrong way. Maybe they wanted to go to the *top* of Zarechuff's mysterious inner workings, not down into the torture dungeons.

Seph kept her eyes peeled for any kind of movement. She was now thoroughly convinced that the man in the video was still here somewhere, wandering this sweltering darkness, searching for stupid, trespassing girls to drag back to that machine and turn into his mutilated brides.

But the only things moving were small creatures that fluttered unseen through the darkness like bats. And although she remained wary of them, like the mosquito-like bugs and the little jellyfish creatures, they didn't seem remotely interested in human flesh. In fact, they seemed to avoid their lights completely.

"Do you hear anything?" she asked, eager for anything to get her mind off that horrid video and the little bat monsters that were probably just waiting for a better opportunity to swarm them and pluck out their eyeballs or suck out their spinal fluid.

Piper glanced around, her spirit ears rotating back and forth, listening for the sounds that only they could hear. "Nothing." Although truth be told, she wasn't exactly disappointed. The last thing she wanted was to follow another noise back to that awful chamber. Or worse, to a brand-new horror. "You?"

"Same."

"I wish you'd hurry up and figure out what you did in Covengale."

"Me too." It *would* be nice to be able to see in this darkness. There were plenty of wide-open spaces down here if she could see. She'd probably feel a lot less scared.

Either that, or she'd be able to see enough to know that there was *plenty* to be afraid of down here…

They continued up, higher and higher into the darkness.

The gravity of this world continued to drag them down. Their legs burned. Their stomach muscles ached. And by now they were both positively drenched in sweat.

Their coughing had eased a little, though. Was the air getting a little cleaner? Or were they just getting used to it?

"I wish I knew if Connor was okay," gasped Piper as she trudged up the endless stairs.

Seph wished so, too. But there was nothing they could do about it. They just had to trust that the Keeper knew what he was doing when he set all this nonsense up.

She kept thinking about how things just seemed to work themselves out again and again. Her gaining access to a higher level of prophet sight just when she needed it to escape the jabberwock. The fact that Hugh had all that extra weight to counteract the weird time flow of the library. The timely arrival of those Ahns to save her from the wretch when the scythe failed her. Even the way the monstrous minions of Tane and Gispuknya kept clashing at just the right times, allowing them to escape certain doom. It was as if every detail had been thoroughly choreographed to make sure they kept going exactly where they needed to go.

It was more than a little convenient, if you asked her.

The Ahns told them that there would always be a way. They had only to find it. Was that what they were talking about? Did the Keeper *make sure* there was always a way?

She paused, distracted, as she passed a rickety walkway stretching out into the darkness. "What is that?"

Piper paused and looked back, concerned. "What's what?"

"Over there." Seph pointed out across the walkway. "There's a light. Do you see it?"

She squinted into the darkness. "No."

"Really?"

"There's nothing there."

Seph took off her glasses and cleaned the fog off them again. She wasn't imagining it. She couldn't see what it was from this distance, but there was definitely a faint, bluish light out there. "Huh…"

"We checking it out?"

"I guess we have to." She stepped out onto the walkway. It seemed sturdy enough beneath her feet, even with her added weight, but the railings were loose. They wobbled back and forth when she tested them. "*That* doesn't make me feel very secure..."

Piper looked down into the darkness below. They'd been climbing for a while now, so it was a long way down. If something snapped halfway across it, there'd be nothing to grab onto. It'd be a long, terrifying fall with no chance of picking themselves back up again.

She couldn't help but wonder how much harder she'd hit the ground in this heavy gravity, too.

Seph took a deep breath and let it out again. "Okay..." she sighed. "You hang back here until I'm across. Just in case."

Piper bit her lip and glanced around. She didn't like the idea of being left alone in the dark, even for a minute, but she couldn't argue that doubling the weight on this deathtrap walkway was probably a bad idea.

It's fine, Seph thought. One foot in front of the other. Focus on the walkway, itself, not the deadly drop below it. But it wasn't long before her confidence began to wane. The farther out she went, the less sturdy it felt. It swayed back and forth beneath her feet. The bolts holding it together groaned in the silence.

Ahead of her, she could see that one of the railings had completely rusted through.

She tried to focus on that soft, blue glow in the distance. Maybe one of the rooms up there had working lights, like those giant orbs hanging in the library.

But something beneath her popped loudly and she froze. Her heart stalled in her chest for a moment. Was that a bolt breaking? A piece of the metal snapping? A vital support beam failing? She stood there, holding her breath, praying the whole thing didn't fall apart beneath her feet.

Then one of the bat-things swooped past her face, a flapping, fluttering thing in the darkness, and she screamed. Then she tipped a little, her balance going. She grabbed for the railing, but it broke apart and dropped into the darkness.

Piper screamed.

Seph dropped onto her hands and knees, trembling, and tried to calm herself.

A moment later, the broken railing crashed to the floor with a loud, echoing clang.

"Are you okay?" squeaked Piper.

She tried to say that she was okay, but her voice seemed to get lost on its way past her lips. All that came out was a pitiful sort of whispered whimpering.

"Persephone?"

"I'm okay," she said, the words actually making it out of her mouth this time.

"Please be careful!"

Very slowly, she rose to her feet and forced herself to walk again. One foot after the other. Slowly. Carefully.

She could see the other side now. She was past the halfway point.

The walkway groaned and creaked beneath her, but didn't break.

Just a little farther.

She stepped through the doorway at the far end and into an empty hallway, where she leaned against the wall, clutching at her chest, willing her poor heart to slow down.

God, that was scary…

"It should be okay," she called back, her voice echoing in the vast emptiness. "Just be careful."

"No problem," said Piper from right behind her.

Seph turned and stared at her, surprised.

Piper stared right back at her. "What? I figured if *you* made it, *I* could make it."

Seph's brow furrowed. She squinted at her.

"Oh! Not that I think you're heavier than me or anything!"

"*What?*"

"That… That didn't sound right," she fretted, her face flushing red. "I just…you know. We're about the same size, right? I figured…it was…it was okay…to come across…" She bit her lip and fidgeted. "*Meg's* the one who says you're fat!" she blurted. "I don't think so at all! I think you're perfect!"

"*What the hell?*"

"I panicked…" she whimpered, wringing her hands. "You keep looking at me like that… It's scary!"

She turned and walked away, shaking her head.

"*Sorry!*"

"Just come on."

The source of the glowing wasn't as far away as she first thought. It was coming from the wall at the end of this corridor. Seph walked up to it, examining it closer.

It was some kind of glowing worm.

"So where'd you see that light?" asked Piper.

Seph looked back at her, confused. "Huh?"

"You said you saw a light."

"Uh…*yeah. This* one."

"Huh?"

Seph looked down at the worm again. "Wait…you can't see it."

"See what?"

She leaned closer, surprised. Now she saw it. The worm wasn't glowing at all. Instead, it was like Piper's spirit ears. It only seemed to shine like that because everything around it was so dark. In fact, the tiny little beast was entirely translucent, as if it were nothing more than a ghost.

She lifted her hand, curious to see whether it was as intangible as Piper's ears, but she couldn't bring herself to try touching the thing. Instead, she shined her light at it and said, "Put your hand right there."

Piper looked at her, confused, but then reached out and touched the wall. As expected, her fingers passed right through it. It was as if it were a hologram. "There's nothing there."

Having passed that test, Seph reached out to try it herself, but even so she couldn't bear it. She snatched her hand back instead.

"What is it?" asked Piper.

"Some kind of…spirit *caterpillar*, I guess?"

"Huh?"

"Ghostly little glowworm thing."

"Aw. Sounds pretty."

"Pretty" wasn't a word Seph used for creepy crawlies, no matter what color they glowed. She turned away from it and looked around. The hallway curved to the right just ahead. There was a doorway there.

She walked into the next room to find hundreds of those strange, ghostly worms glowing in the darkness.

The far wall of this room was lined with dirty glass cases, like the ones in the reptile exhibit at the zoo. (Or, at least, the ones she remembered from her school trip way back when she was in fifth grade, since that was the first and *only* time she ever went inside *that* house of horrors.)

She walked over and shined her light into several of them. Most were completely empty, but a few contained small bones or creepy-looking shells.

Next to the door through which they entered, the wall was a single, massive pane of glass, this one far dirtier than the others. It was smeared almost entirely with mud and grime.

She shined her light through a gap and found piles of bones inside.

A big animal of some sort?

Then she saw it. That wasn't mud. It was *paper.*

This case was like the office in Pappy Stan's Diner.

This was a *hive.*

Chapter 73

There didn't appear to be any wasps inside, or any other creepy crawly things. Like whatever was in the other cases, they'd long ago died, perhaps starved to death when the place was abandoned.

Seph stepped away from the glass, her skin crawling, and turned to the door on the far side of the room. She was starting to get a really bad feeling. And she didn't want to say what she was thinking out loud. She didn't want to give it a voice. She didn't *dare* give it a voice, for fear that speaking it may somehow be the thing that made it so.

She wiped at the sweat on her forehead, cleared her itching throat and then crossed the room and opened the next door. The space behind it was filled with heavy, metal cages. About twenty of them were sitting on the floor, each one about the size of a small, one-car garage, easily big enough to hold a full-grown tusker with room to pace.

Many more much smaller cages dangled from the ceiling by chains. Hundreds of them. Like little bird cages. It was like some kind of bizarre art installation. An eccentric artist's attempt to convey the helplessness of society, perhaps? (Or maybe that was just the artist in her.)

There were even more of those glowing worms in here, crawling over the bars, clinging to the chains, slithering over the walls.

They didn't seem to like the floor for some reason. There were none down where they could be stepped on, which seemed weird because they seemed to be immune to being squashed.

(Seph wasn't warming to them at all, by the way.)

There was an office in the corner of the room. Something about it seemed to call to her. She walked over to it, opened the door and went inside. There was a desk there, steel, like everything else, its legs covered in rust. The chair was falling apart.

There was a screen built into the top of the desk, not unlike a computer monitor, perhaps this world's version of the laptop, but unlike the screen by the freaky machine where the naked man was tortured, it wouldn't turn on.

She wasn't the least bit disappointed.

But there was a dusty, black folder lying next to the screen, bound with rubber bands that had almost completely rotted. They crumbled and fell away as she picked it up.

"What is it?" asked Piper, peering over her shoulder.

Seph hesitated a moment, sure that she was about to see something terrible. She had to remind herself that Connor didn't have time for her to keep being squeamish before she could bring herself to open it. Inside was a pile of orange-tinted papers covered in unreadable writing and, among them, a pile of photographs.

"Oh god…" she gasped as she thumbed through them.

Piper covered her mouth.

Half of the pictures showed people being torn apart by large, white, wolf-like creatures. The other half showed people writhing in agony under a swarm of giant, copper-colored wasps.

"It's them, isn't it?" said Piper.

Seph nodded. There didn't seem to be any denying it.

Hounds and wasps…and a tortured flickering man…

She'd always assumed that Gispuknya's creations were just that: creations. Just things that it made up, designed to hunt down the seekers and destroy the Hands of the Architects forever.

She stared at the white hounds. She'd recognize the shape of those monsters anywhere. Although the ones that attacked them in Nora's Lilac Grove were black and shadowy, their shape was exactly the same.

She dropped the file onto the table and looked out at all those awful cages.

"This is where Gispuknya was born…"

Piper stared at the black folder. "Wait… Does that mean we're in the Black World right now? The one that was created after Tane obtained two of the three Hands?"

Seph felt the hair on the back of her neck prickle at the very thought of setting foot in such a world. But… "No. Louann told me once that Gispuknya was born *from* that world, but not *in* it." She said it was born afterward, but from the same *sins* of that world. A product of it. That's what made it so terrifying. It was proof that the evil born of a black world wouldn't die with it.

Piper turned and shined her light back out at those huge cages. It was far too easy to imagine those awful, white hounds snapping and snarling behind those bars, eager to sink their teeth into anyone careless enough to wander too close.

Seph closed the folder and dropped it back onto the desk. "I don't think it's any coincidence that this file was just lying here."

"And it's a little too convenient that machine downstairs showed us what they did to the flickering man," agreed Piper. She remembered the wire that had been wound around the switch that started that horror show. It was left for them like that, ready to start right at the beginning of that video.

"Someone wants us to see these things," agreed Seph.

"The Keeper?"

She could think of no one else who should be able to have that sort of power, but… "But why?"

"It's like Covengale," recalled Piper. "Those flashbacks. It was like that whole place was put there just to show me the horrors that happened there."

Seph couldn't wrap her head around it. "Let's get out of here. Those cages are making me feel sick."

They left the office and made their way to the next doorway, which opened into a long, concrete corridor with small, metal doors set into the wall on one side at regular intervals. Seph's gaze washed over these doors as she walked.

Why did they make her think of a *morgue*? What was *wrong* with her brain?

She couldn't help but watch those doors as they walked by them, half-expecting one to creak open and something terrible to crawl out of it.

But nothing like that happened. Zarechuff seemed to be holding back whatever terrors it still contained, waiting, perhaps, to unleash them all at once when they finally dared to let their guard down.

Another large room awaited them at the far end of the corridor. A huge, round, concrete and steel structure took up most of the floor, at least fifty yards in diameter, with round, porthole-like windows set into its sides all the way around it. Thousands of small tubes ran from the sides of the structure and snaked up into the darkness above. Massive, steel pipes were rising off the top of it.

Piper pointed to a box mounted to the wall next to one of those little windows. There was another video screen there, like the one in the flickering chamber. "That's still running," she whispered. She could "hear" it making that strange, thrumming, ticking sensation. One of the switches even had a wire wound around it, showing them which one to flip to start the show. She looked over at Seph, a dreadful expression on her face. "Do we…?"

Seph wasn't looking at the screen. She was aiming her flashlight at the window next to it. Her hand was trembling. She was pale. She shook her head. "No…" Her voice was very small. "I'm not watching that… I don't care what the Keeper says… I won't…"

Piper turned and aimed her own flashlight at the window.

There were unsettling, black handprints smeared on the inside of the glass.

Little handprints.

She had to cover her mouth to keep from screaming.

They didn't need to watch the footage to know that this was where the black-eyed children were born.

Seph moved on without stopping. To hell with the Keeper if he thought she was going to turn on that awful screen. She wouldn't watch it. Not now. Not *ever*. Not for any reason. She didn't even want to believe that such a thing existed.

She *never* wanted to know what kinds of terrible horrors went on inside that chamber.

Chapter 74

They left the room with the awful machine and stepped out onto another walkway overlooking another huge, gaping hole of a room. More steel stairs descended into darkness, overlooking a wall of great, black pipes, monstrously huge gears and gigantic chains.

Piper dropped the bag and leaned against the wall, still pressing her hand against her mouth, holding back the sobs that were welling up inside her. Fat tears streaked down her face. She couldn't seem to get the image of those small, bloody handprints out of her head.

Seph, herself, felt numb. There were so many emotions. She, too, wanted to weep for the poor souls who found themselves stuffed into that horrid machine. But she also felt angry. *Furious.* The idea that anyone could be so cruel and heartless as to do something so horrid to a *child*... She hoped the people who ran this hellhole died fitting, horrible deaths. She hoped they suffered a hundred times over for every innocent person they tortured.

But she also felt utterly hopeless. All the terrible things that had happened in her own world, in just *recent* history, were bad enough. Not to mention all the cruelties human beings had committed over the millennia... To think that there were countless other universes out there, all with the same sickening stories of torture and deprivation.

What were they even trying to save?

She turned and hugged Piper as she wept.

For a long time, they stood there like that.

Yes, they needed to hurry…but sometimes you just had to stop and take a moment. Sometimes that was the only way to keep your sanity.

One of the bat creatures fluttered down and landed on a nearby railing. It wasn't a bat *or* a bird, now that Seph was looking at one. It looked *reptilian*. Or maybe *amphibian*, as its skin wasn't scaly, but smooth. It was about the size of a crow, with short little bird-like legs and talons, but long, leathery wings that folded up like a pair of umbrellas behind its back. Its head was sort of toad-like, with a wide, flat mouth and beady little eyes. It had two, bright yellow crests on top of its skull. It stood there a moment, regarding the two of them, and then unfolded its wings and flew off again.

It was odd how peaceful this place was. Where were all the things that should be trying to kill them? Where were the monsters? Where were the vengeful spirits?

Why had the horrors ended in this place while they lived on eternally inside the rotting walls of Covengale? What was the difference?

"I'm okay," sniffled Piper, turning away. "Sorry."

Seph stepped back and crossed her arms. "It's fine," she said, feeling awkward. She wasn't all that good at comforting people. She was much better at making fun of people.

"I just can't understand it."

"I know. I can't either."

"Why would anyone do things like this?"

She wished she had an answer for her. "Come on. Let's keep going."

Piper wiped at her eyes and picked up the bag again. It hadn't gotten any lighter yet.

Seph led the way. She had her choice. She could take the walkway around the room to see if there was another door on that side. Or she could head down the steps into the black mystery below. She decided to go down. At least that way the farther they went, the less distance they'd have to fall when they finally stepped on something that wouldn't hold their weight.

And as it turned out, the darkness wasn't all that deep this time. They descended for less than a minute before the light struck the crusty floor.

It was a lot messier in this area. A portion of one of the walls had fallen in at some point, scattering bricks and knocking down a section of steel pipe.

They made their way to the floor and then walked through a nearby doorway. This part of the building was far older. The walls were dingy brick and the concrete floor—or whatever material it was made from—was cracked and crumbled almost to dirt in places. Steel beams—or some manner of metal, anyway—crisscrossed overhead, casting eerie shadows across the low ceiling as they walked around.

There was litter all over the floor down here. Old, orange-tinted papers were scattered everywhere. A wall of shelves on one side of the room had collapsed, spilling books and boxes of papers into a pile on the floor.

In the far corner of the room, just visible in the beams of their flashlights, was a six-sided, stone structure with an iron gate for a door. The perfect place, Seph assumed, for containing something you didn't want wandering free.

This prison-like structure was made all the more unsettling by the glass enclosure in the center of the room.

She walked up to it, shining her light through the warped, foggy glass. There was a large, metal slab inside, mounted to the floor on two strong legs. Large, disk-like lamps dangled by chains from the ceiling directly over the slab. There was a large cabinet against one of the glass walls, no doubt where they kept all manner of horrible tools, devices and chemicals.

Seph didn't think this was where the employees gathered to put together jigsaw puzzles during breaks. That was an operating room of some sort. The sort of place where the sort of people who shoved terrified, naked people into hellish, flickering chambers likely came to take things apart…and perhaps to put them back together again.

And this larger room…

She turned and shined her light out into the open space surrounding the glass. There was a row of old chairs lined up on one side of the makeshift operating room, as if for an audience. And behind those chairs, a large, darkened window was set high into the wall, overlooking it all.

This wasn't just an operating room. It was an operating *theater.* The glass walls allowed the people in charge to observe without getting dirty.

She looked down at the orange papers on the floor. They weren't just scattered litter. A closer look revealed that they were photographs taken of that glass room. A half-dozen men in long, gray gowns and masks were gathered around the slab. There was a frightening array of machines and cabinets crowded in there with them, far more equipment than was in there now. It looked like there was barely enough room for all those people to move. Bright lights were shining down around them, giving the entire scene a haunting glow while, all around the glass room, the space around it was gloomy.

The thing on the slab… It was much bigger than the men. A great, brown, hulking thing.

She bent and picked up one of the photos. A familiar pair of branching horns were protruding from one end.

She'd know that gnarled shape anywhere. It was the devil that attacked them in Nora's Lilac Grove. The one who murdered poor Amethyst…

Her gaze drifted over to the cell at the far end of the room. For a moment, she was filled with disgust. That monster plunged its mutant hand right through her friend's chest. It deserved whatever horrors it was suffering in this picture. But that faded quickly enough as she realized that these were taken a long, long, *long* time ago. And the real monsters were the inhuman savages gathered around that operating table.

And the ones that watched from the shadows like cowards, of course.

Piper picked up another photograph and looked at it. It was a closeup of the devil's strange, twisted hand. "Did this thing start out as human?" she wondered.

Does it matter? wondered Seph. She dropped the photograph back onto the floor and looked out across the empty room.

She started to walk away, but one of the photographs on the floor caught her eye. It was mostly hidden, buried under several other pictures. Only a corner of it was sticking out. But Someone had written something on it. She picked it up and stared at it. The picture was of the operating theater from right about where she was standing. She could see the men inside the glass room, crowded around the slab. There was a splash of blood on the inside of one of the panes. And she could even see part of the row of chairs. At least two men were sitting there in the shadows, watching the show.

The words scrawled on the photograph were written in English.

"'Do you see it, yet?'" she read, confused.

Piper gasped and snatched the picture from her hand.

Seph looked up at her, surprised. "What?"

"That's what the tall man kept asking me in Covengale."

The tall man? The ghost who Piper claimed saved her from being possessed by the psychotic old hag? She looked down at the photograph again. "What does it mean? See *what* yet?"

"I don't know. He wouldn't say."

For this message to be written in English, it had to be meant for them. But who could've entered this place? Did the Keeper leave it for them? That didn't seem much like something he would do... He was notoriously stingy with clues.

Piper's spirit ears perked up and rotated toward the far corner of the room. "Do you hear that?"

"Hear what?"

She handed Seph back the photograph and then turned and walked in that direction, following the mysterious sound. "It's like the noise I heard from that flickering machine."

Seph looked at the message one last time. (*Do you see it yet?*) Then she dropped it and followed Piper.

Chapter 75

They left the operating theater and made their way down a long, concrete corridor. They passed several rooms, each one containing some monstrous conglomeration of rusted steel.

Were they *all* instruments of horrendous torture, wondered Seph, or just some of them? Did this place have other purposes? Did it generate electricity for the masses? Did it clean the foul stench out of the drinking water? Even as the question crossed her mind, she found that she knew it didn't.

People who built places like this didn't care about basic human rights. This was a weapons research and manufacturing facility. And the worst kinds of weapons, at that. Chemical. Biological. Maybe even nuclear.

Or worse. This was a whole different universe, with entirely different laws governing it. They could've harnessed something far worse than nuclear power for all she knew.

Was this entire facility designed solely to manufacture inhuman ways of killing people? Was its only purpose to spread *misery*?

She shined her light into a door as she passed it and spied a large machine that looked like a giant, rust-encrusted golf ball with thousands of fine, green wires leading off it. She'd never seen a real doomsday device before, but she suspected it would probably look a lot like that.

Just in case, she made a mental note to steer clear of any big red buttons she might come across.

Piper felt a familiar twinge deep inside her stomach. It was almost time to eat again. Her hand went to the bag at her hip. Inside were the rest of the snacks Seph bought for her in Fathom Lake. She should take one and eat it now, while nothing terrifying was happening, but although the monster that lurked inside her was insisting it was time for its regularly scheduled sacrifice of flesh, her appetite was on a completely different clock. She could barely stand the idea of eating anything after the horrors she'd witnessed. She still couldn't get those bloody pictures of the operating theater out of her head.

And those awful, tiny handprints…

The Ahn inside her could wait a little longer.

She wiped the sweat from her face and pushed on through the sweltering darkness.

A moment later, the corridor ended. A single, iron door stood open before them, an oppressive darkness looming just beyond it.

They paused here and exchanged an uncertain glance. What now?

But they didn't have time to linger. Seph wiped at the sweat on her brow and stepped through the doorway.

There was a rack of hooks mounted to the wall just inside the door. Hanging from these hooks were several black, rubber masks with thick, dingy goggles and fat, cylindrical filters protruding from their snouts.

Gas masks.

"That's…unsettling," she groaned.

Piper clasped her hands over her mouth. Did those have something to do with the foul air in this place? Did the people here do something? Was there some sort of chemical leak? The awful possibilities were endless.

Seph didn't bother taking one off the hooks. First of all, Connor told them that the Hands were supposed to be protecting them from anything hazardous in the environment. Secondly, those things were all so ancient and rotten that there was no way they'd do them any good even if the filters still worked. And finally, the next door was already standing open. Anything poisonous in there had already escaped.

The worst part was probably that she was freshly reminded of how irritating the air was. They'd mostly grown used to it. But now she caught herself sniffing at the air, paranoid about lingering poisons, and that awful itching in her throat had started her coughing again.

She stepped through the next doorway and descended a narrow set of stairs into another open chamber.

It was the same as before. A huge pane of glass separated them from the far side of the room. On the other side was darkness. On this side were nine more folding chairs, just like the ones set up outside the operating theater behind them. There was even another of those dark windows set into the wall behind and above the chairs, overlooking the entire, horrific setting.

Hesitantly, she crossed the room and shined her light through the dingy glass.

The floor on the other side was under water. Or…under *some kind of liquid*, anyway. As her light passed over it, she saw the glistening rainbow of an oily slick floating on its surface and her thoughts immediately returned to the foul, irritating stench of the water in that first reservoir.

Several large pipes jutted out from the walls of the enclosed room.

Before she had time to consider what any of it meant, a monitor flickered on in the darkness.

A blurry image of this room appeared there. A woman was standing behind the glass, naked and covered in filth. She had long, black hair and huge, terrified eyes. She was screaming and banging her small fists on the glass, pleading to be let out.

But Seph already knew that no one was going to let her out. Her stomach churned at the fresh memory of those rotten gas masks hanging by the doorway.

She didn't want to see this. Whatever was about to happen was going to be nightmare fuel. She turned away from it and shined her light around the room. There was another doorway on the other side. They could just move on and let the horror movie play by itself.

But Piper was walking toward the monitor, horrified, her gaze fixed on the choppy image.

It was her.

She knew that slight silhouette anywhere.

Somewhere overhead, a speaker crackled and a man's voice boomed over the silence in a language neither of them—and indeed no one born throughout the history of their entire universe—had ever heard before.

Then, after about thirty seconds of incomprehensible droning, the man fell silent and the woman's terrible screams filled the room for the first time in untold ages.

Piper covered her ears and cried out. No. She didn't want to be hearing this. She couldn't stand it.

She was human once. Ages and ages ago, in a universe long dead, the marsh woman was an *ordinary woman.* She lived and breathed and loved just like anyone else.

Until they threw her in that glass cage and locked the doors…

The sound on the speakers was out of sync with the video on the monitor. For some reason that made the whole ordeal even worse. It threw the horrors of the scene even further into chaos.

Seph shined her light up at the ceiling, then around at the walls. There didn't seem to be any way to turn the speakers off.

On the monitor, foul, greenish water began rushing from the pipes in the walls.

Overhead, the woman's screams were already growing more intense. They could hear her hammering her fists against the glass.

Piper turned her back on it. She couldn't watch this. She *wouldn't.* It was inhuman! "Make it stop!" she cried.

Seph snatched up one of the folding chairs and tried to smash the monitor, but the screen was too thick. It didn't even shudder.

She didn't try again. She grabbed Piper's hand and ran for the door. "This way!" Together, they fled the room and ran down another narrow corridor, away from the horrible images playing on the monitor.

But the *sounds* of the woman's strangled cries of terror and agony couldn't be escaped. There were speakers in this ceiling as well. They couldn't get away.

They ran up a flight of stairs, down another corridor, through another room filled with those awful, rusty cages, and across another frightfully rickety walkway to a long, narrow passageway lined with more of those creepy, morgue-like doors. And *still* the audio of the unfortunate woman's hideous fate played.

On and on and on it went, a hellish symphony of suffering, as if someone had lowered a microphone all the way into the blistering bowels of hell itself.

Piper kept her hands pressed over her ears. Tears streamed down her face. She couldn't stand it. Those poor people! First Covengale and now this?

What kinds of monsters lived in these worlds?

The woman's screams didn't even sound human anymore. It was like listening to the shrieks of a wounded animal. A wretched, guttural howl of utter agony.

What was even happening to her? What could make a human being utter such horrible noises? How much could one person possibly suffer?

Maybe Gispuknya was right. Maybe mankind didn't deserve to keep going. Why bother building a new universe to save a species with this kind of capacity for evil?

Then, after a gut-wrenching eternity of screaming, the woman's cries became muffled and a new series of horrible noises took their place. Hideous, strangling, *gurgling* noises.

Then, finally, as they neared the end of the morgue-like corridor, the speakers shut off.

Piper stopped running and dropped to her knees. She was exhausted. Both physically *and* emotionally.

Seph stumbled a few steps ahead and then she, too, stopped. She leaned against the wall, careful not to touch any of those small doors, just in case this really was some sort of morgue…which wouldn't be all that unusual, given that they actually freaking *killed people* in this horrible place!

"Why?" coughed Piper. "Why would anyone do these things?"

Seph shook her head. "I don't know," she gasped, trying to catch her breath through the sour air.

"What kind of an awful world was this?"

Seph stared at her. She wasn't sure what to say. Was *their* world any different? Just look at the Holocaust. The Inquisition. The Salem witch trials. There was evil in the world. It was just the way things were.

"Come on. We have to keep moving. Connor's waiting for us."

Piper looked up at her. She'd almost forgotten about poor Connor. How long had they been gone? It felt like days, though it could only have been a few hours at most…right?

She struggled back to her feet, coughed on the foul air and tugged at the strap of her bag.

She hoped he was still okay. She desperately didn't want to end up trapped in this awful world forever.

Chapter 76

The farther they went, the older and more deteriorated everything became. And the dirtier everything became, too. By now, every surface was covered in that thick, limestone-like crust. It covered almost every inch of the floor and had climbed all the way to the ceiling in places.

How long had they been walking this time? An hour? Two? Twelve? To Seph, it felt like days. Her feet and legs were killing her.

That corridor with the morgue doors had seemed to go on for miles. And then they'd wandered through a labyrinth of pipes and cables for what felt like miles more. Several times they'd heard the unearthly flapping of those creepy lizard-bird things and once they'd had to pass through a dense cloud of those tiny, transparent jellyfish creatures, which Seph still wasn't sure she could've done if Piper hadn't been there to wave them away, opening a path for her to dart through.

Here and there, she'd caught fleeting glimpses of those glowing spirit worms wriggling around deep in the shadows between the machinery.

But even with all the horrors Zarechuff had committed in its time, still nothing dangerous attacked them.

Seph wondered if that was why her prophet sight refused to work. Did it only activate when she was in mortal danger? Was it an automatic reaction to dire peril? She wished someone would tell her how these things worked.

But at least they finally seemed to be making progress. Their surroundings were changing. There was a distinct difference in the atmosphere. The air felt cleaner. An occasional, cool draft blew past them that felt amazingly good after all this time in the sweltering heat, but came with a subtle and unpleasant new smell.

Something was different here.

And when they finally reached the end of the long corridor, they immediately knew what it was.

The Wood had invaded Zarechuff.

They were standing in a large chamber filled with giant, unidentifiable machinery. It wasn't very different from many of the other rooms they'd encountered, except that a large portion of it had collapsed. The entire far side of the room was in ruins. Huge piles of bricks and heavy steel beams had spilled onto the floor. Countless pipes had been ripped from the ceiling and lay broken and crushed among the rubble. Entire machines had been toppled, leaving wires and tubes dangling from the ceiling and walls.

And those bizarre, black trees had crowded into the room, seemingly bursting right through the concrete, transforming the floor into a landscape of broken boulders. Their roots snaked up through the cracks and wrapped themselves around support beams and posts, ripping cables right out of the floor. Meanwhile, their coiled, alien branches had wrapped around every exposed surface, seemingly in an attempt to strangle the iron monstrosities that stood between them and the rest of the facility.

The whole scene created a surreal landscape of fused forest and industry that Seph found both fascinating and terrifying. She stood staring at it for a moment. The artist in her wanted to sit down and draw it, though she wouldn't dare spend that much time in this place.

Then she remembered her phone. She pulled it out and snapped several pictures of it.

She cursed herself for not remembering it sooner. This wasn't just another dirty hole under Sukmukwe Mounds State Park, after all. This was Zarechuff. This was a relic from a long-dead universe.

She pocketed the phone, making a mental note to not forget it again, and then glanced at Piper. "Where to now?"

Piper glanced back, worried. Then she pointed toward a door in the middle of the adjacent wall, near where the trees began. "There's a sound coming from over there."

Seph stared into that darkness. "You remember that those things stole your sweater, right?"

Piper shot her a dirty look. "I think I remember that, yes."

"Just checking."

"Come on. We'll try to stay close to the wall. Maybe they won't be able to reach us there."

Seph didn't like it, but she didn't see much other choice. They still hadn't found the lock yet and the sounds Piper was hearing were all that they had to go on.

They circled around to the far wall and made their way toward the invading Wood.

There was a doorway down there. Something was glowing inside.

"They're not moving," observed Seph.

"The other one didn't move much either," recalled Piper. "Until it tried to grab us."

That was true. But even then, she'd detected *some* movement. These trees were completely motionless. "Just go fast," she whispered.

They hurried on, slipping under the still, snake-like branches of the slumbering night trees and ducking into the room without incident.

Here, they found themselves standing before a large, circular opening in the wall. On either side was half of a heavy, iron disk. Clearly, the two were designed to slide into place over the opening, creating a nearly impenetrable vault door.

This was either where they kept things they *really* didn't want stolen or, more likely, where they kept something they *really* didn't want getting out. Something far more dangerous than the devil with its measly stone prison.

Another video screen was mounted to the wall to the right of the door. It was on. Silent static was playing.

Before they could decide what to do next, the screen switched automatically to an image of a man lying on the floor, as if sleeping. Except if he was asleep, it was a fitful sleep. He kept twitching.

There was no sound, like in the marsh woman's cell, but there was nonetheless something deeply unsettling about the man in this image. For one thing, his arms and legs appeared to be badly broken.

They stared in terrified anticipation, expecting another horror show like the flickering man. Instead, a second screen switched on to the left of the door. On *this* screen, the man was shown from a different angle, and he wasn't just lying there. He was thrashing around on the floor, screaming like a madman.

A third screen turned on then, a larger one, mounted to a machine on the wall to their left. This screen showed four men dressed like the ones in the photographs of the operating theater in the room with him. Three of them were holding him down while the fourth bent over him while he screamed in agony.

A pool of blood was slowly spreading beneath him.

Several smaller screens flickered on around the bigger screen.

Most of them revealed more of the man being tortured. One simply showed the man's face as he stared up into the camera, his eyes hauntingly dark and empty.

Seph turned and looked around as more and more video screens came to life, each one showing new horrors.

And as the horrible pictures played, his hair and beard grew longer. His flesh grew paler. His eyes sank deeper. Then, little by little, his hair began to fall out.

Piper covered her eyes. She couldn't take it anymore. It was too horrible.

Seph *wished* she could turn away. But she seemed to be frozen in horror.

How long? How long did they torture him? How many years did he spend in this horrible place?

Finally, she turned away, only to find herself staring at a screen mounted above the door they came in. There, a loop was playing over and over again. It was a shot of these doors standing open, and the unfortunate man lying on the floor inside, bound by chains around his crooked ankles, his dead eyes staring back at them.

She knew that shape.

The wretch.

This was where they made him.

This was how he was born.

At the end of the loop, the chains pulled taught and he was dragged into the darkness by his mangled legs, his broken body twisting and stretching unnaturally, making him look more serpent-like than human.

Below the screen, across the top of the door, someone had left them a message:

DO YOU SEE IT YET?

Chapter 77

Outside the room, something heavy crashed to the floor, wrenching startled screams from both of them.

Piper shined her light at the doorway and caught sight of several small, coiling branches snaking around the jamb. "The light!" she gasped, remembering Maria's warning about the night trees. "That's what wakes them up."

Seph snapped off her light, only to realize that it did nothing. The monitors were making most of the light, and she had no idea how to shut any of them off.

A large crack shot up the wall. An eerie groaning noise pervaded the silence.

Piper backed away from the doorway, her blue eyes wide with fear.

There was another door behind them. Seph grabbed her hand and fled through it as something much heavier crashed to the floor outside.

They ran up a narrow set of stairs, around a corner and then up more stairs and down a long corridor lined with windows overlooking a vast and unsettling darkness. She didn't think about where she was going. She didn't think about how to get back. They couldn't go back that way anyway now. She just ran. She didn't look at the awful machinery she was passing. She didn't look in the empty little rooms with steel bars for doors. She refused to look at any more of Zarechuff's horrors.

Then, finally, she stepped through a door and found herself in a large office space filled with rusty, metal desks and rotting chairs.

In the far back of the room was another set of steps and a door leading into another office.

There was a light on in there.

She stared at it. Something up there seemed to be calling out to her.

In fact, she became suddenly certain that something had been calling out to her since she left the wretch's awful prison. This was where they were supposed to be. This was what they were looking for.

She let go of Piper's hand and walked across the room. She climbed the steps. She pushed open the door.

Connor was waiting for them.

He was standing with his back to the window, facing her, a shadow of a crooked smile on his face. "Long time, no see." Then he tilted his head to one side. "Or was it? Time works funny here, don't it?"

Piper scrunched her face at him, confused. "Wait…how're *you* here? We left you way back…" She turned and frowned at the door. How far away was that first room now? How long had it been since they left him there? How many rusty miles had they traveled in that time?

Maybe they'd circled back?

"How are you not *dying*?" asked Seph.

"It's complicated," replied Connor.

"I'm sure it is."

"But don't worry." He lifted his arm and showed them the wounds. "See? All healed now."

"How?" asked Piper, amazed.

"I'm a very fast healer. *Very* fast. It's just somethin' I've always been able to do. There're a lot of people like me out there. You'd be surprised what some of us are capable of survivin'."

"So you're, like, Wolverine or something?" said Seph.

"Sort of. Yes. But not nearly as interestin', I'm sure."

"Were you the one who left us those messages?" asked Piper.

"You mean, 'Do you see it yet?' Naw. That was someone else."

"The Keeper?" guessed Seph.

"No. The Keeper don't care if you see it or not."

"Then who?" pressed Piper.

"You don't really understand what's goin' on at all, do you?"

Seph's eyes narrowed. "Who are you really?"

"I'm exactly who I told you I was," he replied. "I'm the Trash Man of Pobsick Spring and the custodian of the gate to Zarechuff."

"*And…*?" pressed Seph.

"*And…*" he relented, "…I'm a messenger. For Janon Tane."

Piper gasped and covered her mouth.

Seph lifted her hands, meaning to raise the scythe, but she forgot that it wouldn't work in here.

"Oh, calm yerselves," sighed Connor. "I'm not gonna hurt you. I'm the *messenger*, not one of his creepy enforcers."

"And why would we listen to anything *he* says?" challenged Seph.

"Uh…'cause if you want me to let you out of here, you have to listen to what I've got to say."

Piper crossed her arms and stuck out her lip. "That's not very nice."

"In case you hadn't noticed, this isn't a very nice place."

She wrinkled her nose at him, but said nothing more. She *had* noticed, after all. And it definitely wasn't somewhere she wanted to be trapped forever. She couldn't wait to be out of this foul air. Her throat was raw.

Seph's eyes drifted to the rifle strapped to his back. She'd already seen that thing blow a scraper's droopy face off. She knew it would do the same to her if he chose to turn it on them.

"I'm not gonna *shoot* you, either," said Connor. "Tane wants you *informed*, not *dead*."

"Okay," grumbled Seph. "Spit it out, then."

Connor reached down and opened a black folder that was lying on the desk. "I'm guessin' you've figured out by now what this place is, right?"

"It's where they made Gispuknya," said Seph.

He took out several photographs and laid them on the desk in front of them one at a time. There was a screenshot of the man in the flickering chamber. There was a picture taken through the bars of the devil's cell of him chained to the wall inside. Another showed an old man bound by wires to some sort of nightmarish treadmill, seemingly running himself to death. A fourth showed those white wolf-like creatures tearing a person to pieces. A fifth showed them the cowering, naked form of the suffering woman lying half-submerged in that foul water. Another revealed a swarm of blood-red bugs crawling over several lifeless corpses. The next was a wide shot of a room teeming with those foul men in the long, gray coats bustling about a very large, shallow tank containing a very familiar, manta-ray-shaped creature. And the last image revealed a glimpse of the horror they'd hoped to never see more than any other: small bodies lying motionless on a blood-spattered floor.

Both of them turned away at this point and refused to look at any more.

Connor didn't push them. He'd made his point. "Zarechuff was the culmination of humanity's darkest and most depraved ambitions." He turned and gestured out the window behind him. "Out there is all that remains of the universe that came *after* the Black World." He looked back at them again. "Let that sink in. This was the *very end*…of the *next* universe. That's how deep the evils of the Black World sank into mankind's soul."

Piper shuddered at the thought.

"No one knows exactly what took place in the Black World anymore. What *is* known is that the people who lived in that world created terrible, ungodly machines."

Seph felt gooseflesh prickling up her arms in spite of the heat as she remembered Annice once telling them about Gispuknya's origins in the Black World. "Where greed and malice built the first of those awful machines," she'd said.

"And the people of *this* universe…" Connor thrust his finger at the window again. "They couldn't be happy leavin' those evil things behind. Some of that dark research was salvaged by those who fled that world durin' the exodus, to be recreated in *this* world. Others, they say, actually ventured out into the Wood to bring some of those machines back. Which, in case you don't know, is pretty much the craziest shit you could possibly do, for the most messed-up reason you can imagine."

"What did the machines do?" asked Piper.

"No one knows anymore, but you're standin' in what those psychopaths built from 'em. This place conducted experiments with exotic energies, for one thing. Not just psychic, spiritual and magical energies, neither. *Really* dark stuff. Really *old* stuff. Combined with things mined from this world's Tartarus."

"Are we supposed to understand any of that?" asked Piper. "Because I think I got stuck on 'magic energy.'"

"And they didn't stop here," Connor went on, ignoring her. "There's been people out there tryin' to recreate the horrors of those machines ever since. There're people still tryin' to rebuild them today! Right now!"

Seph's gaze was drawn to the photos on the table again. New machines? New horrors like these? Happening right now? In her own world? What was wrong with people?

He shoved another photograph at them. "*These* were the creeps in charge of Zarechuff. Look familiar?"

Seph picked it up and stared at it. It was a picture of the operating theater, taken from behind the row of chairs. Nine shadowy figures were sitting there, watching the procedure.

He pushed another photograph toward them, this one taken from *inside* the operating room. Through the dingy glass, those nine figures were little more than distorted shadows.

He laid a third picture on top of it, this one a sort of security camera shot from inside the marsh woman's cruel execution chamber. It showed the nine shadowy figures looming outside the glass, staring in at her as she writhed in that foul, toxic muck.

The next picture was a blown-up closeup of the same image, showing the distorted, gas mask-covered faces.

"The black council," sighed Seph. She remembered distinctly the way those horrible creatures had looked when they turned around to face her in that room inside the cabin they built on the Ahns' stolen property. Their only distinguishing features had been their distorted eyes.

It was just the way they might've appeared to someone looking out from one of these torture chambers, their vision failing, the fumes twisting everything into monstrous shapes. Between that and the gas masks, it would've been impossible to even be sure how many eyes were staring back at you.

She shuddered at the thought.

"And overseein' *them*..." He held out one last picture, making her take it from him. This one was of one of the windows overlooking the black council's chairs. There was a light on inside. A blurry image of a woman was standing there, staring out. "The Empress of Zarechuff, herself."

Piper stared at the picture. Someone *above* the black council? Someone even higher up?

"This entire facility is one big machine, designed and operated by *these evil bastards*, with the sole purpose of collectin' all the bad things that ever existed here and turnin' it into somethin'...*horrifying*..."

"This is insane," said Seph. "I can't even imagine—"

"Cain't you?" He turned and walked over to a switch on the wall. "Haven't you been wonderin' why it's so quiet here? Haven't you been wonderin' where all the scary stuff went?" He flipped the switch. Outside the windows, several powerful search lights flickered on, all of them aimed at an enormous, towering structure.

Seph and Piper walked over to the window and stared, horrified.

Something gigantic had torn a hole right through the metal wall of the structure.

"It ain't here," said Connor, "'cause it *escaped*."

Chapter 78

"There ain't any scary things in Zarechuff 'cause they're all out there in *our* universe." Connor pressed his finger against the glass. "That right there is where the thing that would one day become Gispuknya escaped into the dyin' universe. And when that universe took its last breath and was swallowed by the Wood, the monster cocooned itself in the ruins, rottin' away in the wreckage 'til it was woke by its own hatred."

"Jeez," said Piper.

"Okay," said Seph. "But what are *we* supposed to do?"

Connor smiled that strange smile again. "There's a reason Gispuknya's shadows spawn in those forms. It's the same reason you can kill 'em. They're reflections of *real things.* Gispuknya is bound by the dark reality that spawned it. And it feeds off that same kind of darkness. It'll feed off the darkness of *our* universe as it dies, too, and wake up even more powerful in the *next* universe."

"There's more, isn't there?" said Piper. "Those messages. 'Do you see it yet?' The tall man in Covengale kept asking me that, every time I got caught in one of those freaky flashbacks and had to watch what those people did to each other. You're not just telling us so we know about the dark things that happened in *this* universe, are you?"

He chuckled. "I knew you'd catch on."

"Darkness is a part of the cycle. It's going to happen again." She looked at Seph, then at Connor again. "Darkness takes over as the universe dies, doesn't it?"

His smile faded away. "These trials ain't just a tool for unlockin' the doors to Tartarus. They're here to make sure you understand what your role is as seekers. Your job is to awaken the Architects and kickstart the creation of the next universe. But by doin' that, you have to understand that you'll also be kickstartin' a process that will kill the universe that exists now."

Seph frowned. "Wait… We're going to *destroy* the universe?"

"That's…not what we signed up for," said Piper.

Seph glanced over at her. "We never *signed up* for *anything*."

"Oh yeah…"

"The cycle doesn't just birth a brand-new universe. It *cannibalizes* key energies from the old universe to support the new one. Even the *spirit highways* are severed in the process. Anyone left behind after the exodus ain't just denied the new world, they're denied entrance to whatever lies beyond death. They're shut out of paradise. They're denied all hope. *Forever.*"

"My god…" sighed Seph.

"What are we supposed to do then?" asked Piper. "Awakening the Architects is our job. If we don't, Gispuknya will never stop hunting us."

"And the world is pretty much guaranteed to die anyway," said Connor. "Eventually. It's still flawed."

"So…we *should* wake up the Architects?" Piper pushed her mouth to one side as she processed this. It was all so confusing. "Which one is it?"

"What's the point?" asked Seph.

"The point," he replied, "is that you have to be the ones who make the choice. That's why the trials are here. It was part of the bargain."

"What bargain?" asked Seph.

"The rules the Keeper abides by," he explained. "As agreed upon when the cycle was created. It states that the Keeper controls the process of the cycle, but demands the condition that the seekers be made aware of all costs and consequences associated with the cycle. *He* ain't allowed to make the decisions that directly affect the cycle. Those must be left to humans alone. He cain't wake the Architects himself, or force you to do it for him. He must allow you to decide for yerself whether or not to do it."

"But it's not much of a choice," reasoned Piper. "If we don't do it, the bad guys win…don't they?"

Connor smiled again. "That all depends on who you see as the bad guy, don't it?"

They stared at him, confused.

"Things ain't as simple as they seem. It ain't never black and white."

Piper frowned. Maria told her something like that before letting her out of Covengale.

(*You should be careful who you trust. Things are rarely black and white.*)

"The Keeper ain't what you've been led to believe. There's no good side and bad side. That's the message Tane wants me to give you."

"So he thinks we should just trust *him* instead?" challenged Seph.

"No. He knows you don't trust him. He wants you to ask yerselves how much you should really be trustin' *anybody*."

She glanced over at Piper, concerned.

Somewhere in the building, something crashed.

"Time's runnin' out," he said, looking out the window. "The night trees're wakin' up. They'll bring all of Zarechuff down on top of us if we stay too long."

"Wait!" said Seph. "We haven't found the third lock yet!"

"The third lock's already opened," said Connor. "Tartarus is unchained and waitin' for you."

Piper looked around, confused. "Is…this that thing where we already found it and then forgot about it again?"

He smiled another curious smile. "No. This is the part where the lock wasn't yours to open."

"Huh?"

"It's time for you two to go. When you arrive back in Pobsick Spring, look for an exit to your left. *Don't* go back to the warehouse. And don't let yerselves be seen."

"Wait…" said Piper. "Aren't you coming with us?"

"No. I'll be stayin' here."

"That's insane!" gasped Seph. "You'll be trapped here! And you said yourself that this place is coming down…"

"True enough, but that was the deal I made with Tane. All us custodians want somethin', after all."

It was true. The clones wanted a peaceful life and a place to call home… Maria wanted to escape the hellish justice she earned in life…

"There's somethin' in Zarechuff I need," explained Connor. "Somethin' the people here made."

"But everything the people made here is *evil*," argued Seph.

"No. Everything here was *used* for evil. But if I can find what I'm lookin' for, I might just be able to use it to *undo* a terrible evil."

Seph shook her head. Undo an evil? "What are you talking

about?"

"I'm talkin' about somethin' very bad that happened when I was a kid. I made a mistake. I lost someone important to me."

Piper shook her head. He was trying to save someone?

"She was my best friend…" He was smiling that curious smile again. A strange, sad, nostalgic kind of smile, she realized. The smile of a man who's traveled a hard and trying road for a long, long time and is finally nearing its end. But as she watched, it slowly melted away. "She was taken from me," he explained. "By somethin' *I* let free. And she wasn't the only one. It's taken dozens of kids since then. Maybe hundreds. It drags 'em off, takes 'em where no one can ever find 'em…"

Seph and Piper exchanged a horrified look.

"There're more monsters out there than you can possibly imagine. *So many more*… And one of 'em…" He shook his head. "One of 'em's all my fault. I have to find it. I have to *end* it. And thanks to Tane…and this awful place, ironically…I have a chance to undo some of the darkness in this universe. I can literally make the world a better place. The means to do that is right here."

"But you'll be trapped forever!" gasped Piper.

"No. There's another way out of the compendium. I'll be just fine." Again, he smiled that curious, bittersweet smile. "But I doubt we'll ever see each other again."

Seph shook her head. "No… You can't trust Tane! He's a liar!"

Connor spread his arms apart. "Everyone lies. There *is* no good and evil. The sooner you learn to understand that, the sooner you'll understand *everything*."

Somewhere below them, a loud crash shook the building.

"Time to go," said Connor. "Think about what I said. And good luck out there. Oh, and you might wanna brace yerselves."

"Wait!" said Seph. She didn't even know where they were supposed to go next. But Connor didn't answer any more questions.

Darkness enveloped them.

A moment later, the two of them were lying on the smooth Tartarus stone of the tunnel hidden under the scrapyard.

"Connor?" said Piper, shining her light back at the mysterious, iron door.

Seph shined her light the other way. "I think he's gone…" She wasn't even sure how to feel. On one hand, he was the custodian. His job was to get them in and back out again, and he'd done precisely that. On the other hand, he was sent here by *Tane.* And Tane was *evil.*

Wasn't he?

There is *no good and evil,* she thought. *The sooner you learn to understand that, the sooner you'll understand* everything…

Piper was equally confused. If what she'd been told was true, then Tane gave Connor the opportunity to do something truly good in the universe. In contrast, the Keeper may have unleashed an unspeakable evil into the world.

She turned and looked at Seph. "So…did we do it?"

"I guess."

"Who unlocked the last Tartarus lock, then?"

Seph didn't have any answers. "Come on. We should go see if it's still today."

Chapter 79

"It's so quiet," observed Piper as they knelt in front of the van doors, listening. "I don't hear the storm anymore." She leaned forward, those glowing ears on top of her head twitching back and forth. She couldn't hear the buzzing of Gispuknya's shadows, either. "Do you think the good guys won?"

Seph wasn't even sure who the good guys *were* anymore. What if Connor was telling them the truth? What if they couldn't trust the Keeper?

But what was the alternative? Tane couldn't be the good guy. He'd been deceiving her for years. He tried to burn half of Piper's face off! He sent that psychotic ringmaster to kill them!

Piper leaned a little closer, still listening, and whispered, "What if something's waiting for us out there?"

She looked down at her hand. The water of the scythe was swirling around her fingers, ready to spring open.

Piper stared at it for a moment, then nodded. She adjusted the strap on her shoulder and then closed her hand around the wheel. "Let's go."

Seph took a deep breath and held it for a few seconds, bracing herself for whatever was lurking out there. Then she let it out and opened the van doors.

There was no one here.

The scrapyard was empty. The warehouse was silent.

The sun was shining.

Seph shielded her eyes from the blinding glare and stepped out into the open, searching all around her.

"Storm's moved off," observed Piper, pointing at the threatening clouds to the north.

"Nothing's wet," said Seph.

Piper looked down at the ground. She was right. The dust wasn't even settled. Everything was completely dry. Was it already tomorrow?

Or the next day?

How long were they gone this time?

Seph took her phone out of her pocket and pressed the display button. Then she frowned at the screen. "No… It says it's still Thursday. Unless the Keeper's stupid time magic broke it."

Piper's eyes grew wide. "You don't think we were in there a whole *year*, do you?"

"No. The year hasn't changed." She shook her head. "It's just the phone. It's messed up."

And yet, she couldn't help but wonder what it would mean if they'd actually been gone a whole year. What would've happened to their lives? What about her mom? Piper's family? Their apartment?

If time could scrunch down to just a few minutes or hours after all the time they spent inside one of those last two gates, then why couldn't it stretch the other way so that months or even years could go by in this world?

Piper grabbed her by the arm, dragging her out of her thoughts and back into the open van doors. "Persephone!" she whispered.

"*What*?" But she saw it even before Piper pointed to it. A great, black shadow swooping through the sky. "Wait… *That* thing's still here?"

Piper tilted her head to one side and tried to listen. That familiar buzzing was there again. It was very faint, but it was definitely getting louder as she listened.

"What the hell is going on out here?" whispered Seph.

She pointed to a path between the scrap mounds, just on the other side of a large pile of old appliances. "Connor said to go left."

"Even if we get out of here, we still don't know where we're going," Seph reminded her as they hurried across the dusty ground.

"We'll figure it out once we're out of here. *Oh no*!" She ducked behind an old dryer, her spirit ears laid flat against her head.

Seph saw them, too. Four teethers trudging along the side of the building, dragging their makeshift weapons behind them, as if on patrol. She'd nearly forgotten about those little freaks.

Piper peered over the junk pile at the monsters. They didn't seem to have noticed them, so she continued on around the garbage, crouching low and out of sight.

Seph followed after her, her gaze washing over the yard. There were more teethers in front of the warehouse. Lots more.

They must've returned to their patrol after everything calmed down.

But…what happened to everybody? Where did Jarrett and the others go? Where were the Ahns? Where were the stampeding tuskers?

Where had the thunderbird gone?

Were those freaky white sisters still here somewhere?

The Sugnog swooped low over the garbage, sending scrap metal crashing to the ground somewhere in the scrap yard.

Was it still looking for them?

Seriously, what was going on? How much time had gone by since they followed Connor through those van doors?

Somewhere in the distance, they heard a muffled crash.

Was that a voice on the wind? Was someone still fighting out there somewhere?

And the whole time that eerie buzzing in Piper's spirit ears continued to swell.

They reached the end of the appliance pile. There was a gap between them and the path Connor said would lead them out of here. For a few desperate seconds, they were going to be in full view of all those teethers. If just one of them caught sight of them and gave chase, they would probably all come after them.

Piper clutched her pendant and took a deep breath, then she darted across the opening and ducked behind a pile of tire rims.

Seph followed after her, her heart racing, and crouched down beside her. "Did they see us?"

"I don't think so. I really hate this kind of thing."

"Me too. Let's get out of here already."

But as they backed away, their attention focused on the army of teethers gathered around the warehouse, there was a clattering of metal behind them. They twirled around to see three teethers scurrying down the side of the scrap pile, almost right on top of them.

Seph thrust her hand out, reaping the nearest of the three with ease, but when she lashed out at the second one, the scythe stuttered and splashed harmlessly into the dust. "Not now!" she gasped.

The beast jumped off the crumpled remains of a wrecked trailer and launched itself at Piper.

She stumbled backward, clutching at the pendant.

Then Connor was there. He stepped in front of her and swung an iron bar like a baseball bat, striking the monster's skull with an audible crack and sending it flying backward into the scrap pile.

"Connor!" gasped Piper. "You made it out after all!"

Connor looked back at her, surprised. "Do I know you?"

Piper blinked at him, confused. "Huh?"

"Look out!" squealed Seph.

The third teether took advantage of his distraction and pounced on him, sinking its huge teeth into his forearm. He let out a painful grunt and then thrust the little beast against the ground and impaled it with the iron rod. It opened its mouth, letting go of his arm to let out a wail of agony that probably would've alerted every monster in Pobsick Spring of their presence, but fortunately only came out in a soft, strangled gurgle.

"I am *so* sorry!" gasped Piper.

Connor stood up, clutching at his bleeding arm. "I'll be fine. I heal fast."

"Right," said Piper, staring at the blood dripping off his arm. "You *did* say that…"

"I did?"

"Uh, yeah. In Zarechuff."

"Zarechuff?" His eyes widened. He looked back and forth between them, as if he'd suddenly recognized them. "You're the seekers!"

"Duh," said Seph, baffled.

He didn't seem to hear her. "That explains the…" He pointed up at the sky as the Sugnog circled past. "Whatever *that* is…"

"Sugnog," said Piper.

"If you say so. I was over by the crusher when I saw it circling. I figured it had to have something to do with the gate, so I was hurrying back here to check on it."

Seph and Piper exchanged a confused glance. He was by the crusher? But they just left him inside Zarechuff.

He watched the Sugnog soar out of sight and then turned his gaze in the direction of the van. "So it's finally time to open the gate…"

Piper tilted her head to one side. What was wrong with him? Had he lost all his memories of what happened in that awful factory?

Seph squinted at him. He *looked* the same. He was dressed the same. The only difference she could see was… "Where's your gun?" The last time she saw it, he had it slung over his shoulder. She assumed he'd taken it with him to… Uh… To *where*? Where did he go after he sent them back? And what was he doing back here now? Had he already found what he was looking for? Did the time crunch of the Keeper's compendium spit them out at the same time?

Connor only stared at her, confused. "What?"

She stared back at him. Had he really forgotten all about them?

"What *are* these things anyway?" he asked, clutching his bloody arm against his shirt. It was soaking into the fabric, staining it.

"They're…teethers…" she told him. She thought he already knew that. He told them that it was teethers that gave him that *last* injury, the one that healed while they were exploring the horrors of Zarechuff.

She was about to say something more when Piper abruptly turned and faced her. Her eyes had gone black again. "Get down," snapped Warner.

Seph crouched down obediently. "Where have *you* been?" she sneered.

"Quiet! Don't let them see you."

Her heart leaped. "The teethers!" She'd forgotten about all the monsters surrounding the warehouse.

"Not *them*," said Warner. He (she?) crouched down and crept over to the scrap pile. "*Them*," he said, pointing.

Piper's eyes blinked back to blue as Seph peered over her shoulder. "Huh? What just…?" She leaned forward, squinting at the place where she was still pointing, her thoughts scattered. "How…? What am I looking at?"

On the other side of the clearing, across from the warehouse's front door, were *another* Seph and Piper.

"Oh boy…" sighed Seph.

"What's happening?" whispered Piper. "Who *are* they?"

"They're us," she realized. "It's the Keeper's weird time magic. This time we came out *before* we went in."

"That doesn't make any sense!"

Actually, it sort of did. That was why the ground wasn't wet when they came out of the gate. It was why the same storm seemed to be brewing in the skies to the north. It was why the Sugnog was still flying around, why there was no sign of the Shawbeck Ranch trucks or the tuskers and why the van doors were already open when they first got here. And it was why Connor was here and why he didn't seem to know who they were. He hadn't met them yet.

She turned and looked at him, at the blood dripping down his arm. That wasn't a *new* injury. It was the same one! He even told them it was a teether. (And now that she knew what was happening, she understood those strange looks he was giving them when they first met him; he was trying to wrap his head around answering the same questions they'd literally just answered for *him*.)

Piper stared at the other version of her from across the field, fascinated. "Oh my gosh… That helmet was *not* flattering on me!"

"Never mind that!" grumbled Seph. "We need to get out of here." Connor—the Connor from before…no, from *later*…no… *Whatever*.

The Connor they talked to *inside Zarechuff* told them to take the path on the left and to stay out of the warehouse. Now she understood why. He didn't want them to risk running into themselves. He even told them specifically to not let themselves be seen. They thought he meant by those monsters, but he was talking about their past doubles.

"I look like a bobblehead," groaned Piper.

"Forget about the stupid helmet!" hissed Seph.

"Who's that?" whispered Connor.

Seph stared at him for a moment. "Uh… Those are the seekers."

"I thought you said *you* were the seekers."

"Well, *obviously* it's a little complicated!"

He nodded. "Right. Sorry."

Seph looked back and watched as the other Seph lashed out with the scythe, dispatching three teethers with a single slash. "Wow. I kind of rock, don't I?"

"*Eep*! *Look out*!" squealed Piper, barely managing to stifle her voice.

On the other side of the warehouse, the Sugnog was swooping down the aisle behind them, almost on top of them. The other Piper suddenly perked up, startled, and then turned and shoved the other Seph to the ground.

Seph watched as the great beast climbed back up into the sky and rubbed at her forehead. "That *really* hurt."

Piper flapped her hand at her. "Oh my gosh, I said I was sorry!" She stared at the other version of her as she stood up again. She remembered something catching the attention of her spirit ears, warning her of the incoming danger. Was it possible that what they heard was her own voice just now?

This was *so* weird!

Seph watched as the other Piper grabbed the other Seph's hand and ran for the warehouse while the teethers were still scattered. She frowned. "Do I always run like such a girl?"

"You *are* a girl," replied Piper. "And you're cute when you run."

She scowled at her. "I don't want to be cute."

Piper rolled her eyes and watched as their past selves ran behind the building and out of sight. She sort of wished she hadn't been wearing the stupid helmet. It would've been *extra* weird to see her own face out there. "That was *super* trippy."

Seph stepped back away from the scrap pile and stood up straight. The coast was clear. The teethers had all run to the front of the building. They weren't in any danger of being seen by themselves now. They'd be inside that office. And from there they'd wander into the main warehouse… Phoenix would call…

She'd nearly forgotten about that…

The idea that her three oldest friends could be on Tane's payroll… But why not? Tane might not even be the bad guy. Maybe the Keeper was the real bad guy.

This was all so frustrating!

Phoenix would call and then—

Her eyes flashed wide as she remembered what was waiting for them in the warehouse. She turned and looked at Connor. "You have to get in there!" she told him. "We're going to need you to save us from those scrapers!"

Piper gasped. "That's right!"

"Scrapers?" said Connor, confused.

"They're inside the warehouse. A bunch of them! They attacked us."

Connor seemed to be struggling to take it all in, but he nodded.

"Okay."

"You'll need your gun," Seph recalled.

"My gun?"

"You *do* have a gun, right?"

"Uh…sure. Several. I'll…grab my pistol."

"No. The big one."

He stared at her again. "The big'n, then."

"Oh! The Sugnog!"

"The what?"

Seph pointed up into the sky as the massive creature circled overhead. Soon it would roost itself atop the entrance to the Keeper's gate. "You can't take us outside too soon. That thing's going to block the doors. You have to wait for the storm or we'll never make it. Once you're at the back door, wait until the second lightning strike, no matter what we say."

"Got it," he said, nodding. "The second lightnin' strike." He didn't *look* like he had it, but she knew he did. Because…well, because he *did.*

This was *so* confusing…

"Don't just stand there!" she snapped. "*Go*!"

He stood up straight. "Yes, ma'am!" Then he turned and fled, still clutching his bleeding arm against him.

She rubbed at her temples. This was all too much. *She* was the one who told him to wait for the second lightning strike?

Then she frowned. Wait… If *she* told *him* those things were called "scrapers"…and *she* heard they were called "scrapers" from *him*…then who named the stupid things?

Like she needed a freaking *time paradox* to go with everything else she was dealing with!

Piper stared after him. “I hope he’ll be all right.”

Seph turned and made a face at her. “You already *know* how it turned out!”

She blinked, confused. “Oh yeah…” She narrowed her eyes and stared off into space. “Trippy…” she whispered.

Chapter 80

Lightning flashed across the sky, thunder rolled over the desert and wind whipped through the valleys of rust and decay as the thunderbird drew nearer.

So far, the ringmaster's monsters and Gispuknya's shadows didn't seem to have noticed them, except for those three teethers they stirred up right before they ran into Past Connor. Seph was hopeful that the weird time loop would confuse everyone long enough for them to escape. But she also knew that there was a hell of a storm coming, and she wasn't too keen on being trapped out in the open in it. They had to hurry.

"So where do we go next?" asked Piper.

"Away from here. We'll worry about what comes next *then*."

"Okay."

"Right now we just have to figure out *how* to get out of here. We're in the middle of the desert and our truck is parked under a mountain of garbage."

"We have to steal a car," said Piper, nodding as if it were the most casual suggestion in the world.

"What? *No.* We're not stealing a car."

"Do you have a better idea?"

"Um…*any* idea? Do you know how much trouble we'd be in for

that? I do *not* want to be sitting in a jail cell somewhere the next time Gispuknya comes looking for us."

"You just said we can't *walk* out of here. I really don't think we can just call an Uber."

Seph sighed. "Where would we even find a car to steal?"

"Um…there're cars *everywhere*."

"Yeah, but none of them work! That's why they're in a scrapyard!"

"I'm sure *some* of them do."

"If they worked, they wouldn't be here!"

"Well Connor must have a car around here somewhere, right? Who *knows* when he'll even come back to this world? Or *if*."

Seph supposed that was true…but they had no way of knowing where he might've parked.

A brilliant flash of lightning split the sky, accompanied by a nearly simultaneous crack of thunder that startled Piper and made her scream.

"Quiet!" hissed Seph.

"Sorry!" She turned and looked back the way they came. Was that the first bolt of lightning that Seph told Connor to wait for? It was so weird to imagine that *right now* the two of them were back in that warehouse.

Somewhere nearby, a diesel engine roared.

"Is that Jarrett?" asked Piper. "Maybe they'll let us borrow one of their trucks!"

"I think they'll probably need their trucks to haul their monsters home in."

"Oh yeah…"

The path they were following curved to the right and Seph finally caught sight of the office and front gate about a hundred yards ahead of them. That was their way out of here.

Piper pointed. "Tow truck!"

The tow truck… Seph stared at it as they hurried along. She was right. That might just work.

"I told you there'd be something we could steal."

"It's not stealing! We're just going to borrow it!"

"Whatever, Persephone-Goody-Goody."

"What're you talking abou—"

The second lightning bolt crashed down, wrenching a second startled scream from Piper.

"Oh my god! Shut up!"

"I can't help it! Stop yelling at me!"

Seph didn't dare slow down, but she risked a look up as she ran. If that really *was* the second lightning strike, then…

A tremendous shape passed overhead, its outstretched wings reaching nearly to the horizons on either side of it.

There was no way the Sugnog was any match for that thing.

Right?

More lightning split the sky, making Piper scream again. "This is *so* not safe!" she squealed.

Seph was far less worried about being struck by lightning than she was about being spotted by the ringmaster's creeps again. She'd always heard that lightning always struck the highest object, first. And that it was attracted to metal. As long as they were on the ground between the scrap piles, they should be fairly safe. It was no different than running through that row of lightning rods leading to the warehouse at Shawbeck Ranch where the scythe was hidden.

At least, she hoped so…

Another bolt of lightning flashed in front of them, close enough to have no delay between it and the deafening crack of thunder, and bright enough to leave an afterimage burned into her eyes when she closed them.

She felt the first of a great many raindrops splash against her skin. She recalled the weather as they fled into the open van doors and picked up her pace.

They didn't have long before the sky *really* let loose.

They still didn't see any teethers or demon-winged black-eyed children or face-biting little flits, but as they neared the front gate, a single tusker thundered around the corner and charged down the aisle toward them, having apparently broken away from Jarrett's main herd.

This time, it was Seph who let out a squeal as she darted behind several rusty barrels and out of the way of the shaggy beast.

It swung its head as it plowed past them, as if it knew they were there and wasn't happy about it, but it made no other attempt to attack them.

"*Wow* those things stink," observed Piper.

"Keep moving!" hissed Seph as she hurried on toward the office.

They crossed the drive and reached the tow truck without any further encounters. Even better, they found the vehicle unlocked.

Seph couldn't help but remember the last time she was inside a tow truck. It was when those weird sisters from that creepy gas station rescued them from the depths of the fringe road.

Ironically, that, too, came right after an encounter with a tusker… She might've found that considerably stranger two years ago, but now she knew that life was simply strange. In a world full of Keepers and Ahns and Warners and ringmasters and time loops, she wasn't even sure if she believed in coincidences anymore.

Piper tossed the bag into the seat, then jumped in after it and slammed and locked the door behind her. "If this thing can make helmets and fire alarms," she reasoned, holding up the pendant and gazing through its strange, gleaming ring, "I'll bet it can make keys, too!"

Seph started the engine and shifted the truck into gear. "What?"

Piper pouted. "Or…you can just use the one Connor left in the ignition, I guess…"

"I don't like it," said Seph as she turned the wheel and lumbered toward the gate. "Things are never this easy."

The words were barely out of her mouth when a scraper burst out of the office door and sank its long, hooked claws into the truck's fender.

Piper screamed.

"See?" shrieked Seph as she stomped on the accelerator and lurched forward. "That's exactly what I was just talking about!"

"Your pessimism is going to get us killed!" shouted Piper.

"My pessimism doesn't *make* these things happen! These things happening *makes me pessimistic*!"

A loud thump announced the appearance of a second scraper as it jumped onto the back of the truck.

"Get us out of here!" squealed Piper.

"I'm going!" shouted Seph.

A third scraper darted in front of the truck, its freakish claws raised, only to be plowed under.

"*Why do they keep running out in front of us*?" screamed Seph.

"*I don't know*!"

The scraper on the fender of the truck reached out and dug its claws into the hood, pulling itself upward.

"Persephone!"

"I see it!" She cut the wheel to the right, steering the truck toward the fencepost. "Sorry Connor!" She ground the side of the vehicle along the post, tearing away paint and the side mirror along with the nasty, droopy-faced monster.

Its claws tore long strips along the metal as it was dragged off the side of the vehicle and vanished.

"We are *really* hard on cars this week!" said Piper, covering her ears from the sound of tearing metal outside her window.

Seph jerked the wheel to the left and sped off down the road, kicking up dust and mud as the rain fell harder.

"There's still one out there!" said Piper, pointing out the back window.

"I see it!" she grunted. It was in the rearview, climbing up onto the bed. "Hold on."

Piper thrust her hands against the dashboard. "I hate it when you say that!"

Seph stomped the brake and brought the truck to a skidding halt. The monster tumbled forward with one of those piercing shrieks. Then she accelerated again and the scraper rolled off the truck, its claws flailing for something to hold onto for a split second before it vanished into the storm.

"Is that all of them?"

Piper pressed her forehead to her window and looked around, then she turned around, sat up in the seat on her knees and squinted out the back window. "I think so. I don't see anything else."

"Where're the windshield wipers on this thing? I can't see." It was really pouring now. The world in front of them was a washed-out, muddy blur. And the lightning was striking so rapidly now that the sky practically strobed with it, disorienting her.

Piper held onto the headrest and leaned toward Seph, squinting out her side of the truck. "Do you think that fence will keep those things in?"

"I don't know. Turn around and put your seatbelt on. *There* they are!" The wiper blades came to life at once, slashing back and forth, carving brief windows through the pouring rain, revealing a world utterly drenched. "Jeez…"

The truck rattled in the raging wind. She could feel it in the wheel.

Piper buckled herself in, but continued turning back and forth in her seat, peering out the passenger-side window, then the back window, then back again, watching for any more lurking scrapers. So far, they seemed to have gotten away, but she didn't intend to drop her guard until Pobsick Spring was well out of sight.

Seph leaned forward, squinting through her glasses. Something thick and black had dropped onto the top of the windshield and as it washed down into the path of the wiper blades, they smeared it across the glass before the pounding rain washed it away. "What *is* that?"

Piper turned and looked at her. "What's what?"

Another glob fell onto the glass. Then another.

Seph leaned over the steering wheel for a better look.

The Sugnog crashed down onto the road in front of them, driven to the ground by the thunderbird.

"*Holy kaiju*!" screamed Seph, jerking the wheel to the right and veering out of the way, only narrowly missing the Sugnog's oily, thrashing wings as they pounded the earth.

Piper cried out and covered her face as if the terrifying spectacle before them were nothing more than a scary movie trailer.

The tow truck bounced over the ditch and out into the desert, plowing through the low scrub and kicking up mud.

The rain continued to beat down on the windshield. The wind

shoved at the sides of the truck. Lightning flashed tirelessly. Thunder shook the ground. And great, monstrous roars filled the air as the titans battled.

A great glob of black gore splashed onto them, painting the driver-side window black.

"*Persephone*!" shrieked Piper, her finger mashed against the passenger-side window.

"Kind of busy here!"

"Tornado!"

"*What*?" She turned, her eyes wide, and stared through the window. There, rising from the muddy haze, was a great, swirling funnel.

She knew that the thunderbird had been known to spawn tornados. The last time they saw the monster, it leveled one of the ranch's outbuildings. But she was still stunned to actually find herself staring at one. It was utterly surreal.

A large chunk of twisted metal came reeling out of the clouds and bounced over the hood of the tow truck.

Seph jerked the wheel to the left, away from the twister, and tried to speed away from it, but a few seconds later, a great, black wing slammed down in front of them, forcing her to veer again.

She looked out her side window to see a sheet of crumpled tin flying through the air. And as she watched it soar overhead, she caught sight of the thunderbird's long, quicksilver tail whipping across the sky. Lightning crashed to the ground in its wake, almost as if it were dripping from those long, ghostly tailfeathers. Arcs of white-hot electricity leapt through the air, snatching at the scrapyard fence and the tow truck's protruding hook. "Don't touch anything metal!"

Piper looked down at the door handle next to her and snatched her hand away from it as if it were a coiled snake.

Something large passed overhead, creating a brief gap in the pouring rain and allowing Seph to see that she was speeding straight toward the scrapyard fence. She let out a startled "Whoa!" and jerked the wheel to the right again.

Piper looked out her window in time to see the Sugnog's enormous, skeletal maw reaching out for them out of the storm, its massive teeth glistening, black gore dripping to the ground.

Then the thunderbird's invisible claw parted the mist and shoved the hideous, gigantic face down into the ground, spraying mud and shadowy, black blood onto the glass. "I want to go home, please!" she cried, her eyes huge. "I don't want to do this anymore!"

"Shut up and hold onto something!"

Later, this would probably make for some great artistic inspiration, but right now Seph really just wanted to be as far from this place as possible.

Piper turned and looked out the back window again. "Was that a pig?"

"What?"

"I swear a *pig* just flew by!"

"Where would a *pig* come from?"

"It wasn't a *real* pig. It was, like—" A flash of lightning and an explosion of fire and sparks cut her off. She cried out, startled, and spun around in her seat. "*What was that*?"

"Probably a transformer." She added downed power lines to her list of things to be careful of until they were clear of the storm.

More of that black gore splashed onto the windshield. It wasn't doing her any favors. It was already hard enough to see. But hopefully it meant that the thunderbird was winning. Because if the thunderbird couldn't kill that thing, what kind of chance did they stand?

As Seph drove past the last of the scrapyard's chain-link fence and into the open desert, Piper turned around to see a great cloud of rain and mud and shadows writhing across the storm-torn landscape. "I think we might finally be past it."

"God, I hope so!" gasped Seph. It felt as if her heart was thundering even louder than the storm.

Then the hail came.

Chapter 81

Seph plowed on through the storm, determined to keep moving forward and away from the horrors of Pobsick Spring. The hail and rain raged on for more than five full minutes before they finally emerged from it, miraculously intact and unscathed. The truck, however, was not as lucky. There were gashes in the hood and fender, violent scars down the passenger's side and, of course, a significant amount of hail damage.

Hopefully Connor would understand when and if he returned from his mysterious task in Zarechuff.

Maybe they could pass it off as tornado damage…

Five minutes farther down the road, it was impossible to even tell that there had ever been a storm. The landscape here was parched. The clouds opened up and the sunshine poured down. Even the temperature inside the tow truck had risen at least ten degrees.

Piper turned around and looked at the dangerous skies they were leaving behind them. The buzzing of the Gispuknya shadows had faded almost completely away again, but still she was worried. "Do you think everyone will be okay back there?"

"They'll be fine," she replied, as if she had any idea. In all honesty, she couldn't imagine *anyone* being okay in all that chaos. There were *tornados* on the ground back there!

But the folks at Shawbeck Ranch knew what they were doing. Right? They were the keepers of the thunderbird. They *had* to know how to take care of themselves in a tornado.

Piper faced forward again and slouched down in her seat. She had her phone out again. There were missed calls and messages from Kaitlyn, Alton *and* Phoenix now, but no word from Meg. "Wanda says she's still asking around, but no one's seen or heard anything from Meg. It's like she just vanished off the face of the earth."

"No way we're that lucky," replied Seph. "She'll turn up."

"I hope so…"

Seph hoped so, too. The truth was that she was worried. The longer Meg remained quiet, the more she feared that they'd find her waiting for them at the next stop, chained up inside a wooden crate.

Or worse.

And speaking of the next stop…where exactly *was* it? No one had told them where to go yet. Were they supposed to have figured it out for themselves? Surely they wouldn't be expected to drive all the way back to Missouri to ask Sandy. She was *sick* of driving.

And Nora's Lilac Grove was the last place she ever wanted to see again. It'd be far too painful to have to return to the place where Amethyst—

She pushed the thought away and wiped at a tear. She didn't have time for this. She needed to focus.

Ahead of them, someone was standing in the road.

Seph felt her heart leap. "What *now*?" she groaned.

Piper looked up, alarmed.

It appeared to be a man in a navy hoodie. He was standing in the middle of the road, facing them, his hood up, his head down and his hands stuffed into his pockets.

"That's not suspicious at all," grumbled Seph as she slowed the tow truck to a crawl.

"You think it's Warner?"

"Warner doesn't play games like this. He just shows up with his crappy attitude."

"Maybe it's someone from the ranch?"

Seph shook her head. "I don't like it."

"Just…go around him?"

"Yeah." She veered the truck all the way onto the right shoulder, taking care to give the mysterious stranger plenty of room, never taking her eyes off him until he was well behind her.

But as soon as she pressed down on the accelerator to speed away, an explosion rocked the front of the truck.

"What happened?" cried Piper.

"I don't know! A flutter?" She pressed down on the accelerator again, but the truck only lurched forward a few inches and made an angry sort of grinding noise. "I don't think we're going any farther in this thing."

How ironic was it that the tow truck survived a tornado and the most violent electrical storm she'd ever seen just to be taken out by a kamikaze butterfly?

"Persephone?"

Seph looked up to find that skitters had appeared in front of them. Hundreds of them. No…*thousands*. They'd formed an enormous ring around the broken truck and the mysterious hoodie-wearing stranger.

"What do we do?" whispered Piper.

Seph looked up at the rearview mirror. The stranger was standing in the same place, but he'd turned around. He was facing them. "So it's him…" She opened the door and stepped out into the warm sunshine. She let the water of the scythe envelop her hands.

Piper leaned out after her, confused. "Him who?"

"The ringmaster." Even from where she stood, she could see the grin that spread across his face as she walked toward him.

Piper jumped out of the truck and ran to Seph's side. "Are you sure about this?"

"Do we have any other options?"

She pouted. Of course they didn't. They were out in the middle of the desert, completely surrounded by venomous skeleton bugs and about to stand face-to-face with the insane man responsible for half the monstrosities that had attacked them since Tane first revealed himself in that nightmare hallway.

Wow, but that seemed like a long time ago…

Seph glared at the man in the hoodie. "Okay," she sneered. "You got us out here. Now what?"

The man reached up and pushed back his hood. Beneath it was the face of a withered little man with dark, sunken eyes and thin skin stretched across the curves of his skull. He looked like a man on the verge of death.

Seph tilted her head to one side, surprised. "Huh… I kinda thought he was going to turn out to be someone we've met before. Like when Lyla Shawbeck turned out to be Amethyst? Or when the incubus turned out to be Ian? Or when my boss turned out to be Tane who also turned out to be my high school art teacher? Kind of had a pattern going there."

But Piper lifted her hand and pointed a slender finger at the man. "I *know* you," she sighed.

She glanced over at her. "You do?"

"You were in Covengale!"

Seph looked back over at the ringmaster. "Oh. Well. There you go. Apparently, I was just sleeping through that part of the movie."

Piper stared at him. She couldn't believe it. How long had it been? How many thousands or millions of years had passed? And yet she was certain it was him. He didn't look any older, only much frailer, but she knew that face anywhere. It was the same face that looked up at her as he lay on the floor of that strange room, scrawling those mysterious symbols all over the place.

It was the scribbling man.

"I saw you…" she sighed. "What you did to those women… You're a *psychopath*!"

"Uh, *yeah*," said Seph. "He made the *teethers*. And he made them *without pants*. Of course he's psycho."

The ringmaster never stopped grinning at them. "I remember you, too," he said. His voice was as weak as his body, faint, almost lost in the wind.

Piper blinked. "Wait…what?"

"You were there that night," he said. "You came to my study while I was working. In the time after the others left. I saw you standing there… That was the exact moment I realized that what I was looking for was in the Oblivion."

Oblivion? Piper stared at him. She remembered now. She'd turned her back to look out the window…and when she looked back, he was staring up at her. And while their eyes were locked, he said that one word to her. "But…that was just a flashback… It was just a glimpse of the past. I didn't…really go back in time… Did I?"

He shrugged. "Maybe you didn't. Maybe it was *me* who traveled to *you*. Strange things can happen when you dabble with the sorts of things

I was dabbling with in those ruins."

"Isn't the Oblivion some kind of toxic wasteland at the far edges of reality?" asked Seph, recalling what she learned from the Architects' disk last summer in Fibbel Marsh. It was supposedly where the Great Enemy was born, to whom Tane had some close relation.

"Oh, it's far more than a wasteland," wheezed the ringmaster. "It's the eventual final destination of all things. Even *secrets*."

"Secrets like…how to escape a dying world and become an immortal *creep*?" guessed Seph.

"Yeah!" said Piper. "How are you here? I thought you were trapped in that house with the other spirits."

"A lot of people died in that house," he informed her, "but I wasn't among them. I went there only in search of the immense spiritual power that resided there." He raked his gray tongue over his withered lips and grinned a slimy sort of grin. "But I *did* plant some seeds in that garden before I left."

Piper stared at him, horrified. Plant some seeds? *That* was how he was going to put it. He *murdered* those women! He *tortured* them!

"Covengale was an evil place. And evil is an all-consuming thing. It corrupts *everything* it touches. There are no exceptions. *Everyone* that enters a place like that takes in a little bit of that evil and carries it forever. Even *you*."

Piper shook her head. "Never."

"Deny it all you want, but it's there, inside you somewhere."

"You're wrong."

"Whatever you say."

Piper crossed her arms and scowled at him. "What do you want, anyway?"

The creepy little man never stopped grinning. "The two of you don't have anything I want."

This caught them by surprise. "What?" said Seph.

Piper unfolded her arms and touched the pendant. "You're…not after the third Hand?"

"*Tane* wants the Hand. Personally, I have no use for them. They're unsuitable for my needs. All I want is the resources to continue my research, which Tane has been kind enough to exchange in return for my services these past few eons."

"That's all this is about?" said Seph. "Research?"

"I'm a scientist. I seek the knowledge of the universe. Nothing more."

"And that's all those women were?" challenged Piper, disgusted. "*Research*?"

Now that grin slipped away, replaced by a look of genuine confusion. "Of course. What else would they have been?"

Piper stared at him, gaping. These were *people* he was talking about. Human beings.

"Those women were merely the first of countless. I've accumulated more knowledge than any civilization ever built in any age. I'm practically a *god*."

"But you work for Tane?" challenged Seph.

That slimy grin returned. "As I said, he provides resources. Resources that are hard to come by."

"So he expects us to just give it to you?" said Piper.

"Don't be naïve. The Hands are bound to their seekers. He expects me to bring *the two of you* to him."

Seph glanced around. The skitters had moved a little closer. She wasn't liking the way this was going down. She wasn't sure she could cut her way through that many of them even if the scythe wasn't acting so glitchy. "But you've been trying to kill us since we started."

"Yes. About that… As I said, I work for resources. And my *friends* come at a price, as you can probably see." He gestured at his withered face. "Making them eats away at my soul."

"That explains the Crypt Keeper thing you've got going on there," said Seph.

"Tane pays me very well to bring you to him." That creepy smile spread all the way across his pale face. "But I've recently received a *better* offer."

Seph and Piper exchanged an uneasy look.

The ringmaster turned and began walking away. "My *new* benefactor isn't interested in the Architects or the cycle. He has *other* interests. So it turns out you're not needed anymore."

"Wait…" said Piper. "What?"

Around them, the patient skitters began to move, closing in around them.

Seph tried to raise the scythe, but it sputtered and splashed into the dirt again.

"Skitter venom is fairly quick-acting," the ringmaster called back at them, "but utterly excruciating. So it'll be a fast death, but not a pleasant one, I'm afraid."

Piper turned around, panic welling up inside her. "No!"

"You're really going to betray Tane?" shouted Seph.

"Tane doesn't frighten me," he replied as he walked unharmed through the sea of bony skitters that were closing in around them. "There are *far* greater gods than him out there."

"Bastard!" she growled.

"What do we do?" asked Piper.

Seph tried again to make the scythe appear and again it sputtered and splattered. "What is *wrong* with this thing?"

Piper clutched at the pendant. "Come on, spinning wheel, I could use a *really* big can of bug spray right about now!"

They crowded together as the skitters closed in around them, their bony mandibles snapping together.

This was going to be a terrible way to die.

Chapter 82

The sound of thousands of skitters clicking their mandibles together was to Seph eerily like a pit full of angry rattlesnakes, which didn't make the situation any better at all.

"Persephone?"

"I'm thinking!" The Ahns told them there would always be a way. It was the will of the universe, after all, but no matter how she approached it, she simply couldn't think of a way out of this mess.

She tried again to form the scythe, but again it slipped through her fingers and splashed into the dirt.

"Do something, you stupid wheel!" exclaimed Piper, shaking her pendant at the skitters. "*Please*?"

Then Seph caught sight of something strange.

The sky was boiling.

She squinted up at it, unsure of what it was that she was looking at. Was it something the ringmaster was doing? It appeared to be centered almost directly over where he was walking.

The last time she saw something like that was when Amethyst opened that portal that she nearly fell through, except that this was much, *much* larger.

As she watched, an enormous shadow appeared in the middle of the boiling part of the sky.

The ringmaster stopped and looked up at it. Even from this distance, he appeared surprised.

What happened next was every bit as surreal as Old Fred rising from Fathom Lake and the great, stormy battle between the thunderbird and the Sugnog.

A *skyscraper* fell from the sky.

Or…the *top half* of a skyscraper, anyway…

Thirty stories of steel, stone, concrete, glass and brick came plummeting down from the boiling heavens, remaining completely intact right up until the moment it struck the ground and exploded into a cloud of dust and debris.

It wasn't a *new* skyscraper. Seph watched it as it fell. It was old and dark and empty.

She had no idea who opened the portal, but it had obviously torn a hole between this universe and one where the ruins of an old city were standing, cutting that building in half and dropping the top of it directly onto the ringmaster, crushing him flat almost before he knew what hit him.

Around them, the skitters curled up as if in pain. Then they just sort of melted into dust.

Did that mean the ringmaster was dead? Or had he merely lost his concentration? (A jumbo-sized version of the fate of the Wicked Witch of the East *would* probably do that, Seph supposed.) She was *really* hoping he was gone forever, because if he wasn't, he was probably going to be seriously pissed.

She watched the great cloud of dust swell before them, swallowing the top of the skyscraper as it came crashing down, burying the ringmaster.

Then the cloud seemed to reverse itself and began to shrink. After a few seconds, she realized that another portal had opened *under* the rubble, swallowing the entire mess and taking the ringmaster, dead or alive, with it.

"That was random…" said Piper.

Seph stared into the dust as it settled. Someone was in the middle of it, walking toward them.

It wasn't the ringmaster. That creep was short and hunched, frail, sort of gnomish. This shape was tall and strong, with a distinctively feminine walk.

Seph shook her head. Her brain wanted to tell her it was Amethyst. That portal was exactly like hers, after all, but Amethyst was dead. She'd watched that devil monster plunge its hideous hand through her chest. This was someone else. Someone with the same strange ability.

But the closer the mystery woman came, the more she looked like Amethyst. Her hair was the same. Long and dark and curly. Even the way she walked was the same.

She began walking toward the stranger, stifling the tears that sprang to her eyes. This was no time to be thinking crazy. This person just saved their lives, but that didn't mean she was a friend. The ringmaster had betrayed Tane. This was just another of his enforcers, here to punish the traitor and drag them back to her master.

Except…it *wasn't* crazy.

Amethyst smiled that familiar smile at her.

Seph ran the rest of the way and wrapped her arms around her.

"Oh my gosh!" cried Piper. "We thought you were dead!"

"Yeah. I get that sometimes. Sorry I was gone for so long."

Seph pulled away and smacked her arm. "*Why would you do that to me? You're such a pain in the ass*!" Then she hugged her again. "*Stupid*!"

Amethyst chuckled. "I missed you, too."

"Don't make it weird!" she snapped, her voice muffled against her ample chest.

"Right," she replied, still smiling. "I'll try."

"Is this real?" asked Piper. She looked down at the ground around them. They were standing in an enormous depression. The desert soil here was flat and level and fresh. That second portal had opened just beneath the surface and everything above this perfect, featureless plane fell into another world.

"Seriously, you two," said Amethyst, "I am *so* sorry! I told you I was going to stay with you and then I let that shadow take me by surprise."

"We're okay," said Piper.

Seph let go of her and stepped away, wiping at her eyes. "How are you even alive?" she demanded. "I *saw* you die. That thing stabbed you through the chest."

"Yes, you did," admitted Amethyst. "And that's, admittedly, a little weird. But look." Then, without warning, she crossed her arms in front of her and in one smooth motion, yanked up her shirt and bra, flashing them.

"Whoa!" said Seph, turning away.

"Wowza…" said Piper, staring at her. "Those're huge…"

Amethyst rolled her eyes. "Not *those*," she sighed. She let go of her shirt and covered herself, lifting and separating her breasts to better let them see what she was trying to show them. "The *scar*?"

Seph dared a peek. There, right between her breasts, was a large, ugly scar. "That's where that thing…?"

She turned around and lifted the back of her shirt up, revealing the matching scar on her back. "I've got a ton of these, actually."

It was true. There were several long, jagged scars on her back, as well as a suspiciously *bullet-shaped* mark just below the right side of her ribcage.

"I was trying to tell you I'd be okay, but it's hard to speak when your lungs aren't attached to your throat."

"I guess it would be…" agreed Piper.

Seph recalled standing in front of her, that bloody, spade-shaped claw protruding from her chest. Her mouth had been moving, almost as if she were trying to say something before she could lose consciousness… Something that apparently amounted to, "Oh, by the way, I can't die, so I'll catch up to you later."

"So you're like Connor," guessed Piper. "You have accelerated healing."

He did say there were lots of people like him out there. It shouldn't even be surprising that they'd already known someone like that.

"Well, I haven't found anything I can't survive *so far*." She turned around, covering herself with one hand and pointing at various other scars on her front. Most of them were very faint. "I got this one," she said, pointing to one just above the one the devil gave her, "the same day I got this one." She pointed to the scar on her face.

"You said you got that one when you were a kid," said Seph.

"Technically, yes," she replied as she wrestled her formidable bosom back into her bra. "I was sixteen." She yanked down her shirt and bit her lip. "And I didn't get it falling off my bike. A soldier gave it to me during the French Revolution."

Seph gaped at her. "*How old are you?*"

She shrugged her shoulders, embarrassed. "Two hundred and thirty-seven."

She stared at her, shocked.

"Wow…" said Piper. "You look *amazing*."

"Thank you."

Seph shook her head. "But you're *my* age!"

Amethyst sighed. "You have to have figured out that I was older than I said I was, right? I mean, I had the resources to become your college roommate."

"I guess…"

"And did you really think a twenty-five-year-old would be in charge of the secrets of Shawbeck Ranch?"

She stared at her. Was this real?

"I've been there for eighty years."

"That does make a weird sort of sense," admitted Piper.

"Does it?" huffed Seph. She remembered Amethyst telling her that Stanford Shawbeck deeded the ranch to her family about eighty years ago, but she'd neglected to mention that he signed it over to her, specifically, instead making it sound like her parents and grandparents had run the ranch before her.

But she supposed it made more sense now that she took Shawbeck's name. That little detail *had* nagged at her a little…

"I mean, I hired Mr. Hallet when he was, like, *eleven*."

"Wow…" sighed Piper. "I can't even imagine that."

Seph turned away and rubbed at her temples. This was all so much to process.

"I know," said Amethyst. "You hate all my lies. But it's *embarrassing*, okay? I'm older than dirt. Don't act like you won't crack granny jokes at my expense the first chance you get now."

Seph glared at her, but she didn't deny it.

"Besides, I was honest with you that there were still things I wasn't ready to share with you. You said you were okay with that."

She sighed. "I know."

Amethyst spread her arms apart. "Please don't be mad at me?"

Seph groaned, but she hugged her again. "I'm just glad you're okay."

"Yay..." sighed Amethyst.

"I have, like, *a ton* of questions," said Piper.

Amethyst laughed. "I'll do my best. But right now, you two have a job to do."

"Right," said Seph. She stepped back and wiped at her eyes again. "We unlocked all the Tartarus locks."

"So now we have to go to the actual Tartarus," reasoned Piper. "Right?"

"Exactly."

"So we just need to know *where* Tartarus is," said Seph.

Amethyst crossed her arms and shifted her weight. "That part's easy. Tartarus' gate is hidden in the forests of Arkansas, pretty much centered between the three locks."

"Oh," said Piper. "Well that *was* easy."

"However," added Amethyst. "Tane is also well aware of the location of the gate. He's always known. There's a top-secret Vertical Industries research facility built right on top of it."

"Then what're we supposed to do?" asked Seph.

Amethyst gave her a crooked half-smile. "You're going to love *and* hate this."

Chapter 83

"There's no way in or out of the research center grounds," explained Amethyst as she led them back to her parked truck on the far side of the depression left by her cleanup portal. "It's one of their higher-level sites, completely sealed off from the outside. It's one of those places where you literally can't get there from here. It's accessible only through a network of interconnected gates built into every Vertical Industries site. If you can get to the gate in *any* of their buildings, you can use it to transport yourself into any *other* facility, including the research center at the Tartarus location."

"So we just have to find another Vertical Industries business?" said Piper.

"Not just any business. You'll need one you're familiar with and that you'll be able to move around in relatively unnoticed."

Seph groaned. "I have to go back to Vertical Design?"

Amethyst smiled an apologetic smile. "Yeah. That's the part I knew you'd hate."

"But I don't work there anymore." And if Tane wasn't bluffing, she technically never did, which was something she simply didn't have the time to process right now.

"He's been as busy as you these past few days," said a small, sweet voice from behind them. They turned to find an old woman walking toward them out of the desert. She was a very dainty little woman in a bright red, flowered dress she was busily straightening as she walked. She had disheveled hair and smudges on her face. "I don't think he'll have informed very many people of your status change. You should still be able to get in without drawing too much attention." She stopped in front of them, bent over and yanked at her stockings. "Pardon me," she said. Then she stood up straight again and smiled. "I'm Annabeth."

"You're an Ahn," said Piper, staring at her.

Annabeth gave her a sweet smile. "I am," she replied in that sugary-sweet voice. "And a *nasty* one at that."

"*Oh…*" was all she could think to say.

Seph thought it was pretty obvious that she was an Ahn. She'd clearly just crossed the desert in her monster form. She even recognized the dress. She was one of the three that saved them from the wretch in the scrapyard.

Annabeth turned her sweet smile on Seph. "It's good to see you both again. I'm so happy you're still safe."

Seph stared at her. "You were at my mom's apartment that day," she realized. After their ordeal in Avelby. She was there along with all the other old women who showed up to help Buffy back onto her feet. She remembered Lillyanna introducing them as they walked in, but after all that had happened and as tired as she was that day, she couldn't remember which Ann was which five minutes later, much less after ten months.

"How *is* your mother?" she asked.

"Like nothing ever happened."

Her smile practically beamed at this. "Perfect."

Piper stared at her.

An Ahn…

Did Annabeth know anything about her bloodline? Did she know the identity of the Ahn she was descended from? She wanted to ask, but she wasn't sure how to bring it up. Would it be a delicate topic? Would she resist answering her? Would she get angry with her for bringing it up? The Ahns had kept it a secret all this time. Maybe they didn't want her to know the truth. Maybe they had a good reason for not telling her.

And yet, no matter their reasoning, didn't she deserve to know the truth?

"How is everyone back there?" asked Amethyst, gazing back in the direction of the scrapyard.

"We've managed to expel the shadows. The Sugnog and that filthy snake-man are both dead."

Seph stared at her. So they *had* managed to kill the wretch. That was good news. She was worried it might've gotten away after those white sisters attacked. And she never wanted to see that freaky thing again, especially now that she'd seen what the pitiful man looked like when he was still alive. She couldn't stand the thought of seeing that thing's face again after watching it on those awful video screens.

"Any casualties?"

Annabeth's smile melted away. "Roseann."

"Oh no!" gasped Amethyst.

Piper stared at her, surprised. The Ahns could *die*?

"And we're not entirely sure if Annalee will pull through, either. She's a tough old bird, but she's pretty badly banged up. That was a difficult battle."

"The white sisters were that strong?" gasped Seph. That they might've bested *one* Ahn was surprising enough, but *two*?

"They are," she replied. "They're extremely powerful. If Warner hadn't been there, I really don't think any of us would've survived. And even he might've been in trouble if they hadn't fled when they did."

Amethyst nodded. "It was kind of suspicious," she recalled. "They just sort of vanished for no real reason."

"And they never made any move for the girls," added Annabeth. "I found that odd, too."

"Right. Like Tane wanted to keep us from noticing what they were doing." She shook her head. "We never saw them leave the compendium. I only knew where they were because I had one of my visions." She turned her gaze on Seph. "I caught a glimpse of you in terrible danger and came looking for you."

"A good thing you did," agreed Annabeth. "It looks like Tane was hoping to snag the seekers while we were preoccupied."

"Except the ringmaster betrayed Tane," recalled Seph. "He had no intention of capturing us. He was going to kill us."

Annabeth nodded. "That certainly would've made a mess of things." Then her smile brightened and she turned to face them again. "But it was all worth it."

"Was it?" asked Piper. She wasn't so sure. An Ahn was *dead.* And another might be on death's doorstep right now.

"It was. We know what we're fighting for. All of us understand and accept the risks. And now you've opened all three locks of Tartarus. We're so close. Just one more job remains."

"Tartarus, itself," agreed Amethyst.

Seph stared at her, Connor's message from Tane ringing in her head.

He wants you to ask yourselves how much you should really be trusting anybody.

It isn't black and white.

What if he was right? What if the Keeper was deceiving them? Weren't the Ahns and Amethyst working for him? Could *they* be deceiving them, too?

"Are you coming with us?" asked Seph.

Amethyst reached into the back of the truck and lifted out a bag much like the one Piper was still carrying. "I'd *definitely* draw too much attention. As much as I hate it, I won't be able to go in with you. But I *can* take you back to Cakwetak on the fringe road." She held out the bag. "And I brought you another change of clothes."

"Oh," sighed Piper, distracted. She took the bag from her and looked down at it. "Awesome."

"I'm just glad you found the other bag behind the seat. When Reid told me where he left it, I was sure you wouldn't find it."

"You had Reid put it there?" asked Seph, confused.

"After I woke up in Sandy's trailer," she explained, "I rushed back to the ranch to check in with Annalisa. Reid found that bag in the back of your Jeep while making sure all the fires were out. He thought you might need it, so I sent him to Waybel Valley to give it to you."

"Reid was in Waybel Valley?" said Piper, still processing the fact that the bag behind the seat of the ranch truck didn't just *look* like the bag Wanda stashed in the back of her Jeep, but was, in fact, the very same bag.

"I gave him specific instructions to avoid any unnecessary encounters with monsters, so when he found the town overrun with Tane's puppets, he stashed the bag and came back to report to me." She sighed. "By the time I got there, you were already gone again."

"*You* were in Waybel Valley, too?" asked Seph.

"Was Hugh and the others okay?" asked Piper.

Amethyst looked embarrassed. "I only talked to one person. Wilbur, was it? He said he was the custodian and told me you'd already done your job and left. I…honestly didn't even know there was anyone else there."

Piper pinched her lip as she processed this. She hoped the others were okay. Especially Hugh, who'd endured the time magic of Lodblin's library. But if Wilbur was still there, then at least she knew that they didn't all vanish the moment Horace died. That, alone, was a tremendous relief.

"You could've left us a note or something," grumbled Seph. "Let us know you weren't really *dead*."

"I know. I'm sorry. I wanted to talk to you in person. I wasn't sure you'd believe it otherwise. Things can get so *confusing*."

That *was* true. But she still wasn't happy about it. She opened the bag while Piper held it. The clothes inside were business casual. Skirts and blouses. Dress flats. *Pantyhose*? She frowned. That didn't look nearly as comfortable as Wanda's athleisurewear… And why was it all so *colorful*?

"There's also some of Mr. Hallet's homemade jerky and some bottled waters in the side pocket, plus a fresh first aid kit."

"Homemade jerky?" said Piper, her ears perked up. She could feel her stomach growl at the thought.

"It's *good*," said Amethyst.

"So we're just supposed to walk back into Vertical Design like nothing ever happened?" said Seph. "Just pretend I still work there?"

"Pretty much," she replied.

"Then what? Where do we even find the gate? I've never seen anything like it." Then she frowned. "I don't think. I mean…I don't know what one looks like, I guess."

"It'll probably be located in the most secure area of the building," said Annabeth. "Somewhere Tane can keep a close eye on it. His office would be my guess, on the top floor."

She shook her head. "His office is on the third floor, at the end of the hall."

"That would be Millard Carrol's office," she corrected.

"Uh…yeah. Tane *is* Mr. Carrol."

"Yes," she admitted. "But Carrol and Tane are two different people in the greater inner workings of Vertical Industries. Carrol's office will be near the art studio where you worked, to efficiently do *Carrol's* job. But *Tane's* office will be in a place of much greater power. He *is* one of the Twelve Teeth of the Great Enemy."

"Still," said Seph, shaking her head again. "I've been on the fifth floor. There aren't any offices there."

"The *top* floor, dear," said Annabeth. "Vertical Industries' *real* business takes place where most people can't see it."

Seph gaped at her. "There's…more than five floors?"

"You'll need to get inside the upper levels of the Cakwetak tower," explained Amethyst. "Get inside Tane's office and find the gate."

The Cakwetak *tower*?

"And we're supposed to know how to use the gate when we find it?"

"Warner will be waiting for you," Annabeth assured her. "Plus, we have someone on the inside."

"Someone on the inside…" sighed Seph. Sneak into the hidden tower? Infiltrate Tane's office? Access the secret gate network? When did this turn into *Mission Impossible*?

"As far as Vertical Industries facilities go," Annabeth assured her, "The Cakwetak tower isn't very high-level. Security isn't very tight. You shouldn't have too much trouble finding what you're looking for."

"I guess we should get it over with," relented Seph.

Annabeth turned and looked at Piper. "You look like a girl with something on her mind," she observed.

Piper blinked, surprised. She hadn't realized she'd been staring at her. "I'm sorry. I just… Uh…"

"Something happened while we were in Waybel Valley," said Seph.

That sweet smile softened a little. "So it's out of the bag, is it?"

She stared at her, surprised. "You knew?"

"Of course we knew."

"So…one of you…?"

"Most of us have had children at some point or another," she admitted. "It's not uncommon. And with very few exceptions, our descendants live perfectly normal, human lives."

Piper stared at her. "I think I might be one of those exceptions."

Seph nodded. "We're pretty sure, actually."

Annabeth shrugged her shoulders and smiled. "It does occasionally happen."

"What happened?" asked Amethyst.

"Remember *The Exorcist*?"

She nodded.

"Sort of a cross between that and *The Howling*."

"Oh!"

Piper covered her face. "*Stop*!"

Annabeth giggled. "It's not so bad."

"It's *horrible*! I almost *ate* her!"

"Well, yes, that can happen…"

"That's a pretty serious side effect," worried Amethyst.

Seph nodded.

"But you can control it," Annabeth assured her. "You already know that."

"I guess so… But who is she? Ahns live, like, *forever*, right? So, do I have a grandma somewhere I've never met? Or *have* I met her?"

Annabeth's smile softened again. "We'll tell you all about her when this is over. You have my word on it. Right now, though, you both still have a job to do."

Piper glanced over at Seph. She didn't *want* to do this job. She wanted to know where the monster inside her came from. She wanted answers.

"If we dawdle too much longer, Tane might get suspicious."

"That's true," agreed Amethyst. "The Ahns will be organizing an attack on the research facility to draw Tane's attention. Timing is critical."

"With the ringmaster dead, you can bet the white sisters will be there," said Annabeth. "And we have a score to settle with those two witches!"

"Oh!" said Piper, surprised.

"Come on," said Amethyst. "Let's get you two back to Cakwetak so we can finally finish this."

Chapter 84

Amethyst dropped them off two blocks east of Vertical Design and wished them luck. Then she drove away, leaving them alone with the daunting task before them.

It all felt so surreal to Seph. First, Amethyst was just Amethyst. Then she *wasn't* Amethyst. Then she was *dead.* Then she *wasn't* again…

She straightened the wrinkles in her skirt and checked her hair in her cell phone. It needed a good washing, but it'd have to do. The makeup Amethyst bought for her didn't do much to cover up the scabs on her nose and forehead from those stupid flit bites. And then there were the various bruises and scratches on her hands and wrists. They were supposed to blend in, but if anyone looked very closely at her at all, she was going to stand out. She looked like she'd been in an accident. Or that someone was abusing her. And she wasn't sure anyone would even *have* to look closely. Amethyst gave her a bright red blouse and white skirt and blazer. Anyone who knew her at all knew she never wore such colors!

She was obviously an impostor.

And she kept tugging at the skirt. "Why's it so short?" she grumbled.

"It's fine," insisted Piper. Her skirt and blazer were powder blue, with a white top, but otherwise identical. Unlike Seph, she looked right at home in the outfit. She withdrew a makeup mirror from her purse and looked herself over.

"Fine for *you* maybe. And why do I have to wear pantyhose?" She bent down and pulled at them, uncomfortable. "I *hate* these things!"

"They help cover all the bruises on our legs," replied Piper as she touched up her lipstick. "*Mine* are all scraped up because *someone* made me fall through a rotten floor."

"I don't remember any such thing."

"No, you were too busy being drunk and hitting on me."

Seph shot her a dirty look. "I did *not* hit on you."

"If you say so."

She tucked her cell phone into her blazer pocket with her wallet. She'd opted to leave her purse behind, not wanting to carry it all the way into Tartarus. Piper, on the other hand, chose to keep her purse, which was stuffed nearly to bursting with meat snacks from that Fathom Lake convenience store and Mr. Hallet's homemade jerky. "I was obviously just teasing you. You need to learn how to take a joke."

"Whatever."

"Shut up. Let's just get this over with."

The two of them rounded the corner and made their way down the sidewalk, trying hard to look natural, even though there probably wasn't anybody to worry about out here.

Seph could already see the Vertical Design building. Never before had her walk to work felt so ominous, but of course, never before had her boss turned out to be a murderous maniac hell bent on recreating the universe into a nightmare hellscape. She stared at it as she approached, wondering if there really were invisible floors looming above what she could see.

How did such a thing even work? Wasn't that the whole point of her prophet sight? Wasn't seeing things that were hidden supposed to be her special power? How had she been coming to work here every day for the past eighteen months and never once even glimpsed what was hidden? How was Tane able to keep such a secret from her?

But then again, there were plenty of things that had been difficult for her to see. And that meant that there were probably even more things out there she'd walked right past. The really scary thing was that Tane knew who she was and what she could do, and he was still ballsy enough to put it all right under her nose like this.

There was something chillingly *cocky* about the whole situation, when she really thought about it. He clearly had a far better grasp of her limitations than she did.

Piper's phone rang. She snatched it out of her purse, still hoping to hear from Meg, but it was only Kaitlyn again. She let it go to voicemail with the other dozen or so messages she and Alton and Phoenix had left there.

It was still so strange to think about. Kaitlyn was such a sweet-natured girl. Piper didn't want to believe that she was just another of Tane's monsters. But she could think of no way that any ordinary person could possibly have known all the places they'd been.

On the way over here, Seph asked Amethyst if *she* knew anything about it, but she seemed genuinely confused by the idea of Seph's three college friends being involved in any way.

How deep into their lives did Tane's filthy fingers reach? How much power did he have over them?

What other surprises did he have for them?

They crossed the street and Seph caught sight of her truck sitting in the parking lot. That surreal feeling only grew stronger. She could hardly believe it'd been two days ago that she left it there, never suspecting that she wouldn't be back for it at the end of the day.

So much had changed in just that short amount of time. She was now unemployed. Amethyst was apparently *immortal.* Kaitlyn, Alton and Phoenix were probably working for her enemy. And her best friend was a human-monster hybrid capable of literally *eating* her.

It felt like her entire life was slipping through her fingers, like trying to hold onto a fistful of water…not unlike what the scythe kept doing, she realized…

She could see the main entrance waiting for them up ahead.

She took a deep breath and tried to calm herself.

"You going to be okay?" asked Piper.

Seph nodded. "Just…a little bit scared, I guess."

"I get it. I mean, I always thought this place was kind of intimidating *before* I found out it was, like, an evil lair."

She glanced over at her, surprised. "What?"

She shrugged. "It's all *businessy.*"

"I don't think that's a word."

"Like, everyone there's so serious. It's always so *quiet.* Every time I've ever gone in there to meet you for lunch, I've always felt totally out of place. I'd walk in those doors and I'd sit in one of those chairs in the lobby and I just…I felt *small.* Like I was some silly little girl in this big, gloomy office. I was always kind of afraid someone was going to yell at me and tell me I didn't belong there."

Seph frowned. Piper thought the people she worked with were too serious? Sure, they were all pretty serious about their work, but most of the people here were *goofballs.* "How is my job too serious? The people in there are literally drawing pictures for *video game boxes* right now."

Piper shrugged. "I don't know." She stared at the doors as they drew closer. "It's, like, a *real* job. You work in an *office building*. It's so...*grown up*. And all I want to do is keep working at the mall. Every time I go in here, it always makes me wonder why you even bother hanging out with me."

Seph stopped walking and turned to face her. "Because you're my best friend."

"You're just so much *cooler* than me."

She stared at her for a second, surprised. Then she laughed. "That's the most ridiculous thing I've ever heard. If anyone's not cool enough it's *me*. I'm freaking *pathetic*! I mean, I started *crying* the last time I saw a spider in our apartment and you weren't home to rescue me."

Piper smiled. "I *do* like rescuing people from spiders."

They started walking again.

"And for the record," added Seph, "I was a pretty big mess without you in that library, okay?"

"Same when I thought I lost you in Covengale."

"I really don't know why anyone thought *we'd* make good seekers."

"I know, right?"

They walked up to the doors and paused there. On the other side of the glass was the Vertical Design lobby.

Sitting at the desk, her nose buried in her cell phone, was Stacy Getledder.

Both of them turned and darted back out of sight again.

"What's *she* doing back?" asked Seph.

"I thought you reaped her!"

"I thought I did, too!" It wasn't something she could easily forget. It was a fairly traumatizing experience, reaping a coworker. Especially one she hadn't previously fantasized about reaping, like that sexist creep, Leddy, on the second floor. *Him* she wouldn't have minded reaping, whether he'd turned out to be a monster or not. "How many of her does Tane have?"

"What, like he has a receptionist *cloner*?"

"I don't know!" Seph leaned over and peered in the door. Stacy was right where they left her, still staring at her phone. "Maybe that's the *real* one?"

"There's a real one?" asked Piper.

"I don't know! Maybe?" The Stacy she thought she knew was such a chatterbox, always telling her *way* more than she ever wanted to know about her life. She sure *seemed* real. She wanted to believe that the Stacy she reaped was a monstrous *copy* of a *real* Stacy that Tane had given the day off when he decided he was ready to introduce them to his basement of horrors. Surely all those long-winded stories weren't just made up.

And yet she couldn't gamble that the Stacy sitting at the reception desk right now was just going to sit there and ignore them. If she *was* another monster like the last one, she couldn't rely on the scythe working when she needed it to. The stupid thing seemed to be getting more glitchy the more she tried to use it.

Besides, if she *was* another of Tane's monsters, how could they be sure confronting Stacy wouldn't immediately alert him to their plan?

"Is there a back door?" asked Piper.

Before Seph could reply, there was a muffled crash from the other side of the door.

They turned and peered through the glass again.

Stacy was gone. Her cell phone was lying on the floor in front of the desk.

"What just happened," asked Piper. "Where'd she go?"

Seph shook her head. "Warner, maybe?" Annabeth said he'd be here with them. It made sense. "Who cares? Let's just get in there and find that stupid gate. Are you ready?"

Piper put her hand over the spinning wheel. "As ready I'll ever be, I guess."

Seph paused just a few seconds longer. She took a deep breath…let it out slowly… Then she clenched her fists and marched through the front door of Vertical Design for the last time.

Chapter 85

Stacy Getledder didn't jump out from behind the desk. She didn't come crashing down through the ceiling tiles or burst from the restroom. She seemed to have simply disappeared into thin air.

But Seph didn't trust it. She held her hands out in front of her as she stepped into the room and let the scythe unfurl itself, ready to strike down anything that moved.

Piper stood behind her, still clutching her pendant. "Quiet," she observed.

Seph stopped in front of the desk and nodded. They seemed to be alone.

Then Chip Galasso, the building's network administrator, came around the corner and walked straight toward them.

Seph quickly withdrew the scythe and hid her hands behind her back.

"Hello there," he said. His attention was fixed on his cell phone, as usual, so he didn't notice the disappearing scythe or Seph's not-so-inconspicuous behavior. Chip was fairly tall, about her own age, with a thick, immaculately trimmed beard and one of those ridiculous handlebar mustaches.

"Hey Chip," said Seph, her hands still crossed behind her back. She didn't dare let her guard down in case he was another Stacy monster in disguise, but she had no intention of reaping the *actual* Chip, in the event that he wasn't a monster, either.

He walked up to the desk and finally looked up from his phone to find the receptionist gone. He glanced around the room, as if she might be hiding behind one of the chairs or standing in a corner somewhere. "Where's Stacy?"

"Not sure," replied Seph, not at all lying. "Restroom, maybe?"

He nodded. "Probably." He turned and looked back toward the hallway behind him, in case she was hurrying back.

Piper took the opportunity to stoop down and scoop up Stacy's cell phone that was lying on the floor. Then she stood up again and stashed it in her pocket before he turned around again.

"I'll just leave these here, then." He reached out to lay some folders on the desk, but stopped and turned his head toward them.

His eyes had gone black.

"Tane's not here," Warner informed them. "I've taken care of his guard dog for you."

Guard dog? Was he talking about Stacy?

"Make your way to his office. Quickly."

"How do we get there?" asked Seph. "The elevator and stairs only go to the fifth floor." She'd been all over this building since she came to work here. It wasn't as if she simply hadn't bothered going up to see what was on the sixth floor. The stairs literally ended on the fifth. And the elevator buttons only went to five.

"The elevator goes to *all* floors. You just have to look closer."

"Look closer," she replied, nodding.

Chip blinked and stared at her. "Look at what?" Then he looked down at the papers in his hand, confused about why he was still holding them. He dropped them onto Stacy's desk and started to turn away.

Then he paused and looked back. "You look different today."

Seph looked down at the clothes Amethyst gave her. "Oh… Yeah… It's…uh…"

"Looks nice. That's a good color on you." Then he walked away and disappeared down the hall.

Piper slapped her shoulder. "*See*? You *can* pull off things other than black."

"Will you give it a rest already!"

They crossed the lobby and made their way down the hallway to the elevator and stairwell. Seph couldn't suppress a shudder at the memory of the last time she was standing in this spot, just after Mr. Carrol revealed that he was Janon Tane all along, and just before that first Stacy turned into a monster and the first of those awful teethers came loping out of the elevator after them.

Piper reached out to push the button, but hesitated. "Last time we got in this thing…"

"I remember." The elevator ignored the button they pushed and took them instead down past the basement and into Tane's own, personal level of hell. "But Warner *said* to take the elevator." She reached out and pushed the button. "So that's what we're doing."

"Okay. I hope he's right."

"He said Tane's not here right now," Seph reminded her. "If he doesn't know we're here, there's no reason he'd try to trap us again."

Piper nodded. She had a point, she guessed. But she still cringed a little when the elevator dinged and the doors slid open. She wasn't entirely convinced that Tane would let them simply walk into his office just because he didn't happen to be in the building at the moment. The man wasn't even human. He was one of the Twelve Teeth of the Great Enemy. She wasn't entirely sure what that meant, but it was fairly obvious that it was a pretty big deal.

They stepped inside and stood there as the doors closed.

"Now what?" asked Seph, staring at the control panel. This was the part where she typically just pressed the button marked "4" and let the machine do its thing. But she didn't want to go to the fourth floor today. She wanted to go somewhere that didn't seem to be an option.

"Warner said you just have to look closer," Piper reminded her.

"I know what he said," huffed Seph. "It was like *a minute ago*."

"I'm just trying to *help*," she grumbled.

Seph leaned closer to the panel, looking it over. Look closer... She assumed he was talking about her prophet sight, that there was something inside this elevator that couldn't be seen by normal people. But she'd used this elevator hundreds of times and not once did she ever see anything in this car that didn't belong. Not even when it kidnapped them and carried them down to Tane's torture chamber. Whatever it was, it was clearly hidden better than most of the things her prophet sight showed her.

She squinted at the panel. Maybe the top half was invisible, so that all she could see was the bottom nine buttons?

She didn't even know how many floors the real building had. Annabeth called it a "tower," but that didn't necessarily tell them anything. Technically, a tower was any structure significantly taller than it was wide. At five stories tall, with a fairly small base, the Vertical Design building she'd always known was already sort of tower-like.

She scratched absently at the sting on the back of her neck and leaned back to see if a wider view revealed anything unusual.

It didn't.

She turned and looked at the other three walls of the car, but again she saw nothing.

"This is *hard*," she grumbled.

Was she doing it wrong again? Was she trying too hard? Did she need to relax and find the right mindset? She wasn't sure she could do that. How long before Tane realized they weren't heading for the research center and came to see where they'd gone? And how long before another Stacy turned up? Or some other monstrous thing?

Piper reached out and placed her hand against the wall next to the buttons. She tilted her head to one side, then the other, trying to listen.

"You hear something?"

"I'm not sure. Maybe?" She slid her hand higher up the wall. "I feel like…like there's some kind of energy here…or *something*."

"Energy?" Seph turned her gaze back to the control panel. That *could* make sense, she supposed. It was an elevator that was supposed to take you to the *unreachable* floors of the building.

"Or maybe…" Slowly, her eyes slid up toward the ceiling. "…maybe more of a *vibration*?" She turned around and stared up at the ceiling. "It's kind of like that pipe in Zarechuff. The one that led us to the flickering chamber."

Seph stared up at the ceiling, too. "That sounds like the sort of trouble we're trying to get into."

Piper's spirit ears were fixed on a spot in the back corner. Seph fixed her gaze there and tried to relax. It made sense. Although she'd used this elevator countless times, she'd never really *looked* at it before today. She always just did what you did when you got on an elevator. You walk in. You face forward. You stand still. She had no idea *why* that was what you did on an elevator, why it had to be so strangely formal. But that's what she did. She'd probably never bothered looking at anything more than the control panel and the doors. So it came as no surprise when she suddenly realized that there was a little door up there.

She reached up and turned the latch. The door swung down, revealing a new button. She didn't give herself time to think about whether this button might be a trap of some sort, that it might set off an alarm or trigger a grisly trap. If she hesitated, she knew she'd just struggle over what to do. So she pressed the button.

The control panel with its nine buttons swung open on hidden hinges and a new control panel took its place, this one with buttons leading up *twenty-five* floors.

"Wow," said Piper. "This place is huge."

It was so surreal to think that there were twenty floors sitting on top of her modest workplace that she'd never seen…and she wasn't entirely sure *why*. It didn't *surprise* her. Shawbeck Ranch. The fringe road. The swamp hidden in Fibbel Marsh. The Ahns' playground. Nora's Lilac Grove. The Keeper's compendium… She'd seen *far* stranger. It wouldn't have surprised her if there was an entire city hidden in the break room fridge.

Staring at all those buttons, she slowly began to realize that it was *personal* this time. This wasn't some mysterious place she'd never set foot until today. This was familiarity. This was the elevator that she rode every day on her way to and from her desk in the studio. This was her *job*. This was her *life*. It was like when she found out that Amethyst had been lying to her about who she really was. An entire part of her life was being turned upside down again.

And it made her feel very *angry*.

"You okay?" asked Piper.

"Yeah. I'm fine. Just…distracted." She shook it off and focused on the task in front of her. "Annabeth said his office would be on the top floor, right?"

Piper nodded.

"Let's get it over with."

But before she could press the button, the panel snapped closed again and the elevator began moving. "What's happening?" Had she set off a trap of some sort? Had Tane returned and found them here? Were they going to end up back in another freaky, monster-infested basement level?

But before she could begin to prepare herself for whatever was about to happen, the elevator car rumbled to a stop on the second floor and dinged. The doors slid open. And there stood Gina Sarrelli.

Seph stared at her. The last time she saw Gina was precisely like this. She was waiting for the elevator when they returned from Tane's dungeon. She remembered feeling particularly bad about leaving her here, not just because she'd discovered that a monster was running the place, but because she'd always genuinely liked Gina and she didn't think she'd ever see her again.

"Hi Seph," said Gina. Her voice, as always, was small, quiet and sleepy. She stepped into the elevator with them and turned to face the doors as they slid closed again. "Did you finish taking care of your emergency?"

"Huh?" said Seph, confused. Then she remembered telling her last time that she had to leave early because of an emergency. "Oh! Yeah. Uh… It's…all taken care of."

"That's good. I hope it wasn't anything too bad."

"No. Not too bad." She frowned. "You…going to pick a floor?"

Gina glanced back at her, that small face puzzled. "I'm going to the same floor you are."

Seph looked over at the control panel. The elevator was just sitting here, assuming it was empty because no one had chosen a floor yet. Gina must have assumed that she was on her way up to the studio, but now it was looking as if she'd just been hanging out in the elevator like a weirdo. "Oh…" she said, trying to think. "It's…uh…I guess it's still…acting a little weird…I guess…" She reached out to select the fourth floor.

Gina turned and looked forward again. "Not there," she said. "The *other* panel."

Chapter 86

Seph and Piper exchanged a surprised look. The other panel? How did Gina know about the other panel?

"Warner?" asked Piper.

Gina turned and looked at her. Her eyes were soft and brown and, as far as she could tell, perfectly human. "No. Warner's not here right now. I'm just Gina." She lifted a small hand and pointed at the button in the ceiling. "Open the other panel. We don't have a lot of time."

"Wait…" said Piper. "Annabeth said they had someone on the inside."

Seph stared at her. Annabeth *did* say that…but *Gina*?

"Did the Ahns send you?" asked Piper.

"I don't know what that is," replied Gina. "I was sent here by a goddess."

"A goddess?" said Seph. She kept hearing about a goddess… First by Harv Tottlestep, who said a goddess gave him his humming chicken, then by Wilbur and the other clones who said a goddess gave them their job and quiet life in Waybel Valley. "Who *is* the goddess?"

Gina looked genuinely surprised at this question. "The goddess is the Great Beholder."

Piper shook her head. "That's even more confusing than 'goddess,' actually…"

"I don't really know. I'm sorry. I don't remember much about meeting her. The whole thing was kind of a blur. I know she was very beautiful. And *very* wise. She seemed to know everything that ever happened to me, even things I'd completely forgotten. She gave me this job to do, about a year and a half ago, and said if I did good, I'd finally find what I've been looking for."

Seph glanced over at Piper again. A year and a half ago. About the same time all this started. And about the same time Tane hired her for this job. Gina started just a few weeks after her, she recalled. She could still remember some of her other coworkers gossiping about how there wasn't even an opening, but Mr. Carrol hired her anyway, based apparently on a very impressive recommendation. "What are you looking for?"

"It's kind of private," replied Gina. "Sorry."

"Right. No, that's fine. Sorry to pry." But she wasn't *that* sorry. What was with everybody and their secrets?

Again, she lifted that small hand and pointed at the door in the ceiling of the elevator car. "Please?" she pressed. "We really don't have a lot of time. And eventually someone else is going to want to use this elevator."

"Huh? *Oh*! Sorry." Seph reached up and opened it, then pushed the button, letting the fake five-story panel swing open to reveal the *real* twenty-five-story panel behind it again. "Top floor, right?"

"No. Seventh floor."

Piper pinched her lip, confused. "I thought Annabeth said Tane's office was on the top floor."

"It is. But there's security on the upper floors. There's a good chance we'll be noticed if we ride this elevator all the way to the top."

"But this is the *only* elevator," said Seph, pressing the button for the seventh floor.

"It's the only elevator accessible from the public floors," corrected Gina. "There're two more in the *real* building."

Seph shook her head. "This is *so* weird." Not just the idea of a much larger, invisible structure attached to the office building she'd been working in all these months, but simply listening to Gina talk about this stuff. The two of them had never really been very close, mostly because she'd seemed so painfully shy, but she liked to think that they'd become friends. Was everyone she'd ever grown even a little bit close to mixed up in all this strangeness?

"The elevator won't stop on the first five floors if it's going any higher than that," explained Gina. "Unless you know how to signal that you're also going up there." She turned and looked at Seph with that sleepy expression she always had. "You have to hold the call button down for at least ten seconds."

"Oh," was all Seph could think to say. She remembered how people had been complaining about the elevator for as long as she'd been here. They claimed it was always behaving strangely, taking forever to pick them up, sometimes cruising right past them while they stood there waiting for it. She'd never thought to question it. She just assumed, like everyone else, that it was just old and glitchy.

She watched the number on the display switch from five to six. A small part of her was still stubborn enough to feel a little surprised. At this point in time, was that a sign of lingering sanity? Or precisely the opposite? She couldn't help but wonder.

The six became a seven. It dinged as if stopping on floors that didn't exist was something it did every day. (Which it probably was.) And the doors slid open to reveal a very quiet and dimly lit corridor.

Piper leaned out and peered in both directions. "We couldn't have picked a less spooky floor?"

Gina stepped out into the hallway and turned left. "It's the quietest floor this time of day."

"What's on this floor?" wondered Seph.

"Various things," she replied. "But much of it is conducted during the evening and night hours. There *are* still people working here, though, so we need to be careful. Try to act like you belong here."

"How do you know all this?" asked Seph.

"Warner gave me some of the information. He told me the safest route to Tane's office. And how to use the elevator. The rest I just sort of...*feel*."

Piper tilted her head to one side. "'Feel?' What, like you're psychic or something?"

Gina paused as they approached a large window overlooking a surprisingly high-tech-looking computer room. There were workstations in there for at least twenty people, but there were only four in there right now. She turned and pressed her finger to her lips and then continued walking.

Seph and Piper followed her, their eyes washing over that room. There were three men and one woman. Two of the men had their backs turned to them. The third was facing left and busily typing at his keyboard. The woman, however, was facing them, her eyes fixed on her computer screen, one hand wrapped around a coffee mug. Seph had never seen any of these people before, but that didn't exactly surprise her. The majority of the people who used these upper floors probably didn't enter or leave through the visible Vertical Design building. And Amethyst told them that, regardless of what might go on unseen in this place, the part that she worked in was a legitimate graphic design business. Millard Carrol and Stacy Getledder might have been monsters, but she was fairly confident that most of the people she worked with were perfectly ordinary people simply doing the job they were hired to do.

The woman didn't look up from her screen as they walked by.

Even if she had, Seph suspected that she wouldn't have taken any notice of them. Gina didn't seem too concerned. She'd motioned for them to be quiet, but she didn't make them get down on their hands and knees and crawl past the window, below the woman's line of sight.

"It *is* sort of like a psychic sense," replied Gina once they were past the computer room. "It's something I've had for as long as I can remember. Kind of a *connection* to the universe around me. I'm *aware* of things that I shouldn't have any way of knowing. I'm good at finding lost or hidden things. I can feel when someone is nearby, even if they're hiding or in the next room. I always seem to know who's at the door or on the phone. And I know things about people as soon as I meet them. Like how you guys have a really important job to do. And how you're not entirely human."

Piper's ears perked up and a slight flush filled her cheeks. "You can tell that?"

"Of course. It's pretty rare to come across people like you two."

They reached the end of the hallway and turned the corner. Seph paused and looked both ways. The seventh floor was much larger than the lower five. Was that one of those special things, like how the black council's cabin in the Ahns' playground was much larger on the inside than on the outside? Or was the architecture of the tower more complex than she'd expected? Maybe it got bigger as it went up? Or maybe there were hidden areas branching off the lower floors, too?

Thinking about it too much made her head hurt.

Ahead of them, a woman with long, black hair turned the corner and walked straight toward them. She was dressed a lot like them, black skirt and blouse and beige blazer, but she was giving off a far more confident aura in her tall heels and gaudy jewelry. Unlike most of the people they encountered here, she wasn't looking at her phone or any other device. She was carrying a stack of folders and a coffee mug. But she didn't seem remotely concerned about the three of them as she walked past them.

Apparently, Amethyst really did know what she was doing when she dressed them like this. (Although Seph liked that woman's skirt and blouse *much* better than this bright red nonsense.)

"Are there a lot of people like you out there?" asked Piper once the woman was out of sight, still stuck on the idea that someone could just look at her and know that she wasn't entirely human.

"I don't know," replied Gina. "There are a lot of people out there with special abilities. A lot more than you know. Most of those people don't even know it themselves."

Piper wasn't surprised. She still wouldn't know about her spirit ears if she hadn't met Seph.

"But I've never been able to find anyone exactly like me," Gina went on. "I guess I'm—" she stopped in the middle of the hallway and stared straight ahead. "We need to hide."

"What is it?" whispered Seph.

Gina turned and opened the nearest door. Inside was a meeting room of some sort. There was a large table surrounded by swiveling office chairs. A large television screen was mounted to the wall on one side. "In here!" she whispered. "Hurry!"

They crowded into the room and she quietly closed the door behind them. Then she backed away.

All three of them stood in the gloom, their eyes glued to the window in the door.

The thing that passed behind the glass looked like an ordinary man. He was a little larger than average, with broad shoulders and short, black hair. But he didn't *feel* human. The air in the room took on a strange, shivery sort of feeling that they felt not so much on their skin as in their *veins*, as if the thing's mere presence caused the temperature of their *blood* to lower.

"What the heck was *that*?" whispered Piper as she rubbed at the gooseflesh that was suddenly covering her arms.

"I can't say," said Gina. "I can't even begin to describe the feelings I get from those things. But they're *bad*. We definitely don't want to get caught by one."

"How many of them are there?" asked Seph.

"A lot. Come on. We have to hurry." She opened the door, peered both ways to make sure it was clear, then hurried on down the hallway. "This way."

They turned down an adjacent corridor and stepped through an open door, onto a long balcony overlooking the street.

Seph stopped and stared. For the first time, she could see what the Vertical Design building really looked like.

Chapter 87

The Vertical Design she knew wasn't merely the first five stories of a much taller building. It was little more than a cornerstone of a structure far more massive than she'd imagined. Towering walls of steel and glass rose high up into the sky above them and stretched for what looked like the entire length of the block.

Seph tried to remember exactly what buildings surrounded Vertical Design and how they were laid out to allow for such a building to exist here, but she couldn't quite recall.

"How is all of this here?" asked Piper as she walked over to the balcony railing and looked out over the city. The building was utterly out of place. It towered over everything around it, seemingly impossible to miss, yet she'd never seen such a structure before, and she'd lived in Cakwetak her entire life.

"It's not just that people can't *see* it," explained Gina. "They're completely unaware of the space it takes up and the extra time and distance it requires to walk or drive around it."

Seph stared at her. She remembered Violet saying something like that back in July. When she was describing the hidden places in Avelby. She said they weren't just invisible, but utterly *ignored.* Were these places all the same?

Piper looked down at the street below. "That's where those

teethers attacked my Jeep!"

Seph stepped up beside her and peered over the edge. There was another balcony located off the second floor, directly over the street. That explained why the stupid monsters seemed to be falling right out of the sky and onto the vehicle. They must've been jumping over that lower railing. It also explained where they got those weapons, like the stapler and the potted plant. They probably snatched them from whatever rooms they passed through on their way out of the building.

Except for the axe, she supposed… Did they snatch that out of one of those "In Case of Fire, Break Glass" cases? Did places even still have those anymore? She couldn't remember for sure if she'd ever even seen one of those in real life. But then again, she had no idea what might be located in the building's hidden areas. Maybe it was more of an "In Case of Mutant Zombie Monster Escape, Break Glass" sort of thing…

She supposed it didn't matter.

She looked up and down the street as it twisted alongside the building and wound between the various houses and small businesses crowded around it. "I guess that explains why the back streets were always so confusing," she realized.

Gina nodded. "There're lots of places like this in the world, and it's like people completely ignore their existence, even in photographs or videos. They don't even show up on maps."

"*So* trippy…" sighed Piper. She looked out over the city, wondering what other towering structures might exist out there that her silly human brain simply refused to acknowledge.

"We should keep moving," said Gina. She turned and continued walking, following the balcony past the next several doors.

Piper followed, but her gaze kept drifting out over all those rooftops, still wondering.

Was the entire world like this? Or was it only certain places?

Seph, on the other hand, wasn't thinking about the rest of the world. She could barely handle what was right in front of her face right now. Was this really the reality of Vertical Design? How did that boring, gray rectangle of a building she drove to five days a week turn into this towering monstrosity that loomed over Cakwetak? And how was quiet, timid little *Gina Sarrelli* the one guiding them to Tane's office?

She didn't *have* to turn her gaze out over the city to see that the world had been turned upside down. It was as if everything she'd ever known went topsy-turvy after her father died.

She couldn't help but wonder what part of her life was going to turn out to be a lie next…

"In here," said Gina. She opened a door and stepped inside.

There was a strange smell in this part of the building. A musty and earthy scent, not at all unlike the many underground places they'd visited on this long journey they'd traveled. But this was the seventh floor of a towering high-rise in the middle of the city. They shouldn't be anywhere near anything underground.

And yet that smell only grew stronger as they made their way down the long, empty hallway.

Piper's cell phone rang again. It was Alton. She stuffed it back into her purse without answering it. She couldn't decide what was more disturbing, the fact that Kaitlyn, Alton and Phoenix were the bad guys and were now stalking them or the fact that she still hadn't heard from Meg.

Seph glanced back at her. She didn't ask who it was. She already knew.

At this point in time, she wasn't sure it would surprise her if her own *mother* turned out to be involved in all this.

But these things only seemed to revolve around Seph. It was *her* college friends and roommate. *Her* high school art teacher and boss. Maybe Tane really didn't have any idea who Piper was until the day she and Seph met at the mall and faced that first wraith.

Was it really some kind of divine fate that led to her being here today, or was it only blind chance and dumb luck that she was the one to end up standing by Seph's side in this insane journey?

What were the odds, Piper had often pondered, that she could've died in that restroom that day and that some other poor soul with spirit ears could have been the one to travel with Seph to Messing Knob?

Was it strange that the idea of dying that day didn't bother her quite as much as the thought of some *other* strange person ending up as Seph's partner on this journey? There was an odd and rather childish jolt of jealousy at the thought.

Seph was *her* best friend, after all. She trusted no one more than her.

But that wouldn't have happened. It wasn't just that she had spirit ears, after all. She was a direct descendant of an Ahn. That probably made a difference. Right?

She reached up and rubbed at her temples. She needed to focus. She'd been through a lot in the past few days. Or was it weeks? She still had no idea how long they spent in any of those stupid trials… But she felt tired and emotional and kind of ditsy right now. She needed to focus on the task at hand.

Gina pushed open another door and led them through a wide, open room that appeared to be some sort of science lab. And here, the source of that strong, earthy smell was finally revealed.

Steph stopped, surprised, and stared.

It had been broken into three pieces and then reassembled, held up by several hydraulic arms, but it was quite clearly one of the Architects' disks.

The first one they found beyond the hidden passage in the Muntony City Library eighteen months ago, guarded by the enormous, undead worm. It was carved with the image of the three Architects standing over a newly formed universe. The second was at the end of that flooded chamber under the pyramid in the swamp hidden in Fibbel Marsh, guarded by that army of hairy, alien zombies. It was carved with an illustration of the life cycle of the universes. This was neither of those disks. The image carved on the broken surface of this one was a strange, circular diagram, like an overly complicated clock face, with a swirly sort of symbol at its center. Various lines, some straight, some wavy, others sort of wobbly or broken, all led away from that symbol, connecting it to one of many other curious, alien symbols arranged around the outside of it. A mandala of some sort, perhaps?

"Where did they get that?" sighed Seph.

"Hard to say," replied Gina. "A lot of strange things pass through here."

She walked toward it, curious. Even from here, she could see the mysterious words etched into the lines.

"Were we supposed to find that?" asked Piper. "If the Ahns didn't cheat and give me the wheel? Would that have been waiting for us along the way somewhere?" She pinched her lip between her thumb and forefinger and twisted it as she pondered the thought. The outer edges of the disk were covered in soil and mud, not all of it completely dried. When Tane discovered that she already possessed the final Hand, did he go and dig it up? "Can you read it?"

Seph stopped walking and squinted at it. It was odd. She found that she didn't have to be right under it to read those mysterious words hidden in those carved lines. They were just as clear to her from where she was standing, still twenty feet away. "Something about…a *prophecy*? Is that right?"

"Why not?" said Piper, letting go of her lip and crossing her arms in front of her. "We've had everything else."

"The number twelve…" said Seph. "Over and over again. Groups of twelve. I see the Twelve Teeth…"

"Tane and his…*brothers*, I guess…" reasoned Piper.

Seph nodded. "But also twelve…" She shook her head. "*Some-things*."

"We don't have time," said Gina. "We need to keep moving."

But Seph was fascinated. She stared at the center of the circle, at the swirly symbol that had been carved there. It was the same symbol she was somehow able to read in that study room inside Lodblin's library. "Tartarus."

Piper's spirit ears perked up. She turned, frowning, and looked across the room at one of the doors.

"Twelve *knights*?" read Seph. "Is that right? That sounds kind of right. And twelve… I don't think I know that word…"

From somewhere on the other side of the doorway Piper was staring at came a loud click, as if a heavy door had just opened.

Gina jumped at the sound and turned her small face toward it. "Seph!" she whispered. "We have to go!"

But Seph barely heard her. "Sixes, too," she realized. "But in pairs, making twelve again." She pointed at the symbols around the door. "Six guardians… Six…doors?"

Piper couldn't say for sure what it was her spirit ears were hearing. It wasn't the buzzing sensation that Gispuknya's shadows filled her head with. This was *far* more unpleasant. It was more like the sensation of touching your tongue to the connectors on a nine-volt battery, except that instead of being concentrated on her tongue, it was dissipated throughout her entire head. It was incredibly unpleasant, and rapidly growing stronger. "*Persephone*!" she hissed.

But Seph still didn't move. Her attention was fixed on the mandala. There was something about it, something about the greater meaning laid out in those mysterious symbols carved between the lines, something…*important*…

Gina grabbed her hand and pulled her toward the door she'd been leading them to.

Behind that other door, heavy footsteps were approaching. They echoed across the silent room. And that awful, uncomfortable, low-voltage sensation in Piper's brain was rapidly growing into something *painful*. It made her lips tingle and her fingers feel numb.

Seph let herself be dragged away. Somewhere deep down, she knew that it was important for them to leave. She could hear the approaching footfalls. She could even sense that unsettling feeling of something terribly *wrong* drawing nearer, but she couldn't seem to drag her eyes from those symbols.

She could see something there, she was sure of it. But she just couldn't seem to wrap her head around it.

"Hurry!" gasped Gina. For the first time, her timid demeanor seemed to falter, replaced with mounting terror.

Seph could feel the terror, too. She didn't know what was about to walk through that door, but she *did* know that she shouldn't be here when it did. And yet, she couldn't pull her eyes from the broken disk.

Deception, she thought as she stumbled away from it. *Destruction. Ruin.*

The thing was at the door.

Broken.

Now Piper had her other hand. The two of them were dragging her toward the next door.

On the other side of the room, the knob turned.

The door began to open.

End.

Seph's heart was already racing, but now it suddenly leaped into her throat. End… Not just *an* end. *The* end. Ultimate finality. The end of *everything.*

The third disk contained a terrible warning! But she didn't have time to fully comprehend it!

The man who stepped into the room looked just like any ordinary man, but he was no such thing. Anyone who approached him knew it. He was one of the "higher-ups," as those who'd worked here a while liked to call them. Crossing him was unthinkable. People who crossed the "higher-ups" tended to suffer unthinkable luck. And very little ever got by them.

As the man entered the room, he heard the far door click closed.

He didn't so much walk across the room as sort of shift there. It was an indescribable sort of motion, more like a glitch than a physical action, over well before it could be perceived.

He opened the door and filled the hallway with his searing gaze.

But there was no one there.

He stood there anyway. He watched. He listened.

And the longer he stood there, the darker the hallway became, as if his very presence were draining away the light as it radiated from the fluorescent fixtures in the ceiling.

"I know you're there," he growled.

Chapter 88

Piper stood there, her heart racing. Her body was squeezed into the small supply closet with both Seph and Gina mashed against her. She had to bite her lip to keep back the whimpers of fear that were trying so hard to bubble up her throat.

It took every ounce of willpower she had not to cry out when the evil thing called out like that. (*I know you're there.*) But somehow she managed not to make a sound.

Not that it mattered one bit. If that monster knew they were here, there was nothing stopping it from walking over here, opening the door and dragging them out of this closet.

They were trapped.

"Stop screening my calls, dammit!" He turned away, his phone pressed to his ear, and walked back into the lab. "You're the one who wanted to be kept in the loop on this!" he growled as the door swung closed again.

"Oh my gosh…" gasped Piper. Her knees wobbled beneath her. Her head felt light. "I honestly don't know how many more things like this I can take!"

"We need to get out of here," said Gina, her voice muffled between them.

Seph opened the door and leaned out into the hallway. They were alone again.

"Curious," said Gina. "I feel like this closet shouldn't be here."

"I think I made it," said Piper as she stepped out and straightened her skirt. "With my spinning wheel." She reached up and pulled it from her shirt, looking at it. "I guess that's what it does."

Gina stared at it for a moment. "Oh," was all she said. Then she turned and looked around again. "We should keep going before something like that happens again."

Piper tucked the pendant back into her blouse and followed after her. "Persephone?" she whispered.

"I'm coming," Seph assured her. Her heart was still pounding from that close call, but she still couldn't stop thinking about the words on that disk. Or, more precisely, that *one* word.

End.

It wasn't just the word. It was the imagery that went with it. A vast, lifeless darkness. A churning black sea. An eternal forest of death. An expanse of utter darkness without a single living soul cowering within it.

What did it mean?

What were the Architects trying to tell her?

The three of them turned the corner at the next hallway and Seph stopped, startled at the sight of a man sweeping the floor in front of them. "Empty people!" she gasped.

Piper's heart jumped again. "What?" The man in front of them didn't look any different from anyone else, but then again, neither did the empty people in Waybel Valley until they began chasing after them with those weird, falsely furious expressions.

To Seph, however, that emptiness behind its eyelids and lips was unmistakable. She closed her hands around the scythe's watery handle, ready to strike at the creature.

"He won't hurt us," Gina assured them. She never hesitated. She walked right past the hollow janitor as if he were nothing. "They're only programmed to clean."

Sure enough, Piper and Seph walked past him without any trouble. He never stopped sweeping. He never even looked up. It was impossible to tell if he even realized they were there.

"The elevator's up ahead," reported Gina.

Seph turned and watched the empty janitor as they hurried on their way, refusing to trust it. It may have looked like any ordinary person to everyone else, but she could see behind its hollow eyelids and lips to that creepy darkness that was all that was inside the monster.

But the monster just went about pushing its dust mop along the floor, patiently doing its one job.

Nothing more stood between them and the elevator. Gina ran up to it and pressed the button to go up.

Then they stood and waited.

Time ticked on.

The empty janitor carried on.

Piper's cell phone alerted her to yet another text from Kaitlyn. (*Are you home?*) Followed almost immediately by a second. (*Let's meet somewhere.*) And then a third. (*Are you guys ignoring us?*)

Then Alton texted her, too. (*It's not nice to keep secrets.*)

Piper groaned and switched her phone to Do Not Disturb Mode. "Those guys are really starting to creep me out."

Then Phoenix texted Seph's phone. (*I know you're up to something!*) It, too, was followed by a second message. (*Don't think I won't find out what it is!*) She silenced it and stuffed it back into her purse. She felt like crying. Why did it have to be them, too? Did the universe really have to take *everything* from her?

The elevator dinged and the doors slid open.

There was an attractive woman standing in the car, wearing a gray business suit and heels, busily swiping at the screen of a small tablet. Seph and Piper both froze, but Gina didn't hesitate. She stepped inside the elevator, pressed the button for the top floor and motioned for them to hurry and get on.

They did as they were told, half expecting the woman to turn into a monster and attack them the second the doors slid shut, or at the very least take one look at them and sound an alarm. But the woman barely acknowledged their existence. The four of them rode upward in awkward silence.

Seph kept one wet hand behind her back, ready for anything.

Piper fiddled with her pendant.

The elevator stopped on floor thirteen, opening the door to reveal a strange, mirrored corridor. Two short, pudgy men stepped into the car with them, chattering away in what sounded to Seph like Italian, but she wasn't sure.

Like the woman with her tablet, the two men utterly ignored them. They merely went on about their conversation as if they were alone. The doors slid closed again and the car continued up the shaft.

Piper recalled Annabeth telling them that the Cakwetak tower wasn't a very high-level facility and that security wasn't very tight. But shouldn't it be a little harder than this to sneak around?

Not that she was complaining, of course.

The elevator stopped on floor fifteen and the doors opened onto a room that looked like something out of a movie. A huge, sprawling room filled with dozens of cluttered desks encircled a large bank of enormous television screens all tuned to various *other* large rooms filled with *other* cluttered desks and even *more* enormous television screens. People were bustling about, shouting across the floor at each other in various languages, banging away at keyboards and yelling into their phones.

Seph was reminded of the organized chaos of the New York Stock Exchange. Or of busy newsrooms in the movies.

There were even several more of those empty janitors bustling about, delivering memos and coffee and picking up errant papers.

She had no idea what the purpose of this room was, but she found that it unsettled her. The Ahns told them that Vertical Design had their evil hands in pretty much everything. And this looked like the sort of place where someone could get their hands *very* dirty.

The attractive woman and the two pudgy men exited the elevator and walked off in separate directions while a nervous-looking man with thick glasses stepped in and pushed the button for the twenty-first floor.

Like the other three people, he didn't seem to notice them. He merely stood there, wringing his hands and muttering to himself, his gaze fixed on some far-off place.

Seph and Piper exchanged an uncertain glance. Something seemed off about all of this. It made sense that the business that went down here might not be of the most secure nature, but the whole damn building was invisible. Shouldn't there be more security than this? If nothing else, shouldn't Tane have foreseen the possibility of them returning here in order to infiltrate the research facility?

The whole thing seemed a little sketchy, if you asked Seph.

On floor twenty-one, the elevator doors opened to a brilliant, white emptiness. As they watched, the nervous-looking man walked out of the elevator and was immediately swallowed by it, as if into a dense fog.

Seph and Piper stared after him as the elevator doors slid closed.

Then, finally, they were alone again.

"This place is *freaky*!" gasped Piper. "I feel like we're sneaking into the Ministry of Magic!"

"We're almost there," said Gina as she stared up at the numbers on the display. Twenty-three. Twenty-four. Twenty-five.

The elevator dinged.

The doors slid open to reveal a long, blood-red hallway leading to a big, fancy door.

"That's it," said Gina as she stepped out of the elevator and started walking toward the door. "Janon Tane's office."

Seph and Piper stepped out and followed her. Seph still had her hand closed around the scythe. Piper was still clutching her pendant.

"Where's Warner?" wondered Piper. They hadn't seen him since he released control of the network administrator in the lobby.

"He should be near," reasoned Gina. "His job is to watch over you two and make sure our path remains clear."

Piper hoped so. She wasn't confident that the two of them would be any kind of match for any surprises Tane might've left them in this place. They'd barely encountered anyone on their trip up here, but twice she'd felt the presence of something utterly terrifying.

Seph looked around. She was reminded of that hallway they encountered way down in Tane's dungeon. That one was much longer than this one. And it wasn't painted the color of blood. But just like that hallway, there were no doors on either side. There were only the elevator doors behind them and the office door in front of them. It seemed like a colossal waste of space.

Gina walked up to the door and put her small hand on the door handle. There, she paused. “You guys ready for this?”

“As ready as we’ll ever be,” replied Piper.

Seph nodded. “Yeah. Let’s get it over with.”

Gina turned the knob.

Seph had just a moment to ponder the fact that this was the office of Janon Tane. One of the Twelve Teeth of the Great Enemy. Head of this entire, enormous tower of horrors.

Shouldn’t the door be locked?

She pulled the door open.

Tane was standing there, grinning his smug grin at them.

Chapter 89

Seph grabbed Piper's hand and turned to flee, but there was nowhere to run. A blood-red wall now stood blocking their way back, the hammer's crimson flames still flickering upon its newly shaped surface.

She twirled back around and thrust her hands out, unfurling the scythe's crystal blade in an instant, but once again, it sputtered and fell apart, splashing onto the carpet at Tane's feet.

He looked down at it, a puzzled expression on his face. "What have you done to your Hand?" he asked.

"What are you doing here?" Seph demanded, shaking off her hands and clenching them again. The water swirled around her fingers, but it refused to take form.

He raised an eyebrow at her. "This is my office," he replied. "I basically *live* here."

Seph turned and glared at Gina. "What's the deal?" she demanded. "You said he wasn't here!"

Gina stared back at her, cowering, those timid eyes wide. "I was told he'd be gone!" she cried. "And I never once sensed him! I swear!"

"She's telling the truth," said Tane. "She was following Warner's orders to the letter. And I'm not so stupid that I can't hide my presence from one little psychic girl." He turned his gaze on her. "You're fired, by the way."

She shrank away from him, tears gleaming in her frightened eyes. "Okay…" was all she was able to say.

She'd been so confident this whole time, seemingly certain about every move she made. But now she appeared to have come completely unglued. She was starting to cry. She was wringing her hands. She was trembling. She looked pale, as if she might throw up at any second.

Piper found that she could barely blame her. She'd just attempted to sneak the seekers into Tane's office, only to find him waiting here for them. This was no man. This was the architect of the Black World. The man responsible for the near eradication of humanity. If all he did was fire her, she was getting off lucky. She reached out and put her arm around her, pulling her close. At the same time, she reached up with her other hand and held up the pendant as if it were a crucifix and Tane were a vampire, praying it would protect them both from Tane's fiery fury.

"We won't let you take the wheel," growled Seph. But she wasn't sure how she was going to stop him. Again, she tried to form the scythe and again it splashed through her fingers.

But Tane only stared at her. "Why would I want to take the wheel from her?"

Piper squinted at him from behind what she hoped was the safety of her pendant. "Because…that's…what you've been after…this whole time? Wasn't it?"

"Yes," he replied, "but you and it are a matching set. It's not much good without you."

Seph glanced over at the pendant. The ringmaster said something similar when he had them cornered. She still didn't understand it.

"Come on in," sighed Tane as he turned away. "Make yourselves at home."

"We're not going anywhere!" snapped Seph.

He glanced back at her, that eyebrow raised again. "Or I guess you could just stand there forever…" he replied.

She looked back at that wall again. He was right. There didn't appear to be any other options.

"Besides," he added, turning away again, "you've come this far. Aren't you ready to finally get all of this done and over with?"

Seph stared after him. He'd called this his office, but what she saw on the other side of the door was like no office she'd ever seen. She took a cautious step forward and peered in after him.

A lush, green lawn was spread out before her. A stepping stone path curved through it, leading to a small, cozy cottage with a single, large shade tree growing next to it. A tall, wooden fence encircled the entire lawn.

It looked as if Tane had used his great power to build himself a quiet home right on Vertical Design's roof, which didn't even seem all that crazy, when she thought about it. Rich and powerful people did ridiculous stuff like that all the time. Except for the fact that the entire scene was set beneath a brilliant night sky ablaze with shining stars and the biggest full moon she'd ever seen.

It was only late afternoon. The moon was supposed to be *half* that size. *And* it shouldn't have been full. In fact, it was almost the *new* moon, if Seph remembered correctly.

There was a small patio with an arrangement of lawn furniture set out. Tane made his way there and took a seat in the shadows beneath the shade tree's branches.

(Unless it was night all the time in this wonky dimension, in which case maybe it wasn't so much a *shade* tree as…well…just a tree, she guessed…)

"Come on, now," he called back to them. "Have a seat. I'd offer you something to drink, but you'll just think I'm trying to poison you."

Seph stepped through the doorway and peered up at that blazing moon.

Piper took Gina's hand and followed close behind her, gazing up at the gorgeous sky. "Also very trippy…" she whispered.

Gina merely whimpered. This hadn't gone at all as Warner said it would and now she was utterly terrified of what Tane might decide to do to her before she was allowed to escape this place.

Seph turned her attention to Tane. Once again, she tried to form the scythe. This time, it obeyed her. The long, crystalline blade curled over her, glistening in the moonlight.

Tane sighed. "You can put that away. I already told you once, the owners of the Hands can't harm each other. The scythe can't hurt me. The hammer can't hurt *you*." He pointed his finger at them. At the same moment, a great ball of fire erupted behind Seph and directly in front of Piper's face.

Seph cried out, terrified. The scythe splashed through her fingers as she spun around, certain that Tane had just murdered her best friend.

But Piper was still standing there. With one arm, she held Gina against her, protecting her. With the other, she held a great, shining, golden shield. "Whoa…" she sighed.

"See?" said Tane. "The spinning wheel is bonded to her now, just like the hammer is bound to me and the scythe is bound to you. I couldn't take it from her if I wanted to. So there's no reason for us to fight anymore."

Seph turned and glared at him. "You bastard! You could've just *told us* that!"

"True. But she needed a shock to make her unlock it from that ridiculous necklace form."

Piper looked down to find that the pendant had vanished. Only the naked, golden chain remained around her neck.

And now that she was looking, the shield sort of looked like a grown-up version of the pendant. It was a great, round disk of shining gold, with a ring of small stones of various colors set into its rim.

As she looked at it, it began to melt into a brilliant, golden light that slowly enveloped her hand. It was just like the way the water enveloped Piper's hand when she summoned the scythe, and the way Tane's hand burned with those red flames.

She stared at her hand, flexing her fingers, watching it. This was Rumpelstiltskin's spinning wheel… This was the third Hand of the Architects… It was like Seph's scythe…except this was *her* treasure…

"Are you okay?" asked Seph.

Piper glanced up at her, those blue eyes wide with wonder. "*Everything's* so trippy…" she sighed.

"You're welcome," said Tane.

"Piss off," growled Seph.

Tane chuckled. He stretched his hand out toward the other chairs. "Sit. We're finally nearing the end of our adventure together. Let's take a moment and talk."

"Why?" demanded Seph. "So you can find some other way to steal the Hands from us?"

He spread his arms apart. "We've already established that we can't harm each other," he reminded her. "The Hands are gathered. They're activated. They've chosen their owners. Tartarus stands unlocked. There's nothing more to do but walk into the nexus and awaken the Architects. There's literally nothing I can do to you."

Seph walked up to one of the chairs, but she didn't sit. She stared at him. "We both know there are still plenty of things you can do to us."

He tilted his head to one side. "I'm not sure I understand you."

She pointed to Gina, who was still clinging to Piper with tears flowing down her cheeks. She flinched at the mere motion, as if she might lash out and strike her. "You can still harm *her*."

Gina whimpered and buried her face against Piper's blazer.

"Or anyone else we care about."

"True," he admitted.

"What did you do to Meg?" she demanded.

Piper had been staring at the glowing light emanating from her hand. Now she looked up. Meg… She'd forgotten about her in all the excitement.

But Tane merely looked confused. "Who's Meg?"

"Don't play stupid," growled Seph. "Our roommate. We played this game with that incubus last summer. This is the part where you show us our friend and we have to do things your way or you do something terrible to her."

Tane stared at her. "I guess that *would* certainly be one strategy…" he admitted.

"I know you've been watching us. Stacy knew how to catch Pea off guard by telling her there was an emergency involving her sister." (God, but that felt like forever ago!) "That means you weren't just spying on me at work, but at home, too."

"Fine," he said. "I'll admit it. I've been watching you. Not just recently, either. For *years*." He held his hand out to the side of his chair, palm down. "Since you were just a *little* thing. I know everything about you."

"That's just *creepy*," said Piper.

"But it was no more than those nosy Ahns were doing."

"That doesn't make it better," grumbled Seph. She crossed her arms. The thought of this guy hovering around while she was hanging out at home was unsettling. It was far too easy to imagine him watching her change or shower.

What a creep!

"Just give her back," said Piper. Then she looked down at her glowing hand. She leaned toward Seph and whispered, "How do I use this thing?"

"I'm sorry," said Tane, "but I don't have your roommate." Then he propped his elbow on the arm of his chair and rested his chin on his knuckles, a thoughtful expression crossing his face. "Meg's her name, you said? Why would I pick *her*? From what I've seen, you don't even *like* your roommate."

"That's beside the point," muttered Seph.

"We still want her back," agreed Piper.

Seph tilted her head to one side. "I mean, if you've got her gagged somewhere, I'm not saying you can't leave her like that…"

Piper shot her a dirty look. "Persephone!"

Seph shrugged. "But yeah, we still want her back. I guess."

Tane chuckled. "I see. Well, I'm sorry to disappoint you, but I'm not like that demon. I don't take hostages. I'm afraid wherever your roommate's gone, I had nothing to do with it. Are you sure she was actually taken?"

Seph stared at him, unsure what to say. Of course she wasn't sure. Didn't she keep saying that Meg was fine? That she was just off somewhere doing something stupid?

"I *do* hope you find her," said Tane. "But for now, can we please get down to business?"

Seph looked down at the chair, but still she didn't quite dare to sit. She didn't want to let her guard down around him, not for a single second.

"Gina, my dear," said Tane, his eyes still fixed on Seph. "Make yourself useful, would you?"

Gina stared at him, her eyes filled with terror. "What?"

"Don't you touch her!" shouted Piper. She put her arms around her, shielding her.

"I'm not going to hurt her," sighed Tane. "She's for our *other* guest." He raised his voice and called out, "Any time now, Warner."

Gina let go of Piper and stepped forward, her eyes suddenly black, and sat down in one of the chairs without speaking.

Piper stared at her. "Warner?"

"Sit," said Warner.

Seph still didn't want to sit, but if *Warner* was telling them to do it... Well, she didn't exactly want to do it because *he* said so, either. She hated when he bossed them around. But Warner was supposed to be on their side in this. Surely he wouldn't let Tane do anything to them. Right?

She glanced over at Piper, uncertain. Then, reluctantly, both of them sat down.

"Warner?" said Seph. "What's going on?"

Why was he just sitting there like that? This was the enemy. Shouldn't he be *attacking* Tane?

Warner turned Gina's expressionless face toward her. "Relax. Everything is according to plan."

"What plan?" Demanded Seph. "What're you talking about?"

"It's time for the seekers to enter Tartarus and restart the cycle.

But first, the parameters of the agreement must be met."

"Agreement?" asked Piper.

"The Agreement of the Three," explained Tane. "The law laid down by the three great powers that govern the process of the cycle."

"Three great powers?" She glanced over at Seph. Connor mentioned a bargain. He told them that the Keeper controlled the cycle, but had to allow the seekers to understand what they were doing and make all the actual decisions along the way. But she didn't fully understand what that meant.

"The First Three," explained Tane. "The oldest and wisest of all living things." He leaned forward, his eyebrows raised. "Gods, for lack of a better word."

Piper stared at him. Gods? Plural?

"Or perhaps *elder gods* would be a better term. There've been *many* who took the title of god since them."

"This is the part," said Warner, "where we make sure everything is on the table. It's the part where we make sure everyone is following the rules."

"The *rules*," scoffed Tane. "The Keeper only cares about the rules when they suit him."

"The Keeper is bound by the rules just as we are," growled Warner.

"Don't tell me what he is and isn't bound to," snarled Tane.

A rumble of thunder rolled across the rooftop. Seph and Piper looked up to see that storm clouds had begun to gather all around them.

"The thunderbird again?" wondered Piper.

"The weather in Tane's office tends to reflect his mood," explained Warner. "He has some strong feelings toward the Keeper, so it's likely to get a little stormy in here."

"My apologies in advance," grumbled Tane.

"Why are we even here?" demanded Seph. "The Ahns said that Tane wouldn't be here. We were just supposed to sneak in and use the gate to get to Tartarus."

"They lied," replied Warner. "It was a necessary precaution. Otherwise, there's a good chance you wouldn't have made it here."

"As soon as I realized that you'd been given the wheel early," explained Tane, "I knew we wouldn't have much time. I asked Warner to do whatever was necessary to bring you to me."

"Wait…" said Piper. "You're working for *him* now?"

"I don't *work* for anyone," growled Warner. "Bringing you to Tane was *always* a part of the plan. We just didn't expect to have to do it so soon."

"The Ahns cheated again," said Tane, his lip curling into a sinister sort of sneer that brought with it another rumble of thunder. "They could've ruined everything!"

"But why would you bring us to *him*?" wondered Seph.

"As per the agreement," Warner explained. "The seekers must understand the choices they'll have to make before entering Tartarus."

"But why *him*?" stressed Seph, glaring at Tane again.

Warner gave Gina's head an inquisitive tilt. "Because he's as much a part of this as the two of you."

"What do you mean? What does he have to do with *any* of this? All he wants is to steal the power of the Architects for himself!"

"You really haven't figured it out yet?" asked Tane. "Surely you've stopped to do the math, haven't you?"

"What math?" asked Piper. "What are you talking about?"

"Think about it," said Warner. "Three Hands. Three Architects."

“Three locks,” said Tane. “Three *trials*.”

Seph stared at him. Another piece of the puzzle finally fell into place. In Zarechuff, Connor told them that the lock was never theirs to open… “Three *seekers*,” she realized.

“Each one chosen by one of the First Three.”

“You…” sighed Piper, her eyes fixed on Tane. “*You're* the third seeker.”

Chapter 90

"I'm the third seeker," confirmed Tane. "I've been with you every step of the way. It was *I* who blinded the monster in Lodblin's library."

Seph gaped at him. *He* did that? She'd only narrowly escaped the jabberwock's teeth and claws as it was. If not for it having recently been blinded, there was no way she would've survived against that thing. Did she really have this man…or *whatever* the hell he really was…to thank for that?

"*I* was the tall man in Covengale," he went on.

Piper gasped. The tall man? The one who frightened off the bloody woman and ripped the spirit of that murderous hag from Seph's body?

"And *I* was the one who showed you the true nature of the cycle in Zarechuff," he finished.

"All those awful video screens," realized Piper. All of them set to show them the many horrors of that awful world. "All those pictures…" The mere memory of those horrible files made her feel sick. "You were the one who laid all that stuff out for us?"

"All proof of the horrors the *Keeper* brings into the world *every time* the cycle restarts."

Piper shivered. *Do you see it now?* she thought.

"The rules clearly state that all seekers must be made fully aware of exactly what they're fighting for," explained Tane. "I already know, of course, because I've done this all before. The trials were designed to put the truth in front of your face without actually telling you anything. That's his loophole. He wants you to miss it. He wants you to misinterpret it. But I won't let him get away with it. That's why I'm here. It's why I was given the job as the third seeker. I'll make sure you see the truth about the Keeper."

Seph shook her head. "No. Those things in Zarechuff… They came from the *Black World*. The universe *you* made happen when you stole the spinning wheel and tried to remake the universe in *your* image."

"Is that what they told you?" Tane sneered. Another rumble of thunder rolled over them. "First of all, I've already told you, I can't just *take* the spinning wheel. I never *stole* anything. Five cycles ago, one of the seekers learned the truth that everyone else refuses to believe. He came to me of his own free will. And together, we tried to finally put an end to the horrors. And it *should've* been the end of it. We had a plan. No more leeching the vital energies of the old universe to feed the new. No more ripping open the fragile boundaries and setting loose the horrors of Oblivion. No more darkness. No more madness. No more severing the spirit highways and leaving the remaining souls to the brutal eternity of the Wood."

Seph stared at him. Connor had already told them about the spirit highways and those left behind, but she still didn't want to believe it. It made no sense. Why? There had to be a better way to rebuild the universe than to sacrifice not only the lives but also the very *souls* of those left behind.

"But the Keeper wouldn't have it. He accused me of breaking his precious rules and he *sabotaged* the birth of the next world." He sat up in his chair, his eyes blazing. "The Black World was *his* creation, not mine."

Piper looked over at Gina with her creepy, black eyes. "Warner?"

"I was born in the Black World," said Warner, "like the wraiths and the shadow races. And of course those vile things that would one day become the Ahns. So I can't speak of the events that led to that universe's creation. I wasn't there. And to be honest, I can't even remember most of my existence *during* that universe. That era of my life is mostly a haze. All I know for certain is that I was…something *different* than I am now."

"The death of a universe is a thing of such massive cosmic importance that it breaks time, itself," explained Tane. "Details of those bygone worlds aren't just forgotten. They're literally *lost.* Deleted forever, sometimes even *changing* things in the present. So much has been destroyed that even *I* can't remember where we all began anymore."

"Even the Beholder's all-seeing eye can only peer back so far," agreed Warner.

The Beholder… That was what Gina called the goddess who sent her to Vertical Design. Was *she* one of those three great powers that Tane mentioned?

"I *can* confirm that the shift from the old universe to the new one is…*horrific*," admitted Warner. "He's not wrong about that. But his solution to draw the necessary energy from the Oblivion, instead…" He shook Gina's head. "It's *dangerous* to tamper with things in the Oblivion. They're too often rotten and corrupted."

"But breaking the spirit highways is acceptable?" challenged Tane.

"For the good of the many," replied Warner.

"Bullshit!" A bolt of lightning split the sky above them. Thunder boomed. "That's the *worst* kind of human thinking!"

"The rules must be followed."

"The rules?" scoffed Tane. "The Keeper does a lot of hideous things in the name of a bunch of rules he's constantly bending. He gave my Hand to those *monsters* dressed as old women."

"It wasn't time for you to claim it yet," replied Warner.

Tane pointed at Piper. "And what about giving *hers* to her without a proper bonding journey?"

"Things changed," growled Warner. "Gispuknya was on the verge of—"

"Oh yes, that's right. The *bug*. The one that was created from the sins of the Black World that the Keeper, himself, poisoned because I dared to challenge him."

More lightning flashed. The wind was picking up.

Piper looked up at the sky above her. Were they about to get rained on?

"That's not what happened," snarled Warner. "And if you'd like to start throwing accusations, why don't you tell them who manipulated the shepherd and that incubus into trying to steal the Hands?"

"That was *you*?" said Seph. "Those creeps nearly killed us!"

"*And* Wanda!" Piper reminded her. "*And* your mom!"

But Tane waved a dismissive hand at her as if it were nothing. "That was to spur the Keeper into action. We both know he wasn't going to let anything happen to his precious seekers. Or would you rather have drawn this whole mess out for another forty or fifty years? The Keeper isn't known for getting in any hurry about things."

"Oh!" gasped Piper. She held up a bright, pink umbrella that wasn't there a moment ago. "Look what I did!"

Seph stared at her. "Seriously?"

"*What*? It's going to rain in a minute." She looked up at the churning sky above them again. "And I have to learn to use this Hand thing, don't I?" She turned it over in her hands, looking it over. Now how did it open?

"We're wasting time," said Warner.

"I agree," said Tane. "This is the time and place for *facts.* And the first fact is that when we enter Tartarus, we'll kickstart the birth of a brand-new universe and *simultaneously* doom this one to a dark and hellish demise."

"True," admitted Warner. "But another fact is that this universe, like all that came before it is *flawed.* It's going to end whether the Architects build a new one or not."

"Also true," allowed Tane. "But time after time the universe is rebuilt with the *same* flaws. We're just dooming ourselves to repeat the whole process over and over again instead of doing something to eliminate the flaw in the *next* universe!"

"But if we're not careful," warned Warner, "*this* could end up being our last universe."

Piper's umbrella popped open, startling a surprised scream from her.

"Seriously?" hissed Seph. "You're embarrassing me in front of the bad guy!"

"Sorry!"

Tane sighed and waved an impatient hand at the sky. The storm clouds immediately blew away, leaving only that beautiful night sky shining down on them. "Better?" he grumbled.

Piper sat there, holding her new umbrella without a single raincloud in sight, feeling perfectly silly. "Yes, thank you," she replied in a very small voice.

"This is the struggle we face every cycle," explained Warner. "This is the two sides of the debate."

Seph lifted her glasses and rubbed at her eyes. "But what are *we* expected to do about it? I mean, we're just here to wake up the Architects, aren't we?"

"The whole reason seekers are chosen in the first place," explained Tane, "is to inject our free will into the cycle. We don't just *wake them up*. We infuse them with a little bit of ourselves. A little bit of us lives on forever inside the Architects." He turned his gaze on Warner. "Which *I* believe was meant as a means by which the process would *evolve*, making each universe *better* than the last."

Piper leaned over the arm of her chair, still holding the umbrella, and whispered at Seph, "How do I make it go away again?"

"How should I know?" The scythe only *erased* things. It didn't *make* them.

"The Keeper is stagnating the process," Tane went on. "He refuses to see that the flaw is only getting worse!"

Piper couldn't figure out how to close the umbrella, so she turned around and placed it on the ground behind her, still open.

"The *Keeper* is the flaw in the system," insisted Tane.

"Is he?" challenged Warner. "Or is it that they let a creature like *you* be the third seeker?"

"Oh my god!" shouted Seph. "Shut up, *both of you*!" She took off her glasses and rubbed at the bridge of her nose. She was so tired. She just wanted all of this to be done and over with. "What is it you want us to do?"

"Merely to understand," replied Tane.

She returned her glasses to her face and glared at him. "I understand that you've *lied* to me more times than I can count throughout my entire life! I understand that you've pretended to be my high school art teacher and my boss and I don't even know how many *other* people."

"That's true," he admitted. His expression showed no sign of remorse for his actions.

"And you tried to burn my face off!" said Piper, thrusting a slender finger at him.

"That was a bluff," replied Tane. "I was merely trying to scare you. I wanted to test Seph's control over the scythe. I wouldn't have actually hurt you."

Piper rubbed at her cheek and glared at him. It didn't hurt anymore, but those flames *did* smart for a while.

"So, more lies," said Seph. "Is that all you know how to do?"

"*And* he said all that awful stuff about you not being a good artist," Piper reminded her.

"Yeah, thanks," she replied. "I wanted to be reminded of that."

Piper pinched her lip and looked away. "Sorry…" she muttered.

Tane didn't even take his eyes off her. "I've been around a long time," he said. "I've dealt with a lot of people. I've found that a vast majority of the time, fear, anger, resentment and betrayal make far better motivators than all the niceties in the world."

Seph stared right back at him. "*Or*…you're just a dick."

He shrugged. "Whatever makes you feel better."

"Regardless of whatever bitterness may exist between you," said Warner, "you're going to have to do this final step *together*. And I suggest you all get on with it before the *bug* finishes licking its wounds."

Piper sat up in her chair. Gispuknya. She'd almost forgotten about him. Shawbeck Ranch won the battle against the shadows in Pobsick Spring, according to Annabeth, but the bug, itself, was still out there.

Tane stood up. "I agree. There's nothing left to talk about. All my cards are on the table now. All I'm asking is that, when the time comes, you consider very carefully how you should proceed."

Warner nodded and also rose to his feet. "Agreed."

Seph and Piper stood up as well. "I still don't understand *anything*," whined Piper.

"The only thing you need to understand is the consequences of your actions," explained Tane.

"In the end, only *you* can decide what you give back to the Architects when they awaken," said Warner.

Give back to the Architects? What did that mean? What did *any* of this mean? This whole situation seemed utterly pointless. They just sat here and listened to the ancient evil dude responsible for the Black World argue with the mysterious shadow-thing wearing Seph's coworker's body… There was no *understanding* something like that!

Tane turned and gestured toward a door on the side of his little cottage. "That's the gate," he told them. "It will take us all inside the research facility in Arkansas where the gate is hidden. Just like the gates leading into the Keepers compendium, we'll only be able to open it twice."

Seph stared at the doorway. "We always had to do this together, didn't we?"

He nodded.

Piper looked over at her, confused. "So then…why did we go through all the trouble of sneaking in here? Why not just call Tane up and say, 'Hey, we're ready to go to Tartarus now,' and save us all that trouble?"

Seph stood there for a moment, considering it all, then she turned and looked at Warner. "Yeah… What's up with that? Why did Gina even have to be involved in any of this?"

Warner stared back at them from behind Gina's face. "Because

Gispuknya isn't the only one with an interest in ending the cycle."

"Specifically my *brother*," said Tane. "Turms."

"Brother?" said Piper. Another of the Twelve Teeth of the Great Enemy?

"We all have our jobs," explained Tane. "Mine is to oversee the preservation of the cycle."

Warner nodded. "Caduceus Turms is the tooth responsible for Vertical Industries. The entire corporation is a tool for manipulating the world's economies and amassing fortunes. Even his name is a reference to the Etruscan god of commerce, if that gives you some idea of how massive his ego is."

Piper didn't know anything about Etruscan gods, whatever those were, but she knew that the caduceus was the name of the staff the Greek god of commerce, Hermes, carried. Like the Roman "Mercury," "Turms" was most likely just another name for him.

"He's probably the one who bought the ringmaster," said Tane. "Although it's possible it could've been one of my other 'siblings.' In case you can't tell, we're not exactly a close-knit family."

"Vertical Design and the Cakwetak tower belong to Turms," said Warner. "And he wasn't happy about handing control of it over to Tane in the first place. If given the chance, he'll seize the Hands for himself and to hell with the cycle."

"The Ahns' attack on the research center is to distract Turms, not me," explained Tane. "They'll make sure his people don't have time to get in our way."

"And Gina?" asked Seph.

Tane turned and looked at the girl Warner had borrowed for the sake of this conversation. "She showed up shortly after I hired you with a letter from the Beholder."

The goddess. Very possibly the very *same* goddess who sent the clones to Waybel Valley and gave Harv Tottlestep that queer, humming chicken.

"She told me the girl would be able to sneak you into my office when the time came without Turms noticing you, on the condition that I not let any harm come to her."

"And you really won't hurt her?" asked Seph. She still didn't like seeing her like that, with Warner's eerie black eyes staring out of her face.

"I gave her my word. I have no intention of going back on it."

Piper turned and looked at Seph. "Do you think this Turms guy could've been the one who took Meg?"

There was an awful thought…

"It's not impossible," reasoned Tane. "My brother's something of a bastard."

Seph sighed. If Janon Tane thought Caduceus Turms was a bastard, then she certainly hoped to never meet him.

"You should get going," said Warner. "The Ahns will be converging on the facility about now. Turms will be distracted."

Tane nodded. "Yes. The sooner we get inside Tartarus, the sooner we can be done with this business and the sooner you can go looking for your missing roommate." He gestured toward the door again. "Shall we?"

Seph stared at Gina. "You'll make sure she gets out safely?"

"I will," promised Warner.

She still wasn't entirely sure how much she trusted anyone. Tane was supposed to be the bad guy here, but what if he was telling the truth? Warner admitted that the death of a universe was every bit as horrific as he'd described. What if there really *was* a better way to reboot everything? A way that didn't involve severing the spirit highways and abandoning all hope for anyone left behind?

She couldn't help but think about the trials they'd endured. In the end, the custodian Tane chose sought to undo a terrible evil, while in contrast, the Keeper's custodian was quite possibly a very dangerous spirit who'd done unspeakable things and only wanted to escape her well-deserved eternity in hell…

Why was everything suddenly so confusing?

She turned and looked at the unassuming cottage door that was, in reality, a gateway capable of transporting them to any Vertical Industries location in the world, including the research center where the gate to Tartarus was hidden. "Fine," she sighed. "Let's finish this."

Chapter 91

Stepping through the gate was weird. It wasn't like when they entered the Keeper's gates or the Ahn's playground. In most of those instances, they'd simply blacked out for a moment and awakened on the floor. This was like grabbing hold of an electric fence. Or…at least what Piper *imagined* grabbing hold of an electric fence might feel like, since she'd never actually done it before. It sent a jolt all the way through her body, making her stumble a little as she stepped out the other side of it, and leaving her fingertips and the tip of her nose feeling strangely numb for a few seconds afterward.

The three of them were now standing in a room that could best be described as *underwhelming*. They were supposed to be inside Vertical Industries' top-secret research facility. Seph, for one, was expecting to find herself in a futuristic laboratory surrounded by computer terminals and glowing machinery. A setting right out of *Stargate*, perhaps… Instead, she was standing in the middle of an empty room, surrounded by naked concrete and cinderblocks, with a single, stark-naked lightbulb and an ordinary door without so much as a retinal scanner lock to secure the room. In fact, the door wasn't even closed all the way.

"Not exactly Fort Knox, is it?" she grumbled.

"There're multiple gates leading in and out of the facility," said Tane as he pulled open the door and stepped out into an empty, dimly lit hallway. "This particular one doesn't directly access anything but the Tartarus gate, and since I'm the only one who can open it, there's not much point in elaborate security, is there?"

Piper turned and looked back as she stepped through the door. She could see no sign of the gate they'd just walked through. There was no swirling vortex of light, no framed opening, not even a control panel to tell it where you wanted to go… There was no sign of any machinery of any sort. As far as she could tell, it was simply an empty room. She couldn't even begin to guess at how such a thing should possibly work.

It was the same back at Tane's weird cottage. The door he led them to hadn't contained anything, either. It'd looked to her as if Tane were trying to get them to walk into an empty closet, as if he intended to simply lock them up after all that time they spent sitting on his moonlit patio furniture, listening to him and Warner bicker. She wouldn't have done it if he hadn't gone first. And sure enough, as she stood there and watched, Tane stepped inside and vanished into thin air.

"Definitely not what I expected," said Seph. The place looked more like a deserted asylum than a high-tech research facility. The hallway floor was covered in dust. The walls were bare. The naked lightbulbs had been upgraded to cheap, fluorescent fixtures, but only about half of them were working. The rest had either burned out or were doing that creepy flickering thing they always did in horror movies.

(Totally cliché.)

They turned left at the end of the hall and found themselves walking past a long set of rusty iron bars that separated them from several heavy, prison-like doors.

"Guest rooms?" grumbled Seph.

"Temporary storage," replied Tane. "For transport between other facilities. Not so different from what your Shawbeck Ranch does. Except the things that end up in these cells are far more dangerous."

Seph tried to peer into the darkness of the cells, but without much luck. Most of them were either empty or whatever was inside was keeping out of sight. It wasn't until she passed the eighth cell that she caught a glimpse of something standing behind the bars. She paused and stared at it for a moment, trying to comprehend what she was seeing. It looked like a writhing mass of wriggling, brown eels arranged in a vaguely bipedal shape. A long, hairy neck jutted from the general area of its shoulders, but there was no discernable head attached to it. It just sort of ended in a rounded stump.

Piper didn't care to stop and stare at the squirmy-looking monster. It gave her the creeps. Instead, she walked on past it, curious about what else there was to see.

There was an extremely filthy naked man in a cell a little farther down who was muttering to himself and making little balls of fire rain down around him from the ceiling. In the next cell there appeared to be some kind of large, ape-like creature sitting with its hairy back against the bars. And a few doors down from that there was a large, gnarled hand with far too many fingers wrapped around the bar, attached to a long, bony arm that reached out from the darkness at the back of the cell.

Did something just whisper her name?

She didn't dare pause to listen for it a second time. She kept moving, unnerved.

It wasn't until she neared the end of the hallway that she stopped, startled by the sight of a small shape sitting on the floor and peering out from behind the bars. "There're children in there!" she exclaimed.

"I assure you they're not," said Tane without looking back.

Piper stared at the little girl in the cell. She wasn't one of the black-eyed children. Even from here she could see that she had big, blue eyes and long, blonde pigtails. She was about eight years old, dressed in ordinary blue jeans and a tee shirt with a cartoon unicorn on it. She was staring back at her, her small hands clutching the bars. She *looked* like a child. And yet, even as she watched, the little girl grinned a strangely evil-looking grin and something that looked like a long, black tail flicked in the darkness behind her.

Piper decided that he was probably right. That *wasn't* a child sitting in that cell. And she very much did *not* want anyone to let it out, whatever it was.

The three of them moved on to the end of the hallway and turned the corner. There was a row of narrow, barred windows, letting rectangles of sunlight shine down onto the naked concrete floor. And at the far end of the hallway was another half-open door.

Tane walked on toward it, but Seph and Piper found themselves drawn to the windows, instead.

Something was going on out there. Strange noises drifted through the thick glass. It sounded like shouting…but there were other sounds as well, like the roars and snarls of wild animals.

The windows were high up, and difficult to see through, especially with the blinding sunlight.

A shadow passed over them.

Something let out a terrible shriek.

Then dark blood splashed onto the glass.

"Those windows look out onto the main courtyard," explained Tane without turning around. "That commotion will be the Ahns engaging in combat with the white sisters."

Piper gasped. "The white sisters are here, too?"

"Of course they are."

"Those things tried to steal my pendant!"

"Yes, they did." Tane opened the door all the way and then paused and looked back at them. "They were attempting to lure out the Ahns."

"They were after the Ahns?" asked Seph.

"I summoned the white sisters for the sole purpose of keeping the Ahns busy," explained Tane. "They were never after *you*. *Or* the wheel."

"Those monsters *killed* Roseann!" cried Piper. "Maybe Annalee, too!"

Seph didn't point out that Piper didn't even know who Roseann was. She was pretty sure Annalisa introduced them to an Annalee ten months ago in her mother's apartment, but she couldn't remember which one she was. "Are you really *that* petty about them cheating you out of a few centuries of quality time with your stupid hammer?" she demanded.

Tane glared at her. "The Ahns are monsters, too, remember. And they've done plenty of awful things themselves in the past." He raised an eyebrow at them. "Or haven't they told you about that?"

Seph glanced over at Piper, uncertain.

"Cheating me was the least of their sins," he growled. "But it was the final straw for me."

"You have to stop them!" shouted Piper. "Make them go away!"

"There's no stopping them," said Tane. "They'll fight until they've eradicated the Ahns from existence, or until they, themselves are beaten back. And it doesn't look like they have Warner to protect them this time, I'm afraid. He'll be busy getting that girl who was so important to you out of Vertical Design."

"No…" Piper turned and squinted through the window. She

wished she could see what was going on out there.

"But look at the bright side," said Tane. "The Keeper seems pretty fond of those hags. Maybe he'll send his pets to help them. His hunter wraiths might be a fair match for my white sisters."

Both of them turned to stare at him.

"What?" said Seph.

"The mall wraiths?" said Piper.

A wicked sort of grin touched Tane's lips as he said, "Or didn't you know that it was *him* who first set those monsters after you all those months ago?"

"The *Keeper* sent the wraiths?" Seph shook her head. She thought it was the shepherd who set the wraiths on their trail. "No... Warner said..." What was it Warner told them that day, back when all this first began? That the wraiths answered to an "unspeakable evil" that wanted them dead? She still wasn't sure how trustworthy the Keeper was, but she didn't think he was an "unspeakable evil." And if he'd wanted them dead, she was fairly sure he'd have done it a long time ago.

"Warner doesn't know everything," replied Tane. "The hunter wraiths are mercenaries. Like that that traitor ringmaster. They work for whoever has something they want. And the Keeper *always* has something you want."

"No," said Piper. "Why would he do that?"

"You can't think of why he might do such a thing? Really?" He cocked his head to one side. "Why he'd send a pack of monsters after you who can only be stopped with the very weapon he wanted you to find?"

Seph stared at him. That made a terrible amount of sense, actually. But the wraiths were the ones who killed the first two spirit-eared people she saw. That barista at that coffee shop in Madison...Coby Bilk, his name was…and then that rude businessman in Cakwetak…Baxter Winger… Their bodies were found broken and mangled in plain sight of busy, public areas… Could the Keeper have really been responsible for those horrible deaths?

She turned and looked at Piper. It horrified her to remember how close she came to walking away when she first saw *her* spirit ears. She was in a hurry. She had an important job interview to get to. And it wasn't like the pretty blonde girl with the invisible animal ears was going to believe anything she said anyway. She had no kind of proof. If she hadn't changed her mind and gone back…

Was it really always supposed to be Piper by her side today? Or was it only because of the decision she made that day?

She pushed the thought from her head. It made her sick to think too much about it. And her thoughts turned instead to the slaughtered black-eyed children at Fathom Lake and the wraith perched on the roof of the pickup.

If not for that wraith, what would've happened on the shores of that lake after they landed?

And for that matter, wasn't there always someone there to save them from the wraiths? Warner saved them from the wraith at the mall that day. Lillyanna saved them from another one in that Taco Bell drive-through. Even the shepherd saved them from several of those things in Muntony, while he was pretending to be the librarian.

Thinking about it, why *wouldn't* the Keeper do something like that? With so many powerful forces protecting them, was there ever really any danger of the wraiths succeeding?

"For someone who adheres so vehemently to the rules," said Tane, "the Keeper sure seems to do a lot of *interfering*, don't you think?"

She squinted up at the window again. She was so confused…

What was she supposed to do? She wasn't even sure whose side she should be on at this point.

"Come on," said Tane. "Tartarus is just beyond this door. Regardless of what questions you still have, I know you're eager to get it over with."

Seph stared at him.

He wasn't wrong. But still, she was afraid.

Piper reached out and took her hand. "We'll do it together," she said.

Seph nodded.

Tane turned and walked through the doorway and Seph and Piper followed him.

Chapter 92

The gate to Tartarus wasn't like the gate that transported them from Tane's office. Nor was it precisely like the gates that took them into the Keeper's compendium. The room Seph and Piper found themselves in wasn't so much a room as a concrete dome built around a set of smooth, black steps leading down to what appeared to be a solid wall of Tartarus stone.

There was a single symbol carved into the surface for Seph to read. It was a very simple symbol, a single line, starting at the center and spiraling outward twice, then curving back on itself at the top and snaking upward briefly before it trailed off.

It wasn't the first time she saw this symbol. On the seventh floor of Vertical Design, on the third disk, the same symbol had been carved at the center of that strange mandala.

It was the ancient symbol for Tartarus. For the nexus from which the Architects would begin building the next universe.

And it wasn't just a symbol. She knew it as soon as she saw it. Tane was already descending the black stairs, walking straight toward it. Not just toward the symbol, but toward Tartarus itself. It was disorienting to think about, but in this case, the symbol and the thing it symbolized were very much one and the same.

Tane reached out to place his palm on the symbol and Seph took hold of the back of his jacket with one hand and Piper's hand with the other.

She didn't remember his hand actually touching the symbol. In an instant, she was lying on the floor, enveloped in perfect darkness. Her fingers were still enlaced with Piper's. She could see those spectral ears twitching this way and that, searching for sounds of danger in this unsettling blackness.

But her other hand was empty.

Where was Tane?

She sat up and fished out the flashlight she'd stashed in the pocket of her blazer. Beside her, Piper rummaged in her purse for her own. The effort, however, was scarcely worth the results. As soon as she turned it on, she found herself surrounded by nothing but that light-devouring Tartarus stone, reducing her vision to mere inches, even with the light.

"Are you okay?"

"So far…" whispered Piper.

Seph stood up and shined her light around. They appeared to be standing in a tunnel of pitch-black Tartarus stone. "Tane?"

Her voice sounded funny in this place. It didn't echo, exactly, but the sound was amplified somehow, and seemed to come back to her own ears from every direction at once.

Piper finally managed to locate her own flashlight. She switched it on. "Where'd he go?" she asked, wincing at the sound of her own voice as it flooded over her.

"I'm here," replied Tane. But where "here" was remained a mystery. Voices didn't seem to work the same way here, as strange as it seemed. It was impossible to follow them back to their source.

"Where?"

Then a heavy hand fell on her shoulder and she let out a scream.

"Relax," said Tane.

Piper turned and shined her light at him. His face looked strange. There was an odd sort of darkness bleeding from the shadows cast by his features that moved with her light. And his eyes had turned into smoldering, golden disks. She gasped and took a step back.

"What are you?" asked Seph.

"You didn't think one of the Twelve Teeth would be human, did you?" he asked them, managing to sound offended by their reaction to his freakish face.

Both of them stood there, shining their lights at him, watching the shadows as they danced across his skin.

There was something wrong with his hair, too. It almost looked as if something were moving around in it.

"It's difficult for me to hold my form inside Tartarus," he explained.

Seph leaned forward. Was it just a trick of the light, or did he have *two* noses? One *inside* the other? And…did his *ear* just *blink*?

"Would you please get those lights out of my face?"

Piper dropped hers immediately. "Sorry!"

But Seph only leaned a little closer. "Just a minute…" she said, staring at the strange shape of his lips.

Tane pushed the light aside and glared at her. "Can we please get down to business?"

"Fine!" she snapped. "Somebody's a little *sensitive* about how he looks without makeup…"

"Just follow me," he growled, pushing past them. "And stay close. Tartarus isn't very big, but it's comprised of an infinite number of infinite rings."

"Come again?" said Piper. "Infinite…*infinite*…?"

"If you're not careful, you'll only go in circles," he grumbled.

"Oh…"

A black wall materialized from the gloom and Tane turned right. Then he turned left at another wall. Then past several dark openings in the stone and then left again.

Seph squinted into the darkness ahead of them. Were they inside a labyrinth of black stone? Or were they weaving through an endless forest of black pillars? It was difficult to tell for sure.

Something caught Piper's eye and she shined her light down at Tane's butt. "Did you know you have a tail?" she asked.

"Focus please."

"Or…*three* tails, I think…"

"At least four," said Seph, pointing her own light at his butt.

"Do you *want* to be caught in an endless loop for all eternity?"

Piper stuck her tongue out at him.

"It's so dark…" said Seph. "I can barely see anything."

"Flashlights won't do you much good here," said Tane. "You should be using your gifts."

"Our gifts?" said Piper. "You mean like how Persephone was able to see in the dark in the library and Covengale?"

"Her prophet sight, yes."

Seph frowned. "But I wasn't able to make it work inside Zarechuff."

"And how would it help *me*?" asked Piper. "*I* don't have prophet sight."

"I have no idea how you could come this far and not know how to use your gifts," grumbled Tane. "But I suppose it doesn't matter. I know the way."

But he suddenly stopped.

"What's wrong?" asked Seph.

Tane didn't reply. He turned and leaned toward the wall. "What…?" he muttered.

Seph shined her light at the place he was looking. "What is it?" she asked, concerned.

He reached out with his fingertips—he suddenly had eight of them on that hand—and wiped at a spider web that was clinging there.

Behind him, Piper suddenly turned and looked behind her, her spirit ears perked and alert. "What was that?"

Seph turned and shined her light back that way, but it was pointless. It was swallowed up by the black stone almost as soon as it left the lens of the flashlight. "What was what? Did you hear something?"

She stared into the darkness, confused. "I'm…not sure," she replied. It wasn't a sound, exactly. It wasn't even one of those bizarre *not* sounds that she was used to hearing with her spirit ears. It was more like a brief flash of an image in her mind. A flicker of something, like a subliminal message on a television screen.

Tane turned and looked ahead of them. "This isn't right…" he murmured.

Seph turned her light on him again. Those shadows that had looked like tails before were churning in the darkness, as if agitated. "What is it?" Her heart was pounding again. He was right. Something was wrong. She could feel it. But what was it?

Piper gasped and turned, shining her light into an opening beside her.

A flash of movement, felt, not seen, another flicker of an image passing through her head.

"We're not alone," said Tane.

Seph turned in a circle, shining her useless light in every direction. She didn't understand what was happening. "I thought you said only the three of us could get in here."

He crept forward, peering at the walls ahead of him. There were more cobwebs here. *Lots* more. "Sometimes things sneak in," he explained. "Like the way Warner and the shepherd were able to sneak into the vault where the scythe was kept. Any number of creatures could've sneaked in with us. It would've taken something *very* powerful for me not to notice it, something on par with the Keeper, himself, but it's possible. The thing is..." He reached out and raked his fingers—now only three of them—through a dense film of gray cobwebs. "...that doesn't seem to be the case this time." He squinted into the darkness ahead of them, at the cobweb-covered Tartarus stone stretched out before him. "Something *beat us here.*"

Seph tried to process this. "But you said you were the only person with the power to open it!"

"I *am.*" He continued onward. The cobwebs grew thicker and thicker.

Piper turned and shined her light into the darkness behind her again. Something was moving over there, she was sure of it.

Several somethings.

She turned and peered down an opening to her left, then spun around and looked the other way. "Guys..." she whimpered.

Seph's heart was racing at full speed now. She stepped in front of Piper and tried to form the scythe. The water lurched from her hand in a great, thick, gooey glob. She cried out and shook her hands, splattering it against the walls. "What was that?" she squealed.

Tane reached out and tore away a curtain of heavy cobwebs.

"What do we do?" asked Piper.

Seph glanced back at Tane. "Whatever it is, you can handle it, right? I mean you're supposed to be one of the Twelve Teeth of the Great Enemy, right?"

"I am," he replied. "Although, for the record, it was the Ahns who coined the term 'Great Enemy.' It was called the 'Great Father' before they turned it into something *evil*."

"Whatever. But you're, like, *tough*. Right?"

He brushed aside another curtain of cobwebs, uncovering another opening in the Tartarus stone. "That depends entirely on what manner of thing was able to enter the nexus of the universe on its own."

Piper screamed, startled, and twirled around again. "There's something right over there!" she said, pointing into the shadows.

Seph turned to look, but she couldn't see anything. Again, she tried to take out the scythe. It lurched out, briefly taking the shape of the handle, but then it splattered onto the ground and oozed from her hand. She cursed and wiped it on the wall.

This was a new level of broken. Why was it all goopy? What was wrong with it? If ever there was a time that she needed it, it was now.

She turned and looked at Piper. "Use the wheel!"

Piper looked over at her, then down at her hand. Immediately, her fingers began glowing. It was brighter than her flashlight, but still not bright enough to see by. "What do I make?"

"I don't know! Something to help us see!"

She looked up at her again. "Like what? Flashlights don't work!"

"I don't know!"

But Piper looked down and found that she was suddenly holding a burning highway flare. "Oh. Okay then."

Seph stared at it, puzzled. That was like some kind of magic trick. She couldn't quite wrap her head around it.

Piper turned and threw the flare back the way they came. As it bounced across the black floor, several small things could be seen scuttling away from it.

Seph's already racing heart suddenly leapt into her throat.

Bugs…

Big ones…

She backed away, fresh terror filling her.

Why were there bugs here?

"Tane?"

Piper cried out again and turned to look behind her. Again, she held up a lit flare and threw it. Again, several things on scurrying bug legs darted from its path.

Seph closed her eyes and tried to calm her frantic heart.

Tane pushed his way through the cobwebs. Something was there. He could almost see it. "I have a bad feeling about this," he said.

"Is this supposed to be happening?" squealed Piper. "Because I really don't get the feeling that this is supposed to be happening!"

When Seph opened her eyes again, she found that the darkness had gone away. She was still surrounded by black stone, but suddenly it was as if everything else had begun to glow with an eerie, white light.

There were bugs everywhere she looked. Fat, squatty things on spindly, cricket legs, about the size of large housecats, with sharp little crab claws and huge, needle-like teeth protruding from bizarre, fish-like faces, like an unholy fusion of a beetle, a scorpion and a deep-sea anglerfish.

She turned around as Tane ripped aside one final curtain of cobwebs and revealed a sinister shadow standing at the far end of the corridor.

She stared at it. She knew that silhouette…

It looked just like the picture Connor showed them. The shadow in the window overlooking the black council's chairs that were themselves overlooking that horrific operating theater.

"The Empress of Zarechuff…" she breathed.

Chapter 93

"It couldn't have gotten in on its own," said Tane.

Piper turned and squinted into the darkness. "What got in? What's happening? I can't see anything!"

"Tartarus is sealed absolutely when the new universe is completed. If Gispuknya is here now…"

"Gispuknya's *here*?"

"…then it must've *always* been here…" Tane went on, "…sealed away since the end of this world's creation, biding its time, feeding off the energy of Tartarus itself…" He took a step back and shook his head. "No wonder it grew so powerful in this universe!"

…it was never this strong before… Seph thought, remembering the words of the slime lady she encountered in Avelby ten months ago. *…never in all the worlds that came before…something about this world…gave it new strength…made it…more dangerous…*

Seph stared at the woman standing before them. She couldn't make out her face from here. Even with her prophet sight working at full power again, she couldn't peer through the darkness that enveloped her head and neck. Below her neck, however, her flesh shined almost white in this weird new light.

She was simultaneously naked and *not* naked. Seph could see the shapes of her arms and her breasts and her belly. But below the woman's waist, her body was all wrong. The color and texture of her skin continued all the way down to the shadows that concealed her feet, but her lower half had the *shape* of a long dress. It was as if the monster had taken the shape of the woman who used to be the Empress of Zarechuff, but didn't realize that the dress she was wearing wasn't a part of her body, resulting in a horrific sort of *skin skirt*. And there was something deeply, *deeply* unsettling about it.

"This is *really* bad," said Tane. "That thing is *far* more powerful than it has any right to be. It's saturated in Tartarus energy."

Piper stared into the darkness, trying to make out the shadow that Tane and Seph were staring at. Seph called it the Empress of Zarechuff, referring to that picture Connor showed them of that evil woman who was supposedly the ultimate ruler of that horrible place, the one who commanded even the black council. So she had a pretty good idea of what must be looming there in the gloom. But she couldn't hear that buzzing sound that accompanied Gispuknya's other shadows. Was it because this empress thing was so powerful? Or did it have something to do with this strange place? Something about all the Tartarus stone, perhaps?

"What do we do?" asked Seph.

Tane's hands burst into flames. The hammer flickered into existence, burning away the cobwebs around him. "You two get to the nexus. I'll push her back and meet you there."

Seph turned and looked around. The empress' bugs were closing in all around them. "Um…"

"*Go*!" shouted Tane as he rushed forward.

The empress raised her arms. *All* of her arms. Great, shadowy, spider-like legs emerged from the darkness behind her, curling around her body.

"Oh, *hell no*!" gasped Seph, backing away. She was *not* dealing with *that*. She took Piper's hand and darted into an opening, hoping to circle around the freaky spider lady while Tane distracted her.

"What's happening?" cried Piper.

"Just come on! We have to get to the nexus!"

"I don't even know what a nexus is!"

"It can't be that hard to find!" Seph reasoned. "It's probably the only thing here!"

Ahead of them, several of those awful bugs scurried into the path. "Persephone!"

"I see them," Seph assured her. "This way!" She turned and darted between two black columns.

"You can see?"

"I can." She could see everything. The world had opened up before her. Her head was clear. Again, she tried to take out her scythe, but again, it refused. The water wouldn't even form around her hand. There was only that gross, oozing goo. It dripped from her hand in greasy globs and splattered onto the black stone at her feet. "Oh my god! What's wrong with this thing?" It was the only weapon she had. Why was it doing this? What was she doing wrong? "Can *you* make any weapons?"

"What kind of weapon?"

"*Any* kind of weapon!"

"I don't know." She looked down at her glowing hand, but nothing was happening. "It's hard! I don't know anything about weapons!"

Seph turned a corner and stumbled to a stop. One of the bugs was rushing toward her, its pincers and teeth snapping together, threatening her. She cried out, horrified, and thrust her hands out at it in pure reflex. A great glob of goo sloshed from her fingers and splattered on the floor in front of the bug.

To her surprise, it stopped. In fact, it backed away from the goo, refusing to go near it.

She looked down at the sludge dripping from her hand. What just happened? Was this some new bug-repellant form the scythe had taken?

She lifted both of her hands, curious, and flicked them at the bug, splashing the strange scythe sludge at it. The thing turned and fled. "Okay…" she said. "Weird…but I'll take it."

"I still don't know what's going on!" whined Piper.

Seph wiped her hands on her skirt and hurried onward. "Just come on!"

Piper followed her as she wove between the Tartarus stone pillars, through the otherworldly, black labyrinth, dodging those hideous monsters that kept darting out in front of them, forcing them to change direction. Strange and unsettling things kept flashing through her mind, glimpses of her confusing surroundings and those freaky, fish-faced bugs. She didn't understand this at all. Everything was happening so fast and she couldn't see anything.

Somewhere along the way, she took a wrong turn.

She'd been trying to follow the sound of Seph's startled cries as she dodged those awful bugs, but the sounds in this place were still wrong. Suddenly she was all alone and she had no idea which way she needed to go to catch back up.

She bumped into a wall and stumbled, dropping her flashlight. She bent to pick it up but another of those weird visions flashed through her brain and she snatched her hand back just in time to avoid losing her fingers to a pair of those hideous jaws.

She screamed and backed away, bumping into another wall.

Then she saw another image, this one of one of those sharp claws right next to her foot. She jumped back, blind, but not before a sharp pain blossomed above her left ankle. She cried out and turned to flee, feeling her way along the Tartarus stone.

This was bad. She was trapped in this darkness all alone, surrounded by monsters. It was only a matter of time before they overwhelmed her.

Somewhere, Seph was calling out for her. She could hear her. But where was she? It was like the "sounds" she heard with her spirit ears. It had no volume. It was impossible to discern how far away Seph was. But unlike her spirit ears, she couldn't even determine which *direction* her voice was coming from.

"*Persephone*!" she cried.

"*Where are you*?" called Seph.

But she didn't know where she was. There was nothing here to even describe her location because everything in this place was the same kind of nothing.

Another image flashed through her head: two of those little monsters, scuttling across the floor in front of her. She stopped and backed away, but another image showed her a third right behind her. Too close. Too late. Another of those nasty claws snapped shut on her right calf, sending a bolt of pain all the way up her leg and making her scream.

"*Pea*!" shouted Seph.

Piper backed away from the monsters and into another opening in the walls, her hands groping at the Tartarus stone behind her.

Another of those flashes showed a bug there on the wall, but again, too late. She felt those awful teeth chomp down on her fingers and screamed again. She jerked her hand back, sobbing, and turned around, her eyes wide open, trying to somehow peer through the blind darkness. Another of those claws reached out and sank into her right thigh. When she jumped away, something else bit into her other leg.

She pressed her knees together and wrapped her arms around herself, trying to become as small as possible. Somehow, in the midst of all this terror, she managed to wonder if this was the kind of fear that Seph felt every time she saw a bug. Was this why she sometimes froze up? Was this why she couldn't get into the water that day in the swamp? Was this why she lost her wits when she stumbled into that cobweb-infested tunnel under Adderbell's in Avelby last summer?

Then, as tears streamed down her face, she closed her eyes, too afraid to move, and another image flashed through her head.

But this was more than a flash. It wasn't there and then gone, like the others. The image that flooded her brain opened like a great eye and *stayed open*. Suddenly, she could see!

No…not *see*, exactly. This was different.

She'd backed herself into a corner. She could see the curve of the Tartarus stone, the layout of the floor around her. There were two bugs clinging to the wall right in front of her and three more on the floor scuttling toward her.

She could see *all* the bugs, even the ones moving around behind the pillars where she shouldn't be able to see.

And she could see in every direction at once.

She could even see Seph. She was only about thirty feet away, desperately trying to find her while dodging those awful bugs.

It was a strange sort of vision. There was no color. No brightness or darkness. No light or shadows. And yet everything looked strangely shiny, as if every surface were wet and slippery.

This wasn't any kind of vision at all, she realized. This was her spirit ears. This was her brain piecing together the information they were gathering and presenting it to her in a way that she could envision.

This was her version of Seph's prophet sight overdrive that let her see even in perfect darkness.

"*Pea*!" cried Seph. "*Where are you*?"

There were tears in her voice.

Piper looked down at her hand. She was suddenly holding a large, golden mallet. "I'm here!" she called out. "I'm coming!"

These stupid bugs weren't nearly as frightening when she could see where they all were. They couldn't jump out and surprise her anymore. They couldn't hide in the darkness. They couldn't ambush her exposed ankles again.

One by one she began mashing the little beasts. They made strangely satisfying little cries when she hit them, something between a hiss and a squeak.

It felt like the world's largest game of Whack-A-Mole.

Seph would be so proud of her if she could see her now!

"Where?" shouted Seph. She peered around a black pillar. She could see everything clearly, and all the way to the end of every little passageway, but she couldn't see through the Tartarus stone. And it was still impossible to tell where Piper's voice was coming from. Was she even going in the right direction?

Fortunately, the bugs didn't seem all that aggressive. They kept fleeing from her path as she moved around. They didn't seem to like the scythe goo, which was weird because that was literally the only thing keeping her from forming the scythe and chopping the little freaks into pieces.

But she was still lost.

And worse still, she'd lost Piper! Was she okay? She'd heard her screaming a moment ago. She sounded terrified. If something happened to her…

Then she turned a corner and saw her. She was moving toward her, pausing every few steps to crush one of the empress' foul bugs with a fat hammer. "Pea?"

Piper didn't look at her. Her eyes were closed, as if she were concentrating very hard on listening, but she walked straight toward her, dodging the Tartarus stone where it jutted out into her path and pausing every few steps to pound another of those nasty bugs into mush.

"You okay?" she asked.

The mallet melted back into that brilliant, golden light and Piper reached out and grabbed her hand without opening her eyes. "I'm fine. Are *you* okay?"

"I'm okay."

She tilted her head to one side and then the other. Those spectral ears swiveled back and forth, taking in every "sound" of Tartarus. Then she pointed. "There's something different over there," she reported. "Steps, I think."

"How do you know that?"

"I think my spirit ears gave me *echolocation*."

"Oh. Well *that's* pretty cool…"

"I know, right? Come on." Clinging tightly to Seph's hand, she made her way through the stone to a great, shadowy archway, where there was, indeed, a set of black steps ascending into more darkness.

"This has to be it, right?" said Seph. "I mean, it's the only thing here."

"The nexus," agreed Piper.

But before either of them could begin to climb the steps, Tane's beaten and bloody body thudded onto the floor behind them.

Chapter 94

The empress crawled out of the darkness above them, descending the walls of Tartarus on her countless spider legs, drawing ever closer.

"What the heck *is* that thing?" asked Piper. It was still far too dark to see anything with her human eyes. And her spirit ears didn't show her the frightful woman-shaped monstrosity that Seph was staring at. In fact, it didn't show her anything she could comprehend. Its shape kept changing. All she saw was a bizarre, twisting, *bristling* form crawling down those strange, shiny walls.

Seph, on the other hand, could see the empress just fine. Far better than she wanted to, in fact. She wasn't a spider, she realized. Not exactly, anyway. She had far more than eight of those shadowy legs, first of all. And she had no discernable spider-like shape, just that weird skin skirt that seemed to taper into a strange, fleshy tail.

Just looking at her made Seph's skin crawl.

Tane grunted and sat up. "That's Gispuknya, herself," he replied. "The bug's very consciousness. Its *soul*, you might say."

Seph stared at the hideous form. Tane had caused it *some* damage, at least. She could make out gashes in its body from which black blood was oozing. Several of those spindly legs seemed to have been broken. And even from this distance she could see that the burning hammer had left blisters on her pale skin. But she didn't seem to have slowed down at all.

In contrast, Tane wasn't looking good. (*What she could see of him*, at least; his body was still shifting in and out of view, making it impossible for her to fully understand what she was seeing, even with her prophet sight.) He was covered in blood and the parts of his strangely shifting body that she *could* make out appeared battered and broken.

"It looks like we aren't going to have a choice for this one," he groaned. He turned and looked up at them, his face a twisted mix of shadow and light and warped features. "Listen to me. My job, as the Tooth of the Cycle, was to make sure that no one used the rebuilding of the universe as a weapon to use against the Great Father. But over time I became disgusted at the increasing horrors of the murdered universes. I really did want to create a better cycle. But at this point, there's a real danger of it all ending…" He turned his gaze back to the approaching empress. "That thing isn't going to let us all enter the nexus."

"What do we do?" asked Piper.

"There's only one thing we *can* do," replied Tane. He reached out and pointed one of his many fingers at her heart. A ball of crimson fire erupted between them.

She let out a startled yelp and slapped at her chest. "Ow! Hot!"

"Stop it!" gasped Seph, pulling her away from him.

Piper stared down at her chest.

The golden chain on which the pendant Annalisa gave her once hung was no longer just a chain. A new pendant was hanging from it, this one a great, teardrop-shaped lump of smoking, black glass. She lifted the chain and let it dangle in front of her face as she looked at it. "Is this…?"

"Noah's hammer," confirmed Tane. "Take it to the nexus. I'll hold the bug bitch off as long as I can. Wake the Architects now! Before we lose our chance forever!"

"Wait..." said Seph. "*What?*"

But Tane was already on his feet and stumbling toward the empress. "And about what I said the other morning...about your talent as an artist? I lied. I want you to know that...just in case I don't get another chance to tell you."

She stared at him, surprised.

"I told you...I've been watching you a long time." He paused and glanced back at her. For the moment, his face was human again. It was the face of Mr. Pealmonger, her old art teacher. "Say what you will about me...but in all that time...I did become a little attached to you..."

She shook her head. "What...?"

"Now go!" he shouted.

And then Janon Tane turned into something awful. His body unraveled itself into a great, black, churning shape that seemed to pass in and out of existence before her eyes. It sprang up into the air like something fired from a cannon and collided with the empress with enough force to shatter the Tartarus stone behind her, sending up a great cloud of dust and raining debris down around them.

One of the monsters let out a terrible screech, but she wasn't sure which one.

"Come on!" said Piper. "We have to go!" She didn't need to stay and watch. She could "see" the whole thing clearly enough even with her back turned. Two very distinct and very terrible shapes were colliding over and over again.

Seph turned and followed her up the steps. She was so confused. She had no idea how she was supposed to feel right now.

And neither did Piper. She "watched" as those two shapes behind them crashed through another pillar of Tartarus stone. On one hand, Tane was the enemy. He'd done terrible things. But he'd just entrusted her with returning Noah's hammer to the nexus while he held off Gispuknya's empress…

Was he a bad guy or was he a good guy?

Things are rarely black and white, Maria had warned her. And later, in Zarechuff, Connor echoed those words.

It wasn't black and white. It wasn't good and evil.

Then what was it?

What were they supposed to do?

It was all so confusing…

And now, on top of everything else, it was all going terribly wrong. Gispuknya was literally the bug in the machine. It'd somehow crept into Tartarus eons ago, way back when the Architects were last awake, and allowed itself to be sealed away in this unearthly realm of darkness and stone. It used the mysterious energy of Tartarus to grow stronger and stronger, allowing it to do things that should've been impossible, like stealing the Ahns' playground and shattering the vault where the hammer was slumbering.

Did Sandy know that all this was going to happen? She couldn't help but wonder. Way back at the beginning of their journey, when she warned them about the devil and the wretch, did she know that the empress would be waiting for them when they entered this place?

And what about the Keeper? He was the Keeper of the Cycle, after all. The Keeper of Tartarus. The Keeper of *lots of things*. Did *he* know the bug was here? Surely the Keeper of the Nexus and all its strange, broken time should've at least been able to sense the foul thing in here.

Right?

But she didn't understand anything. How could she? How were

they supposed to know what was right from what was wrong in all these worlds of broken clocks and amber threads?

They climbed the steps until their legs burned and they could barely breathe, but finally they reached the top. Here, set into the wall before them, was a fourth and final Architects' disk. This one's surface was utterly blank, even to Seph's prophet sight, except for three small holes, one round, one teardrop-shaped and one crescent-shaped.

"This is it?" scoffed Seph. "Just fit the shapes in their stupid holes? All the crap we went through and it really just leads up to a cosmic *preschool toy*?"

Piper shrugged. It *did* seem a little anticlimactic, she supposed... But she wasn't about to complain about something finally being *easy*. She lifted the chain over her head and then held it up in front of her, letting Tane's strange pendant dangle in front of her face. Besides...while this one should be easy enough to insert into the disk, she had no idea how to turn the wheel back into that little, golden ring to make it fit in the hole.

Seph frowned. She'd never seen the scythe take a form like that. She assumed it somehow turned into a crescent-shaped pendant. That was basic process of elimination. Plus, it kind of made sense, given the shape of a scythe, she guessed...

Piper continued to stare at the hammer's stone, both with her real eyes in the golden light of the wheel emanating from her hand and with her trippy new spirit vision. The two at once should've been strange and disorienting, but they worked surprisingly well together, giving it a weirdly three-dimensional quality...which was also weird because it was already a three-dimensional object...

So strange.

There was a soft, red glow deep inside the stone, like a glowing ember just waiting there for Tane to command the flames again.

The strangest feeling passed through her, a faint but certain sense that this object dangling from her fingers *didn't like her.*

From somewhere in the darkness came a great, rumbling crash and a distant cry of pain.

"Hurry up and put it in!" gasped Seph. She turned and looked back the way they came. Maybe if the hammer's Architect awakened, it would rush to Tane's aid and help him defeat the empress.

Piper took hold of the pendant and reached out toward the hole with it, but at that very moment, the darkness of Tartarus was filled with a terrible, wailing roar of a scream and the black stone violently cracked in her hand.

She cried out, startled, and snatched it back. "What happened?"

Seph stared at it, her heart sinking. "Did Tane just…?"

Piper's heart leapt. She turned and looked back the way they came.

Something was coming.

And it wasn't Tane.

She turned and placed the cracked crystal into the disk. It would probably still work. Right? Maybe it was only the outer part of the crystal that was attached to Tane. Maybe that glowing ember inside was the *real* hammer and it would still work just fine.

The Architect would awaken. It would slaughter the spider empress and heal Tane and the cycle would continue and they could go back to living their lives in peace and quiet.

She just had to figure out how to put the wheel back into that little pendant…

But before she could even begin to ponder how to do such a thing, the hammer's stone exploded and the disk around it shattered.

All around them, the Tartarus stone began to crack and crumble.

The thing on the stairs was getting closer. Seph could see those long, black legs probing at the trembling walls.

"*Persephone*?" squealed Piper.

Seph stepped forward and tried once again to take out the scythe. Instead, a great, gelatinous mass belched from her hands and splattered on the floor at her feet. She took a step backward, surprised, and slipped, nearly falling. She looked down to find that she was covered in that strange, gray sludge. It seemed to ooze from every pore, cold and slimy. It dripped from her fingers. It oozed down her cheeks. Her hair and clothes were plastered to her skin. "What's happening?"

Piper stood there, terrified. What *was* happening? The scythe had turned to goo? The hammer had broken? And Tane… Could he really be *dead*?

Where did they go wrong?

"Pea…" gasped Seph. The goo was filling her mouth, making it harder and harder to breathe, much less talk. "Help me…"

But Piper didn't know how to help her. She looked down at her glowing hand. What did she do? How did she make everything right again?

Behind her, the disk cracked again. A large chunk broke off of it and crashed onto the ground.

And when she looked back over at the stairs, the empress was there, her shadowy, blank face peering back at her from the gloom.

There was something there, she realized, something she couldn't quite see with either her human eyes *or* her spirit vision, but rather *sensed* somehow.

There was something *inhuman* where her face should've been. Something *bug-like*.

Seph sank to her knees, coughing and spitting.

Piper stood over her, trembling with fear. "*What do I do*?" she cried.

The empress' empty face expanded into a gaping darkness and she made a horrible hissing noise.

This was the end, she realized. They'd lost. The bug had laid a trap for them and they walked right into its web.

A terrified sob escaped her. It wasn't fair.

This was cheating.

Gispuknya cheated.

Why did everyone keep cheating?

Chapter 95

The Ahns cheated by giving Piper the spinning wheel. The Keeper cheated by giving the Ahns the hammer. Tane cheated by involving the shepherd and the incubus. And now Gispuknya had cheated by building a nest inside Tartarus and killing a seeker.

Piper found herself wondering for some reason if *they'd* ever cheated, too. It wouldn't have been hard. It wasn't as if anyone ever explained the rules to them. They just ran from one place to the next, trying to find things they didn't know existed while running away from things that kept trying to kill them. They did so much running… They ran from Cakwetak to Messing Knob to Harv Tottlestep's humming chicken farm. They ran all the way to Muntony and Fathom Lake in South Dakota, through the depths of the terrifying fringe road all the way to Shawbeck Ranch. They ran to the mounds of Sukmukwe, to the strange tunnels of Avelby and into the terrifying waters of Fibbel Marsh. The Ahn's playground in Tennessee. Nora's Lilac Grove in Missouri. Waybel Valley in Florida. The depths of Fathom Lake and the nightmarish battle of Pobsick Spring. The heights of Vertical Design and the empty gateway floor of the Arkansas research facility.

So much running…

It was bound to happen, she supposed. Eventually they were going to end up somewhere they couldn't run away from.

And then they'd never leave that place ever again.

As she stared into that awful, cavernous darkness that was slowly opening in the shadowy depths where the empress' face should've been, she couldn't help but wonder if it was all a lie. If they were always meant to end up like this.

Sandy and her amber threads… Did all the threads lead here? Was this their inescapable destiny the whole time? Did she know from the very beginning that she was sending them to their doom?

The Ahns' insistence that there would always be a way… Well she didn't see a way out of this one, no matter how many ways she had of looking at it.

Surprisingly, she found that she wasn't even bitter. She was afraid. She was *terrified*. But she wasn't bitter. If anything, she was just sad.

Her friends.

Her parents.

Her *sister*… Penny… She wished she could've seen her again, just one more time.

"…Tartarus…is broken…" came a strange voice over the sounds of cracking stone and the empress' creepy hissing.

Piper turned and looked around, confused. Neither her human eyes nor her shiny new spirit vision could determine the source of the voice.

"…the Tooth…is dead…"

Seph spat onto the floor and then lifted her head. That voice… That goopy, oozing, drip-drop sort of voice…

"…the cycle…is forever…ended…"

She *knew* that voice.

Piper lowered her hand, aiming the wheel's golden glow at the floor in front of Seph.

That strange, gooey slime was *moving.*

"...the time...has finally come...for a *new* ending..."

"You..." gasped Seph.

A lean, slender form stood up before her, the form of a woman, her body glistening in the weird light of her prophet sight. Globs of grayish slime oozed off of her, dripping from her fingertips.

The slime lady... The last time Seph saw her, she was a ghoulish figure in filthy rags sliding toward her in the darkness of a locked storm drain, a hideous monster she was convinced was going to devour her. But instead, she was thrust into a pitch-black dream world where she was told about the existence of the black council and given clues about how to find the Ahns' stolen property and defeat the bug god.

She had no idea what manner of creature the slime lady was, but she claimed to be a sworn enemy of Gispuknya, and therefore her ally in this struggle. And in the end, she'd been right. Her clues successfully led them to the second Architects' disk and then to the Ahns' playground, where the Ahns were able to defeat the black council, temporarily crippling the bug so that the hammer could be safely retrieved.

Seph recalled floating in that strange dream world, listening to the slime lady's mysterious words. When she was done speaking, she'd pressed her slimy body against her and enveloped her. She awoke gasping, believing that she was going to drown in that cold, gray ooze, only to find the slime lady gone.

Now she realized that it wasn't a dream at all. The slime lady really did envelop her. More than that, she'd somehow seeped *inside her*! She'd been lurking there since that day, biding her time, waiting for the moment she'd be able to stand against Gispuknya here in Tartarus.

No wonder the scythe had been so glitchy!

And now that she thought about it, weren't the clues there all along? She remembered looking at her hands when it first began acting up and thinking that the water looked muddy for a moment. And how many times did she encounter that gray slime? She put her hand in it when she was hanging out the back of the old Ram, trying to reap the wretch, and again in the scrap yard while climbing over the junk the Sugnog spilled. She slipped on some of it in Pappy Stan's kitchen. Some had even landed on her hand way back at Shawbeck Ranch, when they were running from those flutters. She'd mistaken it for exploding butterfly guts.

"What is that?" gasped Piper. It was too dark to see the shape that was standing before her with her human eyes and her spirit ears couldn't seem to make any sense of it. It was just a blurry, mushy sort of thing without any proper outline. "What's happening?"

"…listen…for their voices…" said the slime lady, her voice oozing through the weird atmosphere of Tartarus. "…let them…guide you…" And with that, she threw herself at that gaping, hissing darkness swirling within the empress' face and both the spider and the slime lady went tumbling down the stairs with a furious screech.

Seph rose to her feet. Her heart was still racing and she was still trembling, but that awful slime that covered her body a moment ago had all dried up, like when the scythe retracted and left her completely dry in spite of having just been soaking wet. All that remained was a fine, sticky residue that made her feel dirty. "We have to go!"

"Go *where?*"

Seph didn't know. But the slime lady just told them that Tartarus was broken and the cycle had ended. That meant that they'd failed in their mission. She looked back at the crumbling disk. There was no awakening the Architects now. The only thing left to do was find a way out of this black hell before it all came crashing down on top of them.

She turned and scanned the room. "There!" she said, grabbing Piper's hand and leading her toward a narrow passage in the Tartarus stone.

Piper looked back over her shoulder at the stairs that brought them here. Another fight was going on over there, and this time it seemed to be the empress that was outmatched. She let out another terrible screech. Black gore and slime splattered against the wall.

This was like something out of a nightmare. Was there even a way out of here? Opening the other gates required the custodian, both to enter and to leave. This time, Tane had acted as the custodian. Only he could do it. That was why the doors weren't locked. There was no point.

So did that mean they were trapped here? After everything they'd done, were they just going to die in this horrible darkness?

It didn't seem fair.

Seph stumbled to a stop and held out her arm. "Whoa!" she cried.

The two of them stood at the edge of a sheer drop, staring down at the cracked floor several stories below them.

"Other way!"

Piper turned and looked back the way they came. "How do we get out of here?"

But Seph didn't know. "Just keep going!" she cried.

Around them, slime had begun to drip from the walls. It was oozing from the very cracks, slowly coating every surface.

The slime lady wasn't just another monster. She was something far more powerful. Was she like the Keeper, Seph wondered. Or was she something even greater?

Piper slipped and fell.

Seph stopped and helped her back up. "Are you okay?"

"Slippery…" she groaned, rubbing at her butt.

Seph turned and looked around. This was pointless. They weren't getting anywhere. They couldn't just run away. Tane warned them that Tartarus was filled with an infinite number of infinite rings. If they tried to flee blindly, they'd only run in circles.

They needed to stop and think.

There had to be an answer.

But did there really? Did the Ahns' assertation that there would always be a way, no matter how dire the situation, really extend to this level of messed up? One of the Hands was destroyed! One of the seekers was *dead*! And worst of all, the cycle was broken. There wasn't going to be another universe. The world was doomed to end and there would never be another one and it was all their fault!

This sucked on such an epic scale that she could scarcely even begin to comprehend it…

Maybe it was better this way. After all, how were they really supposed to go back and face the Ahns and Warner now? How could they face the Keeper? Surely he'd be furious at them for screwing this up.

Maybe it was better if they just never came back at all…

As she stood up, Piper's cell phone rang. She frowned and reached into her purse. "How do I have service in here?" But when she looked at the screen, it was dark.

Yet the ringing continued…

She looked up at Seph, confused, then reached into her pocket and pulled out a second phone. She'd forgotten about this one. It was Stacy Getledder's…the one that was lying on the floor in the Vertical Design lobby after Warner made her disappear…the one she picked up and stuffed in her pocket so the network administrator with the silly mustache wouldn't see it and become suspicious.

But the call wasn't for Stacy. There was no name or number displayed for the caller, but the screen was glowing the same bright gold as the spinning wheel's curious energy.

She put it on speaker and held it between them. "Hello?"

Seph's voice drifted up to them from the speaker: "It's just like the tomb in Amethyst's warehouse," she said. "It's the gateway. We're the key."

Seph frowned. "Was that *me*?"

Then Piper's voice came out of the golden phone. "But what about the gate? Amethyst isn't here to open it."

Piper stared at the screen. "What?"

Seph cocked her head. This conversation sounded familiar.

Then Wanda's voice came over the line: "You don't need a gate to open it. You have the scythe."

No… Not Wanda. It was her voice, but not her words.

Piper pointed at the phone. "This is us and Warner outside the church that last morning in Avelby, isn't it?" Right after they'd defeated the incubus and right before they lost the hammer to Tane. "We were talking about the Ahns' vault. The one in the weeping angel rock."

Another terrible shriek filled the air and the ground beneath their feet shook as if a bomb had gone off. Behind them, close enough to make their hearts stutter in their chests, a great chunk of Tartarus stone crashed to the ground.

"Will that work?" asked Seph's voice from inside the phone and ten months ago.

"No reason it shouldn't," replied Warner in Wanda's voice. "The Hands are pretty much all-powerful."

Then the screen cracked in her hand and went dark. It refused to turn back on.

"That was when Warner was telling us that we didn't need a vault guard to enter the vault, remember?"

Piper tossed the phone away. It was dead and its owner was gone. There didn't seem to be any reason to hold onto it. "So…is the wheel trying to tell us that we never needed a custodian to open the Keeper's gates?"

"I don't know, but I think it's trying to tell us that we don't need *Tane* to open *Tartarus*." She looked down at her hands. The water was flowing over them, clean and clear and free of the slime lady's gray goop.

Piper frowned. "Why would the Hands care about saving us? We messed up."

Another explosion shook the grounds. A large crack split the Tartarus stone directly over their heads.

Seph stared up at the crack. "Maybe they just don't want to get buried here forever. Who cares?" She pushed past her and hurried back down the passageway to the chamber with the broken disk. It was nice and open here. There should be enough room.

She thrust her arms out and the scythe sprang from her palms, its blade shining like sunlight to her prophet sight. "That's the way it's supposed to feel!" she exclaimed. Then she lifted the scythe and turned to face the cracked disk.

"Are you sure about this?" gasped Piper.

"We don't have time to be sure of anything!" She swung the scythe. Its watery tip sank deep into a crack in the Tartarus stone, opening a great, glowing fissure. She grunted and pushed at the handle, but this stuff was harder than it looked. "Help me!"

"How?"

"I don't know! Just do something!"

Another terrible shriek shook the floor. Seph had no idea what was going on over there, but somehow she found that she knew the empress wasn't winning this battle. Whatever that slime woman was, she was a force far greater than any bug god.

Piper stepped forward and thrust her hand out. A great, golden rod wedged itself in the crack beneath the scythe's blade, splitting the stone even more.

Shining, white light poured out.

"Keep going!" grunted Seph.

"The blade!" cried Piper.

Seph saw it, too. The blade of the scythe was beginning to crack, just like the walls around them.

The rod, too, was beginning to crack.

"*Persephone*!"

"*I see it*!"

It shouldn't have been possible. First of all, these were the Hands of the Architects. They were supposed to be indestructible! How could they be cracking? And secondly, how was it possible for *water* and *light* to crack?

"Do we stop?"

"We can't! We'll be trapped here if we don't open it!"

"But the Hands!"

"We don't have a choice!" cried Seph. "The Architects told us to use the Hands! It's the only way!" And even as she said this, she knew that this was the will of the Architects. She could hear a voice inside her head, very faint but also very powerful, urging her to push on.

This was the will of the Architects.

This was how it had to be.

Piper, too, heard the voice speaking to her through the spinning wheel. It was strangely comforting. It told her to keep pushing and that everything would be okay. And she really did feel like it was going to be okay. Even as Tartarus fell apart all around her, she found herself confident that everything would work out just fine.

The cracks in the blade and the rod spread.

Then there was a tremendous explosion of blinding light and everything went white.

Chapter 96

When they opened their eyes, the chaos of Tartarus had vanished. They were lying on their backs again, staring up through a curtain of softly fluttering tree branches at a clear, blue sky.

"Pea?" said Seph.

"Uh huh," said Piper.

"You still okay?"

"Uh huh."

"That's good."

"Is it over?"

"I'm...not sure."

Both of them sat up and looked around. They were in the middle of a forest, without a single structure in sight.

"Where are we?" asked Piper.

But Seph didn't even have a guess. She didn't know much about nature. Her father had tried to teach her on various occasions, but she'd never been very good at listening. She was always far too distracted by all the stupid *bugs*.

Even now, she jumped to her feet and brushed herself off, convinced that she'd been lying there long enough to be covered in ticks and spiders and all manner of gross things.

"You're back in Arkansas," said a familiar voice.

Both of them turned to find a grubby-looking man with a shaggy beard and a deeply lined face sitting at the base of an old oak tree. He looked just the way he did the last time Seph saw him, a year and a half ago. He was even still wearing the same tattered coat and dirty sock cap.

"The research facility is just beyond the hill to the north."

"You…" said Piper. She was still sitting on the ground, far less concerned with all the bugs she might be sharing it with than Seph was. She was just happy to sit for a while. "You're the Keeper…"

"I am," replied the man. Except he wasn't a man at all. Seph's supercharged prophet sight seemed to have switched back off again the moment they entered this sunny forest, but as she stood staring at him, it flickered inside her head a few times, giving her a fleeting glimpse of something much stranger.

"We failed," said Piper, lowering her head. "We messed up bad. Tane is…"

"He is gone," said the Keeper. "The tooth is pulled. I'm aware."

"We weren't able to awaken the Architects," explained Seph. "Gispuknya was there. That woman from Zarechuff… She…"

"I'm aware of that, too," said the Keeper.

Seph stared at him, confused. "You are?"

Again, her prophet sight flickered. He wasn't really sitting beneath the tree. He was standing. He was just much smaller than he appeared…

"And I'm aware that the Hands have all been broken."

Seph's heart leaped in her chest. The scythe! She looked down at her hands, but they remained dry. She remembered those impossible cracks in the watery blade. And then that great blast of white light.

Piper looked down at her own hand. It didn't glow for her. "Aw… I barely even got to play with mine," she pouted.

"It's okay," he assured them. (*It* assured them?) "Everything has gone exactly according to my plan."

Piper looked up at him. "Your…plan…?"

Seph took off her glasses and rubbed at her eyes. *This* was according to plan? The scythe was broken, Tane was dead and the cycle had ended!

Even with her eyes closed, her prophet sight continued to show her glimpses of the creature that stood before her. It wasn't wearing a tattered coat at all. It was merely that its skin was all droopy and leathery. It hung around its small waist like a fleshy skirt. It also dangled around its small hands and from its jowls. It even hung from his forehead in gross, fatty folds that covered its eyes.

She'd never seen anything like this creature…and she'd seen a *lot* of strange things.

"I don't understand," said Piper. "That doesn't make sense. How did us *failing* go according to plan?"

Seph returned her glasses to her face and then shook her head. "*Nothing* makes sense. I don't even know who's the good guy anymore! Tane *saved* us back there… And he said *you* were the one who sent the wraiths after us!"

"And that *you* created the Black World, not him," added Piper.

"Who are we supposed to trust?" demanded Seph.

"Very well," said the Keeper. "You've more than earned the truth. Five cycles ago, Janon Tane managed to corrupt the seeker of the spinning wheel, convincing him to join him in altering the Architects' blueprints. His actions weren't entirely malicious. He wasn't seeking to end the cycle, only to turn it to his own utopian vision. It was a greedy ambition, one that gave him ultimate power, but if he'd accomplished what he set out to do, he *would* have put an end to the euthanization of the old universes. A noble goal. But his insistence on using energies mined from the Oblivion instead of the existing universe was his undoing. There are things built into the universe that even the teeth aren't aware of, and some of those things don't react well when exposed to the Oblivion. Therefore, while he might've saved the previous universe, he would've doomed the new one, and then *everything* would've died. I was forced to cut open the spirit highway myself to preserve the cycle, and in the end, both universes suffered. In that regard, he was correct. *I* created the Black World. But at least one of the worlds *lived*."

Piper pinched her lip. That sounded like it fit right in with what Tane said. If he was too stubborn to admit that his way of doing thing wouldn't work…or if he simply didn't have all the information required to *know* that his plan was doomed, then to him it really might have seemed as if the Keeper simply wrecked his plans out of spite.

"More importantly, those events allowed me to realize that the cycle was damaged beyond repair. Tane was right. A change was necessary or the universes would only become more fragile with the passing of each cycle. It already wouldn't survive another Black World. Unfortunately, I was bound to the Agreement of the Three. Direct interference was strictly forbidden. I was going to have to find a loophole if I was going to make a change."

"A loophole…" said Seph. Now he was starting to sound like a lawyer.

"It has taken the lifespan of five universes…but I've finally done it."

"Wow…" said Piper. "And I don't have the patience to get through a jigsaw puzzle on my own."

Seph barely heard her. "So…you *meant* for us to fail today?"

"I did."

"But without the cycle," said Piper, "won't all life go extinct?"

"The cycle was already broken," explained the Keeper. "Sometimes, when a thing is broken, people have this way of insisting on fixing it, even when it's well beyond fixing. Then you end up with this imperfect, broken thing that only gets worse and worse. Eventually, there comes a point where the only sensible thing left to do is break the thing once and for all and start over new."

Seph stared at him. "So *you're* the one who let the empress into Tartarus during the last creation."

"Yes."

"You're the one who made that monster so powerful."

"True. But I didn't make the monster. That was mankind's own capacity for evil."

Seph could barely grasp all that was going on right now. She was so confused. What were they even talking about? Saving humanity? Or why humanity deserved to be extinguished? "And that slime lady… Was she a part of your plan all along, too?"

"I have no power over her. She does as she wills. But yes. I accounted for her. I even gave her the means to sneak into Tartarus."

"You mean you told her to stow away inside me like that."

"I did."

She frowned. "Is she trapped in Tartarus forever now?"

"No. She will bury the bug and then seep through the cracks and go back to where she came from again. That is what she does."

That was a relief. After all, it was the slime lady who saved them down there. If not for her, they never would've had the chance to break free and they would've ended up buried there as well.

"So *did* you send the wraiths to kill us?" asked Piper. "Was Tane telling the truth about that?"

"He was," replied the Keeper. "I did. It was necessary. You wouldn't have succeeded in your journey without the extreme motivation they provided."

"'Extreme motivation,'" growled Seph. "Seriously? Those things *murdered* two people! And they nearly murdered *us* a bunch of times!"

"They couldn't have succeeded in harming you," he insisted. "You were protected."

"By Warner and the Ahns?" asked Piper. They *had*, admittedly, protected them time and time again.

"And that slime lady," recalled Seph. She wondered what became of her. Did she win her battle with the empress? Was she able to escape the black depths of Tartarus?

(It didn't go unnoticed by either of them, by the way, that the strange little monster had just skipped over the fact that he allowed two men to be killed by the wraiths he set loose.)

"And others who remained unnoticed," added the Keeper.

Piper stared at him. There were people helping them that they never saw? She supposed it made sense. Why not? Who would give such a task to a couple of clueless girls and then just leave them to it? Of course there'd be people watching over things. That was probably why everything was so messed-up and confusing all the time.

"Things will happen faster now," said the Keeper. "With the cycle broken, so is the agreement that kept me from interfering. It won't be an easy road. The Great Enemy and his other teeth will be furious. Others who were bound by the contract will now undoubtedly seek to interfere. But I have no doubt that this will be the age in which the prophecy finally comes true."

"Prophecy?" said Seph. She recalled the broken disk on the seventh floor of Vertical Design. The mandala with the symbol for Tartarus at its center.

"The wheels are already turning," the Keeper told her. "The first of the doors are open. Three have already been knighted. And the first of the new goddesses has already begun her journey. And you've pulled the first of the Great Enemy's teeth."

Piper shook her head. "Wait… How much more are we expected to do?"

"As of today, your job is done," the Keeper assured her. "You are free to return to your lives in peace."

"But what about the Architects?" asked Piper.

"The Hands may be broken," he replied, "but the Architects still live."

"But I thought the Hands *were* the Architects," said Piper. "This is confusing!"

"The Hands were merely physical manifestations that allowed them to be obtained by the seekers. They still exist, in some form or another. And they will awaken when the time comes around again. And this time, they'll build a world that will last *forever*."

Seph stared at him. "Is that possible?"

"It *must* be," replied the Keeper.

"Because of some *prophecy*?"

The man the Keeper was pretending to be grinned. "Why not?"

She stared at him. She wasn't entirely sure how to answer that.

"Now return to your lives," said the Keeper. "The battle with the white sisters is over. The Ahns are waiting for you."

Piper looked out into the woods. Which way did he say the research center was? North? "The Ahns?"

Seph turned and scanned their surroundings, trying to catch sight of the facility through the trees. "They beat the white sisters?"

"I believe it was a draw."

When they turned to face the Keeper again, he was gone.

"I guess we're done here," grumbled Seph. "Now I know how Commissioner Gordon always feels."

Piper turned and gave her that blank stare. "Who?"

"In Batman," replied Seph. "He always…" She sighed and shook her head. "Never mind. Forget it."

Chapter 97

"Okay," said Piper. She turned and looked around again. "Which way do you think north is?"

Seph reached into her pocket. "There's a compass on our phones."

"Oh yeah!" Piper opened her purse. "I always forget that."

Seph groaned as soon as she looked at her screen. "Kaitlyn and the others have been blowing up my phone the whole time we've been gone." She frowned. They never did figure out who put them up to everything. Could it have been Turms? She ignored them and checked her compass. "That way," she said, pointing straight ahead.

Almost immediately, the screen switched over to an incoming call. It was Kaitlyn.

"I'm done with this crap," she growled. She accepted the call and put it to her ear. "It's over!" she said. "Tane's dead. The Hands are *gone.* So you can tell whoever you're working for that there's nothing left!"

There was silence on the line for several seconds. Then Kaitlyn said, "What the heck are you talking about?"

"*You,*" she snapped. "And Alton and Phoenix all *stalking* us!"

"We're not *stalking* you!"

"We just want to know what the heck you're doing," said Alton.

"Who the hell's Tane?" asked Phoenix. "And what happened to

his hands?"

Apparently, they were all gathered together and had her on speaker.

"You're being *super* weird," said Alton.

"Like, *way* weirder than usual," agreed Kaitlyn. "Like, there's cool Seph weird and then there's *this* weird."

"What are you and Peppy up to?" pressed Phoenix. "I just bet it's something *super* juicy."

"How am *I* the one being weird? You've been totally *stalking* us!"

"We just want to know why you're running all over the freaking *country*," said Alton. "I mean, we're your friends, aren't we? Why are you keeping secrets from us? Like, why are you in *Arkansas* right now?"

Seph was so confused. They didn't sound like evil minions… They sounded the same as ever. Except for the fact that they knew where she was all the time. "How do you know where we are?"

"Buddy Finder," replied Kaitlyn.

Seph frowned. "What the hell is 'Buddy Finder'?"

Piper was standing beside her, looking at her own phone. As soon as she heard this, she gasped and clapped her hands over her mouth, her eyes opening wide.

Seph stared at her. "*What?*"

"I totally forgot about that!" said Piper.

"The app on my phone," replied Kaitlyn. "It lets me see where everybody is. I asked Peeps to be my buddy on it. Like, a year ago or something."

Seph stared at her. "You let her follow you on *Buddy Finder*?"

"I called her because she never got back to me about the weekend and she didn't answer, so I checked Buddy Finder to see where she was. I figured if she was at work or something, I wouldn't bother her again.

But it said she was in *Nebraska* of all places. Naturally, I got curious, but then she was totally lying to me about it. I even called Meg, but she said you guys were in *Madison*, so either she was lying for you guys or you were lying to her, too."

"Well, we *always* lie to Meg," said Seph. "So, you know…"

"So of course we weren't going to rest until we found out what you two were up to," said Phoenix.

"When Kaitlyn called and told us you were being weird, we couldn't resist," agreed Alton.

Seph reached under her glasses and rubbed her eyes. "*That's* what all this was about?"

"What else would it be about?" asked Alton. "You should've known we wouldn't leave you alone if we found out you were keeping secrets from us."

"So spill it," said Phoenix. "What *are* you two up to?"

"Yeah," said Alton. "What did you mean when you said 'Tane's dead' and 'the hands are gone'?"

"And why did you think we were working for someone?" asked Kaitlyn.

"Kaitlyn thinks you two quit your jobs and became traveling meth dealers," said Phoenix.

"I never said *meth*!"

"*I* still think it's gotta be something *way* more scandalous," squealed Phoenix.

Seph sighed. On one hand, she had no idea what to tell them. It wasn't like they were going to believe the truth. She didn't even have any kind of evidence. Until a few minutes ago, she could've just whipped out the scythe and showed them, but it looked like she didn't even have that anymore… And she really didn't *want* to tell them the truth. She liked having *normal* friends.

"Lesbian lover's retreat?" guessed Phoenix.

"Stop it!" groaned Kaitlyn.

"I'm just saying. They're being *awful* suspicious, so it *has* to be something *naughty*."

"It doesn't *have* to be something naughty," sighed Alton. "I bet they're on some sort of crazy, Davinci Code treasure hunt or something."

"Ooh!" cooed Kaitlyn. "I like that one! Is it that one?"

Well… Maybe "normal" wasn't the right word…

On the other hand, she was just relieved to know that her friends were who they said they were and that their relationship hadn't been a lie since day one.

"Look, I'm totally exhausted right now. Can we please talk about it this weekend?"

"Oh come on!" groaned Phoenix. "You've kept us waiting long enough!"

"You promise?" asked Kaitlyn.

"No!" squealed Phoenix.

"I promise."

"The truth?" pressed Alton.

"I'm not hanging up until I have an answer!"

"It's *my* phone," said Kaitlyn. "I'll hang it up whenever I want to hang it up."

"The truth," promised Seph. Although in all honesty, she wasn't sure she *could* tell them the truth. Certainly not the *whole* truth. The truth was dangerous. The truth came with certain consequences. The truth could be embarrassing or unpleasant or downright ugly. The fact was that the truth sometimes complicated things.

She frowned as it suddenly occurred to her that she might finally understand Amethyst's point of view on this subject…

"*Tell me now*!" whined Phoenix.

"Fine!" she replied. "We had to unlock three doors to the gates of Tartarus and fight an apocalyptic bug goddess to save the future of the universe."

A silence fell over the line for a moment at that.

Piper stared at her, those blue eyes wide with shock.

Then Phoenix said, "Fine, if you're just going to make fun of us, you can tell us this weekend."

"I'll message Peeps tomorrow, okay?" said Kaitlyn.

"Sounds good," replied Seph. "Bye."

"Bye bye!" chirped Kaitlyn.

"See ya," said Alton.

"No more secrets!" shouted Phoenix.

Then the call was disconnected.

Seph shook her head. "Well, I guess that answers *that* question." She scrolled down through all her missed calls and messages, almost all of them from those three. "Now we just have to figure out what happened to Meg. I mean, if they weren't working for some bad guy, then obviously *they* didn't do anything to her."

When Piper didn't respond, she turned and looked at her. "What?" she asked. "What's wrong? Why're you making that face?"

Piper stood there, her lips pursed and her cheeks tight, as if she'd just bitten into a lemon. She was staring at her phone, her eyebrows knitted together. "I got a text from Meg."

"She's okay?"

"She's fine." She scrolled down the screen. "She sent me the whole story." She kept scrolling down. "More of a book, really. She's up at her parents' cabin again."

Seph wrinkled her nose. "Is she revenge-weekending with someone's *else's* boyfriend now?"

Piper shook her head. "Remember River's new boyfriend that she, uh…?"

"I remember, yeah."

"Turns out River doesn't have a boyfriend."

Seph blinked, confused. "So then…who'd she sleep with?"

"Her little brother."

"Oh." Then she frowned. "*Oh…*"

"Who she apparently made a *really* good impression on, because *he* was the one who was stalking her all that time."

"Seriously?"

"She thought it was River Lobnetter blowing up her phone, but it was *Richard* Lobnetter. I guess that makes sense… And it looks like he had all his friends out looking for her, but she was all spooked and running away from everyone. I guess the guy staring at her and talking on his phone at the Starbucks was one of his friends, calling him to say he'd spotted her."

"That's not creepy at all," said Seph.

"I know, right? I guess he finally tracked her down at Banned Dave's, just before she could find Wanda."

"And she just ran off with him?"

Piper continued scrolling down the page. "Looks like it. Apparently, she thinks the whole thing's really romantic now."

Seph stuck out her tongue and made a gagging face.

"She thinks she's in love."

"Meg's a freak."

"Yeah."

The two of them walked north, through the trees and up the hill. As soon as they started down the other side, they could see the research complex looming ahead of them.

Both of them continued scrolling through their missed messages.

"That still doesn't explain the poisoned candy, though," said Piper, lowering her phone.

Seph laughed at her phone. "No, but *this* does."

Piper looked over at her, eyebrows raised.

"My mom sent me a text asking if we liked the cookies she dropped off for us. She says she's especially proud of the *orange cranberry cookies.*"

She stared at her. "So the box of candy from her secret admirer and would-be assassin…"

"Weren't even for her. Right." She should've known. Buffy had recently taken up baking. The Ahns had given her a ton of recipes to try and she was always making treats and sharing them. *And* she had a key to their apartment.

Meg wasn't very reliable when it came to details. If she hadn't kept telling them it was a box of "candy" instead of a box of "cookies," she might have guessed they came from her mom.

Piper shook her head. "That idiot."

Seph scrolled on. "She says she stopped by the apartment yesterday and dropped off another box…" Then she laughed again. "And she says she cut her finger trying to open the tape with one of our kitchen knives. Meg must've come home at the exact moment she was in the bathroom looking for a bandage. It's like the plot of a bad sitcom!"

They made their way carefully down the hillside and through the last of the trees. Immediately, they caught sight of a trio of Ahns prowling the grounds outside the facility in their monster forms.

"I really hope they can get us a ride home," sighed Seph.

Piper nodded.

The Ahns noticed them and came bounding toward them, tentacles waving. It was hard not to cringe as they bore down on them. They were frightful-looking things, after all. But as they leaped the last ten feet to close the distance, all three of them twisted and snapped back into the familiar shapes of Annalisa, Lillyanna and Arianna and landed gracefully on their feet in spite of their elderly appearances, especially Lillyanna, who sported an especially small and frail-looking shape.

"Thank goodness you're both safe!" exclaimed Annalisa as the three of them straightened their clothes and fussed with their hair.

"Is everyone okay?" asked Piper. "We heard the white sisters attacked."

All three of them seemed to deflate a little. "It was a devastating battle," said Annalisa. "We lost seven."

The news shocked Seph. "*Seven Ahns were killed?*"

"Annabelle and Carolann among them," reported Arianna.

"Oh no!" gasped Piper.

They'd met Carolann several times. She was one of the Ahns who regularly checked up on Buffy. And Annabelle was the Ahn that Seph first met all the way back in Sukmukwe State Park, the one who gave her the hint about looking for the ancient city's footprint. And she was one of the four who saved them from the black council.

"But you beat the white sisters, right?" said Piper, trying to find a ray of hope in such bad news.

"Not exactly," said Arianna.

"They just suddenly stopped fighting and fled," recalled Lillyanna.

Seph looked over at Piper. "Tane was the one who summoned them to attack the Ahns," she said. "I guess they quit fighting for him the moment he died."

The Ahns all looked shocked at this news. "Janon Tane is *dead*?" exclaimed Arianna.

"Impossible!" exclaimed Lillyanna. "He was one of the Twelve Teeth!"

"And a seeker!" Arianna added. "If he's dead it'd mean…"

Seph nodded. "Tartarus is destroyed. And so are the Hands."

Ten months ago, when she told these women that they'd failed and Noah's hammer had fallen to Tane, they surprised them by revealing that they knew all along that it would end that way. She expected the same sort of result this time. And indeed it seemed that they'd known all along about Tane being the third seeker. However, they looked horrified by the news that they'd failed to awaken the Architects.

Clearly, the Keeper hadn't shared his plan with the Ahns.

"What in the world happened in there?" asked Annalisa.

Chapter 98

"Her name was Annamarie."

Piper took the old photograph from Annalisa and stared at it. "She was beautiful." The woman in the picture appeared to be in her late sixties, wearing a long, flowing dress and a big sun hat. She was standing in front of a tree, barefoot in the summer grass, the wind blowing about her. Her blonde hair hung in a braid all the way down to her knees.

Seph leaned over and peered at it. "She really was."

"You should've seen her back in the days when we took younger forms," said Louann.

"Hell, you should've seen *me* in those days," said Annabeth, her small, wrinkled face spreading into a mischievous grin. "I was *hot*."

Amethyst laughed. "I'll bet you were."

Piper giggled. "Annamarie…" She glanced over at Seph. "it's almost the same as your mom's name."

"It is, isn't it?" Buffy was the name she gave herself. Her real name was Marianne. "That's kind of funny."

"She was your mom's dad's mom," recalled Annalisa.

Piper stared at the photo, enchanted. "How did she die?"

"There was a little town in New Mexico back in the sixties," replied Louann. "A fissure opened up there. Random bad luck, really.

Half the town was swallowed up in the middle of the night, never to be seen again. Annamarie went in with a few others to try to help and never made it back."

"She was brave," said Lillyanna. "And she had an enormous heart."

Piper smiled. It still made her sad to find out that her great-grandmother wasn't still among the Ahns. It would've been wonderful to sit and talk with her, to hear stories about her grandfather's childhood, to hear how she ended up married to her great-grandfather. But this picture was nice, too. She didn't think she'd ever seen a picture of her before. Her dad had pictures of his grandparents on his side of the family. And she thought she might have seen a few from her mom's *mom's* side of the family, but this was something she didn't have before now.

It was nice.

And she really was lovely. Even if that *wasn't* what she really looked like.

"That's really cool," said Wanda, leaning over the back of the couch for a better look.

Seph couldn't remember ever having this many people in their apartment. She was surprised everybody fit.

It'd been three days since they returned from Arkansas after failing to awaken the Architects. The world hadn't ended yet. But then again, it wasn't scheduled to for some time, so that wasn't really any surprise.

There *were* a number of small changes, though.

Seph had finally managed to forgive Amethyst for lying to her for all those years, for one thing. That was nice. That stressful tension between them was completely gone, and Piper, for one, found it utterly refreshing.

Seph hadn't returned to Vertical Design since they left Tane's freaky office. Amethyst had managed to confirm that Tane wasn't lying about never entering her into the company's computer. A quick reference check confirmed that there was no record of a Persephone Kipp ever working there. It was as if she'd never existed. But Annalisa had suggested, given how he protected them with his life inside Tartarus, that it could have been less an act of maliciousness than a way to protect her from his brother, Turms, which made a certain amount of sense, given that he ran the company and was the one who tried to buy the ringmaster's loyalty and have them killed.

At least they didn't have to worry about anyone coming after the Hands anymore. Seph hadn't been able to make the water appear since they left Tartarus. She was really going to miss all those little things she'd learned to do with the scythe, like slicing open envelopes and snipping sculpting materials with her fingertips, but she supposed it was worth it to not have a big target painted on her back.

Besides, her prophet sight still worked. She could still see Piper's spirit ears. Right now, they were perked straight up, twitching happily toward every friendly voice in the room.

The best change of all, however, was that Meg was moving out again. (Big "yay" there.) Apparently, she was already *engaged* to Richard Lobnetter…which was weird on *so* many levels!

And she wasn't moving back in this time. There really wasn't going to be room.

"I think she kind of looks like you, even," said Gina, who was sitting next to Piper, also looking at the picture. "I mean, a little bit."

It turned out that Gina wasn't all that sad about losing her job at Vertical Design. She didn't exactly want to be there in the first place, knowing the truth about the building and the monstrous things that passed through there. She only took the job because the goddess wanted her to watch over Seph in the first place. But she didn't have a lot of money saved up and she wasn't going to be able to afford to keep her apartment without a steady paycheck.

Seph wasted no time offering to let her stay with them. She liked Gina a lot more than she liked Meg, and that ridiculous engagement couldn't possibly last forever, so they jumped at the opportunity to fill the space she was vacating.

And as it turned out, Gina had a talent and a passion for drawing comic books. She had tons of notebooks full of ideas and was looking for a partner to help her create and publish independently, which was something Seph had never seriously considered and she wasn't entirely sure why. It sounded like a lot of fun.

And they almost had Piper convinced to be their writer, too. It was going to be great. She just knew it.

Of course, she and Gina would probably need to find real jobs, too. They'd cross that bridge later. Right now, Seph just wanted to enjoy not being chased by monsters for a little while.

Annalisa and the other Ahns told them there probably wasn't anything more to do. Their job was to awaken the Architects. It was what the seekers had always done for as long as anyone could remember. But the Keeper himself, for reasons no one quite understood, plotted to end the cycle now. No one knew what he was up to, but the Ahns were all in agreement that the Keeper was, among other things, the Keeper of the Cycle, meaning he must have a plan of some sort.

But when she asked them, no one knew anything about any prophecy.

She wished she'd taken a picture of that broken disk, although she was sure she wouldn't have been able to read it in a picture anyway, since that was how those other Tartarus stone messages had worked. What did it all mean? Who were the twelve knights? And the six guardians? And…what else did he say? Goddesses and doors?

She should probably forget about it. It made her head hurt, anyway. And it probably wouldn't ever concern them. They were the seekers. Their job was to seek out the Hands and take them to Tartarus. And they'd done that. Whatever came next was someone else's problem.

They'd earned some peace and quiet.

She looked over at Piper. Then she looked around the room at all her friends. She was happy like this. She hoped nothing ever changed.

"I knew you weren't a hundred percent human," said Gina, "but I didn't know what that other part of you was. This is really cool."

Piper smiled. "Yeah. I kind of think so, too."

"As long as you *never* miss a meal again," said Seph.

"It's really rare for our descendants to even carry any of our monster genes," said Louann. "Much less to such an extent as to actually be able to partially *transform*. I'm really surprised."

"I'm just lucky, I guess," grumbled Piper.

Gina leaned over and looked at Seph. "By the way, do you have any idea what *you* are?"

Seph stared back at her for a second. "What?"

"Well, *neither* of you are fully human."

She continued to stare at her. "I'm not…?" She turned her gaze on Piper, then at the Ahns gathered around them. "I'm not human, either?"

"Well, it's not surprising," reasoned Annalisa. "After all, you're the heir to the prophet sight. I don't think that's just a title."

Louann nodded. "Likely it's passed down through the generations."

"Goddess blood, perhaps?" guessed Annabeth.

"Or something even more rare," said Lillyanna.

Seph stared at them all. "You guys are joking, right? I mean…"

"I wouldn't worry about it," said Louann. "Lots of people aren't pure human. It doesn't make any difference."

It made a difference to *her*. What was she, then, if she wasn't human? How was she different? Was there a possibility *she* could turn into a monster someday?

Piper reached over and took her hand. "Don't worry about it. If anything ever happens, we'll deal with it together. 'Cause we're a kickass team."

She laughed. "Yeah. I guess we are."

"Enough talking!" exclaimed Louann. "Lyla brought us a whole cooler full of Mr. Hallet's famous ribs and I can't wait another minute!"

"*Ooh*!" sighed Piper. "*Yes*!"

Everyone else stood up and began moving toward the kitchen, but Seph and Piper lingered there for a moment, their eyes fixed on the picture of Annamarie.

"Thanks," said Piper.

"For what?"

"For everything. For saving me from that mall wraith. For always having my back. For being my best friend." She rolled her eyes. "Even after I tried to *eat* you."

Seph smiled. "Same to you. Except, I guess replace, 'tried to eat you' with 'hit on you like a drunk sorority girl.'"

Piper giggled. "That was pretty funny, looking back on it."

"Just promise never to tell Phoenix. She'll *never* let me live it down."

"I promise." Then she frowned. "By the way, what *are* we going to tell her and Kaitlyn and Alton? They're not going to let us blow them off forever."

Seph sighed. "I don't know. We'll figure something out." They didn't believe the truth when she told them, so that probably wasn't an option… "Right now, let's just eat."

"Yeah. That sounds good." Piper squeezed her hand and then both of them stood up.

Neither of them noticed the wet handprint that Seph left on the cushion of the couch.

ABOUT THE AUTHOR

Brian Harmon grew up in rural Missouri and now lives in Southern Wisconsin with his wife, Guinevere, and their three children.

For more about Brian Harmon and his work, visit www.BrianHarmonBooks.com

www.ingramcontent.com/pod-product-compliance
Lightning Source LLC
Chambersburg PA
CBHW070339030726
47504CB00001B/2